Murder International

Murder International

INCLUDING

SO MANY STEPS TO DEATH

DEATH COMES AS THE END

EVIL UNDER THE SUN

By Agatha Christie

DODD, MEAD & COMPANY
New York

Printed in the United States of America

Contents

So Many Steps to Death

CHAPTER I

THE MAN BEHIND the desk moved a heavy glass paper weight four inches to the right. His face was not so much thoughtful or abstracted as expressionless. He had the pale complexion that comes from living most of the day in artificial light. This man, you felt, was an indoor man. A man of desks and files. The fact that to reach his office you had to walk through long twisting underground corridors was somehow strangely appropriate. It would have been difficult to guess his age. He looked neither old nor young. His face was smooth and unwrinkled, and in his eyes was a great tiredness.

The other man in the room was older. He was dark with a small military moustache. There was about him an alert nervous energy. Even now, unable to sit still, he was pacing up and down, from time to time throwing off a remark in a jerky manner.

"Reports!" he said explosively. "Reports, reports and more reports, and none of them any damn good!"

The man at the desk looked down at the papers in front of him. On top was an official card headed, "Betterton, Thomas Charles." After the name was an interrogation mark. The man at the desk nodded thoughtfully. He said,

"You've followed up these reports and none of them any good?"

The other shrugged his shoulders.

"How can one tell?" he asked.

The man behind the desk sighed.

"Yes," he said, "there is that. One can't tell really."

The older man went on with a kind of machine gun volley abruptness,

"Reports from Rome; reports from Touraine; seen on the Riviera; noticed in Antwerp; definitely identified in Oslo; positively seen in Biarritz; observed behaving suspiciously in Strasburg; seen on the beach at Ostend with a glamorous blonde; noticed walking in the streets in Brussels with a greyhound! Hasn't been seen yet in the Zoo with his arm round a zebra, but I daresay that will come!"

"You've no particular fancy yourself, Wharton? Personally I had hopes of the Antwerp report, but it hasn't led to anything. Of course by now . . ." the young man stopped speaking and seemed to go into a coma. Presently

he came out of it again and said cryptically, "Yes, probably . . . and yet—
I wonder?"

Colonel Wharton sat down abruptly on the arm of a chair.

"But we've got to find out," he said insistently. "We've got to break the
back of all this *how* and *why* and *where?* You can't lose a tame scientist
every month or so and have no idea *how* they go or *why* they go or *where!*
Is it where we think—or isn't it? We've always taken it for granted that it
is, but now I'm not so sure. You've read all the last dope on Betterton from
America?"

The man behind the desk nodded.

"Usual Left Wing tendencies at the period when everyone had them.
Nothing of a lasting or permanent nature as far as can be found out. Did
sound work before the war though nothing spectacular. When Mannheim
escaped from Germany Betterton was assigned as Assistant to him, and
ended by marrying Mannheim's daughter. After Mannheim's death he carried on, on his own, and did brilliant work. He leaped into fame with the
startling discovery of ze Fission. ze Fission was a brilliant and absolutely
revolutionary discovery. It put Betterton absolutely tops. He was all set for
a brilliant career over there, but his wife had died soon after their marriage and he was all broken up over it. He came to England. He has been
at Harwell for the last eighteen months. Just six months ago he married
again."

"Anything there?" asked Wharton sharply.

The other shook his head.

Not that we can find out. She's the daughter of a local solicitor. Worked
in an insurance office before her marriage. No violent political affinities so
far as we've been able to discover."

"ze Fission," said Colonel Wharton gloomily, with distaste. "What they
mean by all these terms beats me. I'm old fashioned. I never really even
visualised a molecule, but here they are nowadays splitting up the universe!
Atom bombs, Nuclear fission, ze Fission, and all the rest of it. And Betterton was one of the splitters in chief! What do they say of him at Harwell?"

"Quite a pleasant personality. As to his work, nothing outstanding or
spectacular. Just variations on the practical applications of zef."

Both men were silent for a moment. Their conversation had been desultory, almost automatic. The security reports lay in a pile on the desk and
the security reports had had nothing of value to tell.

"He was thoroughly screened on arrival here, of course," said Wharton.

"Yes, everything was quite satisfactory."

"Eighteen months ago," said Wharton thoughtfully. "It gets 'em down,
you know. Security precautions. The feeling of being perpetually under the
microscope, the cloistered life. They get nervy, queer. I've seen it often

enough. They begin to dream of an ideal world. Freedom and brother-hood, and pool-all-secrets and work for the good of humanity! That's ex-actly the moment when someone who's more or less the dregs of humanity, sees his chance and takes it!" He rubbed his nose. "Nobody's so gullible as the scientist," he said. "All the phony mediums say so. Can't quite see why."

The other smiled, a very tired smile.

"Oh, yes," he said, "it would be so. They think they *know*, you see. That's always dangerous. Now, our kind are different. We're humble minded men. We don't expect to save the world, only pick up one or two broken pieces and remove a monkey wrench or two when it's jamming up the works." He tapped thoughtfully on the table with his finger. "If I only knew a little more about Betterton," he said. "Not his life and actions, but the revealing, everyday things. What sort of jokes he laughed at. What made him swear. Who were the people he admired and who made him mad."

Wharton looked at him curiously.

"What about the wife—you've tried her?"

"Several times."

"Can't she help?"

The other shrugged his shoulders.

"She hasn't so far."

"You think she knows something?"

"She doesn't admit, of course, that she knows anything. All the estab-lished reactions: worry, grief, desperate anxiety, no cue or suspicion be-forehand, husband's life perfectly normal, no stress of any kind—and so on and so on. Her own theory is that he's been kidnapped."

"And you don't believe her?"

"I'm handicapped," said the man behind the desk bitterly. "I never be-lieve anybody."

"Well," said Wharton slowly, "I suppose one has to keep an open mind. What's she like?"

"Ordinary sort of woman you'd meet any day playing bridge."

Wharton nodded comprehendingly.

"That makes it more difficult," he said.

"She's here to see me now. We shall go over all the same ground again."

"It's the only way," said Wharton. "I couldn't do it, though. Haven't got the patience." He got up. "Well, I won't keep you. We've not got much further, have we."

"Unfortunately, no. You might do a special check up on that Oslo re-port. It's a likely spot."

Wharton nodded and went out. The other man raised the receiver by his elbow and said:

"I'll see Mrs. Betterton now. Send her in."

He sat staring into space until there was a tap on the door and Mrs. Betterton was shown in. She was a tall woman, about twenty-seven years of age. The most noticeable thing about her was a most magnificent head of auburn red hair. Beneath the splendour of this, her face seemed almost insignificant. She had the blue eyes and light eyelashes that so often go with red hair. She was wearing no make-up, he noticed. He considered the significance of that while he was greeting her, settling her comfortably in a chair near the desk. It inclined him very slightly to the belief that Mrs. Betterton knew more than she had said she knew.

In his experience, women suffering from violent grief and anxiety did not neglect their make-up. Aware of the ravages grief made in their appearance, they did their best to repair those ravages. He wondered if Mrs. Betterton calculatingly abstained from make-up, the better to sustain the part of the distracted wife. She said now, rather breathlessly,

"Oh, Mr. Jessop, I do hope—is there any news?"

He shook his head and said gently,

"I'm so sorry to ask you to come up like this, Mrs. Betterton. I'm afraid we haven't got any definite news for you."

Olive Betterton said quickly,

"I know. You said so in your letter. But I wondered if—since then—oh! I was glad to come up. Just sitting at home wondering and brooding—that's the worst of it all. Because there's nothing one *can* do!"

The man called Jessop said soothingly:

"You mustn't mind, Mrs. Betterton, if I go over the same ground again and again, ask you the same questions, stress the same points. You see it's always possible that some small point *might* arise. Something that you hadn't thought of before, or perhaps hadn't thought worth mentioning."

"Yes. Yes, I understand. Ask me all over again about everything."

"The last time you saw your husband was on the 23rd of August?"

"Yes."

"That was when he left England to go to Paris to a Conference there."

"Yes."

Jessop went on rapidly,

"He attended the first two days of the Conference. The third day he did not turn up. Apparently he had mentioned to one of his colleagues that he was going instead for a trip on a *bateau mouche* that day."

"A *bateau mouche*? What's a *bateau mouche*?"

Jessop smiled.

"One of those small boats that go along the Seine." He looked at her sharply. "Does that strike you as unlike your husband?"

She said doubtfully,

"It does, rather. I should have thought he'd be so keen on what was going on at the Conference."

"Possibly. Still the subject for discussion on this particular day was not one in which he had any special interest, so he might reasonably have given himself a day off. But it doesn't strike you as being quite like your husband?"

She shook her head.

"He did not return that evening to his hotel," went on Jessop. "As far as can be ascertained he did not pass any frontier, certainly not on his own passport. Do you think he could have had a second passport, in another name perhaps?"

"Oh, no, why should he?"

He watched her.

"You never saw such a thing in his possession?"

She shook her head with vehemence.

"No, and I don't believe it. I don't believe it for a moment. I don't believe he went away deliberately as you all try to make out. Something's happened to him, or else—or else perhaps he's lost his memory."

"His health had been quite normal?"

"Yes. He was working rather hard and sometimes felt a little tired, nothing more than that."

"He'd not seemed worried in any way or depressed?"

"He wasn't worried or depressed about *anything!*" With shaking fingers she opened her bag and took out her handkerchief. "It's all so awful." Her voice shook. "I can't believe it. He'd never have gone off without a word to me. Something's happened to him. He's been kidnapped or he's been attacked perhaps. I try not to think it but sometimes I feel that that must be the solution. He must be dead."

"Now please, Mrs. Betterton, please—there's no need to entertain that supposition yet. If he's dead, his body would have been discovered by now."

"It might not. Awful things happen. He might have been drowned or pushed down a sewer. I'm sure anything could happen in Paris."

"Paris, I can assure you, Mrs. Betterton, is a very well policed city."

She took the handkerchief away from her eyes and stared at him with sharp anger.

"I know what you think, but it isn't so! Tom wouldn't sell secrets or betray secrets. He wasn't a Communist. His whole life is an open book."

"What were his political beliefs, Mrs. Betterton?"

"In America he was a Democrat, I believe. Here he voted Labour. He wasn't interested in politics. He was a scientist, first and last." She added defiantly, "He was a brilliant scientist."

"Yes," said Jessop, "he was a brilliant scientist. That's really the crux of the whole matter. He might have been offered, you know, very considerable inducements to leave this country and go elsewhere."

"It's not true." Anger leaped out again. "That's what the papers try to make out. That's what you all think when you come questioning me. It's not true. He'd never go without telling me, without giving me some idea."

"And he told you—nothing?"

Again he was watching her keenly.

"Nothing. I don't know where he is. I think he was kidnapped, or else, as I say, dead. But if he's dead, I must know. I must know soon. I can't go on like this, waiting and wondering. I can't eat or sleep. I'm sick and ill with worry. Can't you help me? Can't you help me *at all?*"

He got up then and moved round his desk. He murmured,

"I'm so very sorry, Mrs. Betterton, so very sorry. Let me assure you that we are trying our very best to find out what has happened to your husband. We get reports in every day from various places."

"Reports from where?" she asked sharply. "What do they say?"

He shook his head.

"They all have to be followed up, sifted and tested. But as a rule, I am afraid, they're vague in the extreme."

"I must *know,*" she murmured brokenly again. "I can't go on like this."

"Do you care for your husband very much, Mrs. Betterton?"

"Of course I care for him. Why, we've only been married six months. Only six months."

"Yes, I know. There was—forgive me for asking—no quarrel of any kind between you?"

"Oh, *no!*"

"No trouble over any other woman?"

"Of course not. I've told you. We were only married last April."

"Please believe that I'm not suggesting such a thing is likely, but one has to take every possibility into account that might allow for his going off in this way. You say he had not been upset lately, or worried—not on edge—not nervy in any way?"

"No, no, *no!*"

"People do get nervy, you know, Mrs. Betterton, in such a job as your husband had. Living under exacting security conditions. In fact—" he smiled, "—it's almost normal to be nervy."

She did not smile back.

"He was just as usual," she said stolidly.

"Happy about his work? Did he discuss it at all with you?"

"No, it was all so technical."

"You don't think he had any qualms over its—destructive possibilities, shall I say? Scientists do feel that sometimes."

"He never said anything of the kind."

"You see, Mrs. Betterton," he leaned forward over the desk, dropping some of his impassiveness, "what I am trying to do is to get a picture of your husband. The sort of man he was. And somehow you're not helping me."

"But what more can I say or do? I've answered all your questions."

"Yes, you've answered my questions, mostly in the negative. I want something positive, something constructive. Do you see what I mean? You can look for a man so much better when you know what kind of a man he is."

She reflected for a moment. "I see. At least, I suppose I see. Well, Tom was cheerful and good-tempered. And clever, of course."

Jessop smiled.

"That's a list of qualities. Let's try and get more personal. Did he read much?"

"Yes, a fair amount."

"What sort of books?"

"Oh, biographies. Book Society recommendations, crime stories if he was tired."

"Rather a conventional reader, in fact. No special preferences? Did he play cards or chess?"

"He played bridge. We used to play with Dr. Evans and his wife once or twice a week."

"Did your husband have many friends?"

"Oh, yes, he was a good mixer."

"I didn't mean just that. I mean was he a man who—cared very much for his friends?"

"He played golf with one or two of our neighbours."

"No special friends or cronies of his own?"

"No. You see, he'd been in the U.S.A. for so long, and he was born in Canada. He didn't know many people over here."

Jessop consulted a scrap of paper at his elbow.

"Three people visited him recently from the States, I understand. I have their names here. As far as we can discover, these three were the only people with whom he recently made contact from *outside*, so to speak. That's why we've given them special attention. Now first, Walter Griffiths. He came to see you at Harwell."

"Yes, he was over in England on a visit and he came to look up Tom."

"And your husband's reactions?"

"Tom was surprised to see him, but very pleased. They'd known each other quite well in the States."

"What did this Griffiths seem like to you? Just describe him in your own way."

"But surely you know all about him?"

"Yes, we know all about him. But I want to hear what you thought of him."

She reflected for a moment.

"Well, he was solemn and rather long-winded. Very polite to me and seemed very fond of Tom and anxious to tell him about things that had happened after Tom had come to England. All local gossip I suppose. It wasn't very interesting to me because I didn't know any of the people. Anyway, I was getting dinner ready while they were reminiscing."

"No question of politics came up?"

"You're trying to hint that he was a Communist," Olive Betterton's face flushed. "I'm sure he was nothing of the sort. He had some government job —in the District Attorney's office, I think. And anyway when Tom said something laughing about witch hunts in America, he said solemnly that we didn't understand over here. They were *necessary*. So that shows he *wasn't* a Communist!"

"Please, please, Mrs. Betterton, now don't get upset."

"Tom wasn't a Communist! I keep telling you so and you don't believe me."

"Yes, I do, but the point is bound to come up. Now for the second contact from abroad, Dr. Mark Lucas. You ran across him in London in the Dorset."

"Yes. We'd gone up to do a show and we were having supper at the Dorset afterwards. Suddenly this man, Luke or Lucas, came along and greeted Tom. He was a research chemist of some kind and the last time he had seen Tom was in the States. He was a German refugee who'd taken American nationality. But surely you . . ."

"But surely I know that? Yes, I do, Mrs. Betterton. Was your husband surprised to see him?"

"Yes, very surprised."

"Pleased?"

"Yes, yes—I think so—"

"But you're not sure?" He pressed her.

"Well, he was a man Tom didn't much care about, or so he told me afterwards, that's all."

"It was just a casual meeting? There was no arrangement made to meet at some future date?"

"No, it was just a casual encounter."

"I see. The third contact from abroad was a woman, Mrs. Carol Speeder, also from the States. How did that come about?"

"She was something to do with UNO, I believe. She'd known Tom in

America, and she rang him up from London to say she was over here, and asked if we could come up and lunch one day."

"And did you?"

"No."

"*You* didn't, but your husband did!"

"What!" She stared.

"He didn't tell you?"

"No."

Olive Betterton looked bewildered and uneasy. The man questioning her felt a little sorry for her, but he did not relent. For the first time he thought he might be getting somewhere.

"I don't understand it," she said uncertainly. "It seems very odd he shouldn't have said anything about it to me."

"They lunched together at the Dorset where Mrs. Speeder was staying, on Wednesday August 12th."

"August 12th?"

"Yes."

"Yes, he did go to London about then. . . . He never said anything—" she broke off again, and then shot out a question. "What is she like?"

He answered quickly and reassuringly.

"Not at all a glamorous type, Mrs. Betterton. A competent young career woman of thirty-odd, not particularly good-looking. There's absolutely no suggestion of her ever having been on intimate terms with your husband. That is just why it's odd that he didn't tell you about the meeting."

"Yes, yes, I see that."

"Now think carefully, Mrs. Betterton. Did you notice any change in your husband about that time? About the middle of August, shall we say? That would be about a week before the conference."

"No—No, I noticed nothing. There was nothing to notice."

Jessop sighed.

The instrument on his desk buzzed discreetly. He picked up the receiver.

"Yes," he said.

The voice at the other end said,

"There's a man who's asking to see someone in authority about the Betterton case, sir."

"What's his name?"

The voice at the other end coughed discreetly.

"Well, I'm not exactly sure how you pronounce it, Mr. Jessop. Perhaps I'd better spell it."

"Right. Go ahead."

He jotted down on his blotter the letters as they came over the wire.

"Polish?" he said interrogatively, at the end.

"He didn't say, sir. He speaks English quite well, but with a bit of an accent."

"Ask him to wait."

"Very good, sir."

Jessop replaced the telephone. Then he looked across at Olive Betterton. She sat there quite quietly with a disarming, hopeless placidity. He tore off the leaf on his desk pad with the name he had just written on it, and shoved it across to her.

"Know anybody of that name?" he asked.

Her eyes widened as she looked at it. For a moment he thought she looked frightened.

"Yes," she said. "Yes, I do. He wrote to me."

"When?"

"Yesterday. He's a cousin of Tom's first wife. He's just arrived in this country. He was very concerned about Tom's disappearance. He wrote to ask if I had had any news and—and to give me his most profound sympathy."

"You'd never heard of him before that?"

She shook her head.

"Ever hear your husband speak of him?"

"No."

"So really he mightn't be your husband's cousin at all?"

"Well, no, I suppose not. I never thought of that." She looked startled. "But Tom's first wife was a foreigner. She was Professor Mannheim's daughter. This man seemed to know all about her and Tom in his letter. It was very correct and formal and—and foreign, you know. It seemed quite genuine. And anyway, what would be the point—if he weren't genuine, I mean?"

"Ah, that's what one always asks oneself." Jessop smiled faintly. "We do it so much here that we begin to see the smallest thing quite out of proportion!"

"Yes, I should think you might." She shivered suddenly. "It's like this room of yours, in the middle of a labyrinth of corridors, just like a dream when you think you will never get out. . . ."

"Yes, yes, I can see it might have a claustrophobic effect," said Jessop pleasantly.

Olive Betterton put a hand up and pushed back her hair from her forehead.

"I can't stand it much longer, you know," she said. "Just sitting and waiting. I want to get away somewhere for a change. Abroad for choice. Somewhere where reporters won't ring me up all the time, and people stare at me. I'm always meeting friends and they keep asking if I have had any news?" She paused, then went on, "I think—I think I'm going to break down. I've tried to be brave, but it's too much for me. My doctor agrees. He says I ought to go right away somewhere for three or four weeks. He wrote me a letter. I'll show you."

She fumbled in her bag, took out an envelope and pushed it across the desk to Jessop.

"You'll see what he says."

Jessop took the letter out of the envelope and read it.

"Yes," he said. "Yes, I see."

He put the letter back in the envelope.

"So—so it would be all right for me to go?" Her eyes watched him nervously.

"But of course, Mrs. Betterton," he replied. He raised surprised eyebrows. "Why not?"

"I thought you might object."

"Object—why? It's entirely your own business. You'll arrange it so that I can get in touch with you while you're away in case any news should come through."

"Oh, of course."

"Where were you thinking of going?"

"Somewhere where there is sun and not too many English people. Spain or Morocco."

"Very nice. Do you a lot of good, I'm sure."

"Oh, thank you. Thank you very much."

She rose, excited, elated—her nervousness still apparent.

Jessop rose, shook hands with her, pressed the buzzer for a messenger to see her out. He went back to his chair and sat down. For a few moments his face remained as expressionless as before, then very slowly he smiled. He lifted the phone.

"I'll see Major Glydr now," he said.

CHAPTER II

"MAJOR GLYDR?" JESSOP hesitated a little over the name.

"It is difficult, yes." The visitor spoke with humorous appreciation. "Your compatriots, they have called me Glider in the war. And now, in the States, I shall change my name to Glyn, which is more convenient for all."

"You come from the States now?"

"Yes, I arrive a week ago. You are—excuse me—Mr. Jessop?"

"I'm Jessop."

The other looked at him with interest.

"So," he said. "I have heard of you."

"Indeed? From whom?"

The other smiled.

"Perhaps we go too fast. Before you permit that I should ask you some questions, I present you first this letter from the U.S. Embassy."

He passed it with a bow. Jessop took it, read the few lines of polite introduction, put it down. He looked appraisingly at his visitor. A tall man, carrying himself rather stiffly, aged thirty or thereabouts. The fair hair was close cropped in the continental fashion. The stranger's speech was slow and careful with a very definite foreign intonation, though grammatically correct. He was, Jessop noticed, not at all nervous or unsure of himself. That in itself was unusual. Most of the people who came into this office were nervous or excited or apprehensive. Sometimes they were shifty, sometimes vehement.

This was a man who had complete command of himself, a man with a poker face who knew what he was doing and why, and who would not be easily tricked or betrayed into saying more than he meant to say. Jessop said pleasantly,

"And what can we do for you?"

"I came to ask if you had any further news of Thomas Betterton, who disappeared recently in what seems a somewhat sensational manner. One cannot, I know, believe exactly what one reads in the press, so I ask where I can go for reliable information. They tell me—*you*."

"I'm sorry we've no definite information about Betterton."

"I thought perhaps he might have been sent abroad on some mission." He paused and added, rather quaintly, "You know, hush-hush."

"My dear sir." Jessop looked pained. "Betterton was a scientist, not a diplomat or a secret agent."

"I am rebuked. But labels are not always correct. You will want to inquire my interest in the matter. Thomas Betterton was a relation of mine by marriage."

"Yes. You are the nephew, I believe, of the late Professor Mannheim."

"Ah, that you knew already. You are well informed here."

"People come along and tell us things," murmured Jessop. "Betterton's wife was here. She told me. You had written to her."

"Yes, to express my condolences and to ask if she had had any further news."

"That was very correct."

"My mother was Professor Mannheim's only sister. They were much attached. In Warsaw when I was a child I was much at my uncle's house, and his daugher, Elsa, was to me like a sister. When my father and mother died my home was with my uncle and cousin. They were happy days. Then came the war, the tragedies, the horrors. . . . Of all that we will not speak. My uncle and Elsa escaped to America. I myself remained in the underground Resistance, and after the war ended I had certain assignments. One visit I paid to America to see my uncle and cousin, that was all. But there came a time when my commitments in Europe are ended. I intend to reside in the States permanently. I shall be, I hope, near my uncle and my cousin and her husband. But alas—" he spread out his hands, "—I get there and my uncle, he is dead, my cousin, too, and her husband he has come to this country and has married again. So once more I have no family. And then I read of the disappearance of the well-known scientist Thomas Betterton, and I come over to see what can be done." He paused and looked enquiringly at Jessop.

Jessop looked expressionlessly back at him.

"Why did he disappear, Mr. Jessop?"

"That," said Jessop pleasantly, "is just what we'd like to know."

"Perhaps you do know?"

Jessop appreciated with some interest how easily their roles might become reversed. In this room he was accustomed to ask questions of people. This stranger was not the inquisitor. Still smiling pleasantly, Jessop replied,

"I assure you we do not."

"But you suspect?"

"It is possible," said Jessop cautiously, "that the thing follows a certain pattern. . . . There have been occurrences of this kind before."

"I know." Rapidly the visitor cited a half dozen cases. "All scientists," he said, with significance.

"Yes."

"They have gone beyond the Iron Curtain?"

"It is a possibility, but we do not know."

"But they have gone of their own free will?"

"Even that," said Jessop, "is difficult to say."

"It is not my business you think?"

"Oh, please."

"But you are right. It is of interest to me only because of Betterton."

"You'll forgive me," said Jessop, "if I don't quite understand your interest.

After all, Betterton is only a relation by marriage. You didn't even know him."

"That is true. But for us Poles, the family is very important. There are obligations." He stood up and bowed stiffly. "I regret that I have trespassed upon your time, and I thank you for your courtesy."

Jessop rose also.

"I'm sorry we cannot help you," he said, "but I assure you we are completely in the dark. If I do hear of anything can I reach you?"

"Care of the U.S. Embassy will find me. I thank you." Again he bowed formally.

Jessop touched the buzzer. Major Glydr went out. Jessop lifted the receiver.

"Ask Colonel Wharton to come to my room."

When Wharton entered the room Jessop said:

"Things are moving—at last."

"How?"

"Mrs. Betterton wants to go abroad."

Wharton whistled.

"Going to join hubby?"

"I'm hopeful. She came provided with a convenient letter from her medical adviser. Complete need of rest and change of scene."

"Looks good!"

"Though, of course, it may be true." Jessop warned him. "A simple statement of fact."

"We never take that view here," said Wharton.

"No. I must say she does her stuff very convincingly. Never slips up for a moment."

"You got nothing further from her, I suppose?"

"One faint lead. The Speeder woman with whom Betterton lunched at the Dorset."

"Yes?"

"He didn't tell his wife about the lunch."

"Oh." Wharton considered. "You think that's relevant?"

"It might be. Carol Speeder was had up before the Committee for the investigation of un-American Activities. She cleared herself, but all the same . . . yes, all the same she was, or they thought she was, tarred with that brush. It *may* be a possible contact. The only one we've found for Betterton so far."

"What about Mrs. Betterton's contacts—any possible contact lately who could have instigated the going abroad business?"

"No personal contact. She had a letter yesterday from a Pole. A cousin of Betterton's first wife. I had him here just now asking for details, etc."

"What's he like?"

"Not real," said Jessop. "All very foreign and correct, got all the 'gen,' curiously unreal as a personality."

"Think he's been the contact to tip her off?"

"It could be. I don't know. He puzzles me."

"Going to keep tabs on him?"

Jessop smiled.

"Yes. I pressed the buzzer twice."

"You old spider—with your tricks." Wharton became businesslike again. "Well, what's the form?"

"Janet, I think, and the usual. Spain, or Morocco."

"Not Switzerland?"

"Not this time."

"I should have thought Spain or Morocco would have been difficult for them."

"We mustn't under-estimate our adversaries."

Wharton flipped the security files disgustedly with his nail.

"About the only two countries where Betterton *hasn't* been seen," he said with chagrin. "Well, we'll lay it all on. My God, if we fall down on the job this time—"

Jessop leaned back in his chair.

"It's a long time since I've had a holiday," he said. "I'm rather sick of this office. I *might* take a little trip abroad. . . ."

CHAPTER III

"FLIGHT 108 TO PARIS. Air France. This way please."

The persons in the lounge at Heathrow Airport rose to their feet. Hilary Craven picked up her small, lizard skin travelling case and moved in the wake of the others, out onto the tarmac. The wind blew sharply cold after the heated air of the lounge.

Hilary shivered and drew her furs a little closer round her. She followed the other passengers across to where the aircraft was waiting. This was it! She was off—escaping! Out of the greyness, the coldness, the dead numb misery. Escaping to sunshine and blue skies and a new life. She would leave all this weight behind, this dead weight of misery and frustration. She went up the gangway of her plane, bending her head as she passed inside and was shown by the steward to her seat. For the first time in months she savoured relief from a pain that had been so sharply acute as almost to be physical. "I shall get away," she said to herself, hopefully. "I *shall* get away."

The roaring and the revolutions of the plane excited her. There seemed a kind of elemental savagery in it. Civilised misery, she thought, is the worst misery. Grey and hopeless. "But now," she thought, "I shall escape."

The plane taxied gently along the runway. The air hostess said:

"Fasten your belts, please."

The plane made a half turn and stood waiting its signal to depart. Hilary thought, "Perhaps the plane will crash. . . . Perhaps it will never rise off the ground. Then that will be the end, that will be the solution to everything." They seemed to wait for ages out on the airfield. Waiting for the signal to start off to freedom, Hilary thought, absurdly; "I shall never get away, never. I shall be kept here—a prisoner. . . ."

Ah, at last.

A final roar of engines, then the plane started forward. Quicker, quicker, racing along. Hilary thought; "It won't rise. It can't. . . . This is the end." Ah, they were above the ground now, it seemed. Not so much that the plane rose as that the earth was falling away, dropping down, thrusting its problems and its disappointments and its frustrations beneath the soaring creature rising up so proudly into the clouds. Up they went, circling round, the aerodrome looking like a ridiculous child's toy beneath. Funny little roads, strange little railways with toy trains on them. A ridiculous childish world where people loved and hated and broke their hearts. None of it mattered because they were all so ridiculous and so pettily small and unimportant. Now there were clouds below them, a dense, greyish-white mass. They must be over the Channel now. Hilary leaned back, closing her eyes. Escape. Escape. She had left England, left Nigel, left the sad little mound that was Brenda's grave. All left behind. She opened her eyes, closed them again with a long sigh. She slept. . . .

II

When Hilary awoke, the plane was coming down. "Paris," thought Hilary, as she sat up in her seat and reached for her handbag. But it was not Paris. The air hostess came down the car saying, with that nursery governess brightness that some travellers found so annoying:

"We are landing you at Beauvais as the fog is very thick in Paris."

The suggestion in her manner was: "Won't that be nice, children?" Hil-

ary peered down through the small space of window at her side. She could
see little. Beauvais also appeared to be wreathed in fog. The plane was
circling round slowly. It was some time before it finally made its landing.
Then the passengers were marshalled through cold, damp mist into a rough
wooden building with a few chairs and a long wooden counter.

Depression settled down on Hilary but she tried to fight it off. A man
near her murmured:

"An old war aerodrome. No heating or comforts here. Still, fortunately
being the French, they'll serve us out some drinks."

True enough, almost immediately a man came along with some keys and
presently passengers were being served with various forms of alcoholic re-
freshment to boost their morale. It helped to buoy the passengers up for the
long and irritating wait.

Some hours passed before anything happened. Other planes appeared
out of the fog and landed, also diverted from Paris. Soon the small room was
crowded with cold, irritable people grumbling about the delay.

To Hilary it all had an unreal quality. It was as though she was still in a
dream, mercifully protected from contact with reality. This was only a delay, only a matter of waiting. She was still on her journey—her journey of
escape. She was still getting away from it all, still going towards that spot
where her life would start again. Her mood held. Held through the long,
fatiguing delay, held through the moments of chaos when it was announced, long after dark, that buses had come to convey the travellers to
Paris.

There was then a wild confusion, of coming and going, passengers, officials, porters all carrying baggage, hurrying and colliding in the darkness.
In the end Hilary found herself, her feet and legs icy cold, in a bus slowly
rumbling its way through the fog towards Paris.

It was a long weary drive taking four hours. It was midnight when they
arrived at the Invalides and Hilary was thankful to collect her baggage
and drive to the hotel where accommodation was reserved for her. She was
too tired to eat—just had a hot bath and tumbled into bed.

The plane to Casablanca was due to leave Orly Airport at ten thirty the
following morning, but when they arrived at Orly everything was confusion. Planes had been grounded in many parts of Europe, arrivals had
been delayed as well as departures.

A harassed clerk at the departure desk shrugged his shoulders and said:

"Impossible for Madame to go on the flight where she had reservations!
The schedules have all had to be changed. If Madame will take a seat for
a little minute, presumably all will arrange itself." In the end she was summoned and told that there was a place on a plane going to Dakar which nor-

mally did not touch down at Casablanca but would do so on this occasion. "You will arrive three hours later, that is all, Madame, on this later service."

Hilary acquiesced without protest and the official seemed surprised and positively delighted by her attitude.

"Madame has no conceptions of the difficulties that have been made to me this morning," he said. *"Enfin,* they are unreasonable, Messieurs the travellers. It is not I who made the fog! Naturally it has caused the disruptions. One must accommodate oneself with the good humour—that is what I say, however displeasing it is to have one's plans altered. *Après tout,* Madame, a little delay of an hour or two hours or three hours, what does it matter? How can it matter by what plane one arrives at Casablanca."

Yet on that particular day it mattered more than the little Frenchman knew when he spoke those words. For when Hilary finally arrived and stepped out into the sunshine onto the tarmac, the porter who was moving beside her with his piled-up trolley of luggage observed:

"You have the lucky chance, Madame, not to have been on the plane before this, the regular plane for Casablanca."

Hilary said: "Why, what happened?"

The man looked uneasily to and fro, but after all, the news could not be kept secret. He lowered his voice confidentially and leaned towards her.

"Mauvaise affaire!" he muttered. "It crashed—landing. The pilot and the navigator are dead and most of the passengers. Four or five were alive and have been taken to hospital. Some of those are badly hurt."

Hilary's first reaction was a kind of blinding anger. Almost unprompted there leaped into her mind the thought, "Why wasn't *I* in that plane? If I had been, it would have been all over now—I should be dead, out of it all. No more heartaches, no more misery. The people in that plane wanted to live. And I—I don't care. Why shouldn't it have been me?"

She passed through the Customs, a perfunctory affair, and drove with her baggage to the hotel. It was a glorious, sunlit afternoon, with the sun just sinking to rest. The clear air and golden light—it was all as she had pictured it. She had arrived! She had left the fog, the cold, the darkness of London; she had left behind her misery and indecision and suffering. Here there was pulsating life and colour and sunshine.

She crossed her bedroom and threw open the shutters, looking out into the street. Yes, it was all as she had pictured it would be. Hilary turned slowly away from the window and sat down on the side of the bed. Escape, escape! That was the refrain that had hummed incessantly in her mind ever since she left England. Escape. Escape. And now she knew—knew with a horrible, stricken coldness, *that there was no escape.*

Everything was just the same here as it had been in London. She herself, Hilary Craven, was the same. It was from Hilary Craven that she was trying to escape, and Hilary Craven was Hilary Craven in Morocco just as much as she had been Hilary Craven in London. She said very softly to herself:

"What a fool I've been—what a fool I *am*. Why did I think that I'd feel differently if I got away from England?"

Brenda's grave, that small pathetic mound, was in England and Nigel would shortly be marrying his new wife, in England. Why had she imagined that those two things would matter less to her here? Wishful thinking, that was all. Well, that was all over now. She was up against reality. The reality of herself and what she could bear, and what she could *not* bear. One could bear things, Hilary thought, so long as there was a *reason* for bearing them. She had borne her own long illness, she had borne Nigel's defection and the cruel and brutal circumstances in which it had operated. She had borne these things because there was Brenda. Then had come the long, slow, losing fight for Brenda's life—the final defeat. . . . Now there was nothing to live for any longer. It had taken the journey to Morocco to prove that to her. In London she had had a queer, confused feeling that if only she could get somewhere else she could forget what lay behind her and start again. And so she had booked her journey to this place which had no associations with the past, a place quite new to her which had the qualities she loved so much: sunlight, pure air and the strangeness of new people and things. Here, she had thought, things will be different. But they were not different. They were the same. The facts were quite simple and unescapable. She, Hilary Craven, had no longer any wish to go on living. It was as simple as that.

If the fog had not intervened, if she had travelled on the plane on which her reservations had been made, then her problem might have been solved by now. She might be lying now in some French official mortuary, a body broken and battered with her spirit at peace, freed from suffering. Well, the same end could be achieved, but she would have to take a little trouble.

It would have been so easy if she had had sleeping stuff with her. She remembered how she had asked Dr. Grey and the rather queer look on his face as he had answered:

"Better not. Much better to learn to sleep naturally. Maybe hard at first, but it will come."

A queer look on his face. Had he known then or suspected that it would come to this? Oh well, it should not be difficult. She rose to her feet with decision. She would go out now to a chemist's shop.

III

Hilary had always imagined that drugs were easy to buy in foreign cities. Rather to her surprise, she found that this was not so. The chemist she went to first supplied her with only two doses. For more than that amount, he said, a doctor's prescription would be advisable. She thanked him smilingly and nonchalantly and went rather quickly out of the shop, colliding as she did so with a tall, rather solemn-faced young man, who apologised in English. She heard him asking for toothpaste as she left the shop.

Somehow that amused her. Toothpaste. It seemed so ridiculous, so normal, so everyday. Then a sharp pang pierced her, for the toothpaste he had asked for was the brand that Nigel had always preferred. She crossed the street and went into a shop opposite. She had been to four chemists' shops by the time she returned to the hotel. It had amused her a little that in the third shop the owlish young man had again appeared, once more asking obstinately for his particular brand of toothpaste which evidently was not one commonly stocked by French chemists in Casablanca.

Hilary felt almost lighthearted as she changed her frock and made up her face before going down for dinner. She purposely went down as late as possible since she was anxious not to encounter any of her fellow travellers or the *personnel* of the aeroplane. That was hardly likely in any case, since the plane had gone on to Dakar, she thought that she had been the only person put off at Casablanca.

The restaurant was almost empty by the time she came into it, though she noticed that the young Englishman with the owl-like face was just finishing his meal at the table by the wall. He was reading a French newspaper and seemed quite absorbed in it.

Hilary ordered herself a good meal with a half bottle of wine. She was feeling a heady kind of excitement. She thought to herself, "What is this after all, but the last adventure?" Then she ordered a bottle of Vichy water to be sent up to her room and went straight up after leaving the dining room.

The waiter brought the Vichy, uncapped it, placed it on the table, and wishing her goodnight, left the room. Hilary drew a sigh of relief. As he closed the door after him, she went to it and turned the key in the lock. She took from the drawer of the dressing table the four little packets she had obtained from the chemists, and unwrapped them. She laid the tablets out on the table and poured herself out a glass of Vichy water. Since the drugs were in tablet form, she had only to swallow them, and wash them down with the Vichy water.

She undressed, wrapped her dressing gown round her and came back to sit by the table. Her heart beat faster. She felt something like fear now, but the fear was half fascination and not the kind of flinching that would have tempted her to abandon her plan. She was quite calm and clear about that. This was escape at last—real escape. She looked at the writing table, debating whether she would leave a note. She decided against it. She had no relations, no close or dear friends, there was nobody to whom she wished to say goodbye. As for Nigel, she had no wish to burden him with useless remorse even if a note from her would have achieved that object. Nigel would read presumably in the paper that a Mrs. Hilary Craven had died of an overdose of sleeping tablets in Casablanca. It would probably be quite a small paragraph. He would accept it at its face value. "Poor old Hilary," he would say, "bad luck"—and it might be that, secretly, he would be rather relieved. Because she guessed that she was, slightly, on Nigel's conscience, and he was a man who wished to feel comfortable with himself.

Already Nigel seemed very far away and curiously unimportant. There was nothing more to be done. She would swallow the pills and lie down on her bed and sleep. From that sleep she would not wake. She had not, or thought she had not, any religious feeling. Brenda's death had shut down on all that. So there was nothing more to consider. She was once again a traveller as she had been at Heathrow Airport, a traveller waiting to depart for an unknown destination, unencumbered by baggage, unaffected by farewells. For the first time in her life she was free, entirely free, to act as she wished to act. Already the past was cut away from her. The long aching misery that had dragged her down in her waking hours was gone. Yes. Light, free, unencumbered! Ready to start on her journey.

She stretched out her hand towards the first tablet. As she did so there came a soft, discreet tap on the door. Hilary frowned. She sat there, her hand arrested in mid-air. Who was it—a chambermaid? No, the bed had already been turned down. Somebody, perhaps, about papers or passport? She shrugged her shoulders. She would not answer the door. Why should she bother? Presently whoever it was would go away and come back at some further opportunity.

The knock came again, a little louder this time. But Hilary did not move. There could be no real urgency, and whoever it was would soon go away.

Her eyes were on the door, and suddenly they widened with astonishment. The key was slowly turning backwards round the lock. It jerked forward and fell on the floor with a metallic clang. Then the handle turned, the door opened and a man came in. She recognised him as the solemn, owlish young man who had been buying toothpaste. Hilary stared at him. She was too startled for the moment to say or do anything. The young man turned round, shut the door, picked the key up from the floor, put it into the lock and turned it. Then he came across towards her and sat down in a chair the other side of the table. He said, and it seemed to her a most incongruous remark:

"My name's Jessop."

The colour rose sharply in Hilary's face. She leaned forward. She said with cold anger,

"What do you think you're doing here, may I ask?"

He looked at her solemnly—and blinked.

"Funny," he said. "I came to ask you that." He gave a quick sideways nod towards the preparations on the table. Hilary said sharply:

"I don't know what you mean."

"Oh yes, you do."

Hilary paused, struggling for words. There were so many things she wanted to say. To express indignation. To order him out of the room. But strangely enough, it was curiosity that won the day. The question rose to her lips so naturally that she was almost unaware of asking it.

"That key," she said, "it turned, of itself, in the lock?"

"Oh, that!" The young man gave a sudden boyish grin that transformed his face. He put his hand into his pocket, and taking out a metal instrument, he handed it to her to examine.

"There you are," he said, "very handy little tool. Insert it into the lock the other side, it grips the key and turns it." He took it back from her and put it in his pocket. "Burglars use them," he said.

"So you're a burglar?"

"No, no, Mrs. Craven, do me justice. I did knock, you know. Burglars don't knock. Then, when it seemed you weren't going to let me in, I used this."

"But why?"

Again her visitor's eyes strayed to the preparations on the table.

"I shouldn't do it if I were you," he said. "It isn't a bit what you think, you know. You think you just go to sleep and you don't wake up. But it's not quite like that. All sorts of unpleasant effects. Convulsions sometimes, gangrene of the skin. If you're resistant to the drug, it takes a long time to work, and someone gets to you in time and then all sorts of unpleasant things happen. Stomach pump. Castor oil, hot coffee, slapping and pushing. All very undignified, I assure you."

Hilary leaned back in her chair, her eyelids narrowed. She clenched her hands slightly. She forced herself to smile.

"What a ridiculous person you are," she said. "Do you imagine that I was committing suicide, or something like that?"

"Not only imagine it," said the young man called Jessop, "I'm quite sure of it. I was in that chemist, you know, when you came in. Buying toothpaste, as a matter of fact. Well, they hadn't got the sort I like, so I went to another shop. And there you were, asking for sleeping pills again. Well, I thought that was a bit odd, you know, so I followed you. All those sleeping pills at different places. It could only add up to one thing."

His tone was friendly, offhand, but quite assured. Looking at him Hilary Craven abandoned pretence.

"Then don't you think it is unwarrantable impertinence on your part to try and stop me?"

He considered the point for a moment or two. Then he shook his head.

"No. It's one of those things that you can't *not* do—if you understand."

Hilary spoke with energy. "You can stop me for the moment. I mean you can take the pills away—throw them out of the window or something like that—but you can't stop me from buying more another day or throwing myself down from the top floor of the building, or jumping in front of a train."

The young man considered this.

"No," he said. "I agree I can't stop you doing any of those things. But it's a question, you know, whether you will do them. Tomorrow, that is."

"You think I shall feel differently tomorrow?" asked Hilary, faint bitterness in her tone.

"People do," said Jessop, almost apologetically.

"Yes, perhaps," she considered. "If you're doing things in a mood of hot despair. But when it's cold despair, it's different. I've nothing to live for, you see."

Jessop put his rather owlish head on one side, and blinked.

"Interesting," he remarked.

"Not really. Not interesting at all. I'm not a very interesting woman. My husband, whom I loved, left me, my only child died very painfully of meningitis. I've no near friends or relations. I've no vocation, no art or craft or work that I love doing."

"Tough," said Jessop appreciatively. He added, rather hesitantly: "You don't think of it as—wrong?"

Hilary said heatedly: "Why should it be wrong? It's *my* life."

"Oh yes, yes," Jessop repeated hastily. "I'm not taking a high moral line myself, but there *are* people, you know, who think it's wrong."

Hilary said,

"I'm not one of them."

Mr. Jessop said, rather inadequately,

"Quite."

He sat there looking at her, blinking his eyes thoughtfully. Hilary said: "So perhaps now, Mr.—er—"

"Jessop," said the young man.

"So perhaps now, Mr. Jessop, you will leave me alone."

But Jessop shook his head.

"Not just yet," he said. "I wanted to know, you see, just what was behind it all. I've got it clear now, have I? You're not interested in life, you don't want to live any longer, you more or less welcome the idea of death?"

"Yes."

"Good," said Jessop, cheerfully. "So now we know where we are. Let's go on to the next step. Has it got to be sleeping pills?"

"What do you mean?"

"Well, I've already told you that they're not as romantic as they sound. Throwing yourself off a building isn't too nice, either. You don't always die at once. And the same applies to falling under a train. What I'm getting at is that there *are* other ways."

"I don't understand what you mean."

"I'm suggesting another method. Rather a sporting method, really. There's some excitement in it, too. I'll be fair with you. There's just a hundred to one chance that you mightn't die. But I don't believe under the circumstances, that you'd really object by that time."

"I haven't the faintest idea what you're talking about."

"Of course you haven't," said Jessop. "I've not begun to tell you about it yet. I'm afraid I'll have to make rather a thing about it—tell you a story, I mean. Shall I go ahead?"

"I suppose so."

Jessop paid no attention to the grudgingness of the assent. He started off in his most owl-like manner.

"You're the sort of woman who reads the papers and keeps up with things generally, I expect," he said. "You'll have read about the disappearance of various scientists from time to time. There was that Italian chap about a year ago, and about two months ago a young scientist called Thomas Betterton disappeared."

Hilary nodded. "Yes, I read about that in the papers."

"Well, there's been a good deal more than has appeared in the papers. More people, I mean, have disappeared. They haven't always been scientists. Some of them have been young men who were engaged in important medical research. Some of them have been research chemists, some of them have been physicists, there was one barrister. Oh, quite a lot here and there and everywhere. Well, ours is a so-called free country. You can leave it if you like. But in these peculiar circumstances we've got to know why these people left it and where they went, and, also important, *how* they went. Did they go of their own free will? Were they kidnapped? Were they blackmailed into going? What route did they take—what kind of organisation is it that sets this in motion and what is its ultimate aim? Lots of questions. We want the answer to them. You might be able to help get us that answer."

Hilary stared at him.

"Me? How? Why?"

"I'm coming down to the particular case of Thomas Betterton. He disappeared from Paris just over two months ago. He left a wife in England. She was distracted—or said she was distracted. She swore that she had no idea why he'd gone or where or how. That may be true, or it may not. Some people—and I'm one of them—think it wasn't true."

Hilary leaned forward in her chair. In spite of herself she was becoming interested. Jessop went on.

"We prepared to keep a nice, unobtrusive eye on Mrs. Betterton. About a fortnight ago she came to me and told me she had been ordered by her doctor to go abroad, take a thorough rest and get some distraction. She was doing no good in England, and people were continually bothering her— newspaper reporters, relations, kind friends."

Hilary said drily: "I can imagine it."

"Yes, tough. Quite natural she would want to get away for a bit."

"Quite natural, I should think."

"But we've got nasty, suspicious minds in our department, you know. We arranged to keep tabs on Mrs. Betterton. Yesterday she left England as arranged, for Casablanca."

"Casablanca?"

"Yes—*en route* to other places in Morocco, of course. All quite open and above board, plans made, bookings ahead. But it may be that this trip to Morocco is where Mrs. Betterton steps off into the unknown."

Hilary shrugged her shoulders.

"I don't see where I come in to all this."

Jessop smiled.

"You come into it because you've got a very magnificent head of red hair, Mrs. Craven."

"*Hair?*"

"Yes. It's the most noticeable thing about Mrs. Betterton—her hair. You've heard, perhaps, that the plane before yours today crashed on landing."

"I know. I should have been on that plane. I actually had reservations for it."

"Interesting," said Jessop. "Well, Mrs. Betterton *was* on that plane. She wasn't killed. She was taken out of the wreckage still alive, and she is in hospital now. But according to the doctor, she won't be alive tomorrow morning."

A faint glimmer of light came to Hilary. She looked at him enquiringly.

"Yes," said Jessop, "perhaps now you see the form of suicide I'm offering you. I'm suggesting that Mrs. Betterton goes on with her journey. I'm suggesting that you should become Mrs. Betterton."

"But surely," said Hilary, "that would be quite impossible. I mean, they'd know at once she wasn't me."

Jessop put his head on one side.

"That, of course, depends entirely on who you mean by 'they.' It's a very vague term. Who is or are 'they?' Is there such a thing, are there such persons as 'they?' We don't know. But I can tell you this. If the most popular explanation of 'they' is accepted, then these people work in very close, self-contained cells. They do that for their own security. If Mrs. Betterton's journey had a purpose and is planned, then the people who were in charge of it here will know nothing about the English side of it. At the appointed moment they will contact a certain woman at a certain place, and carry on from there. Mrs. Betterton's passport description is five-feet-seven, red hair, blue eyes, mouth medium, no distinguishing marks. Good enough."

"But the authorities here. Surely they—"

Jessop smiled. "That part of it will be quite all right. The French have lost a few valuable young scientists and chemists of their own. They'll co-operate. The facts will be as follows. Mrs. Betterton, suffering from concussion, is taken to hospital. Mrs. Craven, another passenger in the crashed plane will also be admitted to hospital. Within a day or two *Mrs. Craven will die in hospital,* and Mrs. Betterton will be discharged, suffering slightly from concussion, but able to proceed on her tour. The crash was genuine, the concussion is genuine, and concussion makes a very good cover for you. It excuses a lot of things like lapses of memory and various unpredictable behaviour."

Hilary said:

"It would be madness!"

"Oh, yes," said Jessop, "it's madness, all right. It's a very tough assignment and if our suspicions are realised, you'll probably cop it. You see, I'm being quite frank, but according to you, you're prepared and anxious to cop it. As an alternative to throwing yourself in front of a train or something like that, I should think you'd find it far more amusing."

Suddenly and unexpectedly Hilary laughed.

"I do believe," she said, "that you're quite right."

"You'll do it?"

"Yes. Why not."

"In that case," said Jessop, rising in his seat with sudden energy, "there's absolutely no time to be lost."

CHAPTER IV

IT WAS NOT really cold in the hospital but it felt cold. There was a smell of antiseptics in the air. Occasionally in the corridor outside could be heard the rattle of glasses and instruments as a trolley was pushed by. Hilary Craven sat in a hard iron chair by a bedside.

In the bed, lying flat under a shaded light with her head bandaged, Olive Betterton lay unconscious. There was a nurse standing on one side of the bed and the doctor on the other. Jessop sat in a chair in the far corner of the room. The doctor turned to him and spoke in French.

"It will not be very long now," he said. "The pulse is very much weaker."

"And she will not recover consciousness?"

The Frenchman shrugged his shoulders.

"That I cannot say. It may be, yes, at the very end."

"There is nothing you can do—no stimulant?"

The doctor shook his head. He went out. The nurse followed him. She was replaced by a nun who moved to the head of the bed, and stood there, fingering her rosary. Hilary looked at Jessop and in obedience to a glance from him came to join him.

"You heard what the doctor said?" he asked in a low voice.

"Yes. What is it you want to say to her?"

"If she regains consciousness I want any information you can possibly get, any password, any sign, any message, *anything*. Do you understand? She is more likely to speak to you than to me."

Hilary said with sudden emotion:

"You want me to betray someone who is dying?"

Jessop put his head on one side in the birdlike manner which he sometimes adopted.

"So it seems like that to you, does it?" he said, considering.

"Yes, it does."

He looked at her thoughtfully.

"Very well then, you shall say and do what you please. For myself I can have no scruples! You understand that?"

"Of course. It's your duty. You'll do whatever questioning you please, but don't ask *me* to do it."

"You're a free agent."

"There is one question we shall have to decide. Are we to tell her that she is dying?"

"I don't know. I shall have to think it out."

She nodded and went back to her place by the bed. She was filled now with a deep compassion for the woman who lay there dying. The woman who was on her way to join the man she loved. Or were they all wrong? Had she come to Morocco simply to seek solace, to pass the time until perhaps some definite news could come to her as to whether her husband were alive or dead? Hilary wondered.

Time went on. It was nearly two hours later when the click of the nun's beads stopped. She spoke in a soft impersonal voice.

"There is a change," she said. "I think, Madame, it is the end that comes. I will fetch the doctor."

She left the room. Jessop moved to the opposite side of the bed, standing back against the wall so that he was out of the woman's range of vision. The eyelids flickered and opened. Pale incurious blue eyes looked into Hilary's. They closed, then opened again. A faint air of perplexity seemed to come into them.

"Where . . . ?"

The word fluttered between the almost breathless lips, just as the doctor entered the room. He took her hand in his, his finger on the pulse, standing by the bed looking down on her.

"You are in hospital, Madame," he said. "There was an accident to the plane."

"To the plane?"

The words were repeated dreamily in that faint breathless voice.

"Is there anyone you want to see in Casablanca, Madame? Any message we can take?"

Her eyes were raised painfully to the doctor's face. She said:

"No."

She looked back again at Hilary.

"Who—who—"

Hilary bent forward and spoke clearly and distinctly.

"I came out from England on a plane, too—if there is anything I can do to help you, please tell me."

"No—nothing—nothing—unless—"

"Yes?"

"Nothing."

The eyes flickered again and half closed—Hilary raised her head and looked across to meet Jessop's imperious commanding glance. Firmly, she shook her head.

Jessop moved forward. He stood close beside the doctor. The dying woman's eyes opened again. Sudden recognition came into them. She said: "I know *you*."

"Yes, Mrs. Betterton, you know me. Will you tell me anything you can about your husband?"

"No."

Her eyelids fell again. Jessop turned quietly and left the room. The doctor looked across at Hilary. He said very softly,

"*C'est la fin!*"

The dying woman's eyes opened again. They travelled painfully round the room, then they remained fixed on Hilary. Olive Betterton made a very faint motion with her hand, and Hilary instinctively took the white cold hand between her own. The doctor, with a shrug of his shoulders and a little bow, left the room. The two women were alone together. Olive Betterton was trying to speak:

"Tell me—tell me—"

Hilary knew what she was asking, and suddenly her own course of action opened clearly before her. She leaned down over the recumbent form.

"Yes," she said, her words clear and emphatic. "You are dying. That's what you want to know, isn't it? Now listen to me. I am going to try and reach your husband. Is there any message you want me to give him if I succeed?"

"Tell him—tell him—to be careful. Boris—Boris—dangerous. . . ."

The breath fluttered off again with a sigh. Hilary bent closer.

"Is there anything you can tell me to help me—help me in my journey, I mean? Help me to get in contact with your husband?"

"*Snow.*"

The word came so faintly that Hilary was puzzled. Snow? *Snow?* She repeated it uncomprehendingly. A faint, ghostlike little giggle came from Olive Betterton. Faint words came tumbling out:

> "*Snow, snow, beautiful snow!*
> *You slip on a lump, and over you go!*"

She repeated the last word. "Go . . . Go? Go and tell him about Boris. I didn't believe it. I *wouldn't* believe it. But perhaps it's true. . . . If so, if so . . ." a kind of agonised question came into her eyes which stared up into Hilary's. ". . . take care. . . ."

A queer little rattle came to her throat. Her lips jerked.
Olive Betterton died.

II

The next five days were strenuous mentally, though inactive physically.
Immured in a private room in the hospital, Hilary was set to work. Every
evening she had to pass an examination on what she had studied that
day. All the details of Olive Betterton's life, as far as they could be ascertained, were set down on paper and she had to memorise and learn
them by heart. The house she had lived in, the daily women she had employed, her relations, the names of her pet dog and her canary, every detail
of the six months of her married life with Thomas Betterton. Her wedding,
the names of her bridesmaids, their dresses, the patterns of curtains, car-
pets and chintzes. Olive Betterton's tastes, predilections and day by day
activities. Her preferences in food and drink. Hilary was forced to marvel
at the amount of seemingly meaningless information that had been massed
together. Once she said to Jessop;
"Can any of this possibly *matter*?"
And to that he had replied quietly:
"Probably not. But you've got to make yourself into the authentic article.
Think of it this way, Hilary. You're a writer. You're writing a book about
a woman. The woman is Olive. You describe scenes of her childhood, her
girlhood; you describe her marriage, the house she lived in. All the time
that you do it she becomes more and more of a real person to you. Then
you go over it a second time. You write it this time as an autobiography.
You write it *in the first person*. Do you see what I mean?"
She nodded slowly, impressed in spite of herself.
"You can't think of yourself as Olive Betterton until you *are* Olive Betterton. It would be better if you had time to learn it up, but *we can't afford
time*. So I've got to cram you. Cram you like a schoolboy—like a student
who is going in for an important examination." He added, "You've got a
quick brain and a good memory, thank the Lord."
He looked at her in cool appraisement.
The passport descriptions of Olive Betterton and Hilary Craven were
almost identical, but actually the two faces were entirely different. Olive
Betterton had had a quality of rather commonplace and insignificant
prettiness. She had looked obstinate but not intelligent. Hilary's face had
power and an intriguing quality. The deep set bluish-green eyes under
dark level brows had fire and intelligence in their depths. Her mouth
curved upwards in a wide and generous line. The plane of the jaw was

unusual—a sculptor would have found the angles of the face interesting.

Jessop thought: "There's passion there—and guts—and somewhere, damped but not quenched, there's a gay spirit that's tough—and that enjoys life and searches out for adventure."

"You'll do," he said to her. "You're an apt pupil."

This challenge to her intellect and her memory had stimulated Hilary. She was becoming interested now, keen to achieve success. Once or twice objections occurred to her. She voiced them to Jessop.

"You say that I shan't be rejected as Olive Betterton. You say that they won't know what she looks like, except in general detail. But how sure can you be of that?"

Jessop shrugged his shoulders.

"One can't be sure—of anything. But we do know a certain amount about the set up of these shows, and it does seem that internationally there is very little communication from one country to another. Actually, that's a great advantage to *them*. If we come upon a weak link in England (and, mind you, in every organisation there always will be a weak link), that weak link in the chain knows nothing about what's going on in France, or Italy, or Germany, or wherever you like, we are brought up short by a blank wall. They know their own little part of the whole—no more. The same applies the opposite way round. I dare swear that all the cell operating here knows is that Olive Betterton will arrive on such and such a plane and is to be given such and such instructions. You see, it's not as though she were important in *herself*. If they're bringing her to her husband, it's because her husband wants her brought to him and because they think they'll get better work out of him if she joins him. She herself is a mere pawn in the game. You must remember too, that the idea of substituting a false Olive Betterton is definitely a spur of the moment improvisation— occasioned by the plane accident and the colour of your hair. Our plan of operation was to keep tabs on Olive Betterton and find out where she went, *how* she went, whom she met—and so on. That's what the other side will be on the look out for."

Hilary asked:

"Haven't you tried all that before?"

"Yes. It was tried in Switzerland. Very unobtrusively. And it failed as far as our main objective was concerned. *If* anyone contacted her there we didn't know about it. So the contact must have been very brief. Naturally they'll expect that someone will be keeping tabs on Olive Betterton. They'll be prepared for that. It's up to us to do our job more thoroughly than last time. We've got to try and be rather more cunning than our adversaries."

"So you'll be keeping tabs on me?"

"Of course."

"How?"

He shook his head.

"I shan't tell you that. Much better for you not to know. What you don't know you can't give away."

"Do you think I would give it away?"

Jessop put on his owl-like expression again.

"I don't know how good an actress you are—how good a liar. It's not easy, you know. It's not a question of *saying* anything indiscreet. It can be anything, a sudden intake of the breath, the momentary pause in some action—lighting a cigarette, for instance. Recognition of a name or a friend. You could cover it up quickly, but just a flash might be enough!"

"I see. It means—being on your guard for every single split second."

"Exactly. In the meantime, on with the lessons! Quite like going back to school, isn't it? You're pretty well word-perfect on Olive Betterton, now. Let's go on to the other."

Codes, responses, various properties. The lesson went on, the questioning, the repetition, the endeavour to confuse her, to trip her up; then hypothetical schemes and her own reactions to them. In the end, Jessop nodded his head and declared himself satisfied.

"You'll do," he said. He patted her on the shoulder in an avuncular manner. "You're an apt pupil. And remember this, however much you may feel at times that you're all alone in this, you're probably not. I say *probably*—I won't put it higher than that. These are clever devils."

"What happens," said Hilary, "if I reach journey's end?"

"You mean?"

"I mean when at last I come face to face with Tom Betterton."

Jessop nodded grimly.

"Yes," he said. "That's the danger moment. I can only say that at that moment, *if all has gone well*, you *should* have protection. If, that is to say, things have gone as we *hope*; but the very basis of this operation, as you may remember, was that there wasn't a very high chance of survival."

"Didn't you say one in a hundred?" said Hilary drily.

"I think we can shorten the odds a little. I didn't know what you were like."

"No, I suppose not." She was thoughtful. "To you, I suppose, I was just . . ."

He finished the sentence for her:

"A woman with a noticeable head of red hair and who hadn't the pluck to go on living."

She flushed.

"That's a harsh judgment."

"It's a true one, isn't it? I don't go in for being sorry for people. For one thing it's insulting. One is only sorry for people when they're sorry for themselves. Self-pity is one of the biggest stumbling blocks in the world today."

Hilary said thoughtfully:

"I think perhaps you're right. Will you permit yourself to be sorry for me when I've been liquidated or whatever the term is, in fulfilling this mission?"

"Sorry for you? No. I shall curse like hell because we've lost someone who's worth while taking a bit of trouble over."

"A compliment at last." In spite of herself she was pleased.

She went on in a practical tone:

"There's just one other thing that occurred to me. You say nobody's likely to know what Olive Betterton looks like, but what about being recognised as *myself?* I don't know anyone in Casablanca, but there are the people who travelled here with me in the plane. Or one may of course run across somebody one knows among the tourists here."

"You needn't worry about the passengers in the plane. The people who flew with you from Paris were business men who went on to Dakar and a man who got off here who has since flown back to Paris. You will go to a different hotel when you leave here, the hotel for which Mrs. Betterton had reservations. You will be wearing her clothes and her style of hair-dressing and one or two strips of plaster at the sides of your face will make you look very different in feature. We've got a doctor coming to work upon you, by the way. Local anaesthetic, so it won't hurt, but you will have to have a few genuine marks of the accident."

"You're very thorough," said Hilary.

"Have to be."

"You've never asked me," said Hilary, "whether Olive Betterton told me anything before she died."

"I understood you had scruples."

"I'm sorry."

"Not at all. I respect you for them. I'd like to indulge in them myself— but they're not in the schedule."

"She did say something that perhaps I ought to tell you. She said 'Tell him'—Betterton, that is—'tell him to be careful—Boris—dangerous—'"

"Boris." Jessop repeated the name with interest. "Ah! Our correct foreign Major Boris Glydr."

"You know him? Who is he?"

"A Pole. He came to see me in London. He's supposed to be a cousin of Tom Betterton by marriage."

"Supposed?"

"Let us say, more correctly, that if he is who he says he is, he is a cousin of the late Mrs. Betterton. But we've only his word for it."

"She was frightened," said Hilary, frowning. "Can you describe him? I'd like to be able to recognise him."

"Yes. It might be as well. Six foot. Weight roughly 160 lbs. Fair—rather wooden poker face—light eyes—foreign stilted manner—English very correct, but a pronounced accent, military bearing."

He added:

"I had him tailed when he left my office. Nothing doing. He went straight to the U.S. Embassy—quite correctly—he'd brought me an introductory letter from there. The usual kind they send out when they want to be polite but non-committal. I presume he left the Embassy either in somebody's car or by the back entrance disguised as a footman or something. Anyway he evaded us. Yes—I should say that Olive Betterton was perhaps right when she said that Boris Glydr was dangerous."

CHAPTER V

IN THE SMALL formal salon of the Hotel St. Louis, three ladies were sitting, each engaged in her particular occupation. Mrs. Calvin Baker, short, plump, with well blued hair, was writing letters with the same driving energy she applied to all forms of activity. No one could have mistaken Mrs. Calvin Baker for anything but a travelling American, comfortably off, with an inexhaustible thirst for precise information on every subject under the sun.

In an uncomfortable Empire type chair, Miss Hetherington who again could not have been mistaken for anything but travelling English, was knitting one of those melancholy shapeless looking garments that English ladies of middle age always seem to be knitting. Miss Hetherington was tall and thin with a scraggy neck, badly arranged hair, and a general expression of moral disapprovement of the Universe.

Mademoiselle Jeanne Maricot was sitting gracefully in an upright chair, looking out of the window and yawning. Mademoiselle Maricot was a brunette dyed blonde, with a plain but excitingly made-up face. She was wearing chic clothes and had no interest whatsoever in the other occupants of the room whom she dismissed contemptuously in her mind as being exactly what they were! She was contemplating an important change in her sex life and had no interest to spare for these animals of tourists!

Miss Hetherington and Mrs. Calvin Baker, having both spent a couple of nights under the roof of the St. Louis, had become acquainted. Mrs. Calvin Baker, with American friendliness, talked to everybody. Miss Hetherington, though just as eager for companionship, talked only to English and Americans of what she considered a certain social standing. The French she had no truck with unless guaranteed of respectable family life as evidenced by little ones who shared the parental table in the dining room.

A Frenchman looking like a prosperous business man glanced into the salon, was intimidated by its air of female solidarity and went out again with a look of lingering regret at Mademoiselle Jeanne Maricot.

Miss Hetherington began to count stitches *sotto voce*.

"Twenty-eight, twenty-nine—now what can I have— Oh, I see."

A tall woman with red hair looked into the room and hesitated a moment before going on down the passage towards the dining room.

Mrs. Calvin Baker and Miss Hetherington were immediately alert. Mrs. Baker slewed herself round from the writing table and spoke in a thrilled whisper.

"Did you happen to notice that woman with red hair who looked in, Miss Hetherington? They say she's the only survivor of that terrible plane crash last week."

"I saw her arrive this afternoon," said Miss Hetherington, dropping another stitch in her excitement. "*In an ambulance.*"

"Straight from the hospital, so the Manager said. I wonder now if it was wise—to leave hospital so soon. She's had concussion, I believe."

"She's got strapping on her face, too—cut, perhaps, by the glass. What a mercy she wasn't burned. Terrible injuries from burning in these air accidents, I believe."

"It just doesn't bear thinking about. Poor young thing. I wonder if she had a husband with her and if he was killed?"

"I don't think so," Miss Hetherington shook her yellow grey head. "It said in the paper, one woman passenger."

"That's right. It gave her name, too. A Mrs. Beverly—no, Betterton, that was it."

"Betterton," said Miss Hetherington reflectively. "Now what does that remind me of? Betterton. In the papers. Oh, dear, I'm sure that was the name."

"*Tant pis pour Pierre,*" Mademoiselle Maricot said to herself. "*Il est vraiment insupportable! Mais le petit Jules, lui il est bien gentil. Et son père est tres bien placé dans les affaires. Enfin, je me decide!*"

And with long graceful steps Mademoiselle Maricot walked out of the small salon and out of the story.

II

Mrs. Thomas Betterton had left the hospital that afternoon five days after the accident. An ambulance had driven her to the Hotel St. Louis.

Looking pale and ill, her face strapped and bandaged, Mrs. Betterton was shown at once to the room reserved for her, a sympathetic manager hovering in attendance.

"What emotions you must have experienced, Madame!" he said, after enquiring tenderly as to whether the room reserved suited her, and turning on all the electric lights quite unnecessarily. "But what an escape! What a miracle! What good fortune. Only three survivors, I understand, and one of them in a critical condition still."

Hilary sank down on a chair wearily.

"Yes, indeed," she murmured. "I can hardly believe it myself. Even now I can remember so little. The last twenty-four hours before the crash are still quite vague to me."

The manager nodded sympathetically.

"Ah, yes. That is the result of the concussion. That happens once to a sister of mine. She was in London in the war. A bomb came, she was knocked unconscious. But presently she gets up, she walks about London and she takes a train from the station of Euston and, *figurez-vous*, she wakes up at Liverpool and she cannot remember anything of the bomb, of going across London, of the train or of getting there! The last thing she remembers is hanging up her skirt in the wardrobe in London. Very curious these things, are they not?"

Hilary agreed that they were, indeed. The manager bowed and departed. Hilary got up and looked at herself in the glass. So imbued was she now with her new personality that she positively felt the weakness in her limbs which would be natural to one who had just come out of hospital after a severe ordeal.

She had already enquired at the desk, but there had been no messages or letters for her there. The first steps in her new role had to be taken very much in the dark. Olive Betterton might perhaps have been told to ring a certain number or to contact a certain person at Casablanca. As to that there was no clue. All the knowledge she had to go on was Olive Betterton's passport, her letter of credit, and her book of Cook's tickets and reservations. These provided for two days in Casablanca, six days in Fez and five days in Marrakesh. These reservations were now, of course, out of date, and would have to be dealt with accordingly. The passport, the Letter of Credit and the accompanying Letter of Identification had been suitably dealt with. The photograph on the passport was now that of Hilary, the signature on the Letter of Credit was *Olive Betterton* in Hilary's handwriting. Her credentials were all in order. Her task was to play her part adequately and to wait. Her master card must be the plane accident, and its resultant loss of memory and general haziness.

It had been a genuine accident and Olive Betterton had been genuinely on board the plane. The fact of concussion would adequately cover her failure to adopt any measures in which she might have been instructed. Bewildered, dazed, weak, Olive Betterton would await orders.

The natural thing to do would be to rest. Accordingly she lay down on the bed. For two hours she went over in her mind all that she had been taught. Olive's luggage had been destroyed in the plane. Hilary had a few things with her supplied at the hospital. She passed a comb through her hair, touched her lips with a lipstick and went down to the hotel dining room for dinner.

She was looked at, she noticed, with a certain amount of interest. There were several tables occupied by business men and these hardly vouchsafed a glance at her. But at other tables, clearly occupied by tourists, she was conscious of a murmur and a whisper going on.

"That woman over there—the one with the red hair—she's a survivor of the plane crash, my dear. Yes, came from hospital in an ambulance. I saw her arrive. She looks terribly ill still. I wonder if they ought to have let her out so soon. What a frightful experience. What a merciful escape!"

After dinner Hilary sat for a short while in the small formal salon. She wondered if anyone would approach her in any way. There were one or two other women scattered about the room, and presently a small, plump, middle-aged woman with well-blued white hair, moved to a chair near hers. She opened proceedings in a brisk, pleasant American voice.

"I do hope you'll excuse me, but I just felt I had to say a word. It's you, isn't it, who had the *wonderful* escape from that air crash the other day?"

Hilary put down the magazine she was reading.

"Yes," she said.

"My! Isn't that terrible? The crash I mean. Only three survivors, they say. Is that right?"

"Only two," said Hilary. "One of the three died in hospital."

"My! You don't say! Now, if you don't mind my asking, Miss—Mrs. . . ."

"Betterton."

"Well, if you don't mind my asking, just where were you sitting in that plane? Were you up at the front or near the tail?"

Hilary knew the answer to that one and gave it promptly.

"Near the tail."

"They always say, don't they, that's the safest place. I just insist now on always having a place near the rear doors. Did you hear that, Miss Hetherington?" She turned her head to include another middle-aged lady. This one was uncompromisingly British with a long, sad, horselike face. "It's just as I was saying the other day. Whenever you go into an aeroplane, don't you let those air hostesses take you right up to the front."

"I suppose someone has to sit at the front," said Hilary.

"Well, it won't be me," said her new American friend promptly. "My name's Baker, by the way, Mrs. Calvin Baker."

Hilary acknowledged the introduction and Mrs. Baker plunged on, monopolising the conversation easily.

"I've just come here from Mogador and Miss Hetherington has come from Tangier. We became acquainted here. Are you going to visit Marrakesh, Mrs. Betterton?"

"I'd arranged to do so," said Hilary. "Of course, this accident has thrown out all my time schedule."

"Why, naturally, I can see that. But you really mustn't miss Marrakesh, wouldn't you say so, Miss Hetherington?"

"Marrakesh is terribly expensive," said Miss Hetherington. "This miserable travel allowance makes everything so difficult."

"There's a wonderful hotel, the Mamounia," continued Mrs. Baker.

"Wickedly expensive," said Miss Hetherington. "Out of the question for *me*. Of course, it's different for you, Mrs. Baker—dollars, I mean. But someone gave me the name of a small hotel there, really very nice and clean, and the food, they say, is not at all bad."

"Where else do you plan to go, Mrs. Betterton?" asked Mrs. Calvin Baker.

"I would like to see Fez," said Hilary, cautiously. "I shall have to get fresh reservations, of course."

"Oh, yes, you certainly oughtn't to miss Fez or Rabat."

"You've been there?"

"Not yet. I'm planning to go there shortly, and so is Miss Hetherington."

"I believe the old city is quite unspoiled," said Miss Hetherington.

The conversation continued in desultory fashion for some time further. Then Hilary pleaded fatigue from her first day out of the hospital and went up to her bedroom.

The evening so far had been quite indecisive. The two women who had talked to her had been such well-known travelling types that she could hardly believe that they were other than they seemed. Tomorrow, she decided, if she had received no word or communication of any kind, she would go to Cook's and raise the question of fresh reservations at Fez and Marrakesh.

There were no letters, messages or telephone calls the following morning and about eleven o'clock she made her way to the travel agency. There was somewhat of a queue, but when she at last reached the counter and began talking to the clerk, an interruption occurred. A somewhat more senior clerk with glasses elbowed the young man aside. He beamed at Hilary through his glasses.

"It is Madame Betterton, is it not? I have all your reservations made."

"I am afraid," said Hilary, "that they will be out of date. I have been in hospital and . . ."

"Ah, *mais oui*, I know all that. Let me congratulate you on your escape, Madame. But I got your telephone message about fresh reservations, and we have them here ready for you."

Hilary felt a faint quickening of her pulse. As far as she knew no one had phoned the travel agency. Here then were definite signs that Olive Betterton's travelling arrangements were being supervised. She said,

"I wasn't sure if they had telephoned or not."

"But yes, Madame. Here, I will show you."

He produced railway tickets, and vouchers for hotel accommodation, and a few minutes later the transactions were completed. Hilary was to leave for Fez on the following day.

Mrs. Calvin Baker was not in the restaurant either for lunch or dinner. Miss Hetherington was. She acknowledged Hilary's bow as the latter passed to her table, but made no attempt to get into conversation with her. On the following day, after making some necessary purchases of clothes and underclothing, Hilary left by train for Fez.

III

It was on the day of Hilary's departure that Mrs. Calvin Baker coming into the hotel in her usual brisk fashion, was accosted by Miss Hetherington whose long thin nose was quivering with excitement.

"I've remembered about the name *Betterton*—the disappearing scientist. It was in all the papers. About two months ago."

"Why, now I do remember something. A British scientist—yes—he'd been at some conference in Paris."

"Yes—that's it. Now I wonder, do you think—this could possibly be his *wife*. I looked in the register and I see her address is Harwell—Harwell, you know, is the Atom Station. I do think all these atom bombs are very wrong. And Cobalt. Such a lovely colour in one's paint-box and I used it a lot as a child; the worst of all, I understand *nobody* can survive. We weren't meant to do these experiments. Somebody told me the other day that her cousin who is a very shrewd man, said the whole world might go *radio-active.*"

"My, my," said Mrs. Calvin Baker.

CHAPTER VI

CASABLANCA HAD VAGUELY disappointed Hilary by being such a prosperous-looking French town with no hint of the orient or mystery about it, except for the crowds in the streets.

The weather was still perfect, sunny and clear, and she enjoyed looking out of the train at the passing landscape as they journeyed northward. A small Frenchman who looked like a commercial traveller sat opposite to her, in the far corner was a somewhat disapproving-looking nun telling her beads, and two Moorish ladies with a great many packages who conversed gaily with one another, completed the complement of the carriage. Offering a light for her cigarette, the little Frenchman opposite soon entered into conversation. He pointed out things of interest as they passed, and gave her various information about the country. She found him interesting and intelligent.

"You should go to Rabat, Madame. It is a great mistake not to go to Rabat."

"I shall try to do so. But I have not very much time. Besides," she smiled. "Money is short. We can only take so much with us abroad, you know."

"But that is simple. One arranges with a friend here."

"I'm afraid I haven't got a convenient friend in Morocco."

"Next time you travel, Madame, send me a little word. I will give you my card. And I arrange everything. I travel often in England on business and you repay me there. It is all quite simple."

"That's very kind of you, and I hope I shall pay a second visit to Morocco."

"It must be a change for you, Madame, to come here from England. So cold, so foggy, so disagreeable."

"Yes, it's a great change."

"I, too, I travelled from Paris three weeks ago. It was then fog, rain and all of the most disgusting. I arrive here and all is sunshine. Though, mind you, the air is cold. But it is pure. Good pure air. How was the weather in England when you left?"

"Much as you say," said Hilary. "Fog."

"Ah yes, it is the foggy season. Snow—you have had snow this year?"

"No," said Hilary, "there has been no snow." She wondered to herself, amusedly, if this much-travelled little Frenchman was following what he considered to be the correct trend of English conversation, dealing principally with the weather. She asked him a question or two about the political situation in Morocco and in Algiers, and he responded willingly, showing himself to be well informed.

Glancing across at the far corner, Hilary observed the nun's eyes fixed disapprovingly on her. The Moroccan ladies got out and other travellers got in. It was evening when they arrived at Fez.

"Permit me to assist you, Madame."

Hilary was standing, rather bewildered at the bustle and noise of the station. Arab porters were seizing her luggage from her hands, shouting, yelling, calling, recommending different hotels. She turned gratefully to her new French acquaintance.

"You are going to the Palais Jamail, n'est-ce-pas, Madame?"

"Yes."

"That is right. It is eight kilometres from here, you understand."

"Eight kilometres?" Hilary was dismayed. "It's not in the town, then."

"It is by the old town," the Frenchman explained. "Me, I stay here at the hotel in the commercial new city. But for the holiday, the rest, the enjoyment, naturally you go to the Palais Jamail. It was a former residence, you understand, of the Moroccan nobility. It has beautiful gardens, and you go straight from it into the old city of Fez which is untouched. It does not seem as though the hotel had sent to meet this train. If you permit, I will arrange for a taxi for you."

"You're very kind, but . . ."

The Frenchman spoke in rapid Arabic to the porters and shortly afterwards Hilary took her place in a taxi, her baggage was pushed in, and the Frenchman told her exactly what to give the rapacious porters. He also dismissed them with a few sharp words of Arabic when they protested that the remuneration was inadequate. He whipped a card from his pocket and handed it to her.

"My card, Madame, and if I can be of assistance to you at any time, tell me. I shall be at the Grand Hotel here for the next four days."

He raised his hat and went away. Hilary looked down at the card which she could just see before they moved out of the lighted station.

Monsieur Henri Laurier

The taxi drove briskly out of the town, through the country, up a hill. Hilary tried to see, looking out of the windows, where she was going, but darkness had set in now. Except when they passed a lighted building nothing much could be seen. Was this, perhaps, where her journey diverged from the normal and entered the unknown? Was Monsieur Laurier an emissary from the organisation that had persuaded Thomas Betterton to leave his work, his home and his wife? She sat in the corner of the taxi, nervously apprehensive, wondering where it was taking her.

It took her, however, in the most exemplary manner to the Palais Jamail. She dismounted there, passed through an arched gateway and found herself, with a thrill of pleasure, in an oriental interior. There were long divans, coffee tables, and native rugs. From the reception desk she was taken through several rooms which led out of each other, out onto a terrace, passing by orange trees and scented flowers, and then up a winding staircase and into a pleasant bedroom, still oriental in style but equipped with all the *conforts modernes* so necessary to twentieth-century travellers.

Dinner, the porter informed her, took place from seven-thirty. She unpacked a little, washed, combed her hair and went downstairs through the long oriental smoking room, out on the terrace and across and up some steps to a lighted dining room running at right angles to it.

The dinner was excellent, and as Hilary ate, various people came and went from the restaurant. She was too tired to size them up and classify them this particular evening, but one or two outstanding personalities took her eye. An elderly man, very yellow of face, with a little goatee beard. She noticed him because of the extreme deference paid to him by the staff. Plates were whisked away and placed for him at the mere raising of his head. The slightest turn of an eyebrow brought a waiter rushing to his table. She wondered who he was. The majority of diners were clearly touring on pleasure trips. There was a German at a big table in the centre, there was a middle-aged man with a fair, very beautiful girl whom she thought might be Swedes, or possible Danes. There was an English family with two children, and various groups of travelling Americans. There were three French families.

After dinner she had coffee on the terrace. It was slightly cold but not unduly so and she enjoyed the smell of scented blossoms. She went to bed early.

Sitting on the terrace the following morning in the sunshine under the red striped umbrella that protected her from the sun, Hilary felt how fantastic the whole thing was. Here she sat, pretending to be a dead woman, expecting something melodramatic and out of the common to occur. After all, wasn't it only too likely that poor Olive Betterton had come abroad merely to distract her mind and heart from sad thoughts and feelings.

Probably the poor woman had been just as much in the dark as everybody else.

Certainly the words she had said before she died admitted of a perfectly ordinary explanation. She had wanted Thomas Betterton warned against somebody called Boris. Her mind had wandered—she had quoted a strange little jingle—she had gone on to say that she couldn't believe it at first. Couldn't believe what? Possibly only that Thomas Betterton had been spirited away the way he had been.

There had been no sinister undertones, no helpful clues. Hilary stared down at the terrace garden below her. It was beautiful here. Beautiful and peaceful. Children chattered and ran up and down the terrace, French mammas called to them or scolded them. The blonde Swedish girl came and sat down by a table and yawned. She took out a pale pink lipstick and touched up her already exquisitely painted lips. She appraised her face seriously, frowning a little.

Presently her companion—husband, Hilary wondered, or it might possibly be her father—joined her. She greeted him without a smile. She leaned forward and talked to him, apparently expostulating about something. He protested and apologised.

The old man with the yellow face and the little goatee came up the terrace from the gardens below. He went and sat at a table against the extreme wall, and immediately a waiter darted forth. He gave an order and the waiter bowed before him and went away, in all haste to execute it. The fair girl caught her companion excitedly by the arm and looked towards the elderly man.

Hilary ordered a Martini, and when it came she asked the waiter in a low voice,

"Who is the old man there against the wall?"

"Ah!" The waiter leaned forward dramatically, "That is Monsieur Aristides. He is enormously—but yes, enormously—rich."

He sighed in ecstasy at the contemplation of so much wealth and Hilary looked over at the shrivelled up, bent figure at the far table. Such a wrinkled, dried up, mummified old morsel of humanity. And yet, because of his enormous wealth, waiters darted and sprang and spoke with awe in their voices. Old Monsieur Aristides shifted his position. Just for a moment his eyes met hers. He looked at her for a moment, then looked away.

"Not so insignificant after all," Hilary thought to herself. Those eyes, even at that distance, had been wonderfully intelligent and alive.

The blonde girl and her escort got up from their table and went into the dining room. The waiter who now seemed to consider himself as Hilary's guide and mentor, stopped at her table as he collected glasses and gave her further information.

"*Ce Monsieur là,* he is a big business magnate from Sweden. Very rich, very important. And the lady with him she is a film star—another Garbo, they say. Very chic—very beautiful—but does she make him the scenes, the histories! Nothing pleases her. She is, as you say, 'fed up' to be here, in Fez, where there are no jewellers' shops—and no other expensive women to admire and envy her toilettes. She demands that he should take her somewhere more amusing tomorrow. Ah, it is not always the rich who can enjoy the tranquillity and peace of mind."

Having uttered this last in a somewhat sententious fashion, he saw a beckoning forefinger and sprang across the terrace as though galvanised.

"Monsieur?"

Most people had gone in to lunch, but Hilary had had breakfast late and was in no hurry for her midday meal. She ordered herself another drink. A good-looking young Frenchman came out of the bar and across the terrace, cast a swift, discreet glance at Hilary which, thinly disguised, meant: "Is there anything doing here, I wonder?" and then went down the steps to the terrace below. As he did so he half sang, half hummed a snatch of French opera,

> "*Le long des lauriers roses,*
> *Revant de douces choses.*"

The words formed a little pattern on Hilary's brain. *Le long des lauriers roses.* Laurier. *Laurier?* That was the name of the Frenchman in the train. Was there a connection here or was it coincidence? She opened her bag and hunted in it for the card he had given her. *Mons. Henri Laurier, 3 Rue des Croissants, Casablanca.* She turned the card over and there seemed to be faint pencil marks on the back of it. It was as though something had been written on it and then rubbed out. She tried to decipher what the marks were. "*Où sont,*" the message began, then something which she could not decipher, and finally she made out the words "*D'antan.*" For a moment she had thought that it might be a message, but now she shook her head and put the card back in her bag. It must have been some quotation that he had once written on it and then rubbed out.

A shadow fell on her and she looked up, startled. Mr. Aristides was standing there between her and the sun. His eyes were not on her. He was looking across over the gardens below towards the silhouette of hills in the distance. She heard him sigh and then he turned abruptly towards the dining room and as he did so, the sleeve of his coat caught the glass on her table and sent it flying to the terrace where it broke. He wheeled round quickly and politely.

"Ah. *Mille pardons, Madame.*"

Hilary assured him smilingly in French that it did not matter in the least. With the swift flick of a finger he summoned a waiter. The waiter as usual came running. He ordered a replacement of Madame's drink and then, once more apologising, he made his way into the restaurant.

The young Frenchman, still humming, came up the steps again. He lingered noticeably as he passed Hilary, but as she gave no sign, he went on into lunch with a slight philosophic shrug of the shoulders.

A French family passed across the terrace, the parents calling to their young.

"*Mais viens, donc, Bobo. Qu'est ce que tu fais? Dépêches toi!*"

"*Laisse ta balle, cherie, on va dejeuner.*"

They passed up the steps and into the restaurant, a happy contented little nucleus of family life. Hilary felt suddenly alone and frightened.

The waiter brought her drink. She asked him if M. Aristides was all alone here?

"Oh, Madame, naturally, anyone so rich as M. Aristides would never travel *alone*. He has here his valet and two secretaries and a chauffeur."

The waiter was quite shocked at the idea of M. Aristides travelling un-accompanied.

Hilary noted, however, when she at last went into the dining room that the old man sat at a table by himself as he had done on the previous eve-ning. At a table nearby sat two young men whom she thought were probably the secretaries since she noticed that one or the other of them was always on the alert and looked constantly towards the table where M. Aris-tides, shrivelled and monkey-like, ate his lunch and did not seem to notice their existence. Evidently to M. Aristides, secretaries were not human!

The afternoon passed in a vague dreamlike manner. Hilary strolled through the gardens, descending from terrace to terrace. The peace and the beauty seemed quite astounding. There was the splash of water, the gleam of the golden oranges, and innumerable scents and fragrances. It was the oriental atmosphere of seclusion about it that Hilary found so satisfying. *As a garden enclosed is my sister, my spouse* . . . This was what a garden was meant to be, a place shut away from the world—full of green and gold—

If I could stay here, thought Hilary. If I could stay here always . . .

It was not the actual garden of the Palais Jamail that was in her thoughts, it was the state of mind it typified. When she no longer looked for peace, she had found it. And peace of mind had come to her at a mo-ment when she was committed to adventure and danger.

But perhaps there was no danger and no adventure . . . Perhaps she could stay here awhile and nothing would happen . . . and then . . .

And then—what?

A little cold breeze sprang up and Hilary gave a quick shiver. You strayed into the garden of peaceful living, but in the end you would be betrayed from within. The turmoil of the world, the harshness of living, the regrets and despairs, all these she carried within her.

And it was late afternoon, and the sun had lost its power. Hilary went up the various terraces and into the hotel.

In the gloom of the Oriental Lounge, something voluble and cheerful resolved itself, as Hilary's eyes got attuned to the dimness, into Mrs. Calvin Baker, her hair newly blued, and her appearance immaculate as ever.

"I've just got here by air," she explained. "I simply can't stand these trains—the time they take! And the people in them, as often as not, quite unsanitary! They've no idea at all of hygiene in these countries. My dear, you should see the meat in the *souks*—all smothered in flies. They just seem to think it's *natural* to have flies settling on everything."

"I suppose it is really," said Hilary.

Mrs. Calvin Baker was not going to allow such a heretical statement to pass.

"I'm a great believer in the Clean Food movement. At home everything perishable is wrapped in cellophane—but even in London your bread and cakes just stand about unwrapped. Now tell me, have you been getting around? You've been doing the old city today, I expect?"

"I'm afraid I haven't 'done' anything," said Hilary, smiling. "I've just been sitting about in the sun."

"Ah, of course—you're just out of hospital. I forgot." Clearly only recent illness was accepted by Mrs. Calvin Baker as an excuse for failure to sightsee. "How could I be so stupid? Why, it's perfectly true, after concussion you ought to lie down and rest in a dark room most of the day. By and by we can make some expeditions together. I'm one of those people who likes a real packed day—everything planned and arranged. Every minute filled."

In Hilary's present mood, this sounded like a foretaste of hell, but she congratulated Mrs. Calvin Baker on her energy.

"Well, I will say that for a woman of my age I get around pretty well. I hardly ever feel fatigue. Do you remember Miss Hetherington at Casablanca? An Englishwoman with a long face. She'll be arriving this evening. She prefers train to flying. Who's staying in the hotel? Mostly French, I suppose. And honeymoon couples. I must run along now and see about my room. I didn't like the one they gave me and they promised to change it."

A miniature whirlwind of energy, Mrs. Calvin Baker departed.

When Hilary entered the dining room that evening, the first thing she saw was Miss Hetherington at a small table against the wall eating her dinner with a book propped up in front of her.

The three ladies had coffee together after dinner and Miss Hetherington displayed a pleasurable excitement over the Swedish magnate and the blonde film star.

"Not married, I understand," she breathed, disguising her pleasure with a correct disapproval. "One sees so much of that sort of thing abroad. That seemed a nice French family at the table by the window. The children seemed so fond of their papa. Of course, French children are allowed to sit up far too late. Ten o'clock sometimes before they go to bed, and they go through every course on the menu instead of just having milk and biscuits as children should."

"They seem to look quite healthy on it," said Hilary laughing.

Miss Hetherington shook her head and uttered a cluck of disapproval.

"They'll pay for it later," she said with grim foreboding, "their parents even let them drink *wine*."

Horror could go no further.

Mrs. Calvin Baker began making plans for the next day.

"I don't think I shall go to the old city," she said. "I did that very thoroughly last time. Most interesting and quite a labyrinth, if you know what I mean. So quaint and old world. If I hadn't had the guide with me, I don't think I should have found my way back to the hotel. You just kind of lose your sense of direction. But the guide was a very nice man and told me quite a lot of interesting things. He has a brother in the States—in Chicago, I think he said. Then when we'd finished with the town, he took me up to a kind of eating house or tea room, right up on the hillsides looking down over the old city—a marvellous view. I had to drink that dreadful mint tea, of course, which is really very nasty. And they wanted me to buy various things, some quite nice, but some just rubbish. One has to be very firm, I find."

"Yes, indeed," said Miss Hetherington.

She added rather wistfully, "And, of course, one can't really spare the money for souvenirs. These money restrictions are so worrying."

CHAPTER VII

HILARY HOPED TO avoid having to see the old city of Fez in the depressing company of Miss Hetherington. Fortunately the latter was invited by Mrs. Baker to come with her on an expedition by car. Since Mrs. Baker made it clear that she was going to pay for the car, Miss Hetherington, whose travelling allowance was dwindling in an alarming manner, accepted with avidity. Hilary, after inquiry at the desk, was supplied with a guide, and set forth to see the city of Fez.

They started from the terrace, going down through the succession of terraced gardens until they reached an enormous door in the wall at the bottom. The guide produced a key of mammoth proportions, unlocked the door which swung slowly open, and motioned Hilary to pass through.

It was like stepping into another world. All about her were the walls of Old Fez. Narrow winding streets, high walls, and occasionally, through a doorway, a glimpse of an interior or a courtyard, and moving all around her were laden donkeys, men with their burdens, boys, women veiled and unveiled, the whole busy secret life of this Moorish city. Wandering through the narrow streets she forgot everything else, her mission, the past tragedy of her life, even herself. She was all eyes and ears, living and walking in a dream world. The only annoyance was the guide who talked unceasingly, and urged her into various establishments into which she had no particular wish to go.

"You look, lady. This man have very nice things, very cheap, really old, really Moorish. He have gowns and silks. You like very nice beads?"

The eternal commerce of East selling to West went on, but it hardly disturbed the charm for Hilary. She soon lost all sense of place or direction. Here within this walled city she had little idea of whether she was walking north or south or whether she were retracing her steps over the same streets through which she had already passed. She was quite exhausted when the guide made his final suggestion, which was evidently part of the routine.

"I take you very nice house, now, very superior. Friends of mine. You have mint tea there and they show you plenty lovely things."

Hilary recognised the well-known gambit which Mrs. Calvin Baker had described. However, she was willing to see, or be taken to see, anything that was suggested. Tomorrow, she promised herself, she would come into the Old City alone and wander around without a guide chattering by her elbow. So she allowed herself to be guided through a gateway and up a winding path climbing up more or less outside the city walls. They arrived at last at a garden surrounding an attractive house built in native style.

Here in a big room with a fine view out over the city, she was urged to sit down at a small coffee table. In due course glasses of mint tea were brought. To Hilary who did not like sugar with her tea, it was somewhat of an ordeal to drink it. But by banishing the idea of tea from her mind, and merely thinking of it as a new kind of lemonade, she managed almost to enjoy it. She enjoyed, too, being shown rugs and beads and draperies, embroideries and various other things. She made one or two small purchases more out of good manners than for any other reason. The indefatigable guide then said,

"I have car ready now and take you very nice short drive. One hour, not more, see very beautiful scenery and country. And then back to hotel." He added, assuming a suitably discreet expression, "This girl here, she take you first to very nice ladies' toilet."

The girl who had served the tea was standing by them smiling, and said at once in careful English,

"Yes, yes, Madame. You come with me. We have very fine toilet, oh very fine. Just like the Ritz Hotel. Same as in New York or Chicago. You see!"

Smiling a little, Hilary followed the girl. The toilet hardly rose to the heights claimed for it, but it did at least have running water. There was a wash basin and a small cracked mirror which had such distorting proportions that Hilary almost shrank back in alarm at the sight of her own face. When she had washed and dried her hands, which she did on her own handkerchief, not much caring for the appearance of the towel, she turned to leave.

In some way, however, the door of the toilet appeared to have stuck. She turned and rattled the handle unavailingly. It would not move. Hilary wondered whether it had been bolted or locked from the outside. She grew angry. What was the idea of shutting her in there? Then she noticed that there was another door in a corner of the room. Going to it she turned the handle. This time the door opened easily enough. She passed through.

She found herself in a small eastern looking room with light that came only from slits high in the wall. Sitting there on a low divan, smoking, was the little Frenchman she had met in the train, M. Henri Laurier.

II

He did not rise to greet her. He merely said, and the timbre of his voice was slightly changed,

"Good afternoon, Mrs. Betterton."

For a moment Hilary stood motionless. Astonishment held her in its grip. So this—was *it!* She pulled herself together. "This is what you've been expecting. Act as you think *she* would act." She came forward and said eagerly,

"You have news for me? You can help me?"

He nodded, then said reproachfully:

"I found you, Madame, somewhat obtuse upon the train. Perhaps you are too well accustomed to talk of the weather."

"The weather?" She stared at him, bewildered.

What had he said about weather on the train? Cold? Fog? Snow?

Snow. That was what Olive Betterton had whispered as she lay dying. And she had quoted a silly little jingle—what was it?

> *Snow, snow, beautiful snow,*
> *You slip on a lump and over you go.*

Hilary repeated it falteringly now.

"Exactly—why did you not respond with that immediately as ordered?"

"You don't understand. I have been ill. I was in a plane crash and afterwards in hospital with concussion. It's affected my memory in all sorts of ways. Everything long ago is clear enough, but there are terrible blanks—great gaps." She let her hands rise to her head. She found it easy enough to go on with a real tremor in her voice. "You can't understand how frightening that is. I keep feeling that I've forgotten important things—really important things. The more I try to get them back, the less they will come."

"Yes," said Laurier, "the aeroplane crash was unfortunate." He spoke in a cold businesslike way. "It is going to be a question of whether you have the necessary stamina and courage to continue your journey."

"Of course I'm going to continue my journey," cried Hilary. "My husband—" her voice broke.

He smiled, but not a very pleasant smile. Faintly catlike.

"Your husband," he said, "is, I understand, awaiting you with eagerness." Hilary's voice broke.

"You have no idea," she said, "no idea what it's been like these months since he went away."

"Do you think the British authorities came to a definite conclusion as to what you did or did not know?"

Hilary stretched out her hands with a wide gesture.

"How do I know—how can I tell? They *seemed* satisfied."

"All the same . . ." he stopped.

"I think it quite possible," said Hilary slowly, "that I have been followed here. I can't pick out any one particular person but I have had the feeling ever since I left England that I am under observation."

"Naturally," said Laurier, coldly. "We expected no less."

"I thought I ought to warn you."

"My dear Mrs. Betterton, we are not children. We understand what we are doing."

"I'm sorry," said Hilary, humbly. "I'm afraid I'm very ignorant."

"It does not matter if you are ignorant so long as you are obedient."

"I shall be obedient," said Hilary in a low voice.

"You were closely watched in England, I have no doubt, ever since the day of your husband's departure. Nevertheless, the message came to you, did it not?"

"Yes," said Hilary.

"Now," said Laurier in a businesslike manner, "I will give you your instructions, Madame."

"Please do."

"From here you will proceed to Marrakesh the day after tomorrow. That is as you planned and in accordance with your reservations."

"Yes."

"The day after you arrive there you will receive a telegram from England. What it will say I do not know, but it will be sufficient for you to make plans immediately to return to England."

"I am to *return to England?*"

"Please listen. I have not finished. You will book a seat on a plane leaving Casablanca the following day."

"Supposing I cannot get reservations—supposing the seats are all booked?"

"They will not be all booked. Everything is arranged for. Now, you understand your instructions?"

"I understand."

"Then please return to where your guide is waiting. You have been long enough in this ladies' toilet. By the way, you have become friendly with an American woman and an English woman who are now staying at the Palais Jamail?"

"Yes. Has that been a mistake? It has been difficult to avoid."

"Not at all. It suits our plans admirably. If you can persuade one or other of them to accompany you to Marrakesh, so much the better. Goodbye, Madame."

"Au revoir, Monsieur."

"It is unlikely," Monsieur Laurier told her with a complete lack of interest, "that I shall meet you again."

Hilary retraced her steps to the ladies' toilet. This time she found the other door unfastened. A few minutes later she had rejoined the guide in the tea room.

"I got very nice car waiting," said the guide. "I take you now for very pleasant instructive drive."

The expedition proceeded according to plan.

III

"So you're leaving for Marrakesh tomorrow," said Miss Hetherington. "You haven't made a very long stay in Fez, have you? Wouldn't it have been much easier to go to Marrakesh first and then to Fez, returning to Casablanca afterwards?"

"I suppose it would really," said Hilary, "but reservations are rather difficult to obtain. It's pretty crowded here."

"Not with English people," said Miss Hetherington, rather disconsolately. "It really seems dreadful nowadays the way one meets hardly *any* of one's fellow countrymen." She looked round her disparagingly and said, "It's all the French."

Hilary smiled faintly. The fact that Morocco was a French colonial possession did not seem to count much with Miss Hetherington. Hotels anywhere abroad she regarded as the prerogative of the English travelling public.

"The French and the Germans *and* the Greeks," said Mrs. Calvin Baker, with a little cackle of laughter. "That scruffy little old man is a Greek, I believe."

"I was told he was Greek," said Hilary.

"Looks like a person of importance," said Mrs. Baker. "You see how the waiters fly about for him."

"They give the English hardly any attention nowadays," said Miss Hetherington, gloomily. "They always give them the most terrible back bedrooms—the ones maids and valets used to have in the old days."

"Well, I can't say I've found any fault with the accommodation I've had since I came to Morocco," said Mrs. Calvin Baker. "I've managed to get a most comfortable room and bath every time."

"You're an American," said Miss Hetherington, sharply, and with some venom in her voice. She clicked her knitting needles furiously.

"I wish I could persuade you two to come to Marrakesh with me," said Hilary. "It's been so pleasant meeting you and talking to you here. Really, it's very lonely travelling all by oneself."

"I've *been* to Marrakesh," said Miss Hetherington in a shocked voice.

Mrs. Calvin Baker, however, appeared to be somewhat sold on the idea.

"Well, it certainly is an idea," she said. "It's over a month since I was in Marrakesh. I'd be glad to go there again for a spell, and I could show you around, too, Mrs. Betterton and prevent you being imposed upon. It's not until you've been to a place and looked around it that you learn the ropes. I wonder now. I'll go to the office and see what I can fix up."

Miss Hetherington said acidly, when she had departed;

"That's exactly like these American women. Rushing from place to place, never settling down anywhere. Egypt one day, Palestine the next. Sometimes I really don't think they know what country they're in."

She shut her lips with a snap and rising and gathering up her knitting carefully, she left the Turkish room with a little nod to Hilary as she went. Hilary glanced down at her watch. She felt inclined not to change this evening for dinner, as she usually did. She sat on there alone in the low, rather dark room with its oriental hangings. A waiter looked in, then went away after turning on two lamps. They did not give out very much light and the room seemed pleasantly dim. It had an Eastern sort of serenity. Hilary sat back on the low divan, thinking of the future.

Only yesterday she had been wondering if the whole business upon which she had been engaged was a mare's nest. And now—now she was on the point of starting on her real journey. She must be careful, very careful. She must make no slip. She must be Olive Betterton, moderately well educated, inartistic, conventional but with definite Left Wing sympathies, and a woman who was devoted to her husband.

"I must make no mistake," said Hilary to herself, under her breath.

How strange it felt to be sitting here alone in Morocco. She felt as though she had got into a land of mystery and enchantment. That dim lamp beside her! If she were to take the carved brass between her hands and rub, would a Djin of the Lamp appear? As the thought came to her, she started. Materialising quite suddenly from beyond the lamp, she saw the small wrinkled face and pointed beard of M. Aristides. He bowed politely before sitting down beside her, saying;

"You permit, Madame?"

Hilary responded politely.

Taking out his cigarette case he offered her a cigarette. She accepted and he lit one himself also.

"It pleases you, this country, Madame?" he asked after a moment or two.

"I have been here only a very short time," said Hilary. "I find it so far quite enchanting."

"Ah. And you have been into the old city? You liked it?"

"I think it is wonderful."

"Yes, it is wonderful. It is the past there—the past of commerce, of intrigue, of whispering voices, shuttered activities, all the mystery and passion of a city enclosed in its narrow streets and walls. Do you know what I think of, Madame, when I walk through the streets of Fez?"

"No?"

"I think of your Great West Road in London. I think of your great factory buildings on each side of the road. I think of those buildings lit throughout with their neon lighting and the people inside, that you see so clearly from the road as you drive along in your car. There is nothing hidden, there is nothing mysterious. There are not even curtains to the windows. No, they do their work there with the whole world observing them if it wants to do so. It is like slicing off the top of an anthill."

"You mean," said Hilary, interested, "that it is the contrast that interests you?"

Mr. Aristides nodded his elderly, tortoiselike head.

"Yes," he said. "There everything is in the open and in the old streets of Fez nothing is *à jour*. Everything is hidden, dark. . . . *But—*" he leaned forward and tapped a finger on the little brass coffee table "—but the same things go on. The same cruelties, the same oppressions, the same wish for power, the same bargaining and haggling."

"You think that human nature is the same everywhere?" Hilary asked.

"In every country. In the past as in the present there are always the two things that rule. Cruelty and benevolence! One or the other. Sometimes both." He continued with hardly a change of manner, "They have told me, Madame, that you were in a very bad aeroplane accident the other day at Casablanca?"

"Yes, that is true."

"I envy you," Mr. Aristides said unexpectedly.

Hilary looked at him in an astonished manner. Again he waggled his head in vehement assertion.

"Yes," he added, "you are to be envied. You have had an experience. I should like the experience of having come so near to death. To have that, yet survive—do you not feel yourself different since then, Madame?"

"In a rather unfortunate way," said Hilary. "I had concussion and that gives me very bad headaches, and it also affects my memory."

"Those are mere inconveniences," said Mr. Aristides with a wave of the hand, "but it is an adventure of the spirit you have passed through, is it not?"

"It is true," said Hilary slowly, "that I have passed through an adventure of the spirit."

She was thinking of a bottle of Vichy water and a little heap of sleeping pills.

"I have never had that experience," said Mr. Aristides in his dissatisfied voice. "So many other things, but not that."

He rose, bowed, said, "*Mes homages, Madame,*" and left her.

CHAPTER VIII

How ALIKE, HILARY thought to herself, all airports were! They had a strange anonymity about them. They were all at some distance from the town or city they served, and in consequence you had a queer, stateless feeling of existing nowhere. You could fly from London to Madrid, to Rome, to Istanbul, to Cairo, to anywhere you liked and if your journey was a through one by air, you would never have the faintest idea of what any of these cities looked like! If you caught a glimpse of them from the air, they were only a kind of glorified map, something built with a child's box of bricks.

And why, she thought vexedly, looking round her, does one always have to be at these places so much too early?

They had spent nearly half an hour in the waiting room. Mrs. Calvin Baker, who had decided to accompany Hilary to Marrakesh had been talking non-stop ever since their arrival. Hilary had answered almost mechanically. But now she realised that the flow had been diverted. Mrs. Baker had now switched her attention to two other travellers who were sitting near her. They were both tall, fair young men. One an American with a broad, friendly grin, the other a rather solemn looking Dane or Norwegian. The Dane talked heavily, slowly, and rather pedantically in careful English. The American was clearly delighted to find another American traveller. Presently, in conscientious fashion, Mrs. Calvin Baker turned to Hilary.

"Mr—? I'd like to have you know my friend, Mrs. Betterton."

"Andrew Peters—Andy to my friends."

The other young man rose to his feet, bowed rather stiffly and said, "Torquil Ericsson."

"So now we're all acquainted," said Mrs. Baker happily. "Are we all going to Marrakesh? It's my friend's first visit there—"

"I, too," said Ericsson. "I, too, for the first time go."

"That goes for me too," said Peters.

The loud speaker was suddenly switched on and a hoarse announcement in French was made. The words were barely distinguishable but it appeared to be their summons to the plane.

There were four passengers besides Mrs. Baker and Hilary. Besides

Peters and Ericsson, there was a thin, tall Frenchman, and a severe-looking nun.

It was a clear, sunny day and flying conditions were good. Leaning back in her seat with half closed eyes, Hilary studied her fellow passengers, seeking to distract herself that way from the anxious questionings which were going on in her mind.

One seat ahead of her, on the other side of the aisle, Mrs. Calvin Baker in her grey travelling costume looked like a plump and contented duck. A small hat with wings was perched on her blue hair and she was turning the pages of a glossy magazine. Occasionally she leaned forward to tap the shoulder of the man sitting in front of her, who was the cheerful-looking fair young American, Peters. When she did so he turned round, displaying his good-humoured grin, and responding energetically to her remarks. How very good natured and friendly Americans were, Hilary thought to herself. So different from the stiff travelling English. She could not imagine Miss Hetherington, for instance, falling into easy conversation with a young man even of her own nation, on a plane, and she doubted if the latter would have responded as good-naturedly as this young American was doing.

Across the aisle from her was the Norwegian, Ericsson.

As she caught his eye, he made her a stiff little bow and leaning across offered her his magazine, which he was just closing. She thanked him and took it. In the seat behind him was the thin, dark Frenchman. His legs were stretched out and he seemed to be asleep.

Hilary turned her head over her shoulder. The severe-faced nun was sitting behind her, and the nun's eyes, impersonal, incurious, met Hilary's with no expression in them. She sat immovable, her hands clasped. It seemed to Hilary an odd trick of Time that a woman in traditional mediae-val costume should be travelling by air in the twentieth century.

Six people, thought Hilary, travelling together for a few hours, travelling to different places with different aims, scattering perhaps at the end of that few hours and never meeting again. She had read a novel which had hinged on a similar theme and where the lives of those six people were followed up. The Frenchman, she thought, must be on a holiday. He seemed so tired. The young American was perhaps a student of some kind. Ericsson was perhaps going to take up a job. The nun was doubtless bound for her convent.

Hilary closed her eyes and forgot her fellow travellers. She puzzled, as she had done all last night, over the instructions that had been given her. She was to return to England! It seemed crazy! Or could it be that in some way she had been found wanting, was not trusted: had failed to supply certain words or credentials that the real Olive would have supplied. She sighed and moved restlessly. "Well," she thought, "I can do no more than I am doing. If I've failed—I've failed. At any rate, I've done my best."

Then another thought struck her. Henri Laurier had accepted it as natural and inevitable that a close watch was being kept upon her in Morocco—was this a means of disarming suspicion? With the abrupt return of Mrs. Betterton to England it would surely be assumed that she had *not* come to Morocco in order to "disappear" like her husband. Suspicion would relax—she would be regarded as a *bona fide* traveller.

She would leave for England, going by Air France via Paris—and perhaps in Paris—

Yes, of course—in Paris. In Paris where Tom Betterton had disappeared. How much easier to stage a disappearance there. Perhaps Tom Betterton had never left Paris. Perhaps—tired of profitless speculation Hilary went to sleep. She woke—dozed again, occasionally glancing without interest, at the magazine she held. Awakening suddenly from a deeper sleep, she noticed that the plane was rapidly losing height and circling round. She glanced at her watch, but it was still some time earlier than the estimated time of arrival. Moreover, looking down through the window, she could not see any signs of an aerodrome beneath.

For a moment a faint qualm of apprehension struck her. The thin, dark Frenchman rose, yawned, stretched his arms and looked out and said something in French which she did not catch. But Ericsson leaned across the aisle and said,

"We are coming down here, it seems—but why?"

Mrs. Calvin Baker, leaning out of her seat, turned her head and nodded brightly as Hilary said,

"We seem to be landing."

The plane swooped round in ever lower circles. The country beneath them seemed to be practically desert. There were no signs of houses or villages. The wheels touched with a decided bump, bouncing along and taxiing until they finally stopped. It had been a somewhat rough landing, but it was a landing in the middle of nowhere.

Had something gone wrong with the engine, Hilary wondered, or had they run out of petrol? The pilot, a dark-skinned, handsome young man, came through the forward door and along the plane.

"If you please," he said, "you will all get out."

He opened the rear door, let down a short ladder and stood there waiting for them all to pass out. They stood in a little group on the ground, shivering a little. It was chilly here, with the wind blowing sharply from the mountains in the distance. The mountains, Hilary noticed, were covered with snow and singularly beautiful. The air was crisply cold and intoxicating. The pilot descended too, and addressed them, speaking French:

"You are all here? Yes? Excuse, please, you will have to wait a little minute, perhaps. Ah, no, I see it is arriving."

He pointed to where a small dot on the horizon was gradually growing nearer. Hilary said in a slightly bewildered voice:

"But why have we come down here? What is the matter? How long shall we have to be here?"

The French traveller said,

"There is, I understand, a station wagon arriving. We shall go on in that."

"Did the engine fail?" asked Hilary.

Andy Peters smiled cheerfully.

"Why no, I shouldn't say so," he said, "the engine sounded all right to me. However, they'll fix up something of that kind, no doubt."

She stared, puzzled. Mrs. Calvin Baker murmured,

"My, but it's chilly, standing about here. That's the worst of this climate. It seems so sunny but it's cold the moment you get near sunset."

The pilot was murmuring under his breath, swearing, Hilary thought. He was saying something like:

"*Toujours des retards insupportables.*"

The station wagon came towards them at a breakneck pace. The Berber driver drew up with a grinding of brakes. He sprang down and was immediately engaged by the pilot in angry conversation. Rather to Hilary's surprise, Mrs. Baker intervened in the dispute—speaking in French.

"Don't waste time," she said peremptorily. "What's the good of arguing? We want to get out of here."

The driver shrugged his shoulders, and going to the station wagon, he unhitched the back part of it which let down. Inside was a large packing case. Together with the pilot and with help from Ericsson and Peters, they got it down onto the ground. From the effort it took, it seemed to be heavy. Mrs. Calvin Baker put her hand on Hilary's arm and said, as the man began to raise the lid of the case,

"I shouldn't watch, my dear. It's never a pretty sight."

She led Hilary a little way away, on the other side of the wagon. The Frenchman and Peters came with them. The Frenchman said in his own language,

"What is it then, this manoeuvre there that they do?"

Mrs. Baker said,

"You are Dr. Barron?"

The Frenchman bowed.

"Pleased to meet you," said Mrs. Baker. She stretched out her hand, rather like a hostess welcoming him to a party. Hilary said in a bewildered tone,

"But I don't understand. What is in that case? Why is it better not to look?"

Andy Peters looked down on her consideringly. He had a nice face, Hilary thought. Something square and dependable about it. He said,

"I know what it is. The pilot told me. It's not very pretty perhaps, but I guess it's necessary." He added quietly, "There are bodies in there."

"Bodies!" She stared at him.

"Oh, they haven't been murdered or anything," he grinned reassuringly. "They were obtained in a perfectly legitimate way for research—medical research, you know."

But Hilary still stared.

"I don't understand."

"Ah. You see, Mrs. Betterton, this is where the journey ends. One journey, that is."

"Ends?"

"Yes. They'll arrange the bodies in that plane and then the pilot will fix things and presently, as we're driving away from here, we shall see in the distance the flames going up in the air. Another plane that has crashed and come down in flames, *and no survivors!*"

"But why? How fantastic!"

"But surely—" It was Dr. Barron now who spoke to her. "But surely you know where we are going?"

Mrs. Baker, drawing near, said cheerfully,

"Of course she knows. But maybe she didn't expect it quite so soon."

Hilary said, after a short bewildered pause,

"But you mean—all of us?" She looked round.

"We're fellow travellers," said Peters gently.

The young Norwegian, nodding his head, said with an almost fanatical enthusiasm,

"Yes, we are all fellow travellers."

CHAPTER IX

THE PILOT CAME up to them.

"You will start now, please," he said. "As soon as possible. There is much to be done, and we are late on schedule."

Hilary recoiled for a moment. She put her hand nervously to her throat. The pearl choker she was wearing broke under the strain of her fingers. She picked up the loose pearls and crammed them into her pocket.

They all got into the station wagon. Hilary was on a long bench crowded up with Peters one side of her and Mrs. Baker the other. Turning her head towards the American woman, Hilary said,

"So you—so you—are what you might call the liaison officer, Mrs. Baker?"

"That hits it off exactly. And though I say it myself, I'm well qualified. Nobody is surprised to find an American woman getting around and travelling a lot."

She was still plump and smiling, but Hilary sensed, or thought she sensed, a difference. The slight fatuity and surface conventionality had gone. This was an efficient, probably ruthless woman.

"It will make a fine sensation in the headlines," said Mrs. Baker. She laughed with some enjoyment. "*You,* I mean, my dear. Persistently dogged by ill-luck, they'll say. First nearly losing your life in the crash at Casablanca, then being killed in this further disaster."

Hilary realised suddenly the cleverness of the plan.

"These others?" she murmured. "Are they who they say they are?"

"Why yes. Dr. Barron is a bacteriologist, I believe. Mr. Ericsson a very brilliant young physicist, Mr. Peters is a research chemist, Miss Needheim, of course, isn't a nun, she's an endocrinologist. Me, as I say, I'm only the liaison officer. I don't belong in this scientific bunch." She laughed again as she said, "That Hetherington woman never had a chance."

"Miss Hetherington—was she—was she—"

Mrs. Baker nodded emphatically.

"If you ask me, she's been tailing you. Took over in Casablanca from whoever followed you out."

"But she didn't come with us today although I urged her to?"

"That wouldn't have been in character," said Mrs. Baker. "It would have looked a little too obvious to go back again to Marrakesh after having been there already. No, she'll have sent a telegram or a phone message through and there'll be someone waiting at Marrakesh to pick you up when you arrive. When you arrive! That's a good laugh, isn't it? Look! Look there now! Up she goes."

They had been driving rapidly away across the desert, and now as Hilary craned forward to look through the little window, she saw a great glow behind them. A faint sound of an explosion came to her ears. Peters threw his head back and laughed. He said:

"Six people die when plane to Marrakesh crashes!"

Hilary said almost under her breath:

"It's—it's rather frightening."

"Stepping off into the unknown?" It was Peters who spoke. He was serious enough now. "Yes, but it's the only way. We're leaving the Past and stepping out towards the Future." His face lit up with sudden enthusiasm. "We've got to get quit of all the bad, mad old stuff. Corrupt governments and the warmongers. We've got to go into the new world—the world of science, clean away from the scum and the driftwood."

Hilary drew a deep breath.

"That's like the things my husband used to say," she said, deliberately.

"Your husband?" He shot her a quick glance. "Why, was he *Tom* Betterton?"

Hilary nodded.

"Well that's great. I never knew him out in the States, though I nearly met him more than once. ZE Fission is one of the most brilliant discoveries of this age—yes, I certainly take my hat off to him. Worked with old Mannheim, didn't he?"

"Yes," said Hilary.

"Didn't they tell me he'd married Mannheim's daughter. But surely *you're* not—"

"I'm his second wife," said Hilary, flushing a little. "He—his—Elsa died in America."

"I remember. Then he went to Britain to work there. Then he riled them by disappearing." He laughed suddenly. "Walked slap out of some Paris Conference into nowhere." He added, as though in further appreciation, "Lord, you can't say they don't organise well."

Hilary agreed with him. The excellence of their organisation was sending a cold pang of apprehension through her. All the plans, codes, signs that had been so elaborately arranged were going to be useless now, for now there would be no trail to pick up. Things had been so arranged that everyone on the fatal plane had been fellow travellers bound for the Unknown Destination where Thomas Betterton had gone before them. There would be no trace left. Nothing. Nothing but a burnt-out plane. Could they—was it possible that Jessop and his organisation could guess that she, Hilary, was *not* one of those charred bodies? She doubted it. The accident had been so convincing, so clever—there would even be charred bodies in the plane.

Peters spoke again. His voice was boyish with enthusiasm. For him there were no qualms, no looking back, only eagerness to go forward.

"I wonder," he said, "where do we go from here?"

Hilary, too, wondered, because again much depended on that. Sooner or later there *must* be contacts with humanity. Sooner or later, if investigation was made, the fact that a station wagon with six people in it resembling the description of those who had left that morning by plane, might possibly be noted by someone. She turned to Mrs. Baker, and asked, trying to make her tone the counterpart of the childish eagerness of the young American beside her,

"Where are we going—what happens next?"

"You'll see," said Mrs. Baker, and for all the pleasantness of her voice, there was something somehow ominous in those words.

They drove on. Behind them the flare of the plane still showed in the sky, showed all the more clearly because the sun was now dropping below the horizon. Night fell. Still they drove. The going was bad since they were obviously not on any main road. Sometimes they seemed to be on field tracks, at other times they drove over open country.

For a long time Hilary remained awake, thoughts and apprehensions turning round in her head excitedly. But at last, shaken and tossed from side to side, exhaustion had its way and she fell asleep. It was a broken sleep. Various ruts and jars in the road awoke her. For a moment or two she would wonder confusedly where she was, then reality would come back to her. She would remain awake for a few moments, her thoughts racing round in confused apprehension, then once more her head would drop forward and nod, and once again she would sleep.

She was awakened suddenly by the car coming to an abrupt stop. Very gently Peters shook her by the arm.

"Wake up," he said, "we seem to have arrived somewhere."

Everyone got out of the station wagon. They were all cramped and weary. It was still dark and they seemed to have drawn up outside a house surrounded by palm trees. Some distance away they could see a few dim lights as though there were a village there. Guided by a lantern they were ushered into the house. It was a native house with a couple of giggling Berber women who stared curiously at Hilary and Mrs. Calvin Baker. They took no interest in the nun.

The three women were taken to a small upstairs room. There were three mattresses on the floor and some heaps of coverings, but no other furniture.

"I'll say I'm stiff," said Mrs. Baker. "Gets you kind of cramped, riding along the way we've been doing."

"Discomfort does not matter," said the nun.

She spoke with a harsh, guttural assurance. Her English, Hilary found, was good and fluent, though her accent was bad.

"You're living up to your part, Miss Needheim," said the American woman. "I can just see you in the convent, kneeling on the hard stones at four in the morning."

Miss Needheim smiled contemptuously.

"Christianity has made fools of women," she said. "Such a worship of weakness, such snivelling humiliation! Pagan women had strength. They rejoiced and conquered! And in order to conquer, no discomfort is unbearable. Nothing is too much to suffer."

"Right now," said Mrs. Baker, yawning, "I wish I was in my bed at the Palais Jamail at Fez. What about you, Mrs. Betterton? That shaking hasn't done your concussion any good, I'll bet."

"No, it hasn't," Hilary said.

"They'll bring us something to eat presently, and then I'll fix you up with some aspirin and you'd better get to sleep as fast as you can."

Steps were heard coming up the stairs outside and giggling female voices. Presently the two Berber women came into the room. They carried a tray with a big dish of semolina and meat stew. They put it down on the floor, came back again with a metal basin with water in it and a towel. One of them felt Hilary's coat, passing the stuff between her fingers and speaking to the other woman who nodded her head in rapid agreement, and did the same to Mrs. Baker. Neither of them paid any attention to the nun.

"Shoo," said Mrs. Baker, waving them away. "Shoo, shoo."

It was exactly like shooing chickens. The women retreated, still laughing, and left the room.

"Silly creatures," said Mrs. Baker, "it's hard to have patience with them. I suppose babies and clothes are their only interest in life."

"It is all they are fit for," said Fraulein Needheim, "they belong to a slave race. They are useful to serve their betters, but no more."

"Aren't you a little harsh?" said Hilary, irritated by the woman's attitude.

"I have no patience with sentimentality. There are those that rule, the few; and there are the many that serve."

"But surely . . ."

Mrs. Baker broke in in an authoritative manner.

"We've all got our own ideas on these subjects, I guess," she said, "and very interesting they are. But this is hardly the time for them. We'll want to get what rest we can."

Mint tea arrived. Hilary swallowed some aspirin willingly enough, since her headache was quite a genuine one. Then the three women lay down on the mattresses and fell asleep.

They slept late into the following day. They were not to go on again until the evening, so Mrs. Baker informed them. From the room in which they had slept, there was an outside staircase leading onto a flat roof where they had a certain amount of view over the surrounding country. A little distance away was a village, but here where they were, the house was isolated in a large palm garden. On awakening, Mrs. Baker had indicated three heaps of clothing which had been brought and laid down just inside the door.

"We're going native for the next lap," she explained, "we leave our other clothes here."

So the smart little American woman's neat suiting and Hilary's tweed coat and skirt and the nun's habit were all laid aside and three native Moroccan women sat on the roof of the house and chatted together. The whole thing had a curiously unreal feeling.

Hilary studied Miss Needheim more closely now that she had left the anonymity of her nun's habit. She was a younger woman than Hilary had thought her, not more, perhaps, than thirty-three or thirty-four. There was a neat spruceness in her appearance. The pale skin, the short stubby fingers, and the cold eyes in which burned from time to time the gleam of the fanatic, repelled rather than attracted. Her speech was brusque and uncompromising. Towards both Mrs. Baker and Hilary she displayed a certain amount of contempt as towards people unworthy to associate with her. This arrogance Hilary found very irritating. Mrs. Baker, on the other hand, seemed hardly to notice it. In a queer way Hilary felt far nearer and more in sympathy with the two giggling Berber women who brought them food, than with her two companions of the Western world. The young German woman was obviously indifferent to the impression she created. There was a certain concealed impatience in her manner, and it was obvious that she was longing to get on with her journey and that she had no interest in her two companions.

Appraising Mrs. Baker's attitude, Hilary found more difficult. At first Mrs. Baker seemed a natural and normal person after the inhumanity of the German woman specialist. But as the sun sank lower in the sky she felt almost more intrigued and repelled by Mrs. Baker than by Helga Needheim. Mrs. Baker's social manner was almost robotlike in its perfection. All her comments and remarks were natural, normal, everyday currency, but one had a suspicion that the whole thing was like an actor playing a part for perhaps the seven hundredth time. It was an automatic performance, completely divorced from what Mrs. Baker might really have been thinking or feeling. Who was Mrs. Calvin Baker, Hilary wondered? Why had she come to play her part with such machinelike perfection? Was she, too, a fanatic? Had she dreams of a brave new world—was she in violent revolt against the capitalist system? Had she given up all normal life because of her political beliefs and aspirations? Impossible to tell.

They resumed their journey that evening. It was no longer the station wagon. This time it was an open touring car. Everyone was in native dress, the men with white djellabos round them, the women with their faces hidden. Packed tightly in, they started off once more, driving all through the night.

"How are you feeling, Mrs. Betterton?"

Hilary smiled up at Andy Peters. The sun had just risen and they had stopped for breakfast. Native bread, eggs, and tea made over a primus.

"I feel as though I were taking part in a dream," said Hilary.

"Yes, it has rather that quality."

"Where are we?"

He shrugged his shoulders.

"Who knows? Our Mrs. Calvin Baker, no doubt, but no other."

"It's a very lonely country."

"Yes, practically desert. But then it would have to be, wouldn't it."

"You mean so as to leave no trace?"

"Yes. One realises, doesn't one, that the whole thing must be very carefully thought out. Each stage of our journey is, as it were, quite independent of the other. A plane goes up in flames. An old station wagon drives through the night. If anyone notices it, it has on it a plate stating that it belongs to a certain archaeological Expedition that is excavating in these parts. The following day there is a touring car full of Berbers, one of the commonest sights on the road to be seen. For the next stage—" he shrugged his shoulders "—who knows?"

"But where are we going?"

Andy Peters shook his head.

"No use to ask. We shall find out."

The Frenchman, Dr. Barron, had joined them.

"Yes," he said, "we shall find out. But how true it is that we cannot but ask? That is our western blood. We can never say 'sufficient for the day.' It is always tomorrow, tomorrow with us. To leave yesterday behind, to proceed to tomorrow. That is what we demand."

"You want to hurry the world on, Doctor, is that it?" asked Peters.

"There is so much to achieve," said Dr. Barron, "life is too short. One must have more time. More time, more time." He flung out his hands in a passionate gesture.

Peters turned to Hilary.

"What are the four freedoms you talk about in your country? Freedom from want, freedom from fear . . ."

The Frenchman interrupted. "Freedom from fools," he said bitterly. "That is what *I* want! That is what my work needs. Freedom from incessant, pettifogging economies! Freedom from all the nagging restrictions that hamper one's work!"

"You are a bacteriologist, are you not, Dr. Barron?"

"Yes, I am a bacteriologist. Ah, you have no idea, my friend, what a fascinating study that is! But it needs patience, infinite patience, repeated experiment—and *money*—much money! One must have equipment, assistants, raw materials! Given that you have all you ask for, what can one not achieve?"

"Happiness?" asked Hilary.

He flashed her a quick smile, suddenly human again.

"Ah, you are a woman, Madame. It is women who ask always for happiness."

"And seldom get it?" asked Hilary.

He shrugged his shoulders.

"That may be."

"Individual happiness does not matter," said Peters seriously, "there must be the happiness of *all*, the brotherhood of the spirit! The workers, free and united, owning the means of production, free of the warmongers, of the greedy, insatiable men who keep everything in their own hands. Science is for *all*, and must not be held jealously by one power or the other."

"So!" said Ericsson appreciatively, "you are right. The scientists must be masters. They must control and rule. They and they alone are the Supermen. It is only the Supermen who matter. The slaves must be well treated, but they *are* slaves."

Hilary walked a little way away from the group. After a minute or two Peters followed her.

"You look just a little scared," he said humorously.

"I think I am." She gave a short, breathless laugh. "Of course what Dr. Barron said was quite true. I'm only a woman. I'm not a scientist, I don't do research or surgery, or bacteriology. I haven't, I suppose, much mental ability. I'm looking, as Dr. Barron said, for happiness—just like any other fool of a woman."

"And what's wrong with that?" said Peters.

"Well, maybe I feel a little out of my depth in this company. You see, I'm just a woman who's going to join her husband."

"Good enough," said Peters. "You represent the fundamental."

"It's nice of you to put it that way."

"Well, it's true." He added in a lower voice, "You care for your husband very much?"

"Would I be here if I didn't?"

"I suppose not. You share his views? I take it that he's a Communist?"

Hilary avoided giving a direct answer.

"Talking of being a Communist," she said, "has something about our little group struck you as curious?"

"What's that?"

"Well, that although we're all bound for the same destination, the views of our fellow travellers don't seem really alike."

Peters said thoughtfully,

"Why, no. You've got something there. I hadn't thought of it quite that way—but I believe you're right."

"I don't think," said Hilary, "that Dr. Barron is politically minded at all! He wants money for his experiments. Helga Needheim talks like a Fascist, not a Communist. And Ericsson—"

"What about Ericsson?"

"I find him frightening—he's got a dangerous kind of single-mindedness. He's like a mad scientist in a film!"

"And I believe in the Brotherhood of men, and you're a loving wife, and our Mrs. Calvin Baker—where would you place her?"

"I don't know. I find her more hard to place than anyone."

"Oh, I wouldn't say that. I'd say she was easy enough."

"How do you mean?"

"I'd say it was money all the way with her. She's just a well-paid cog in the wheel."

"She frightens me, too," said Hilary.

"Why? Why on earth does she frighten you? No touch of the mad scientist about her."

"She frightens me because she's so ordinary. You know, just like anybody else. And yet she's mixed up in all this."

Peters said grimly,

"The Party is realistic, you know. It employs the best man or woman for the job."

"But is someone who only wants money the best person for the job? Mightn't they desert to the other side?"

"That would be a very big risk to take," said Peters, quietly. "Mrs. Calvin Baker's a shrewd woman. I don't think she'd take that risk."

Hilary shivered suddenly.

"Cold?"

"Yes. It is a bit cold."

"Let's move around a little."

They walked up and down. As they did so Peter stooped and picked up something.

"Here. You're dropping things."

Hilary took it from him.

"Oh, yes, it's a pearl from my choker. I broke it the other day—no, yesterday. What ages ago that seems already."

"Not real pearls, I hope."

Hilary smiled.

"No, of course not. Costume jewellery."

Peters took a cigarette case from his pocket.

"Costume jewellery," he said, "what a term!"

He offered her a cigarette.

"It does sound foolish—here." She took a cigarette. "What an odd case. How heavy it is."

"Made of lead, that's why. It's a war souvenir—made out of a bit of a bomb that just failed to blow me up."

"You were—in the war then?"

"I was one of the backroom boys who tickled things to see if they'd go bang! Don't let's talk about wars. Let's concentrate on tomorrow."

"Where are we going?" asked Hilary. "Nobody's told me anything. Are we—"

He stopped her.

"Speculations," he said, "are not encouraged. You go where you're told and do what you're told."

With sudden passion Hilary said,

"Do you like being dragooned, being ordered about, having no say of your own?"

"I'm prepared to accept it if it's necessary. And it is necessary. We've got to have World Peace, World Discipline, World Order."

"Is it possible? Can it be got?"

"Anything's better than the muddle we live in. Don't you agree to that?"

For a moment, carried away by fatigue, by the loneliness of her surroundings and the strange beauty of the early morning light, Hilary nearly burst out into a passionate denial.

She wanted to say,

"Why do you decry the world we live in? There are good people in it. Isn't muddle a better breeding ground for kindliness and individuality than a world order that's imposed, a world order that may be right today and wrong tomorrow? I would rather have a world of kindly, faulty, human beings, than a world of superior robots who've said goodbye to pity and understanding and sympathy."

But she restrained herself in time. She said instead, with a deliberate subdued enthusiasm,

"How right you are. I was tired. We must obey and go forward."

He grinned.

"That's better."

CHAPTER X

A DREAM JOURNEY. So it seemed; more so every day. It was as though, Hilary felt, she had been travelling all her life with these five strangely assorted companions. They had stepped off from the beaten track into the void. In one sense this journey of theirs could not be called a flight. They were all, she supposed, free agents; free, that is, to go where they chose. As far as she knew they had committed no crime, they were not wanted by the police. Yet great pains had been taken to hide their tracks. Sometimes she wondered why this was, since they were not fugitives. It was as though they were in process of becoming not themselves but someone else.

That indeed was literally true in her case. She who had left England as Hilary Craven had become Olive Betterton, and perhaps her strange feeling of unreality had something to do with that. Every day the glib political slogans seemed to come more easily to her lips. She felt herself becoming earnest and intense, and that again she put down to the influence of her companions.

She knew now that she was afraid of them. She had never before spent any time in close intimacy with people of genius. This was genius at close quarters, and genius had that something above normal in it that was a great strain upon the ordinary mind and feeling. All five were different from each other, yet each had that curious quality of burning intensity, the single-mindedness of purpose that made such a terrifying impression. She did not know whether it were a quality of brain or rather a quality of outlook, of intensity. But each of them, she thought, was in his or her way a passionate idealist. To Dr. Barron life was a passionate desire to be once more in his laboratory, to be able to calculate and experiment and work with unlimited money and unlimited resources. To work for what? She doubted if he ever put that question to himself. He spoke to her once of the powers of destruction that he could let loose on a vast continent, which could be contained in one little phial. She had said to him,

"But could you ever *do* that? Actually really do it?"

And he replied, looking at her with faint surprise,

"Yes. Yes, of course, if it became necessary."

He had said it in a merely perfunctory fashion. He had gone on,

"It would be amazingly interesting to see the exact course, the exact progress." And he had added with a deep half sigh, "You see, there's so much more to know, so much more to find out."

For a moment Hilary understood. For a moment she stood where he stood, impregnated with that single-hearted desire for knowledge which swept aside life and death for millions of human beings as essentially unimportant. It was a point of view and in a way a not ignoble one. Towards Helga Needheim she felt more antagonistic. The young woman's superb arrogance revolted her. Peters she liked but was from time to time repulsed and frightened by the sudden fanatical gleam in his eye. She said to him once,

"It is not a new world you want to create. It is destroying the old one that you will enjoy."

"You're wrong, Olive. What a thing to say."

"No, I'm not wrong. There's hate in you. I can feel it. Hate. The wish to destroy."

Ericsson she found the most puzzling of all. Ericsson, she thought, was a dreamer, less practical than the Frenchman, further removed from destructive passion than the American. He had the strange, fanatical idealism of the Norseman.

"We must conquer," he said, "we must conquer the world. Then we can rule."

"We?" she asked.

He nodded, his face strange and gentle with a deceptive mildness about the eyes.

"Yes," he said, "we few who count. The brains. That is all that matters."

Hilary thought, where are we going? Where is all this leading. These people are mad, but they're not mad in the same way as each other. It's as though they were all going towards different goals, different mirages. Yes, that was the word. *Mirages*. And from them she turned to a contemplation of Mrs. Calvin Baker. Here there was no fanaticism, no hate, no dream, no arrogance, no aspiration. There was nothing here that Hilary could find or take notice of. She was a woman, Hilary thought, without either heart or conscience. She was the efficient instrument in the hands of a big unknown force.

It was the end of the third day. They had come to a small town and alighted at a small native hotel. Here, Hilary found, they were to resume European clothing. She slept that night in a small, bare, whitewashed room, rather like a cell. At early dawn Mrs. Baker woke her.

"We're going off right now," said Mrs. Baker. "The plane's waiting."

"The plane?"

"Why yes, my dear. We're returning to civilized travelling, thank the Lord."

They came to the airfield and the plane after about an hour's drive. It looked like a disused army airfield. The pilot was a Frenchman. They flew for some hours, their flight taking them over mountains. Looking down from the plane Hilary thought what a curious sameness the world has, seen from above. Mountains, valleys, roads, houses. Unless one was really an aerial expert all places looked alike. That in some the population was denser than in others, was about all that one could say. And half of the time one saw nothing owing to travelling over clouds.

In the early afternoon they began to lose height and circle down. They were in mountainous country still but coming down in a flat plain. There was a well-marked aerodrome here and a white building beside it. They made a perfect landing.

Mrs. Baker led the way towards the building. Beside it were two powerful cars with chauffeurs standing by them. It was clearly a private aerodrome of some kind, since there appeared to be no official reception.

"Journey's end," said Mrs. Baker cheerfully. "We all go in and have a good wash and brush up. And then the cars will be ready."

"Journey's end?" Hilary stared at her. "But we've not—we haven't crossed the sea at all."

"Did you expect to?" Mrs. Baker seemed amused. Hilary said confusedly, "Well, yes. Yes, I did. I thought . . ." She stopped.

Mrs. Baker nodded her head.

"Why, so do a lot of people. There's a lot of nonsense talked about the Iron Curtain, but what I say is an Iron Curtain can be anywhere. People don't think of that."

Two Berber servants received them. After a wash and freshening up they sat down to coffee and sandwiches and biscuits. Then Mrs. Baker glanced at her watch.

"Well, so long, folks," she said. "This is where I leave you."

"Are you going back to Morocco?" asked Hilary, surprised.

"That wouldn't quite do," said Mrs. Calvin Baker, "with me being supposed to be burnt up in a plane accident! No, I shall be on a different run this time."

"But someone might still recognise you," said Hilary. "Someone, I mean, who'd met you in hotels in Casablanca or Fez."

"Ah," said Mrs. Baker, "but they'd be making a mistake. I've got a different passport now, though it's true enough that a sister of mine, a Mrs. Calvin Baker, lost her life that way. My sister and I are supposed to be very alike." She added, "And to the casual people one comes across in hotels one travelling American woman is very like another."

Yes, Hilary thought, that was true enough. All the outer, unimportant characteristics were present in Mrs. Baker. The neatness, the trimness, the carefully arranged blue hair, the highly monotonous, prattling voice. Inner characteristics, she realised, were carefully masked or, indeed, absent. Mrs. Calvin Baker presented to the world and to her companions a façade, but what was behind the façade was not easy to fathom. It was as though she had deliberately extinguished those tokens of individuality by which one personality is distinguishable from another.

Hilary felt moved to say so. She and Mrs. Baker were standing a little apart from the rest.

"One doesn't know," said Hilary, "in the least what you're really like?"

"Why should you?"

"Yes. Why should I? And yet, you know, I feel I ought to. We've travelled together in rather intimate circumstances and it seems odd to me that I know nothing about you. Nothing, I mean, of the essential you, of what you feel and think, of what you like and dislike, of what's important to you and what isn't."

"You've such a probing mind, my dear," said Mrs. Baker. "If you'll take my advice, you'll curb that tendency."

"I don't even know what part of the United States you come from."

"That doesn't matter either. I've finished with my own country. There are reasons why I can never go back there. If I can pay off a grudge against that country, I'll enjoy doing it."

For just a second or two malevolence showed both in her expression and in the tone of her voice. Then it relaxed once more into cheerful tourist tones.

"Well, so long, Mrs. Betterton, I hope you have a very agreeable reunion with your husband."

Hilary said helplessly,

"I don't even know where I am, what part of the world, I mean."

"Oh, that's easy. There needs to be no concealment about that now. A remote spot in the High Atlas my dear. That's near enough—"

Mrs. Baker moved away and started saying goodbye to the others. With a final gay wave of her hand she walked out across the tarmac. The plane had been refuelled and the pilot was standing waiting for her. A faint cold chill went over Hilary. Here, she felt, was her last link with the outside world. Peters, standing near her, seemed to sense her reaction.

"The place of no return," he said softly. "That's us, I guess."

Dr. Barron said softly,

"Have you still courage, Madame, or do you at this moment want to run after your American friend and climb with her into the plane and go back—back to the world you have left?"

"Could I go if I wanted to?" asked Hilary.

The Frenchman shrugged his shoulders.

"One wonders."

"Shall I call to her?" asked Andy Peters.

"Of course not," said Hilary sharply.

Helga Needheim said scornfully,

"There is no room here for women who are weaklings."

"She is not a weakling," said Dr. Barron softly, "but she asks herself questions as any intelligent woman would do." He stressed the word "intelligent" as though it were a reflection upon the German woman. She, however, was unaffected by his tone. She despised all Frenchmen and was happily assured of her own worth. Ericsson said, in his high nervous voice,

"When one has at last reached freedom, can one even contemplate going back?"

Hilary said,

"But if it is not possible to go back, or to choose to go back, then it is not freedom!"

One of the servants came to them and said,

"If you please, the cars are ready now to start."

They went out through the opposite door of the building. Two Cadillac cars were standing there with uniformed chauffeurs. Hilary indicated a preference for sitting in front with the chauffeur. She explained the swinging motion of a large car occasionally made her feel car sick. This explanation seemed to be accepted easily enough. As they drove along Hilary made a little desultory conversation from time to time. The weather, the excellence of the car. She spoke French quite easily and well, and the chauffeur responded agreeably. His manner was entirely natural and matter of fact.

"How long will it take us?" she asked presently.

"From the aerodrome to the hospital? It is a drive of perhaps two hours, Madame."

The words struck Hilary with faintly disagreeable surprise. She had noted, without thinking much about it, that Helga Needheim had changed at the rest house and was now wearing a hospital nurse's kit. This fitted in.

"Tell me something about the hospital," she said to the chauffeur.

His reply was enthusiastic.

"Ah, Madame, it is magnificent. The equipment, it is the most up-to-date in the world. Many doctors come and visit it, and all of them go away full of praise. It is a great thing that is being done there for humanity."

"It must be," said Hilary, "yes, yes, indeed it must."

"These miserable ones," said the chauffeur, "they have been sent in the past to perish miserably on a lonely island. But here this new treatment of Dr. Kolini's cures a very high percentage. Even those who are far gone."

"It seems a lonely place to have a hospital," said Hilary.

"Ah, Madame, but you would have to be lonely in the circumstances. The authorities would insist upon it. But it is good air here, wonderful air. See, Madame, you can see now where we are going." He pointed.

They were approaching the first spurs of a mountain range, and on the side of it, set flat against the hillside, was a long gleaming white building.

"What an achievement," said the chauffeur, "to raise such a building out here. The money spent must have been fantastic. We owe much, Madame, to the rich philanthropists of this world. They are not like governments who do things always in a cheap way. Here money has been spent like water. Our patron, he is one of the richest men in the world, they say. Here truly he has built a magnificent achievement for the relief of human suffering."

He drove up a winding track. Finally they came to rest outside great barred iron gates.

"You must dismount here, Madame," said the chauffeur. "It is not permitted that I take the car through these gates. The garages are a kilometre away."

The travellers got out of the car. There was a big bell pull at the gate, but before they could touch it the gates swung slowly open. A white-robed figure with a black, smiling face bowed to them and bade them enter. They passed through the gate; at one side screened by a high fence of wire, there was a big courtyard where men were walking up and down. As these men turned to look at the arrivals, Hilary uttered a gasp of horror.

"But they're lepers!" she exclaimed. "Lepers!"

A shiver of horror shook her entire frame.

CHAPTER XI

THE GATES OF the Leper Colony closed behind the travellers with a metallic clang. The noise struck on Hilary's startled consciousness with a horrible note of finality. *Abandon hope,* it seemed to say, *all ye who enter here* . . . This, she thought, was the end . . . really the end. Any way of retreat there might have been was now cut off.

She was alone now amongst enemies, and in, at most, a very few minutes, she would be confronted with discovery and failure. Subconsciously, she supposed, she had known that all day, but some undefeatable optimism of the human spirit, some persistence in the belief that that entity one-self could not possibly cease to exist, had been masking that fact from her. She had said to Jessop in Casablanca "And when do I reach Tom Better-ton?" and he had said then gravely that that was when the danger would become acute. He had added that he hoped that by then he might be in a position to give her protection, but that hope, Hilary could not but realise, had failed to materialise.

If "Miss Hetherington" had been the agent on whom Jessop was re-lying, "Miss Hetherington" had been outmanoeuvred and left to confess failure at Marrakesh. But in any case, what could Miss Hetherington have done?

The party of travellers had arrived at the place of no return. Hilary had gambled with death and lost. And she knew now that Jessop's diagnosis had been correct. She no longer wanted to die. She wanted to live. The zest of living had come back to her in full strength. She could think of Nigel, of the little mound that was Brenda's grave, with a sad wondering pity, but no longer with the cold lifeless despair that had urged her on to seek oblivion in death. She thought: "I'm alive again, sane, whole . . . and now I'm like a rat in a trap. If only there were some way out. . . ."

It was not that she had given no thought to the problem. She had. But it seemed to her, reluctantly, that once confronted with Betterton, there could be no way out. . . .

Betterton would say: "But that's not my wife—" And that would be that! Eyes turning towards her . . . realisation . . . a spy in their midst. . . .

Because what other solution could there be? Supposing she were to get in first? Supposing she were to cry out, before Tom Betterton could get in a word—"Who are you? You're not my husband!" If she could simulate indignation, shock, horror, sufficiently well—might it, just credibly, raise a doubt? A doubt whether Betterton was Betterton—or some other scientist sent to impersonate him. A spy, in other words. But if they believed that, then it might be rather hard on Betterton! But, she thought, her mind turning in tired circles, if Betterton was a traitor, a man willing to sell his country's secrets, could anything be 'hard on him'? How difficult it was, she thought, to make any appraisement of loyalties—or indeed any judgments of people or things. . . . At any rate it might be worth trying. To create a doubt—

With a giddy feeling, she returned to her immediate surroundings. Her thoughts had been running underground with the frenzied violence of a rat caught in a trap. But during that time her surface stream of consciousness had been playing its appointed part.

The little party from the outside world had been welcomed by a big handsome man—a linguist, it would seem, since he had said a word or two to each person in his or her own language.

"*Enchanté de faire votre connaisance, mon cher docteur,*" he was murmuring to Dr. Barron, and then turning to her:

"Ah, Mrs. Betterton, we're very pleased to welcome you here. A long confusing journey, I'm afraid. Your husband's very well and, naturally, awaiting you with impatience."

He gave her a discreet smile; it was a smile, she noticed, that did not touch his cold pale eyes.

"You must," he added, "be longing to see him."

The giddiness increased—she felt the group round her approaching and receding like the waves of the sea. Beside her, Andy Peters put out an arm and steadied her.

"I guess you haven't heard," he said to their welcoming host. "Mrs. Betterton had a bad crash at Casablanca—concussion. This journey's done her no good. Nor the excitement of looking forward to meeting her husband. I'd say she ought to lie down right now in a darkened room."

Hilary felt the kindness of his voice, of the supporting arm. She swayed a little more. It would be easy, incredibly easy, to crumple at the knees, to drop flaccidly down . . . to feign unconsciousness—or at any rate near unconsciousness. To be laid on a bed in a darkened room—to put off the moment of discovery just a little longer. . . . But Betterton would come to her there—any husband would. He would come there and lean over the bed in the dim gloom and at the first murmur of her voice, the first dim outline of her face as his eye became accustomed to the twilight he would realise that she was not Olive Betterton.

Courage came back to Hilary. She straightened up. Colour came into her cheeks. She flung up her head.

If this were to be the end, let it be a gallant end! She would go to Betterton and when he repudiated her, she would try out the last lie, come out with it confidently, fearlessly:

"No, of course I'm not your wife. Your wife—I'm terribly sorry, it's awful—she's dead. I was in hospital with her when she died. I promised her I'd get to you somehow and give her her last messages. I wanted to. You see, I'm in sympathy with what you did—with what all of you are doing. I agree with you politically. I want to help. . . ."

Thin, thin, all very thin . . . And such awkward trifles to explain—the faked passport—the forged letter of credit. Yes, but people did get by some-times with the most audacious lies—if one lied with sufficient confidence—if you had the personality to put a thing over. One could at any rate go down fighting.

She drew herself up, gently freeing herself from Peters' support.

"Oh, no. I must see Tom," she said. "I must go to him—now—at once—please."

The big man was hearty about it. Sympathetic. (Though the cold eyes were still pale and watchful.)

"Of course, of course, Mrs. Betterton. I quite understand how you are feeling. Ah, here's Miss Jennsen."

A thin spectacled girl had joined them.

"Miss Jennsen, meet Mrs. Betterton, Fraulein Needheim, Dr. Barron, Mr. Peters, Dr. Ericsson. Show them into the Registry, will you? Give them a drink. I'll be with you in a few minutes. Just take Mrs. Betterton along to her husband. I'll be with you again shortly."

He turned to Hilary again, saying:

"Follow me, Mrs. Betterton."

He strode forward, she followed. At a bend in the passage, she gave a last look over her shoulder. Andy Peters was still watching her. He had a faintly puzzled unhappy look—she thought for a moment he was going to come with her. He must have realised, she thought, that there's something wrong, realised it from *me*, but he doesn't know what it is.

And she thought, with a slight shiver: 'It's the last time, perhaps, that I'll ever see him. . . .'

And so, as she turned the corner after her guide, she raised a hand and waved a goodbye. . . .

The big man was talking cheerfully.

"This way, Mrs. Betterton. I'm afraid you'll find our buildings rather confusing at first, so many corridors, and all rather alike."

Like a dream, Hilary thought, a dream of hygienic white corridors along which you pass forever, turning, going on, never finding your way out. . . .

She said:

"I didn't realise it would be a—a hospital."

"No, no, of course. You couldn't realise anything, could you?"

There was a faint sadistic note of amusement in his voice.

"You've had, as they say, to 'fly blind.' My name's Van Heidem, by the way. Paul Van Heidem."

"It's all a little strange—and rather terrifying," said Hilary. "The lepers . . ."

"Yes, yes, of course. Picturesque—and usually so very unexpected. It does upset newcomers. But you'll get used to them—oh yes, you'll get used to them in time."

He gave a slight chuckle.

"A very good joke, I always think myself."

He paused suddenly.

"Up one flight of stairs—now don't hurry. Take it easy. Nearly there now."

Nearly there—nearly there . . . so many steps to death . . . up—up—deep steps, deeper than European steps. And now another of the hygienic passages and Van Heidem was stopping by a door. He tapped, waited, and then opened it.

"Ah, Betterton—here we are at last. Your wife!"

He stood aside with a slight flourish.

Hilary walked into the room. No holding back. No shrinking. Chin up. Forward to doom.

A man stood half turned from the window, an almost startlingly good-looking man. She noted that, recognising his fair handsomeness with a feeling almost of surprise. He wasn't, somehow, her idea of Tom Betterton. Surely, the photograph of him that she had been shown wasn't in the least—

It was that confused feeling of surprise that decided her. She would go all out for her first desperate expedient.

She made a quick movement forward, then drew back. Her voice rang out, startled, dismayed . . .

"But—that isn't Tom. That isn't my husband. . . ."

It was well done, she felt it herself. Dramatic, but not over dramatic. Her eyes met Van Heidem's in bewildered questioning.

And then Tom Betterton laughed. A quiet, amused, almost triumphant laugh.

"Pretty good, eh, Van Heidem?" he said, "if even my own wife doesn't know me!"

With four quick steps he had crossed to her and gathered her tightly into his arms.

"Olive, darling. Of course you know me. I'm Tom all right even if I haven't got quite the same face as I used to have."

His face pressed against hers, his lips by her ear, she caught the faint whispered addition,

"Play up. For God's sake. Danger."

He released her for a moment, caught her to him again.

"Darling! It's seemed years—years and years. But you're here at last!"

She could feel the warning pressure of his fingers below her shoulder blades, admonishing her, giving their urgent message.

Only after a moment or two did he release her, push her a little from him and look into her face.

"I still can't quite believe it," he said with an excited little laugh. "Still, you know it's me now, don't you?"

His eyes, burning into hers, still held that message of warning.

She didn't understand it—couldn't understand it. But it was a miracle from heaven and she rallied to play her part.

"Tom!" she said, and there was a catch in her voice that her listening ears approved. "Oh, Tom—but what—"

"Plastic surgery! Hertz of Vienna is here. And he's a living marvel. Don't say you regret my old crushed nose."

He kissed her again, lightly, easily, this time, then turned to the watching Van Heidem with a slight apologetic laugh.

"Forgive the transports, Van," he said.

"But naturally, naturally—" the Dutchman smiled benevolently.

"It's been so long," said Hilary, "and I—" she swayed a little, "I—please, can I sit down."

Hurriedly Tom Betterton eased her into a chair.

"Of course, darling. You're all in. That frightful journey. And the plane accident. My God, what an escape!"

(So there was full communication. They knew all about the plane crash.)

"It's left me terribly woolly-headed," said Hilary, with an apologetic little laugh. "I forget things and get muddled up, and have awful headaches. And then, finding you looking like a total stranger, I'm a bit of a mess, darling. I hope I won't be a bother to you!"

"You a bother? Never. You'll just have to take it easy for a bit, that's all. There's all the—time in the world here."

Van Heidem moved gently towards the door.

"I will leave you now," he said. "After a little you will bring your wife to the Registry, Betterton? For the moment you will like to be alone."

He went out, shutting the door behind him.

Immediately Betterton dropped on his knees by Hilary and buried his face on her shoulder.

"Darling, darling," he said.

And once again she felt that warning pressure of the fingers. The whisper, so faint as hardly to be heard, was urgent and insistent.

"Keep it up. There might be a microphone—one never knows."

That was it, of course. One never knew. . . . Fear—uneasiness—uncertainty—danger—always danger—she could feel it in the atmosphere.

Tom Betterton sat back on his haunches.

"It's so wonderful to see you," he said softly. "And yet, you know, it's like a dream—not quite real. Do you feel like that, too?"

"Yes, that's just it—a dream—being here—with you—at last. It doesn't seem real, Tom."

She had placed both hands on his shoulders. She was looking at him, a faint smile on her lips. (There might be a spy hole as well as a microphone.)

Coolly and calmly she appraised what she saw. A nervous good-looking man of thirty-odd who was badly frightened—a man nearly at the end of his tether—a man who had, presumably, come here full of high hopes and had been reduced—to this.

Now that she had surmounted her first hurdle, Hilary felt a curious exhilaration in the playing of her part. She must *be* Olive Betterton. Act as Olive would have acted, feel as Olive would have felt. And life was so unreal that that seemed quite natural. Somebody called Hilary Craven had died in an aeroplane accident. From now on she wouldn't even remember her.

Instead, she rallied her memories of the lessons she had studied so assiduously.

"It seems such ages since Firbank," she said. "Whiskers—you remember Whiskers? She had kittens—just after you went away. There are so many things, silly everyday little things, you don't even know about. That's what seems so odd."

"I know. It's breaking with an old life and beginning a new one."

"And—it's all right here? You're happy?"

A necessary wifely question that any wife would ask.

"It's wonderful." Tom Betterton squared his shoulders, threw his head back. Unhappy, frightened eyes looked out of a smiling confident face. "Every facility. No expense spared. Perfect conditions to get on with the job. And the organisation! It's unbelievable."

"Oh, I'm sure it is. My journey—did you come the same way?"

"One doesn't talk about that. Oh, I'm not snubbing you, darling. But—you see, you've got to learn about everything."

"But the lepers? Is it really a Leper Colony?"

"Oh, yes. Perfectly genuine. There's a team of medicos doing very fine work in research on the subject. But it's quite self-contained. It needn't worry you. It's just—clever camouflage."

"I see." Hilary looked round her. "Are these our quarters?"

"Yes. Sitting room, bathroom there, bedroom beyond. Come, I'll show you."

She got up and followed him through a well-appointed bathroom into a good-sized bedroom with twin beds, big built-in cupboards, a dressing table, and a bookshelf near the beds. Hilary looked into the cupboard space with some amusement.

"I hardly know what I'm going to put in here," she remarked. "All I've got is what I stand up in."

"Oh that. You can fit yourself out with all you want. There's a fashion model department and all accessories, cosmetics, everything. All first class. The Unit is quite self-contained—all you want on the premises. No need to go outside ever again."

He said the words lightly, but it seemed to Hilary's sensitive ear that there was despair concealed behind the words.

No need to go outside ever again. No chance of ever going outside again. *Abandon hope all ye who enter here* . . . The well-appointed cage! Was if for this, she thought, that all these varying personalities had abandoned their countries, their loyalties, their everyday lives? Dr. Barron, Andy Peters, young Ericsson with his dreaming face, the overbearing Helga Needheim? Did they know what they were coming to find? Would they be content? Was this what they had wanted?

She thought: "I'd better not ask too many questions . . . If someone is listening."

Was someone listening? Were they being spied upon? Tom Betterton evidently thought it might be so. But was he right? Or was it nerves—hysteria? Tom Betterton, she thought, was very near to a breakdown.

"Yes," she thought grimly, "and so may you be, my girl, in six months' time . . ."

What did it do to people, she wondered, living like this?

Tom Betterton said to her:

"Would you like to lie down—to rest?"

"No—" she hesitated. "No, I don't think so."

"Then perhaps you'd better come with me to the Registry."

"What's the Registry?"

"Everyone who clocks in goes through the Registry. They record everything about you. Health, teeth, blood pressure, blood group, psychological reactions, tastes, dislikes, allergies, aptitudes, preferences."

"It sounds very military—or do I mean medical?"

"Both," said Tom Betterton. "Both. This organisation—it's really formidable."

"One's always heard so," said Hilary. "I mean that everything behind the Iron Curtain is really properly planned."

She tried to put a proper enthusiasm into her voice. After all, Olive Betterton had presumably been a sympathiser with the Party, although, perhaps by order, she had not been known to be a Party member.

Betterton said evasively,

"There's a lot for you to—understand." He added quickly: "Better not try to take in too much at once."

He kissed her again, a curious, apparently tender and even passionate kiss, that was actually cold as ice, murmured very low in her ear, "Keep it up," and said aloud, "And now, come down to the Registry."

CHAPTER XII

THE REGISTRY WAS presided over by a woman who looked like a strict nursery governess. Her hair was rolled into a rather hideous bun and she wore some very efficient-looking pince-nez. She nodded approval as the Bettertons entered the severe office-like room.

"Ah," she said. "You've brought Mrs. Betterton. That's right."

Her English was perfectly idiomatic but it was spoken with a stilted precision which made Hilary believe that she was probably a foreigner. Actually, her nationality was Swiss. She motioned Hilary to a chair, opened a drawer beside her and took out a sheaf of forms upon which she commenced to write rapidly. Tom Betterton said rather awkwardly:

"Well then, Olive, I'll leave you."

"Yes, please, Dr. Betterton. It's much better to get through all the formalities straight away."

Betterton went out, shutting the door behind him. The Robot, for as such Hilary thought of her, continued to write.

"Now then," she said, in a businesslike way. "Full name, please. Age. Where born. Father's and mother's names. Any serious illnesses. Tastes. Hobbies. List of any jobs held. Degrees at any university. Preferences in food and drink."

It went on, a seemingly endless catalogue. Hilary responded vaguely, almost mechanically. She was glad now of the careful priming she had received from Jessop. She had mastered it all so well that the responses came automatically, without having to pause or think. The Robot said finally, as she made the last entry,

"Well, that seems to be all for this department. Now we'll hand you over to Doctor Schwartz for medical examination."

"Really!" said Hilary. "Is all this necessary? It seems most absurd."

"Oh, we believe in being thorough, Mrs. Betterton. We like to have everything down in the records. You'll like Dr. Schwartz very much. Then from her you go on to Doctor Rubec."

Dr. Schwartz was fair and amiable and female. She gave Hilary a meticulous physical examination and then said,

"So! That is finished. Now you go to Dr. Rubec."

"Who is Dr. Rubec?" Hilary asked. "Another doctor?"

"Dr. Rubec is a psychologist."

"I don't want a psychologist. I don't like psychologists."

"Now please don't get upset, Mrs. Betterton. You're not going to have treatment of any kind. It's simply a question of an intelligence test and of your type-group personality."

Dr. Rubec was a tall, melancholy Swiss of about forty years of age. He greeted Hilary, glanced at the card that had been passed on to him by Dr. Schwartz and nodded his head approvingly.

"Your health is good, I am glad to see," he said. "You have had an aeroplane crash recently, I understand?"

"Yes," said Hilary. "I was four or five days in hospital at Casablanca."

"Four or five days are not enough," said Dr. Rubec reprovingly. "You should have been there longer."

"I didn't want to be there longer. I wanted to get on with my journey."

"That, of course, is understandable, but it is important with concussion that plenty of rest should be had. You may appear quite well and normal after it but it may have serious effects. Yes, I see your nerve reflexes are not quite what they should be. Partly the excitement of the journey and partly, no doubt, due to concussion. Do you get headaches?"

"Yes. Very bad headaches. And I get muddled up every now and then and can't remember things."

Hilary felt it well to continually stress this particular point. Dr. Rubec nodded soothingly.

"Yes, yes, yes. But do not trouble yourself. All that will pass. Now we will have a few association tests, so as to decide what type of mentality you are."

Hilary felt faintly nervous but all appeared to pass off well. The test seemed to be of a merely routine nature. Dr. Rubec made various entries on a long form.

"It is a pleasure," he said at last, "to deal with someone (if you will excuse me, Madame, and not to take amiss what I am going to say), to deal with someone who is not in any way a genius!"

Hilary laughed.

"Oh, I'm certainly not a genius," she said.

"Fortunately for you," said Dr. Rubec. "I can assure you your existence will be far more tranquil." He sighed. "Here, as you probably understand, I deal mostly with keen intellects, but with the type of sensitive intellect that is apt to become easily unbalanced, and where the emotional stress is strong. The man of science, Madame, is not the cool, calm individual he is made out to be in fiction. In fact," said Dr. Rubec, thoughtfully, "between a first-class tennis player, an operatic prima-donna and a nuclear physicist there is really very little difference as far as emotional instability goes."

"Perhaps you are right," said Hilary, remembering that she was supposed to have lived for some years in close proximity to scientists. "Yes, they *are* rather temperamental sometimes."

Dr. Rubec threw up a pair of expressive hands.

"You would not believe," he said, "the emotions that arise here! The quarrels, the jealousies, the *touchiness!* We have to take steps to deal with all that. But you, Madame," he smiled. "You are in a class that is in a small minority here. A fortunate class, if I may so express myself."

"I don't quite understand you. What kind of a minority?"

"Wives," said Dr. Rubec. "We have not many wives here. Very few are permitted. One finds them, on the whole, refreshingly free from the brainstorms of their husbands and their husbands' colleagues."

"What do wives do here?" asked Hilary. She added apologetically, "You see it's all so new to me. I don't understand anything yet."

"Naturally not. Naturally. That is bound to be the case. There are hobbies, recreations, amusements, instructional courses. A wide field. You will find it, I hope, an agreeable life."

"As you do?"

It was a question, and rather an audacious one and Hilary wondered a moment or two later whether she had been wise to ask it. But Dr. Rubec merely seemed amused.

"You are quite right, Madame," he said. "I find life here peaceful and interesting in the extreme."

"You don't ever regret—Switzerland?"

"I am not homesick. No. That is partly because, in my case, my home conditions were bad. I had a wife and several children. I was not cut out, Madame, to be a family man. Here conditions are infinitely more pleasant. I have ample opportunity of studying certain aspects of the human mind which interest me and on which I am writing a book. I have no domestic cares, no distractions, no interruptions. It all suits me admirably."

"And where do I go next?" asked Hilary, as he rose and shook her courteously and formally by the hand.

"Mademoiselle La Roche will take you to the dress department. The result, I am sure—" he bowed "—will be admirable."

After the severe robotlike females she had met so far, Hilary was agreeably surprised by Mademoiselle La Roche. Mademoiselle La Roche had been a *vendeuse* in one of the Paris houses of *haute couture* and her manner was thrillingly feminine.

"I am delighted, Madame, to make your acquaintance. I hope that I can be of assistance to you. Since you have just arrived and since you are, no doubt, tired, I would suggest that you select now just a few essentials. Tomorrow and indeed during the course of next week, you can examine what we have in stock at your leisure. It is tiresome I always think, to have to select things rapidly. It destroys all the pleasure of *la toilette*. So I would suggest, if you agree, just a set of underclothing, a dinner dress, and perhaps a *tailleur*."

"How delightful it sounds," said Hilary. "I cannot tell you how odd it feels to own nothing but a toothbrush and a sponge."

Mademoiselle La Roche laughed cheeringly. She took a few rapid measures and led Hilary into a big apartment with built-in cupboards. There were clothes here of every description, made of good material and excellent cut and in a large variety of sizes. When Hilary had selected the essentials of *la toilette*, they passed on to the cosmetics department where Hilary made a selection of powders, creams and various other toilet accessories. These were handed to one of the assistants, a native girl with a shining dark face, dressed in spotless white, and she was instructed to see that they were delivered to Hilary's apartment.

All these proceedings had seemed to Hilary more and more like a dream.

"And we shall have the pleasure of seeing you again shortly, I hope," said Mademoiselle La Roche, gracefully. "It will be a great pleasure, Madame, to assist you to select from our models. *Entre nous* my work is sometimes disappointing. These scientific ladies often take very little interest in *la toilette*. In fact, not half an hour ago I had a fellow traveller of yours."

"Helga Needheim?"

"Ah yes, that was the name. She is, of course, a *Boche*, and the *Boches* are not sympathetic to us. She is not actually bad looking if she took a little care of her figure; if she chose a flattering line she could look very well. But no! She has no interest in clothes. She is a doctor, I understand. A specialist of some kind. Let us hope she takes more interest in her patients than she does in her *toilette*— Ah, that one, what man will look at her twice?"

Miss Jennsen, the thin, dark, spectacled girl who had met the party on arrival, now entered the fashion salon.

"Have you finished here, Mrs. Betterton?" she asked.

"Yes, thank you," said Hilary.

"Then perhaps you will come and see the Deputy Director."

Hilary said "au revoir" to Mademoiselle La Roche and followed the earnest Miss Jennsen.

"Who is the Deputy Director?" she asked.

"Doctor Nielson."

Everybody, Hilary reflected, in this place was doctor of something.

"Who exactly is Doctor Nielson?" she asked. "Medical, scientific, what?"

"Oh, he's not medical, Mrs. Betterton. He's in charge of Administration. All complaints have to go to him. He's the administrative head of the Unit. He always has an interview with everyone when they arrive. After that I don't suppose you'll ever see him again unless something very important should arise."

"I see," said Hilary, meekly. She had an amused feeling of having been put severely in her place.

Admission to Dr. Nielson was through two antechambers where stenographers were working. She and her guide were finally admitted into the inner sanctum where Dr. Nielson rose from behind a large executive's desk. He was a big florid man with an urbane manner. Of trans-Atlantic origin, Hilary thought, though he had very little American accent.

"Ah!" he said, rising and coming forward to shake Hilary by the hand! "This is—yes—let me see—yes, Mrs. Betterton. Delighted to welcome you here, Mrs. Betterton. We hope you'll be very happy with us. Sorry to hear of the unfortunate accident during the course of your journey, but I'm glad it was no worse. Yes, you were lucky there. Very lucky indeed. Well, your husband's been awaiting you impatiently and I hope now you've got here you will settle down and be very happy amongst us."

"Thank you, Dr. Nielson."

Hilary sat down in the chair he drew forward for her.

"Any questions you want to ask me?" Dr. Nielson leaned forward over his desk in an encouraging manner. Hilary laughed a little.

"That's a most difficult thing to answer," she said, "The real answer is, of course, that I've got so many questions to ask that I don't know where to begin."

"Quite, quite. I understand that. If you'll take my advice—this is just advice, you know, nothing more—I shouldn't ask anything. Just adapt yourself and see what comes. That's the best way, believe me."

"I feel I know so little," said Hilary. "It's all so—so very unexpected."

"Yes. Most people think that. The general idea seems to have been that one was going to arrive in Moscow." He laughed cheerfully. "Our desert home is quite a surprise to most people."

"It was certainly a surprise to me."

"Well, we don't tell people too much beforehand. They mightn't be discreet, you know, and discretion's rather important. But you'll be comfortable here, you'll find. Anything you don't like—or particularly would like to have . . . just put in a request for it and we'll see what can be managed. Any artistic requirement, for instance. Painting, sculpture, music, we have a department for all that sort of thing."

"I'm afraid I'm not talented that way."

"Well, there's plenty of social life too, of a kind. Games, you know. We have tennis courts, squash courts. It takes a week or two, we often find, for people to find their feet, especially the wives, if I may say so. Your husband's got his job and he's busy with it and it takes a little time, sometimes, for the wives to find—well—other wives who are congenial. All that sort of thing. You understand me."

"But does one—does one—stay here?"

"Stay here? I don't quite understand you, Mrs. Betterton."

"I mean, does one stay here or go on somewhere else?"

Dr. Nielson became rather vague.

"Ah," he said. "That depends on your husband. Ah, yes, yes, that depends very much on him. There are possibilities. Various possibilities. But it's better not to go into all that just now. I'd suggest, you know, that you—well—come and see me again perhaps in three weeks' time. Tell me how you've settled down. All that kind of thing."

"Does one—go out at all?"

"Go out, Mrs. Betterton?"

"I mean outside the walls. The gates."

"A very natural question," said Dr. Nielson. His manner was now rather heavily beneficent. "Yes, very natural. Most people ask it when they come here. But the point of our Unit is that it's a world in itself. There is nothing, if I may so express myself, to go out to. Outside us there is only desert. Now I'm not blaming you, Mrs. Betterton. Most people feel like that when they first get here. Slight claustrophobia. That's how Dr. Rubec puts it. But I assure you that it passes off. It's a hangover, if I may so express it, from the world that you have left. Have you ever observed an ant hill, Mrs. Betterton? An interesting sight. Very interesting and very instructive. Hundreds of little black insects hurrying to and fro, so earnest, so eager, so purposeful. And yet the whole thing's such a muddle. That's the bad old world you have left. Here there is leisure, purpose, infinite time. I assure you," he smiled, "an earthly paradise."

CHAPTER XIII

"IT'S LIKE A school," said Hilary.

She was back once more in her own *suite*. The clothes and accessories she had chosen were awaiting her in the bedroom. She hung the clothes in the cupboard and arranged the other things to her liking.

"I know," said Betterton, "I felt like that at first."

Their conversation was wary and slightly stilted. The shadow of a possible microphone still hung over them. He said in an oblique manner,

"I think it's all right, you know. I think I was probably imagining things. But all the same . . ."

He left it at that, and Hilary realised that what he had left unsaid was, "but all the same, we had better be careful."

The whole business was, Hilary thought, like some fantastic nightmare. Here she was, sharing a bedroom with a strange man, and yet so strong was the feeling of uncertainty, and danger, that to neither of them did the intimacy appear embarrassing. It was like, she thought, climbing a Swiss mountain where you share a hut in close proximity with guides and other climbers as a matter of course. After a minute or two Betterton said,

"It all takes a bit of getting used to, you know. Let's just be very natural. Very ordinary. More or less as if we were at home still."

She realised the wisdom of that. The feeling of unreality persisted and would persist, she supposed, some little time. The reasons for Betterton leaving England, his hopes, his disillusionment could not be touched upon between them at this moment. They were two people playing a part with an undefined menace hanging over them, as it were. She said presently,

"I was taken through a lot of formalities. Medical, psychological and all that."

"Yes. That's always done. It's natural I suppose."

"Did the same happen to you?"

"More or less."

"Then I went in to see the—Deputy Director I think they called him?"

"That's right. He runs this place. Very capable and a thoroughly good administrator."

"But he's not really the head of it all?"

"Oh no, there's the Director himself."

"Does one—do I—shall I see the Director?"

"Sooner or later I expect. But he doesn't often appear. He gives us an address from time to time—he's got a wonderfully stimulating personality."

There was a faint frown between Betterton's brows and Hilary thought it wise to abandon the subject. Betterton said, glancing at a watch,

"Dinner is at eight. Eight to eight-thirty, that is. We'd better be getting down, if you're ready?"

He spoke exactly as though they were staying in a hotel.

Hilary had changed into the dress she had selected. A soft shade of grey-green that made a good background for her red hair. She clasped a necklace of rather attractive costume jewellery round her neck and said she was ready. They went down the stairs and along corridors and finally into a large dining room. Miss Jennsen came forward and met them.

"I have arranged a slightly larger table for you, Tom," she said to Betterton. "A couple of your wife's fellow travellers will sit with you—and the Murchisons, of course."

They went along to the table indicated. The room contained mostly small tables seating four, eight or ten persons. Andy Peters and Ericsson were already sitting at the table and rose as Hilary and Tom approached. Hilary introduced her "husband" to the two men. They sat down, and presently they were joined by another couple. These Betterton introduced as Dr. and Mrs. Murchison.

"Simon and I work in the same lab," he said, in an explanatory fashion.

Simon Murchison was a thin, anaemic-looking young man of about twenty-six. His wife was dark and stocky. She spoke with a strong foreign accent and was, Hilary gathered, an Italian. Her Christian name was Bianca. She greeted Hilary politely but, or so it seemed to Hilary, with a certain reserve.

"Tomorrow," she said, "I will show you around the place. You are not a scientist, no?"

"I'm afraid," said Hilary, "that I have had no scientific training." She added, "I worked as a secretary before my marriage."

"Bianca has had legal training," said her husband. "She has studied economics and commercial law. Sometimes she gives lectures here but it is difficult to find enough to do to occupy one's time."

Bianca shrugged her shoulders.

"I shall manage," she said. "After all, Simon, I came here to be with you and I think that there is much here that could be better organised. I am studying conditions. Perhaps Mrs. Betterton, since she will not be engaged on scientific work, can help me with these things."

Hilary hastened to agree to this plan. Andy Peters made them all laugh by saying ruefully,

"I guess I feel rather like a homesick little boy who's just gone to boarding school. I'll be glad to get down to doing some work."

"It's a wonderful place for working," said Simon Murchison with enthusiasm. "No interruptions and all the apparatus you want."

"What's your line?" asked Andy Peters.

Presently the three men were talking a jargon of their own which Hilary found difficult to follow. She turned to Ericsson who was leaning back in his chair, his eyes abstracted.

"And you?" she asked. "Do you feel like a homesick little boy too?"

He looked at her as though from a long way away.

"I do not need a home," he said. "All these things; home, ties of affection, parents, children; all these are a great hindrance. To work one should be quite free."

"And you feel that you will be free here?"

"One cannot tell yet. One hopes so."

Bianca spoke to Hilary.

"After dinner," she said, "there is a choice of many things to do. There is a card room and you can play bridge; or there is a cinema or three nights a week theatrical performances are given and occasionally there is dancing."

Ericsson frowned disapprovingly.

"All these things are unnecessary," he said. "They dissipate energy."

"Not for us women," said Bianca. "For us women they are necessary."

He looked at her with an almost cold and impersonal dislike.

Hilary thought: "To him women are unnecessary, too."

"I shall go to bed early," said Hilary. She yawned deliberately. "I don't think I want to see a film or play bridge this evening."

"No, dear," said Tom Betterton hastily. "Much better to go to bed really early and have a good night's rest. You've had a very tiring journey, remember."

As they rose from the table, Betterton said:

"The air here is wonderful at night. We usually take a turn or two on the roof garden after dinner, before dispersing to recreations or study. We'll go up there for a little and then you'd better go to bed."

They went up in a lift manned by a magnificent-looking native in white robes. The attendants were darker-skinned and of a more massive build than the slighter Berbers—a desert type, Hilary thought. She was startled by the unexpected beauty of the roof garden, and also by the lavish expenditure that must have gone to create it. Tons of earth must have been brought and carried up here. The result was like an Arabian Nights fairy tale. There was the plash of water, tall palms, the tropical leaves of bananas and other plants and paths of beautiful coloured tiles with designs of Persian flowers.

"It's unbelievable," said Hilary. "Here in the middle of the desert." She spoke out what she had felt: "It's an Arabian Nights fairy tale."

"I agree with you, Mrs. Betterton," said Murchison. "It looks exactly as though it has come into being by conjuring up a Djin! Ah well—I suppose even in the desert there's nothing you can't do, given water and money—plenty of both of them."

"Where does the water come from?"

"Spring tapped deep in the mountain. That's the *raison d'être* of the Unit."

A fair sprinkling of people was on the roof garden, but little by little they dwindled away. The Murchisons excused themselves. They were going to watch some ballet.

There were few people left now. Betterton guided Hilary with his hand on her arm to a clear space near the parapet. The stars showed above them and the air was cold now, crisp and exhilarating. They were alone here. Hilary sat down on the low concrete, and Betterton stood in front of her.

"Now then," he said in a low nervous voice, *"Who the hell are you?"*

She looked up at him for a moment or two without answering. Before she replied to his question there was something that she herself had got to know.

"Why did you recognise me as your wife?" she asked.

They looked at each other. Neither of them wished to be the first to answer the other's question. It was a duel of wills between them, but Hilary knew that whatever Tom Betterton had been like when he left England, his will was now inferior to her own. She had arrived here fresh in the self-confidence of organising her own life—Tom Betterton had been living a planned existence. She was the stronger.

He looked away from her at last, and muttered sullenly:

"It was—just an impulse. I was probably a damned fool. I fancied that you might have been sent—to get me out of here."

"You want to get out of here, then?"

"My God, can you ask?"

"How did you get here from Paris?"

Tom Betterton gave a short unhappy laugh.

"I wasn't kidnapped or anything like that, if that's what you mean. I came of my own free will, under my own steam. I came keenly and enthusiastically."

"You knew that you were coming here?"

"I'd no idea I was coming to Africa, if that's what you mean. I was caught by the usual lure. Peace on earth, free sharing of scientific secrets amongst the scientists of the world; suppression of capitalists and war-mongers—all the usual jargon! That fellow Peters who came with you is the same, he's swallowed the same bait."

"And when you got here—it wasn't like that?"

Again he gave that short bitter laugh.

"You'll see for yourself. Oh, perhaps it *is* that, more or less! But it's not the way you thought it would be. It's not—*freedom.*"

He sat down beside her frowning to himself.

"That's what got me down at home, you know. The feeling of being watched and spied upon. All the security precautions. Having to account for one's actions, for one's friends . . . All necessary, I daresay, but it gets you down in the end . . . And so when someone comes along with a proposition—well, you listen . . . It all sounds fine . . ." He gave a short laugh. "And one ends up—here!"

Hilary said slowly:

"You mean you've come to exactly the same circumstances as those from which you tried to escape? You're being watched and spied upon in just the same way—or worse?"

Betterton pushed his hair back nervously from his forehead.

"I don't know," he said. "Honestly. I don't know. I can't be sure. It may be all going on in my own mind. I don't know that I'm being watched at all. Why should I be? Why should they bother? They've got me here—in prison."

"It isn't in the least as you imagined it?"

"That's the odd thing. I suppose it *is* in a way. The working conditions are perfect. You've every facility, every kind of apparatus. You can work for as long a time as you like or as short a time. You've got every comfort and accessory. Food, clothes, living quarters, but you're conscious all the time that you're in prison."

"I know. When the gates clanged behind us today as we came in it was a horrible feeling." Hilary shuddered.

"Well," Betterton seemed to pull himself together. "I've answered your question. Now answer mine. What are you doing here pretending to be Olive?"

"Olive—" she stopped, feeling for words.

"Yes? What about Olive? What's happened to her? What are you trying to say?"

She looked with pity at his haggard nervous face.

"I've been dreading having to tell you."

"You mean—something's happened to her?"

"Yes. I'm sorry, terribly sorry. . . . Your wife's dead. . . . She was coming to join you and the plane crashed. She was taken to hospital and died two days later."

He stared straight ahead of him. It was as though he was determined to show no emotion of any kind. He said quietly:

"So Olive's dead? I see . . ."

There was a long silence. Then he turned to her.

"All right. I can go on from there. You took her place and came here, why?"

This time Hilary was ready with her response. Tom Betterton had believed that she had been sent "to get him out of here" as he had put it. That was not the case. Hilary's position was that of a spy. She had been sent to gain information not to plan the escape of a man who had placed himself willingly in the position he now was. Moreover she could command no means of deliverance, she was a prisoner as much as he was.

To confide in him fully would, she felt, be dangerous. Betterton was very near a breakdown. At any moment he might go completely to pieces. In those circumstances it would be madness to expect him to keep a secret.

She said,

"I was in the hospital with your wife when she died. I offered to take her place and try and reach you. She wanted to get a message to you very badly."

He frowned.

"But surely—"

She hurried on—before he could realise the weakness of the tale.

"It's not so incredible as it sounds. You see I had a lot of sympathy with all these ideas—the ideas you've just been talking about. Scientific secrets shared with all nations—a new World Order. I was enthusiastic about it all. And then my hair—if what they expected was a red-haired woman of the right age, I thought I'd get through. It seemed worth trying anyway."

"Yes," he said. His eyes swept over her head. "Your hair's exactly like Olive's."

"And then, you see, your wife was so insistent—about the message she wanted me to give to you."

"Oh, yes, the message. What message?"

"To tell you to be careful—very careful—that you were in danger—from someone called Boris?"

"Boris? Boris Glydr, do you mean?"

"Yes, do you know him?"

He shook his head.

"I've never met him. But I know him by name. He's a relation of my first wife's. I know about him."

"Why should he be dangerous?"

"What?"

He spoke absently.

Hilary repeated her question.

"Oh, that." He seemed to come back from far away. "I don't know why he should be dangerous to *me*, but it's true that by all accounts he's a dangerous sort of chap."

"In what way?"

"Well, he's one of those half balmy idealists who would quite happily kill off half humanity if they thought for some reason it would be a good thing."

"I know the sort of person you mean."

She felt she did know—vividly. (But why?)

"Had Olive seen him? What did he say to her?"

"I can't tell you. That's all she said. About danger—oh yes, she said she couldn't believe it."

"Believe what?"

"I don't know." She hesitated a minute and then said, "You see—she was dying . . ."

A spasm of pain convulsed his face.

"I know . . . I know . . . I shall get used to it in time. At the moment I can't realise it. But I'm puzzled about Boris. How could he be dangerous to me *here*? If he'd seen Olive he was in London, I suppose?"

"He was in London, yes."

"Then I simply don't get it. . . . Oh well, what does it matter? What the hell does anything matter? Here we are, stuck in this bloody Unit surrounded by a lot of inhuman Robots . . ."

"That's just how they felt to me."

"And we can't get out." He pounded with his fist on the concrete. "*We can't get out.*"

"Oh, yes, we can," said Hilary.

He turned to stare at her in surprise.

"What on earth do you mean?"

"We'll find a way," said Hilary.

"My dear girl," his laugh was scornful. "You haven't the faintest idea what you're up against in this place."

"People escaped from the most impossible places during the war," said Hilary stubbornly. She was not going to give in to despair. "They tunnelled, or something."

"How can you tunnel through sheer rock? And where to? It's desert all round."

"Then it will have to be 'or something.'"

He looked at her. She smiled with a confidence that was dogged rather than genuine.

"What an extraordinary girl you are. You sound quite sure of yourself."

"There's always a way. I daresay it will take time, and a lot of planning."

His face clouded over again.

"Time," he said. "Time . . . That's what I can't afford."

"Why?"

"I don't know whether you'll be able to understand . . . It's like this. I can't really—do my stuff here."

She frowned.

"How do you mean?"

"How shall I put it? I can't work. I can't *think*. In my stuff one has to have a high degree of concentration. A lot of it is—well—*creative*. Since coming here I've just lost the urge. All I can do is good sound hack work. The sort of thing any twopenny-halfpenny scientific chap can do. But that's not what they brought me here for. They want original stuff and I can't *do* original stuff. And the more nervous and afraid I get, the less I'm fit to turn out anything worth turning out. And it's driving me off my rocker, do you see?"

Yes, she saw now. She recalled Dr. Rubec's remarks about prima donnas and scientists.

"If I can't deliver the goods, what is an outfit like this going to do about it? They'll liquidate me."

"Oh, no."

"Oh, yes, they will. They're not sentimentalists here. What's saved me so far is this plastic surgery business. They do it a little at a time, you know. And naturally a fellow who's having constant minor operations can't be expected to concentrate. But they've finished the business now."

"But why was it done at all? What's the point?"

"Oh, that! For safety. My safety, I mean. It's done if—if you're a 'wanted' man."

"Are you a 'wanted' man, then?"

"Yes, didn't you know? Oh, I suppose they wouldn't advertise the fact in the papers. Perhaps even Olive didn't know. But I'm wanted right enough."

"You mean for—*treason* is the word, isn't it? You mean you've sold them atom secrets?"

He avoided her eyes.

"I didn't sell anything. I gave them what I knew of our processes—gave it freely. If you can believe me, I *wanted* to give it to them. It was part of the whole setup—the pooling of scientific knowledge. Oh, can't you understand?"

She could understand. She could understand Andy Peters doing just that. She could see Ericsson with his fanatical dreamer's eyes betraying his country with a high-souled enthusiasm.

Yet it was hard for her to visualise Tom Betterton doing it—and she realised with a shock that all that showed was the difference between Betterton a few months ago, arriving in all the zeal of enthusiasm, and Betterton now, nervous, defeated, down to earth—an ordinary badly frightened man.

Even as she accepted the logic of that, Betterton looked round him nervously and said:

"Everyone's gone down. We'd better—"

She rose.

"Yes. But it's all right, you know. They'll think it quite natural—under the circumstances."

He said awkwardly:

"We'll have to go on with this now, you know. I mean—you'll have to go on being—my wife."

"Of course."

"And we'll have to share a room and all that. But it will be quite all right. I mean, you needn't be afraid that—"

He swallowed in an embarrassed manner.

"How handsome he is," thought Hilary, looking at his profile, "and how little it moves me . . ."

"I don't think we need worry about that," she said cheerfully. "The important thing is to get out of here alive."

CHAPTER XIV

IN A ROOM at the Hotel Mamounia, Marrakesh, the man called Jessop was talking to Miss Hetherington. A different Miss Hetherington this, from the one that Hilary had known at Casablanca and at Fez. The same appearance, the same twin set, the same depressing hair-do. But the manner had changed. It was a woman now both brisk, competent, and seeming years younger than her appearance.

The third person in the room was a dark stocky man with intelligent eyes. He was tapping gently on the table with his fingers and humming a little French song under his breath.

". . . and as far as you know," Jessop was saying, "those are the only people she talked to at Fez?"

Janet Hetherington nodded.

"There was the Calvin Baker woman, whom we'd already met at Casablanca. I'll say frankly I still can't make up my mind about her. She went out of her way to be friendly with Olive Betterton, and with me for that matter. But Americans are friendly, they do enter into conversation with people in hotels, and they like joining them on trips."

"Yes," said Jessop, "it's all a little too overt for what we're looking for."

"And besides," went on Janet Hetherington, "*she* was on this plane, too."

"You're assuming," said Jessop, "that the crash was planned." He looked sideways towards the dark, stocky man. "What about it, Leblanc?"

Leblanc stopped humming his tune, and stopped his little tattoo on the table for a moment or two.

"*Ça ce peut,*" he said. "There may have been sabotage to the machine and that is why it crashed. We shall never know. The plane crashed and went up in flames and everyone on board was killed."

"What do you know of the pilot?"

"Alcadi? Young, reasonably competent. No more. Badly paid." He added the two last words with a slight pause in front of them.

Jessop said:

"Open therefore to other employment, but presumably not a candidate for suicide?"

"There were seven bodies," said Leblanc. "Badly charred, unrecognisable, but seven bodies. One cannot get away from that."

Jessop turned back to Janet Hetherington.

"You were saying?" he said.

"There was a French family at Fez that Mrs. Betterton exchanged a few words with. There was a rich Swedish business man with a glamour girl. And the rich oil magnate, Mr. Aristides."

"Ah," said Leblanc, "that fabulous figure himself. What must it feel like, I have often asked myself, to have all the money in the world? For me," he added frankly, "I would keep race horses and women, and all the world has to offer. But old Aristides shuts himself up in his castle in Spain —literally his castle in Spain, *mon cher*—and collects, so they say, Chinese potteries of the Sung period. But one must remember," he added, "that he is at least seventy. It is possible at that age that Chinese potteries are all that interest one."

"According to the Chinese themselves," said Jessop, "the years between sixty and seventy are the most rich in living and one is then most appreciative of the beauty and delight of life."

"*Pas moi!*" said Leblanc.

"There were some Germans at Fez, too," continued Janet Hetherington, "but as far as I know they didn't exchange any remarks with Olive Betterton."

"A waiter or a servant, perhaps," said Jessop.

"That's always possible."

"And she went out into the old town alone, you say?"

"She went with one of the regular guides. Someone may have contacted her on that tour."

"At any rate she decided quite suddenly to go to Marrakesh."

"Not suddenly," she corrected him. "She already had her reservations."

"Ah, I'm wrong," said Jessop. "What I mean is that Mrs. Calvin Baker decided rather suddenly to accompany her." He got up and paced up and down. "She flew to Marrakesh," he said, "and the plane crashed and came down in flames. It seems ill-omened, does it not, for anyone called Olive Betterton to travel by air. First the crash near Casablanca, and then this one. Was it an accident or was it contrived? If there were people who wished to get rid of Olive Betterton, there would be easier ways to do it than by wrecking a plane, I should say."

"One never knows," said Leblanc. "Understand me, *mon cher*. Once you have got into that state of mind where the taking of human lives no longer counts, then if it is simpler to put a little explosive package under a seat in a plane, than to wait about at the corner on a dark night and stick a knife into someone, then the package will be left and the fact that six other people will die also is not even considered."

"Of course," said Jessop, "I know I'm in a minority of one, but I still think there's a third solution—that they faked the crash."

Leblanc looked at him with interest.

"That could be done, yes. The plane could be brought down and it could be set on fire. But you cannot get away from the fact, *mon cher* Jessop, that there were *people* in the plane. The charred bodies were actually *there*."

"I know," said Jessop. "That's the stumbling block. Oh, I've no doubt my ideas are fantastic, but it's such a neat ending to our hunt. Too neat. That's what I feel. It says finish to us. We write down R.I.P. in the margin of our report and it's ended. There's no further trail to take up." He turned again to Leblanc. "You are having that search instituted?"

"For two days now," said Leblanc. "Good men, too. It's a particularly lonely spot, of course, where the plane crashed. It was off its course, by the way."

"Which is significant," Jessop put in.

"The nearest villages, the nearest habitations, the nearest traces of a car, all those are being investigated fully. In this country as well as in yours, we fully realise the importance of the investigation. In France, too, we have lost some of our best young scientists. In my opinion, *mon cher*, it is easier to control temperamental opera singers than it is to control a scientist. They are brilliant, these young men, erratic, rebellious; and finally and dangerously, they are most completely credulous. What do they imagine goes on *là-bas?* Sweetness and light and desire for truth and the millennium? Alas, poor children, what disillusionment awaits them."

"Let's go over the passenger list once more," said Jessop.

The Frenchman reached out a hand, picked it out of a wire basket and set it before his colleague. The two men pored over it together.

"Mrs. Calvin Baker, American. Mrs. Betterton, English. Torquil Ericsson, Norwegian—what do you know of him, by the way?"

"Nothing that I can recall," said Leblanc. "He was young, not more than twenty-seven or twenty-eight."

"I know his name," said Jessop, frowning. "I think—I am almost sure—that he read a paper before the Royal Society."

"Then there is the *religieuse*," Leblanc said, turning back to the list. "Sister Marie something or other. Andrew Peters, also American. Dr. Barron. That is a celebrated name, *le docteur Barron*. A man of great brilliance. An expert on virus diseases."

"Biological warfare," said Jessop. "It fits. It all fits."

"A man poorly paid and discontented," said Leblanc.

"How many going to St. Ives?" murmured Jessop.

The Frenchman shot him a quick look and he smiled apologetically.

"Just an old nursery rhyme," he said. "For St. Ives read question mark. Journey to nowhere."

The telephone on the table buzzed and Leblanc picked up the receiver.

"Allo?" he said. "*Qu'est ce qu'il y a?* Ah, yes, send them up." He turned his head towards Jessop. His face was suddenly alive, vigorous. "One of my men reporting," he said. "They have found something. *Mon cher collègue*, it is possible—I say no more—possible that your optimism is justified."

A few moments later two men entered the room. The first bore a rough resemblance to Leblanc, the same type, stocky, dark, intelligent. His manner was respectful but exhilarated. He wore European clothes badly stained and marked, covered with dust. He had obviously just arrived from a journey. With him was a native wearing the white local dress. He had the dignified composure of the dweller in remote places. His manner was courteous but not subservient. He looked with a faint wonder round the room whilst the other man explained things in rapid French.

"The reward was offered and circulated," the man explained, "and this fellow and his family and a great many of his friends have been searching diligently. I let him bring you the find himself as there may be questions you want to ask him."

Leblanc turned to the Berber—

"You have done good work," he said, speaking now in the man's own language. "You have the eyes of the hawk, my father. Show us then what you have discovered."

From a fold in his white robe the man took out a small object, and stepping forward laid it on the table before the Frenchman. It was rather a large sized pinkish grey synthetic pearl.

"It is like the one shown to me and shown to others," he said. "It is of value and I have found it."

Jessop stretched out a hand and took the pearl. From his pocket he drew out another exactly like it and examined both. Then he walked across the room to the window, and examined them both through a powerful lens.

"Yes," he said, "the mark is there." There was jubilation now in his voice and he came back to the table. "Good girl," he said, "good girl, good girl! She managed it!"

Leblanc was questioning the Berber in a rapid exchange of Arabic. Finally he turned to Jessop.

"I make my apologies, *mon cher collègue*," he said. "This pearl was found at a distance of nearly *half a mile* from the flaming plane."

"Which shows," said Jessop, "that Olive Betterton was a survivor, and that though seven people left Fez in the plane and seven charred bodies were found, one of those charred bodies was definitely not hers."

"We extend the search now," said Leblanc. He spoke again to the Berber and the man smiled back happily. He left the room with the man who had brought him in. "He will be handsomely rewarded as promised," said Leblanc, "and there will be a hunt now all over the countryside for these pearls. They have hawk eyes, these people, and the knowledge that these are worth good money in reward will pass round like a grapevine. I think —I think, *mon cher collègue*, that we shall get results! If only they have not tumbled to what she was doing."

Jessop shook his head.

"It would be such a natural occurrence," he said. "The sudden breaking of a necklace of costume jewellery such as most women wear, the picking up apparently of what loose pearls she can find and stuffing them into her pocket, then a little hole in the pocket. Besides, why should they suspect her? She is Olive Betterton, anxious to join her husband."

"We must review this matter in a new light," said Leblanc. He drew the passenger list towards him. "Olive Betterton. Dr. Barron," he said, ticking off the two names. "Two at least who are going—wherever they are going. The American woman, Mrs. Calvin Baker. As to her we keep an open mind. Torquil Ericsson you say has read papers before the Royal Society. The American, Peters, was described on his passport as a Research Chemist. The *religieuse*—well, it would make a good disguise. In fact, a whole cargo of people cleverly shepherded from different points to travel in that one plane on that particular day. And then the plane is discovered in flames and inside it the requisite number of charred bodies. How did they manage that, I wonder? *Enfin, c'est colossal!*"

"Yes," said Jessop. "It was the final convincing touch. But we know now that six or seven people have started off on a fresh journey, and we know where their point of departure is. What do we do next—visit the spot?"

"But precisely," said Leblanc. "We take up advanced headquarters. If I mistake not, now that we are on the track, other evidence will come to light."

"If our calculations are exact," Leblanc said, "there should be results."

The calculations were many and devious. The rate of progress of a car, the likely distance where it would refuel, possible villages where travellers might have stayed the night. The tracks were many and confusing, disappointments were continual, but every now and then there came a positive result.

"*Voila, mon capitaine!* A search of the latrines, as you ordered. In a dark corner of the latrine a pearl embedded in a little piece of chewing gum in the house of one Abdul Mohammed. He and his sons have been interrogated. At first they denied, but at last they have confessed. A carload of six people said to be from the German archaeological expedition spent a night in his house. Much money was paid, and they were not to mention this to anyone, the excuse being that there was some illicit digging in prospect. Children in the village of El Kaif also have brought in two more pearls. We know now the direction. There is more, *Monsieur le Capitaine*. The hand Fatma has been seen as you foretold. This type here, he will tell you about it."

"This type" was a particularly wild-looking Berber.

"I was with my flocks," he said, "at night and I heard a car. It passed me and as it did so I saw the sign. The hand of Fatma was outlined on one side of it. It gleamed, I tell you, in the darkness."

"The application of phosphorus on a glove can be very efficacious," murmured Leblanc. "I congratulate you, *mon cher*, on that idea."

"It's effective," said Jessop, "but it's dangerous. It's too easily noticed by the fugitives themselves, I mean."

Leblanc shrugged his shoulders.

"It could not be seen in daylight."

"No, but if there was a halt and they alighted from the car in the darkness—"

"Even then—it is a notable Arab superstition. It is painted often on carts and wagons. It would only be thought that some pious Moslem had painted it in luminous paint on his vehicle."

"True enough. But we must be on our guard. For if our enemies did notice it, it is highly possible that they will lay a false trail for us, of hands of Fatma in phosphorous paint."

"Ah, as to that I agree with you. One must indeed be on one's guard. Always, always on one's guard."

On the following morning Leblanc had another exhibit of three false pearls arranged in a triangle, stuck together by a little piece of chewing gum.

"This should mean," said Jessop, "that the next stage of the journey was by plane."

He looked enquiringly at Leblanc.

"You are absolutely right," said the other. "This was found on a disused army airfield, in a remote and desolate place. There were signs that a plane landed and left there not long ago." He shrugged his shoulders. "An unknown plane," he said, "and once again they took off for a destination unknown. That brings us once more to a halt and we do not know where next to take up the trail."

CHAPTER XV

"IT'S INCREDIBLE," THOUGHT Hilary to herself, "incredible that I've been here ten days!" The frightening thing in life, Hilary thought, was how easily you adapted yourself. She remembered once being shown in France some peculiar torture arrangement of the Middle Ages, an iron cage wherein a prisoner had been confined and in which he could neither lie, stand nor sit. The guide had recounted how the last man imprisoned there had lived in it for eighteen years, had been released and had lived for another twenty after that, before dying, an old man. That adaptability, thought Hilary, was what differentiated man from the animal world. Man could live in any climate and on any food and under any conditions. He could exist slave or free.

She had felt first, when introduced into the Unit, a blinding panic, a horrible feeling of imprisonment and frustration, and the fact that the imprisonment was camouflaged in circumstances of luxury had somehow made it seem all the more horrible to her. And yet now, already, even after a week here she had begun insensibly to accept the conditions of her life as natural. It was a queer, dreamlike existence. Nothing seemed particularly real, but already she had the feeling that the dream had gone on a long time and would go on for a long time more. It would, perhaps, last forever. . . . She would always live here in the Unit, this was life, and there was nothing outside.

This dangerous acceptance, she thought, came partly from the fact that she was a woman. Women were adaptable by nature. It was their strength and their weakness. They examined their environment, accepted it, and like realists settled down to make the best of it. What interested her most were the reactions of the people who had arrived here with her. Helga Needheim she hardly ever saw except sometimes at meals. When they met, the German woman vouchsafed her a curt nod, but no more. As far as she could judge, Helga Needheim was happy and satisfied. The Unit obviously lived up to the picture she had formed in her mind of it. She was the type of woman absorbed by her work, and was comfortably sustained by her natural arrogance. The superiority of herself and her fellow scientists was the first article of Helga's creed. She had no views of a brotherhood of man, of an era of peace, of liberty of mind and spirit. For her the future was narrow but all conquering. The super race, herself a member of it; the rest of the world in bondage, treated, if they behaved, with condescending kindness. If her fellow workers expressed different views, if their ideas were Communist rather than Fascist, Helga took little notice. If their work was good they were necessary, and their ideas would change.

Dr. Barron was more intelligent than Helga Needheim. Occasionally Hilary had brief conversations with him. He was absorbed in his work, deeply satisfied with the conditions provided for him, but his enquiring Gallic intellect led him to speculate and ponder on the media in which he found himself.

"It was not what I expected. No, frankly," he said one day, "*entre nous,* Mrs. Betterton, I do not care for prison conditions. And these *are* prison conditions, though the cage, let us say, is heavily gilded."

"There is hardly the freedom here that you came to seek?" Hilary suggested.

He smiled at her, a quick, rueful smile.

"But no," he said, "you are wrong. I did not really seek liberty. I am a civilised man. The civilised man knows there is no such thing. Only the younger and cruder nations put the word *Liberty* on their banner. There must always be a planned framework of security. And the essence of civilisation is that the way of life should be a moderate one. The middle way. Always one comes back to the middle way. No. I will be frank with you. I came here for money."

Hilary in her turn smiled. Her eyebrows rose.

"And what good is money to you here?"

"It pays for very expensive laboratory equipment," said Dr. Barron. "I am not obliged to put my hand into my own pocket, and so I can serve the cause of science and satisfy my own intellectual curiosity. I am a man who loves his work, true, but I do not love it for the sake of humanity. I have usually found that those who do so are somewhat woolly headed, and often incompetent workers. No, it is the pure intellectual joy of research that I appreciate. For the rest, a large sum of money was paid to me before I left France. It is safely banked under another name and in due course, when all this comes to an end, I shall have it to spend as I choose."

"When all this comes to an end?" Hilary repeated. "But why should it come to an end?"

"One must have the common sense," said Dr. Barron, "nothing is permanent, nothing endures. I have come to the conclusion that this place is run by a madman. A madman, let me tell you, can be very logical. If you are rich and logical and also mad, you can succeed for a very long time in living out your illusion. But in the end—" he shrugged, "—in the end this will break up. Because, you see, it is not reasonable, what happens here! That which is not reasonable must always pay the reckoning in the end. In the meantime—" again he shrugged his shoulders, "—it suits me admirably."

Torquil Ericsson, whom Hilary expected to be violently disillusioned, appeared to be quite content in the atmosphere of the Unit. Less practical than the Frenchman, he existed in a single-minded vision of his own. The world in which he lived was one so unfamiliar to Hilary that she could not even understand it. It engendered a kind of austere happiness, an absorption in mathematical calculations, and an endless vista of possibilities. The strange, impersonal ruthlessness of his character frightened Hilary. He was the kind of young man, she thought, who in a moment of idealism could send three quarters of the world to their death in order that the remaining quarter should participate in an impractical Utopia that existed only in Ericsson's mind.

With the American, Andy Peters, Hilary felt herself far more in accord.

Possibly, she thought, it was because Peters was a man of talents but not a genius. From what others said, she gathered he was a first-class man at his job, a careful and skilled chemist, but not a pioneer. Peters, like herself, had at once hated and feared the atmosphere of the Unit.

"The truth is that I didn't know where I was going," he said. "I thought I knew, but I was wrong. The Party has got nothing to do with this place. We're not in touch with Moscow. This is a lone show of some kind—a Fascist show possibly."

"Don't you think," said Hilary, "that you go in too much for labels?"

He considered this.

"Maybe you're right," he said. "Come to think of it, these words we throw around don't mean much. But I do know this. I want to get out of here and I mean to get out of here."

"It won't be easy," said Hilary, in a low voice.

They were walking together after dinner near the splashing fountains of the roof garden. With the illusion of darkness and the starlit sky they might have been in the private gardens of some sultan's palace. The functional concrete buildings were veiled from their sight.

"No," said Peters, "it won't be easy, but nothing's impossible."

"I like to hear you say that," said Hilary. "Oh, how I like to hear you say that!"

He looked at her sympathetically.

"Been getting you down?" he asked.

"Very much so. But that's not what I'm really afraid of."

"No? what then?"

"I'm afraid of getting used to it," said Hilary.

"Yes." He spoke thoughtfully. "Yes, I know what you mean. There's a kind of mass suggestion going on here. I think perhaps you're right about that."

"It would seem to me much more natural for people to rebel," said Hilary.

"Yes. Yes, I've thought the same. In fact I've wondered once or twice whether there's not a little hocus-pocus going on."

"Hocus-pocus? What do you mean by that?"

"Well, to put it frankly, dope."

"Do you mean a drug of some kind?"

"Yes. It might be possible, you know. Something in the food or drink, something that induces—what shall I say—docility?"

"But is there such a drug?"

"Well, that's not really my line of country. There are things that are given to people to soothe them down, to make them acquiescent before operations and that. Whether there is anything that can be administered steadily over a long period of time—and which at the same time does not impair efficiency—that I don't know. I'm more inclined to think now that the effect is produced mentally. I mean that I think some of these organisers and administrators here are well-versed in hypnosis and psychology and that, without our being aware of it, we are continually being offered suggestions of our well being, of our attaining our ultimate aim (whatever it is), and that all this *does* produce a definite effect. A lot can be done that way, you know, if it's done by people who know their stuff."

"But we mustn't acquiesce," cried Hilary, hotly. "We mustn't feel for one moment that it's a good thing to be here."

"What does your husband feel?"

"Tom? I—oh, I don't know. It's so difficult. I—" she lapsed into silence.

The whole fantasy of her life as she lived it she could hardly communicate to the man who was listening to her. For ten days now she had lived in an apartment with a man who was a stranger to her. They shared a bedroom and when she lay awake at night she could hear him breathing in the other bed. Both of them accepted the arrangement as inevitable. She was an impostor, a spy, ready to play any part and assume any personality. Tom Betterton she quite frankly did not understand. He seemed to her a terrible example of what could happen to a brilliant young man who had lived for some months in the enervating atmosphere of the Unit. At any rate there was in him no calm acceptance of his destiny. Far from taking pleasure in his work, he was, she thought, increasingly worried by his inability to concentrate on it. Once or twice he had reiterated what he had said on that first evening.

"I can't think. It's just as though everything in me has dried up."

Yes, she thought, Tom Betterton, being a real genius, needed liberty more than most. Suggestion had failed to compensate him for the loss of freedom. Only in perfect liberty was he able to produce creative work.

He was a man, she thought, very close to a serious nervous breakdown. Hilary herself he treated with curious inattention. She was not a woman to him, not even a friend. She even doubted whether he realised and suffered from the death of his wife. The thing that preoccupied him incessantly was the problem of confinement. Again and again he had said,

"I must get away from here. I must, I must." And sometimes, "I didn't know. I'd no idea what it was going to be like. How *am* I going to get out of here? How? I've got to. I've simply got to."

It was in essence very much what Peters had said. But it was said with a great deal of difference. Peters had spoken as a young, energetic, angry, disillusioned man, sure of himself and determined to pit his wits against the brains of the establishment in which he found himself. But Tom Betterton's rebellious utterances were those of a man at the end of his tether, a man almost crazed with the need for escape. But perhaps, Hilary thought suddenly, that was where she and Peters would be in six months' time. Perhaps what began as healthy rebellion and a reasonable confidence in one's own ingenuity, would turn at last into the frenzied despair of a rat in a trap.

She wished she could talk of all this to the man beside her. If only she could say: "Tom Betterton isn't my husband. I know nothing about him. I don't know what he was like before he came here and so I'm in the dark. I can't help him, for I don't know what to do or say." As it was she had to pick her words carefully. She said,

"Tom seems like a stranger to me now. He doesn't—tell me things. Sometimes I think the confinement, the sense of being penned up here, is driving him mad."

"It's possible," said Peters drily, "it could act that way."

"But tell me—you speak so confidently of getting away. How *can* we get away—what earthly chance is there?"

"I don't mean we can walk out the day after tomorrow, Olive. The thing's got to be thought out and planned. People have escaped, you know, under the most unpromising conditions. A lot of our people, and a lot your side of the Atlantic, too, have written books about escape from fortresses in Germany."

"That was rather different."

"Not in essence. Where there's a way in, there's a way out. Of course tunnelling is out of the question here, so that knocks out a good many methods. But as I say, where there's a way in, there's a way out. With ingenuity, camouflage, playing a part, deception, bribery and corruption, one ought to manage it. It's the sort of thing you've got to study and think about. I'll tell you this. I *shall* get out of here. Take it from me."

"I believe you will," said Hilary, then she added, "but shall I?"

"Well, it's different for you."

His voice sounded embarrassed. For a moment she wondered what he meant. Then she realised that presumably her own objective had been attained. She had come here to join the man she had loved, and having joined him her own personal need for escape should not be so great. She was almost tempted to tell Peters the truth—but some instinct of caution forbade that.

She said goodnight and left the roof.

CHAPTER XVI

"Good evening, Mrs. Betterton."

"Good evening, Miss Jennsen."

The thin spectacled girl was looking excited. Her eyes glinted behind the thick lenses.

"There will be a Reunion this evening," she said. "The *Director himself* is going to address us!"

She spoke in an almost hushed voice.

"That's good," said Andy Peters who was standing close by. "I've been waiting to catch a glimpse of this Director."

Miss Jennsen threw him a glance of shocked reproof.

"The Director," she said austerely, "is a very wonderful man."

As she went away from them down one of the inevitable white corridors, Andy Peters gave a low whistle.

"Now did I, or did I not, catch a hint of the Heil Hitler attitude there?"

"It certainly sounded like it."

"The trouble in this life is that you never really know where you're going. If I'd known when I left the States all full of boyish ardour for the good old Brotherhood of Man that I was going to land myself in the clutches of yet another Heavenborn Dictator—" he threw out his hands.

"You don't know that yet," Hilary reminded him.

"I can smell it—in the air," said Peters.

"Oh," cried Hilary, "how glad I am that you're here."

She flushed, as he looked at her quizzically.

"You're so nice and ordinary," said Hilary desperately.

Peters looked amused.

"Where I come from," he said, "the word ordinary doesn't have your meaning. It can stand for being just plain mean."

"You know I didn't mean it that way. I mean you're like everybody else. Oh dear, that sounds rude, too."

"The common man, that's what you're asking for? You've had enough of the genius?"

"Yes, and you've changed, too, since you came here. You've lost that streak of bitterness—of hatred."

But immediately his face grew rather grim.

"Don't count on that," he said. "It's still there—underneath. I can still hate. There are things, believe me, that *should* be hated."

The Reunion, as Miss Jennsen had called it, took place after dinner. All members of the Unit assembled in the large lecture room.

The audience did not include what might be called the technical staff: the laboratory assistants, the corps de ballet, the various service personnel, and the small assembly of handsome prostitutes who also served the Unit as purveyors of sex to those men who had no wives with them and had formed no particular attachments with the female workers.

Sitting next to Betterton, Hilary awaited with keen curiosity the arrival on the platform of that almost mythical figure, the Director. Questioned by her, Tom Betterton had given unsatisfactory, almost vague answers, about the personality of the man who controlled the Unit.

"He's nothing much to look at," he said. "But he has tremendous impact. Actually I've only seen him twice. He doesn't show up often. He's remarkable, of course, one feels that, but honestly I don't know *why*."

From the reverent way Miss Jennsen and some of the other women spoke about him, Hilary had formed a vague mental figure of a tall man with a golden beard wearing a white robe—a kind of godlike abstraction.

She was almost startled when, as the audience rose to their feet, a dark rather heavily built man of middle age came quietly onto the platform. In appearance he was quite undistinguished, he might have been a business man from the Midlands. His nationality was not apparent. He spoke to them in three languages, alternating one with the other, and never exactly repeating himself. He used French, German and English, and each was spoken with equal fluency.

"Let me first," he began, "welcome our new colleagues who have come to join us here."

He then paid a few words of tribute to each of the new arrivals.

After that he went on to speak of the aims and beliefs of the Unit.

Trying to remember his words later, Hilary found herself unable to do so with any accuracy. Or perhaps it was that the words, as remembered, seemed trite and ordinary. But listening to them was a very different thing.

Hilary remembered once being told by a friend who had lived in Germany in the days before the war, how she had gone to a meeting in mere curiosity to listen "to that absurd Hitler"—and how she had found herself crying hysterically, swept away by intense emotion. She had described how wise and inspiring every word had seemed, and how, afterwards, the remembered words in their actuality had seemed commonplace enough.

Something of the same kind was happening now. In spite of herself,

Hilary was stirred and uplifted. The Director spoke very simply. He spoke primarily of Youth. With Youth lay the future of mankind.

"Accumulated Wealth, Prestige, influential Families—those have been the forces of the past. But today, power lies in the hands of the young. Power is in Brains. The brains of the chemist, the physicist, the doctor . . . From the laboratories comes the power to destroy on a vast scale. With that power you can say 'Yield—or perish!' That power should not be given to this or that nation. Power should be in the hands of those who create it. This Unit is a gathering place for the Power of all the world. You come here from all parts of the globe, bringing with you your creative scientific knowledge. And with you, you bring *Youth!* No one here is over forty-five. When the day comes, we shall create a Trust. The Brains Trust of Science. And we shall administer world affairs. We shall issue our orders to Capitalists and Kings and Armies and Industries. We shall give the World the *Pax Scientifica*."

There was more of it—all the same heady intoxicating stuff—but it was not the words themselves—it was the power of the orator that carried away an assembly that could have been cold and critical had it not been swayed by that nameless emotion about which so little is known.

When the Director had ended abruptly:

"Courage and Victory! Goodnight!" Hilary left the Hall, half stumbling in a kind of exalted dream, and recognised the same feeling in the faces around her. She saw Ericsson in particular, his pale eyes gleaming, his head tossed back in exultation.

Then she felt Andy Peters' hand on her arm and his voice said in her ear:

"Come up on the roof. We need some air."

They went up in the lift without speaking and stepped out among the palm trees under the stars. Peters drew a deep breath.

"Yes," he said. "This is what we need. Air to blow away the clouds of glory."

Hilary gave a deep sigh. She still felt unreal.

He gave her arm a friendly shake.

"Snap out of it, Olive."

"Clouds of glory," said Hilary. "You know—it *was* like that!"

"Snap out of it, I tell you. Be a woman! Down to earth and basic realities! When the effects of the Glory Gas poisoning pass off you'll realise that you've been listening to the same old Mixture as Before."

"But it was fine—I mean a fine ideal."

"Nuts to ideals. Take the facts. Youth and Brains—glory glory Alleluia! And what are the youth and brains? Helga Needheim, a ruthless egoist. Torquil Ericsson, an impractical dreamer. Dr. Barron who'd sell his grandmother to the knacker's yard to get equipment for his work. Take me, an ordinary guy, as you've said yourself, good with the test-tube and the microscope but with no talent whatever for efficient administration of an office, let alone a World! Take your own husband—yes, I'm going to say it—a man whose nerves are frayed to nothing and who can think of nothing but the fear that retribution will catch up with him. I've given you those people we know best—but they're all the same here—or all that I've come across. Geniuses, some of them, damned good at their chosen jobs—but as Administrators of the Universe—hell, don't make me laugh! Pernicious nonsense, that's what we've been listening to."

Hilary sat down on the concrete parapet. She passed a hand across her forehead.

"You know," she said. "I believe you're right . . . But the clouds of glory are still trailing. How does he do it? Does he believe it himself? He must."

Peters said gloomily,

"I suppose it always comes to the same thing in the end. A madman who believes he's God."

Hilary said slowly,

"I suppose so. And yet—that seems curiously unsatisfactory."

"But it happens, my dear. Again and again throughout history it happens. And it gets one. It nearly got me, tonight. It *did* get you. If I hadn't whisked you up here—" his manner changed suddenly. "I suppose I shouldn't have done that. What will Betterton say? He'll think it odd."

"I don't think so. I doubt if he'll notice."

He looked at her questioningly.

"I'm sorry, Olive. It must be all pretty fair hell for you. Seeing him go down the hill."

Hilary said passionately,

"We must get out of here. We must. We must."

"We shall."

"You said that before—but we've made no progress."

"Oh, yes, we have. I've not been idle."

She looked at him in surprise.

"No precise plan, but I've initiated subversive activities. There's a lot of dissatisfaction here, far more than our godlike Herr Director knows. Amongst the humbler members of the Unit, I mean. Food and money and luxury and women aren't everything, you know. I'll get you out of here yet, Olive."

"And Tom, too."

Peters' face darkened.

"Listen, Olive, and believe what I say. Tom will do best to stay on here. He's—" he hesitated, "—safer here than he would be in the outside world."

"Safer? What a curious word."

"Safer," said Peters. "I use the word deliberately."

Hilary frowned.

"I don't really see what you mean. Tom's not—you don't think he's becoming mentally unhinged?"

"Not in the least. He's het up, but I'd say Tom Betterton's as sane as you or I."

"Then why are you saying he'd be safer here?"

Peters said slowly,

"A cage, you know, is a very safe place to be."

"Oh, no," cried Hilary. "Don't tell me you're going to believe that too. Don't tell me that mass hypnotism, or suggestion, or whatever it is, is working on you. Safe, tame, content! We *must* rebel still! We must want to be free!"

Peters said slowly,

"Yes, I know. But—"

"Tom, at any rate, wants desperately to get away from here."

"Tom mayn't know what's good for him."

Suddenly Hilary remembered what Tom had hinted at to her. If he had disposed of secret information he would be liable, she supposed, to prosecution under the Official Secrets Act— That, no doubt, was what Peters was hinting at in his rather embarrassed way—but Hilary was clear in her own mind. Better to serve a prison sentence even than remain on here. She said, obstinately,

"Tom must come, too."

She was startled when Peters said suddenly, in a bitter tone,

"Have it your own way. I've warned you. I wish I knew what the hell makes you care for that fellow so much?"

She stared at him in dismay. Words sprang to her lips, but she checked them. She realised that what she wanted to say was, "I don't care for him. He's nothing to me. He was another woman's husband and I've a responsibility to her." She wanted to say, "You fool, if there's anybody I care about, it's *you* . . ."

II

"Been enjoying yourself with your tame American?"

Tom Betterton threw the words at her as she entered their bedroom. He was lying on his back on his bed, smoking.

Hilary flushed slightly.

"We arrived here together," she said, "and we seem to think alike about certain things."

He laughed.

"Oh! I don't blame you." For the first time he looked at her in a new and appraising way. "You're a good-looking woman, Olive," he said.

From the beginning Hilary had urged him always to call her by his wife's name.

"Yes," he continued, his eyes raking her up and down. "You're a damned good-looking woman. I'd have noticed that once. As it is, nothing of that kind seems to register with me any more."

"Perhaps it's just as well," said Hilary drily.

"I'm a perfectly normal man, my dear, or I used to be. God knows what I am now."

Hilary sat down by him.

"What *is* the matter with you, Tom?" she said.

"I tell you. I can't concentrate. As a scientist I'm shot to pieces. This place—"

"The others—or most of them—don't seem to feel like you?"

"Because they're a damned insensitive crowd, I suppose."

"Some of them are temperamental enough," said Hilary, drily. She went on, "If only you had a friend here—a real friend."

"Well, there's Murchison. Though he's a dull dog. And I've seen a good deal of Torquil Ericsson lately."

"Really?" For some reason Hilary felt surprised.

"Yes. My God, he's brilliant. I wish I had *his* brains."

"He's an odd sort of person," said Hilary. "I always find him rather frightening."

"Frightening? Torquil? He's as mild as milk. Like a child in some ways. No knowledge of the world."

"Well *I* find him frightening," repeated Hilary obstinately.

"Your nerves must be getting upset, too."

"Not yet. I suspect they will, though. Tom—don't get too friendly with Torquil Ericsson."

He stared at her.

"Why ever not?"

"I don't know. It's a feeling I have."

CHAPTER XVII

LEBLANC SHRUGGED HIS shoulders.

"They have left Africa, it is certain."

"Not *certain*."

"The probabilities point that way." The Frenchman shook his head. "After all, we know, do we not, for where they are bound?"

"If they are bound for where we think, why start the journey from Africa? Anywhere in Europe would be simpler."

"That is true. But there is the other side of it. No one would expect them to assemble and start from here."

"I still think there's more to it than that." Jessop was gently insistent. "Besides, only a small plane could have used that airfield. It would have to come down and refuel before crossing the Mediterranean. And where they refuelled some trace should have been left."

"*Mon cher*, we have instituted the most searching enquiries—everywhere there has been—"

"The men with the Geiger counters must get results in the end. The number of planes to be examined is limited. Just a trace of radio-activity and we shall know that is the plane we are looking for—"

"If your agent has been able to use the spray. Alas! Always so many 'ifs' . . ."

"We shall get there," said Jessop obstinately. "I wonder—"

"Yes?"

"We have assumed they are going *north*—towards the Mediterranean—suppose instead, they flew *south*."

"Doubled back on their tracks? But where, then, could they be flying *to*? There are the mountains of the High Atlas—and after that the desert sands."

II

"Sidi, you swear to me that it will be as you have promised? A petrol station in America, in Chicago? It is certain?"

"It is certain, Mohammed, if we get out of here, that is."

"Success depends on the will of Allah."

"Let us hope, then, that it is the will of Allah that you should have a petrol station in Chicago. Why Chicago?"

"Sidi, the brother of my wife went to America, and he has there a petrol pump in Chicago. Do I want to remain in a backward part of the world all my days? Here there is money and much food and many rugs and women—but it is not modern. It is not America."

Peters looked thoughtfully into the dignified black face. Mohammed in his white robes was a magnificent sight. What strange desires rose in the human heart!

"I don't know that you're wise," he said with a sigh, "but so be it. Of course, if we are found out—"

A smile on the black face revealed beautiful white teeth.

"Then it is death—for me certainly. Perhaps not for you, Sidi, since you are valuable."

"They deal out death rather easily here, do they?"

The shoulders of the other man rose and fell contemptuously.

"What is death? That, too, is the will of Allah."

"You know what you have to do?"

"I know, Sidi. I am to take you to the roof after dark. Also I am to put in your room clothing such as I and the other servants wear. Later—there will be other things."

"Right. You'd better let me out of the lift now. Somebody may notice we're riding up and down. It may give them ideas."

III

There was dancing going on. Andy Peters was dancing with Miss Jennsen. He held her close to him, and seemed to be murmuring in her ear. As they revolved slowly near where Hilary was standing he caught her eye and immediately gave her an outrageous wink.

Hilary, biting her lip to avoid a smile, averted her eyes quickly.

Her glance fell on Betterton who was standing just across the room talking to Torquil Ericsson. Hilary frowned a little as she watched them.

"Have a turn with me, Olive?" said Murchison's voice at her elbow.

"Yes, of course, Simon."

"Mind you, I'm not very hot at dancing," he warned her.

Hilary concentrated on keeping her feet where he could not possibly tread on them.

"It's exercise, that's what I say," said Murchison, panting slightly. He was an energetic dancer.

"Awfully jolly frock you've got on, Olive."

His conversation seemed always to come out of an old-fashioned novel.

"I'm glad you like it," said Hilary.

"Get it out of the Fashion Department?"

Resisting the temptation to reply: "Where else?" Hilary merely said, "Yes."

"Must say, you know," panted Murchison as he capered perseveringly round the floor, "they do you jolly well here. Said so to Bianca only the other day. Beats the Welfare State every time. No worries about money, or income tax—or repairs or upkeep. All the worrying done for you. Must be a wonderful life for a woman, I should say."

"Bianca finds it so, does she?"

"Well, she was restless for a bit, but now she's managed to get up a few committees and organise one or two things—debates, you know, and lectures. She's complaining that you don't take as much part as you might in things."

"I'm afraid I'm not that kind of person, Simon. I've never been very public spirited."

"Yes, but you girls have got to keep yourselves amused one way or another. At least I don't mean *amused* exactly—"

"Occupied?" suggested Hilary.

"Yes—I mean the modern woman wants to get her teeth into something. I quite realise that women like you and Bianca have made a definite sacrifice coming here—you're neither of you scientists, thank goodness—really, these scientific women! Absolutely the limit, most of them! I said to Bianca, 'Give Olive time, she's got to get tuned in.' It takes a little time getting used to this place. To begin with, one gets a kind of claustrophobic feeling. But it wears off—it wears off . . ."

"You mean—one can get used to anything?"

"Well, some people feel it more than others. Tom, now, seems to take it hard. Where's old Tom tonight? Oh yes, I see, over there with Torquil. Quite inseparable, those two."

"I wish they weren't. I mean, I shouldn't have thought they had very much in common."

"Young Torquil seems fascinated by your husband. He follows him round everywhere."

"I've noticed it. I wondered—why?"

"Well, he's always got some outlandish theory to get off his chest—it's beyond my power to follow him—his English isn't too good, as you know. But Tom listens and manages to take it all in."

The dance ended. Andy Peters came up and claimed Hilary for the next one.

"I observed you suffering in a good cause," he said. "How badly did you get trampled?"

"Oh, I was fairly agile."

"You noticed me doing my stuff?"

"With the Jennsen?"

"Yes. I think I may say without undue modesty that I have made a hit, a palpable hit in that quarter. These plain angular short-sighted girls respond immediately when given the treatment."

"You certainly gave the impression of having fallen for her."

"That was the idea. That girl, Olive, properly handled, can be very useful. She's in the know about all the arrangements here. For instance, tomorrow there's a party of various V.I.P.'s due here. Doctors and a few Government officials and a rich patron or two."

"Andy—do you think there might be a chance . . ."

"No, I don't. I bet *that's* going to be taken care of. So don't cherish false hopes. But it will be valuable because we'll get an idea of the procedure. And on the next occasion—well, there might be something doing. So long as I can keep the Jennsen eating out of my hand, I can get a lot of miscellaneous information out of her."

"How much do the people who are coming know?"

"About *us*—the Unit, I mean—nothing at all. Or so I gather. They just inspect the settlement and the medical research laboratories. This place has been deliberately built like a labyrinth, just so that nobody coming into it can possibly guess its extent. I gather there are kinds of bulkheads that close, and that shut off our area."

"It all seems so incredible."

"I know. Half the time one feels one must be dreaming. One of the unreal things here is never seeing any children about. Thank goodness there aren't! You must be thankful you haven't got a child."

He felt the sudden stiffening of her body.

"Here—I'm sorry—I said the wrong thing!" He led her off the dance floor and to a couple of chairs.

"I'm very sorry," he repeated. "I hurt you, didn't I?"

"It's nothing—no, really not your fault. I did have a child—and it died—that's all."

"You had a child?—" he stared, surprised. "I thought you'd only been married to Betterton six months?"

Hilary flushed. She said quickly,

"Yes, of course. But I was—married before. I divorced my first husband."

"Oh, I see. That's the worst of this place. One doesn't know anything about people's lives before they came here, and so one goes and says the wrong thing. It's odd to realise sometimes that I don't know anything about you at all."

"Or I anything about you. How you were brought up—and where—your family—"

"I was brought up in a strictly scientific atmosphere. Nourished on test tubes, you might say. Nobody ever thought or talked of anything else. But I was never the bright boy of the family. Genius lay elsewhere."

"Where exactly?"

"A girl. She was brilliant. She might have been another Madame Curie. She could have opened up new horizons . . ."

"She—what happened to her?"

He said shortly:

"She was killed."

Hilary guessed at some wartime tragedy. She said gently,

"You cared for her?"

"More than I have ever cared for anybody."

He roused himself suddenly.

"What the heck—we've got enough troubles in the present, right here and now. Look at our Norwegian friend. Apart from his eyes, he always looks as though he were made from wood. And that wonderful little stiff bow of his—as though you'd pulled a string."

"It's because he's so very tall and thin."

"Not so very tall. About my height—five foot eleven or six foot, not more."

"Height is deceptive."

"Yes, it's like descriptions on passports. Take Ericsson. Height six foot, fair hair, blue eyes, face long, demeanour wooden, nose medium, mouth ordinary. Even add what a passport wouldn't—speaks correctly but pedantically—you still wouldn't have the first idea what Torquil really looked like. What's the matter?"

"Nothing."

She was staring across the room at Ericsson. That description of Boris Glydr! Almost word for word as she had heard it from Jessop. Was *that* why she had always felt nervous of Torquil Ericsson? Could it possibly be that—Turning abruptly to Peters she said,

"I suppose he *is* Ericsson? He couldn't be someone else?"

Peters looked at her in astonishment.

"Someone else? Who?"

"I mean—at least I think I mean—could he have come here pretending to be Ericsson?"

Peters considered.

"I suppose—no, I don't think that would be feasible. He'd have to be a scientist . . . and anyway, Ericsson is quite well known."

"But nobody here seems ever to have met him before—or I suppose he could be Ericsson, but be someone else as well."

"You mean Ericsson could have been leading some kind of double life? That's possible, I suppose. But it's not very likely."

"No," said Hilary. "No, of course it isn't likely."

Of course Ericsson was not Boris Glydr. But why should Olive Betterton have been so insistent on warning Tom against Boris? Could it have been because she knew that Boris was on his way to the Unit? Supposing the man who had come to London calling himself Boris Glydr was not Boris Glydr at all? Supposing that he was really Torquil Ericsson. The description fitted. Ever since he arrived at the Unit, he had focussed his attention on Tom. Ericsson, she was sure, was a dangerous person,—you didn't know what went on behind those pale dreamy eyes . . .

She shivered.

"Olive—what's the matter? What is it?"

"Nothing. Look. The Deputy Director is going to make an announcement."

Dr. Neilson was holding up his hand for silence. He spoke into the microphone on the platform of the Hall.

"Friends and colleagues. Tomorrow you are asked to remain in the Emergency Wing. Please assemble at 11:00 A.M. when there will be roll call. Emergency orders are for twenty-four hours only. I much regret the inconvenience. A notice had been posted on the board."

He retired smiling. The music began again.

"I must pursue the Jennsen again," said Peters. "I see her looking earnest by a pillar. I want to hear just what these Emergency quarters consist of."

He moved away. Hilary sat thinking. Was she an imaginative fool? Torquil Ericsson? Boris Glydr?

IV

Roll call was in the big lecture room. Everyone was present and answered to his or her name. Then they were marshalled into a long column and marched off.

The route was, as usual, through a maze of winding corridors. Olive, walking by Peters, knew that he had concealed in his hand, a tiny compass. From this, unobtrusively, he was calculating their direction.

"Not that it helps," he observed ruefully in a low tone. "Or at any rate it doesn't help at the moment. But it may do—some time."

At the end of the corridor they were following was a door and there was a momentary halt as the door was opened.

Peters took out his cigarette case—but immediately Van Heidem's voice was raised peremptorily.

"No smoking, please. That has already been told you."

"Sorry, sir."

Peters paused with the cigarette case in his hand. Then they all went forward again.

"Just like sheep," said Hilary disgustedly.

"Cheer up," Peter murmured. "Baa, baa, black sheep is among the flock, thinking up devilry hard."

She flashed him a grateful glance and smiled.

"Women's dormitory to the right," said Miss Jennsen. She shepherded the women off in the direction indicated.

The men were fallen off to the left.

The dormitory was a large room of hygienic appearance rather like a hospital ward. It had beds along the walls with curtains of plastic material that could be pulled for privacy. There was a locker by each bed.

"You will find arrangements rather simple," said Miss Jennsen, "but not too primitive. The bathroom accommodation is through there to the right. The communal living room is through the door at the end."

The communal living room where they all met again was plainly furnished rather like an airport waiting room—there was a bar and snack counter at one side. Along the other side was a row of book shelves.

The day passed quite agreeably. There were two cinema performances shown on a small portable screen.

The lighting was of the daylight type which tended to obscure the fact that there were no windows. Towards evening a fresh set of bulbs came on—soft and discreet night lighting.

"Clever," said Peters appreciatively. "It all helps to minimise the feeling of being walled up alive."

How helpless they all were, thought Hilary. Somewhere, quite near them, were a party from the outside world. And there was no means of communicating with them, of appealing for help. As usual, everything had been ruthlessly and efficiently planned.

Peters was sitting with Miss Jennsen. Hilary suggested to the Murchisons that they should play bridge. Tom Betterton refused. He said he couldn't concentrate, but Dr. Barron made a fourth.

Oddly enough, Hilary found the game enjoyable. It was half past eleven when their third rubber came to an end, with herself and Dr. Barron the winners.

"I enjoyed that," she said. She glanced at her watch. "It's quite late. I suppose the V.I.P.'s will have left now—or do they spend the night here?"

"I don't really know," said Simon Murchison. "I believe one or two of the specially keen medicos stay over. Anyway, they'll all have gone by tomorrow midday."

"And that's when we're put back in circulation?"

"Yes. About time, too. It upsets all one's routine, this sort of thing."

"But it is well arranged," said Bianca with approval.

She and Hilary got up and said goodnight to the two men.

Hilary stood back a little to allow Bianca to precede her into the dimly lit dormitory. As she did so, she felt a soft touch on her arm.

She turned sharply to find one of the tall dark-faced servants standing beside her.

He spoke in a low urgent voice in French.

"*S'il vous plait, Madame*, you are to come."

"Come? Come where?"

"If you will please follow me."

She stood irresolute for a moment.

Bianca had gone on into the dormitory. In the communal living room the few persons left were engaged in conversation with each other.

Again she felt that soft urgent touch on her arm.

"You will follow me please, Madame."

He moved a few steps and stood, looking back, beckoning to her. A little doubtfully Hilary followed him.

She noticed that this particular man was far more richly dressed than most of the native servants. His robes were embroidered heavily with gold thread.

He led her through a small door in a corner of the communal living room, then once more along the inevitable anonymous white corridors. She did not think it was the same way by which they had come to the Emergency Wing, but it was always difficult to be sure because of the similarity of the passages. Once she turned to ask a question but the guide shook his head impatiently and hurried on.

He stopped finally at the end of a corridor and pressed a button in the wall. A panel slid back disclosing a small lift. He gestured her in, followed her, and the lift shot upwards.

Hilary said sharply:

"Where are you taking me?"

The dark eyes held hers in a kind of dignified reproof.

"To the Master, Madame. It is for you a great honour."

"To the Director, you mean?"

"To the Master . . ."

The lift stopped. He slid back the doors and motioned her out. Then they walked down another corridor and arrived at a door. Her guide rapped on the door and it was opened from inside. Here again were white robes, gold embroidery and a black, impassive face.

The man took Hilary across the small red-carpeted anteroom and drew aside some hangings at the further side. Hilary passed through. She found herself, unexpectedly, in an almost oriental interior. There were low couches, coffee tables, one or two beautiful rugs hanging on the walls. Sitting on a low divan was a figure at whom she stared with complete incredulity. Small, yellow, wrinkled, old, she stared unbelievingly into the smiling eyes of Mr. Aristides.

CHAPTER XVIII

"Asseyez vous, chère Madame," said Mr. Aristides.

He waved a small clawlike hand, and Hilary came forward in a dream and sat down upon another low divan opposite him. He gave a gentle little cackle of laughter.

"You are surprised," he said. "It is not what you expected, eh?"

"No, indeed," said Hilary. "I never thought—I never imagined—"

But already her surprise was subsiding.

With her recognition of Mr. Aristides, the dream world of unreality in which she had been living for the past weeks shattered and broke. She knew now that the Unit had seemed unreal to her—because it *was* unreal. It had never been what it pretended to be. The Herr Director with his spellbinder's voice had been unreal too—a mere figurehead of fiction set up to obscure the truth. The truth was here in this secret oriental room. A little old man sitting there and laughing quietly. With Mr. Aristides in the centre of the picture, everything made sense—hard, practical everyday sense.

"I see now," said Hilary. "This—is all yours, isn't it?"

"Yes, Madame."

"And the Director? The so-called Director?"

"He is very good," said Mr. Aristides appreciatively. "I pay him a very high salary. He used to run Revivalist meetings."

He smoked thoughtfully for a moment or two. Hilary did not speak.

"There is Turkish Delight beside you, Madame. And other sweetmeats if you prefer them." Again there was a silence. Then he went on, "I am a philanthropist, Madame. As you know, I am rich. One of the richest men —possibly the richest man in the world today. With my wealth I feel under the obligation to serve humanity. I have established here, in this remote spot, a colony of lepers and a vast assembly of research into the problem of the cure of leprosy. Certain types of leprosy are curable. Others, so far, have proved incurable. But all the time we are working and obtaining good results. Leprosy is not really such an easily communicated disease. It is not half so infectious or so contagious as smallpox or typhus or plague or any of these other things. And yet, if you say to people, "a leper colony" they will shudder and give it a wide berth. It is an old, old fear that. A fear that you can find in the Bible, and which has existed all down through the years. The horror of the leper. It has been useful to me in establishing this place."

"You established it for that reason?"

"Yes. We have here also a Cancer Research department, and important work is being done on tuberculosis. There is virus research, also—for curative reasons, *bien entendu*—biological warfare is not mentioned. All humane, all acceptable, all redounding greatly to my honour. Well-known physicians, surgeons and research chemists come here to see our results from time to time as they have come today. The building has been cunningly constructed is such a way that a part of it is shut off and unapparent even from the air. The more secret laboratories have been tunnelled right into the rock. In any case, I am above suspicion." He smiled and added simply: "I am so very rich, you see."

"But why?" demanded Hilary. "Why this urge for destruction?"

"I have no urge for destruction, Madame. You wrong me."

"But then—I simply don't understand."

"I am a business man," said Mr. Aristides simply. "I am also a collector. When wealth becomes oppressive, that is the only thing to do. I have collected many things in my time. Pictures—I have the finest art collection in Europe. Certain kinds of ceramics. Philately—my stamp collection is famous. When a collection is fully representative, one goes on to the next thing. I am an old man, Madame, and there was not very much more for me to collect. So I came at last to collecting brains."

"Brains?" Hilary queried.

He nodded gently.

"Yes, it is the most interesting thing to collect of all. Little by little, Madame, I am assembling here all the brains of the world. The young men, those are the ones I am bringing here. Young men of promise, young men of achievement. One day the tired nations of the world will wake up and realise that their scientists are old and stale, and that the young brains of the world—the doctors, the research chemists, the physicists, the surgeons, are all here in my keeping. And if they want a scientist, or a plastic surgeon, or a biologist, they will have to come and buy him from me!"

"You mean . . ." Hilary leaned forward, staring at him. "You mean that this is all a gigantic financial operation?"

Again Mr. Aristides nodded gently.

"Yes," he said. "Naturally. Otherwise—it would not make sense, would it?"

Hilary gave a deep sigh.

"No," she said. "That's just what I've felt."

"After all, you see," said Mr. Aristides almost apologetically, "it is my profession. I am a financier."

"And you mean there is no political side to this at all? You don't want World Power—?"

He threw up his hand in rebuke.

"I do not want to be God," he said. "I am a religious man. That is the occupational disease of Dictators: wanting to be God. So far I have not contracted that disease." He reflected a moment and said: "It may come. Yes, it may come . . . But as yet, mercifully—no."

"But how do you get all these people to come here?"

"I buy them, Madame. In the open market. Like any other merchandise. Sometimes I buy them with money. More often, I buy them with ideas. Young men are dreamers. They have ideals. They have beliefs. Sometimes I buy them with safety—those that have transgressed the law."

"That explains it," said Hilary. "Explains, I mean, what puzzled me so on the journey here."

"Ah! It puzzled you on the journey, did it?"

"Yes. The difference in aims. Andy Peters, the American, seemed completely Left Wing. But Ericsson was a fanatical believer in the Superman. And Helga Needheim was a Fascist of the most arrogant and pagan kind. Dr. Barron—" she hesitated.

"Yes, he came for money," said Aristides. "Dr. Barron is civilised and cynical. He has no illusions, but he has a genuine love of his work. He wanted unlimited money, so as to pursue his researches further." He added: "You are intelligent, Madame. I saw that at once in Fez."

He gave a gentle little cackle of laughter.

"You did not know it, Madame, but I went to Fez simply to observe you—or rather I had you brought to Fez in order that I might observe you."

"I see," said Hilary.

She noted the oriental rephrasing of the sentence.

"I was pleased to think that you would be coming here. For, if you understand me, I do not find many intelligent people in this place to talk to." He made a gesture. "These scientists, these biologists, these research chemists, they are not interesting. They are geniuses perhaps at what they do, but they are uninteresting people with whom to converse."

"Their wives," he added thoughtfully, "are usually very dull, too. We do not encourage wives here. I permit wives to come for only one reason."

"What reason?"

Mr. Aristides said drily,

"In the rare cases where a husband is unable to do his work properly because he is thinking too much of his wife. That seemed to be the case with your husband, Thomas Betterton. Thomas Betterton is known to the world as a young man of genius, but since he has been here he has done only mediocre and second class work. Yes, Betterton has disappointed me."

"But don't you find that constantly happening? These people are, after all, in prison here. Surely they rebel? At first, at any rate?"

"Yes," Mr. Aristides agreed. "That is only natural and inevitable. It is so when you first cage a bird. But if the bird is in a big enough aviary; if it has all that it needs; a mate, seed, water, twigs, all the material of life, it forgets in the end that it was ever free."

Hilary shivered a little.

"You frighten me," she said. "You really frighten me."

"You will grow to understand many things here, Madame. Let me assure you that though all these men of different ideologies arrive here and are disillusioned and rebellious, they will all toe the line in the end."

"You can't be sure of that," said Hilary.

"One can be absolutely sure of nothing in this world. I agree with you there. But it is a ninety-five per cent certainty all the same."

Hilary looked at him with something like horror.

"It's dreadful," she said. "It's like a typists' pool! You've got a pool here of brains."

"Exactly. You put it very justly, Madame."

"And from this pool, you intend, one day, to supply scientists to whoever pays you best for them?"

"That is, roughly, the general principle, Madame."

"But you can't send out a scientist just as you can send out a typist."

"Why not?"

"Because once your scientist is in the free world again, he could refuse to work for his new employer. He would be free again."

"True up to a point. There may have to be a certain—conditioning, shall we say?"

"Conditioning—what do you mean by that?"

"You have heard of lobotomy, Madame?"

Hilary frowned.

"That's a brain operation, isn't it?"

"But yes. It was devised originally for the curing of melancholia. I put it to you not in medical terms, Madame, but in such terms as you and I understand. After the operation the patient has no more desire to commit suicide, no further feelings of guilt. He is carefree, conscienceless and in most cases obedient."

"It hasn't been a hundred per cent success, has it?"

"In the past, no. But here we have made great strides in the investigation of the subject. I have here three surgeons: one Russian, one Frenchman and an Austrian. By various operations of grafting and delicate manipulation of the brain, they are arriving gradually at a state where docility can be assured and the will can be controlled without necessarily affecting mental brilliance. It seems possible that we may in the end so condition a human being that while his powers of intellect remain unimpaired, he will exhibit perfect docility. Any suggestion made to him he will accept."

"But that's horrible," cried Hilary. "Horrible!"

He corrected her serenely.

"It is useful. It is even in some ways beneficent. For the patient will be happy, contented, without fears or longings or unrest."

"I don't believe it will ever happen," said Hilary defiantly.

"*Chère Madame,* forgive me if I say you are hardly competent to speak on the subject."

"What I mean is," said Hilary, "that I do not believe a contented, suggestible animal will ever produce creative work of real brilliance."

Aristides shrugged his shoulders.

"Perhaps. You are intelligent. You may have something there. Time will show. Experiments are going on all the time."

"Experiments! On human beings, do you mean?"

"But certainly. That is the only practical method."

"But—what human beings?"

"There are always the misfits," said Aristides. "The ones who do not adapt themselves to life here, who will not co-operate. They make good experimental material."

Hilary dug her fingers into the cushions of the divan. She felt a deep horror of this smiling, yellow-faced little man with his inhuman outlook. Everything he said was so reasonable, so logical and so businesslike, that it made the horror worse. Here was no raving madman, just a man to whom his fellow creatures were so much raw material.

"Don't you believe in God?" she said.

"Naturally I believe in God." Mr. Aristides raised his eyebrows. His tone was almost shocked. "I have told you already. I am a religious man. God has blessed me with supreme power. With money and opportunity."

"Do you read your Bible?" asked Hilary.

"Certainly, Madame."

"Do you remember what Moses and Aaron said to Pharaoh? 'Let my people go.'"

He smiled.

"So—I am Pharaoh?— And you are Moses and Aaron in one? Is that what you are saying to me, Madame? To let these people go, all of them, or just—one special case?"

"I'd like to say—all of them," said Hilary.

"But you are well aware, chère Madame," he said, "that that would be a waste of time. So instead, is it not your husband for whom you plead?"

"He is no good to you," said Hilary. "Surely by now you must realise that."

"Perhaps, it is true what you say, Madame. Yes, I am very much disappointed in Thomas Betterton. I hoped that your presence here might restore him to his brilliance, for undoubtedly he has brilliance. His reputation in America leaves no doubt as to that. But your coming seems to have had little or no effect. I speak not of my own knowledge, of course, but from the reports of those fitted to know. His brother scientists who have been working with him." He shrugged his shoulders. "He does conscientious, mediocre work. No more."

"There are birds that cannot sing in captivity," said Hilary. "Perhaps there are scientists who cannot attain creative thought under certain circumstances. You must admit that that is a reasonable possibility."

"It may be so. I do not deny it."

"Then write off Thomas Betterton as one of your failures. Let him return to the outer world."

"That would hardly do, Madame. I am not yet prepared to have knowledge of this place broadcast to the globe."

"You could swear him to secrecy. He would swear never to breathe a word."

"He would swear—yes. But he would not keep that word."

"He would! Oh, indeed, he would!"

"There speaks a wife! One cannot take the word of wives on this point. Of course," he leaned back in his chair, and brought the tips of his yellow fingers together, "of course, he might leave a hostage behind him, and that might tie his tongue."

"You mean?"

"I mean you, Madame. . . . If Thomas Betterton went, and you remained as a hostage, how would that bargain strike you? Would you be willing?"

Hilary stared past him into the shadows. Mr. Aristides could not know the pictures that rose before her eyes. She was back in a hospital room, sitting by a dying woman. She was listening to Jessop and memorising his instructions. If there was a chance, now, that Thomas Betterton might go free, whilst she remained, would not that be the best way to fulfil her mission? For she knew (what Mr. Aristides did not), that there would be no hostage in the usual meaning of the word, left behind. She herself meant nothing to Thomas Betterton. The wife he had loved was already dead.

She raised her head and looked across at the little old man on the divan.

"I should be willing," she said.

"You have courage, Madame, and loyalty and devotion. They are good qualities. For the rest—" He smiled. "We will talk of it again some other time."

"Oh, no, no!" Hilary suddenly buried her face in her hands. Her shoulders shook. "I can't bear it! I can't bear it! It's all too inhuman."

"You must not mind so much, Madame." The old man's voice was tender, almost soothing. "It has pleased me tonight to tell you my aims and my aspirations. It has been interesting to me to see the effect upon a mind totally unprepared. A mind like yours, well balanced, sane and intelligent. You are horrified. You are repulsed. Yet I think that to shock you in this way is a wise plan. At first you repel the idea, then you think of it, you reflect on it, and in the end it will seem to you natural; as though it has always existed, a commonplace."

"Never that!" cried Hilary. "Never that! Never! Never!"

"Ah," said Mr. Aristides. "There speaks the passion and the rebellion that go with red hair. My second wife," he added reflectively, "had red hair. She was a beautiful woman, and she loved me. Strange, is it not? I have always admired red-haired women. Your hair is very beautiful. There are other things I like about you. Your spirit, your courage; the fact that you have a mind of your own." He sighed. "Alas! Women as women interest me very little nowadays. I have a couple of young girls here who please me sometimes, but it is the stimulus of mental companionship that I now prefer. Believe me, Madame, your company has refreshed me greatly."

"Supposing I repeat all that you have told me to—my husband?"

Aristides smiled indulgently.

"Ah yes, supposing you do? But will you?"

"I don't know. I—oh, I don't know."

"Ah!" said Mr. Aristides. "You are wise. There is some knowledge women should keep to themselves. But you are tired—and upset. From time to time, when I pay my visits here, you shall be brought to me, and we will discuss many things."

"Let me leave this place—" Hilary stretched her hands out to him. "Oh, let me go away. Let me leave with you when you go. Please! Please!"

He shook his head gently. His expression was indulgent, but there was a faint touch of contempt behind it.

"Now you are talking like a child," he said reprovingly. "How could I let you go? How could I let you spread the story round the world of what you have seen here?"

"Wouldn't you believe me if I swore I wouldn't say a word to anyone?"

"No indeed, I should not believe you," said Mr. Aristides. "I should be very foolish if I believed anything of the kind."

"I don't want to be here. I don't want to stay here in this prison. I want to get out."

"But you have your husband. You came here to join him, deliberately, of your own free will."

"But I didn't know what I was coming to. I'd no idea."

"No," said Mr. Aristides, "you had no idea. But I can assure you this particular world you have come to is a much pleasanter world than the life beyond the Iron Curtain. Here you have everything you need! Luxury, a beautiful climate, distractions . . ."

He got up and patted her gently on the shoulder.

"You will settle down," he said, confidently. "Ah yes, the red-headed bird in the cage will settle down. In a year, in two years certainly, you will be very happy! Though possibly," he added thoughtfully, "less interesting."

CHAPTER XIX

HILARY AWOKE THE following night with a start. She raised herself on her elbow, listening.

"Tom, do you hear?"

"Yes. Aircraft—flying low. Nothing in that. They come over from time to time."

"I wondered—" She did not finish her sentence.

She lay awake thinking, going over and over that strange interview with Aristides.

The old man had got some kind of capricious liking for her.

Could she play upon that?

Could she in the end prevail upon him to take her with him, out into the world again?

Next time he came, if he sent for her, she would lead him on to talk of his dead red-haired wife. It was not the lure of the flesh that would captivate him. His blood ran too coldly now in his veins for that. Besides he had his "young girls." But the old like to remember, to be urged on to talk of times gone by . . .

Uncle George, who had lived at Cheltenham . . .

Hilary smiled in the darkness, remembering Uncle George.

Were Uncle George and Aristides, the man of millions, really very different under the skin? Uncle George had had a housekeeper—"such a nice safe woman, my dear, not flashy or sexy or anything like that. Nice and plain and safe." But Uncle George had upset his family by marrying that nice plain woman. She had been a very good listener . . .

What had Hilary said to Tom? "I'll find a way of getting out of here?" Odd, if the way should prove to be Aristides . . .

II

"A message," said Leblanc. "A message at last."

His orderly had just entered and, after saluting, had laid a folded paper before him. He unfolded it, then spoke excitedly.

"This is a report from one of our reconnaissance pilots. He has been operating over one of the selected squares of territory. When flying over a certain position in a mountainous region he observed a signal being flashed. It was in Morse and was twice repeated. Here it is."

He laid the enclosure before Jessop.

C.O.G.L.E.P.R.O.S.I.E.S.L.

He separated off the last two letters with a pencil.

"SL—that is our code for 'Do not acknowledge.'"

"And COG with which the message starts," said Jessop, "is our recognition signal."

"Then the rest is the actual message." He underlined it. "LEPROSIE." He surveyed it dubiously.

"Leprosy?" said Jessop.

"And what does that mean?"

"Have you any important Leper Settlements? Or unimportant ones for that matter?"

Leblanc spread out a large map in front of him. He pointed with a stubby forefinger stained with nicotine.

"Here," he marked it off, "is the area over which our pilot was operating. Let me see now. I seem to recall . . ."

He left the room. Presently he returned.

"I have it," he said. "There is a very famous medical Research station, founded and endowed by well known philanthropists and operating in that area—a very deserted one, by the way. Valuable work has been done there in the study of Leprosy. There is a Leper Settlement there of about two hundred people. There is also a Cancer Research Station, and a Tubercular Sanatorium. But understand this, it is all of the highest authenticity. Its reputation is of the highest. The President of the Republic himself is its patron."

"Yes," said Jessop appreciatively. "Very nice work, in fact."

"But it is open to inspection at any time. Medical men who are interested in these subjects visit there."

"And see nothing they ought not to see! Why should they? There is no better camouflage for dubious business, than an atmosphere of the highest respectability."

"It could be," Leblanc said dubiously, "I suppose, a halting place, for parties of people bound on a journey. One or two of the mid-European doctors, perhaps, have managed to arrange something like that. A small party of people, like the one we are tracking, could lie *perdu* there for a few weeks before continuing their journey."

"I think it might be something more than that," said Jessop. "I think it might be—Journey's End."

"You think it is something—big?"

"A Leper Settlement seems to me very suggestive . . . I believe, under modern treatment, leprosy nowadays is treated at home."

"In civilised communities, perhaps. But one could not do that in this country."

"No. But the word Leprosy still has its association with the Middle Ages when the Leper carried his bell to warn away people from his path. Idle curiosity does not bring people to a Leper Settlement; the people who come are, as you say, the medical profession, interested only in the medical research done there, and possibly the social worker, anxious to report on the conditions under which the Lepers live—all of which are no doubt admirable. Behind that façade of philanthropy and charity—anything might go on. Who, by the way, owns the place? Who are the philanthropists who endowed it and set it up?"

"That is easily ascertained. A little minute."

He turned shortly, an official reference book in his hand.

"It was established by private enterprise. By a group of philanthropists of whom the chief is Aristides. As you know, he is a man of fabulous wealth, and gives generously to charitable enterprises. He has founded hospitals in Paris and also in Seville. This is, to all intents and purposes, his show—the other benefactors are a group of his associates."

"So—it's an Aristides enterprise. And Aristides was in Fez when Olive Betterton was there."

"Aristides!" Leblanc savoured the full implication. *"Mais—c'est colossal!"*

"Yes."

"C'est fantastique!"

"Quite."

"Enfin—c'est formidable!"

"Definitely."

"But do you realise how formidable it is?" Leblanc shook an excited forefinger in the other's face. "This Aristides, he has a finger in every pie. He is behind nearly everything. The banks, the Government, the manufacturing industries, armaments, transport! One never sees him, one hardly hears of him! He sits in a warm room in his Spanish castle, smoking, and sometimes he scrawls a few words on a little piece of paper and throws it on the ground, and a secretary crawls forward and picks it up, and a few days later an important banker in Paris blows his brains out! It is like that!"

"How wonderfully dramatic you are, Leblanc. But it is really not very surprising. Presidents and Ministers make important pronouncements, bankers sit back behind their sumptuous desks and roll out opulent statements—but one is never surprised to find out that behind the importance and magnificence there is somewhere some scrubby little man who is the real motive power. It is really not at all surprising to find that Aristides is behind all this disappearing business—in fact if we'd had any sense we'd have thought of it before. The whole thing's a vast commercial ramp. It's not political at all. The question is," he added, "What are we going to do about it?"

Leblanc's face grew gloomy.

"It is not going to be easy, you understand. If we are wrong—I dare not think of it! And even if we are right—we have got to prove we are right. If we make investigations—those investigations can be called off—at the highest level, you understand? No, it is not going to be easy. . . . But," he wagged an emphatic stubby forefinger, "it will be done."

CHAPTER XX

THE CARS SWEPT up the mountain road and stopped in front of the great gate set in the rock. There were four cars. In the first car was a French Minister and the American Ambassador, in the second car was the British Consul, a Member of Parliament and the Chief of Police. In the third car were two members of a former Royal Commission and two distinguished journalists. The complement of these three cars was made up with the necessary satellites. The fourth car contained certain people not known to the general public, but sufficiently distinguished in their own sphere. They included Captain Leblanc and Mr. Jessop. The chauffeurs, immaculately garbed, were now opening car doors and bowing as they assisted the distinguished visitors to alight.

"One hopes," murmured the Minister, apprehensively, "that there will be no possibility of a contact of any kind."

One of the satellites immediately made soothing noises.

"*Du tout, M. le Ministre*. Every suitable precaution is taken. One inspects only from a distance."

The Minister, who was elderly and apprehensive, looked relieved. The Ambassador said something about the better understanding and treatment of these diseases nowadays.

The great gates were flung open. On the threshold stood a small party bowing to welcome them. The Director, dark, thickset, the Deputy Director, big and fair, two distinguished doctors and a distinguished Research Chemist. The greetings were French, florid and prolonged.

"And *ce cher* Aristides," demanded the Minister. "I sincerely hope ill health has not prevented him from fulfilling his promise to meet us here."

"M. Aristides flew from Spain yesterday," said the Deputy Director. "He awaits you within. Permit me, Your Excellency—M. le Ministre, to lead the way."

The party followed him. M. le Ministre, who was slightly apprehensive, glanced through the heavy railings to his right. The lepers were drawn up to attention in a serried row as far as possible from the grating. The Minister looked relieved. His feelings about leprosy were still mediaeval.

In the well furnished modern lounge Mr. Aristides was awaiting his guests. There were bows, compliments, introductions. Aperitifs were served by the dark-faced servants dressed in their white robes and turbans.

"It's a wonderful place you have here, sir," said one of the younger journalists to Aristides.

The latter made one of his oriental gestures.

"I am proud of this place," he said. "It is, as you might say, my swan song. My final gift to humanity. No expense has been spared."

"I'll say that's so," said one of the doctors on the staff, heartily. "This place is a professional man's dream. We do pretty well in the States, but what I've seen since I came here . . . and we're getting results! Yes, sir, we certainly are getting results."

His enthusiasm was of a contagious kind.

"We must make all acknowledgements to private enterprise," said the Ambassador, bowing politely to Mr. Aristides.

Mr. Aristides spoke with humility.

"God has been very good to me," he said.

Sitting hunched up in his chair he looked like a small yellow toad. The Member of Parliament murmured to the member of the Royal Commission who was very old and deaf, that he presented a very interesting paradox.

"That old rascal has probably ruined millions of people," he murmured, "and having made so much money, he doesn't know what to do with it, so he pays it back with the other hand."

The elderly judge to whom he spoke, murmured,

"One wonders to what extent results justify increased expenditure. Most of the great discoveries that have benefited the human race have been discovered with quite simple equipment."

"And now," said Aristides, when the civilities were accomplished and the aperitifs drunk, "you will honour me by partaking of a simple repast which awaits you. Dr. Van Heidem will act as your host. I myself am on a diet and eat very little these days. After the repast you will start on your tour of our building."

Under the leadership of the genial Dr. Van Heidem, the guests moved enthusiastically into the dining room. They had had two hours' flight followed by an hour's drive by car and they were all sharp set. The food was delicious and was commented on with special approval by the Minister.

"We enjoy our modest comforts," said Van Heidem. "Fresh fruit and vegetables are flown to us twice a week, arrangements are made for meat and chicken and we have, of course, substantial deep freezing units. The body must claim its due from the resources of science."

The meal was accompanied by choice vintages. After it Turkish coffee was served. The party was then asked to start on its tour of inspection. The tour took two hours and was most comprehensive. The Minister, for one, was glad when it finished. He was quite dazed by the gleaming laboratories, the endless white, shining corridors, and still more dazed by the mass of scientific detail handed out to him.

Though the Minister's interest was perfunctory, some of the others were more searching in their enquiries. Some curiosity was displayed as to the living conditions of the personnel and various other details. Dr. Van Heidem showed himself only too willing to show the guests all there was to see. Leblanc and Jessop, the former in attendance on the Minister and the latter accompanying the British Consul, fell a little behind the others as they all returned to the lounge.

"There is no trace here, nothing," murmured Leblanc in an agitated manner.

"Not a sign."

"*Mon cher,* if we have, as your saying is, barked up the wrong tree, what a catastrophe. After the weeks it has taken to arrange all this! As for me—it will finish my career."

"We're not licked yet," said Jessop. "Our friends are here, I'm sure of it."

"There is no trace of them."

"Of course there is no trace. They could not afford to have a trace of them. For these official visits everything is prepared and arranged."

"Then how are we to get our evidence? I tell you, without evidence no one will move in the matter. They are sceptical, all of them. The Minister, the American Ambassador, the British Consul—they say all of them, that a man like Aristides is above suspicion."

"Keep calm, Leblanc, keep calm. I tell you we're not licked yet."

Leblanc shrugged his shoulders.

"You have the optimism, my friend," he said. He turned for a moment to speak to one of the immaculately arrayed moon-faced young men who formed part of the *entourage,* then turned back to Jessop and asked suspiciously: "Why are you smiling?"

"Heard of a Geiger counter?"

"Naturally. But I am not a scientist, you understand."

"No more am I. It is a very sensitive detector of radio-activity."

"And so?"

"Our friends are here. The Geiger counter tells me that. It imparts a message to say that our friends are here. This building has been purposely built in a confusing manner. All the corridors and the rooms so resemble each other that it is difficult to know where one is or what the plan of the building can be. There is a part of this place that we have not seen. It has not been shown to us."

"But you deduce that it is there because of some radio-active indication?"

"Exactly."

"In fact, it is the pearls of Madame all over again?"

"Yes. We're still playing Hansel and Gretel, as you might say. But the signs left here cannot be so apparent or so crude as the beads of a pearl necklace, or a hand of phosphoric paint. They cannot be seen, but they can be sensed . . . by our radio-active detector—"

"But, *mon Dieu,* Jessop, is that enough?"

"It should be," said Jessop. "What one is afraid of . . ." He broke off. Leblanc finished the sentence for him.

"What you mean is that these people will not want to believe. They have been unwilling from the start. Oh yes, that is so. Even your British Consul is a man of caution. Your government at home is indebted to Aristides in many ways. As for our government," he shrugged his shoulders. "M. le Ministre, I know, will be exceedingly hard to convince."

"We won't put our faith in governments," said Jessop. "Governments and diplomats have their hands tied. But we've got to have them here, because they're the only ones with authority. But as far as believing is concerned, I'm pinning my faith elsewhere."

"And on what in particular do you pin your faith, my friend?"

Jessop's solemn face suddenly relaxed into a grin.

"There's the press," he said. "Journalists have a nose for news. They don't want it hushed up. They're ready always to believe anything that remotely can be believed. The other person I have faith in," he went on, "is that very deaf old man."

"Aha, I know the one you mean. The one who looks as though he crumbles to his grave."

"Yes, he's deaf and infirm and semi-blind. But he's interested in truth. He's a former Lord Chief Justice, and though he may be deaf and blind and shaky on his legs, his mind's as keen as ever—he's got that keen sense that legal luminaries acquire—of knowing when there's something fishy about and someone's trying to prevent it being brought into the open. He's a man who'll listen, and will want to listen, to evidence."

They had arrived back now in the lounge. Both tea and aperitifs were provided. The Minister congratulated Mr. Aristides in well-rounded periods. The American Ambassador added his quota. It was then that the Minister, looking round him, said in a slightly nervous tone of voice,

"And now, gentlemen, I think the time has come for us to leave our kind host. We have seen all there is to see . . ." his tone dwelt on those last words with some significance, "all here is magnificent. An establishment of the first class! We are most grateful for the hospitality of our kind host, and we congratulate him on the achievement here. So we say our farewells now and depart. I am right, am I not?"

The words were, in a sense, conventional enough. The manner, too, was conventional. The glance that swept round the assembly of guests might have been no more than courtesy. Yet in actuality the words were a plea. In effect, the Minister was saying, "You've seen, gentlemen, there is nothing here, nothing of what you suspected and feared. That is a great relief and we can now leave with a clear conscience."

But in the silence a voice spoke. It was the quiet, deferential, well-bred English voice of Mr. Jessop. He spoke to the Minister in a Britannic though idiomatic French.

"With your permission, sir," he said, "and if I may do so, I would like to ask a favour of our kind host."

"Certainly, certainly. Of course, Mr.—ah—Mr. Jessop—yes, yes?"

Jessop addressed himself solemnly to Dr. Van Heidem. He did not look ostensibly to Mr. Aristides.

"We've met so many of your people," he said, "Quite bewildering. But there's an old friend of mine here that I'd rather like to have a word with. I wonder if it could be arranged before I go?"

"A friend of yours?" Dr. Van Heidem said politely, surprised.

"Well, two friends really," said Jessop. "There's a woman, Mrs. Betterton. Olive Betterton. I believe her husband's working here. Tom Betterton. Used to be at Harwell and before that in America. I'd very much like to have a word with them both before I go."

Dr. Van Heidem's reactions were perfect. His eyes opened in wide and polite surprise. He frowned in a puzzled way.

"Betterton—Mrs. Betterton—no, I'm afraid we have no one of that name here."

"There's an American, too," said Jessop. "Andrew Peters. Research chemistry, I believe, is his line. I'm right, sir, aren't I?" He turned deferentially to the American Ambassador.

The Ambassador was a shrewd, middle-aged man with keen blue eyes. He was a man of character as well as diplomatic ability. His eyes met Jessop's. He took a full minute to decide, and then he spoke.

"Why, yes," he said. "That's so. Andrew Peters. I'd like to see him."

Van Heidem's polite bewilderment grew. Jessop unobtrusively shot a quick glance at Aristides. The little yellow face betrayed no knowledge of anything amiss, no surprise, no disquietude. He looked merely uninterested.

"Andrew Peters? No, I'm afraid, Your Excellency, you've got your facts wrong. We've no one of that name here. I'm afraid I don't even know the name."

"You know the name of Thomas Betterton, don't you?" said Jessop.

Just for a second Van Heidem hesitated. His head turned very slightly towards the old man in the chair, but he caught himself back in time.

"Thomas Betterton," he said. "Why, yes, I think—"

One of the gentlemen of the press spoke up quickly on that cue.

"Thomas Betterton," he said. "Why, I should say he was pretty well big news. Big news six months ago when he disappeared. Why, he's made headlines in the papers all over Europe. The police have been looking for him here, there and everywhere. Do you mean to say he's been here in this place all the time?"

"No." Van Heidem spoke sharply. "Someone, I fear, has been misinforming you. A hoax, perhaps. You have seen today all our workers at the Unit. You have seen everything."

"Not quite everything I think," said Jessop, quietly. "There's a young man called Ericsson, too," he added, "and Dr. Louis Barron, and possibly Mrs. Calvin Baker."

"Ah." Dr. Van Heidem seemed to receive enlightenment. "But those people were killed in Morocco—in a plane crash. I remember it perfectly now. At least I remember Ericsson was in the crash and Dr. Louis Barron. Ah, France sustained a great loss that day. A man such as Louis Barron is hard to replace." He shook his head. "I do not know anything about a Mrs. Calvin Baker, but I do seem to remember that there was an English or American woman on that plane. It might well perhaps have been this Mrs. Betterton, of whom you speak. Yes, it was all very sad." He looked across enquiringly at Jessop. "I do not know, Monsieur, why you should suppose that these people were coming here. It may possibly be that Dr. Barron mentioned at one time that he hoped to visit our settlement here while he was in North Africa. That may possibly have given rise to a misconception."

"So you tell me," said Jessop, "that I am mistaken? That these people are none of them here."

"But how can they be, my dear sir, since they were all killed in this plane accident. The bodies were recovered, I believe."

"The bodies recovered were too badly charred for identification." Jessop spoke the last words with deliberation and significance.

There was a little stir behind him. A thin, precise, very attenuated voice said,

"Do I understand you to say that there was no precise identification?" Lord Alverstoke was leaning forward, his hand to his ear. Under bushy, overhanging eyebrows his small keen eyes looked into Jessop's.

"There could be no formal identification, my lord," said Jessop, "and I have reason to believe these people survived that accident."

"Believe?" said Lord Alverstoke, with displeasure in his thin, high voice.

"I should have said I had evidence of survival."

"Evidence? Of what nature, Mr.—er—er—Jessop."

"Mrs. Betterton was wearing a choker of false pearls on the day she left Fez for Marrakesh," said Jessop. "One of these pearls was found at a distance of half a mile from the burnt out plane."

"How can you state positively that the pearl found actually came from Mrs. Betterton's necklace?"

"Because all the pearls of that necklace had had a mark put upon them invisible to the naked eye, but recognisable under a strong lens."

"Who put that mark on them?"

"I did, Lord Alverstoke, in the presence of my colleague, here, Monsieur Leblanc."

"You put those marks—you had a reason in marking those pearls in that special fashion?"

"Yes, my lord. I had reason to believe that Mrs. Betterton would lead me to her husband, Thomas Betterton, against whom a warrant is out." Jessop continued. "Two more of these pearls came to light. Each on stages of a route between where the plane was burnt out and the settlement where we now are. Enquiries in the places where these pearls were found resulted in a description of six people, roughly approximating to those people who were supposed to have been burnt in the plane. One of these passengers had also been supplied with a glove impregnated with luminous, phosphorous paint. That mark was found on a car which had transported these passengers part of the way here."

Lord Alverstoke remarked in his dry, judicial voice,

"Very remarkable."

In the big chair Mr. Aristides stirred. His eyelids blinked once or twice rapidly. Then he asked a question.

"Where were the last traces of this party of people found?"

"At a disused airfield, sir." He gave precise location.

"That is many hundreds of miles from here," said Mr. Aristides, "Granted that your very interesting speculations are correct, that for some reason the accident was faked, these passengers, I gather, then took off from this disused airport for some unknown destination. Since that airport is many hundreds of miles from here, I really cannot see on what you base your belief that these people are here. Why should they be?"

"There are certain very good reasons, sir. A signal was picked up by one of our searching aeroplanes. The signal was brought to Monsieur Leblanc here. Commencing with a special code recognition signal, it gave the information that the people in question were at a Leper Settlement."

"I find this remarkable," said Mr. Aristides. "Very remarkable. But it seems to me that there is no doubt that an attempt has been made to mislead you. These people are not here." He spoke with a quiet, definite decision. "You are at perfect liberty to search the settlement if you like."

"I doubt if we should find anything, sir," said Jessop, "not, that is, by a superficial search, although," he added deliberately, "I am aware of the area at which the search should begin."

"Indeed! And where is that?"

"In the fourth corridor from the second laboratory turning to the left at the end of the passage there."

There was an abrupt movement from Dr. Van Heidem. Two glasses crashed from the tables to the floor. Jessop looked at him, smiling.

"You see, Doctor," he said, "we are well informed."

Van Heidem said sharply, "It's preposterous. Absolutely preposterous! You are suggesting that we are detaining people here against their will. I deny that categorically."

The Minister said uncomfortably,

"We seem to have arrived at an *impasse*."

Mr. Aristides said gently,

"It has been an interesting theory. But it is only a theory." He glanced at his watch. "You will excuse me, gentlemen, if I suggest that you should leave now. You have a long drive back to the airport, and there will be alarm felt if your plane is overdue."

Both Leblanc and Jessop realised that it had come now to the showdown. Aristides was exerting all the force of his considerable personality. He was daring these men to oppose his will. If they persisted, it meant that they were willing to come out into the open against him. The Minister, as per his instructions, was anxious to capitulate. The Chief of Police was anxious only to be agreeable to the Minister. The American Ambassador was not satisfied, but he, too, would hesitate for diplomatic reasons to insist. The British Consul would have to fall in with the other two.

The journalists—Aristides considered the journalists—the journalists could be attended to! Their price might come high but he was of the opinion that they could be bought. And if they could not be bought—well, there were other ways.

As for Jessop and Leblanc, they knew. That was clear, but they could not act without authority. His eyes went on and met the eyes of a man as old as himself, cold, legal eyes. This man, he knew, could not be bought. But after all . . . His thoughts were interrupted by the sound of that cold, clear, far away little voice.

"I am of the opinion," said the voice, "that we should not unduly hurry our departure. For there is a case here that it seems to me would bear further enquiry. Grave allegations have been made and should not, I consider, be allowed to drop. In fairness every opportunity should be given to rebut them."

"The onus of proof," said Mr. Aristides, "is on you." He made a graceful gesture towards the company. "A preposterous accusation has been made, unsupported by any evidence."

"Not unsupported."

Dr. Van Heidem swung round in surprise. One of the Moroccan servants had stepped forward. He was a fine figure of a man in white embroidered robes with a white turban surrounding his head, his face gleamed black and oily.

What caused the entire company to gaze at him in speechless astonishment was the fact that from his full rather Negroid lips a voice of purely trans-Atlantic origin was proceeding.

"Not unsupported," that voice said, "you can take my evidence here and now. These gentlemen have denied that Andrew Peters, Torquil Ericsson, Mr. and Mrs. Betterton and Dr. Louis Barron are here. That's false. They're all here—and I speak for them." He took a step forward towards the American Ambassador. "You may find me a bit difficult to recognise at the moment, sir," he said, "but I am Andrew Peters."

A very faint, sibilant hiss issued from Aristides' lips; then he settled back in his chair, his face impassive once more.

"There's a whole crowd of people hidden away here," said Peters. "There's Schwartz of Munich: there's Helga Needheim; there are Jeffreys and Davidson, the English scientists; there's Paul Wade from the U.S.A.; there are the Italians, Ricochetti and Bianco; there's Murchison. They're all right here in this building. There's a system of closing bulkheads that's quite impossible to detect by the naked eye. There's a whole network of secret laboratories cut right down into the rock."

"God bless my soul," ejaculated the American Ambassador. He looked searchingly at the dignified African figure, and then he began to laugh. "I wouldn't say I'd recognise you even now," he said.

"That's the injection of paraffin in the lips, sir, to say nothing of black pigment."

"If you're Peters, what's the number you go under in the F.B.I.?"

"813471, sir."

"Right," said the Ambassador, "and the initials of your other name?"

"B.A.B.D.G. sir."

The Ambassador nodded.

"This man is Peters," he said. He looked towards the Minister.

The Minister hesitated, then cleared his throat.

"You claim," he demanded of Peters, "that people are being detained here against their will?"

"Some are here willingly, Excellence, and some are not."

"In that case," said the Minister, "statements must be taken—er—yes, yes, statements must certainly be taken."

He looked at the Prefect of Police. The latter stepped forward.

"Just a moment, please." Mr. Aristides raised a hand. "It would seem," he said, in a gentle, precise voice, "that my confidence here has been greatly abused." His cold glance went from Van Heidem to the Director and there was implacable command in it. "As to what you have permitted yourselves to do, gentlemen, in your enthusiasm for science, I am not as yet quite clear. My endowment of this place was purely in the interests of research. I have taken no part in the practical application of its policy. I would advise you, Monsieur le Directeur, if this accusation is borne out by facts, to produce immediately those people who are suspected of being detained here unlawfully."

"But, Monsieur, it is impossible. I—it will be—"

"Any experiment of that kind," said Mr. Aristides, "is at an end." His calm, financier's gaze swept over his guests. "I need hardly assure you, Messieurs," he said, "that if anything illegal is going on here, it has been no concern of mine."

It was an order, and understood as such because of his wealth, because of his power and because of his influence. Mr. Aristides, that world-famous figure, would not be implicated in this affair. Yet, even though he himself escaped unscathed, it was nevertheless defeat. Defeat for his purpose, defeat for that brains pool from which he had hoped to profit so greatly. Mr. Aristides was unperturbed by failure. It had happened to him occasionally in the course of his career. He had always accepted it philosophically and gone on to the next *coup*.

He made an oriental gesture of his hand.

"I wash my hands of this affair," he said.

The Prefect of Police bustled forward. He had had his cue now, he knew what his instructions were and he was prepared to go ahead with the full force of his official position.

"I want no obstructions," he said. "It is my duty."

His face very pale, Van Heidem stepped forward.

"If you will come this way," he said, "I will show you our reserve accommodation."

CHAPTER XXI

"OH, I FEEL as if I'd woken up out of a nightmare," sighed Hilary.

She stretched her arms wide above her head. They were sitting on the terrace of the hotel in Tangier. They had arrived there that morning by plane. Hilary went on,

"Did it all happen? It can't have!"

"It happened all right," said Tom Betterton, "but I agree with you, Olive, it was a nightmare. Ah well, I'm out of it now."

Jessop came along the terrace and sat down beside them.

"Where's Andy Peters?" asked Hilary.

"He'll be here presently," said Jessop. "He has a bit of business to attend to."

"So Peters was one of your people," said Hilary, "and he did things with phosphorus and a lead cigarette case that squirted radio-active material. I never knew a thing about that."

"No," said Jessop, "you were both very discreet with each other. Strictly speaking, though, he isn't one of my people. He represents the U.S.A."

"That's what you meant by saying that if I actually reached Tom here, you hoped I should have protection? You meant Andy Peters."

Jessop nodded.

"I hope you're not blaming me," said Jessop in his most owl-like manner, "for not providing you with the desired end of your experience."

Hilary looked puzzled. "What end?"

"A more sporting form of suicide," he said.

"Oh, that!" She shook her head incredulously. "That seems just as unreal as anything else. I've been Olive Betterton so long now that I'm feeling quite confused to be Hilary Craven again."

"Ah," said Jessop, "there is my friend, Leblanc. I must go and speak to him."

He left them and walked along the terrace. Tom Betterton said, quickly,

"Do one more thing for me, will you Olive? I call you Olive still—I've got used to it."

"Yes, of course. What is it?"

"Walk along the terrace with me, then come back here and say that I've gone up to my room to lie down."

She looked at him questioningly.

"Why? What are you—"

"I'm off, my dear, while the going's good."

"Off, where?"

"Anywhere."

"But why?"

"Use your head, my dear girl. I don't know what the status is here. Tangier is an odd sort of place not under the jurisdiction of any particular country. But I know what'll happen if I come with the rest of you to Gibraltar. The first thing that'll happen when I get there, I shall be arrested."

Hilary looked at him with concern. In the excitement of their escape from the Unit, she had forgotten Tom Betterton's troubles.

"You mean the Official Secrets Act, or whatever they call it? But you can't really hope to get away can you, Tom? Where can you go?"

"I've told you. Anywhere."

"But is that feasible nowadays? There's money and all sorts of difficulties."

He gave a short laugh.

"The money's all right. It's salted away where I can get at it under a new name."

"So you did take money?"

"Of course I took money."

"But they'll track you down."

"They'll find it hard to do that. Don't you realise, Olive, that the description they'll have of me is quite unlike my present appearance. That's why I was so keen on this plastic surgery business. That's been the whole point, you see. To get away from England, bank some money, have my appearance altered in such a way that I'm safe for life."

Hilary looked at him doubtfully.

"You're wrong," she said. "I'm sure you're wrong. It'd be far better to go back and face the music. After all, it's not war time. You'd only get a short term of imprisonment, I expect. What's the good of being hounded for the rest of your life?"

"You don't understand," he said. "You don't understand the first thing about it all. Come on, let's get going. There's no time to lose."

"But how are you going to get away from Tangier?"

"I'll manage. Don't you worry."

She got up from her seat and walked with him slowly along the terrace. She felt curiously inadequate and tongue-tied. She had fulfilled her obligations to Jessop and also to the dead woman, Olive Betterton. Now there was no more to do. She and Tom Betterton had shared weeks of the closest association and yet she felt they were still strangers to each other. No bond of fellowship or friendship had grown up between them.

They reached the end of the terrace. There was a small side door there through the wall which led out onto a narrow road which curved down the hill to the port.

"I shall slip out this way," Betterton said, "nobody's watching. So long."

"Good luck to you," said Hilary slowly.

She stood there watching Betterton as he went to the door and turned its handle. As the door opened he stepped back a pace and stopped. Three men stood in the doorway. Two of them entered and came towards him. The first spoke formally.

"Thomas Betterton, I have here a warrant for your arrest. You will be held here in custody whilst extradition proceedings are taken."

Betterton turned sharply, but the other man had moved quickly round the other side of him. Instead, he turned back with a laugh.

"It's quite all right," he said, "except that I'm not Thomas Betterton."

The third man moved in through the doorway, came to stand by the side of the other two.

"Oh, yes, you are," he said. "You're Thomas Betterton."

Betterton laughed.

"What you mean is that for the last month you've been living with me and hearing me called Thomas Betterton and hearing me call myself Thomas Betterton. The point is that I'm not Thomas Betterton. I met Betterton in Paris, I came on and took his place. Ask this lady if you don't believe me," he said. "She came to join me, pretending to be my wife, and I recognised her as my wife. I did, didn't I?"

Hilary nodded her head.

"That," said Betterton, "was because not being Thomas Betterton, naturally I didn't know Thomas Betterton's wife from Adam. I thought she was Thomas Betterton's wife. Afterwards I had to think up some sort of explanation that would satisfy her. But that's the truth."

"So that's why you pretended to know me," cried Hilary. "When you told me to play up—to keep up the deception!"

Betterton laughed again, confidently.

"I'm not Betterton," he said. "Look at any photograph of Betterton and you'll see I'm speaking the truth."

Peters stepped forward. His voice when he spoke was totally unlike the voice of the Peters that Hilary had known so well. It was quiet and implacable.

"I've seen photographs of Betterton," he said, "and I agree I wouldn't have recognised you as the man. But you are Thomas Betterton all the same, and I'll prove it."

He seized Betterton with a sudden strong grasp and tore off his jacket.

"If you're Thomas Betterton," he said, "you've got a scar in the shape of a Z in the crook of your right elbow."

As he spoke he ripped up the shirt and bent back Betterton's arm.

"There you are," he said, pointing triumphantly. "There are two lab assistants in the U.S.A. who'll testify to that. I know about it because Elsa wrote and told me when you did it."

"Elsa?" Betterton stared at him. He began to shake nervously. "Elsa? What about Elsa?"

"Ask what the charge is against you?"

The police official stepped forward once more.

"The charge," he said, "is murder in the first degree. Murder of your wife, Elsa Betterton."

CHAPTER XXII

"I'M SORRY, OLIVE. You've got to believe I'm sorry. About you, I mean. For your sake I'd have given him one chance. I warned you that he'd be safer to stay in the Unit and yet I'd come half way across the world to get him, and I meant to get him for what he did to Elsa."

"I don't understand. I don't understand anything. Who are you?"

"I thought you knew that. I'm Boris Andrei Pavlov Glydr, Elsa's cousin. I was sent over to America from Poland, to the University there to complete my education. And the way things were in Europe my uncle thought it best for me to take out American citizenship. I took the name of Andrew Peters. Then, when the war came, I went back to Europe. I worked for the Resistance. I got my uncle and Elsa out of Poland and they got to America. Elsa—I've told you about Elsa already. She was one of the first-class scientists of our time. It was Elsa who discovered ZE Fission. Betterton was a young Canadian who was attached to Mannheim to help him in his experiments. He knew his job, but there was no more to him than that. He deliberately made love to Elsa and married her so as to be associated with her in the scientific work she was doing. When her experiments neared completion and he realised what a big thing ZE Fission was going to be, he deliberately poisoned her."

"Oh, no, no."

"Yes. There were no suspicions at the time. Betterton appeared heart-broken, threw himself with renewed ardour into his work and then announced the ZE Fission discovery as his own. It brought him what he wanted. Fame and the recognition of being a first-class scientist. He thought it prudent after that to leave America and come to England. He went to Harwell and worked there.

"I was tied up in Europe for some time after the war ended. Since I had a good knowledge of German, Russian and Polish, I could do very useful work there. The letter that Elsa had written to me before she died disquieted me. The illness from which she was suffering and from which she died seemed to me mysterious and unaccounted for. When at last I got back to the U.S.A. I started instituting enquiries. We won't go into it all, but I found what I was looking for. Enough, that is, to apply for an Order of Exhumation of the body. There was a young fellow in the District Attorney's office who had been a great friend of Betterton. He was going over on a trip to Europe about that time, and I think that he visited Betterton and in the course of his visit mentioned the exhumation. Betterton got the wind up. I imagine that he'd been already approached by agents of our friend, Mr. Aristides. Anyway he now saw that there lay his best chance to avoid being arrested and tried for murder. He accepted the terms, stipulating that his facial appearance was to be completely changed. What actually happened, of course, was that he found himself in a very real captivity. Moreover, he found himself in a dangerous position there since he was quite unable to deliver the goods—the scientific goods, that is to say. He was not, and never had been, a man of genius."

"And you followed him?"

"Yes. When the newspapers were full of the sensational disappearance of the scientist, Thomas Betterton, I came over to England. A rather brilliant scientist friend of mine had had certain overtures made to him by a woman, a Mrs. Speeder, who worked for UNO. I discovered on arriving in England that she had had a meeting with Betterton. I played up to her, expressing Left Wing views, rather exaggerating perhaps my scientific abilities. I thought, you see, that Betterton had gone behind the Iron Curtain where no one could reach him. Well, if nobody else could reach him, I was going to reach him." His lips set in a grim line. "Elsa was a first-class scientist, and she was a beautiful and gentle woman. She'd been killed and robbed by the man whom she loved and trusted. If necessary I was going to kill Betterton with my own hands."

"I see," said Hilary, "oh, I see now."

"I wrote to you," said Peters, "when I got to England. Wrote to you, that is, in my Polish name, telling you the facts." He looked at her. "I suppose you didn't believe me. You never answered." He shrugged his shoulders. "Then I went to the Intelligence people. At first I went there putting on an act. Polish officer. Stiff, foreign and correctly formal. I was suspicious just then of everybody. However, in the end Jessop and I got together." He paused. "This morning my quest has come to an end. Extradition will be applied for, Betterton will go to the U.S.A. and will stand his trial there. If he's acquitted, I have no more to say." He added grimly, "But he won't be acquitted. The evidence is too strong."

He paused, staring down over the sunlit gardens towards the sea.

"The hell of it is," he said, "that you came out there to join him and I met you and fell in love with you. It has been hell, Olive. Believe me. So there we are. I'm the man who's responsible for sending your husband to the electric chair. We can't get away from it. It's a thing that you'll never be able to forget even if you forgave it." He got up. "Well, I wanted to tell you the whole story from my own lips. This is goodbye." He turned abruptly as Hilary stretched out a hand.

"Wait," she said, "wait. There is something you don't know. I'm not Betterton's wife. Betterton's wife, Olive Betterton, died at Casablanca. Jessop persuaded me to take her place."

He wheeled round staring at her.

"You're not Olive Betterton?"

"No."

"Good Lord," said Andy Peters. "Good Lord!" He dropped heavily into a chair beside her. "Olive," he said, "Olive, my darling."

"Don't call me Olive. My name's Hilary. Hilary Craven."

"Hilary?" He said it questioningly. "I'll have to get used to that." He put his hand over hers.

At the other end of the terrace Jessop, discussing with Leblanc various technical difficulties in the present situation, broke off in the middle of a sentence.

"You were saying?" he asked absently.

"I said, *mon cher*, that it does not seem to me that we are going to be able to proceed against this animal of an Aristides."

"No, no. Aristides always wins. That is to say he always manages to squirm out from under. But he'll have lost a lot of money, and he won't like that. And even Aristides can't keep death at bay for ever. I should say he'll be coming up before the Supreme Justice before very long, from the look of him."

"What was it attracting your attention, my friend?"

"Those two," said Jessop. "I sent Hilary Craven off on a journey to a destination unknown, but it seems to me that her journey's end is the usual one after all."

Leblanc looked puzzled for a moment then he said,

"Aha! Yes! Your Shakespeare!"

"You Frenchmen are so well read," said Jessop.

Death Comes as the End

AUTHOR'S NOTE

THE ACTION OF this story takes place on the west bank of the Nile at Thebes in Egypt about 2000 B.C. Both places and time are incidental to the story. Any other place at any other time would have served as well, but it so happened that the inspiration of both characters and plot was derived from two or three Egyptian letters of the XIth Dynasty, found about forty years ago by the Egyptian Expedition of the Metropolitan Museum of Art, New York, in a rock tomb opposite Luxor, and translated by Professor (then Mr.) Battiscombe Gunn in the Museum's Bulletin.

It may be of interest to the reader to note that an endowment for ka-service—an everyday feature of ancient Egyptian civilization—was very similar in principle to a mediaeval chantry bequest. Property was bequeathed to the ka-priest, in return for which he was expected to maintain the tomb of the testator, and to provide offerings at the tomb on certain feast days throughout the year for the repose of the deceased's soul.

The terms "Brother," "Sister," in Egyptian text regularly meaning "Lover" are frequently interchangeable with "Husband," "Wife." They are so used on occasion in this book.

The agricultural calendar of Ancient Egypt, consisting of three seasons of four months of thirty days, formed the background of peasant life, and with the addition of five intercalary days at the end of the year was used as the official calendar of 365 days to the year. This "year" originally began with the arrival in Egypt of the flood-water of the Nile in the third week of July by our reckoning. The absence of a leap year caused this to lag through the centuries, so that at the time of our story, the official New Year's Day fell about six months earlier than the opening of the agricultural year, i.e., in January instead of July. To save the reader from continually having to make allowance for this six months, however, the dates here used as chapter headings are calculated by the agricultural year of the time, i.e., Inundation—late July to late November; Winter—late November to late March; and Summer—late March to late July.

CHAPTER I

Second Month of Inundation, 20th Day

RENISENB STOOD LOOKING out over the Nile.

In the distance she could hear faintly the upraised voices of her brothers, Yahmose and Sobek, disputing as to whether or not the dykes in a certain place needed strengthening. Sobek's voice was high and confident as always. He had the habit of asserting his views with easy certainty. Yahmose's voice was low and grumbling in tone; it expressed doubt and anxiety. Yahmose was always in a state of anxiety over something or other. He was the eldest son and during his father's absence on the northern estates, the management of the farm lands was more or less in his hands. Yahmose was slow, prudent and prone to look for difficulties where none existed. He was a heavily built, slow-moving man with none of Sobek's gaiety and confidence.

From her early childhood Renisenb could remember hearing these elder brothers of hers arguing in just those selfsame accents. It gave her suddenly a feeling of security. . . . She was at home again. Yes, she had come home. . . .

Yet as she looked once more across the pale, shining river, her rebellion and pain mounted again. Khay, her young husband, was dead. . . . Khay with his laughing face and his strong shoulders. Khay was with Osiris in the Kingdom of the Dead—and she, Renisenb, his dearly loved wife, was left desolate. Eight years they had had together—she had come to him as little more than a child—and now she had returned widowed, with Khay's child, Teti, to her father's house.

It seemed to her at this moment as though she had never been away. . . .

She welcomed that thought. . . .

She would forget those eight years—so full of unthinking happiness, so torn and destroyed by loss and pain.

Yes, forget them, put them out of her mind. Become once more Renisenb, Imhotep the ka-priest's daughter, the unthinking, unfeeling girl. This love of a husband and brother had been a cruel thing, deceiving her by its sweetness. She remembered the strong bronze shoulders, the laughing mouth—now Khay was embalmed, swathed in bandages, protected with amulets in his journey through the other world. No more Khay in this world to sail on the Nile and catch fish and laugh up into the sun whilst she, stretched out in the boat with little Teti on her lap, laughed back at him. . . .

Renisenb thought:

"I will not think of it. It is over! Here I am at home. Everything is the same as it was. I, too, shall be the same presently. It will all be as before. Teti has forgotten already. She plays with the other children and laughs."

Renisenb turned abruptly and made her way back towards the house, passing on the way some loaded donkeys being driven towards the river-bank. She passed by the cornbins and the outhouses and through the gateway into the courtyard. It was very pleasant in the courtyard. There was the artificial lake, surrounded by flowering oleanders and jasmines and shaded by sycamore fig trees. Teti and the other children were playing there now, their voices rising shrill and clear. They were running in and out of the little pavilion that stood at one side of the lake. Renisenb noticed that Teti was playing with a wooden lion whose mouth opened and shut by pulling a string, a toy which she herself had loved as a child. She thought again, gratefully, "I have come home. . . ." Nothing was changed here; all was as it had been. Here life was safe, constant, unchanging. Teti was now the child and she one of the many mothers enclosed by the home walls—but the framework, the essence of things, was unchanged.

A ball with which one of the children was playing rolled to her feet and she picked it up and threw it back, laughing.

Renisenb went on to the porch with its gaily coloured columns, and then through into the house, passing through the big central chamber, with its coloured frieze of lotus and poppies, and so on to the back of the house and the women's quarters.

Upraised voices struck on her ear and she paused again, savouring with pleasure the old familiar echoes. Satipy and Kait—arguing as always! Those well-remembered tones of Satipy's voice, high, domineering and bullying! Satipy was her brother Yahmose's wife, a tall, energetic, loud-tongued woman, handsome in a hard, commanding kind of way. She was eternally laying down the law, hectoring the servants, finding fault with everything, getting impossible things done by sheer force of vituperation and personality. Everyone dreaded her tongue and ran to obey her orders. Yahmose himself had the greatest admiration for his resolute, spirited wife, though he allowed himself to be bullied by her in a way that had often infuriated Renisenb.

At intervals, in the pauses in Satipy's high-pitched sentences, the quiet, obstinate voice of Kait was heard. Kait was a broad, plain-faced woman, the wife of the handsome, gay Sobek. She was devoted to her children and seldom thought or spoke about anything else. She sustained her side of the daily arguments with her sister-in-law by the simple expedient of repeating whatever statement she had originally made with quiet, immovable obstinacy. She displayed neither heat nor passion, and never considered for a moment any side of a question but her own. Sobek was extremely attached to his wife and talked freely to her of all his affairs, secure in the knowledge that she would appear to listen, make comforting sounds of assent or dissent, and would remember nothing inconvenient, since her mind was sure to have been dwelling on some problem connected with the children all the time.

"It's an outrage, that's what I say," shouted Satipy. "If Yahmose had the spirit of a mouse he would not stand it for a moment! Who is in charge here when Imhotep is absent? Yahmose! And as Yahmose's wife it is *I* who should have the first choice of the woven mats and cushions. That hippopotamus of a black slave should be—"

Kait's heavy, deep voice cut in:

"No, no, my little one, do not eat your doll's hair. See, here is something better—a sweet—oh, how *good*. . . ."

"As for you, Kait, you have no courtesy; you don't even listen to what I say—you do not reply—your manners are atrocious."

"The blue cushion has always been mine. . . . Oh, look at little Ankh —she is trying to walk. . . ."

"You are as stupid as your children, Kait, and that is saying a good deal! But you shall not get out of it like this. I will have my rights, I tell you."

Renisenb started as a quiet footfall sounded behind her. She turned with a start and with the old, familiar feeling of dislike at seeing the woman Henet standing behind her.

Henet's thin face was twisted into its usual half-cringing smile.

"Things haven't changed much, you'll be thinking, Renisenb," she said. "How we all bear Satipy's tongue, I don't know! Of course, Kait can answer back. Some of us aren't so fortunate! I know *my* place, I hope—and my gratitude to your father for giving me a home and food and clothing. Ah, he's a good man, your father. And I've always tried to do what I can. I'm always working—giving a hand here and a hand there—and I don't expect thanks or gratitude. If your dear mother had lived it would have been different. *She* appreciated me. Like sisters we were! A beautiful woman she was. Well, I've done my duty and kept my promise to her. 'Look after the children, Henet,' she said when she was dying. And I've been faithful to my word. Slaved for you all, I have, and never wanted thanks. Neither asked for them nor got them! 'It's only old Henet,' people say; 'she doesn't count.' Nobody thinks anything of me. Why should they? I just try to be helpful, that's all."

She slipped like an eel under Renisenb's arm and entered the inner room.

"About those cushions, you'll excuse me, Satipy, but I happened to hear Sobek say—"

Renisenb moved away. Her old dislike of Henet surged up. Funny how they all disliked Henet! It was her whining voice, her continual self-pity and the occasional malicious pleasure she took in fanning the flames of a discussion.

"Oh, well," thought Renisenb, "why not?" It was, she supposed, Henet's way of amusing herself. Life must be dreary for her—and it was true that she worked like a drudge and that no one was ever grateful. You couldn't be grateful to Henet—she drew attention to her own merits so persistently that it chilled any generous response you might have felt.

Henet, thought Renisenb, was one of those people whose fate it is to be devoted to others and to have no one devoted to them. She was unattractive to look at, and stupid as well. Yet she always knew what was going on. Her noiseless way of walking, her sharp ears and quick, peering eyes made it a certainty that nothing could long be a secret from her. Sometimes she hugged her knowledge to herself—at other times she would go round from one person to another whispering and standing back delightedly to observe the results of her tale-telling.

At one time or another everyone in the household had begged Imhotep to get rid of Henet, but Imhotep would never hear of such a thing. He was perhaps the only person who was fond of her; and she repaid his patronage with a fulsome devotion that the rest of the family found quite nauseating.

Renisenb stood uncertainly for a moment, listening to the accelerated clamour of her sisters-in-law, fanned by the flame of Henet's interference, then she went slowly towards the small room where her grandmother, Esa, sat by herself, attended by two little black slave girls. She was busy now inspecting certain linen garments that they were displaying to her and scolding them in a characteristic, friendly fashion.

Yes, it was all the same. Renisenb stood, unnoticed, listening. Old Esa had shrunk a little, that was all. But her voice was the same and the things that she was saying were the same, word for word, almost, as Renisenb could remember them before she herself had left home eight years ago. . . .

Renisenb slipped out again. Neither the old woman nor the two little black slave girls had noticed her. For a moment or two Renisenb paused by the open kitchen door. A smell of roasting ducks, a lot of talking and laughing and scolding; a mound of vegetables waiting to be prepared.

Renisenb stood quite still, her eyes half closed. From where she stood she could hear everything going on at once. The rich, varied noises of the kitchen, the high, shrill note of old Esa's voice, the strident tones of Satipy and, very faintly, the deeper, persistent contralto of Kait. A babel of women's voices—chattering, laughing, complaining, scolding, exclaiming . . .

And suddenly Renisenb felt stifled, encircled by this persistent and clamorous femininity. Women—noisy, vociferous women! A houseful of women—never quiet, never peaceful—always talking, exclaiming, *saying* things—not *doing* them!

And Khay—Khay silent and watchful in his boat, his whole mind bent on the fish he was going to spear. . . .

None of this clack of tongues, this busy, incessant *fussiness*.

Renisenb went swiftly out of the house again into hot, clear stillness. She saw Sobek coming back from the fields and saw in the distance Yahmose going up towards the Tomb.

She turned away and took the path up to the limestone cliffs where the Tomb was. It was the Tomb of the great noble Meriptah, and her father was the mortuary priest responsible for its upkeep. All the estate and land was part of the endowment of the Tomb.

When her father was away the duties of the ka-priest fell upon her brother Yahmose. When Renisenb, walking slowly up the steep path, arrived, Yahmose was in consultation with Hori, her father's man of business and affairs, in a little rock chamber next door to the offering chamber of the Tomb.

Hori had a sheet of papyrus spread out on his knees and Yahmose and he were bending over it.

Both Yahmose and Hori smiled at Renisenb when she arrived and she sat down near them in a patch of shade. She had always been very fond of her brother Yahmose. He was gentle and affectionate to her and had a mild and kindly disposition. Hori, too, had always been gravely kind to the small Renisenb and had sometimes mended her toys for her. He had been a grave, silent young man when she went away, with sensitive, clever fingers. Renisenb thought that though he looked older he had changed hardly at all. The grave smile he gave her was just the same as she remembered.

Yahmose and Hori were murmuring together:

"Seventy-three bushels of barley with Ipi the younger . . ."

"The total then is two hundred and thirty of spelt and one hundred and twenty of barley."

"Yes, but there is the price of the timber, and the crop was paid for in oil at Perhaa. . . ."

Their talk went on. Renisenb sat drowsily content with the men's murmuring voices as a background. Presently Yahmose got up and went away, handing back the roll of papyrus to Hori.

Renisenb sat on in a companionable silence.

Presently she touched a roll of papyrus and asked: "Is that from my father?"

Hori nodded.

"What does it say?" she asked curiously.

She unrolled it and stared at those marks that were so meaningless to her untutored eyes.

Smiling a little, Hori leaned over her shoulder and traced with his finger as he read. The letter was couched in the ornate style of the professional letter writer of Heracleopolis.

"The Servant of the Estate, the ka-servant Imhotep, says:

"May your condition be like that of one who lives a million times. May the God Herishaf, Lord of Heracleopolis and all the Gods that are aid you. May the God Ptah gladden your heart as one who lives long. The son speaks to his mother, the ka-servant to his mother Esa. How are you in your life, safety and health? To the whole household, how are you? To my son Yahmose, how are you in your life, safety and health? Make the most of my land. Strive to the uttermost, dig the ground with your noses in the work. See, if you are industrious I will praise God for you—"

Renisenb laughed.

"Poor Yahmose! He works hard enough, I am sure."

Her father's exhortations had brought him vividly before her eyes—his pompous, slightly fussy manner, his continual exhortations and instructions.

Hori went on:

"Take great care of my son Ipy. I hear he is discontented. Also see that Satipy treats Henet well. Mind this. Do not fail to write about the flax and the oil. Guard the produce of my grain—guard everything of mine, for I shall hold you responsible. If my land floods, woe to you and Sobek."

"My father is just the same," said Renisenb happily. "Always thinking that nothing can be done right if he is not here."

She let the roll of papyrus slip and added softly:

"*Everything is just the same. . . .*"

Hori did not answer.

He took up a sheet of papyrus and began to write. Renisenb watched him lazily for some time. She felt too contented to speak.

By and by she said dreamily:

"It would be interesting to know how to write on papyrus. Why doesn't everyone learn?"

"It is not necessary."

"Not necessary, perhaps, but it would be pleasant."

"You think so, Renisenb? What difference would it make to *you*?"

Renisenb considered for a moment or two. Then she said slowly: "When you ask me like that, truly I do not know, Hori."

Hori said, "At present a few scribes are all that are needed on a large estate, but the day will come, I fancy, when there will be armies of scribes all over Egypt. We are living at the beginning of great times."

"That will be a good thing," said Renisenb.

Hori said slowly: "I am not so sure."

"Why are you not sure?"

"Because, Renisenb, it is so easy and it costs so little labour to write down ten bushels of barley, or a hundred head of cattle, or ten fields of spelt—and the thing that is written will come to seem like the real thing, and so the writer and the scribe will come to despise the man who ploughs the fields and reaps the barley and raises the cattle—but all the same the fields and the barley and the cattle are *real*—they are not just marks of ink on papyrus. And when all the records and all the papyrus rolls are destroyed and the scribes are scattered, the men who toil and reap will go on, and Egypt will still live."

Renisenb looked at him attentively. She said slowly: "Yes, I see what you mean. Only the things that you can *see* and *touch* and *eat* are real. . . . To write down 'I have two hundred and forty bushels of barley' means nothing unless you *have* the barley. One could write down lies."

Hori smiled at her serious face. Renisenb said suddenly:

"You mended my lion for me—long ago, do you remember?"

"Yes, I remember, Renisenb."

"Teti is playing with it now. . . . It is the same lion."

She paused and then said simply:

"When Khay went to Osiris I was very sad. But now I have come home and I shall be happy again and forget—for everything here is the same. Nothing is changed at all."

"You really think that?"

Renisenb looked up at him sharply.

"What do you mean, Hori?"

"I mean there is always change. Eight years is eight years."

"Nothing changes here," said Renisenb with confidence.

"Perhaps, then, there *should* be change."

Renisenb said sharply:

"No, no, I want everything the same!"

"But you yourself are not the same Renisenb who went away with Khay."

"Yes, I am! Or if not, then I soon shall be again."

Hori shook his head.

"You cannot go back, Renisenb. It is like my measures here. I take a half and add to it a quarter, and then a tenth and then a twenty-fourth—and at the end, you see, it is a different quantity altogether."

"But I am just Renisenb."

"But Renisenb has something added to her all the time, so she becomes all the time a different Renisenb!"

"No, no. You are the same Hori."

"You may think so, but it is not so."

"Yes, yes, and Yahmose is the same, so worried and so anxious, and Satipy bullies him just the same, and she and Kait were having their usual quarrel about mats or beads, and presently when I go back they will be laughing together, the best of friends, and Henet still creeps about and listens and whines about her devotion, and my grandmother was fussing with her little maid over some linen! It was all the same and presently my father will come home and there will be a great fuss and he will say, 'Why have you not done this?' and 'You should have done that,' and Yahmose will look worried and Sobek will laugh and be insolent about it, and my father will spoil Ipy, who is sixteen, just as he used to spoil him when he was eight, and nothing will be different at all!" She paused, breathless.

Hori sighed. Then he said gently:

"You do not understand, Renisenb. There is an evil that comes from outside, that attacks so that all the world can see, but there is another kind of rottenness that breeds from within—that shows no outward sign. It grows slowly, day by day, till at last the whole fruit is rotten—eaten away by disease."

Renisenb stared at him. He had spoken almost absently, not as though he were speaking to her, but more like a man who muses to himself.

She cried out sharply:

"What do you mean, Hori? You make me afraid."

"I am afraid myself."

"But what do you *mean*? What is this evil you talk about?"

He looked at her then and suddenly smiled.

"Forget what I said, Renisenb. I was thinking of the diseases that attack the crops."

Renisenb sighed in relief.

"I'm glad. I thought—I don't know what I thought."

CHAPTER II

Third Month of Inundation, 4th Day

I

SATIPY WAS TALKING to Yahmose. Her voice had a high strident note that seldom varied its tone.

"You must assert yourself. That is what I say! You will never be valued unless you assert yourself. Your father says this must be done and that must be done and why have you not done this? And you listen meekly and reply Yes, yes, and excuse yourself for the things that he says should have been done—and which, the Gods know, have often been quite impossible! Your father treats you as a child—as a young, irresponsible boy! You might be the age of Ipy."

Yahmose said quietly:

"My father does not treat me in the least as he treats Ipy."

"No, indeed." Satipy fell upon the new subject with renewed venom. "He is foolish about that spoiled brat! Day by day Ipy gets more impossible. He swaggers round and does no work that he can help and pretends that anything that is asked of him is too hard for him! It is a disgrace. And all because he knows that your father will always indulge him and take his part. You and Sobek should take a strong line about it."

Yahmose shrugged his shoulders.

"What is the good?"

"You drive me mad, Yahmose—that is so like you! You have no *spirit*. You're as meek as a woman! Everything that your father says you agree with at once!"

"I have a great affection for my father."

"Yes, and he trades on that! You go on meekly accepting blame and excusing yourself for things that are no fault of yours! You should speak up and answer him back as Sobek does. Sobek is afraid of nobody!"

"Yes, but remember, Satipy, that it is *I* who am trusted by my father, not Sobek. My father reposes no confidence in Sobek. Everything is always left to *my* judgement, not his."

"And that is why you should be definitely associated as a partner in the estate! You represent your father when he is away, you act as ka-priest in his absence; everything is left in your hands—and yet you have no recognised authority. There should be a proper settlement. You are now a man of nearly middle age. It is not right that you should be treated still as a child."

Yahmose said doubtfully:

"My father likes to keep things in his own hands."

"Exactly. It pleases him that everyone in the household should be dependent upon him—and upon his whim of the moment. It is bad, that, and it will get worse. This time when he comes home you must tackle him boldly—you must say that you demand a settlement in writing, that you insist on having a regularised position."

"He would not listen."

"Then you must *make* him listen. Oh, that I were a man! If I were in your place *I* would know what to do! Sometimes I feel that I am married to a worm."

Yahmose flushed.

"I will see what I can do—I might, yes, I might perhaps speak to my father—ask him—"

"Not *ask*—you must *demand!* After all, you have the whip hand of him. There is no one but you whom he can leave in charge here. Sobek is too wild; your father does not trust him, and Ipy is too young."

"There is always Hori."

"Hori is not a member of the family. Your father relies on his judgement but he would not leave authority except in the hands of his own kin. But I see how it is; you are too meek and mild—there is milk in your veins, not blood! You don't consider me or our children. Not till your father is dead shall we ever have our proper position."

Yahmose said heavily:

"You despise me, don't you, Satipy?"

"You make me angry."

"Listen, I tell you that I will speak to my father when he comes. There, it is a promise."

Satipy murmured under her breath:

"Yes—but *how* will you speak? Like a man—or like a mouse?"

II

Kait was playing with her youngest child, little Ankh. The baby was just beginning to walk and Kait encouraged her with laughing words, kneeling in front of her and waiting with outstretched arms until the child lurched precariously forward and toddled on uncertain feet into her mother's arms.

Kait had been displaying these accomplishments to Sobek, but she realised suddenly that he was not attending, but was sitting with his handsome forehead furrowed into a frown.

"Oh, Sobek—you were not looking. You do not see. Little one, tell your father he is naughty not to watch you."

Sobek said irritably:

"I have other things to think of—yes, and worry about."

Kait leaned back on her heels, smoothing her hair back from her heavy dark brows where Ankh's fingers had clutched it.

"Why? Is there something wrong?"

Kait spoke without quite giving all her attention. The question was more than half mechanical.

Sobek said angrily:

"The trouble is that I am not trusted. My father is an old man, absurdly old-fashioned in his ideas, and he insists on dictating every single action here—he will not leave things to my judgement."

Kait shook her head and murmured vaguely:

"Yes, yes, it is too bad."

"If only Yahmose had a little more spirit and would back me up there might be some hope of making my father see reason. But Yahmose is so timid. He carries out every single instruction my father gives him to the letter."

Kait jingled some beads at the child and murmured:

"Yes, that is true."

"In this matter of the timber I shall tell my father when he comes that I used my judgement. It was far better to take the price in flax and not in oil."

"I am sure you are right."

"But my father is as obstinate over having his own way as anyone can be. He will make an outcry, will shout out, 'I told you to transact the business in oil. Everything is done wrong when I am not here. You are a foolish boy who knows nothing!' How old does he think I am? He doesn't realise that I am now a man in my prime and he is past his. His instructions and his refusals to sanction any unusual transactions mean that we do not do nearly as good business as we might do. To attain riches it is necessary to take a few risks. I have vision and courage. My father has neither."

Her eyes on the child, Kait murmured softly:

"You are so bold and so clever, Sobek."

"But he shall hear some home truths this time if he dares to find fault and shout abuse at me! Unless I am given a free hand, I shall leave. I shall go away."

Kait, her hand stretched out to the child, turned her head sharply, the gesture arrested.

"Go away? Where would you go?"

"Somewhere! It is insupportable to be bullied and nagged at by a fussy, self-important old man who gives me no scope at all to show what I can do."

"No," said Kait sharply. "I say no, Sobek."

He stared at her, recalled by her tone into noticing her presence. He was so used to her as a merely soothing accompaniment to his talk that he often forgot her existence as a living, thinking, human woman.

"What do you mean, Kait?"

"I mean that I will not let you be foolish. All the estate belongs to your father—the lands, the cultivation, the cattle, the timber, the fields of flax—all! When your father dies it will be ours—yours and Yahmose's and our children's. If you quarrel with your father and go off, then he may divide your share between Yahmose and Ipy—already he loves Ipy too much. Ipy knows that and trades on it. You must not play into the hands of Ipy. It would suit him only too well if you were to quarrel with Imhotep and go away. We have our children to think of."

Sobek stared at her. Then he gave a short surprised laugh.

"A woman is always unexpected. I did not know you had it in you, Kait, to be so fierce."

Kait said earnestly:

"Do not quarrel with your father. Do not answer him back. Be wise for a little longer."

"Perhaps you are right—but this may go on for years. What my father should do is to associate us with him in a partnership."

Kait shook her head.

"He will not do that. He likes too much to say that we are all eating his bread, that we are all dependent on him, that without him we should all be nowhere."

Sobek looked at her curiously.

"You do not like my father very much, Kait."

But Kait had bent once more to the toddling baby.

"Come, sweetheart—see, here is your doll. Come, then—come . . ."

Sobek looked down at her black bent head. Then, with a puzzled look, he went out.

III

Esa had sent for her grandson Ipy.

The boy, a handsome, discontented-looking stripling, was standing before her whilst she rated him in a high shrill voice, peering at him out of her dim eyes that were shrewd although they could now see little.

"What is this I hear? You will not do this, and you will not do that? You want to look after the bulls, and you do not like going with Yahmose or seeing to the cultivating? What are things coming to when a child like you says what he will or will not do?"

Ipy said sullenly:

"I am not a child. I am grown now—and why should I be treated as a child? Put to this work or that with no say of my own and no separate allowance! Given orders all the time by Yahmose! Who does Yahmose think he is?"

"He is your older brother and he is in charge here when my son Imhotep is away."

"Yahmose is stupid—slow and stupid. I am much cleverer than he is. And Sobek is stupid too for all that he boasts and talks about how clever he is! Already my father has written and has said that I am to do the work that I myself choose—"

"Which is none at all," interpolated old Esa.

"And that I am to be given more food and drink and that if he hears I am discontented and have not been well treated he will be very angry."

He smiled as he spoke, a sly upcurving smile.

"You are a spoiled brat," said Esa with energy. "And I shall tell Imhotep so."

"No, no, Grandmother, you would not do that."

His smile changed; it became caressing, if slightly impudent.

"You and I, Grandmother, we have the brains of the family."

"The impudence of you!"

"My father relies on your judgement—he knows you are wise."

"That may be—indeed it is so—but I do not need you to tell me so."

Ipy laughed.

"You had better be on my side, Grandmother."

"What is this talk of *sides?*"

"The big brothers are very discontented. Don't you know that? Of course you do. Henet tells you everything. Satipy harangues Yahmose all day and all night whenever she can get hold of him. And Sobek has made a fool of himself over the sale of the timber and is afraid my father will be furious when he finds out. You will see, Grandmother, in another year or two I shall be associated with my father and he will do everything that I wish."

"You, the youngest of the family?"

"What does age matter? My father is the one who has the power—and I am the one who knows how to manage my father!"

"This is evil talk," said Esa.

Ipy said softly:

"You are not a fool, Grandmother. . . . You know quite well that my father, in spite of all his big talk, is really a weak man—"

He stopped abruptly, noting that Esa had shifted her head and was peering over his shoulder. He turned his own head to find Henet standing close behind him.

"So Imhotep is a weak man?" said Henet in her soft whining voice. "He will not be pleased, I think, to hear that you have said *that* of him."

Ipy gave a quick uneasy laugh.

"But you will not tell him, Henet. . . . Come now, Henet—promise me. . . . Dear Henet . . ."

Henet glided towards Esa. She raised her voice with its slightly whining note.

"Of course, I never want to make trouble—you know that. . . . I am devoted to all of you. I never repeat anything unless I think it is my *duty*. . . ."

"I was teasing Grandmother, that was all," said Ipy. "I shall tell my father so. He will know I could not have said such a thing seriously."

He gave Henet a short, sharp nod and went out of the room.

Henet looked after him and said to Esa:

"A fine boy—a fine, well-grown boy. And how bravely he speaks!"

Esa said sharply:

"He speaks dangerously. I do not like the ideas he has in his head. My son indulges him too much."

"Who would not? He is such a handsome, attractive boy."

"Handsome is as handsome does," said Esa sharply.

She was silent a moment or two, then she said slowly:

"Henet—I am worried."

"Worried, Esa? What should worry you? Anyway, the master will soon be here and then all will be well."

"Will it? I wonder."

She was silent once more, then she said:

"Is my grandson Yahmose in the house?"

"I saw him coming towards the porch a few moments ago."

"Go and tell him I wish to speak with him."

Henet departed. She found Yahmose on the cool porch with its gaily coloured columns and gave him Esa's message.

Yahmose obeyed the summons at once.

Esa said abruptly:

"Yahmose, very soon Imhotep will be here."

Yahmose's gentle face lighted up.

"Yes, that will indeed be good."

"All is in order for him? Affairs have prospered?"

"My father's instructions have been carried out as well as I could compass them."

"What of Ipy?"

Yahmose sighed.

"My father is overindulgent where that boy is concerned. It is not good for the lad."

"You must make that clear to Imhotep."

Yahmose looked doubtful.

Esa said firmly:

"I will back you up."

"Sometimes," said Yahmose, sighing, "there seem to be nothing but difficulties. But everything will be right when my father comes. He can make his own decisions then. It is hard to act as he would wish in his absence —especially when I have no real authority and only act as his delegate."

Esa said slowly:

"You are a good son—loyal and affectionate. You have been a good husband too; you have obeyed the proverb that says that a man should love his wife and make a home for her, that he should fill her belly and put clothes on her back, and provide expensive ointments for her toilet and that he should gladden her heart as long as she lives. But there is a further precept—it goes like this: *Prevent her from getting the mastery.* If I were you, Grandson, I should take that precept to heart. . . ."

Yahmose looked at her, flushed deeply, and turned away.

CHAPTER III

Third Month of Inundation, 14th Day

I

EVERYWHERE THERE WERE bustle and preparation. Hundreds of loaves had been baked in the kitchen, now ducks were roasting; there was a smell of leeks and garlic and various spices. Women were shouting and giving orders, serving-men ran to and fro.

Everywhere ran the murmur:

"The master—the master is coming. . . ."

Renisenb, helping to weave garlands of poppies and lotus flowers, felt an excited happiness bubbling up in her heart. Her father was coming home! In the last few weeks she had slipped imperceptibly back into the confines of her old life. That first sense of unfamiliarity and strangeness, induced in her, she believed, by Hori's words, had gone. She was the same Renisenb—Yahmose, Satipy, Sobek and Kait were all the same—now, as in the past, there was all the bustle and fuss of preparations for Imhotep's return. Word had come ahead that he would be with them before night-fall. One of the servants had been posted on the riverbank to give warning of the master's approach, and suddenly his voice rang out loud and clear, giving the agreed call.

Renisenb dropped her flowers and ran out with the others. They all hastened towards the mooring place on the riverbank. Yahmose and Sobek were already there in a little crowd of villagers, fishermen and farm labourers, all calling out excitedly and pointing.

Yes, there was the barge with its great square sail coming fast up the river with the north wind bellying out the sail. Close behind it was the kitchen barge crowded with men and women. Presently Renisenb could make out her father sitting holding a lotus flower and with him someone whom she took to be a singer.

The cries on the bank redoubled, Imhotep waved a welcoming hand, the sailors were heaving and pulling on the halyards. There were cries of "Welcome to the master," calls upon the Gods, and thanks for his safe return, and a few moments later Imhotep came ashore, greeting his family and answering the loud salutations that etiquette demanded.

"Praise be to Sobk, the child of Neith, who has brought you safely on the water!" "Praise be to Ptah, south of the Memphite wall, who brings you to us!" "Thanks be to Re who illumines the Two Lands!"

Renisenb pressed forward, intoxicated with the general excitement.

Imhotep drew himself up importantly and suddenly Renisenb thought: "But he is a *small* man. I thought of him as much bigger than that." A feeling that was almost dismay passed over her.

Had her father *shrunk*? Or was her own memory at fault? She had thought of him as rather a splendid being, tyrannical, often fussy, exhorting everybody right and left, and sometimes provoking her to quiet inward laughter, but nevertheless a *personage*. But this small, stout, elderly man, looking so full of his own importance and yet somehow failing to impress— What was wrong with her? What were these disloyal thoughts that came into her head?

Imhotep, having finished the sonorous and ceremonial phrases, had arrived at the stage of more personal greetings. He embraced his sons.

"Ah, my good Yahmose, all smiles, you have been diligent in my absence, I am sure. . . . And Sobek, my handsome son, still given to merriness of heart, I see. And here is Ipy—my dearest Ipy—let me look at you—stand away—so. Grown bigger, more of a man! How it rejoices my heart to hold you again! And Renisenb—my dear daughter—once more in the home. Satipy, Kait, my no less dear daughters. . . . And Henet—my faithful Henet—"

Henet was kneeling, embracing his knees, and ostentatiously wiping tears of joy from her eyes.

"It is good to see you, Henet—you are well—happy? As devoted as ever— that is pleasant to the heart. . . .

"And my excellent Hori, so clever with his accounts and his pen! All has prospered? I am sure it has."

Then, the greetings finished and the surrounding murmur dying down, Imhotep raised his hand for silence and spoke out loud and clear:

"My sons and daughters—friends. I have a piece of news for you. For many years, as you all know, I have been a lonely man in one respect. My wife—your mother, Yahmose and Sobek—and my sister—your mother, Ipy —have both gone to Osiris many years ago. So to you, Satipy and Kait, I bring a new sister to share your home. Behold, this is my concubine, Nofret, whom you shall love for my sake. She has come with me from Memphis in the north and will dwell here with you when I go away again."

As he spoke he drew forward a woman by the hand. She stood there beside him, her head flung back, her eyes narrowed, young, arrogant and beautiful.

Renisenb thought with a shock of surprise: "But she's quite young—perhaps not as old as I am."

Nofret stood quite still. There was a faint smile on her lips—it had more derision in it than any anxiety to please.

She had very straight black brows and a rich bronze skin, and her eyelashes were so long and thick that one could hardly see her eyes.

The family, taken aback, stared in dumb silence. With a faint edge of irritation in his voice, Imhotep said:

"Come now, children, welcome Nofret. Don't you know how to greet your father's concubine when he brings her to his house?"

Haltingly and stumblingly the greetings were given.

Imhotep, affecting a heartiness that perhaps concealed some uneasiness, exclaimed cheerfully:

"That is better! Nofret, Satipy and Kait and Renisenb will take you to the women's quarters. Where are the trunks? Have the trunks been brought ashore?"

The round-topped travelling trunks were being carried from the barge. Imhotep said to Nofret:

"Your jewels and your clothes are here safely. Go and see to their bestowing."

Then, as the women moved away together, he turned to his sons.

"And what of the estate? Does all go well?"

"The lower fields that were rented to Nehkte—" began Yahmose, but his father cut him short.

"No details now, good Yahmose. They can wait. Tonight is rejoicing. Tomorrow you and I and Hori here will get to business. Come here, Ipy, my boy, let us walk to the house. How tall you have grown—your head is above mine."

Scowling, Sobek walked behind his father and Ipy. Into Yahmose's ear he murmured:

"Jewels and clothes—did you hear? That is where the profits of the northern estates have gone. *Our* profits."

"Hush," whispered Yahmose. "Our father will hear."

"What if he does? I am not afraid of him as you are."

Once in the house, Henet came to Imhotep's room to prepare the bath. She was all smiles.

Imhotep abandoned a little of his defensive heartiness.

"Well, Henet, and what do you think of my choice?"

Although he had determined to carry things off with a high hand, he had known quite well that the arrival of Nofret would provoke a storm

—at least in the women's part of the house. Henet was different—a singularly devoted creature. She did not disappoint him.

"She is beautiful! Quite beautiful! What hair, what limbs! She is worthy of you, Imhotep. What can I say more than that? Your dear wife who is dead will be glad that you have chosen such a companion to gladden your days."

"You think so, Henet?"

"I am sure of it, Imhotep. After mourning her so many years it is time that you once more enjoyed life."

"You knew her well. . . . I, too, felt it was time to live as a man should live. Er—ahem—my sons' wives and my daughter—they will take this with resentment perhaps?"

"They had better not," said Henet. "After all, do they not all depend upon you in this house?"

"Very true, very true," said Imhotep.

"Your bounty feeds and clothes them—their welfare is entirely the result of your efforts."

"Yes, indeed." Imhotep sighed. "I am continually active on their behalf. I sometimes doubt if they realise all they owe to me."

"You must remind them of it," said Henet, nodding her head. "I, your humble devoted Henet, never forget what I owe you—but children are sometimes thoughtless and selfish, thinking, perhaps, that it is *they* who are important and not realising that they only carry out the instructions that *you* give."

"That is indeed most true," said Imhotep. "I have always said you were an intelligent creature, Henet."

Henet sighed.

"If others only thought so."

"What is this? Has anyone been unkind to you?"

"No, no—that is, they do not mean it—it is a matter of course to them that I should work unceasingly—which I am glad to do—but a word of affection and appreciation, that is what makes all the difference."

"That you will always have from me," said Imhotep. "And this is always your home, remember."

"You are too kind, master." She paused and added: "The slaves are ready in the bathroom with the hot water—and when you have bathed and dressed, your mother asks that you should go to her."

"Ah, my mother? Yes—yes, of course. . . ."

Imhotep looked suddenly slightly embarrassed. He covered his confusion by saying quickly:

"Naturally—I had intended that—tell Esa I shall come."

II

Esa, dressed in her best pleated linen gown, peered across at her son with a kind of sardonic amusement.

"Welcome, Imhotep. So you have returned to us—and not alone, I hear."

Imhotep, drawing himself up, replied rather shamefacedly:

"Oh, so you have heard?"

"Naturally. The house is humming with the news. The girl is beautiful, they say, and quite young."

"She is nineteen and—er—not ill-looking."

Esa laughed—an old woman's spiteful cackle.

"Ah, well," she said, "there's no fool like an old fool."

"My dear mother. I am really at a loss to understand what you mean."

Esa replied composedly:

"You always were a fool, Imhotep."

Imhotep drew himself up and spluttered angrily. Though usually comfortably conscious of his own importance, his mother could always pierce the armour of his self-esteem. In her presence he felt himself dwindling. The faint sarcastic gleam of her nearly sightless eyes never failed to disconcert him. His mother, there was no denying, had never had an exaggerated opinion of his capabilities. And although he knew well that his own estimate of himself was the true one and his mother's a maternal idiosyncrasy of no importance—yet her attitude never failed to puncture his happy conceit of himself.

"Is it so unusual for a man to bring home a concubine?"

"Not at all unusual. Men are usually fools."

"I fail to see where the folly comes in."

"Do you imagine that the presence of this girl is going to make for harmony in the household? Satipy and Kait will be beside themselves and will inflame their husbands."

"What has it to do with them? What right have they to object?"

"None."

Imhotep began to walk up and down angrily.

"Can I not do as I please in my own house? Do I not support my sons and their wives? Do they not owe the very bread they eat to me? Do I not tell them so without ceasing?"

"You are too fond of saying so, Imhotep."

"It is the truth. They all depend on me. All of them!"

"And are you sure that that is a good thing?"

"Are you saying that it is not a good thing for a man to support his family?"

Esa sighed.

"They work for you, remember."

"Do you want me to encourage them in idleness? Naturally they work."

"They are grown men—at least Yahmose and Sobek are—more than grown."

"Sobek has no judgement. He does everything wrong. Also he is frequently impertinent, which I will not tolerate. Yahmose is a good obedient boy—"

"A good deal more than a boy!"

"But sometimes I have to tell him things two or three times before he takes them in. I have to think of everything—be everywhere! All the time I am away, I am dictating to scribes—writing full instructions so that my sons can carry them out. . . . I hardly rest—I hardly sleep! And now when I come home, having earned a little peace, there is to be fresh difficulty! Even you, my mother, deny my right to have a concubine like other men. You are angry—"

Esa interrupted him.

"I am not angry. I am amused. There will be good sport to watch in the household—but I say all the same that when you go north again you had best take the girl with you."

"Her place is here, in my household! And woe to any who dare ill-treat her."

"It is not a question of ill-treatment. But remember, it is easy to kindle a fire in dry stubble. It has been said of women that 'the place where they are is not good. . . .'"

Esa paused and said slowly:

"Nofret is beautiful. But remember this: *Men are made fools by the gleaming limbs of women, and lo, in a minute they are become discoloured carnelians. . . .*"

Her voice deepened as she quoted:

"*A trifle, a little, the likeness of a dream, and death comes as the end. . . .*"

CHAPTER IV

Third Month of Inundation, 15th Day

I

IMHOTEP LISTENED TO Sobek's explanations of the sale of the timber in ominous silence. His face had grown very red and a small pulse was beating in his temple.

Sobek's air of easy nonchalance wore a little thin. He had intended to carry things off with a high hand, but in the face of his father's gathering frowns, he found himself stammering and hesitating.

Imhotep finally cut him short impatiently:

"Yes, yes, yes—you thought that you knew more than I did—you departed from my instructions—it is always the same—unless I am here to see to everything." He sighed. "What would become of you boys without me, I cannot imagine!"

Sobek went on doggedly:

"There was a chance of making a much bigger profit—I took the risk. One cannot always be pettifogging and cautious!"

"There is nothing cautious about you, Sobek! You are rash and much too bold and your judgement is always wrong."

"Do I ever have a chance to exercise my judgement?"

Imhotep said drily:

"You have done so this time—against my express orders—"

"*Orders?* Have I always got to take orders? I am a grown man."

Losing control of his temper, Imhotep shouted:

"Who feeds you; who clothes you? Who thinks of the future? Who has your welfare—the welfare of all of you—constantly in mind? When the River was low and we were threatened with famine, did I not arrange for food to be sent south to you? You are lucky to have such a father—who thinks of everything! And what do I ask in return? Only that you should work hard, do your best, and obey the instructions I send you—"

"Yes," shouted Sobek. "We are to work for you like slaves—so that you can buy gold and jewels for your concubine!"

Imhotep advanced towards him, bristling with rage.

"Insolent boy—to speak like that to your father. Be careful or I will say that this is no longer your home—and you can go elsewhere!"

"And if *you* are not careful I *will* go! I have ideas, I tell you—good ideas —that would bring in wealth if I was not tied down by pettifogging caution and never allowed to act as I choose."

"Have you finished?"

Imhotep's tone was ominous. Sobek, a trifle deflated, muttered angrily: "Yes—yes—I have no more to say—*now*."

"Then go and see after the cattle. This is no time for idling."

Sobek turned and strode angrily away. Nofret was standing not far away and as he passed her she looked sideways at him and laughed. At her laugh the blood came up in Sobek's face—he made an angry half-step towards her. She stood quite still, looking at him out of contemptuous half-closed eyes.

Sobek muttered something and resumed his former direction. Nofret laughed again, then walked slowly on to where Imhotep was now turning his attention to Yahmose.

"What possessed you to let Sobek act in that foolish fashion?" he demanded irritably. "You should have prevented it! Don't you know by now that he has no judgement in buying and selling? He thinks everything will turn out as he wants it to turn out."

Yahmose said apologetically:

"You do not realise my difficulties, Father. You told me to entrust Sobek with the sale of the timber. It was necessary therefore that it should be left to him to use his judgement."

"Judgement? Judgement? He has no judgement! He is to do what I instruct him to do—and it is for *you* to see that he does exactly that."

Yahmose flushed.

"I? What authority have I?"

"What authority? The authority I give you."

"But I have no real status. If I were legally associated with you—"

He broke off as Nofret came up. She was yawning and twisting a scarlet poppy in her hands.

"Won't you come to the little pavilion by the lake, Imhotep? It is cool there and there is fruit waiting for you and Keda beer. Surely you have finished giving your orders by now."

"In a minute, Nofret—in a minute."

Nofret said in a soft, deep voice:

"Come *now*. I want you to come now. . . ."

Imhotep looked pleased and a little sheepish. Yahmose said quickly before his father could speak:

"Let us just speak of this first. It is important. I want to ask you—"

Nofret spoke directly to Imhotep, turning her shoulder on Yahmose:

"Can you not do what you want in your own house?"

Imhotep said sharply to Yahmose:

"Another time, my son. Another time."

He went with Nofret and Yahmose stood on the porch looking after them.

Satipy came out from the house and joined him.

"Well," she demanded eagerly, "have you spoken to him? What did he say?"

Yahmose sighed.

"Do not be so impatient, Satipy. The time was not—propitious."

Satipy gave an angry exclamation.

"Oh, yes—that's what you *would* say! That is what you will always say. The truth is you are *afraid* of your father—you are as timid as a sheep— you bleat at him—you will not stand up to him like a man! Do you not re- call the things you promised me? I tell you *I* am the better man of us two! You promise—you say: 'I will ask my father—at once—the very first day.' And what happens—"

Satipy paused—for breath, not because she had finished—but Yahmose cut in mildly:

"You are wrong, Satipy. I began to speak—but we were interrupted."

"Interrupted? By whom?"

"By Nofret."

"Nofret! That woman! Your father should not let his concubine interrupt when he is speaking of business to his eldest son. Women should not con- cern themslves with business."

Possibly Yahmose wished that Satipy herself would live up to the maxim she was enunciating so glibly, but he was given no opportunity to speak. His wife swept on:

"Your father should have made that clear to her at once."

"My father," said Yahmose drily, "showed no signs of displeasure."

"It is disgraceful," Satipy declared. "Your father is completely bewitched by her. He lets her say and do as she pleases."

Yahmose said thoughtfully:

"She is very beautiful. . . ."

Satipy snorted.

"Oh, she has looks of a kind. But no manners! No upbringing! She does not care how rude she is to all of us."

"Perhaps *you* are rude to her?"

"I am the soul of politeness. Kait and I treat her with every courtesy. Oh, she shall have nothing of which to go complaining to your father. We can wait our time, Kait and I."

Yahmose looked up sharply.

"How do you mean—*wait your time?*"

Satipy laughed meaningly as she moved away.

"My meaning is woman's meaning—you would not understand. We have our ways—and our weapons! Nofret would do well to moderate her insolence. What does a woman's life come to in the end, after all? It is spent in the back of the house—amongst the other women."

There was a peculiar significance in Satipy's tone. She added:

"Your father will not always be here. . . . He will go away again to his estates in the north. And then—we shall see."

"Satipy—"

Satipy laughed—a hard-sounding, high laugh—and went back into the house.

II

By the lake the children were running about and playing. Yahmose's two boys were fine, handsome little fellows, looking more like Satipy than like their father. Then there were Sobek's three—the youngest a mere toddling baby. And there was Teti, a grave, handsome child of four years.

They laughed and shouted, threw balls—occasionally a dispute broke out and a childish wail of anger rose high and shrill.

Sitting sipping his beer, with Nofret beside him, Imhotep murmured: "How fond children are of playing by water. It was always so, I remember. But, by Hathor, what a noise they make!"

Nofret said quickly:

"Yes—and it could be so peaceful. . . . Why do you not tell them to go away whilst you are here? After all, when the master of the house wants relaxation a proper respect should be shown. Don't you agree?"

"I—well—" Imhotep hesitated. The idea was new to him but pleasing. "I do not really mind them," he finished doubtfully.

He added rather weakly:

"They are accustomed to play here always as they please."

"When you are away, yes," said Nofret quickly. "But I think, Imhotep, considering all that you do for your family, they should show more sense of your dignity—of your importance. You are too gentle—too easygoing."

Imhotep sighed placidly.

"It has always been my failing. I never insist on the outward forms."

"And therefore these women, your sons' wives, take advantage of your kindness. It should be understood that when you come here for repose, there must be silence and tranquillity. See, I will go and tell Kait to take her children away and the others too. Then you shall have peace and contentment here."

"You are a thoughtful girl, Nofret—yes, a good girl. You are always thinking of my comfort."

Nofret murmured: "Your pleasure is mine."

She got up and went to where Kait was kneeling by the water playing with a little model barge which her second child, a rather spoilt-looking boy, was trying to float.

Nofret said curtly:

"Will you take the children away, Kait?"

Kait stared up at her uncomprehendingly.

"Away? What do you mean? This is where they always play."

"Not today. Imhotep wants peace. These children of yours are noisy."

Colour flamed into Kait's heavy face.

"You should mend your ways of speech, Nofret! Imhotep likes to see his sons' children playing here. He has said so."

"Not today," said Nofret. "He has sent me to tell you to take the whole noisy brood into the house so that he can sit in peace—with me."

"With *you* . . ." Kait stopped abruptly in what she had been about to say. Then she got up and walked to where Imhotep was half-sitting, half-lying. Nofret followed her.

Kait spoke without circumlocution.

"Your concubine says I am to take the children away from here? Why? What are they doing that is wrong? For what reason should they be banished?"

"I should have thought the wish of the master of the house was enough," said Nofret softly.

"Exactly—exactly," said Imhotep pettishly. "Why should I have to give *reasons*? Whose house is this?"

"I suppose it is *she* who wants them away." Kait turned and looked Nofret up and down.

"Nofret thinks of my comfort—of my enjoyment," said Imhotep. "No one else in this house ever considers it—except perhaps poor Henet."

"So the children are not to play here any more?"

"Not when I have come here to rest."

Kait's anger flamed forth suddenly:

"Why do you let this woman turn you against your own blood? Why should she come and interfere with the ways of the house—with what has always been done?"

Imhotep suddenly began to shout. He felt a need to vindicate himself.

"It is *I* who say what is to be done here—not you! You are all in league to do as you choose—to arrange everything to suit yourselves. And when I, the master of the house, come home, no proper attention is paid to my wishes. But I *am* master here, let me tell you! I am constantly planning and working for your welfare—but am I given gratitude, are my wishes respected? No. First, Sobek is insolent and disrespectful, and now you, Kait, try to browbeat me! What am I supporting you all for? Take care—or I shall cease to support you. Sobek talks of going—then let him go and take you and your children with him."

For a moment Kait stood perfectly still. There was no expression at all on her heavy, rather vacant face. Then she said in a voice from which all emotion had been eliminated:

"I will take the children into the house. . . ."

She moved a step or two, pausing by Nofret. In a low voice Kait said: "This is *your* doing, Nofret. I shall not forget. No, I shall not forget. . . ."

CHAPTER V

Fourth Month of Inundation, 5th Day

I

IMHOTEP BREATHED A sigh of satisfaction as he finished his ceremonial duties as mortuary priest. The ritual had been observed with meticulous detail—for Imhotep was in every respect a most conscientious man. He had poured the libations, burnt incense, and offered the customary offerings of food and drink.

Now, in the cool shade of the adjacent rock chamber where Hori was waiting for him, Imhotep became once more the landowner and the man of affairs. Together the two men discussed business matters, prevailing prices, and the profits resulting from crops, cattle, and timber.

After half an hour or so, Imhotep nodded his head with satisfaction.

"You have an excellent head for business, Hori," he said.

The other smiled.

"I should have, Imhotep. I have been your man of affairs for many years now."

"And a most faithful one. Now, I have a matter to discuss with you. It concerns Ipy. He complains that his position is subordinate."

"He is still very young."

"But he shows great ability. He feels that his brothers are not always fair to him. Sobek, it seems, is rough and overbearing—and Yahmose's continual caution and timidity irk him. Ipy is high-spirited. He does not like taking orders. Moreover he says that it is only I, his father, who have the right to command."

"That is true," said Hori. "And it has struck me, Imhotep, that that is a weakness here on the estate. May I speak freely?"

"Certainly, my good Hori. Your words are always thoughtful and well-considered."

"Then I say this. When you are away, Imhotep, there should be someone here who has real authority."

"I trust my affairs to you and to Yahmose—"

"I know that we act for you in your absence—but that is not enough. Why not appoint one of your sons as a partner—associate him with you by a legal deed of settlement."

Imhotep paced up and down, frowning.

"Which of my sons do you suggest? Sobek has an authoritative manner —but he is insubordinate—I could not trust him. His disposition is not good."

"I was thinking of Yahmose. He is your eldest son. He has a gentle and affectionate disposition. He is devoted to you."

"Yes, he has a good disposition—but he is too timid—too yielding. He gives in to everybody. Now if Ipy were only a little older—"

Hori said quickly:

"It is dangerous to give power to too young a man."

"True—true—well, Hori, I will think of what you have said. Yahmose is certainly a good son . . . an obedient son. . . ."

Hori said gently but urgently:

"You would, I think, be wise."

Imhotep looked at him curiously.

"What is in your mind, Hori?"

Hori said slowly:

"I said just now that it is dangerous to give a man power when he is too young. But it is also dangerous to give it to him too late."

"You mean that he has become too used to obeying orders and not to giving them? Well, perhaps there is something in that."

Imhotep sighed.

"It is a difficult task to rule a family! The women in particular are hard to manage. Satipy has an ungovernable temper; Kait is often sulky. But I have made it clear to them that Nofret is to be treated in a proper fashion. I think I may say that—"

He broke off. A slave was coming panting up the narrow pathway.

"What is this?"

"Master—a barge is here. A scribe called Kameni has come with a message from Memphis."

Imhotep got up fussily.

"More trouble," he exclaimed. "As sure as Re sails the Heavens this will be more trouble! Unless I am on hand to attend to things everything goes wrong."

He went stamping down the path and Hori sat quite still looking after him.

There was a troubled expression on his face.

II

Renisenb had been wandering aimlessly along the bank of the Nile when she heard shouts and commotion and saw people running towards the landing stage.

She ran and joined them. In the boat that was pulling to shore stood a young man and just for a moment, as she saw him outlined against the bright light, her heart missed a beat.

A mad, fantastic thought leapt into her mind.

"It is Khay," she thought. "Khay returned from the Underworld."

Then she mocked herself for the superstitious fancy. Because, in her own remembrance, she always thought of Khay as sailing on the Nile, and this was indeed a young man of about Khay's build—she had imagined a fantasy. This man was younger than Khay, with an easy, supple grace, and had a laughing, gay face.

He had come, he told them, from Imhotep's estates in the north. He was a scribe and his name was Kameni.

A slave was despatched for her father and Kameni was taken to the house where food and drink were put before him. Presently her father arrived and there was much consultation and talking.

The gist of it all filtered through into the women's quarters with Henet, as usual, as the purveyor of the news. Renisenb sometimes wondered how it was that Henet always contrived to know all about everything.

Kameni, it seemed, was a young scribe in Imhotep's employ—the son of one of Imhotep's cousins. Kameni had discovered certain fraudulent dispositions—a falsifying of the accounts, and since the matter had many ramifications and involved the stewards of the property, he had thought it best to come south in person to report.

Renisenb was not much interested. It was clever, she thought, of Kameni to have discovered all this. Her father would be pleased with him.

The immediate outcome of the matter was that Imhotep made hurried preparations for departure. He had not meant to leave for another two months, but now the sooner he was on the spot the better.

The whole household was summoned and innumerable exordiums and recommendations were made. This was to be done and that. Yahmose was on no account to do such and such a thing. Sobek was to exercise the utmost discretion over something else. It was all, Renisenb thought, very familiar. Yahmose was attentive, Sobek was sulky. Hori, as usual, was calm and efficient. Ipy's demands and importunities were put aside with more sharpness than usual.

"You are too young to have a separate allowance. Obey Yahmose. He knows my wishes and commands." Imhotep placed a hand on his eldest son's shoulder. "I trust you, Yahmose. When I return we will speak once more of a partnership."

Yahmose flushed quickly with pleasure. He drew himself a little more erect.

Imhotep went on:

"See only that all goes well in my absence. See to it that my concubine is well-treated—and with due honour and respect. She is in your charge. It is for you to control the conduct of the women of the household. See that Satipy curbs her tongue. See also that Sobek duly instructs Kait. Renisenb, also, must act toward Nofret with courtesy. Then I will have no unkindness shown toward our good Henet. The women, I know, find her tiresome sometimes. She has been here long and thinks herself privileged to say many things that are sometimes unwelcome. She has, I know, neither beauty nor wit—but she is faithful, remember, and has always been devoted to my interests. I will not have her despised and abused."

"Everything shall be done as you say," said Yahmose. "But Henet sometimes makes trouble with her tongue."

"Pah! Nonsense! All women do. Not Henet more than another. Now as to Kameni, he shall remain here. We can do with another scribe and he can assist Hori. As for that land that we have rented to the woman Yaii—"

Imhotep went off into meticulous details.

When at last all was ready for the departure Imhotep felt a sudden qualm. He took Nofret aside and said doubtfully:

"Nofret, are you content to remain here? Would it be, perhaps, best if, after all, you came with me?"

Nofret shook her head and smiled.

"You will not be long absent," she said.

"Three months—perhaps four. Who knows?"

"You see—it will not be long. I shall be content here."

Imhotep said fussily:

"I have enjoined upon Yahmose—upon all my sons—that you are to have every consideration. On their heads be it if you have anything of which to complain!"

"They will do as you say, I am sure, Imhotep." Nofret paused. Then she said, "Who is there here whom I can trust absolutely? Someone who is truly devoted to your interests? I do not mean one of the family."

"Hori—my good Hori? He is in every way my right hand—and a man of good sense and discrimination."

Nofret said slowly:

"He and Yahmose are like brothers. Perhaps—"

"There is Kameni. He, too, is a scribe. I will enjoin on him to place himself at your service. If you have anything of which to complain, he will write down your words with his pen and despatch the complaint to me."

Nofret nodded appreciatively.

"That is a good thought. Kameni comes from the north. He knows my father. He will not be influenced by family considerations."

"And Henet," exclaimed Imhotep. "There is Henet."

"Yes," said Nofret reflectively. "There is Henet. Suppose that you were to speak to her now—in front of me?"

"An excellent plan."

Henet was sent for and came with her usual cringing eagerness. She was full of lamentations over Imhotep's departure. Imhotep cut her short with abruptness.

"Yes, yes, my good Henet—but these things must be. I am a man who can seldom count on any stretch of peace or rest. I must toil ceaselessly for my family—little though they sometimes appreciate it. Now I wish to speak to you very seriously. You love me faithfully and devotedly, I know. I can leave you in a position of trust. Guard Nofret here—she is very dear to me."

"Whoever is dear to you, master, is dear to me," Henet declared with fervour.

"Very good. Then you will devote yourself to Nofret's interests?"

Henet turned towards Nofret, who was watching her under lowered lids.

"You are too beautiful, Nofret," she said. "That is the trouble. That is why the others are jealous—but I will look after you—I will warn you of all they say and do. You can count on me!"

There was a pause whilst the eyes of the two women met.

"You can count on me," Henet repeated.

A slow smile came to Nofret's lips—a rather curious smile.

"Yes," she said. "I understand you, Henet. I think I can count on you."

Imhotep cleared his throat noisily.

"Then I think all is arranged—yes—everything is satisfactory. Organisation—that has always been my strong point."

There was a dry cackle of laughter and Imhotep turned sharply to see his mother standing in the entrance of the room. She was supporting her weight on a stick and looked more dried up and malevolent than ever.

"What a wonderful son I have!" she observed.

"I must not delay—there are some instructions to Hori—" Muttering importantly, Imhotep hurried from the room. He managed to avoid meeting his mother's eye.

Esa gave an imperious nod of the head to Henet—and Henet glided obediently out of the room.

Nofret had risen. She and Esa stood looking at each other.

Esa said:

"So my son is leaving you behind? You had better go with him, Nofret."

"He wishes me to stay here."

Nofret's voice was soft and submissive. Esa gave a shrill chuckle.

"Little good that would be if you wanted to go! And why do you not want to go? I do not understand you. What is there for you here? You are a girl who has lived in cities—who has perhaps travelled. Why do you choose the monotony of day after day here—amongst those who—I am frank —do not like you—who in fact dislike you?"

"So you dislike me?"

Esa shook her head.

"No—I do not dislike you. I am old and though I can see but dimly—I can still see beauty and enjoy it. You are beautiful, Nofret, and the sight of you pleases my old eyes. Because of your beauty I wish you well. I am warning you. Go north with my son."

Again Nofret repeated:

"He wishes me to stay here."

The submissive tone was now definitely impregnated with mockery. Esa said sharply:

"You have a purpose in remaining here. What is it, I wonder? Very well, on your own head be it. But be careful. Act discreetly. And trust no one."

She wheeled abruptly and went out. Nofret stood quite still. Very slowly her lips curved upwards in a wide, catlike smile.

CHAPTER VI

First Month of Winter, 4th Day

I

RENISENB HAD GOT into the habit of going up to the Tomb almost every day. Sometimes Yahmose and Hori would be there together, sometimes Hori alone, sometimes there would be no one—but always Renisenb was aware of a curious relief and peace—a feeling almost of escape. She liked it best when Hori was there alone. There was something in his gravity, his incurious acceptance of her coming, that gave her a strange feeling of contentment. She would sit in the shade of the rock chamber entrance with one knee raised and her hands clasped around it, and stare out over the green belt of cultivation to where the Nile showed a pale gleaming blue and beyond it to a distance of pale soft fawns and creams and pinks, all melting hazily into each other.

She had come the first time, months ago now, on a sudden wish to escape from a world of intense femininity. She wanted stillness and companionship—and she had found them here. The wish to escape was still with her but it was no longer a mere revulsion from the stress and fret of domesticity. It was something more definite, more alarming.

She said to Hori one day: "I am afraid. . . ."

"Why are you afraid, Renisenb?" He studied her gravely.

Renisenb took a minute or two to think. Then she said slowly:

"Do you remember saying to me once that there were two evils—one that came from without and one from within?"

"Yes, I remember."

"You were speaking, so you said afterwards, about diseases that attack fruit and crops, but I have been thinking—it is the same with *people*."

Hori nodded slowly.

"So you have found that out. . . . Yes, you are right, Renisenb."

Renisenb said abruptly:

"It is happening now—down there at the house. Evil has come—from outside! And I know who has brought it. It is Nofret."

Hori said slowly:

"You think so?"

Renisenb nodded vigorously.

"Yes, yes, I know what I am talking about. Listen, Hori, when I came up to you here and said that everything was the same even to Satipy and Kait quarrelling—that was true. But those quarrels, Hori, were not *real* quarrels. I mean Satipy and Kait *enjoyed* them—they made the time pass—neither of the women felt any real anger against each other! But now it is different. Now they do not just say things that are rude and unpleasant—they say things that they mean shall *hurt*—and when they have seen that a thing hurts, then they are glad! It is horrid, Hori—horrid! Yesterday Satipy was so angry that she ran a long gold pin into Kait's arm—and a day or two ago Kait dropped a heavy copper pan full of boiling fat over Satipy's foot. And it is the same everywhere—Satipy rails at Yahmose far into the night—we can all hear her. Yahmose looks sick and tired and hunted. And Sobek goes off to the village and stays there with women and comes back drunk and shouts and boasts and says how clever he is!"

"Some of these things are true, I know," said Hori slowly. "But why should you blame Nofret?"

"Because it is her doing! It is always the things she says—little things—clever things—that start it all. She is like the goad with which you prick oxen. She is clever, too, in knowing just *what* to say. Sometimes I think it is Henet who tells her. . . ."

"Yes," said Hori thoughtfully. "That might well be."

Renisenb shivered.

"I don't like Henet. I hate the way she creeps about. She is so devoted to us all, and yet none of us want her devotion. How *could* my mother have brought her here and been so fond of her?"

"We have only Henet's word for that," said Hori drily.

"Why should Henet be so fond of Nofret and follow her round and whisper and fawn upon her? Oh, Hori, I tell you I am *afraid!* I hate Nofret! I wish she would go away. She is beautiful and cruel and *bad!*"

"What a child you are, Renisenb."

Then Hori added quietly:

"Nofret is coming up here now."

Renisenb turned her head. Together they watched Nofret come slowly up the steep path that led up the cliff face. She was smiling to herself and humming a little tune under her breath.

When she reached the place where they were, she looked round her and smiled. It was a smile of amused curiosity.

"So this is where you slip away to every day, Renisenb."

Renisenb did not answer. She had the angry, defeated feeling of a child whose refuge has been discovered.

Nofret looked about her again.

"And this is the famous Tomb?"

"As you say, Nofret," said Hori.

She looked at him, her catlike mouth curving into a smile.

"I've no doubt you find it profitable, Hori. You are a good man of business, so I hear."

There was a tinge of malice in her voice, but Hori remained unmoved, smiling his quiet, grave smile.

"It is profitable to all of us. . . . Death is always profitable. . . ."

Nofret gave a quick shiver as she looked round her, her eyes sweeping over the offering tables, the entrance to the shrine and the false door.

She cried sharply:

"I hate death!"

"You should not." Hori's tone was quiet. "Death is the chief source of wealth here in Egypt. Death bought the jewels you wear, Nofret. Death feeds you and clothes you."

She stared at him.

"What do you mean?"

"I mean that Imhotep is a ka-priest—a mortuary priest—all his lands, all his cattle, his timber, his flax, his barley, are the endowment of a Tomb."

He paused and then went on reflectively:

"We are a strange people, we Egyptians. We love life—and so we start very early to plan for death. That is where the wealth of Egypt goes—into pyramids, into tombs, into tomb endowments."

Nofret said violently:

"*Will* you stop talking about death, Hori! I do not like it!"

"Because you are truly Egyptian—because you love life, because—sometimes—you feel the shadow of death very near. . . ."

"Stop!"

She turned on him violently. Then, shrugging her shoulders, she turned away and began to descend the path.

Renisenb breathed a sigh of satisfaction.

"I am glad she has gone," she said childishly. "You frightened her, Hori."

"Yes. . . . Did I frighten you, Renisenb?"

"N-no." Renisenb sounded a little unsure. "It is true what you said, only I had never thought of it that way before. My father *is* a mortuary priest."

Hori said with sudden bitterness:

"All Egypt is obsessed by death! And do you know why, Renisenb? Because we have eyes in our bodies, but none in our minds. We cannot conceive of a life other than this one—of a life after death. We can visualise only a continuation of what we know. We have no real belief in a God."

Renisenb stared at him in amazement.

"How can you say that, Hori? Why, we have many, *many* Gods—so many that I could not name them all. Only last night we were saying, all of us, which Gods we preferred. Sobek was all for Sakhmet and Kait prays always to Meskhent. Kameni swears by Thoth, as is natural, being a scribe. Satipy is for the falcon-headed Horus and also for our own Meresger. Yahmose says that Ptah is to be worshipped because he made all things. I myself love Isis. And Henet is all for our local God Amûn. She says that there are prophecies amongst the priests that one day Amûn will be the greatest God in all Egypt—so she takes him offerings now while he is still a small God. And there is Re, the Sun God, and Osiris, before whom the hearts of the dead are weighed."

Renisenb paused, out of breath. Hori was smiling at her.

"And what is the difference, Renisenb, between a God and a man?"

She stared at him.

"The Gods are—they are *magic!*"

"That is all?"

"I don't know what you mean, Hori."

"I meant that to you a God is only a man or a woman who can do certain things that men and women cannot do."

"You say such odd things! I cannot understand you."

She looked at him with a puzzled face—then glancing down over the valley, her attention was caught by something else.

"Look," she exclaimed. "Nofret is talking to Sobek. She is laughing. Oh" —she gave a sudden gasp—"no, it is nothing. I thought he was going to strike her. She is going back to the house and he is coming up here."

Sobek arrived looking like a thundercloud.

"May a crocodile devour that woman!" he cried. "My father was more of a fool than usual when he took her for a concubine!"

"What did she say to you?" asked Hori curiously.

"She insulted me as usual! Asked if my father had entrusted me with the sale of any more timber. I'd like to strangle her."

He moved along the platform and, picking up a piece of rock, threw it down to the valley below. The sound of it bouncing off the cliff seemed to please him. He levered up a larger piece, then sprang back as a snake that had been coiled up beneath it raised its head. It reared up, hissing, and Renisenb saw that it was a cobra.

Catching up a heavy staff Sobek attacked it furiously. A well-directed blow broke its back, but Sobek continued to slash at it, his head thrown back, his eyes sparkling, and below his breath he muttered some word which Renisenb only half heard and did not recognise.

She cried out:

"Stop, Sobek, stop—it is dead!"

Sobek paused, then he threw the staff away and laughed.

"One poisonous snake the less in the world."

He laughed again, his good humour restored, and clattered off down the path again.

Renisenb said in a low voice: "I believe Sobek—*likes* killing things!"

"Yes."

There was no surprise in the word. Hori was merely acknowledging a fact which he evidently already knew well. Renisenb turned to stare at him. She said slowly:

"Snakes are dangerous—but how beautiful that cobra looked. . . ."

She stared down at its broken, twisted body. For some unknown reason she felt a pang at her heart.

Hori said dreamily:

"I remember when we were all small children—Sobek attacked Yahmose. Yahmose was a year older, but Sobek was the bigger and the stronger. He had a stone and he was banging Yahmose's head with it. Your mother came running and tore them apart. I remember how she stood looking down at Yahmose—and how she cried out: 'You must not do things like that, Sobek—it is dangerous! I tell you, it is *dangerous!*'" He paused and went on, "She was very beautiful. . . . I thought so as a child. You are like her, Renisenb."

"Am I?" Renisenb felt pleased—warmed. Then she asked:

"Was Yahmose badly hurt?"

"No, it was not as bad as it looked. Sobek was very ill the next day. It might have been something he ate, but your mother said it was his rage and the hot sun—it was the middle of summer."

"Sobek has a terrible temper," said Renisenb thoughtfully.

She looked again at the dead snake and turned away with a shiver.

II

When Renisenb got back to the house Kameni was sitting on the front porch with a roll of papyrus. He was singing and she paused a minute and listened to the words.

"*I will go to Memphis,*" sang Kameni, "*I will go to Ptah, Lord of Truth. I will say to Ptah, 'Give me my sister tonight.' The stream is wine, Ptah is its reeds, Sakhmet its lotus, Earit its bud, Nefertem its flower. I will say to Ptah, 'Give me my sister tonight. The dawn breaks through her beauty. Memphis is a dish of love apples set before the fair of face. . . .'*"

He looked up and smiled at Renisenb.

"Do you like my song, Renisenb?"

"What is it?"

"It is a love song from Memphis."

He kept his eyes on her, singing softly:

"Her arms are full of branches of the persea, her hair is weighed down with unguent. She is like a Princess of the Lord of the Two Lands."

The colour came up in Renisenb's face. She passed on quickly into the house and almost collided with Nofret.

"Why are you in such a hurry, Renisenb?"

Nofret's voice had a sharp edge to it. Renisenb looked at her in faint surprise. Nofret was not smiling. Her face looked grim and tense and Renisenb noticed that her hands were clenched at her sides.

"I am sorry, Nofret. I did not see you. It is dark in here when you come from the light outside."

"Yes, it is dark here. . . ." Nofret paused a moment. "It would be pleasanter outside—on the porch—with Kameni's singing to listen to. He sings well, does he not?"

"Yes—yes, I am sure he does."

"Yet you did not stay to listen? Kameni will be disappointed."

Renisenb's cheeks felt hot again. Nofret's cold, sneering glance made her uncomfortable.

"Do you not like love songs, Renisenb?"

"Does it matter to you, Nofret, what I like or do not like?"

"So little cats have claws."

"What do you mean?"

Nofret laughed. "You are not such a fool as you look, Renisenb. So you find Kameni handsome? Well, that will please him, no doubt."

"I think you are quite odious," said Renisenb passionately.

She ran past Nofret towards the back of the house. She heard the girl's mocking laugh. But through that laugh, sounding clearly in her memory, was the echo of Kameni's voice and the song that he had sung with his eyes watching her face. . . .

III

That night Renisenb had a dream.

She was with Khay, sailing with him in the Barque of the Dead in the Underworld. Khay was standing in the bows of the boat—she could only see the back of his head. Then, as they drew near to sunrise, Khay turned his head and Renisenb saw that it was not Khay but Kameni. And at the same time the prow of the barque, the serpent's head, began to writhe. It was a live serpent, a cobra, and Renisenb thought: *"It is the serpent that comes out in the Tombs to eat the souls of the dead."* She was paralysed with fear. And then she saw that the serpent's face was the face of Nofret and she woke up screaming: "Nofret—Nofret. . . ."

She had not really screamed—it was all in the dream. She lay still, her heart beating, telling herself that none of all this was real. And then she thought suddenly: "That is what Sobek said when he was killing the snake yesterday. He said: *'Nofret'* . . ."

CHAPTER VII

First Month of Winter, 5th Day

I

RENISENB'S DREAM HAD left her wakeful. She slept after it only in snatches, and towards morning she did not sleep at all. She was obsessed by an obscure feeling of impending evil.

She rose early and went out of the house. Her steps led her, as they did so often, to the Nile. There were fishermen out already and a big barge rowing with powerful strokes towards Thebes. There were other boats with sails flapping in the faint puffs of wind.

Something turned over in Renisenb's heart—the stirring of a desire for something she could not name. She thought, "I feel—I feel—" But she did not know what it was that she felt! That is to say, she knew no words to fit the sensation. She thought, "I want—but what do I want?"

Was it Khay she wanted? Khay was dead—he would not come back. She said to herself, "I shall not think of Khay any more. What is the use? It is over, all that."

Then she noticed another figure standing looking after the barge that was making for Thebes—and something forlorn about that figure—some emotion it expressed by its very motionlessness struck Renisenb, even as she recognised Nofret.

Nofret staring out at the Nile. Nofret—alone. Nofret thinking of—what?

With a little shock Renisenb suddenly realised how little they all knew about Nofret. They had accepted her as an enemy—a stranger—without

interest or curiosity in her life or the surroundings from which she had
come.

It must, Renisenb thought suddenly, be sad for Nofret alone here, without friends, surrounded only by people who disliked her.

Slowly Renisenb went forward until she was standing by Nofret's side.
Nofret turned her head for a moment, then moved it back again and resumed her study of the Nile. Her face was expressionless.

Renisenb said timidly:

"There are a lot of boats on the River."

"Yes."

Renisenb went on, obeying some obscure impulse towards friendliness:
"Is it like this, at all, where you come from?"

Nofret laughed, a short, rather bitter laugh.

"No, indeed. My father is a merchant in Memphis. It is gay and amusing
in Memphis. There are music and singing and dancing. Then my father
travels a good deal. I have been with him to Syria—to Byblos beyond the
Gazelle's Nose. I have been with him in a big ship on the wide seas."

She spoke with pride and animation.

Renisenb stood quite still, her mind working slowly, but with growing
interest and understanding.

"It must be very dull for you here," she said slowly.

Nofret laughed impatiently.

"It is dead here—dead—nothing but ploughing and sowing and reaping
and grazing—and talk of crops—and wanglings about the price of flax."

Renisenb was still wrestling with unfamiliar thoughts as she watched
Nofret sideways.

And suddenly, as though it was something physical, a great wave of
anger and misery and despair seemed to emanate from the girl at her side.

Renisenb thought: "She is as young as I am—younger. And she is the
concubine of that old man, that fussy, kindly, but rather ridiculous old
man, my father. . . ."

What did she, Renisenb, know about Nofret? Nothing at all. What was
it Hori had said yesterday when she had cried out, "She is beautiful and
cruel and bad"?

"You are a child, Renisenb." That was what he had said. Renisenb
knew now what he meant. Those words of hers had meant nothing—you
could not dismiss a human being so easily. What sorrow, what bitterness,
what despair lay behind Nofret's cruel smile? What had Renisenb, what
had any of them, done to make Nofret welcome?

Renisenb said stumblingly, childishly:

"You hate us all—I see why—we have not been kind—but now—it is not too late. Can we not, you and I, Nofret, can we not be sisters to each other? You are far away from all you know—you are alone—can I not help?"

Her words faltered into silence. Nofret turned slowly.

For a minute or two her face was expressionless—there was even, Renisenb thought, a momentary softening in her eyes. In that early morning stillness, with its strange clarity and peace, it was as though Nofret hesitated—as though Renisenb's words had touched in her some last core of irresolution.

It was a strange moment, a moment Renisenb was to remember afterwards. . . .

Then, gradually, Nofret's expression changed. It became heavily malevolent, her eyes smouldered. Before the fury of hate and malice in her glance, Renisenb recoiled a step.

Nofret said in a low, fierce voice:

"Go! I want nothing from any of you. Stupid fools, that is what you all are, every one of you. . . ."

She paused a moment, then wheeled round and retraced her steps towards the house, walking with energy.

Renisenb followed her slowly. Curiously enough, Nofret's words had not made her angry. They had opened before her eyes a black abyss of hate and misery—something quite unknown as yet in her own experience, and in her mind was only a confused, groping thought of how dreadful it must be to feel like that.

II

As Nofret entered the gateway and crossed the courtyard, one of Kait's children came running across her path, chasing a ball.

Nofret pushed the child out of her way with an angry thrust that sent the little girl sprawling on the ground. The child set up a wail and Renisenb ran to her and picked her up, saying indignantly:

"You should not have done that, Nofret! You have hurt her, see. She has cut her chin."

Nofret laughed stridently.

"So I should be careful not to hurt these spoiled brats? Why? Are their mothers so careful of my feelings?"

Kait had come running out of the house at the sound of her child's wails. She ran to it, examining the injured face. Then she turned on Nofret.

"Devil and serpent! Evil one! Wait and see what we will do to you."

With all the force of her arm she struck Nofret in the face. Renisenb gave a cry and caught her arm before she could repeat the blow.

"Kait—Kait—you must not do that."

"Who says so? Let Nofret look to herself. She is only one here among many."

Nofret stood quite still. The print of Kait's hand showed clear and red on her cheek. By the corner of the eye, where a bangle Kait wore on her wrist had cut the skin, a small trickle of blood was running down her face.

But it was Nofret's expression that puzzled Renisenb—yes, and frightened her. Nofret showed no anger. Instead there was a queer, exultant look in her eyes, and once more her mouth was curving up in its catlike, satisfied smile.

"Thank you, Kait," she said.

Then she walked on into the house.

III

Humming softly under her breath, her eyelids lowered, Nofret called Henet.

Henet came running, stopped, exclaimed. Nofret cut short her exclamations.

"Fetch me Kameni. Tell him to bring his pen case and ink and papyrus. There is a letter to be written to the master."

Henet's eyes were fixed on Nofret's cheek.

"To the master . . . I see. . . ."

Then she asked:

"Who did—that?"

"Kait." Nofret smiled quietly and reminiscently.

Henet shook her head and clicked her tongue.

"All this is very bad—very bad. . . . Certainly the master must know of it." She darted a quick, sideways look at Nofret. "Yes, certainly Imhotep must know."

Nofret said smoothly:

"You and I, Henet, think alike. . . . I thought that we should do so."

From the corner of her linen robe she detached a jewel of amethyst set in gold and placed it in the woman's hand.

"You and I, Henet, have Imhotep's true welfare at heart."

"This is too good for me, Nofret. . . . You are too generous . . . such a lovely bit of workmanship."

"Imhotep and I appreciate fidelity."

Nofret was still smiling, her eyes narrow and catlike.

"Fetch Kameni," she said. "And come with him. You and he together are witnesses of what has occurred."

Kameni came a little unwillingly, his brow puckered.

Nofret spoke imperiously:

"You remember Imhotep's instructions—before he left?"

"Yes," said Kameni.

"The time has come," said Nofret. "Sit and take ink and write as I tell you." Then as Kameni still hesitated, she said impatiently, "What you write shall be what you have seen with your own eyes and heard with your own ears—and Henet shall confirm all I say. The letter must be despatched with all secrecy and speed."

Kameni said slowly: "I do not like—"

Nofret flashed out at him:

"I have no complaint against Renisenb. Renisenb is soft, weak and a fool, but she has not tried to harm me. Does that content you?"

The colour of Kameni's bronze face deepened.

"I was not thinking of that—"

Nofret said smoothly:

"I think you were. . . . Come now—fulfil your instructions—write."

"Yes, write," said Henet. "I'm so distressed by all this—so terribly distressed. Certainly Imhotep must know about it. It's only right that he should. However unpleasant a thing is, one has to do one's duty. I've always felt that."

Nofret laughed softly.

"I'm sure you have, Henet. You shall do your duty! And Kameni shall do his office. And I—I shall do what it is my pleasure to do. . . ."

But still Kameni hesitated. His face was sullen—almost angry.

"I do not like this," he said. "Nofret, you had better take a little time to think."

"*You* say that to *me!*" Kameni flushed at her tone. His eyes avoided hers, but his sullen expression remained.

"Be careful, Kameni," said Nofret smoothly. "I have great influence with Imhotep. He listens to what I say—so far he has been pleased with you—" She paused significantly.

"Are you threatening me, Nofret?" asked Kameni angrily.

"Perhaps."

He looked angrily at her for a moment or two—then he bent his head.

"I will do as you say, Nofret, but I think—yes, I think—that you will be sorry."

"Are *you* threatening *me*, Kameni?"

"I am warning you. . . ."

CHAPTER VIII

Second Month of Winter, 10th Day

I

DAY FOLLOWED DAY, and Renisenb sometimes felt that she was living in a dream.

She had made no more timid overtures to Nofret. She was, now, afraid of Nofret. There was something about Nofret she did not understand.

After the scene in the courtyard that day, Nofret had changed. There was a complacency about her, an exultation that Renisenb could not fathom. Sometimes she thought that her own vision of Nofret as profoundly unhappy must have been ridiculously wrong. Nofret seemed pleased with life and herself and her surroundings.

And yet, actually, her surroundings had very definitely changed for the worse. In the days following Imhotep's departure, Nofret had quite deliberately, Renisenb thought, set out to sow dissension between the various members of Imhotep's family.

Now that family had closed its ranks solidly against the invader. There were no more dissensions between Satipy and Kait—no railing of Satipy against the unfortunate Yahmose. Sobek seemed quieter and boasted less. Ipy was less impudent and offhand with his elder brothers. There seemed a new harmony between the family—yet this harmony did not bring peace of mind to Renisenb—for with it went a curious, persistent undercurrent of ill-will to Nofret.

The two women, Satipy and Kait, no longer quarrelled with her—they avoided her. They never spoke to her and wherever she came, they immediately gathered the children together and went elsewhere. At the same time, queer, annoying little accidents began to happen. A linen dress of Nofret's was spoilt with an overhot iron—some dyestuff was spilt over another. Sometimes sharp thorns found their way into her clothing—a scorpion was discovered by her bed. The food that was served to her was over-seasoned—or lacking in any seasoning. There was a dead mouse one day in her portion of bread.

It was a quiet, relentless, petty persecution—nothing overt, nothing to lay hold of—it was essentially a woman's campaign.

Then, one day, old Esa sent for Satipy, Kait and Renisenb. Henet was already there, shaking her head and rubbing her hands in the background.

"Ha!" said Esa, peering at them with her usual ironical expression. "So here are my clever granddaughters. What do you think you are doing, all of you? What is this I hear about Nofret's dress being ruined—and her food uneatable?"

Satipy and Kait both smiled. They were not nice smiles.

Satipy said: "Has Nofret complained?"

"No," said Esa. She pushed the wig she always wore even in the house a little awry with one hand. "No, Nofret has not complained. That is what worries me."

"It does not worry *me*," said Satipy, tossing her handsome head.

"Because you are a fool," snapped Esa. "Nofret has twice the brains of any of you three."

"That remains to be seen," said Satipy. She looked good-humoured and pleased with herself.

"What do you think you are all doing?" inquired Esa.

Satipy's face hardened.

"You are an old woman, Esa. I do not speak with any lack of respect—but things no longer matter to you in the way they matter to us who have husbands and young children. We have decided to take matters into our own hands—we have ways of dealing with a woman whom we do not like and will not accept."

"Fine words," said Esa. "Fine words." She cackled. "But a good discourse can be found with slave girls over the millstone."

"A true and wise saying," sighed Henet from the background.

Esa turned on her.

"Come, Henet, what does Nofret say to all this that is going on? You should know—you are always waiting on her."

"As Imhotep told me to do. It is repugnant to me, of course—but I must do what the master ordered. You do not think, I hope—"

Esa cut into the whining voice:

"We know all about you, Henet. Always devoted—and seldom thanked as you should be. What does Nofret say to all this? That is what I asked you."

Henet shook her head.

"She says nothing. She just—smiles."

"Exactly." Esa picked up a jujube from a dish at her elbow, examined it and put it in her mouth. Then she said with sudden, malevolent acerbity:

"You are fools, all of you. The power is with Nofret, not with you. All you are doing is to play into her hands. I dare swear it even pleases her what you are doing."

Satipy said sharply:

"Nonsense. Nofret is alone amongst many. What power has she?"

Esa said grimly:

"The power of a young, beautiful woman married to an ageing man. I know what I am talking about." With a quick turn of her head she said: "Henet knows what I am talking about!"

Henet started. She sighed and began to twist her hands.

"The master thinks a great deal of her—naturally—yes, quite naturally."

"Go to the kitchen," said Esa. "Bring me some dates and some Syrian wine—yes, and honey too."

When Henet had gone, the old woman said:

"There is mischief brewing—I can smell it. Satipy, you are the leader in all this. Be careful that while you are thinking yourself clever, you do not play into Nofret's hands."

She leaned back and closed her eyes.

"I have warned you—now go."

"We in Nofret's power, indeed!" said Satipy with a toss of her head as they went out to the lake. "Esa is so old she gets the most extraordinary ideas into her head. It is we who have got Nofret in *our* power! We will do nothing against her that can be reported—but I think, yes, I think that she will soon be sorry she ever came here."

"You are cruel—cruel—" cried Renisenb.

Satipy looked amused.

"Do not pretend you love Nofret, Renisenb!"

"I do not. But you sound so—so *vindictive*."

"I think of my children—and Yahmose! I am not a meek woman or one who brooks insult—and I have ambition. I would wring that woman's neck with the greatest of pleasure. Unfortunately it is not so simple as that. Imhotep's anger must not be aroused. But I think—in the end—something may be managed."

II

The letter came like a spear thrust to a fish.

Dumbfounded, silent, Yahmose, Sobek and Ipy stared at Hori as he read out the words from the papyrus scroll.

"Did I not tell Yahmose that I would hold him to blame if any harm came to my concubine? As you all live, I am against you and you are against me! I will no longer live with you in one house since you have not respected my concubine Nofret! You are no longer my son of my flesh.

Neither are Sobek and Ipy my sons of my flesh. Each one of you has done harm to my concubine. That is attested by Kameni and Henet. I will turn you out of my house—each of you! I have supported you—now I will no longer support you."

Hori paused and went on:

"The ka-servant Imhotep addresses Hori. To you who have been faithful, how are you in your life, safety and health? Salute my mother Esa for me and my daughter Renisenb, and greet Henet. Look after my affairs carefully until I reach you and see that there be prepared for me a deed whereby my concubine Nofret shall share with me in all my property as my wife. Neither Yahmose nor Sobek shall be associated with me, nor will I support them, and hereby I denounce them that they have done harm to my concubine! Keep all safe till I come. How evil it is when a man's household do evil deeds to his concubine. As for Ipy, let him take warning, and if he does a single hurt to my concubine, he too shall depart from my house."

There was a paralysed silence, then Sobek rose up in a violent rage.

"How has this come about? What has my father heard? Who has been bearing false tales to him? Shall we endure this? My father cannot disinherit us so and give all his goods to his concubine!"

Hori said mildly:

"It will cause unfavourable comment—and it will not be accepted as a right action—but legally it is in his power. He can make a deed of settlement in any way he wishes."

"She has bewitched him—that black, jeering serpent has put a spell upon him!"

Yahmose murmured as though dumbfounded:

"It is unbelievable—it cannot be true."

"My father is mad—mad!" cried Ipy. "He turns even against *me* at this woman's bidding!"

Hori said gravely:

"Imhotep will return shortly—that he says. By then his anger may have abated; he may not really mean to do as he says." There was a short, unpleasant laugh. It was Satipy who had laughed. She stood looking at them from the doorway into the women's quarters.

"So that is what we are to do, is it, most excellent Hori? Wait and see!"

Yahmose said slowly:

"What else can we do?"

"What else?" Satipy's voice rose. She screamed out: "What have you got in your veins, all of you? Milk? Yahmose, I know, is not a man! But you, Sobek—have you no remedy for these ills? A knife in the heart and the girl could do us no more harm."

"Satipy," cried Yahmose. "My father would never forgive us!"

"So you say. But I tell you a dead concubine is not the same as a live concubine! Once she was dead, his heart would return to his sons and their children. And besides, how should he know *how* she died? We could say a scorpion stung her! We are all together in this, are we not?"

Yahmose said slowly:

"My father *would* know. Henet would tell him."

Satipy gave a hysterical laugh.

"Most prudent Yahmose! Most gentle, cautious Yahmose! It is *you* who should look after the children and do woman's work in the back of the house. Sakhmet help me! Married to a man who is not a man. And *you*, Sobek, for all your bluster, what courage have you, what determination? I swear by Re, I am a better man than either of you."

She swung round and went out.

Kait, who had been standing behind her, came a step forward.

She said, her voice deep and shaken:

"It is true what Satipy says! She is a better man than any of you. Yahmose, Sobek, Ipy—will you all sit here doing nothing? What of our children, Sobek? Cast out to starve! Very well, if *you* will do nothing, *I* will. You are none of you *men!*"

As she in turn went out, Sobek sprang to his feet.

"By the Nine Gods of the Ennead, Kait is right! There is a man's work to be done—and we sit here talking and shaking our heads."

He strode towards the door. Hori called after him:

"Sobek, Sobek, where are you going? What are you going to do?"

Sobek, handsome and fierce, shouted from the doorway:

"I shall do *something*—that is clear. And what I do I shall *enjoy* doing!"

CHAPTER IX

Second Month of Winter, 10th Day

I

RENISENB CAME OUT onto the porch and stood there for a moment, shielding her eyes against the sudden glare.

She felt sick and shaken and full of a nameless fear. She said to herself, repeating the words over and over again mechanically:

"I must warn Nofret. . . . I must warn her. . . ."

Behind her, in the house, she could hear men's voices: those of Hori and Yahmose blending into each other, and above them, shrill and clear, the boyish tones of Ipy.

"Satipy and Kait are right. There are no men in this family! But *I* am a man. Yes, I am a man in heart if not in years. Nofret has jeered at me, laughed at me, treated me as a child. I will show her that I am *not* a child. I am not afraid of my father's anger. I know my father. He is bewitched—the woman has put a spell on him. If she were destroyed his heart would come back to me—to *me! I* am the son he loves best. You all treat me as a child—but you shall see. Yes, you shall see!"

Rushing out of the house he collided with Renisenb and almost knocked her down. She clutched at his sleeve.

"Ipy, Ipy, where are you going?"

"To find Nofret. She shall see whether she can laugh at me!"

"Wait a little. You must calm down. We must none of us do anything rash."

"Rash?" The boy laughed scornfully. "You are like Yahmose. Prudence! Caution! Nothing must be done in a hurry! Yahmose is an old woman. And Sobek is all words and boasting. Let go of me, Renisenb."

He twitched the linen of his sleeve from her grasp.

"Nofret, where *is* Nofret?"

Henet, who had just come bustling out from the house, murmured:

"Oh, dear, this is a bad business—a very bad business. What will become of us all? What would my dear mistress say?"

"Where is Nofret, Henet?"

Renisenb cried: "Don't tell him," but Henet was already answering:

"She went out the back way. Down towards the flax fields."

Ipy rushed back through the house and Renisenb said reproachfully: "You should not have told him, Henet."

"You don't trust old Henet. You never have confidence in me." The whine in her voice became more pronounced. "But poor old Henet knows what she is doing. The boy needs time to cool off. He won't find Nofret by the flax fields." She grinned. "Nofret is here—in the pavilion—with Kameni."

She nodded her head across the courtyard.

And she added with what seemed rather disproportionate stress: "With Kameni. . . ."

But Renisenb had already started to cross the courtyard.

Teti, dragging her wooden lion, came running from the lake to her mother and Renisenb caught her up in her arms. She knew, as she held the child to her, the force that was driving Satipy and Kait. These women were fighting for their children.

Teti gave a little fretful cry.

"Not so tight, Mother, not so tight. You are hurting me."

Renisenb put the child down. She went slowly across the courtyard. On the far side of the pavilion Nofret and Kameni were standing together. They turned as Renisenb approached.

Renisenb spoke quickly and breathlessly:

"Nofret, I have come to warn you. You must be careful. You must guard yourself."

A look of contemptuous amusement passed over Nofret's face.

"So the dogs are howling?"

"They are very angry—they will do some harm to you."

Nofret shook her head.

"No one can harm me," she said with a superb confidence. "If they did, it would be reported to your father—and he would exact vengeance. They will know that when they pause to think." She laughed. "What fools they have been—with their petty insults and persecutions! It was *my* game they played all the time."

Renisenb said slowly:

"So you have planned for this all along? And I was sorry for you—I thought we were unkind! I am not sorry any longer. . . . I think, Nofret, that you are *wicked*. When you come to deny the forty-two sins at the hour of judgement you will not be able to say, 'I have done no evil.' Nor will you be able to say, 'I have not been covetous.' And your heart that is being weighed in the scales against the feather of truth will sink in the balance."

Nofret said sullenly:

"You are very pious all of a sudden. But I have not harmed *you*, Renisenb. I said nothing against you. Ask Kameni if that is not so."

Then she walked across the courtyard and up the steps to the porch. Henet came out to meet her and the two women went into the house.

Renisenb turned slowly to Kameni.

"So it was *you*, Kameni, who helped her to do this to us?"

Kameni said eagerly:

"Are you very angry with me, Renisenb? But what could I do? Before Imhotep left he charged me solemnly that I was to write at Nofret's bidding at any time she might ask me to do so. Say you do not blame me, Renisenb. What else could I do?"

"I cannot blame you," said Renisenb slowly. "You had, I suppose, to carry out my father's orders."

"I did not like doing it—and it is true, Renisenb, there was not one word said against *you*."

"As if I cared about that!"

"But I do. Whatever Nofret had told me, I would not have written one word that might harm *you*. Renisenb—please believe me."

Renisenb shook her head perplexedly. The point Kameni was labouring to make seemed of little importance to her. She felt hurt and angry, as though Kameni, in some way, had failed her. Yet he was, after all, a stranger. Though allied by blood, he was nevertheless a stranger whom her father had brought from a distant part of the country. He was a junior scribe who had been given a task by his employer, and who had obediently carried it out.

"I wrote no more than truth," Kameni persisted. "There were no lies set down; that I swear to you."

"No," said Renisenb. "There would be no lies. Nofret is too clever for that."

Old Esa had, after all, been right. That persecution over which Satipy and Kait had gloated had been just exactly what Nofret had wanted. No wonder she had gone about smiling her catlike smile.

"She is bad," said Renisenb, following out her thoughts. "Yes!"

Kameni assented. "Yes," he said. "She is an evil creature."

Renisenb turned and looked at him curiously.

"You knew her before she came here, did you not? You knew her in Memphis?"

Kameni flushed and looked uncomfortable.

"I did not know her well. . . . I had heard of her. A proud girl, they said, ambitious and hard—and one who did not forgive."

Renisenb flung back her head in sudden impatience.

"I do not believe it," she said. "My father will not do what he threatens. He is angry at present—but he could not be so unjust. When he comes he will forgive."

"When he comes," said Kameni, "Nofret will see to it that he does not change his mind. You do not know Nofret, Renisenb. She is very clever and very determined—and she is, remember, very beautiful."

"Yes," admitted Renisenb. "She is beautiful."

She got up. For some reason the thought of Nofret's beauty hurt her. . . .

II

Renisenb spent the afternoon playing with the children. As she took part in their game, the vague ache in her heart lessened. It was not until just before sunset that she stood upright, smoothing back her hair and the pleats of her dress which had got crumpled and disarranged, and wondered vaguely why neither Satipy nor Kait had been out as usual.

Kameni had long gone from the courtyard. Renisenb went slowly across into the house. There was no one in the living room and she passed through to the back of the house and the women's quarters. Esa was nodding in the corner of her room and her little slave girl was marking piles of linen sheets. They were baking batches of triangular loaves in the kitchen. There was no one else about.

A curious emptiness pressed on Renisenb's spirits. Where was everyone?

Hori had probably gone up to the Tomb. Yahmose might be with him or out in the fields. Sobek and Ipy would be with the cattle or possibly seeing to the cornbins. But where were Satipy and Kait, and where, yes, where was Nofret?

The strong perfume of Nofret's unguent filled her empty room. Renisenb stood in the doorway staring at the little wood pillow, at a jewel box, at a heap of bead bracelets and a ring set with a blue glazed scarab. Perfumes, unguents, clothes, linens, sandals—all speaking of their owner, of Nofret who lived in their midst and who was a stranger and an enemy.

Where, Renisenb wondered, could Nofret herself be?

She went slowly towards the back entrance of the house and met Henet coming in.

"Where is everybody, Henet? The house is empty except for my grandmother."

"How should I know, Renisenb? I have been working—helping with the weaving, seeing to a thousand and one things. I have no time for going for walks."

That meant, thought Renisenb, that somebody had gone for a walk. Perhaps Satipy had followed Yahmose up to the Tomb to harangue him further? But where was Kait? Unlike Kait to be away from her children for so long.

And again, a strange disturbing undercurrent, there ran the thought: *"Where is Nofret?"*

As though Henet had read the thought in her mind, she supplied the answer.

"As for Nofret, she went off a long time ago up to the Tomb. Oh, well, Hori is a match for her." Henet laughed spitefully. "Hori has brains too." She sidled a little closer to Renisenb. "I wish you knew, Renisenb, how unhappy I've been over all this. She came to me, you know, that day—with the mark of Kait's fingers on her cheek and the blood streaming down. And she got Kameni to write and me to say what I'd seen—and of course I couldn't say I *hadn't* seen it! Oh, she's a clever one. And I, thinking all the time of your dear mother—"

Renisenb pushed past her and went out into the golden glow of the evening sun. Deep shadows were on the cliffs—the whole world looked fantastic at this hour of sunset.

Renisenb's steps quickened as she took the way to the cliff path. She would go up to the Tomb—find Hori. Yes, find Hori. It was what she had done as a child when her toys had been broken—when she had been uncertain or afraid. Hori was like the cliffs themselves—steadfast, immovable, unchanging.

Renisenb thought confusedly: "Everything will be all right when I get to Hori. . . ."

Her steps quickened—she was almost running.

Then suddenly she saw Satipy coming towards her. Satipy too must have been up to the Tomb.

What a very odd way Satipy was walking, swaying from side to side, stumbling as though she could not see. . . .

When Satipy saw Renisenb she stopped short, her hand went to her breast. Renisenb, drawing close, was startled at the sight of Satipy's face.

"What's the matter, Satipy, are you ill?"

Satipy's voice in answer was a croak, her eyes were shifting from side to side.

"No, no, of course not."

"You look ill. You look frightened. What has happened?"

"What should have happened? Nothing, of course."

"Where have you been?"

"I went up to the Tomb—to find Yahmose. He was not there. No one was there."

Renisenb still stared. This was a new Satipy—a Satipy with all the spirit and resolution drained out of her.

"Come, Renisenb—come back to the house."

Satipy put a slightly shaking hand on Renisenb's arm, urging her back the way she had come and at that touch Renisenb felt a sudden revolt.

"No, I am going up to the Tomb."

"There is no one there, I tell you."

"I like to look out over the River. To sit there."

"But the sun is setting—it is too late."

Satipy's fingers closed vice-like over Renisenb's arm. Renisenb wrenched herself loose.

"Don't! Let me go, Satipy."

"No. Come back. Come back with me."

But Renisenb had already broken loose, pushed past her, and was on her way to the cliff.

There was something—instinct told her there was *something*. . . . Her steps quickened to a run. . . .

Then she saw it—the dark bundle lying under the shadow of the cliff. . . . She hurried along until she stood close beside it.

There was no surprise in her at what she saw. It was as though already she had expected it. . . .

Nofret lay with her face upturned, her body broken and twisted. Her eyes were open and sightless. . . .

Renisenb bent and touched the cold stiff cheek, then stood up again looking down on her. She hardly heard Satipy come up behind her.

"She must have fallen," Satipy was saying. "She has fallen. She was walking along the cliff path and she fell. . . ."

Yes, Renisenb thought, that was what had happened. Nofret had fallen from the path above, her body bouncing off the limestone rocks.

"She may have seen a snake," said Satipy, "and been startled. There are snakes asleep in the sun on that path sometimes."

Snakes. Yes, snakes. *Sobek and the snake.* A snake, its back broken, lying dead in the sun. Sobek, his eyes gleaming . . .

She thought: "*Sobek . . . Nofret . . .*"

Then sudden relief came to her as she heard Hori's voice.

"What has happened?"

She turned with relief. Hori and Yahmose had come up together. Satipy was explaining eagerly that Nofret must have fallen from the path above.

Yahmose said, "She must have come up to find us, but Hori and I have been out to look at the irrigation canals. We have been away at least an hour. As we came back we saw you standing here."

Renisenb said, and her voice surprised her, it sounded so different: *"Where is Sobek?"*

She felt rather than saw Hori's immediate sharp turn of the head at the question. Yahmose sounded merely puzzled as he said:

"Sobek? I have not seen him all the afternoon. Not since he left us so angrily in the house."

But Hori was looking at Renisenb. She raised her eyes and met his. She saw him turn from their gaze and look down thoughtfully at Nofret's body and she knew with absolute certainty exactly what he was thinking.

He murmured questioningly:

"Sobek?"

"Oh, no," Renisenb heard herself saying. "Oh, no . . . Oh, *no* . . ."

Satipy said again urgently: *"She fell from the path.* It is narrow just above here—and dangerous. . . ."

Dangerous? What was it Hori had told her once? A tale of Sobek as a child attacking Yahmose, and of her dead mother prising them apart and saying, "You must not do that, Sobek. It is *dangerous.* . . ."

Sobek liked killing. *"What I do, I shall enjoy doing.* . . ."

Sobek killing a snake . . .

Sobek meeting Nofret on that narrow path . . .

She heard herself murmuring brokenly:

"We don't know—we don't *know* . . ."

And then, with infinite relief, with the sense of a burden taken away, she heard Hori's grave voice giving weight and value to Satipy's asseveration.

"She must have fallen from the path. . . ."

His eyes met Renisenb's. She thought: "He and I know. . . . We shall always know. . . ."

Aloud she heard her voice saying shakily:

"She fell from the path. . . ."

And like a final echo, Yahmose's gentle voice chimed in:

"She must have fallen from the path."

CHAPTER X

Fourth Month of Winter, 6th Day

I

Imhotep sat facing Esa.

"They all tell the same story," he said fretfully.

"That is at least convenient," said Esa.

"Convenient—convenient? What extraordinary words you use!"

Esa gave a short cackle.

"I know what I am saying, my son."

"Are they speaking the truth, that is what I have to decide!" Imhotep spoke portentously.

"You are hardly the goddess Maat. Nor, like Anubis, can you weigh the heart in a balance!"

"Was it an accident?" Imhotep shook his head judicially. "I have to remember that the announcement of my intentions towards my ungrateful family may have aroused some passionate feelings."

"Yes, indeed," said Esa. "Feelings were aroused. They shouted so in the main hall that I could hear what was said in my room here. By the way, were those *really* your intentions?"

Imhotep shifted uneasily as he murmured:

"I wrote in anger—in justifiable anger. My family needed teaching a sharp lesson."

"In other words," said Esa, "you were merely giving them a fright. Is that it?"

"My dear mother, does that matter now?"

"I see," said Esa. "You did not know what you meant to do. Muddled thinking, as usual."

Imhotep controlled his irritation with an effort.

"I simply mean that that particular point no longer arises. It is the facts of Nofret's death that are now in question. If I were to believe that anyone in my family could be so undutiful, so unbalanced in their anger, as wantonly to harm the girl—I—I really do not know what I should do!"

"So it is fortunate," said Esa, "that they all tell the same story! Nobody has hinted at anything else, have they?"

"Certainly not."

"Then why not regard the incident as closed? You should have taken the girl north with you. I told you so at the time."

"Then you *do* believe—"

Esa said with emphasis:

"I believe what I am told unless it conflicts with what I have seen with my own eyes—which is very little nowadays—or heard with my own ears. You have questioned Henet, I suppose? What has she to say of the matter?"

"She is deeply distressed—very deeply distressed. On my behalf."

Esa raised her eyebrows.

"Indeed. You surprise me."

"Henet," said Imhotep warmly, "has a lot of heart."

"Quite so. She has also more than the usual allowance of tongue. If distress at your loss is her only reaction, I should certainly regard the incident as closed. There are plenty of other affairs to occupy your attention."

"Yes, indeed." Imhotep rose with a reassumption of his fussy, important manner. "Yahmose is waiting for me now in the main hall with all sorts of matters needing my urgent attention. There are many decisions awaiting my sanction. As you say, private grief must not usurp the main functions of life."

He hurried out.

Esa smiled for a moment, a somewhat sardonic smile, then her face grew grave again. She sighed and shook her head.

II

Yahmose was awaiting his father with Kameni in attendance. Hori, Yahmose explained, was superintending the work of the embalmers and undertakers who were busy with the first stages of the funeral preparations.

It had taken Imhotep some weeks to journey home after receiving the news of Nofret's death, and the funeral preparations were now completed. The body had received its long soaking in the brine bath, had been restored to some semblance of its normal appearance, had been oiled and rubbed with salts, and duly wrapped in its bandages and deposited in its coffin.

Yahmose explained that he had appointed a small funeral chamber near the rock tomb designed later to hold the body of Imhotep himself. He went into the details of what he had ordered and Imhotep expressed his approval.

"You have done well, Yahmose," he said kindly. "You seem to have shown very good judgement and to have kept your head well."

Yahmose coloured a little at this unexpected praise.

"Ipi and Montu are, of course, expensive embalmers," went on Imhotep. "These canopic jars, for instance, seem to me unduly costly. There is really no need for such extravagance. Some of their charges seem to me much too high. That is the worst of these embalmers who have been employed by the Governor's family. They think they can charge any fantastic prices they like. It would have come much cheaper to go to somebody less well-known."

"In your absence," said Yahmose, "I had to decide on these matters—and I was anxious that all honour should be paid to a concubine for whom you had so great a regard."

Imhotep nodded and patted Yahmose's shoulder.

"It was a fault on the right side, my son. You are, I know, usually most prudent in money matters. I appreciate that in this matter any unnecessary expense was incurred in order to please me. All the same, I am not made of money, and a concubine is—er, ahem!—only a concubine. We will cancel, I think, the more expensive of the amulets—and let me see, there are one or two other ways of cutting down the fees. . . . Just read out the items of the estimate, Kameni."

Kameni rustled the papyrus.

Yahmose breathed a sigh of relief.

III

Kait, coming slowly out from the house to the lake, paused where the children and their mothers were.

"You were right, Satipy," she said. "A live concubine is *not* the same as a dead concubine!"

Satipy looked up at her, her eyes vague and unseeing. It was Renisenb who asked quickly:

"What do you mean, Kait?"

"For a live concubine, nothing was too good—clothes, jewels—even the inheritance of Imhotep's own flesh and blood! But now Imhotep is busy cutting down the cost of the funeral expenses! After all, why waste money on a dead woman? Yes, Satipy, you were right."

Satipy murmured: "What did I say? I have forgotten."

"It is best so," agreed Kait. "I, too, have forgotten. And Renisenb also."

Renisenb looked at Kait without speaking. There had been something in Kait's voice—something faintly menacing, that impressed Renisenb disagreeably. She had always been accustomed to think of Kait as rather a stupid woman—someone gentle and submissive, but rather negligible. It struck her now that Kait and Satipy seemed to have changed places. Satipy the dominant and aggressive was subdued—almost timid. It was the quiet Kait who now seemed to domineer over Satipy.

But people, thought Renisenb, do not really change their characters—or do they? She felt confused. Had Kait and Satipy *really* changed in the last few weeks, or was the change in the one the result of the change in the other? Was it Kait who had grown aggressive? Or did she merely *seem* so because of the sudden collapse of Satipy?

Satipy definitely *was* different. Her voice was no longer upraised in the familiar shrewish accents. She crept round the courtyard and the house with a nervous, shrinking gait quite unlike her usual self-assured manner. Renisenb had put down the change in her to the shock of Nofret's death, but it was incredible that that shock could last so long. It would have been far more like Satipy, Renisenb could not but think, to have exulted openly in a matter-of-fact manner over the concubine's sudden and untimely death. As it was, she shrank nervously whenever Nofret's name was mentioned. Even Yahmose seemed to be exempt from her hectoring and bullying and had, in consequence, begun to assume a more resolute demeanour himself. At any rate, the change in Satipy was all to the good—or at least so Renisenb supposed. Yet something about it made her vaguely uneasy. . . .

Suddenly, with a start, Renisenb became aware that Kait was looking at her, was frowning. Kait, she realised, was waiting for a word of assent to something she had just said.

"Renisenb also," repeated Kait, "has forgotten."

Suddenly Renisenb felt a flood of revolt overwhelm her. Neither Kait, nor Satipy, nor anyone should dictate to her what she should or should not remember. She returned Kait's look steadily with a distinct hint of defiance.

"The women of a household," said Kait, "must stand together."

Renisenb found her voice. She said clearly and defiantly:

"Why?"

"Because their interests are the same."

Renisenb shook her head violently. She thought, confusedly, "I am a person as well as a woman. I am Renisenb."

Aloud she said:

"It is not so simple as that."

"Do you want to make trouble, Renisenb?"

"No. And anyway, what do you mean by trouble?"

"Everything that was said that day in the big hall had best be forgotten."

Renisenb laughed.

"You are stupid, Kait. The servants, the slaves, my grandmother—everyone must have overheard! Why pretend that things did not happen that did happen?"

"We were angry," said Satipy in a dull voice. "We did not mean what we said."

She added with a feverish irritability:

"Stop talking about it, Kait. If Renisenb wants to make trouble, let her."

"I don't want to make trouble," said Renisenb indignantly. "But it is stupid to *pretend*."

"No," said Kait. "It is wisdom. You have Teti to consider."

"Teti is all right."

"Everything is all right—*now that Nofret is dead*." Kait smiled.

It was a serene, quiet, satisfied smile—and again Renisenb felt a tide of revolt rise in her.

Yet what Kait said was quite true. Now that Nofret was dead everything was all right.

Satipy, Kait, herself, the children—all secure—all at peace—with no apprehensions for the future. The intruder, the disturbing, menacing stranger, had departed—for ever.

Then why this stirring of an emotion that she did not understand on Nofret's behalf? Why this feeling of championship for the dead girl whom she had not liked? Nofret was wicked and Nofret was dead. Could she not leave it at that? Why this sudden stab of pity—of something more than pity —something that was almost comprehension?

Renisenb shook her head perplexedly. She sat on there by the water after the others had gone in, trying vainly to understand the confusion in her mind.

The sun was low when Hori, crossing the courtyard, saw her and came to sit beside her.

"It is late, Renisenb. The sun is setting. You should go in."

His grave, quiet voice soothed her, as always. She turned to him with a question.

"*Must* the women of a household stick together?"

"Who has been saying that to you, Renisenb?"

"Kait. She and Satipy—"

Renisenb broke off.

"And you—want to think for yourself?"

"Oh, *think!* I do not know how to think, Hori. Everything is confused in my head. *People* are confused. Everybody is different from what I thought they were. Satipy I always thought was bold, resolute, domineering. But now she is weak, vacillating, even timid. Then which is the real Satipy? People cannot change like that in a day."

"Not in a day—no."

"And Kait—she who was always meek and submissive and let everybody bully her. Now she dominates us all! Even Sobek seems afraid of her. And even Yahmose is different—he gives orders and expects them to be obeyed!"

"And all this confuses you, Renisenb?"

"Yes. Because I do not *understand*. I feel sometimes that even Henet may be quite different from what she appears to be!"

Renisenb laughed as though at an absurdity, but Hori did not join her. His face remained grave and thoughtful.

"You have never thought very much about people, have you, Renisenb? If you had you would realise—" He paused and then went on. "You know that in all tombs there is always a false door?"

Renisenb stared. "Yes, of course."

"Well, people are like that too. They create a false door—to deceive. If they are conscious of weakness, of inefficiency, they make an imposing door of self-assertion, of bluster, of overwhelming authority—and, after a time, they get to believe in it themselves. They think, and everybody thinks, that they *are* like that. But behind that door, Renisenb, is bare rock. . . . And so when reality comes and touches them with the feather of truth— their true self reasserts itself. For Kait gentleness and submission brought her all she desired—a husband and children. Stupidity made life easier for her. But when reality in the form of danger threatened, her true nature appeared. She did not change, Renisenb—that strength and that ruthlessness were always there."

Renisenb said childishly: "But I do not like it, Hori. It makes me afraid. Everyone being different from what I thought them. And what about myself? *I* am always the same."

"Are you?" He smiled at her. "Then why have you sat here all these hours, your forehead puckered, brooding and thinking? Did the old Renisenb—the Renisenb who went away with Khay—ever do that?"

"Oh, no. There was no need—" Renisenb stopped.

"You see? You have said it yourself. That is the word of reality—*need!* You are not the happy, unthinking child you have always appeared to be, accepting everything at its face value. You are not just one of the women of the household. You are Renisenb who wants to think for herself, who wonders about other people. . . ."

Renisenb said slowly: "I have been wondering about Nofret. . . ."

"What have you been wondering?"

"I have been wondering why I cannot forget about her. . . . She was bad and cruel and tried to do us harm and she is dead. Why can I not leave it at that?"

"Can you not leave it at that?"

"No. I try to—but—" Renisenb paused. She passed her hand across her eyes perplexedly. "Sometimes I feel I *know* about Nofret, Hori."

"Know? What do you mean?"

"I can't explain. But it comes to me every now and then—almost as though she were here beside me. I feel—almost—as though I were her. I seem to know what she felt. She was very unhappy, Hori, I know that now, though I didn't at the time. She wanted to hurt us all *because* she was so unhappy."

"You cannot know that, Renisenb."

"No, of course I cannot *know* it, but it is what I *feel*. That misery, that bitterness, that black hate—I saw it in her face once, and I did not understand! She must have loved someone and then something went wrong—perhaps he died . . . or went away—but it left her like that—wanting to hurt—to wound. Oh! You may say what you like. I know I am right! She became a concubine to that old man, my father—and she came here, and we disliked her—and she thought she would make us all as unhappy as she was— Yes, that was how it was!"

Hori looked at her curiously.

"How sure you sound, Renisenb. And yet you did not know Nofret well."

"But I feel it is *true*, Hori. I feel *her*—Nofret. Sometimes I feel her quite close beside me. . . ."

"I see."

There was silence between them. It was almost dark now.

Then Hori said quietly: "You believe, do you not, that Nofret did not die by accident? You think she was thrown down?"

Renisenb felt a passionate repugnance at hearing her belief put into words.

"No, no, don't say it."

"But I think, Renisenb, we had better say it—since it is in your head. You *do* think so?"

"I—yes!"

Hori bent his head thoughtfully. He went on:

"And you think it was Sobek who did it?"

"Who else could it have been? You remember him with the snake? And you remember what he said—that day—the day of her death—before he went out of the great hall?"

"I remember what he said, yes. But it is not always the people who *say* most who *do* most!"

"But don't you believe she *was* killed?"

"Yes, Renisenb, I do. . . . But it is, after all, only an opinion. I have no proof. I do not think there ever can be proof. That is why I have encouraged Imhotep to accept the verdict of accident. Someone pushed Nofret —we shall never know who it was."

"You mean you don't think it *was* Sobek?"

"I do not think so. But as I say, we can never know—so it is best not to think about it."

"But—if it was not Sobek—who do you think it was?"

Hori shook his head.

"If I have an idea—it may be the wrong idea. So it is better not to say. . . ."

"But then—we shall never know!"

There was dismay in Renisenb's voice.

"Perhaps—" Hori hesitated—"perhaps that may be the best thing."

"Not to know?"

"Not to know."

Renisenb shivered.

"But then—oh, Hori, I am afraid!"

CHAPTER XI

First Month of Summer, 11th Day

I

THE FINAL CEREMONIES had been completed and the incantations duly spoken. Montu, a Divine Father of the Temple of Hathor, took the broom of *heden* grass and carefully swept out the chamber whilst he recited the charm to remove the footprints of all evil spirits before the door was sealed up for ever.

Then the Tomb was sealed and all that remained of the embalmers' work, pots full of natron, salt and rags that had been in contact with the body, were placed in a little chamber near by, and that too was sealed.

Imhotep squared his shoulders and took a deep breath, relaxing his devout funeral expression. Everything had been done in a befitting manner.

Nofret had been buried with all the prescribed rites and with no sparing of expense (somewhat undue expense, in Imhotep's opinion).

Imhotep exchanged courtesies with the priests who, their sacred office now finished, reassumed their men-of-the-world manner. Everyone descended to the house, where suitable refreshments were waiting. Imhotep discussed with the principal Divine Father the recent political changes. Thebes was rapidly becoming a very powerful city. It was possible that Egypt might once more be united under one ruler before very long. The Golden Age of the Pyramid builders might return.

Montu spoke with reverence and approval of the King Nebhepet-Re. A first-class soldier and a man of piety also. The corrupt and cowardly north could hardly stand against him. A unified Egypt—that was what was needed. And it would mean, undoubtedly, great things for Thebes. . . .

The men walked together, discussing the future.

Renisenb looked back at the cliff and the sealed tomb chamber.

"So that is the end," she murmured. A feeling of relief swept over her. She had feared she hardly knew what! Some last-minute outburst or accusation? But everything had gone with commendable smoothness. Nofret was duly buried with all the rites of religion.

It was the end.

Henet said below her breath: "I hope so; I'm sure I hope so, Renisenb."

Renisenb turned on her.

"What do you mean, Henet?"

Henet avoided her eyes.

"I just said I hoped it *was* the end. Sometimes what you think is an end is only a beginning. And that wouldn't do at all."

Renisenb said angrily:

"What are you talking about, Henet? What are you hinting at?"

"I'm sure I never hint, Renisenb. I wouldn't do such a thing. Nofret's buried and everyone is satisfied. So everything is as it should be."

Renisenb demanded: "Did my father ask you what *you* thought about Nofret's death?"

"Yes, indeed, Renisenb. Most particular, he was, that I should tell him exactly what I thought about it all."

"And what did you tell him?"

"Well, of course I said it was an accident. What else could it have been? You don't think for a minute, I said, that anyone in your family would harm the girl, do you? They wouldn't dare, I said. They have far too much respect for you. Grumble they might, but nothing more, I said. You can take it from me, I said, that there's been nothing of *that* kind!"

Henet nodded her head and chuckled.

"And my father believed you?"

Again Henet nodded with a good deal of satisfaction.

"Ah, your father knows how devoted I am to his interests. He'll always take old Henet's word for anything. *He* appreciates me if none of the rest of you do. Ah, well, my devotion to all of you is its own reward. I don't expect thanks."

"You were devoted to Nofret too," said Renisenb.

"I'm sure I don't know what gave you that idea, Renisenb. I had to obey orders like everyone else."

"She thought you were devoted to her."

Henet chuckled again.

"Nofret wasn't quite as clever as she thought herself. A proud girl—and a girl who thought she owned the earth. Well, she's got the judges in the Underworld to satisfy now—and a pretty face won't help her there. At any rate we're quit of her. At least," she added under her breath and touching one of the amulets she wore, "I hope so."

II

"Renisenb, I want to talk to you about Satipy."

"Yes, Yahmose?"

Renisenb looked up sympathetically into her brother's gentle, worried face.

Yahmose said slowly and heavily: "There is something very wrong the matter with Satipy. I cannot understand it."

Renisenb shook her head sadly. She was at a loss to find anything comforting to say.

"I have noticed this change in her for some time," went on Yahmose. "She starts and trembles at any unaccustomed noise. She does not eat well. She creeps about as though—as though she were afraid of her own shadow. You must have noticed it, Renisenb?"

"Yes, indeed, we have all noticed it."

"I have asked her if she is ill—if I should send for a physician—but she says there is nothing—that she is perfectly well."

"I know."

"So you have asked her that too? And she has said nothing to you—nothing at all?"

He laid stress on the words. Renisenb sympathised with his anxiety, but she could say nothing to help.

"She insists that she is quite well."

Yahmose murmured: "She does not sleep well at night—she cries out in her sleep. Is she—could she have some sorrow that we know nothing about?"

Renisenb shook her head.

"I do not see how that is possible. There is nothing wrong with the children. Nothing has happened here—except, of course, Nofret's death—and Satipy would hardly grieve for that," she added drily.

Yahmose smiled faintly.

"No, indeed. Quite the contrary. Besides, this has been coming on for some time. It began, I think, before Nofret's death."

His tone was a little uncertain and Renisenb looked at him quickly. Yahmose said with mild persistence:

"*Before* Nofret's death. Don't you think so?"

"I did not notice it until afterwards," said Renisenb slowly.

"And she has said nothing to you—you are sure?"

Renisenb shook her head. "But you know, Yahmose, I do not think Satipy is ill. It seems to me more that she is—afraid."

"Afraid?" exclaimed Yahmose in great astonishment. "But why should Satipy be afraid? And of what? Satipy has always had the courage of a lion."

"I know," said Renisenb helplessly. "We have always thought so—but people change—it is queer."

"Does Kait know anything, do you think? Has Satipy spoken to her?"

"She would be more likely to talk to her than to me—but I do not think so. In fact, I am sure of it."

"What does Kait think?"

"Kait? Kait never thinks about anything."

All Kait had done, Renisenb was reflecting, was to take advantage of Satipy's unusual meekness by grabbing for herself and her children the finest of the newly woven linen—a thing she would never have been allowed to do had Satipy been her usual self. The house would have resounded with passionate disputings! The fact that Satipy had given it up with hardly a murmur had impressed Renisenb more than anything else that could have happened.

"Have you spoken to Esa?" Renisenb asked. "Our grandmother is wise about women and their ways."

"Esa," said Yahmose with some slight annoyance, "merely bids me be thankful for the change. She says it is too much to hope that Satipy will continue to be so sweetly reasonable."

Renisenb said with some slight hesitation:

"Have you asked Henet?"

"Henet?" Yahmose frowned. "No, indeed. I would not speak of such things to Henet. She takes far too much upon herself as it is. My father spoils her."

"Oh, I know that. She is very tiresome. But all the same—well—" Renisenb hesitated—"Henet usually knows things."

Yahmose said slowly:

"Would you ask her, Renisenb? And tell me what she says?"

"If you like."

Renisenb put her query at a moment when she had Henet to herself. They were on their way to the weaving sheds. Rather to her surprise the question seemed to make Henet uneasy. There was none of her usual avidity to gossip.

She touched an amulet she was wearing and glanced over her shoulder.

"It's nothing to do with me, I'm sure. . . . It's not for me to notice whether anyone's themselves or not. I mind my own business. If there's trouble I don't want to be mixed up in it."

"Trouble? What kind of trouble?"

Henet gave her a quick, sideways glance.

"None, I hope. None that need concern us, anyway. You and I, Renisenb, we've nothing to reproach ourselves with. That's a great consolation to me."

"Do you mean that Satipy— What *do* you mean?"

"I don't mean anything at all, Renisenb—and please don't start making out that I do. I'm little better than a servant in this house, and it's not my business to give my opinion about things that are nothing to do with me. If you ask me, it's a change for the better and if it stops at that, well, we'll all do nicely. Now, please, Renisenb, I've got to see that they are marking the date properly on the linen. So careless as they are, these women, always talking and laughing and neglecting their work."

Unsatisfied, Renisenb watched her dart away into the weaving shed. She herself walked slowly back to the house. Her entry into Satipy's room was unheard, and Satipy sprang round with a cry as Renisenb touched her shoulder.

"Oh, you startled me. I thought—"

"Satipy," said Renisenb. "What is the matter? Won't you tell me? Yahmose is worried about you and—"

Satipy's fingers flew to her lips. She said, stammering nervously, her eyes wide and frightened:

"Yahmose? What—what did he say?"

"He is anxious. You have been calling out in your sleep—"

"Renisenb!" Satipy caught her by the arm. "Did I say— What did I say?" Her eyes seemed dilated with terror.

"Does Yahmose think— What did he tell you?"

"We both think that you are ill—or—or unhappy."

"Unhappy?" Satipy repeated the word under her breath with a peculiar intonation.

"*Are* you unhappy, Satipy?"

"Perhaps. . . . I don't know. It is not that."

"No. You're frightened, aren't you?"

Satipy stared at her with sudden hostility.

"Why should you say that? Why should I be frightened? What is there to frighten me?"

"I don't know," said Renisenb. "But it is true, isn't it?"

With an effort Satipy recovered her old arrogant pose. She tossed her head.

"I'm not afraid of anything—of anyone! How dare you suggest such a thing to me, Renisenb? And I won't have you talking me over with Yahmose. Yahmose and I understand each other." She paused and then said sharply, "Nofret is dead—and a good riddance. That's what I say. And you can tell anyone who asks you that that's what I feel about it."

"Nofret?" Renisenb uttered the name questioningly.

Satipy flew into a passion that made her seem quite like her old self.

"Nofret—Nofret—Nofret! I'm sick of the sound of that name. We don't need to hear it any more in this house—and thank goodness for that."

Her voice, which had been raised to its old shrill pitch, dropped suddenly as Yahmose entered. He said, with unusual sternness:

"Be quiet, Satipy. If my father heard you, there would be fresh trouble. How can you behave so foolishly?"

If Yahmose's stern and displeased tone was unusual, so too was Satipy's meek collapse. She murmured: "I am sorry, Yahmose. . . . I did not think."

"Well, be more careful in future! You and Kait made most of the trouble before. You women have no sense!"

Satipy murmured again: "I am sorry. . . ."

Yahmose went out, his shoulders squared, and his walk far more resolute than usual, as though the fact of having asserted his authority for once had done him good.

Renisenb went slowly along to old Esa's room. Her grandmother, she felt, might have some helpful counsel.

Esa, however, who was eating grapes with a good deal of relish, refused to take the matter seriously.

"Satipy? Satipy? Why all this fuss about Satipy? Do you all like being bullied and ordered about by her that you make such a to-do because she behaves herself properly for once?"

She spat out the pips of the grape and remarked:

"In any case, it's too good to last—unless Yahmose can keep it up."

"Yahmose?"

"Yes. I hoped Yahmose had come to his senses at last and given Satipy a good beating. It's what she needs—and she's the kind of woman who would probably enjoy it. Yahmose, with his meek, cringing ways, must have been a great trial to her."

"Yahmose is a dear," cried Renisenb indignantly. "He is kind to everybody—and as gentle as a woman—if women are gentle," she added doubtfully.

Esa cackled.

"A good afterthought, Granddaughter. No, there's nothing gentle about women—or if there is, Isis help them! And there are few women who care for a kind, gentle husband. They'd sooner have a handsome, blustering brute like Sobek—he's the one to take a girl's fancy. Or a smart young fellow like Kameni—hey, Renisenb? The flies in the courtyard don't settle on him for long! He's got a pretty taste in love songs too. Eh? Hee, hee, hee."

Renisenb felt her cheeks going red.

"I don't know what you mean," she said with dignity.

"You all think old Esa doesn't know what's going on! I know all right." She peered at Renisenb with her semi-blind eyes. "I know, perhaps, before you do, child. Don't be angry. It's the way of life, Renisenb. Khay was a good brother to you—but he sails his boat now in the Field of Offerings. The sister will find a new brother who spears his fish in our own River—not that Kameni would be much good. A reed pen and a papyrus roll are his fancy. A personable young man, though—with a pretty taste in songs. But for all that I'm not sure he's the man for you. We don't know much about him—he's a northerner. Imhotep approves of him—but then I've always thought Imhotep was a fool. Anyone can get round him by flattery. Look at Henet!"

"You are quite wrong," said Renisenb with dignity.

"Very well, then, I'm wrong. Your father is *not* a fool."

"I didn't mean that. I meant—"

"I know what you meant, child." Esa grinned. "But you don't know the real joke. You don't know how good it is to sit at ease like I do, and to be done with all this business of brothers and sisters, and loving and hating. To eat a well-cooked fat quail or a reed bird, and then a cake with honey, and some well-cooked leeks and celery and wash it down with wine from Syria—and have never a care in the world. And look on at all the turmoil and the heartaches and know that none of that can affect you any more. To see your son make a fool of himself over a handsome girl, and to see her set the whole place by the ears—it made me laugh, I can tell you! In a way, you know, I liked that girl! She had the devil in her all right—the way she touched them all on the raw. Sobek like a pricked bladder—Ipy made to look a child—Yahmose shamed as a bullied husband. It's like the way you see your face in a pool of water. She made them see just how they looked to the world at large. But why did she hate *you*, Renisenb? Answer me that."

"Did she hate me?" Renisenb spoke doubtfully. "I—tried once to be friends."

"And she'd have none of it? She hated you all right, Renisenb."

Esa paused and then asked sharply:

"Would it be because of Kameni?"

The colour rose in Renisenb's face. "Kameni? I do not know what you mean."

Esa said thoughtfully:

"She and Kameni both came from the north, but it was you Kameni watched cross the courtyard."

Renisenb said abruptly:

"I must go and see to Teti."

Esa's shrill, amused cackle followed her. Her cheeks hot, Renisenb sped across the courtyard towards the lake.

Kameni called to her from the porch:

"I have made a new song, Renisenb. Stay and hear it."

She shook her head and hurried on. Her heart was beating angrily. Kameni and Nofret. Nofret and Kameni. Why let old Esa, with her malicious love of mischief, put these ideas into her head? And why should she care?

Anyway, what did it matter? She cared nothing for Kameni—nothing at all. An impertinent young man with a laughing voice and shoulders that reminded her of Khay.

Khay . . . Khay . . .

She repeated his name insistently—but for once no image came before her eyes. Khay was in another world. He was in the Field of Offerings . . .

On the porch Kameni was singing softly:

"*I will say to Ptah: Give me my sister tonight. . . .*"

III

"Renisenb!"

Hori had repeated her name twice before she heard him and turned from her contemplation of the Nile.

"You were lost in thought, Renisenb. What were you thinking about?"

Renisenb said with defiance:

"I was thinking of Khay."

Hori looked at her for a minute or two—then he smiled.

"I see," he said.

Renisenb had an uncomfortable feeling that he did see!

She said with a sudden rush:

"What happens when you are dead? Does anyone really know? All these texts—all these things that are written on coffins—some of them are so obscure they seem to mean nothing at all. We know that Osiris was killed and that his body was joined together again, and that he wears the white crown, and because of him we need not die—but sometimes, Hori, none of it seems *real*—and it is all so confused. . . ."

Hori nodded gently.

"But what really happens after you are dead—that is what I want to know?"

"I cannot tell you, Renisenb. You should ask a priest these questions."

"He would just give me the usual answers. I want to *know*."

Hori said gently:

"We shall none of us know until we are dead ourselves. . . ."

Renisenb shivered.

"Don't—don't say that!"

"Something has upset you, Renisenb?"

"It was Esa." She paused and then said, "Tell me, Hori, did—did Kameni and Nofret know each other well before—before they came here?"

Hori stood quite still for a moment, then as he walked by Renisenb's side, back towards the house, he said: "I see. So that is how it is. . . ."

"What do you mean—'*that is how it is*'? I only asked you a question."

"To which I do not know the answer. Nofret and Kameni knew each other in the north—how well, I do not know."

He added gently: "Does it matter?"

"No, of course not," said Renisenb. "It is of no importance at all."

"Nofret is dead."

"Dead and embalmed and sealed up in her tomb! And that is that!"

Hori continued calmly:

"And Kameni—does not seem to grieve. . . ."

"No," said Renisenb, struck by this aspect of the question. "That is true." She turned to him impulsively. "Oh, Hori, how—how *comforting* a person you are!"

He smiled.

"I mended little Renisenb's lion for her. Now—she has other toys."

Renisenb skirted the house as they came to it.

"I don't want to go in yet. I feel I hate them all. Oh, not *really*, you understand. But just because I am cross—and impatient and everyone is so *odd.* Can we not go up to your Tomb? It is so nice up there—one is—oh, *above* everything."

"That is clever of you, Renisenb. That is what I feel. The house and the cultivation and the farming lands—all that is below one, insignificant. One looks beyond all that—to the River—and beyond again—to the whole of Egypt. For very soon now Egypt will be one again—strong and great as she was in the past."

Renisenb murmured vaguely:

"Oh—does it matter?"

Hori smiled.

"Not to little Renisenb. Only her own lion matters to Renisenb."

"You are laughing at me, Hori. So it *does* matter to you?"

Hori murmured:

"Why should it? Yes, why should it? I am only a ka-priest's man of business. Why should I care if Egypt is great or small?"

"Look." Renisenb drew his attention to the cliff above them. "Yahmose and Satipy have been up to the Tomb. They are coming down now."

"Yes," said Hori. "There were some things to be cleared away, some rolls of linen that the embalmers did not use. Yahmose said he would get Satipy to come up and advise him what to do about them."

The two of them stood there looking up at the two descending the path above.

It came to Renisenb suddenly that they were just approaching the spot from which Nofret must have fallen.

Satipy was ahead, Yahmose a little way behind her.

Suddenly Satipy turned her head to speak to Yahmose. Perhaps, Renisenb thought, she was saying to him that this must be the place where the accident had occurred.

And then, suddenly, Satipy stiffened in her tracks. She stood as though frozen, staring back along the path. Her arms went up as though at some dreadful sight or as though to ward off a blow. She cried out something, stumbled, swayed, and then, as Yahmose sprang towards her, she screamed, a scream of terror, and plunged forward off the edge headlong to the rocks below. . . .

Renisenb, her hand to her throat, watched the fall unbelievingly.

Satipy lay, a crumpled mass, just where the body of Nofret had lain.

Rousing herself, Renisenb ran forward to her. Yahmose was calling and running down the path.

Renisenb reached the body of her sister-in-law and bent over it. Satipy's eyes were open, the eyelids fluttering. Her lips were moving, trying to speak. Renisenb bent closer over her. She was appalled by the glazed terror in Satipy's eyes.

Then the dying woman's voice came. It was just a hoarse croak.
"*Nofret . . .*"

Satipy's head fell back. Her jaw dropped.

Hori had turned to meet Yahmose. The two men came up together.
Renisenb turned on her brother.

"What did she call out, up there, before she fell?"

Yahmose's breath was coming in short jerks—he could hardly speak. . . .

"She looked past me—*over my shoulder*—as though she saw someone coming along the path—but there was no one—*there was no one there.*"

Hori assented:

"There was no one. . . ."

Yahmose's voice dropped to a low, terrified whisper. "And then she called out—"

"What did she say?" Renisenb demanded impatiently.

"She said—she said"—his voice trembled—"Nofret . . ."

CHAPTER XII

First Month of Summer, 12th Day

"So THAT IS what you meant?"

Renisenb flung the words at Hori more as an affirmation than as a question.

She added softly under her breath with growing comprehension and horror:

"It was Satipy who killed Nofret. . . ."

Sitting with her chin supported by her hands in the entrance to Hori's little rock chamber next to the Tomb, Renisenb stared down at the valley below.

She thought dreamily how true the words were she had uttered yesterday. Was it really only such a short time ago? From up here the house below and the busy hurrying figures had no more significance nor meaning than an ants' nest.

Only the sun, majestic in power, shining overhead—only the slim streak of pale silver that was the Nile in this morning light—only these were eternal and enduring. Khay had died, and Nofret and Satipy—and someday she and Hori would die. But Re would still rule the Heavens and travel by night in his barque through the Underworld to the dawning of the next day. And the River would still flow, flow from beyond Elephantine and down past Thebes and past the village and to lower Egypt where Nofret had lived and been gay and light of heart, and on to the great waters and so away from Egypt altogether.

Satipy and Nofret . . .

Renisenb pursued her thoughts aloud, since Hori had not answered her last demand.

"You see, I was so sure that Sobek—"

She broke off.

Hori said thoughtfully:

"The preconceived idea."

"And yet it was stupid of me," Renisenb went on. "Henet told me, or more or less told me, that Satipy had gone walking this way and she said that Nofret had come up here. I ought to have seen how obvious it was that Satipy had followed Nofret—that they had met on the path—and that Satipy had thrown her down. She had said, only a short while before, that she was a better man than any of my brothers."

Renisenb broke off and shivered.

"And when I met her," she resumed, "I should have known then. She was quite different—she was frightened. She tried to persuade me to turn back with her. She didn't want me to find Nofret's body. I must have been blind not to realise the truth. But I was so full of fear about Sobek . . ."

"I know. It was seeing him kill that snake."

Renisenb agreed eagerly.

"Yes, that was it. And then I had a dream. . . . Poor Sobek—how I have misjudged him. As you say, *threatening* is not *doing*. Sobek has always been full of boastful talk. It was Satipy who was always bold and ruthless and not afraid of action. And then ever since—the way she has gone about like a ghost—it has puzzled us all. Why did we not think of the true explanation?"

She added, with a quick upward glance:

"But you did?"

"For some time," said Hori, "I have felt convinced that the clue to the truth of Nofret's death was in Satipy's extraordinary change of character. It was so remarkable that there had to be something to account for it."

"And yet you said nothing?"

"How could I, Renisenb? What could I ever *prove*?"

"No, of course not."

"Proofs must be solid brick walls of fact."

"Yet once you said," Renisenb argued, "that people did not really change. But now you admit that Satipy *did* change."

Hori smiled at her.

"You should argue in the Nomarch's courts. No, Renisenb, what I said was true enough—people are always themselves. Satipy, like Sobek, was all bold words and talk. She, indeed, might go on from talk to action—but I think she is one of those who cannot know a thing or what it is like until it has happened. In her life up to that particular day, she had never had anything to *fear*. When fear came, it took her unawares. She learned then that courage is the resolution to face the unforeseen—and she had not got that courage."

Renisenb murmured in a low voice:

"*When fear came* . . . Yes, that is what has been with us ever since Nofret died. Satipy has carried it in her face for us all to see. It was there, staring from her eyes when she died . . . when she said 'Nofret . . .' It was as though she saw—"

Renisenb stopped herself. She turned her face to Hori, her eyes wide with a question.

"Hori, what did she see? There on the path. *We* saw nothing! There *was* nothing."

"Not for us—no."

"But for her? It was Nofret she saw—Nofret come to take her revenge. But Nofret is dead and her tomb is sealed. What then did she see?"

"The picture that her own mind showed her."

"You are sure? Because if not—"

"Yes, Renisenb, if not?"

"Hori—" Renisenb stretched out her hand. "Is it ended now? Now that Satipy is dead? Is it truly ended?"

He held her hand in both of his in a comforting clasp.

"Yes, yes, Renisenb—surely. And you at least need not be afraid."

Renisenb murmured under her breath:

"But Esa says that Nofret hated me. . . ."

"Nofret hated *you*?"

"Esa says so."

"Nofret was good at hating," said Hori. "Sometimes I think she hated every person in this house. But you at least did nothing against her."

"No—no, that is true."

"And therefore, Renisenb, there is nothing in *your* mind to rise up against you in judgement."

"You mean, Hori, that if I were to walk down this path alone—at sunset—at that same time when Nofret died—and if I were to turn my head—I should see nothing? I should be safe?"

"You will be safe, Renisenb, because if you walk down the path, I will walk with you and no harm shall come to you."

But Renisenb frowned and shook her head.

"No, Hori. I will walk alone."

"But why, little Renisenb? Will you not be afraid?"

"Yes," said Renisenb, "I think I shall be afraid. But all the same that is what has to be done. They are all trembling and shaking in the house and running to the temples to buy amulets and crying out that it is not well to walk on this path at the hour of sundown. But it was not magic that made Satipy sway and fall—it was fear—fear because of an evil thing that she had done. For it is evil to take away life from someone who is young and strong and who enjoys living. But I have not done any evil thing, and so even if Nofret did hate me, her hate cannot harm me. That is what I believe. And anyway if one is to live always in fear it would be better to die —so I will overcome fear."

"Those are brave words, Renisenb."

"They are perhaps rather braver than I feel, Hori." She smiled up at him. She rose to her feet. "But it has been good to say them."

Hori rose and stood beside her.

"I shall remember these words of yours, Renisenb. Yes, and the way you threw back your head when you said them. They show the courage and the truth that I have always felt were in your heart."

He took her hand in his.

"Look, Renisenb. Look out from here across the valley to the River and beyond. That is Egypt, our land. Broken by war and strife for many long years, divided into petty kingdoms, but now—very soon—to come together and form once more a united land—Upper and Lower Egypt once again welded into one—I hope and believe to recover her former greatness! In those days, Egypt will need men and women of heart and courage—women such as you are, Renisenb. It is not men like Imhotep, forever preoccupied with his own narrow gains and losses, nor men like Sobek, idle and boastful, nor boys like Ipy, who thinks only of what he can gain for himself, no, nor even conscientious, honest sons like Yahmose whom Egypt will need in that hour. Sitting here, literally amongst the dead, reckoning up gains and losses, casting accounts, I have come to see gains that cannot be reckoned in terms of wealth, and losses that are more damaging than loss of a crop. . . . I look at the River and I see the lifeblood of Egypt that has existed before we lived and that will exist after we die. . . . Life and death, Renisenb, are not of such great account. I am only Hori, Imhotep's man of business, but when I look out over Egypt I know a peace—yes, and an exultation that I would not exchange to be Governor of the Province. Do you understand at all what I mean, Renisenb?"

"I think so, Hori—a little. You are different from the others down there —I have known that for some time. And sometimes when I am with you here, I can feel what you feel—but dimly—not very clearly. But I do know what you mean. When I am *here* the things down *there*"—she pointed— "do not seem to matter any longer—the quarrels and the hatreds and the incessant bustle and fuss. Here one escapes from all that."

She paused, her brow puckering, and went on, stammering a little:

"Sometimes I—I am glad to have escaped. And yet—I do not know— there is something—down there—that calls me back."

Hori dropped her hand and stepped back a pace.

He said gently:

"Yes—I see—Kameni singing in the courtyard."

"What do you mean, Hori? I was not thinking of Kameni."

"You may not have been thinking of him. But all the same, Renisenb, I think it is his songs that you are hearing without knowing it."

Renisenb stared at him, her brow puckered.

"What extraordinary things you say, Hori. One could not possibly hear him singing up here. It is much too far away."

Hori sighed gently and shook his head. The amusement in his eyes puzzled her. She felt a little angry and bewildered because she could not understand.

CHAPTER XIII

First Month of Summer, 23rd Day

I

"Can I speak with you a minute, Esa?"

Esa peered sharply towards Henet, who stood in the doorway of the room, an ingratiating smile upon her face.

"What is it?" the old woman asked sharply.

"It's nothing, really—at least I don't suppose so—but I thought I'd just like to ask—"

Esa cut her short.

"Come in, then; come in. And you"—she tapped the little black slave girl, who was threading beads, on the shoulder with her stick—"go to the kitchen. Get me some olives—and make me a drink of pomegranate juice."

The little girl ran off, and Esa beckoned Henet impatiently.

"It's just this, Esa."

Esa peered down at the article Henet was holding out to her. It was a small jewel box with a sliding lid, the top fastened with two buttons.

"What about it?"

"It's *hers*. And I found it now—in her room."

"Who are you talking about? Satipy?"

"No, no, Esa. *The other.*"

"Nofret, you mean? What of it?"

"All her jewels and her toilet vases and her perfume jars—everything—was buried with her."

Esa twirled the string from the buttons and opened the box. In it was a string of small carnelian beads and half of a green glazed amulet which had been broken in two.

"Pooh," said Esa. "Nothing much here. It must have been overlooked."

"The embalmers' men took everything away."

"Embalmers' men aren't any more reliable than anyone else. They forgot this."

"I tell you, Esa—this wasn't in the room when last I looked in."

Esa looked up sharply at Henet.

"What are you trying to make out? That Nofret has come back from the Underworld and is here in the house? You're not really a fool, Henet, though you sometimes like to pretend you're one. What pleasure do you get from spreading these silly magical tales?"

Henet was shaking her head portentously.

"We all know what happened to Satipy—and *why!*"

"Maybe we do," said Esa. "And maybe some of us knew it before! Eh, Henet? I've always had an idea you knew more about how Nofret came to her death than the rest of us."

"Oh, Esa, surely you wouldn't think for a moment—"

Esa cut her short.

"What wouldn't I think? I'm not afraid of thinking, Henet. I've seen Satipy creeping about the house for the last two months looking frightened to death—and it's occurred to me since yesterday that someone might have known what she'd done to Nofret, and that that someone might have been holding the knowledge over her head—threatening maybe to tell Yahmose —or Imhotep himself—"

Henet burst into a shrill clamour of protestations and exclamations. Esa closed her eyes and leaned back in her chair.

"I don't suppose for a moment you'd ever admit you did such a thing. I'm not expecting you to."

"Why should I? That's what I ask you—why should I?"

"I've not the least idea," said Esa. "You do a lot of things, Henet, for which I've never been able to find a satisfactory reason."

"I suppose you think I was trying to make her bribe me to silence. I swear by the Nine Gods of the Ennead—"

"Do not trouble the Gods. You're honest enough, Henet—as honesty goes. And it may be that you knew nothing about how Nofret came to her death. But you know most things that go on in this house. And if I were going to do any swearing myself, I'd swear that you put this box in Nofret's room yourself—though why I can't imagine. But there's some reason behind it. . . . You can deceive Imhotep with your tricks, but you can't deceive me. And don't *whine!* I'm an old woman and I cannot stand people whining. Go and whine to Imhotep. He seems to like it, though Re alone knows why!"

"I will take the box to Imhotep and tell him—"

"I'll hand the box to him myself. Be off with you, Henet, and stop spreading these silly superstitious tales. The house is a more peaceful place without Satipy. Nofret dead has done more for us than Nofret living. But now that the debt is paid, let everyone return to their everyday tasks."

II

"What is all this?" Imhotep demanded as he came fussily into Esa's room a few minutes later. "Henet is deeply distressed. She came to me with the tears running down her face. Why nobody in the house can show that devoted woman the most ordinary kindness—"

Esa, unmoved, gave a cackle of laughter.

Imhotep went on:

"You have accused her, I understand, of stealing a box—a jewel box."

"Is that what she told you? I did nothing of the sort. Here is the box. It seems it was found in Nofret's room."

Imhotep took it from her.

"Ah, yes, it is one I gave her." He opened it. "H'm, nothing much inside. Very careless of the embalmers not to have included it with the rest of her personal belongings. Considering the prices Ipi and Montu charge, one could at least expect no carelessness. Well, this all seems to me a great fuss about nothing—"

"Quite so."

"I will give the box to Kait—no, to Renisenb. She always behaved with courtesy towards Nofret."

He sighed.

"How impossible it seems for a man to get any peace. These women—endless tears or else quarrels and bickerings."

"Ah, well, Imhotep, there is at least one woman less now!"

"Yes, indeed. My poor Yahmose! All the same, Esa—I feel that—er—it may be all for the best. Satipy bore healthy children, it is true, but she was in many ways a most unsatisfactory wife. Yahmose, of course, gave in to her far too much. Well, well, all that is over now. I must say that I have been much pleased with Yahmose's behaviour of late. He seems much more self-reliant—less timid—and his judgement on several points has been excellent—quite excellent. . . ."

"He was always a good, obedient boy."

"Yes, yes—but inclined to be slow and somewhat afraid of responsibility."

Esa said drily:

"Responsibility is a thing you have never allowed him to have!"

"Well, all that will be changed now. I am arranging a deed of association and partnership. It will be signed in a few days' time. I am associating with myself all my three sons."

"Surely not Ipy?"

"He would be hurt to be left out. Such a dear, warmhearted lad."

"There is certainly nothing slow about *him*," observed Esa.

"As you say. And Sobek too—I have been displeased with him in the past, but he has really turned over a new leaf of late. He no longer idles his time away, and he defers more to my judgement and to that of Yahmose."

"This is indeed a hymn of praise," said Esa. "Well, Imhotep, I must say that I think you are doing the right thing. It was bad policy to make your sons discontented. But I still think that Ipy is too young for what you propose. It is ridiculous to give a boy of that age a definite position. What hold will you have over him?"

"There is something in that, certainly." Imhotep looked thoughtful.

Then he roused himself.

"I must go. There are a thousand things to see to. The embalmers are here—there are all the arrangements to make for Satipy's burial. These deaths are costly—very costly. And following so quickly one upon the other!"

"Oh, well," said Esa consolingly, "we'll hope this is the last of them—until my times comes!"

"You will live many years yet, I hope, my dear mother."

"I'm sure you hope so," said Esa with a grin. "No economy over me, if you please! It wouldn't look well! I shall want a good deal of equipment to amuse me in the other world. Plenty of food and drink and a lot of models of slaves—a richly ornamented gaming board, perfume sets and cosmetics, and I insist on the most expensive canopic jars—the alabaster ones."

"Yes, yes, of course." Imhotep changed his position nervously from one foot to the other. "Naturally all respect will be paid when the sad day comes. I must confess that I feel rather differently about Satipy. One does not want a scandal, but really, *in the circumstances—*"

Imhotep did not finish his sentence, but hurried away.

Esa smiled sardonically as she realised that that one phrase "in the circumstances" was the nearest Imhotep would ever get towards admitting that an accident did not fully describe the way his valued concubine had met her death.

CHAPTER XIV

First Month of Summer, 25th Day

I

WITH THE RETURN of the members of the family from the Nomarch's court, the deed of association duly ratified, a general spirit of hilarity was felt. The exception was undoubtedly Ipy who had, at the last moment, been excluded from participation on the ground of his extreme youth. He was sullen in consequence and purposely absented himself from the house.

Imhotep, in excellent spirits, called for a pitcher of wine to be brought out onto the porch where it was placed in the big wine stand.

"You shall drink, my son," he declared, clapping Yahmose on the shoulder. "Forget for the moment your sorrow in bereavement. Let us think only of the good days that are to come."

Imhotep, Yahmose, Sobek and Hori drank the toast. Then word was brought that an ox had been stolen and all four men went hurriedly off to verify the report.

When Yahmose re-entered the courtyard, an hour later, he was tired and hot. He went to where the wine jar still stood in the stand. He dipped a bronze cup into it and sat down on the porch, gently sipping the wine. A little later Sobek came striding in and exclaimed with pleasure.

"Ha," he said. "Now for more wine! Let us drink to our future which is at last well-assured. Undoubtedly this is a joyful day for *us*, Yahmose!"

Yahmose agreed.

"Yes, indeed. It will make life easier in every way."

"You are always so moderate in your feelings, Yahmose."

Sobek laughed as he spoke and dipping a cup in the wine, he tossed it off, smacking his lips as he put it down.

"Let us see now whether my father will be as much of a stick-in-the-mud as ever, or whether I shall be able to convert him to up-to-date methods."

"I should go slowly if I were you," Yahmose counselled. "You are always so hotheaded."

Sobek smiled at his brother affectionately. He was in high good-humour.

"Old slow-and-sure," he said scoffingly.

Yahmose smiled, not at all put out.

"It is the best way in the end. Besides, my father has been very good to us. We must do nothing to cause him worry."

Sobek looked at him curiously.

"You are really fond of our father? You are an affectionate creature, Yahmose! Now I—I care for nobody—for nobody, that is, but Sobek, long life to him!"

He took another draught of wine.

"Be careful," Yahmose said warningly. "You have eaten little today. Sometimes, then, when one drinks wine—"

He broke off with a sudden contortion of the lips.

"What is the matter, Yahmose?"

"Nothing—a sudden pain—I, it is nothing. . . ."

But he raised a hand to wipe his forehead which was suddenly bedewed with moisture.

"You do not look well."

"I was quite all right just now."

"So long as nobody has poisoned the wine." Sobek laughed at his own words and stretched out his arm toward the jar. Then, in the very act, his arm stiffened, his body bent forward in a sudden spasm of agony. . . .

"Yahmose," he gasped. "Yahmose . . . I—too . . ."

Yahmose, slipping forward, was bent double. A half-stifled cry came from him.

Sobek was now contorted with pain. He raised his voice.

"Help. Send for a physician—a physician. . . ."

Henet came running out of the house.

"You called? What was it that you said? What is it?"

Her alarmed cries brought others.

The two brothers were both groaning with pain.

Yahmose said faintly:

"The wine—poison—send for a physician. . . ."

Henet uttered a shrill cry:

"More misfortune. In truth this house is accursed. Quick! Hurry! Send to the Temple for the Divine Father Mersu, who is a skilled physician of great experience."

II

Imhotep paced up and down the central hall of the house. His fine linen robe was soiled and limp, he had neither bathed nor changed. His face was drawn with worry and fear.

From the back of the house came a low sound of keening and weeping—the women's contribution to the catastrophe that had overrun the household—Henet's voice led the mourners.

From a room at the side, the voice of the physician and priest Mersu was heard raised as he strove over the inert body of Yahmose. Renisenb, stealing quietly out of the women's quarters into the central hall, was drawn by the sound. Her feet took her to the open doorway and she paused there, feeling a healing balm in the sonorous words that the priest was reciting.

"O Isis, great of magic, loose thou me, release thou me from all things bad, evil, and red, from the stroke of a God, from the stroke of a Goddess, from dead man or dead woman, from a male foe, or a female foe who may oppose himself to me. . . ."

A faint sigh came fluttering from Yahmose's lips.

In her heart Renisenb joined in the prayer.

"O Isis—O great Isis—save him—save my brother Yahmose—Thou who art great of magic. . . ."

Thoughts passed confusedly through her mind, raised there by the words of the incantation.

"From all things bad, evil, and red. . . . That is what has been the matter with us here in this house—yes, red thoughts, angry thoughts—the anger of a dead woman."

She spoke within the confines of her thoughts, directly addressing the person in her mind.

"It was not Yahmose who harmed you, Nofret—and though Satipy was his wife, you cannot hold him responsible for her actions—he never had any control over her—no one had. Satipy who harmed you is dead. Is that not enough? Sobek is dead—Sobek who only spoke against you, yet never actually harmed you. O Isis, do not let Yahmose also die—save him from the vengeful hatred of Nofret."

Imhotep, pacing distractedly up and down, looked up and saw his daughter and his face relaxed with affection.

"Come here, Renisenb, dear child."

She ran to him and he put his arm round her.

"Oh, Father, what do they say?"

Imhotep said heavily:

"They say that in Yahmose's case there is hope. Sobek—you know?"

"Yes, yes. Have you not heard us wailing?"

"He died at dawn," said Imhotep. "Sobek, my strong, handsome son." His voice faltered and broke.

"Oh, it is wicked, cruel— Could nothing be done?"

"All was done that could be. Potions forcing him to vomit. Administration of the juice of potent herbs. Sacred amulets were applied and mighty incantations spoken. All was of no avail. Mersu is a skilled physician. If he could not save my son—then it was the will of the Gods that he should not be saved."

The priest-physician's voice rose in a final high chant and he came out from the chamber wiping the perspiration from his forehead.

"Well?" Imhotep accosted him eagerly.

The physician said gravely:

"By the favour of Isis your son will live. He is weak but the crisis of the poison has passed. The evil influence is on the wane."

He went on, slightly altering his tone to a more everyday intonation.

"It is fortunate that Yahmose drank much less of the poisoned wine. He sipped his wine, whereas it seems your son Sobek tossed it off at a draught."

Imhotep groaned.

"You have there the difference between them. Yahmose timid, cautious and slow in his approach to everything, even eating and drinking. Sobek, always given to excess, generous, free-handed—alas! imprudent."

Then he added sharply:

"And the wine was definitely poisoned?"

"There is no doubt of that, Imhotep. The residue was tested by my young assistants—of the animals treated with it, all died more or less swiftly."

"And yet I who had drunk of the same wine not an hour earlier have felt no ill effects."

"It was doubtless not poisoned at that time—the poison was added afterwards."

Imhotep struck the palm of one hand with his other hand clenched into a fist.

"No one," he declared, "no one living would dare to poison my sons here under my roof! Such a thing is impossible. No *living* person, I say!"

Mersu inclined his head slightly. His face became inscrutable.

"Of that, Imhotep, you are the best judge."

Imhotep stood scratching nervously behind his ear.

"There is a tale I would like you to hear," he said abruptly.

He clapped his hands and as a servant ran in, he called:

"Bring the herd boy here."

He turned back to Mersu, saying:

"This is a boy whose wits are not of the best. He takes in what people say to him with difficulty and he has not full possession of his faculties. Nevertheless he has eyes and his eyesight is good, and he is moreover devoted to my son Yahmose who has been gentle with him and kindly to his infirmity."

The servant came back, dragging by the hand a thin, almost black-skinned boy, clad in a loincloth, with slightly squinting eyes and a frightened, witless face.

"Speak," said Imhotep sharply. "Repeat what you told me just now."

The boy hung his head, his fingers began kneading the cloth round his waist.

"Speak," shouted Imhotep.

Esa came hobbling in, supported by her stick and peering with her dim eyes.

"You are terrifying the child. Here, Renisenb, give him this jujube. There, boy, tell us what you saw."

The boy gazed from one to the other of them.

Esa prompted him.

"It was yesterday, as you passed the door of the courtyard—you saw— What did you see?"

The boy shook his head, glancing sideways. He murmured:

"Where is my Lord Yahmose?"

The priest spoke with authority and kindliness.

"It is the wish of your Lord Yahmose that you tell us your tale. Have no fear. No one will hurt you."

A gleam of light passed over the boy's face.

"My Lord Yahmose has been good to me. I will do what he wishes."

He paused. Imhotep seemed about to break out, but a look from the physician restrained him.

Suddenly the boy spoke, nervously, in a quick gabble, and with a look from side to side as he spoke, as though he was afraid that some unseen presence would overhear him.

"It was the little donkey—protected by Set and always up to mischief. I ran after him with my stick. He went past the big gate of the courtyard, and I looked in through the gate at the house. There was no one on the porch but there was a wine stand there. And then a woman, a lady of the house, came out upon the porch from the house. She walked to the wine jar and she held out her hands over it and then—and then—she went back into the house, I think. I do not know. For I heard footsteps and turned and saw in the distance my Lord Yahmose coming back from the fields. So I went on seeking the little donkey, and my Lord Yahmose went into the courtyard."

"And you did not warn him," cried Imhotep angrily. "You said nothing."

The boy cried out, "I did not know anything was wrong. I saw nothing but the lady standing there smiling down as she spread out her hand over the wine jar. . . . I saw nothing. . . ."

"Who was this lady, boy?" asked the priest.

With a vacant expression the boy shook his head.

"I do not know. She must have been one of the ladies of the house. I do not know them. I have the herds at the far end of the cultivation. She wore a dress of dyed linen."

Renisenb started.

"A servant, perhaps?" suggested the priest, watching the boy.

The boy shook his head positively.

"She was not a servant. . . . She had a wig on her head and she wore jewels—a servant does not wear jewels."

"Jewels?" demanded Imhotep. "What jewels?"

The boy replied eagerly and confidently as though at last he had overcome his fear and was quite sure of what he was saying.

"Three strings of beads, with gold lions hanging from them in front. . . ."

Esa's stick clattered to the floor. Imhotep uttered a stifled cry.

Mersu said threateningly:

"If you are lying, boy—"

"It is the truth. I swear it is the truth." The boy's voice rose shrill and clear.

From the side chamber where the ill man lay, Yahmose called feebly:

"What is all this?"

The boy darted through the open door and crouched down by the couch on which Yahmose lay.

"Master, they will torture me."

"No, no." Yahmose turned his head with difficulty on the curved, wooden headrest. "Do not let the child be hurt. He is simple but honest. Promise me."

"Of course, of course," said Imhotep. "There is no need. It is clear the boy has told all that he knows—and I do not think he is inventing. Be off with you, child, but do not return to the far herds. Stay near the house so that we can summon you again if we need you."

The boy rose to his feet. He bent a reluctant glance upon Yahmose.

"You are ill, Lord Yahmose?"

Yahmose smiled faintly.

"Have no fear. I am not going to die. Go now—and be obedient to what you have been told."

Smiling happily now, the boy went off. The priest examined Yahmose's eyes and felt the rate at which the blood was coursing under the skin. Then, recommending him to sleep, he went with the others out into the central hall again.

He said to Imhotep:

"You recognise the description the boy gave?"

Imhotep nodded. His deep, bronze cheeks showed a sickly plum colour.

Renisenb said: "Only Nofret ever wore a dress of dyed linen. It was a new fashion she brought with her from the cities in the north. But those dresses were buried with her."

Imhotep said:

"And the three strings of beads with the lions' heads in gold were what I gave her. There is no other such ornament in the house. It was costly and unusual. All her jewellery, with the exception of a trumpery string of carnelian beads, was buried with her and is sealed in her tomb."

He flung out his arms.

"What persecution—what vindictiveness—is this! My concubine whom I treated well, to whom I paid all honour, whom I buried with the proper rites, sparing no expense. I have eaten and drunk with her in friendship— to that all can bear witness. She had had nothing of which to complain—I did indeed more for her than what had been considered right and fitting. I was prepared to favour her to the detriment of my sons who were born to me. Why, then, should she thus come back from the dead to persecute me and my family?"

Mersu said gravely:

"It seems that it is not against you personally that the dead woman wishes evil. The wine when you drank it was harmless. Who in your family did injury to your dead concubine?"

"A woman who is dead," Imhotep answered shortly.

"I see. You mean the wife of your son Yahmose?"

"Yes." Imhotep paused, then broke out: "But what can be done, Reverend Father? How can we counteract this malice? Oh, evil day when I first took the woman into my house!"

"An evil day indeed," said Kait in a deep voice, coming forward from the entrance to the women's quarters.

Her eyes were heavy with the tears she had shed, and her plain face had a strength and resolution which made it noticeable. Her voice, deep and hoarse, was shaken with anger.

"It was an evil day when you brought Nofret here, Imhotep, to destroy the cleverest and most handsome of your sons! She has brought death to Satipy and death to my Sobek, and Yahmose has only narrowly escaped. Who will be next? Will she spare even children—she who struck my little Ankh? Something must be *done*, Imhotep!"

"Something *must* be done," Imhotep echoed, looking imploringly at the priest.

The latter nodded his head with calm assumption.

"There are ways and means, Imhotep. Once we are sure of our facts, we can go ahead. I have in mind your dead wife, Ashayet. She was a woman of influential family. She can invoke powerful interests in the Land of the Dead who can intervene on your behalf and against whom the woman Nofret will have no power. We must take counsel together."

Kait gave a short laugh.

"Do not wait too long. Men are always the same— Yes, even priests! Everything must be done according to law and precedent. But I say, act quickly—or there will be more dead beneath this roof."

She turned and went out.

"An excellent woman," murmured Imhotep. "A devoted mother to her children, a dutiful wife—but her manners, sometimes, are hardly what they should be—to the head of the house. Naturally at such a time I forgive her. We are all distraught. We hardly know what we are doing."

He clasped his hands to his head.

"Some of us seldom do know what we are doing," remarked Esa.

Imhotep shot an annoyed glance at her. The physician prepared to take his leave and Imhotep went out with him onto the porch, receiving instructions for the care of the sick man.

Renisenb, left behind, looked inquiringly at her grandmother.

Esa was sitting very still. She was frowning and the expression on her face was so curious that Renisenb asked timidly:

"What is it that you are thinking, Grandmother?"

"Thinking is the word, Renisenb. Such curious things are happening in this house that it is very necessary for someone to think."

"They are terrible," said Renisenb with a shiver. "They frighten me."

"They frighten *me*," said Esa. "But not perhaps for the same reason."

With the old familiar gesture, she pushed the wig on her head askew.

"But Yahmose will not die now," said Renisenb. "He will live."

Esa nodded.

"Yes, a master physician reached him in time. On another occasion, though, he may not be so lucky."

"You think—there will be other happenings like this?"

"I think that Yahmose and you and Ipy—and perhaps Kait too had better be very careful indeed what you eat and drink. See always that a slave tastes it first."

"And you, Grandmother?"

Esa smiled her sardonic smile.

"I, Renisenb, am an old woman, and I love life as only the old can, savouring every hour, every minute, that is left to them. Of you all I have the best chance of life—because I shall be more careful than any of you."

"And my father? Surely Nofret would wish no evil to my father?"

"Your father? I do not know. . . . No, I do not know. I cannot as yet see clearly. Tomorrow, when I have thought about it all, I must speak once more with that herd boy. There was something about his story—"

She broke off, frowning. Then, with a sigh, she rose to her feet, and helping herself with her stick, limped slowly back to her own quarters.

Renisenb went into her brother's room. He was sleeping and she crept out again softly. After a moment's hesitation she went to Kait's quarters. She stood in the doorway unnoticed, watching Kait sing one of the children to sleep. Kait's face was calm and placid again—she looked so much as usual that for a moment Renisenb felt that the tragic occurrences of the last twenty-four hours were a dream.

She turned slowly away and went to her own apartment. On a table, amongst her own cosmetic boxes and jars, was the little jewel case that had belonged to Nofret.

Renisenb picked it up and stood looking at it as it lay on the palm of her hand. Nofret had touched it, had held it—it was her possession.

And again a wave of pity swept over Renisenb, allied to that queer sense of understanding. Nofret had been unhappy. As she had held this little box in her hand perhaps she had deliberately forced that unhappiness into malice and hatred . . . and even now that hatred was unabated . . . was still seeking revenge. . . . Oh, no, surely not—surely not!

Almost mechanically, Renisenb twisted the two buttons and slid back the lid. The carnelian beads were there and the broken amulet and *something else. . . .*

Her heart beating violently, Renisenb drew out a necklace of gold beads with gold lions in front. . . .

CHAPTER XV

First Month of Summer, 30th Day

I

THE FINDING OF the necklace frightened Renisenb badly.

On the impulse of the minute she replaced it quickly in the jewel box, slid home the lid and tied the string round the buttons again. Her instinct was to conceal her discovery. She even glanced fearfully behind her to make sure that no one had watched what she had been doing.

She passed a sleepless night, twisting to and fro uneasily and settling and resettling her head on the curved wooden headrest of her bed.

By the morning she had decided that she must confide in someone. She could not bear the weight of that disturbing discovery alone. Twice in the night she had started up, wondering if, perhaps, she might perceive Nofret's figure standing menacingly by her side. But there was nothing to be seen.

Taking the lion necklace from the jewel box, Renisenb hid it in the folds of her linen dress. She had only just done so when Henet came bustling in. Her eyes were bright and sharp with the pleasure of having fresh news to impart.

"Just imagine, Renisenb, isn't it terrible? That boy—the herd boy, you know—fast asleep this morning out by the cornbins and everyone shaking him and yelling in his ear—and now it seems that he'll never wake again. It's as though he'd drunk the poppy juice—and maybe he did—but if so, who gave it to him? Nobody here, that I'll be bound. And it's not likely he'd take it himself. Oh, we might have known how it would be yesterday." Henet's hand went to one of the many amulets she wore. "Amûn protect us against the evil spirits of the dead! The boy told what he saw. He told how he saw Her. And so She came back and gave him poppy juice to close his eyes for ever. Oh, She's very powerful, that Nofret! She'd been abroad, you know, out of Egypt. I dare swear She got to know all sorts of outlandish primitive magic. We're not safe in this house—none of us are safe. Your father should give several bulls to Amûn—a whole herd if necessary—this isn't a time for economy. We've got to protect ourselves. We must appeal to your mother—that's what Imhotep is planning to do. The priest Mersu says so. A solemn Letter to the Dead. Hori is busy now drawing up the terms of it. Your father was for addressing it to Nofret—appealing to her. You know: 'Most excellent Nofret, what evil thing have I ever done to you—' etc. But as the Divine Father Mersu pointed out, it needs stronger measures than *that*. Now your mother, Ashayet, was a great lady. Her mother's brother was the Nomarch and her brother was Chief Butler to the Vizier at Thebes. If it's once brought to *her* knowledge, she'll see to it that a mere concubine isn't allowed to destroy her own children! Oh, yes, we'll get justice done. As I say, Hori is drawing up the plea to her now."

It had been Renisenb's intention to seek out Hori and tell him about her finding of the lion necklace. But if Hori were busy with the priests at the Temple of Isis it was hopeless to think of trying to get hold of him alone.

Should she go to her father? Dissatisfied, Renisenb shook her head. Her old childish belief in her father's omnipotence had quite passed away. She realised now how quickly in times of crisis he went to pieces—a fussy pomposity replacing any real strength. If Yahmose were not ill, she could have told him, though she doubted if he would have any very practical counsels to offer. He would probably insist on the matter being laid before Imhotep.

And that, Renisenb felt with increasing urgency, was at all costs to be avoided. The first thing Imhotep would do would be to blazon the whole thing abroad, and Renisenb had a strong instinct for keeping it secret— though for what exact reason she would have been hard put to it to say.

No, it was Hori's advice she wanted. Hori would, as always, know the right thing to do. He would take the necklace from her and at the same time take her worry and perplexity away. He would look at her with those kind grave eyes and instantly she would feel that now all was well. . . .

For a moment Renisenb was tempted to confide in Kait—but Kait was unsatisfactory; she never listened properly. Perhaps if one got her away from the children—no, it wouldn't do. Kait was nice but stupid.

Renisenb thought: "There is Kameni . . . and there is my grandmother."

Kameni . . . ? There was something pleasurable in the thought of telling Kameni. She could see his face quite clearly in her thoughts—its expression changing from a merry challenge to interest—to apprehension on her behalf. . . . Or would it not be on her behalf?

Why this insidious lurking suspicion that Nofret and Kameni had been closer friends than had appeared on the surface? Because Kameni had helped Nofret in her campaign of detaching Imhotep from his family? He had protested that he could not help himself—but was that true? It was an easy thing to say. Everything Kameni said sounded easy and natural and right. His laugh was so gay that you wanted to laugh too. The swing of his body was so graceful as he walked—the turn of his head on those smooth bronze shoulders—his eyes that looked at you—that looked at you— Renisenb's thought broke off confusedly. Kameni's eyes were not like Hori's eyes, safe and kind. They demanded; they challenged.

Renisenb's thoughts had brought blood into her cheeks and a sparkle into her eyes. But she decided that she would not tell Kameni about the finding of Nofret's necklace. No, she would go to Esa. Esa had impressed her yesterday. Old as she was, the old woman had a grasp of things and a shrewd practical sense that was unshared by anyone else in the family.

Renisenb thought: "She is old. But she will know."

II

At the first mention of the necklace, Esa glanced quickly round, placed a finger to her lips, and held out her hand. Renisenb fumbled in her dress, drew out the necklace and laid it in Esa's hand. Esa held it for a moment close to her dim eyes, then stowed it away in her dress. She said in a low, authoritative voice:

"No more now. Talking in this house is talking to a hundred ears. I have lain awake most of the night thinking, and there is much that must be done."

"My father and Hori have gone to the Temple of Isis to confer with the priest Mersu on the drawing up of a petition to my mother for her intervention."

"I know. Well, let your father concern himself with the spirits of the dead. My thoughts deal with the things of this world. When Hori returns, bring him here to me. There are things that must be said and discussed—and Hori I can trust."

"Hori will know what to do," said Renisenb happily.

Esa looked at her curiously.

"You go often up to see him at the Tomb, do you not? What do you talk about, you and Hori?"

Renisenb shook her head vaguely.

"Oh, the River—and Egypt—and the way the light changes and the colours of the sand below and the rocks. . . . But very often we do not talk at all. I just sit there and it is peaceful, with no scolding voices and no crying children and no bustle of coming and going. I can think my own thoughts and Hori does not interrupt them. And then, sometimes, I look up and find him watching me and we both smile. . . . I can be happy up there."

Esa said slowly:

"You are lucky, Renisenb. You have found the happiness that is inside everybody's own heart. To most women happiness means coming and going, busied over small affairs. It is care for one's children and laughter and conversation and quarrels with other women and alternate love and anger with a man. It is made up of small things strung together like beads on a string."

"Has your life been like that, Grandmother?"

"Most of it. But now that I am old and sit much alone and my sight is dim and I walk with difficulty—then I realise that there is a life within as well as a life without. But I am too old now to learn the true way of it—and so I scold my little maid and enjoy good food hot from the kitchen and savour all the many different kinds of bread that we bake and enjoy ripe grapes and the juice from pomegranates. These things remain when others go. The children that I have loved most are now dead. Your father, Re help him, was always a fool. I loved him when he was a toddling little boy but now he irritates me with his airs of importance. Of my grand-children I love you, Renisenb—and talking of grandchildren, where is Ipy? I have not seen him today or yesterday."

"He is very busy superintending the storing of the grain. My father left him in charge."

Esa grinned.

"That will please our young gander. He will be strutting about full of his own importance. When he comes in to eat tell him to come to me."

"Yes, Esa."

"For the rest, Renisenb, *silence*. . . ."

III

"You wanted to see me, Grandmother?"

Ipy stood smiling and arrogant, his head held a little on one side, a flower held between his white teeth. He looked very pleased with himself and with life generally.

"If you can spare a moment of your valuable time," said Esa, screwing her eyes up to see better and looking him up and down.

The acerbity of her tone made no impression on Ipy.

"It is true that I am very busy today. I have to oversee everything since my father has gone to the Temple."

"Young jackals bark loud," said Esa.

But Ipy was quite unperturbable.

"Come, Grandmother, you must have more to say to me than that."

"Certainly I have more to say. And to begin with, this is a house of mourning. Your brother Sobek's body is already in the hands of the embalmers. Yet your face is as cheerful as though this was a festival day."

Ipy grinned.

"You are no hypocrite, Esa. Would you have me be one? You know very well that there was no love lost between me and Sobek. He did everything he could to thwart and annoy me. He treated me as a child. He gave me all the most humiliating and childish tasks in the fields. Frequently he jeered and laughed at me. And when my father would have associated me with him in partnership, together with my elder brothers, it was Sobek who persuaded him not to do so."

"What makes you think it was Sobek who persuaded him?" asked Esa sharply.

"Kameni told me so."

"Kameni?" Esa raised her eyebrows, pushed her wig on one side, and scratched her head. "Kameni indeed. Now I find that interesting."

"Kameni said he had it from Henet—and we all agree that Henet always knows everything."

"Nevertheless," said Esa drily, "this is an occasion when Henet was wrong in her facts. Doubtless both Sobek and Yahmose were of the opinion that you were too young for the business—but it was I—yes, I—who dissuaded your father from including you."

"You, Grandmother?" The boy stared at her in frank surprise. Then a dark scowl altered the expression of his face, the flower fell from his lips. "Why should you do that? What business was it of yours?"

"My family's business is my business."

"And my father listened to you?"

"Not at the moment," said Esa drily. "But I will teach you a lesson, my handsome child. Women work roundabout—and they learn—if they are not born with the knowledge—to play on the weaknesses of men. You may remember I sent Henet with the gaming board to the porch in the cool of the evening."

"I remember. My father and I played together. What of it?"

"This. You played three games. And each time, being a much cleverer player, you beat your father."

"Yes."

"That is all," said Esa, closing her eyes. "Your father, like all inferior players, did not like being beaten—especially by a chit of a boy. So he remembered my words—and he decided that you were certainly too young to be given a share in the partnership."

Ipy stared at her for a moment. Then he laughed—not a very pleasant laugh.

"You are clever, Esa," he said. "Yes, you may be old, but you are clever.

Decidedly you and I have the brains of the family. You have pegged out in the first match on our gaming board. But you will see, I shall win the second. So look to yourself, Grandmother."

"I intend to," said Esa. "And in return for your words, let me advise *you* to look to *yourself*. One of your brothers is dead, the other has been near to death. You also are your father's son—and you may go the same way."

Ipy laughed scornfully.

"There is little fear of that."

"Why not? You also threatened and insulted Nofret."

"Nofret!" Ipy's scorn was unmistakable.

"What is in your mind?" demanded Esa sharply.

"I have my ideas, Grandmother. And I can assure you that Nofret and her spirit tricks will not worry me. Let her do her worst."

There was a shrill wail behind him and Henet ran in crying out:

"Foolish boy—imprudent child. Defying the dead! And after we've all had a taste of her quality! And not so much as an amulet on you for protection!"

"Protection? I will protect myself. Get out of my way, Henet. I've got work to do. Those lazy peasants shall know what it is to have a real master over them."

Pushing Henet aside, Ipy strode out of the room.

Esa cut short Henet's wails and lamentations.

"Listen to me, Henet, and stop exclaiming about Ipy. He may know what he is doing or he may not. His manner is very odd. But answer me this: Did you tell Kameni that it was Sobek who had persuaded Imhotep not to include Ipy in the deed of association?"

Henet's voice dropped to its usual whining key.

"I'm sure I'm far too busy in the house to waste my time running about telling people things—and telling Kameni, of all people. I'm sure I'd never speak a word to him if he didn't come and speak to me. He's got a pleasant manner, as you must admit yourself, Esa—and I'm not the only one who thinks so—oh, dear, no! And if a young widow wants to make a new contract, well, she usually fancies a handsome young man—though what Imhotep would say I'm sure I don't know. Kameni is only a junior scribe, when all is said and done."

"Never mind what Kameni is or isn't! Did you tell him that it was Sobek who opposed Ipy being made a partner in the association?"

"Well, really, Esa, I can't remember what I may or may not have said. I didn't actually go and tell anyone anything, that much is sure. But a word passes here and there, and you know yourself that Sobek was saying—and Yahmose too for that matter, though, of course, not so loud nor so often—

that Ipy was a mere boy and that it would never do—and for all I know Kameni may have heard him say it himself and not got it from me at all. I never gossip—but after all, a tongue is given one to speak with, and I'm not a deaf mute."

"That you most certainly are not," said Esa. "A tongue, Henet, may sometimes be a weapon. A tongue may cause a death—may cause more than one death. I hope *your* tongue, Henet, has not caused a death."

"Why, Esa, the things you say! And what's in your mind? I'm sure I never say a word to anybody that I wouldn't be willing to let the whole world overhear. I'm so devoted to the whole family—I'd die for any one of them. Oh, they underestimate old Henet's devotion. I promised their dear mother—"

"Ha," said Esa, cutting her short, "here comes my plump reed bird, cooked with leeks and celery. It smells delicious—cooked to a turn. Since you're so devoted, Henet, you can take a little mouthful from one side—just in case it's poisoned."

"Esa!" Henet gave a squeal. "Poisoned! How can you say such things! And cooked in our very own kitchen."

"Well," said Esa, "someone's got to taste it—just in case. And it had better be you, Henet, since you're so willing to die for any member of the family. I don't suppose it would be too painful a death. Come on, Henet. Look how plump and juicy and tasty it is. No, thanks, I don't want to lose my little slave girl. She's young and merry. You've passed your best days, Henet, and it wouldn't matter so much what happened to you. Now then—open your mouth. . . . Delicious, isn't it? I declare—you're looking quite green in the face. Didn't you like my little joke? I don't believe you did. Ha ha, he he!"

Esa rolled about with merriment, then composing herself suddenly, she set greedily to work to eat her favourite dish.

CHAPTER XVI

Second Month of Summer, 1st Day

I

THE CONSULTATION AT the Temple was over. The exact form of the petition had been drawn up and amended. Hori and two Temple scribes had been busily employed. Now at last the first step had been taken.

The priest signed that the draft of the petition should be read out.

"To THE MOST EXCELLENT SPIRIT ASHAYET:

"This from your brother and husband. Has the sister forgotten her brother? Has the mother forgotten the children that were born to her? Does not the most excellent Ashayet know that a spirit of evil life menaces her children? Already is Sobek, her son, passed to Osiris by means of poison.

"I treated you in life with all honour. I gave you jewels and dresses, unguents and perfumes and oils for your limbs. Together we ate of good foods, sitting in peace and amity with tables loaded before us. When you were ill, I spared no expense. I procured for you a master physician. You were buried with all honour and with due ceremonies and all things needful for your life in the hereafter were provided for you—servants and oxen and food and drink and jewels and raiment. I mourned for you many years —and after long, long years only did I take a concubine so that I might live as befits a man not yet old.

"This concubine it is that now does evil to your children. Do you not know of this? Perchance you are in ignorance. Surely if Ashayet knows, she will be swift to come to the aid of the sons born to her.

"Is it that Ashayet knows, but that evil is still done because the concubine Nofret is strong in evil magic? Yet surely it is against your will, most excellent Ashayet. Therefore reflect that in the Field of Offerings you have great relatives and powerful helpers. The great and noble Ipi, Chief Butler to the Vizier. Invoke his aid! Also your mother's brother, the great and powerful Meriptah, the Nomarch of the Province. Acquaint him with the shameful truth! Let it be brought before his court. Let witnesses be summoned. Let them testify against Nofret that she has done this evil. Let judgement be given and may Nofret be condemned, and let it be decreed that she do no more evil to this house.

"Oh, excellent Ashayet, if you are angry with this your brother Imhotep in that he did listen to this woman's evil persuasions and did threaten to do injustice to your children that were born of you, then reflect that it is not he alone that suffers, but your children also. Forgive your brother Imhotep aught that he has done for the sake of your children."

The Chief Scribe stopped reading. Mersu nodded approval.

"It is well-expressed. Nothing, I think, has been left out."

Imhotep rose.

"I thank you, Reverend Father. My offering shall reach you before tomorrow's sun sets—cattle, oil and flax. Shall we fix the day after that for the ceremony—the placing of the inscribed bowl in the offering chamber of the tomb?"

"Make it three days from now. The bowl must be inscribed and the preparations made for the necessary rites."

"As you will. I am anxious that no more mischief should befall."

"I can well understand your anxiety, Imhotep. But have no fear. The good spirit Ashayet will surely answer this appeal, and her kinsfolk have authority and power and can deal justice where it is so richly deserved."

"May Isis allow that it be so! I thank you, Mersu—and for your care and cure of my son Yahmose. Come, Hori, we have much that must be seen to. Let us return to the house. Ah—this petition does indeed lift a weight off my mind. The excellent Ashayet will not fail her distracted brother."

II

When Hori entered the courtyard, bearing his rolls of papyrus, Renisenb was watching for him. She came running from the lake.

"Hori!"

"Yes, Renisenb?"

"Will you come with me to Esa? She has been waiting and wants you."

"Of course. Let me just see if Imhotep—"

But Imhotep had been buttonholed by Ipy and father and son were engaged in close conversation.

"Let me put down these scrolls and these other things and I will come with you, Renisenb."

Esa looked pleased when Renisenb and Hori came to her.

"Here is Hori, Grandmother. I brought him to you at once."

"Good. Is the air pleasant outside?"

"I—I think so." Renisenb was slightly taken aback.

"Then give me my stick. I will walk a little in the courtyard."

Esa seldom left the house, and Renisenb was surprised. She guided the old woman with a hand below her elbow. They went through the central hall and out onto the porch.

"Will you sit here, Grandmother?"

"No, child, I will walk as far as the lake."

Esa's progress was slow, but although she limped, she was strong on her feet and showed no signs of tiredness. Looking about her, she chose a spot where flowers had been planted in a little bed near the lake and where a sycamore fig tree gave welcome shade.

Then, once established, she said with grim satisfaction:

"There! Now we can talk and no one can overhear our talk."

"You are wise, Esa," said Hori approvingly.

"The things which have to be said must be known only to us three. I trust you, Hori. You have been with us since you were a little boy. You have always been faithful and discreet and wise. Renisenb here is the dearest to me of all my son's children. No harm must come to her, Hori."

"No harm shall come to her, Esa."

Hori did not raise his voice but the tone of it and the look in his face as his eyes met the old woman's amply satisfied her.

"That is well said, Hori—quietly and without heat—but as one who means what he says. Now tell me what has been arranged today?"

Hori recounted the drawing up of the petition and the gist of it. Esa listened carefully.

"Now listen to me, Hori, and look at this." She drew the lion necklace from her dress and handed it to him. She added: "Tell him, Renisenb, where you found this."

Renisenb did so. Then Esa said: "Well, Hori, what do you think?"

Hori was silent for a moment, then he asked: "You are old and wise, Esa. What do you think?"

Esa said: "You are one of those, Hori, who do not like to speak rash words unaccompanied with facts. You knew, did you not, from the first how Nofret came to her death?"

"I suspected the truth, Esa. It was only suspicion."

"Exactly. And we have only suspicion now. Yet here, by the lake, between us three, suspicion can be spoken—and afterward not referred to again. Now it seems to me that there are three explanations of the tragic things that happened. The first is that the herd boy spoke truth and that what he saw was indeed Nofret's ghost returned from the dead and that she had an evil determination to revenge herself still further by causing increased sorrow and grief to our family. That may be so—it is said by priests and others to be possible and we do know that illnesses are caused by evil spirits. But it seems to me, who am an old woman and who am not inclined to believe all that priests and others say, that there are other possibilities."

"Such as?" asked Hori.

"Let us admit that Nofret was killed by Satipy, that some time afterwards at that same spot Satipy had a vision of Nofret and that, in her fear and guilt, she fell and died. That is all clear enough. But now let us come to another assumption; and that is that after that someone, for a reason we have yet to discover, wished to cause the death of two of Imhotep's sons. That someone counted on a superstitious dread ascribing the deed to the spirit of Nofret—a singularly convenient assumption."

"Who would want to kill Yahmose or Sobek?" cried Renisenb.

"Not a servant," said Esa; "they would not dare. That leaves us with but few people from whom to choose."

"One of *ourselves?* But, Grandmother, that could not be!"

"Ask Hori," said Esa drily. "You notice he makes no protest."

Renisenb turned to him.

"Hori—surely—"

Hori shook his head gravely.

"Renisenb, you are young and trusting. You think that everyone you know and love is just as they appear to you. You do not know the human heart and the bitterness—yes, and evil—it may contain."

"But who—which one—?"

Esa broke in briskly:

"Let us go back to this tale told by the herd boy. He saw a woman dressed in a dyed linen dress wearing Nofret's necklace. Now if it was no spirit, then he saw exactly what he said he did—which means that he saw a woman who was deliberately trying to *appear* like Nofret. It might have been Kait—it might have been Henet—it might have been *you*, Renisenb! From that distance it might have been *anyone* wearing a woman's dress and a wig. Hush—let me go on. The other possibility is that the boy is lying. He told a tale that he had been *taught* to tell. He was obeying someone who had the right to command him and he may have been too dull-witted even to realise the point of the story he was bribed or cajoled to tell. We shall never know now because the boy is dead—in itself a suggestive point. It inclines me to the belief that the boy told a story he had been taught. Questioned closely, as he would have been today, that story could have been broken down—it is easy to discover with a little patience whether a child is lying."

"So you think we have a poisoner in our midst?" asked Hori.

"I do," said Esa. "And you?"

"I think so too," said Hori.

Renisenb glanced from one to the other of them in dismay.

Hori went on:

"But the motive seems to me far from clear."

"I agree," said Esa. "That is why I am uneasy. *I do not know who is threatened next.*"

Renisenb broke in: "But—one of *us?*" Her tone was still incredulous.

Esa said sternly: "Yes, Renisenb—one of us. Henet or Kait or Ipy, or Kameni, or Imhotep himself—yes, or Esa or Hori, or even"—she smiled—"Renisenb."

"You are right, Esa," said Hori. "We must include ourselves."

"But *why?*" Renisenb's voice held wondering horror. *"Why?"*

"If we knew that, we'd know very nearly all we wanted to know," said Esa. "We can only go by who was attacked. Sobek, remember, joined Yahmose unexpectedly after Yahmose had commenced to drink. Therefore it is *certain* that whoever did it wanted to kill Yahmose, less certain that that person wished also to kill Sobek."

"But who could wish to kill Yahmose?" Renisenb spoke with sceptical intonation. "Yahmose, surely, of us all would have no enemies. He is always quiet and kindly."

"Therefore, clearly, the motive was not one of personal hate," said Hori. "As Renisenb says, Yahmose is not the kind of man who makes enemies."

"No," said Esa. "The motive is more obscure than that. We have here either enmity against the family as a whole, or else there lies behind all these things that covetousness against which the Maxims of Ptahotep warn us. It is, he says, a bundle of every kind of evil and a bag of everything that is blameworthy!"

"I see the direction in which your mind is tending, Esa," said Hori. "But to arrive at any conclusion we shall have to make a forecast of the future."

Esa nodded her head vigorously and her large wig slipped over one ear. Grotesque though this made her appearance, no one was inclined to laugh.

"Make such a forecast, Hori," she said.

Hori was silent for a moment or two, his eyes thoughtful. The two women waited. Then, at last, he spoke.

"If Yahmose had died as intended, then the principal beneficiaries would have been Imhotep's remaining sons, Sobek and Ipy—some part of the estate would doubtless have been set aside for Yahmose's children, but the administration of it would have been in their hands—in Sobek's hands in particular. Sobek would undoubtedly have been the greatest gainer. He would presumably have functioned as ka-priest during Imhotep's absences and would succeed to that office after Imhotep's death. But though Sobek benefited, yet Sobek *cannot* be the guilty person, since he himself drank of the poisoned wine so heartily that he died. Therefore, as far as I can see, the deaths of these two can *benefit* only one person—at the moment, that is—and that person is Ipy."

"Agreed," said Esa. "But I note, Hori, that you are farseeing—and I appreciate your qualifying phrase. But let us consider Ipy. He is young and impatient; he has in many ways a bad disposition; he is at the age when the fulfilment of what he desires seems to him the most important thing in life. He felt anger and resentment against his elder brothers and considered that he had been unjustly excluded from participation in the family partnership. It seems, too, that unwise things were said to him by Kameni—"

"Kameni?"

It was Renisenb who interrupted. Immediately she had done so she flushed and bit her lip. Hori turned his head to look at her. The long, gentle, penetrating look he gave her hurt her in some indefinable way. Esa craned her neck forward and peered at the girl.

"Yes," she said. "By Kameni. Whether or not inspired by Henet is another matter. The fact remains that Ipy is ambitious and arrogant, was resentful of his brothers' superior authority and that he definitely considers himself, as he told me long ago, the superior ruling intelligence of the family."

Esa's tone was dry.

Hori asked: "He said that to *you?*"

"He was kind enough to associate me with himself in the possession of a certain amount of intelligence."

Renisenb demanded incredulously:

"You think Ipy deliberately poisoned Yahmose and Sobek?"

"I consider it a possibility, no more. This is suspicion that we talk now —we have not yet come to proof. Men have killed their brothers since the beginning of time, knowing that the Gods dislike such killing, yet driven by the evils of covetousness and hatred. And if Ipy did this thing, we shall not find it easy to get proof of what he did, for Ipy, I freely admit, is clever."

Hori nodded.

"But as I say, it is suspicion we talk here under the sycamore. And we will go on now to considering every member of the household in the light of suspicion. As I say, I exclude the servants because I do not believe for one moment that any one of them would dare do such a thing. But I do not exclude Henet."

"Henet?" cried Renisenb. "But Henet is devoted to us all. She never stops saying so."

"It is as easy to utter lies as truth. I have known Henet for many years. I knew her when she came here as a young woman with your mother. She was a relative of hers—poor and unfortunate. Her husband had not cared for her—and indeed Henet was always plain and unattractive—and had divorced her. The one child she bore died in infancy. She came here professing herself devoted to your mother, but I have seen her eyes watching your mother as she moved about the house and courtyard—and I tell you, Renisenb, there was no love in them. No, sour envy was nearer the mark—and as to her professions of love for you all, I distrust them."

"Tell me, Renisenb," said Hori. "Do you yourself feel affection towards Henet?"

"N-no," said Renisenb unwillingly. "I cannot. I have often reproached myself because I dislike her."

"Don't you think that that is because, instinctively, you know her words are false? Does she ever show her reputed love for you by any real service? Has she not always fomented discord between you all by whispering and repeating things that are likely to wound and cause anger?"

"Yes—yes, that is true enough."

Esa gave a dry chuckle.

"You have both eyes and ears in your head, most excellent Hori."

Renisenb argued:

"But my father believes in her and is fond of her."

"My son is a fool and always has been," said Esa. "All men like flattery —and Henet applies flattery as lavishly as unguents are applied at a banquet! She may be really devoted to him—sometimes I think she is—but certainly she is devoted to no one else in this house."

"But surely she would not—she would not *kill*," Renisenb protested. "Why should she want to poison any of us? What good would it do her?"

"None. None. As to why—I know nothing of what goes on inside Henet's head. What she thinks, what she feels—that I do not know. But I sometimes think that strange things are brewing behind that cringing, fawning manner. And if so, her reasons are reasons that we, you and I and Hori, would not understand."

Hori nodded.

"There is a rottenness that starts from within. I spoke to Renisenb once of that."

"And I did not understand you," said Renisenb. "But I am beginning to understand better now. It began with the coming of Nofret—I saw then how none of us were quite what I had thought them to be. It made me afraid. . . . And now"—she made a helpless gesture with her hands—"everything is fear. . . ."

"Fear is only incomplete knowledge," said Hori. "When we *know*, Renisenb, then there will be no more fear."

"And then, of course, there is Kait," proceeded Esa.

"Not Kait," protested Renisenb. "Kait would not try to kill Sobek. It is unbelievable."

"Nothing is unbelievable," said Esa. "That at least I have learned in the course of my life. Kait is a thoroughly stupid woman and I have always mistrusted stupid women. They are dangerous. They can see only their own immediate surroundings and only one thing at a time. Kait lives at the core of a small world which is herself and her children and Sobek as her children's father. It might occur to her quite simply that to remove Yahmose would be to enrich her children. Sobek had always been unsatisfactory in Imhotep's eyes—he was rash, impatient of control and not amenable. Yahmose was the son on whom Imhotep relied. But with Yahmose gone, Imhotep would *have* to rely on Sobek. She would see it, I think, quite simply like that."

Renisenb shivered. In spite of herself she recognised a true description of Kait's attitude to life. Her gentleness, her tenderness, her quiet loving ways were all directed to her own children. Outside herself and her children and Sobek, the world did not exist for her. She looked at it without curiosity and without interest.

Renisenb said slowly: "But surely she would have realised that it was quite possible for Sobek to come back, as he did, thirsty and also drink the wine?"

"No," said Esa. "I don't think that she would. Kait, as I say, is stupid. She would see only what she wanted to see—Yahmose drinking and dying and the business being put down to the magical intervention of our evil and beautiful Nofret. She would see only one simple thing—not various possibilities or probabilities, and since she did not want Sobek to die, it would never occur to her that he might come back unexpectedly."

"And now Sobek is dead and Yahmose is living! How terrible that must be for her if what you suggest is true."

"It is the kind of thing that happens to you when you are stupid," said Esa. "Things go entirely differently from the way you planned them."

She paused and then went on:

"And now we come to Kameni."

"Kameni?" Renisenb felt it necessary to say the word quietly and without protest. Once again she was uncomfortably aware of Hori's eyes on her.

"Yes, we cannot exclude Kameni. He has no known motive for injuring us—but then what do we really know of him? He comes from the north —from the same part of Egypt as Nofret. He helped her—willingly or unwillingly, who can say?—to turn Imhotep's heart against the children that had been born to him. I have watched him sometimes and in truth I can make little of him. He seems to me, on the whole, a commonplace young man with a certain shrewdness of mind, and also, besides being hand-some, with a certain something that draws after him the eyes of women. Yes, women will always like Kameni and yet I think—I may be wrong—that he is not one of those who have a real hold on their hearts and minds. He seems always gay and lighthearted and he showed no great concern at the time of Nofret's death.

"But all this is outward seeming. Who can tell what goes on in the hu-man heart? A determined man could easily play a part. . . . Does Kameni in reality passionately resent Nofret's death, and does he seek to exact re-venge for it? Since Satipy killed Nofret, must Yahmose, her husband, also die? Yes, and Sobek too, who threatened her—and perhaps Kait, who per-secuted her in petty ways, and Ipy, who also hated her? It seems fantastic, but who can tell?"

Esa paused. She looked at Hori.

"Who can tell, Esa?"

Esa peered at him shrewdly.

"Perhaps you can tell, Hori? You think you know, do you not?"

Hori was silent for a moment, then he said:

"I have an idea of my own, yes, as to who poisoned that wine and why—but it is not as yet very clear—and indeed I do not see—" He paused for a minute, frowning, then shook his head. "No, I could make no definite accusation."

"We talk only suspicion here. Go on, Hori, speak."

Hori shook his head.

"No, Esa. It is only a nebulous thought. . . . And if it were true, then it is better for you not to know. The knowledge might be dangerous. And the same applies to Renisenb."

"Then the knowledge is dangerous to you, too, Hori?"

"Yes, it is dangerous. . . . I think, Esa, that we are all in danger—though Renisenb, perhaps, least."

Esa looked at him for some time without speaking.

"I would give a great deal," she said at last, "to know what is in your mind."

Hori did not reply directly. He said, after a moment or two during which he seemed to be thinking:

"The only clue to what is in people's minds is in their behaviour. If a man behaves strangely, oddly, is not himself—"

"Then you suspect him?" asked Renisenb.

"No," said Hori. "That is just what I mean. A man whose mind is evil and whose intentions are evil is conscious of that fact and he knows that he must conceal it at all costs. He dare not, therefore, afford any unusual behaviour. . . ."

"A man?" asked Esa.

"Man or woman—it is the same."

"I see," said Esa. She threw him a very sharp glance. Then she said: "And what of us? What of suspicion where we three are concerned?"

"That, too, must be faced," said Hori. "I have been much trusted. The making of contracts and the disposal of crops have been in my hands. As scribe I have dealt with all the accounts. It could be that I had falsified them—as Kameni discovered had been done in the north. Then Yahmose, it may be, might have been puzzled, he might have begun to suspect. Therefore it would be necessary for me to silence Yahmose." He smiled faintly at his own words.

"Oh, Hori," said Renisenb, "how can you say such things! No one who knew you would believe them."

"No one, Renisenb, knows anyone else. Let me tell you that yet once more."

"And I?" said Esa. "Where does suspicion point in my case? Well, I am old. When a brain grows old, it turns sick sometimes. It hates where it used to love. I may be weary of my children's children and seek to destroy my own blood. It is an affliction of an evil spirit that happens sometimes to those who are old."

"And I?" asked Renisenb. "Why should I try to kill my brother whom I love?"

Hori said:

"If Yahmose and Sobek and Ipy were dead, then you would be the last of Imhotep's children. He would find you a husband and all here would come to you—and you and your husband would be guardians to Yahmose's and Sobek's children."

Then he smiled.

"But under the sycamore tree, we do not suspect you, Renisenb."

"Under the sycamore tree, or not under the sycamore tree, we love you," said Esa.

CHAPTER XVII

Second Month of Summer, 1st Day

I

"So you have been outside the house?" said Henet, bustling in as Esa limped into her room. "A thing you have not done for almost a year!"

Her eyes looked inquisitively at Esa.

"Old people," said Esa, "have whims."

"I saw you sitting by the lake—with Hori and Renisenb."

"Pleasant company, both of them. Is there ever anything you do *not* see, Henet?"

"Really, Esa, I don't know what you mean! You were sitting there plain enough for all the world to see."

"But not near enough for all the world to hear!"

Esa grinned and Henet bridled angrily.

"I don't know why you're so unkind to me, Esa! You're always suggesting things. I'm much too busy seeing that things are done as they should be in this house to listen to other people's conversations. What do *I* care what people say!"

"I've often wondered."

"If it were not for Imhotep, who *does* appreciate me—"

Esa cut in sharply:

"Yes, if it were not for Imhotep! It is on Imhotep you depend, is it not? If anything were to happen to Imhotep—"

It was Henet's turn to interrupt.

"Nothing will happen to Imhotep!"

"How do you know, Henet? Is there such safety in this house? Something has happened to Yahmose and Sobek."

"That is true—Sobek died—and Yahmose nearly died. . . ."

"Henet!" Esa leaned forward. *"Why did you smile when you said that?"*

"I? Smile?" Henet was taken aback. "You are dreaming, Esa! Is it likely I should smile—at such a moment—talking of such a terrible thing?"

"It is true that I am nearly blind," said Esa. "But I am not quite blind. Sometimes, by a trick of light, by a screwing up of the eyelids, I see very well. It can happen that if anyone is talking to a person they know cannot see well, they are careless. They permit themselves an expression of face that on other occasions they would not allow. So I ask you again: Why do you smile with such secret satisfaction?"

"What you say is outrageous—quite outrageous!"

"Now you are frightened."

"And who would not be with the things going on in this house?" cried Henet shrilly. "We're all afraid, I'm sure, with evil spirits returning from the dead to torment us! But I know what it is—you've been listening to Hori. What did he say about me?"

"What does Hori know about you, Henet?"

"Nothing—nothing at all. You'd better ask what do I know about him?"

Esa's eyes grew sharp.

"Well, what do you know?"

Henet tossed her head.

"Ah, you all despise poor Henet! You think she's ugly and stupid. But I know what's going on! There are a lot of things I know—indeed, there's not much I don't know of what goes on in this house. I may be stupid, but I can count how many beans are planted to a row. Maybe I see more than clever people like Hori do. When Hori meets me anywhere he has a trick of looking as though I didn't exist, as though he saw something behind me, something that isn't there. He'd better look at me, that's what I say! He may think me negligible and stupid—but it's not always the clever ones who know everything. Satipy thought she was clever, and where is she now, I should like to know?"

Henet paused triumphantly—then a qualm seemed to pass over her, and she visibly cringed a little, glancing nervously at Esa.

But Esa seemed lost in some train of thought of her own. She had a shocked, almost frightened look of bewilderment on her face. She said slowly and musingly:

"Satipy . . ."

Henet said in her old whining tone:

"I'm sorry, Esa, I'm sure, for losing my temper. Really, I don't know what came over me. I didn't mean anything of what I've been saying. . . ."

Looking up, Esa cut her short.

"Go away, Henet. Whether you meant what you said or did not mean what you said does not really matter. But you have uttered one phrase which has awakened new thoughts in my mind. . . . Go, Henet, and I warn you. Be careful of your words and actions. *We want no more deaths in this house.* I hope you understand."

II

Everything is fear. . . .

Renisenb had found those words rising to her lips automatically during the consultation by the lake. It was only afterwards that she began to realise their truth.

She set out mechanically to join Kait and the children where they were clustered by the little pavilion, but found that her footsteps lagged and then ceased as if of their own volition.

She was afraid, she found, to join Kait, to look into that plain and placid face, in case she might fancy she saw there the face of a poisoner. She watched Henet bustle out on the porch and back again and her usual sense of repulsion was, she found, heightened. Desperately she turned towards the doorway of the courtyard, and a moment later encountered Ipy striding in, his head held high and a gay smile on his impudent face.

Renisenb found herself staring at him. Ipy, the spoilt child of the family, the handsome, wilful little boy she remembered when she had gone away with Khay. . . .

"Why, Renisenb, what is it? Why are you looking at me so strangely?"

"Was I?"

Ipy laughed.

"You are looking as half-witted as Henet."

Renisenb shook her head.

"Henet is not half-witted. She is very astute."

"She has plenty of malice, that I know. In fact, she's a nuisance about the house. I mean to get rid of her."

Renisenb's lips opened and closed. She whispered, "Get rid of her?"

"My dear sister, what is the matter with you? Have you too been seeing evil spirits like that miserable, half-witted black child?"

"You think everyone is half-witted!"

"That child certainly was. Well, it's true I'm inclined to be impatient of stupidity. I've had too much of it. It's no fun, I can tell you, being plagued with two slow-going elder brothers who can't see beyond their own noses! Now that they are out of the way, and there is only my father to deal with, you will soon see the difference. My father will do what *I* say."

Renisenb looked up at him. He looked unusually handsome and arrogant. There was a vitality about him, a sense of triumphant life and vigour, that struck her as above the normal. Some inner consciousness seemed to be affording him this vital sense of well-being.

Renisenb said sharply:

"My brothers are not both out of the way, as you put it. Yahmose is alive."

Ipy looked at her with an air of contemptuous mockery.

"And I suppose you think he will get quite well again?"

"Why not?"

Ipy laughed.

"Why not? Well, let us say simply that I disagree with you. Yahmose is finished, done for—he may crawl about for a little and sit and moan in the sun. But he is no longer a man. He has recovered from the first effects of the poison, but you can see yourself, he makes no further headway."

"Then why doesn't he?" Renisenb demanded. "The physician said it would only take a little time before he was quite strong and himself again."

Ipy shrugged his shoulders.

"Physicians do not know everything. They talk wisely and use long words. Blame the wicked Nofret if you like—but Yahmose, your dear brother Yahmose, is doomed."

"And have you no fear yourself, Ipy?"

"Fear? I?" The boy laughed, throwing back his handsome head.

"Nofret did not love you overwell, Ipy."

"Nothing can harm me, Renisenb, unless I choose to let it! I am young still, but I am one of those people who are born to succeed. As for you, Renisenb, you would do well to be on my side, do you hear? You treat me, often, as an irresponsible boy. But I am more than that now. Every month will show a difference. Soon there will be no will but mine in this place. My father may give the orders but though his voice speaks them, the brain that conceives them will be mine!" He took a step or two, paused, and said over his shoulder: "So be careful, Renisenb, that I do not become displeased with *you*."

As Renisenb stood staring after him, she heard a footstep and turned to see Kait standing beside her.

"What was Ipy saying, Renisenb?"

Renisenb said slowly:

"He says that he will be master here soon."

"Does he?" said Kait. "I think otherwise."

III

Ipy ran lightly up the steps of the porch and into the house. The sight of Yahmose lying on a couch seemed to please him. He said gaily:

"Well, how goes it, Brother? Are we never to see you back on the cultivation? I cannot understand why everything has not gone to pieces without you!"

Yahmose said fretfully in a weak voice:

"I do not understand it at all. The poison is now eliminated. Why do I not regain my strength? I tried to walk this morning and my legs would not support me. I am weak—weak—and what is worse, I seem to grow weaker every day."

Ipy shook his head with facile commiseration.

"That is indeed bad. And the physicians give no help?"

"Mersu's assistant comes every day. He cannot understand my condition. I drink strong decoctions of herbs. The daily incantations are made to the goddess. Special food full of nourishment is prepared for me. There is no reason, so the physician assures me, why I should not rapidly grow strong. Yet instead, I seem to waste away."

"That is too bad," said Ipy.

He went on, singing softly under his breath till he came upon his father and Hori engaged with a sheet of accounts.

Imhotep's face, anxious and careworn, lightened at the sight of his much-loved youngest son.

"Here is my Ipy. What have you to report from the estate?"

"All goes well, Father. We have been reaping the barley. A good crop."

"Yes, thanks to Re, all goes well outside. Would it went as well inside. Still I must have faith in Ashayet—she will not refuse to aid us in our distress. I am worried about Yahmose. I cannot understand this lassitude —this unaccountable weakness."

Ipy smiled scornfully.

"Yahmose was always a weakling," he said.

"That is not so," said Hori mildly. "His health has always been good."

Ipy said assertively:

"Health depends upon the spirit of a man. Yahmose never had any spirit. He was afraid, even, to give orders."

"That is not so lately," said Imhotep. "Yahmose has shown himself to be full of authority in these last months. I have been surprised. But this weakness in the limbs worries me. Mersu assured me that once the effects of the poison had worn off, recovery should be swift."

Hori moved some of the papyrus aside.

"There are other poisons," he said quietly.

"What do you mean?" Imhotep wheeled round.

Hori spoke in a gentle, speculative voice.

"There are poisons known which do not act at once, with violence. They are insidious. A little taken every day accumulates in the system. Only after long months of weakness, does death come. . . . There is a knowledge of such things among women—they use them sometimes to remove a husband and to make it seem as though his death were natural."

Imhotep grew pale.

"Do you suggest that that—*that*—is what is the matter with Yahmose?"

"I am suggesting that it is a possibility. Though his food is now tasted by a slave before he gets it, such a precaution means nothing, since the amount in any one dish on any one day would cause no ill effect."

"Folly," cried Ipy loudly. "Absolute folly! I do not believe there are such poisons. *I* have never heard of them."

Hori raised his eyes.

"You are very young, Ipy. There are still things you do not know."

Imhotep exclaimed, "But what can we do? We have appealed to Ashayet. We have sent offerings to the Temple—not that I have ever had much belief in temples. It is women who are credulous about such things. What more can be done?"

Hori said thoughtfully:

"Let Yahmose's food be prepared by one trustworthy slave, and let that slave be watched all the time."

"But that means—that *here* in this house—"

"Rubbish," shouted Ipy. "Absolute rubbish."

Hori raised his eyebrows.

"Let it be tried," he said. "We shall soon see if it is rubbish."

Ipy went angrily out of the room. Hori stared thoughtfully after him with a perplexed frown on his face.

IV

Ipy went out of the house in such a rage that he almost knocked over Henet.

"Get out of my way, Henet. You are always creeping about and getting in the way."

"How rough you are, Ipy. You have bruised my arm."

"A good thing. I am tired of you and your snivelling ways. The sooner you are out of this house for good the better—and I shall see that you do go."

Henet's eyes flashed maliciously.

"So you would turn me out, would you? After all the care and love I have bestowed on you all. Devoted, I've been, to the whole family. Your father knows it well enough."

"He's heard about it enough, I'm sure! And so have we! In my opinion you're just an evil-tongued old mischief-maker. You helped Nofret with her schemes—that I know well enough. Then she died and you came fawning round us again. But you'll see—in the end my father will listen to *me* and not to your lying tales."

"You're very angry, Ipy. What has made you angry?"

"Never mind."

"You're not afraid of something, are you, Ipy? There are odd things going on here."

"You can't frighten me, you old cat."

He flung himself past her and out of the house.

Henet turned slowly inwards. A groan from Yahmose attracted her attention. He had raised himself from the couch and was trying to walk. But his legs failed him almost at once and but for Henet's rapid assistance he would have fallen to the ground.

"There, Yahmose, there. Lie back again."

"How strong you are, Henet. One would not think it to look at you." He settled back again with his head on the wooden headrest. "Thank you. But what is the matter with me? Why this feeling as though my muscles were turned to water?"

"The matter is that this house is bewitched. The work of a she-devil who came to us from the north. No good ever came out of the north."

Yahmose murmured with sudden despondency:

"I am dying. Yes, I am dying. . . ."

"Others will die before you," said Henet grimly.

"What? What do you mean?" He raised himself on an elbow and stared at her.

"I know what I am saying." Henet nodded her head several times. "It is not you who will die next. Wait and see."

V

"Why do you avoid me, Renisenb?"

Kameni planted himself directly in Renisenb's way. She flushed and found it difficult to give a suitable answer. It was true that she had deliberately turned aside when she saw Kameni coming.

"Why, Renisenb, tell me why?"

But she had no answer ready—could only shake her head dumbly.

Then she glanced up at him as he stood facing her. She had had a faint dread that Kameni's face too might seem different. It was with a curious gladness that she saw it unchanged, his eyes looking at her gravely and for once no smile upon his lips.

Before the look in his eyes her own fell. Kameni could always disturb her. His nearness affected her physically. Her heart beat a shade faster.

"I know why you avoid me, Renisenb."

She found her voice.

"I—was not avoiding you. I did not see you coming."

"That is a lie." He was smiling now; she could hear it in his voice. "Renisenb, beautiful Renisenb."

She felt his warm, strong hand round her arm and immediately she shook herself free.

"Do not touch me! I do not like to be touched."

"Why do you fight against me, Renisenb? You know well enough the thing that is between us. You are young and strong and beautiful. It is against nature that you should go on grieving for a husband all your life. I will take you away from this house. It is full of deaths and evil spells. You shall come away with me and be safe."

"And suppose I do not want to come?" said Renisenb with spirit.

Kameni laughed. His teeth gleamed white and strong.

"But you do want to come, only you will not admit it! Life is good, Renisenb, when a sister and brother are together. I will love you and make you happy and you shall be a glorious field to me, your lord. See, I shall no longer sing to Ptah, 'Give me my sister tonight' but I shall go to Imhotep and say, 'Give me my sister Renisenb.' But I think it is not safe for you here, so I shall take you away. I am a good scribe and I can enter the household of one of the great nobles of Thebes if I wish, though actually I like the country life here—the cultivation and the cattle and the songs of the men who reap, and the little pleasure craft on the River. I would like to sail with you on the River, Renisenb. And we will take Teti with us. She is a beautiful, strong child and I will love her and be a good father to her. Come, Renisenb, what do you say?"

Renisenb stood silent. She was conscious of her heart beating fast and she felt a kind of languor stealing over her senses. Yet with this feeling of softness, this yielding, went something else—a feeling of antagonism.

"The touch of his hand on my arm and I am all weakness . . ." she thought. "Because of his strength . . . of his square shoulders . . . his laughing mouth . . . But I know nothing of his mind, of his thoughts, of his heart. There is no peace between us and no sweetness. . . . What do I want? I do not know. . . . But not this . . . No, not this . . ."

She heard herself saying, and even to her own ears the words sounded weak and uncertain:

"I do not want another husband. . . . I want to be alone . . . to be myself. . . ."

"No, Renisenb, you are wrong. You were not meant to live alone. Your hand says so when it trembles within mine. . . . See?"

With an effort Renisenb drew her hand away.

"I do not love you, Kameni. I think I hate you."

He smiled.

"I do not mind your hating me, Renisenb. Your hate is very close to love. We will speak of this again."

He left her, moving with the swiftness and easy gait of a young gazelle.

Renisenb went slowly on to where Kait and the children were playing by the lake.

Kait spoke to her, but Renisenb answered at random.

Kait, however, did not seem to notice, or else, as usual, her mind was too full of the children to pay much attention to other things.

Suddenly, breaking the silence, Renisenb said:

"Shall I take another husband? What do you say, Kait?"

Kait replied placidly without any great interest:

"It would be as well, I think. You are strong and young, Renisenb, and you can have many more children."

"Is that all a woman's life, Kait? To busy myself in the back of the house, to have children, to spend afternoons with them by the lake under the sycamore trees?"

"It is all that matters to a woman. Surely you know that. Do not speak as though you were a slave. Women have power in Egypt—inheritance passes through them to their children. Women are the life blood of Egypt."

Renisenb looked thoughtfully at Teti, who was busily making a garland of flowers for her doll. Teti was frowning a little with the concentration of what she was doing. There had been a time when Teti had looked so like Khay, pushing out her underlip, turning her head a little sideways, that Renisenb's heart had turned over with pain and love. But now not only was Khay's face dim in Renisenb's memory, but Teti no longer had that trick of head-turning and pushing out her lip. There had been other moments when Renisenb had held Teti close to her, feeling the child still part of her own body, her own living flesh, with a passionate sense of ownership. "She is mine, all mine," she had said to herself.

Now, watching her, Renisenb thought: "She is *me*—and she is *Khay*. . . ."

Then Teti looked up, and seeing her mother, she smiled. It was a grave, friendly smile, with confidence in it and pleasure.

Renisenb thought: "No, she is not me and she is not Khay—she is *herself*. She is Teti. She is alone, as I am alone, as we are all alone. If there is love between us we shall be friends all our life—but if there is not love she will grow up and we shall be strangers. She is Teti and I am Renisenb."

Kait was looking at her curiously.

"What *do* you want, Renisenb? I do not understand."

Renisenb did not answer. How put into words for Kait the things she hardly understood herself? She looked round her, at the courtyard walls, at the gaily coloured porch of the house, at the smooth waters of the lake and the graceful little pleasure pavilion, the neat flower beds and the clumps of papyrus. All safe, shut in, nothing to fear, with around her the murmur of the familiar home sounds, the babble of children's voices, the raucous, far-off, shrill clamour of women in the house, the distant lowing of cattle.

She said slowly:

"One cannot see the River from here."

Kait looked surprised.

"Why should one want to see it?"

Renisenb said slowly:

"I am stupid. I do not know."

Before her eyes, very clearly, she saw spread out the panorama of green fields, rich and lush, and beyond, far away, an enchanted distance of pale rose and amethyst fading into the horizon, and cleaving the two, the pale silver blue of the Nile. . . .

She caught her breath—for with the vision, the sights and sounds around her faded—there came instead a stillness, a richness, an infinite satisfaction. . . .

She said to herself: "If I turn my head, I shall see Hori. He will look up from his papyrus and smile at me. . . . Presently the sun will set and there will be darkness and then I shall sleep. . . . That will be death."

"What did you say, Renisenb?"

Renisenb started. She was not aware she had spoken aloud. She came back from her vision to reality. Kait was looking at her curiously.

"You said '*death*,' Renisenb. What were you thinking?"

Renisenb shook her head.

"I don't know. I didn't mean—" She looked round her again. How pleasant it was, this family scene, with the splashing water and the children at play. She drew a deep breath.

"How peaceful it is here. One can't imagine anything—horrible—happening here."

But it was by the lake that they found Ipy the next morning. He was sprawled face downwards with his face in the water where a hand had held him while he drowned.

CHAPTER XVIII

Second Month of Summer, 10th Day

I

IMHOTEP SAT HUDDLED down upon himself. He looked very much older, a broken, shrunken old man. On his face was a piteous look of bewilderment.

Henet brought him food and coaxed him to take it.

"Yes, yes, Imhotep, you must keep up your strength."

"Why should I? What is strength? Ipy was strong—strong in youth and beauty—and now he lies in the brine bath . . . My son, my dearly loved son. The last of my sons."

"No, no, Imhotep—you have Yahmose, your good Yahmose."

"For how long? No, he too is doomed. We are all doomed. What evil is this that has come upon us? Could I know that such things would come of taking a concubine into my house? It is an accepted thing to do—it is righteous and according to the law of men and Gods. I treated her with honour. Why, then, should these things come upon me? Or is it Ashayet who wreaks vengeance upon me? Is it she who will not forgive? Certainly she has made no answer to my petition. The evil business still goes on."

"No, no, Imhotep. You must not say that. So short a time has passed since the bowl was placed in the offering-chamber. Does one not know how long affairs of law and justice take in this world—how endless are the delays in the Nomarch's court—and still more when a case goes up to the Vizier? Justice is justice, in this world and the next, a business that moves slowly but is adjusted with righteousness in the end."

Imhotep shook his head doubtfully. Henet went on:

"Besides, Imhotep, you must remember that Ipy was not Ashayet's son —he was born to your sister Ipi. Why, then, should Ashayet concern herself violently on his behalf? But with Yahmose, it will be different—Yahmose will recover because Ashayet will see to it that he does."

"I must admit, Henet, that your words comfort me. . . . There is much in what you say. Yahmose, it is true, recovers strength now every day. He is a good loyal son—but, oh! for my Ipy—such spirit—such beauty!" Imhotep groaned anew.

"Alas! Alas!" Henet wailed in sympathy.

"That accursed girl and her beauty! Would I had never set eyes on her."

"Yes, indeed, dear master. A daughter of Set if I ever saw one. Learned in magic and evil spells, there can be no doubt about it."

There was the tap of a stick on the floor and Esa came limping into the hall. She gave a derisive snort.

"Has no one in this house any sense? Have you nothing better to do than bleat out curses against an unfortunate girl who took your fancy and who indulged in a little feminine spite and malice, goaded by the stupid behaviour of the stupid wives of your stupid sons?"

"A little spite and malice—is that what you call it, Esa? When, of my three sons, two are dead and one is dying! Oh! that my mother should say such things to me!"

"It seems necessary that someone should say them, since you cannot recognise facts for what they are. Wipe out of your mind this silly superstitious belief that a dead girl's spirit is working this evil. It was a *live* hand that held Ipy's head down in the lake to drown, and a live hand that dropped poison into the wine that Yahmose and Sobek drank. You have an enemy, yes, Imhotep, but an enemy here in this house. And the proof is that since Hori's advice was taken and Renisenb herself prepares Yahmose's food, or a slave prepares it while she watches, and that her hand carries it to him, since then, I say, Yahmose has gained health and strength every day. Try to stop being a fool, Imhotep, and moaning and beating your head—in all of which Henet is being extremely helpful—"

"Oh, Esa, how you misjudge me!"

"In which, I say, Henet assists you—either because she is a fool too, or for some other reason—"

"May Re forgive you, Esa, for your unkindness to a poor lonely woman!"

Esa swept on, shaking her stick in an impressive gesture.

"Pull yourself together, Imhotep, and *think*. Your dead wife Ashayet, who was a very lovely woman and *not* a fool, by the way, may exert her influence for you in the other world, but can hardly be expected to do your thinking for you in this one! We have got to *act*, Imhotep, for if we do not, then there will be more deaths."

"A live enemy? An enemy in this house? You really believe that, Esa?"

"Of course I believe it, because it is the only thing that makes sense."

"But then we are all in danger?"

"Certainly we are. In danger, not of spells and spirit hands, but of human agency—of live fingers that drop poison in food and drink, of a human figure that steals up behind a boy who returns late at night from the village and forces his head down into the waters of the lake!"

Imhotep said thoughtfully: "Strength would be needed for that."

"On the face of it, yes, but I am not sure. Ipy had drunk much beer in the village. He was in a wild and boastful mood. It may be that he returned home unsteady on his feet and that, having no fear of the person who accosted him, he bent of his own accord to bathe his face in the lake. Little strength would be needed then."

"What are you trying to say, Esa? That a *woman* did this thing? But it is impossible—the whole thing is impossible—there can be no enemy in this house or we should know it. *I* should know it!"

"There is an evil of the heart, Imhotep, that does not show in the face."

"You mean that one of our servants, or a slave—"

"No servant and no slave, Imhotep."

"One of ourselves? Or else—do you mean Hori or Kameni? But Hori is one of the family. He has proved himself faithful and trustworthy. And Kameni—he is a stranger, true, but he is of our blood and he has proved his devotion by his zeal in my service. Moreover, he came to me only this morning and urged that I should consent to his marriage with Renisenb."

"Oh, he did, did he?" Esa showed interest. "And what did you say?"

"What could I say?" Imhotep was fretful. "Is this a time to talk of marriage? I said as much to him."

"And what did he say to that?"

"He said that in his opinion this *was* the time to talk of marriage. He said that Renisenb was not safe in this house."

"I wonder," said Esa. "I very much wonder. . . . Is she? I thought she was—and Hori thought so—but now . . ."

Imhotep went on.

"Can one have marriages and funeral ceremonies going on side by side? It is not decent. The whole Nome would talk about it."

"This is no time for convention," said Esa. "Especially since it would seem that the embalmers' men are with us permanently. All this must be a blessing to Ipi and Montu—the firm must be doing exceptionally well."

"They have put their charges up by ten per cent!" Imhotep was momentarily diverted. "Iniquitous! They say that labour is more expensive."

"They should give us a cut-rate price for quantity!" Esa smiled grimly at her joke.

"My dear mother." Inhotep looked at her in horror. "This is not a jest."

"All life is a jest, Imhotep—and it is death who laughs last. Do you not hear it at every feast? Eat, drink and be merry, for tomorrow you die? Well, that is very true for us here—it is a question only of *whose* death will come tomorrow."

"What you say is terrible—terrible! What can be done?"

"Trust no one," said Esa. "That is the first, the most vital thing." She repeated with emphasis: "*Trust no one.*"

Henet began to sob.

"Why do you look at *me?* . . . I'm sure if anyone is worthy of trust, I am. I've proved it over all these years. Don't listen to her, Imhotep."

"There, there, my good Henet—naturally I trust you. I know only too well your true and devoted heart."

"You know nothing," said Esa. "None of us know anything. That is our danger."

"You accused *me*," whined Henet.

"I cannot accuse. I have neither knowledge nor proof—only suspicion." Imhotep looked up sharply.

"You have suspicion—of whom?"

Esa said slowly: "I have suspected once—and twice—and a third time. I will be honest. I suspected first Ipy—but Ipy is dead, so that suspicion was false. Then I suspected another person—but, on the very day of Ipy's death, yet a third idea came to me. . . ."

She paused.

"Are Hori and Kameni in the house? Send for them here—yes, and Renisenb too from the kitchen. And Kait and Yahmose. I have something to say and all the house should hear it."

II

Esa looked round at the assembled family. She met Yahmose's grave and gentle glance, Kameni's ready smile, the frightened enquiry in Renisenb's eyes, the placid incurious glance of Kait, the quiet inscrutability of Hori's thoughtful gaze, the irritable fear in Imhotep's twitching face and the avid curiosity and—yes—pleasure in Henet's eyes.

She thought: "Their faces tell me nothing. They show only the outward emotion. Yet surely, if I am right, there must be *some* betrayal."

Aloud she said:

"I have something to say to you all—but first I will speak only to Henet —here in front of all of you."

Henet's expression changed—the avidity and the pleasure went out of it. She looked frightened. Her voice rose in a shrill protest.

"You suspect me, Esa. I knew it! You will make a case against me and how am I, a poor woman with no great wits, to defend myself? I shall be condemned—condemned unheard."

"Not unheard," said Esa with irony, and saw Hori smile.

Henet went on, her voice growing more and more hysterical:

"I have done nothing . . . I am innocent . . . Imhotep, my dearest master, save me. . . ." She flung herself down and clasped him round the knees. Imhotep began to splutter indignantly, meanwhile patting Henet's head.

"Really, Esa, I protest— This is disgraceful. . . ."

Esa cut him short.

"I have made no accusation. I do not accuse without proof. I ask only that Henet shall explain to us here the meaning of certain things she has said."

"I have said nothing—nothing at all. . . ."

"Oh, yes, you have," said Esa. "These are words I heard with my own ears—and my ears are sharp even if my eyes are dim. You said that you knew something about Hori. Now what is it that you know about Hori?"

Hori looked slightly surprised.

"Yes, Henet," he said. "What do you know about me? Let us have it."

Henet sat back on her haunches and wiped her eyes. She looked sullen and defiant.

"I know nothing," she said. "What should I know?"

"That is what we are waiting for you to tell us," said Hori.

Henet shrugged her shoulders.

"I was just talking. I meant nothing."

Esa said:

"I will repeat to you your own words. You said that we all despised you, but that you knew a lot of what was going on in this house—and that you saw more than many clever people saw.

"And then you said this—that when Hori met you, he looked at you as though you didn't exist, as though he saw something behind you—*something that wasn't there.*"

"He always looks like that," said Henet sullenly. "I might be an insect, the way he looks at me—something that practically doesn't matter."

Esa said slowly:

"That phrase has remained in my mind—something behind—*something that wasn't there.* Henet said, 'He should have looked *at* me.' And she went on to speak of Satipy—yes, of Satipy—and of how Satipy was clever, but where was Satipy now? . . ."

Esa looked round.

"Does that mean nothing to any of you? Think of Satipy—Satipy who is dead. . . . And remember one should look *at* a person—not at something that isn't there. . . ."

There was a moment's dead silence and then Henet screamed. It was a high, thin scream—a scream, it would seem, of sheer terror. She cried out incoherently:

"I didn't— Save me—master. Don't let her . . . I've said nothing—nothing."

Imhotep's pent-up rage burst out.

"This is unpardonable," he roared. "I will not have this poor woman terrified and accused. What have you against her? By your own words, nothing at all."

Yahmose joined in without his usual timidity:

"My father is right. If you have a definite accusation to bring against Henet, bring it."

"I do not accuse her," said Esa slowly.

She leaned on her stick. Her figure seemed to have shrunk. She spoke slowly and heavily.

Yahmose turned with authority to Henet.

"Esa is not accusing you of causing the evils that have happened, but if I understand her rightly, she thinks that you have certain knowledge which you are withholding. Therefore, Henet, if there is anything you know, about Hori or another, now is the time to speak. Here, before us all. Speak. What knowledge have you?"

Henet shook her head.

"None."

"Be very sure of what you are saying, Henet. Knowledge is dangerous."

"I know nothing. I swear it. I swear it by the Nine Gods of the Ennead, by the Goddess Maat, by Re himself."

Henet was trembling. Her voice had none of its usual whining affected quality. It sounded awed and sincere.

Esa gave a deep sigh. Her figure bent forward. She murmured:

"Help me back to my room."

Hori and Renisenb came quickly to her.

Esa said:

"Not you, Renisenb. I will have Hori."

She leaned on him as he helped her from the room towards her own quarters. Glancing up at him she saw his face was stern and unhappy.

She murmured:

"Well, Hori?"

"You have been unwise, Esa; very unwise."

"I had to know."

"Yes—but you have taken a terrible risk."

"I see. So you too think the same?"

"I have thought so for some time, but there is no proof—no shadow of proof. And even now, Esa, *you* have no *proof*. It is all in your mind."

"It is enough that I *know*."

"It may be too much."

"What do you mean? Oh, yes, of course."

"Guard yourself, Esa. From now on you are in danger."

"We must try to act quickly."

"That, yes. But what can we do? There must be proof."

"I know."

They could say no more. Esa's little maid came running to her mistress. Hori relinquished her to the girl's care and turned away. His face was grave and perplexed.

The little maid chattered and fussed round Esa, but Esa hardly noticed her. She felt old and ill and cold. . . . Once again she saw that intent circle of faces watching her as she spoke.

Only a look—a momentary flash of fear and understanding. Could she have been wrong? Was she so sure of what she had seen? After all, her eyes were dim. . . .

Yes, she was sure. It was less an expression than the sudden tension of a whole body—a hardening—a rigidity. To one person, and one person only, her rambling words had made sense—that deadly, unerring sense which is truth. . . .

CHAPTER XIX

Second Month of Summer, 15th Day

I

"Now THAT THE matter is laid before you, Renisenb, what have you to say?"

Renisenb looked doubtfully from her father to Yahmose. Her head felt dull and bemused.

"I do not know."

The words fell from her lips tonelessly.

"Under ordinary conditions," went on Imhotep, "there would be plenty of time for discussion. I have other kinsmen, and we could select and reject until we settled upon the most suitable as a husband for you. But as it is, life is uncertain—yes, life is uncertain."

His voice faltered. He went on:

"That is how the matter stands, Renisenb. Death is facing all three of us today. Yahmose, yourself, myself. At which of us will the peril strike next? Therefore it behooves me to put my affairs in order. If anything should happen to Yahmose, you, my only daughter, will need a man to stand by your side and share your inheritance and perform such duties of my estate as cannot be administered by a woman. For who knows at what moment I may be taken from you? The trusteeship and guardianship of Sobek's children, I have arranged in my will, shall be administered by Hori if Yahmose is no longer alive—also the guardianship of Yahmose's children —since that is his wish—eh, Yahmose?"

Yahmose nodded.

"Hori has always been very close to me. He is as one of my own family."

"Quite, quite," said Imhotep. "But the fact remains he is *not* of the family. Now Kameni is. Therefore, all things considered, he is the best husband available at the moment for Renisenb. So what do you say, Renisenb?"

"I do not know," Renisenb repeated again.

She felt a terrible lassitude.

"He is handsome and pleasing, you will agree?"

"Oh, yes."

"But you do not want to marry him?" Yahmose asked gently.

Renisenb threw her brother a grateful glance. He was so resolved that she should not be hurried or badgered into doing what she did not want to do.

"I really do not know what I want to do." She hurried on: "It is stupid, I know, but I am stupid today. It is—it is the strain under which we are living."

"With Kameni at your side you will feel protected," said Imhotep.

Yahmose asked his father:

"Have you considered Hori as a possible husband for Renisenb?"

"Well, yes, it is a possibility. . . ."

"His wife died when he was still a young man. Renisenb knows him well and likes him."

Renisenb sat in a dream while the two men talked. This was her marriage they were discussing, and Yahmose was trying to help her to choose what she herself wanted, but she felt as lifeless as Teti's wooden doll.

Presently she said abruptly, interrupting their speech without even hearing what they were saying:

"I will marry Kameni since you think it is a good thing."

Imhotep gave an exclamation of satisfaction and hurried out of the hall. Yahmose came over to his sister. He laid a hand on her shoulder.

"Do you want this marriage, Renisenb? Will you be happy?"

"Why should I not be happy? Kameni is handsome and gay and kind."

"I know." Yahmose still looked dissatisfied and doubtful. "But your happiness is important, Renisenb. You must not let my father rush you into something you do not want. You know how he is."

"Oh, yes, yes, when he gets an idea into his head we all have to give way to it."

"Not necessarily." Yahmose spoke with firmness. "I will not give way here unless you wish it."

"Oh, Yahmose, you never stand out against our father."

"But I will in this case. He cannot force me to agree with him and I shall not do so."

Renisenb looked up at him. How resolute and determined his usually undecided face was looking!

"You are good to me, Yahmose," she said gratefully. "But indeed I am not yielding to compulsion. The old life here, the life I was so pleased to come back to, has passed away. Kameni and I will make a new life together and live as a good brother and sister should."

"If you are sure—"

"I am sure," said Renisenb, and smiling at him affectionately, she went out of the hall onto the porch.

From there she crossed the courtyard. By the edge of the lake Kameni was playing with Teti. Renisenb drew near very quietly and watched them whilst they were still unaware of her approach. Kameni, merry as ever, seemed to be enjoying the game as much as the child did. Renisenb's heart warmed to him. She thought: "He will make a good father to Teti."

Then Kameni turned his head and saw her and stood upright with a laugh.

"We have made Teti's doll a ka-priest," he said. "And he is making the offerings and attending to the ceremonies at the Tomb."

"His name is Meriptah," said Teti. She was very serious. "He has two children and a scribe like Hori."

Kameni laughed.

"Teti is very intelligent," he said. "And she is strong and beautiful too."

His eyes went from the child to Renisenb and in their caressing glance Renisenb read the thought in his mind—of the children that she would one day bear him.

It sent a slight thrill through her—yet at the same time a sudden piercing regret. She would have liked in that moment to have seen in his eyes only her own image. She thought: "Why cannot it be only Renisenb he sees?"

Then the feeling passed and she smiled at him gently.

"My father has spoken to me," she said.

"And you consent?"

She hesitated a moment before she answered:

"I consent."

The final word was spoken; that was the end. It was all settled. She wished she did not feel so tired and numb.

"Renisenb?"

"Yes, Kameni."

"Will you sail with me on the River in a pleasure boat? That is a thing I have always wanted to do with you."

Odd that he should say that. The very first moment she had seen him she had thought of a square sail and the River and Khay's laughing face. And now she had forgotten Khay's face and in the place of it, against the sail and the River, it would be Kameni who sat and laughed into her eyes.

That was death. That was what death did to you. "I felt this," you said. "I felt that"—but you only said it, you did not now feel anything. The dead were dead. There was no such thing as remembrance. . . .

Yes, but there was Teti. There were life and the renewing of life, as the waters of the yearly inundation swept away the old and prepared the soil for the new crops.

What had Kait said: "The women of the household must stand together"? What was she, after all, but a woman of a household—whether Renisenb or another, what matter? . . .

Then she heard Kameni's voice—urgent, a little troubled.

"What are you thinking, Renisenb? You go so far away sometimes. . . . Will you come with me on the River?"

"Yes, Kameni, I will come with you."

"We will take Teti too."

II

It was like a dream, Renisenb thought—the boat and the sail and Kameni and herself and Teti. They had escaped from death and the fear of death. This was the beginning of new life.

Kameni spoke and she answered as though in a trance. . . .

"This is my life," she thought, "there is no escape. . . ."

Then, perplexed: "But why do I say to myself 'escape'? What place is there to which I could fly?"

And again there rose before her eyes the little rock chamber beside the Tomb and herself sitting there with one knee drawn up and her chin resting on her hand. . . .

She thought: "But that was something outside life. *This* is life—and there is no escape now until death. . . ."

Kameni moored the boat and she stepped ashore. He lifted Teti out. The child clung to him and her hand at his neck broke the string of an amulet he wore. It fell at Renisenb's feet. She picked it up. It was an Ankh sign of electrum and gold.

She gave a little regretful cry.

"It is bent. I am sorry. Be careful"—as Kameni took it from her—"it may break."

But his strong fingers, bending it still further, snapped it deliberately in two.

"Oh, what have you done?"

"Take half, Renisenb, and I will take the other. It shall be a sign between us—that we are halves of the same whole."

He held it out to her, and just as she stretched out her hand to take it, something clicked in her brain and she drew in her breath sharply.

"What is it, Renisenb?"

"*Nofret.*"

"What do you mean—*Nofret?*"

Renisenb spoke with swift certainty.

"The broken amulet in Nofret's jewel box. It was *you* who gave it to her. . . . *You and Nofret.* . . . I see everything now. Why she was so unhappy. And I know who put the jewel box in my room. I know everything. . . . Do not lie to me, Kameni. I tell you, I *know*."

Kameni made no protest. He stood looking at her steadily and his gaze did not falter. When he spoke, his voice was grave and for once there was no smile on his face.

"I shall not lie to you, Renisenb."

He waited a moment, frowning a little as though trying to arrange his thoughts.

"In a way, Renisenb, I am glad that you do know—though it is not quite as you think."

"You gave the broken amulet to her—as you would have given it to me—as a sign that you were halves of the same whole. Those were your words."

"You are angry, Renisenb. I am glad because that shows that you love me. But all the same, I must make you understand. I did not give the amulet to Nofret. *She* gave it to *me*. . . ."

He paused.

"Perhaps you do not believe me, but it is true. I swear that it is true."

Renisenb said slowly:

"I will not say that I do not believe you. . . . That may very well be true."

Nofret's dark, unhappy face rose up before her eyes.

Kameni was going on, eagerly, boyishly . . .

"Try to understand, Renisenb. Nofret was very beautiful. I was flattered and pleased. Who would not be? But I never really loved her—"

Renisenb felt an odd pang of pity. No, Kameni had not loved Nofret—but Nofret had loved Kameni—had loved him despairingly and bitterly. It was at just this spot on the Nile bank that she had spoken to Nofret that morning, offering her friendship and affection. She remembered only too well the dark tide of hate and misery that had emanated from the girl then. The cause of it was clear enough now. Poor Nofret—the concubine of a fussy, elderly man—eating her heart out for love of a gay, careless, handsome young man who had cared little or nothing for her.

Kameni was going on eagerly:

"Do you not understand, Renisenb, that as soon as I came here, I saw you and loved you? That from that moment I thought of no one else? Nofret saw it plainly enough."

Yes, Renisenb thought, Nofret had seen it. Nofret had hated her from that moment—and Renisenb did not feel inclined to blame her.

"I did not even want to write the letter to your father. I did not want to have anything to do with Nofret's schemes any more. But it was difficult —you must try to realise that it was difficult."

"Yes, yes." Renisenb spoke impatiently. "All that does not matter. It is only Nofret that matters. She was very unhappy. She loved you, I think, very much."

"Well, I did not love her." Kameni spoke impatiently.

"You are cruel," said Renisenb.

"No, I am a man, that is all. If a woman chooses to make herself miserable about me, it annoys me, that is the simple truth. I did not want Nofret. I wanted you. Oh, Renisenb, you cannot be angry with me for *that?*"

In spite of herself she smiled.

"Do not let Nofret who is dead make trouble between us who are living. I love you, Renisenb, and you love me and that is all that matters."

Yes, Renisenb thought, that is all that matters. . . .

She looked at Kameni, who stood with his head a little on one side, a pleading expression on his gay, confident face. He looked very young.

Renisenb thought: "He is right. Nofret is dead and we are alive. I understand her hatred of me now—and I am sorry that she suffered—but it was not my fault. And it was not Kameni's fault that he loved me and not her. These things happen."

Teti, who had been playing on the riverbank, came up and pulled at her mother's hand.

"Shall we go home now? Mother—shall we go home?"

Renisenb gave a deep sigh.

"Yes," she said, "we will go home."

They walked towards the house, Teti running a little way in front of them.

Kameni gave a sigh of satisfaction.

"You are generous, Renisenb, as well as lovely. All is the same as it was between us?"

"Yes, Kameni. All is the same."

He lowered his voice.

"Out there on the River—I was very happy. Were you happy too, Renisenb?"

"Yes, I was happy."

"You looked happy. But you looked as though you were thinking of something very far away. I want you to think of *me*."

"I was thinking of you."

He took her hand and she did not draw it away. He sang very softly under his breath:

"*My sister is like the persea tree. . . .*"

He felt her hand tremble in his, and heard the quickened pace of her breathing, and was satisfied at last. . . .

III

Renisenb called Henet to her room.

Henet, hurrying in, came to an abrupt stop as she saw Renisenb standing by the open jewel box with the broken amulet in her hand. Renisenb's face was stern and angry.

"You put this jewel box in my room, didn't you, Henet? You wanted me to find that amulet. You wanted me one day—"

"To find out who had the other half? I see you have found out. Well, it's always as well to know, isn't it, Renisenb?"

Henet laughed spitefully.

"You wanted the knowledge to hurt me," said Renisenb, her anger still at white heat. "You like hurting people, don't you, Henet? You never say anything straight out. You wait and wait—until the best moment comes. You hate us all, don't you? You always have."

"The things you're saying, Renisenb! I'm sure you don't mean them!"

But there was no whine in Henet's voice now, only a sly triumph.

"You wanted to make trouble between me and Kameni. Well, there is no trouble."

"That's very nice and forgiving of you, I'm sure, Renisenb. You're quite different from Nofret, aren't you?"

"Do not let us talk of Nofret."

"No, better not, perhaps. Kameni's lucky as well as being good-looking, isn't he? It was lucky for him, I mean, that Nofret died when she did. She could have made a lot of trouble for him—with your father. She wouldn't have liked his marrying you—no, she wouldn't have liked it at all. In fact, I think she would have found some way of stopping it. I'm quite sure she would."

Renisenb looked at her with cold dislike.

"There is always poison in your tongue, Henet. It stings like a scorpion. But you cannot make me unhappy."

"Well, that's splendid, isn't it? You must be very much in love. Oh, he's a handsome young man is Kameni—and he knows how to sing a very pretty love song. He'll always get what he wants, never fear. I admire him, I really do. He always seems so simple and straightforward."

"What are you trying to say, Henet?"

"I'm just telling you that I admire Kameni. And I'm quite sure that he *is* simple and straightforward. It's not put on. The whole thing is quite like one of those tales the storytellers in the bazaars recite. The poor young scribe marrying the master's daughter and sharing the inheritance with her and living happily ever afterwards. Wonderful, what good luck a handsome young man always has."

"I am right," said Renisenb. "You do hate us."

"Now how can you say that, Renisenb, when you know how I've slaved for you all ever since your mother died?"

But there was still the evil triumph in Henet's voice rather than the customary whine.

Renisenb looked down again at the jewel box and suddenly another certainty came into her mind.

"It was *you* who put the gold lion necklace in this box. Don't deny it, Henet. I know, I tell you."

Henet's sly triumph died. She looked suddenly frightened.

"I couldn't help it, Renisenb. I was afraid. . . ."

"What do you mean—afraid?"

Henet came a step nearer and lowered her voice.

"*She* gave it me—Nofret, I mean. Oh, some time before she died. She gave me one or two—presents. Nofret was generous, you know. Oh, yes, she was generous."

"I dare say she paid you well."

"That's not a nice way of putting it, Renisenb. But I'm telling you all about it. She gave me the gold lion necklace and an amethyst clasp and one or two other things. And then, when that boy came out with his story of having seen a woman with that necklace on—well, I was afraid. I thought maybe they'd think that it was I who poisoned Yahmose's wine. So I put the necklace in the box."

"Is that the truth, Henet? Do you ever speak the truth?"

"I swear it's the truth, Renisenb. I was afraid. . . ."

Renisenb looked at her curiously.

"You're shaking, Henet. You look as though you were afraid now."

"Yes, I am afraid. . . . I've reason to be."

"Why? Tell me."

Henet licked her thin lips. She glanced sideways behind her. Her eyes came back like a hunted animal's.

"Tell me," said Renisenb.

Henet shook her head. She said in an uncertain voice:

"There's nothing to tell."

"You know too much, Henet. You've always known too much. You've enjoyed it, but now it's dangerous. That's it, isn't it?"

Henet shook her head again. Then she laughed maliciously.

"You wait, Renisenb. One day I shall hold the whip in this house—and crack it. Wait and see."

Renisenb drew herself up.

"You will not harm *me*, Henet. My mother will not let you harm me."

Henet's face changed—the eyes burned.

"I hated your mother," she said. "I always hated her. . . . And you who have her eyes—and her voice—her beauty and her arrogance—I hate *you*, Renisenb."

Renisenb laughed.

"And at last—I've made you say it!"

CHAPTER XX

Second Month of Summer, 15th Day

I

OLD ESA LIMPED wearily into her room.

She was perplexed and very weary. Age, she realised, was at last taking toll of her. So far she had acknowledged her weariness of body but had •

been conscious of no weariness of mind. But now she had to admit that the strain of remaining mentally alert was taxing her bodily resources.

If she knew now, as she believed she did, from what quarter danger impended— Yet that knowledge permitted of no mental relaxation. Instead she had to be more than ever on her guard since she had deliberately drawn attention to herself. Proof—proof—she must get proof. But how?

It was there, she realised, that her age told against her. She was too tired to improvise—to make the mental creative effort. All she was capable of was defence—to remain alert, watchful, guarding herself.

For the killer—she had no illusions about that—would be quite ready to kill again.

Well, she had no intention of being the next victim. Poison, she felt sure, was the vehicle that would be employed. Violence was not conceivable, since she was never alone, but was always surrounded by servants. So it would be poison. Well, she could counter that. Renisenb should cook her food and bring it to her. She had a wine stand and jar brought to her room, and after a slave had tasted it, she waited twenty-four hours to make sure that no evil results followed. She made Renisenb share her food and her wine—although she had no fear for Renisenb—yet. It might be that there was no fear for Renisenb—ever. But of that one could not be sure.

Between whiles she sat motionless, driving her weary brain to devise means of proving the truth, or watching her little maid starching and pleating her linen dresses, or restringing necklaces and bracelets.

This evening she was very weary. She had joined Imhotep at his request to discuss the question of Renisenb's marriage before he himself spoke to his daughter.

Imhotep, shrunken and fretful, was a shadow of his former self. His manner had lost its pomposity and assurance. He leaned now on his mother's indomitable will and determination.

As for Esa, she had been fearful—very fearful—of saying the wrong thing. Lives might hang on an injudicious word.

Yes, she said at last, the idea of marriage was wise. And there was no time to go far afield for a husband amongst more important members of the family clan. After all, the female line was the important one—her husband would be only the administrator of the inheritance that came to Renisenb and Renisenb's children.

So it came to a question of Hori—a man of integrity, of old and long-proved friendship, the son of a small landowner whose estate had adjoined their own—or young Kameni, with his claims of cousinship.

Esa had weighed the matter carefully before speaking. A false word now—and disaster might result.

Then she had made her answer, stressing it with the force of her indomitable personality. Kameni, she said, was undoubtedly the husband for Renisenb. Their declarations and the necessary attendant festivities—much curtailed owing to the recent bereavements—might take place in a week's time. That is, if Renisenb was willing. Kameni was a fine young man—together they would raise strong children. Moreover, the two of them loved each other.

Well, Esa thought, she had cast her die. The thing would be pegged out now on the gaming board. It was out of her hands. She had done what she thought expedient. If it was hazardous—well, Esa liked a match at the gaming board quite as well as Ipy had. Life was not a matter of safety—it must be hazarded to win the game.

She looked suspiciously round her room when she returned to it. Particularly she examined the big wine jar. It was covered over and sealed as she had left it. She always sealed it when she left the room, and the seal hung safely round her neck.

Yes—she was taking no risks of that kind. Esa chuckled with malicious satisfaction. Not so easy to kill an old woman. Old women knew the value of life—and knew most of the tricks too.

Tomorrow— She called her little maid.

"Where is Hori? Do you know?"

The girl replied that she thought Hori was up at the Tomb in the rock chamber.

Esa nodded satisfaction.

"Go up to him there. Tell him that tomorrow morning, when Imhotep and Yahmose are out on the cultivation, taking Kameni with them for the counting, and when Kait is at the lake with the children, he is to come to me here. Have you understood that? Repeat it."

The little maid did so, and Esa sent her off.

Yes, her plan was satisfactory. The consultation with Hori would be quite private, since she would send Henet on an errand to the weaving sheds. She would warn Hori of what was to come and they could speak freely together.

When the black girl returned with the message that Hori would do as she said, Esa gave a sigh of relief.

Now, these things settled, her weariness spread over her like a flood. She told the girl to bring the pot of sweet-smelling ointment and massage her limbs.

The rhythm soothed her, and the unguent eased the aching of her bones.

She stretched herself out at last, her head on the wooden pillow, and slept—her fears for the moment allayed.

She woke much later with a strange sensation of coldness. Her feet, her hands, were numbed and dead. . . . It was like a constriction stealing all over her body. She could feel it numbing her brain, paralysing her will, slowing down the beat of her heart.

She thought: "This is death. . . ."

A strange death—death unheralded, with no warning signs.

This, she thought, is how the old die. . . .

And then a surer conviction came to her. This was *not* natural death! This was the enemy striking out of the darkness.

Poison . . .

But how? When? All she had eaten, all she had drunk—tested, secured —there had been no loophole of error.

Then how? When?

With her last feeble flickers of intelligence, Esa sought to penetrate the mystery. She must know—she *must*—before she died.

She felt the pressure increasing on her heart—the deadly coldness—the slow painful indrawing of her breath.

How had the enemy done this thing?

And suddenly, from the past, a fleeting memory came to aid her understanding. The shaven skin of a lamb—a lump of smelling grease—an experiment of her father's—to show that some poisons could be absorbed by the skin. Wool fat—unguents made of wool fat.

That was how the enemy had reached her. Her pot of sweet-smelling unguent, so necessary to an Egyptian woman. The poison had been in that. . . .

And tomorrow—Hori—he would not know—she could not tell him. . . . It was too late.

In the morning a frightened little slave girl went running through the house crying out that her lady had died in her sleep.

II

Imhotep stood looking down on Esa's dead body. His face was sorrowful, but not suspicious.

His mother, he said, had died naturally enough of old age.

"She was old," he said. "Yes, she was old. It was doubtless time for her to go to Osiris, and all our troubles and sorrows have hastened the end. But it seems to have come peacefully enough. Thank Re in his mercy that here is a death unaided by man or by evil spirit. There is no violence here. See how peaceful she looks."

Renisenb wept and Yahmose comforted her. Henet went about sighing and shaking her head, and saying what a loss Esa would be and how devoted she, Henet, had always been to her. Kameni checked his singing and showed a proper mourning face.

Hori came and stood looking down at the dead woman. It was the hour of her summons to him. He wondered what, exactly, she had meant to say.

She had had something definite to tell him.

Now he would never know.

But he thought, perhaps, that he could guess. . . .

CHAPTER XXI

Second Month of Summer, 16th Day

I

"Hori—was she killed?"

"I think so, Renisenb."

"How?"

"I do not know."

"But she was so careful." The girl's voice was distressed and bewildered. "She was always on the watch. She took every precaution. Everything she ate and drank was proved and tested."

"I know, Renisenb. But all the same, I think she was killed."

"And she was the wisest of us all—the cleverest! She was so sure that no harm could befall her. Hori, it *must* be magic! Evil magic, the spell of an evil spirit."

"You believe that because it is the easiest thing to believe. People are like that. But Esa herself would not have believed it. If she knew—before she died, and did not die in her sleep—she knew it was a living person's work."

"And she knew whose?"

"Yes. She had shown her suspicion too openly. She became a danger to the enemy. The fact that she died proves that her suspicion was correct."

"And she told you—who it was?"

"No," said Hori. "She did not tell me. She never mentioned a name.

Nevertheless, her thought and my thought were, I am convinced, the same."

"Then you must tell *me*, Hori, so that I may be on my guard."

"No, Renisenb, I care too much for your safety to do that."

"*Am* I so safe?"

Hori's face darkened. He said: "No, Renisenb, you are not safe. No one is safe. But you are much safer than if you were assured of the truth—for then you would become a definite menace, to be removed at once whatever the risk."

"What about you, Hori? *You* know."

He corrected her. "I *think* I know. But I have said nothing and shown nothing. Esa was unwise. She spoke out. She showed the direction in which her thoughts were tending. She should not have done that— I told her so afterwards."

"But you—Hori . . . If anything happens to you . . ."

She stopped. She was aware of Hori's eyes looking into hers.

Grave, intent, seeing straight into her mind and heart. . . .

He took her hands in his and held them lightly.

"Do not fear for me, little Renisenb. . . . All will be well."

Yes, she thought, all will indeed be well if Hori says so. Strange, that feeling of content, of peace, of clear singing happiness—as lovely and as remote as the far distance seen from the Tomb—a distance in which there was no clamour of human demands and restrictions.

Suddenly, almost harshly, she heard herself saying:

"I am to marry Kameni."

Hori let her hands go—quietly and quite naturally.

"I know, Renisenb."

"They—my father—they think it is the best thing."

"I know."

He moved away.

The courtyard walls seemed to come nearer, the voices within the house and from the cornbins outside sounded louder and noisier.

Renisenb had only one thought in her mind: "Hori is going. . . ."

She called to him timidly:

"Hori, where are you going?"

"Out to the fields with Yahmose. There is much work there to be done and recorded. The reaping is nearly finished."

"And Kameni?"

"Kameni comes with us."

Renisenb cried out: "I am afraid here. Yes, even in daylight with the servants all round and Re sailing across the heavens, I am afraid."

He came quickly back.

"Do not be afraid, Renisenb. I swear to you that you need not be afraid. Not today."

"But after today?"

"Today is enough to live through—and I swear to you you are not in danger today."

Renisenb looked at him and frowned.

"But we *are* in danger? Yahmose, my father, myself? It is not *I* who am threatened first . . . is that what you think?"

"Try not to think about it, Renisenb. I am doing all I can, though it may appear to you that I am doing nothing."

"I see—" Renisenb looked at him thoughtfully. "Yes, I see. It is to be Yahmose first. The enemy has tried twice with poison and failed. There is to be a third attempt. That is why you will be close beside him—to protect him. And after that it will be the turn of my father and myself. Who is there who hates our family so much that—"

"Hush. You would do well not to talk of these things. Trust me, Renisenb. Try to banish fear from your mind."

Renisenb threw her head back. She faced him proudly.

"I do trust you, Hori. You will not let me die. . . . I love life very much and I do not want to leave it."

"You shall not leave it, Renisenb."

"Nor you either, Hori."

"Nor I either."

They smiled at each other and then Hori went away to find Yahmose.

II

Renisenb sat back on her haunches watching Kait.

Kait was helping the children to model toys out of clay, using the water of the lake. Her fingers were busy kneading and shaping, and her voice encouraged the two small serious boys at their task. Kait's face was the same as usual, affectionate, plain, expressionless. The surrounding atmosphere of violent death and constant fear seemed to affect her not at all. . . .

Hori had bidden Renisenb not to think, but with the best will in the world Renisenb could not obey. If Hori knew the enemy, if Esa had known the enemy, then there was no reason why she should not know the enemy too. She might be safer not knowing, but no human creature could be content to have it that way. She wanted to know.

And it must be very easy—very easy indeed. Her father, clearly, could not desire to kill his own children. So that left—who did it leave? It left, starkly and uncompromisingly, two people—Kait and Henet.

Women, both of them . . .

And surely with no reason for killing . . .

Yet Henet hated them all . . . Yes, undoubtedly Henet hated them. She had admitted hating Renisenb. So why should she not hate the others equally?

Renisenb tried to project herself into the dim, tortured recesses of Henet's brain. Living here all these years, working, protesting her devotion, lying, spying, making mischief . . . Coming here, long ago, as the poor relative of a great and beautiful lady. Seeing that lovely lady happy with husband and children. Repudiated by her own husband, her only child dead . . . Yes, that might be the way of it. Like a wound from a spear thrust that Renisenb had once seen. It had healed quickly over the surface, but beneath evil matters had festered and raged and the arm had swollen and had gone hard to the touch. And then the physician had come and, with a suitable incantation, had plunged a small knife into the hard, swollen, distorted limb. It had been like the breaking down of an irrigation dyke. A great stream of evil-smelling stuff had come welling out. . . .

That, perhaps, was like Henet's mind. Sorrow and injury smoothed over too quickly—and festering poison beneath, ever swelling in a great tide of hate and venom.

But did Henet hate Imhotep too? Surely not. For years she had fluttered round him, fawning on him, flattering him. . . . He believed in her implicitly. Surely that devotion could not be wholly feigned?

And if she were devoted to him, could she deliberately inflict all this sorrow and loss upon him?

Ah, but suppose she hated him too—had always hated him? Had flattered him deliberately with a view to bringing out his weaknesses? Supposing Imhotep was the one she hated *most*? Then to a distorted, evil-ridden mind, what better pleasure could there be than this—to let him see his children die off one by one?

"What is the matter, Renisenb?"

Kait was staring at her.

"You look so strange."

Renisenb stood up.

"I feel as though I were going to vomit," she said.

In a sense it was true enough. The picture she had been conjuring up induced in her a strong feeling of nausea. Kait accepted the words at their face value.

"You have eaten too many green dates—or perhaps the fish had turned."

"No, no, it is nothing I have eaten. It is the terrible thing we are living through."

"Oh, that."

Kait's disclaimer was so nonchalant that Renisenb stared at her.

"But, Kait, are you not afraid?"

"No, I do not think so." Kait considered. "If anything happens to Imhotep, the children will be protected by Hori. Hori is honest. He will guard their inheritance for them."

"Yahmose will do that."

"Yahmose will die too."

"Kait, you say that so calmly. Do you not mind at all? I mean, that my father and Yahmose should die?"

Kait considered a moment or two. Then she shrugged her shoulders.

"We are two women together. Let us be honest. Imhotep I have always considered tyrannical and unfair. He behaved outrageously in the matter of his concubine—letting himself be persuaded by her to disinherit his own flesh and blood. I have never liked Imhotep. As to Yahmose—he is nothing. Satipy ruled him in every way. Lately, since she is gone, he takes authority on himself, gives orders. He would always prefer his children before mine—that is natural. So, if he is to die, it is as well for my children that it should be so—that is how I see it. Hori has no children and he is just. All these happenings have been upsetting—but I have been thinking lately that very likely they are all for the best."

"You can talk like that, Kait—so calmly, so coldly—when your own husband, whom you loved, was the first to be killed?"

A faint expression of some indefinable nature passed over Kait's face. She gave Renisenb a glance which seemed to contain a certain scornful irony.

"You are very like Teti sometimes, Renisenb. Really, one would swear, no older!"

"You do not mourn for Sobek." Renisenb spoke the words slowly. "No, I have noticed that."

"Come, Renisenb, I fulfilled all the conventions. I know how a newly made widow should behave."

"Yes—that was all there was to it. . . . So—it means—that you did not love Sobek?"

Kait shrugged her shoulders.

"Why should I?"

"Kait! He was your husband—he gave you children."

Kait's expression softened. She looked down at the two small boys engrossed with the clay and then to where Ankh was rolling about chanting to herself and waving her little legs.

"Yes, he gave me my children. For that I thank him. But what was he, after all? A handsome braggart—a man who was always going to other women. He did not take a sister, decently, into the household, some modest person who would have been useful to us all. No, he went to ill-famed houses, spending much copper and gold there, drinking too and asking for all the most expensive dancing girls. It was fortunate that Imhotep kept him as short as he did and that he had to account so closely for the sales he made on the estate. What love and respect should I have for a man like that? And what are men anyway? They are necessary to breed children, that is all. But the strength of the race is in the women. It is *we*, Renisenb, who hand down to our children all that is ours. As for men, let them breed and die early. . . ."

The scorn and contempt in Kait's voice rose in a note like some musical instrument. Her strong, ugly face was transfigured.

Renisenb thought with dismay:

"Kait is strong. If she is stupid, it is with a stupidity that is satisfied with itself. She hates and despises men. I should have known. Once before I caught a glimpse of this—this *menacing* quality. Yes, Kait is strong—"

Unthinkingly, Renisenb's gaze fell to Kait's hands. They were squeezing and kneading clay—strong, muscular hands, and as Renisenb watched them pushing down the clay, she thought of Ipy and of strong hands pushing his head down into the water and holding it there inexorably. Yes, Kait's hands could have done that. . . .

The little girl, Ankh, rolled over onto a thorny spice and set up a wail. Kait rushed to her. She picked her up, holding her to her breast, crooning over her. Her face now was all love and tenderness.

Henet came running out from the porch.

"Is anything wrong? The child yelled so loud. I thought perhaps—"

She paused, disappointed. Her eager, mean, spiteful face, hoping for some catastrophe, fell.

Renisenb looked from one woman to the other.

Hate in one face. Love in the other. Which, she wondered, was the more terrible?

III

"Yahmose, be careful of Kait."

"Of Kait?" Yahmose showed his astonishment. "My dear Renisenb—"

"I tell you, she is dangerous."

"Our quiet Kait? She has always been a meek, submissive woman, not very clever—"

Renisenb interrupted him.

"She is neither meek nor submissive. I am afraid of her, Yahmose. I want you to be on your guard."

"Against Kait?" He was still incredulous. "I can hardly see Kait dealing out death all round. She would not have the brains."

"I do not think that it is brains that are concerned. A knowledge of poisons—that is all that has been needed. And you know that such knowledge is often found amongst certain families. They hand it down from mother to daughter. They brew these concoctions themselves from potent herbs. It is the kind of lore that Kait might easily have. She brews medicines for the children when they are ill, you know."

"Yes, that is true." Yahmose spoke thoughtfully.

"Henet too is an evil woman," went on Renisenb.

"Henet—yes. We have never liked her. In fact, but for my father's protection—"

"Our father is deceived in her," said Renisenb.

"That may well be." Yahmose added in a matter-of-fact tone: "She flatters him."

Renisenb looked at him for a moment in surprise. It was the first time she had ever heard Yahmose utter a sentence containing criticism of Imhotep. He had always seemed overawed by his father.

But now, she realised, Yahmose was gradually taking the lead. Imhotep had aged by years in the last few weeks. He was incapable now of giving orders, of making decisions. Even his physical activity seemed impaired. He spent long hours staring in front of him, his eyes filmed and abstracted. Sometimes he seemed not to understand what was said to him.

"Do you think that she—" Renisenb stopped. She looked round and began, "Is it she, do you think, who has—who is—?"

Yahmose caught her by the arm.

"Be quiet, Renisenb. These things are better not said—not even whispered."

"Then you too think—"

Yahmose said softly and urgently:

"Say nothing now. We have plans."

CHAPTER XXII

Second Month of Summer, 17th Day

I

THE FOLLOWING DAY was the festival of the new moon. Imhotep was forced to go up to the Tomb to make the offerings. Yahmose begged his father to leave it to him on this occasion, but Imhotep was obdurate. With what seemed now a feeble parody of his old manner, he murmured, "Unless I see to things myself, how can I be sure they are properly done? Have I ever shirked my duties? Have I not provided for all of you, supported you all—"

His voice stopped. "All? *All?* Ah, I forget—my two brave sons—my handsome Sobek—my clever and beloved Ipy—gone from me. Yahmose and Renisenb—my dear son and daughter—you are still with me—but for how long—how long?"

"Many long years, we hope," said Yahmose.

He spoke rather loudly as to a deaf man.

"Eh? What?" Imhotep seemed to have fallen into a coma.

He said suddenly and surprisingly:

"It depends on Henet, does it not? Yes, it depends on Henet."

Yahmose and Renisenb exchanged glances.

Renisenb said gently and clearly:

"I do not understand you, Father."

Imhotep muttered something they did not catch. Then, raising his voice a little, but with dull and vacant eyes, he said:

"Henet understands me. She always has. She knows how great my responsibilities are—how great. Yes, how great. . . . And always ingratitude . . . Therefore there must be retribution. That, I think, is a practice well-established. Presumption must be punished. Henet has always been modest, humble and devoted. She shall be rewarded. . . ."

He drew himself up and said pompously:

"You understand, Yahmose. Henet is to have all she wants. Her commands are to be obeyed!"

"But why is this, Father?"

"Because I say so. Because if what Henet wants is done, there will be no more deaths. . . ."

He nodded his head sagely and went away—leaving Yahmose and Renisenb staring at each other in wonder and alarm.

"What does this mean, Yahmose?"

"I do not know, Renisenb. Sometimes I think my father no longer knows what he does or says."

"No—perhaps not. But I think, Yahmose, that *Henet* knows very well what she is saying and doing. She said to me, only the other day, that it would soon be *she* who would crack the whip in this house."

They looked at each other. Then Yahmose put his hand on Renisenb's arm.

"Do not anger her. You show your feelings too plainly, Renisenb. You heard what my father said? If what Henet wants is done—*there will be no more deaths. . . .*"

II

Henet was crouching down on her haunches in one of the storerooms counting out piles of sheets. They were old sheets, and she held the mark on the corner of one close up to her eyes.

"Ashayet," she murmured. "Ashayet's sheets. Marked with the year she came here—she and I together. . . . That's a long time ago. Do you know, I wonder, what your sheets are being used for now, Ashayet?"

She broke off in the midst of a chuckle and gave a start as a sound made her glance over her shoulder.

It was Yahmose.

"What are you doing, Henet?"

"The embalmers need more sheets. Piles and piles of sheets they've used. Four hundred cubits they used yesterday alone. It's terrible the way these funerals use up the sheeting! We'll have to use these old ones. They're good quality and not much worn. Your mother's sheets, Yahmose. Yes, your mother's sheets. . . ."

"Who said you might take those?"

Henet laughed.

"Imhotep's given everything into my charge. I don't have to ask leave. He trusts poor old Henet. He knows she'll see to everything in the right way. I've seen to most things in this house for a long time. I think—now—I'm going to have my reward!"

"It looks like it, Henet." Yahmose's tone was mild. "My father said"—he paused—"*everything depends on you.*"

"Did he now? Well, that's nice hearing—but perhaps *you* don't think so, Yahmose."

"Well—I'm not quite sure." Yahmose's tone was still mild, but he watched her closely.

"I think you'd better agree with your father, Yahmose. We don't want any more—*trouble*, do we?"

"I don't quite understand. You mean—we don't want any more deaths?"

"There are going to be more deaths, Yahmose. Oh, yes—"

"Who is going to die next, Henet?"

"Why do you think I should know that?"

"Because I think you know a great deal. You knew the other day, for instance, that Ipy was going to die. . . . You are very clever, aren't you, Henet?"

Henet bridled.

"So you're beginning to realise that now! I'm not poor, stupid Henet any longer. I'm the one who *knows*."

"What do you know, Henet?"

Henet's voice changed. It was low and sharp.

"I know that *at last* I can do as I choose in this house. There will be no one to stop me. Imhotep leans upon me already. And *you* will do the same, eh, Yahmose?"

And Renisenb?"

Henet laughed, a malicious, happy chuckle.

"*Renisenb will not be here.*"

"You think it is Renisenb who will die next?"

"What do *you* think, Yahmose?"

"I am waiting to hear what *you* say."

"Perhaps I only meant that Renisenb will marry—and go away."

"What *do* you mean, Henet?"

Henet chuckled.

"Esa once said my tongue was dangerous. Perhaps it is!"

She laughed shrilly, swaying to and fro on her heels.

"Well, Yahmose, what do you say? Am I at last to do as I choose in this house?"

Yahmose studied her for a moment before saying:

"Yes, Henet. You are so clever. You shall do as you choose."

He turned to meet Hori, who was coming from the main hall and who said:

"There you are, Yahmose. Imhotep is awaiting you. It is time to go up to the Tomb."

Yahmose nodded.

"I am coming." He lowered his voice. "Hori—I think Henet is mad—she is definitely afflicted by devils. I begin to believe that *she* has been responsible for all these happenings."

Hori paused a moment before saying in his quiet, detached voice:

"She is a strange woman—and an evil one, I think."

Yahmose lowered his voice still more:

"Hori, I think Renisenb is in danger."

"From Henet?"

"Yes. She has just hinted that Renisenb may be the next to—go."

Imhotep's voice came fretfully:

"Am I to wait all day? What conduct is this? No one considers me any more. No one knows what I suffer. Where is Henet? Henet understands."

From within the storeroom Henet's chuckle of triumph came shrilly.

"Do you hear that, Yahmose? Henet! Henet is the one!"

Yahmose said fiercely:

"Yes, Henet—I understand. You are the powerful one. You and my father and I—we three together. . . ."

Hori went off to find Imhotep. Yahmose spoke a few more words to Henet, who nodded, her face sparkling with malicious triumph.

Then Yahmose joined Hori and Imhotep, apologising for his delay, and the three men went up to the Tomb together.

III

The day passed slowly for Renisenb.

She was restless, passing to and from from the house to the porch, then to the lake and then back again to the house.

At midday Imhotep returned, and after a meal had been served to him, he came out upon the porch and Renisenb joined him.

She sat with her hands clasped round her knees, occasionally looking up at her father's face. It still wore that absent, bewildered expression. Imhotep spoke little. Once or twice he sighed deeply.

Once he roused himself and asked for Henet. But just at that time Henet had gone with linen to the embalmers.

Renisenb asked her father where Hori and Yahmose were.

"Hori has gone out to the far flax fields. There is a tally to be taken there. Yahmose is on the cultivation. It all falls on him now. . . . Alas for Sobek and Ipy. My boys—my handsome boys. . . ."

Renisenb tried quickly to distract him.

"Cannot Kameni oversee the workers?"

"Kameni? Who is Kameni? I have no son of that name."

"Kameni the scribe. Kameni who is to be my husband."

He stared at her.

"You, Renisenb? But you are to marry Khay."

She sighed, but said no more. It seemed cruel to try to bring him back to the present.

After a little while, however, he roused himself and exclaimed suddenly:

"Of course. Kameni! He has gone to give some instructions to the overseer at the brewery. I must go and join him."

He strode away, muttering to himself, but with a resumption of his old manner, so that Renisenb felt a little cheered.

Perhaps this clouding of his brain was only temporary.

She looked round her. There seemed something sinister about the silence of the house and court today. The children were at the far side of the lake. Kait was not with them, and Renisenb wondered where she was.

Then Henet came out onto the porch. She looked round her and then came sidling up to Renisenb. She had resumed her old wheedling, humble manner.

"I've been waiting till I could get you alone, Renisenb."

"Why, Henet?"

Henet lowered her voice.

"I've got a message for you—from Hori."

"What does he say?" Renisenb's voice was eager.

"He asks that you should go up to the Tomb."

"Now?"

"No. Be there an hour before sunset. That was the message. If he is not there then, he asks that you will wait until he comes. It is important, he says."

Henet paused—and then added:

"I was to wait until I got you alone to say this—and no one was to overhear."

Henet glided away again.

Renisenb felt her spirits lightened. She felt glad at the prospect of going up to the peace and quietness of the Tomb. Glad that she would see Hori and be able to talk to him freely. The only thing that surprised her a little was that he should have entrusted his message to Henet.

Nevertheless, malicious though Henet was, she had delivered the message faithfully.

"And why should I fear Henet at any time?" thought Renisenb. "I am stronger than she is."

She drew herself up proudly. She felt young and confident and very much alive. . . .

IV

After giving the message to Renisenb, Henet went once more into the linen storeroom. She was laughing quietly to herself.

She bent over the disordered piles of sheets.

"We'll be needing more of you soon," she said to them gleefully. "Do you hear, Ashayet? I'm the mistress here now and I'm telling you that your linen will bandage yet another body. And whose body is that, do you think? Hee hee! You've not been able to do much about things, have you? You and your mother's brother, the Nomarch! Justice? What justice can you do in *this* world? Answer me that!"

There was a movement behind the bales of linen. Henet half turned her head.

Then a great width of linen was thrown over her, stifling her mouth and nose. An inexorable hand wound the fabric round and round her body, swathing her like a corpse until her struggles ceased. . . .

CHAPTER XXIII

Second Month of Summer, 17th Day

I

RENISENB SAT IN the entrance of the rock chamber staring out at the Nile and lost in a queer dream fantasy of her own.

It seemed to her a very long time since the day when she had first sat here soon after her return to her father's house. That had been the day when she had declared so gaily that everything was unchanged, that all in the home was exactly as it had been when she left it eight years before.

She remembered now how Hori had told her that she herself was not the same Renisenb who had gone away with Khay and how she had answered confidently that she soon would be.

Then Hori had gone on to speak of changes that came from within, of a rottenness that left no outward sign.

She knew now something of what had been in his mind when he said those things. He had been trying to prepare her. She had been so assured, so blind—accepting so easily the outward values of her family.

It had taken Nofret's coming to open her eyes. . . .

Yes, Nofret's coming. It had all hinged on that.

With Nofret had come death. . . .

Whether Nofret had been evil or not, she had certainly brought evil. . . .

And the evil was still in their midst.

For the last time, Renisenb played with the belief that Nofret's spirit was the cause of everything. . . .

Nofret, malicious and dead . . .

Or Henet, malicious and living . . . Henet the despised, the syco-phantic, fawning Henet . . .

Renisenb shivered, stirred, and then slowly rose to her feet.

She could wait for Hori no longer. The sun was on the point of setting. Why, she wondered, had he not come?

She got up, glanced round her, and started to descend the path to the valley below.

It was very quiet at this evening hour. Quiet and beautiful, she thought. What had delayed Hori? If he had come, they would at least have had this hour together. . . .

There would not be many such hours. In the near future, when she was Kameni's wife—

Was she really going to marry Kameni? With a kind of shock Renisenb shook herself free from the mood of dull acquiescence that had held her so long. She felt like a sleeper awakening from a feverish dream. Caught in that stupor of fear and uncertainty, she had assented to whatever had been proposed to her.

But now she was Renisenb again, and if she married Kameni it would be because she wanted to marry him, and not because her family arranged it. Kameni, with his handsome, laughing face! She loved him, didn't she? That was why she was going to marry him.

In this evening hour up here, there were clarity and truth. No con-fusion. She was Renisenb, walking here above the world, serene and un-afraid, herself at last.

Had she not once said to Hori that she must walk down this path alone at the hour of Nofret's death—that whether fear went with her or not, she must still go alone?

Well, she was doing it now. This was just about the hour when she and Satipy had bent over Nofret's body. And it was about this same hour when Satipy in her turn had walked down the path and had suddenly looked back—to see doom overtaking her.

At just about this same point too. What was it that Satipy had heard to make her look suddenly behind her?

Footsteps?

Footsteps . . . but Renisenb heard footsteps now—*following her down the path.*

Her heart gave a sudden leap of fear. It *was* true then! Nofret was behind her, following her. . . .

Fear coursed through her, but her footsteps did not slacken. Nor did they race ahead. She must overcome fear, since there was, in her mind, no evil deed to regret. . . .

She steadied herself, gathered her courage, and, still walking, turned her head.

Then she felt a great throb of relief. It was Yahmose following her. No spirit from the dead, but her own brother. He must have been busied in the offering chamber of the Tomb and have come out of it just after she had passed.

She stopped with a happy little cry.

"Oh, Yahmose, I'm so glad it's you."

He was coming up to her rapidly. She was just beginning another sentence—a recital of her foolish fears—when the words froze on her lips.

This was not the Yahmose she knew—the gentle, kindly brother. His eyes were very bright and he was passing his tongue quickly over dried lips. His hands, held a little in front of his body, were slightly curved, the fingers looking like talons.

He was looking at her, and the look in his eyes was unmistakable. It was the look of a man who had killed and was about to kill again. There was a gloating cruelty, an evil satisfaction in his face.

Yahmose—the hidden enemy was Yahmose! Behind the mask of that gentle, kindly face—*this!*

She had thought that her brother loved her—but there was no love in that inhuman, gloating face.

Renisenb screamed—a faint, hopeless scream.

This, she knew, was death. There was no strength in her to match Yahmose's strength. Here, where Nofret had fallen, where the path was narrow, she too would fall to death. . . .

"Yahmose!" It was a last appeal—in that uttering of his name was the love she had always given to this eldest brother. It pleaded in vain. Yahmose laughed, a soft, inhuman, happy little laugh.

Then he rushed forward, those cruel hands with talons curving as though they longed to fasten round her throat. . . .

Renisenb backed up against the cliff face, her hands outstretched in a vain attempt to ward him off. This was terror—death.

And then she heard a sound, a faint, twanging, musical sound. . . .

Something came singing through the air. Yahmose stopped, swayed, then with a loud cry he pitched forward on his face at her feet. She stared down stupidly at the feather shaft of an arrow.

Then she looked down over the edge—to where Hori stood, the bow still held to his shoulder. . . .

II

"Yahmose . . . Yahmose . . ."

Renisenb, numbed by shock, repeated the name again, and yet again. It was as though she could not believe it. . . .

She was outside the little rock chamber, Hori's arm still round her. She could hardly recollect how he had led her back up the path. She had been only able to repeat her brother's name in that dazed tone of wonder and horror.

Hori said gently:

"Yes, Yahmose. All the time, Yahmose."

"But how? Why? And how *could* it be he? Why, he was poisoned himself. He nearly died."

"No, he ran no risk of dying. He was very careful of how much wine he drank. He sipped enough to make him ill and he exaggerated his symptoms and his pains. It was the one way, he knew, to disarm suspicion."

"But *he* could not have killed Ipy. Why, he was so weak he could not stand on his feet!"

"That, again, was feigned. Do you not remember that Mersu pronounced that once the poison was eliminated, he would regain strength quickly. So he did in reality."

"But *why*, Hori? That is what I cannot make out—why?"

Hori sighed.

"Do you remember, Renisenb, that I talked to you once of the rottenness that comes from within?"

"I remember. Indeed I was thinking of it only this evening."

"You said once that the coming of Nofret brought evil. That was not true. The evil was already here concealed within the hearts of the household. All that Nofret's coming did was to bring it from its hidden place into light. Her presence banished concealment. Kait's gentle motherliness had turned to ruthless egoism for herself and her young. Sobek was no longer the gay and charming young man, but the boastful, dissipated weakling. Ipy was not so much a spoilt, attractive child as a scheming, selfish boy. Through Henet's pretended devotion, the venom began to show clearly. Satipy showed herself as a bully and a coward. Imhotep himself had degenerated into a fussy, pompous tyrant."

"I know—I know." Renisenb's hands went to her eyes. "You need not tell me. I have found out little by little for myself. . . . Why should these things happen? Why should this rottenness come, as you say, working from within?"

Hori shrugged his shoulders.

"Who can tell? It may be that there must always be growth—and that if one does not grow kinder and wiser and greater, then the growth must be the other way, fostering the evil things. Or it may be that the life they all led was too shut in, too folded back upon itself—without breadth or vision. Or it may be that, like a disease of crops, it is contagious, that first one and then another sickened."

"But Yahmose—Yahmose seemed always the same."

"Yes, and that is one reason, Renisenb, why I came to suspect. For the others, by reason of their temperaments, could get relief. But Yahmose has always been timid, easily ruled, and with never enough courage to rebel. He loved Imhotep and worked hard to please him, and Imhotep found him well-meaning but stupid and slow. He despised him. Satipy, too, treated Yahmose with all the scorn of a bullying nature. Slowly his burden of resentment, concealed but deeply felt, grew heavier. The meeker he seemed, the more his inward anger grew.

"And then, just when Yahmose was hoping at last to reap the reward of his industry and diligence, to be recognised and associated with his father, Nofret came. It was Nofret, and perhaps Nofret's beauty, that kindled the final spark. She attacked the manhood of all three brothers. She touched Sobek on the raw by her scorn of him as a fool, she infuriated Ipy by treating him as a truculent child without any claim to manhood, and she showed Yahmose that he was something less than a man in her eyes. It was after Nofret came that Satipy's tongue finally goaded Yahmose beyond endurance. It was her jeers, her taunt that she was a better man than he, that finally sapped his self-control. He met Nofret on this path and—driven beyond endurance—he threw her down."

"But it was Satipy—"

"No, no, Renisenb. That is where you were all wrong. From down below Satipy saw it happen. Now do you understand?"

"But Yahmose was with you on the cultivation."

"Yes, for the last hour. But do you not realise, Renisenb, that Nofret's body was *cold*? You felt her cheek yourself. You thought she had fallen a few moments before—but that was impossible. She had been dead at least two hours; otherwise, in that hot sun, her face could never have felt cold to your touch. Satipy saw it happen. Satipy hung around, fearful, uncertain what to do; then she saw you coming and tried to head you off."

"Hori, when did you know all this?"

"I guessed fairly soon. It was Satipy's behaviour that told me. She was obviously going about in deadly fear of someone or something—and I was fairly soon convinced that the person she feared was *Yahmose*. She stopped bullying him and instead was eager to obey him in every way. It had been, you see, a terrible shock to her. Yahmose, whom she despised as the meekest of men, had actually been the one to kill Nofret. It turned Satipy's world upside down. Like most bullying women, she was a coward. This new Yahmose terrified her. In her fear she began to talk in her sleep. Yahmose soon realised that she was a danger to him. . . .

"And now, Renisenb, you can realise the truth of what you saw that day with your own eyes. It was not a spirit Satipy saw that caused her to fall. She saw what you saw today. She saw in the face of the man following her—her own husband—the intention to throw her down as he had thrown that other woman. In her fear she backed away from him and fell. And when, with her dying lips, she shaped the word *Nofret*, she was trying to tell you that Yahmose killed Nofret."

Hori paused and then went on:

"Esa came on the truth because of an entirely irrelevant remark made by Henet. Henet complained that I did not look *at* her, but as though I saw something behind her that was not there. She went on to speak of Satipy. In a flash Esa saw how much simpler the whole thing was than we had thought. Satipy did not look at something *behind* Yahmose—it was *Yahmose himself* she saw. To test her idea, Esa introduced the subject in a rambling way which could mean nothing to anyone except Yahmose himself—and only to him if what she suspected was true. Her words surprised him and he reacted to them just for a moment, sufficiently for her to know that what she suspected was the truth. But Yahmose knew then that she *did* suspect. And once a suspicion had arisen, things would fit in too well, even to the story the herd boy told—a boy devoted to him who would do anything his Lord Yahmose commanded—even to swallowing a medicine that night which ensured that he would not wake again. . . ."

"Oh, Hori, it is so hard to believe that Yahmose could do such things. Nofret, yes, I can understand that. But why these other killings?"

"It is difficult to explain to you, Renisenb, but once the heart is opened to evil—evil blossoms like poppies amongst the corn. All his life Yahmose had had, perhaps, a longing for violence and had been unable to achieve it. He despised his own meek, submissive rôle. I think that the killing of Nofret gave him a great sense of *power*. He realised it first by Satipy. Satipy, who had browbeaten and abused him, was now meek and terrified. All the grievances that had laid buried in his heart so long reared their heads—as that snake reared up on the path here one day. Sobek and Ipy were, one handsomer, the other cleverer than he—so *they* must go. He, Yahmose, was to be the ruler of the house, and his father's only comfort and stay! Satipy's death increased the actual pleasure of killing. He felt more powerful as a result of it. It was after that that his mind began to give way—from then on evil possessed him utterly.

"You, Renisenb, were not a rival. So far as he still could, he loved you. But the idea that your husband should share with him in the estate was not one to be borne. I think Esa agreed to the idea of accepting Kameni with two ideas in her head—the first that if Yahmose struck again, it would be more likely to be at Kameni than at you—and in any case she trusted me to see that you were kept safe. The second idea—for Esa was a bold woman—was to bring things to a head. Yahmose, watched by me—whom he did not know suspected him—could be caught in the act."

"As you did," said Renisenb. "Oh, Hori, I was so frightened when I looked back and saw him."

"I know, Renisenb. But it had to be. So long as I stuck close to Yahmose's side, you would necessarily be safe—but that could not go on for ever. I knew that if he had an opportunity of throwing you off the path *at that same place,* he would take it. It would revive the superstitious explanation of the deaths."

"Then the message Henet brought me was not from you?"

Hori shook his head.

"I sent you no message."

"But why did Henet—" Renisenb stopped and shook her head. "I cannot understand Henet's part in all this."

"I think Henet knows the truth," said Hori thoughtfully. "She was conveying as much to Yahmose this morning—a dangerous thing to do. He made use of her to lure you up here—a thing she would be willing to do—since she hates you, Renisenb—"

"I know."

"Afterwards—I wonder? Henet would believe her knowledge would give her power. But I do not believe Yahmose would have let her live long. Perhaps even now—"

Renisenb shivered.

"Yahmose was mad," said Renisenb. "He was possessed by evil spirits, but he was not always like that."

"No, and yet— You remember, Renisenb, how I told you the story of Sobek and Yahmose as children, and how Sobek beat Yahmose's head against the ground and how your mother came, all pale and trembling, and said, 'That is dangerous.' I think, Renisenb, that her meaning was that to do such things *to Yahmose* was dangerous. Remember that next day how Sobek was ill—food poisoning, they thought. I think your mother, Renisenb, knew something of the queer self-contained fury that dwelt within the breast of her gentle, meek little son and feared that someday it might be roused."

Renisenb shuddered.

"Is no one what he seems?"

Hori smiled at her.

"Yes, sometimes. Kameni and I, Renisenb. Both of us, I think, are as you believe we are. Kameni and I . . ."

He said the last words with significance, and suddenly Renisenb realised that she stood at a moment of choice in her life.

Hori went on:

"We both love you, Renisenb. You must know that."

"And yet," said Renisenb slowly, "you have let the arrangements be made for my marriage, and you have said nothing—not one word."

"That was for your protection. Esa had the same idea. I must remain disinterested and aloof, so that I could keep constant watch on Yahmose, and not arouse his animosity." Hori added with emotion: "You must understand, Renisenb, that Yahmose has been my friend for many years. I loved Yahmose. I tried to induce your father to give him the status and authority he desired. I failed. All that came too late. But although I was convinced in my heart that Yahmose had killed Nofret, I tried *not* to believe it. I found excuses, even, for his action. Yahmose, my unhappy, tormented friend, was very dear to me. Then came Sobek's death, and Ipy's and finally Esa's. . . . I knew then that the evil in Yahmose had finally vanquished the good. And so Yahmose has come to his death at my hands—a swift, almost painless death."

"Death—always death."

"No, Renisenb. It is not death that faces you today, but life. With whom will you share that life? With Kameni or with me?"

Renisenb stared straight ahead of her out over the valley below and to the silver streak of the Nile.

Before her, very clearly, there rose up the image of Kameni's smiling face as he had sat facing her that day in the boat.

Handsome, strong, gay . . . She felt again the throb and lilt of her blood. She had loved Kameni in that moment. She loved him now. Kameni could take the place that Khay had held in her life.

She thought: "We shall be happy together—yes, we shall be happy. We shall live together and take pleasure in each other and we shall have strong, handsome children. There will be busy days full of work . . . and days of pleasure when we sail on the River. . . . Life will be again as I knew it with Khay. . . . What could I ask more than that? What do I want more than that?"

And slowly, very slowly indeed, she turned her face towards Hori. It was as though, silently, she asked him a question.

As though he understood her, he answered,

"When you were a child, I loved you. I loved your grave face and the confidence with which you came to me, asking me to mend your broken toys. And then, after eight years' absence, you came again and sat here, and brought me the thoughts that were in your mind. And your mind, Renisenb, is not like the minds of the rest of your family. It does not turn in upon itself, seeking to encase itself in narrow walls. Your mind is like my mind, it looks out over the River, seeing a world of changes, of new ideas—seeing a world where all things are possible to those with courage and vision . . ."

"I know, Hori, I know. I have felt these things with you. But not all the time. There will be moments when I cannot follow you, when I shall be alone. . . ."

She broke off, unable to find words to frame her struggling thoughts. What life would be with Hori, she did not know. In spite of his gentleness, in spite of his love for her, he would remain in some respects incalculable and incomprehensible. They would share moments of great beauty and richness together—but what of their common daily life?

She stretched out her hands impulsively to him.

"Oh, Hori, decide for me. Tell me what to do!"

He smiled at her, at the child Renisenb speaking, perhaps, for the last time. But he did not take her hands.

"I cannot tell you what to do with your life, Renisenb—because it is *your* life—and only you can decide."

She realised then that she was to have no help, no quickening appeal to her senses such as Kameni had made. If Hori would only have touched her—but he did not touch her.

And the choice suddenly presented itself to her in the simplest terms—the easy life or the difficult one. She was strongly tempted then to turn and go down the winding path, down to the normal, happy life she already knew—that she had experienced before with Khay. There was safety there —the sharing of daily pleasures and griefs, with nothing to fear but old age and death. . . .

Death. . . . From thoughts of life she had come full circle again to death. Khay had died. Kameni, perhaps, would die, and his face, like Khay's, would slowly fade from her memory. . . .

She looked then at Hori, standing quietly beside her. It was odd, she thought, that she had never really known just what Hori looked like. . . . She had never needed to know. . . .

She spoke then, and the tone of her voice was the same as when she had announced, long before, that she would walk down the path at sunset alone.

"I have made my choice, Hori. I will share my life with you for good or evil, until death comes. . . ."

With his arms round her, with the sudden new sweetness of his face against hers, she was filled with an exultant richness of living.

"If Hori were to die," she thought, "I should *not* forget! Hori is a song in my heart for ever. . . . That means—that there is no more death. . . ."

Evil under the Sun

CHAPTER I

When Captain Roger Angmering built himself a house in the year 1782 on the island off Leathercombe Bay, it was thought the height of eccentricity on his part. A man of good family such as he was should have had a decorous mansion set in wide meadows with, perhaps, a running stream and good pasture.

But Captain Roger Angmering had only one great love, the sea. So he built his house—a sturdy house too, as it needed to be, on the little windswept gull-haunted promontory—cut off from land at each high tide.

He did not marry, the sea was his first and last spouse, and at his death the house and island went to a distant cousin. That cousin and his descendants thought little of the bequest. Their own acres dwindled, and their heirs grew steadily poorer.

In time, when the great cult of the Seaside for Holidays was finally established and the coast of Devon and Cornwall was no longer thought too hot in the summer, Arthur Angmering found his vast inconvenient late Georgian house unsaleable, but he got a good price for the odd bit of property acquired by the seafaring Captain Roger.

The sturdy house was added to and embellished. A concrete causeway was laid down from the mainland to the island. "Walks" and "Nooks" were cut and devised all round the island. There were two tennis courts, sunterraces leading down to a little bay embellished with rafts and divingboards. The Jolly Roger Hotel, Smugglers' Island, Leathercombe Bay came triumphantly into being. And from June till September (with a short season at Easter) the Jolly Roger Hotel was usually packed to the attics. It was enlarged and improved later on by the addition of a cocktail bar, a bigger dining-room and some extra bathrooms. The prices went up.

People said:

"Ever been to Leathercombe Bay? Awfully jolly hotel there, on a sort of island. Very comfortable and no trippers or charabancs. Good cooking and all that. You ought to go."

And people did go.

II

There was one very important person (in his own estimation at least) staying at the Jolly Roger. Hercule Poirot, resplendent in a white duck suit, with a Panama hat tilted over his eyes, his moustaches magnificently befurled, lay back in an improved type of deck-chair and surveyed the bathing beach. A series of terraces led down to it from the hotel. On the beach itself were floats, lilos, rubber and canvas boats, balls and rubber toys. There were a long springboard and three rafts at varying distances from the shore.

Of the bathers, some were in the sea, some were lying stretched out in the sun, and some were anointing themselves carefully with oil.

On the terrace immediately above, the non-bathers sat and commented on the weather, the scene in front of them, the news in the morning papers and any other subject that appealed to them.

On Poirot's left a ceaseless flow of conversation poured in a gentle monotone from the lips of Mrs. Gardener while at the same time her needles clacked as she knitted vigorously. Beyond her, her husband, Odell C. Gardener, lay in a hammock chair, his hat tilted forward over his nose, and occasionally uttered a brief statement when callled upon to do so.

On Poirot's right, Miss Brewster, a tough athletic woman with grizzled hair and a pleasant weatherbeaten face, made gruff comments. The result sounded rather like a sheepdog whose short stentorian barks interrupted the ceaseless yapping of a Pomeranian.

Mrs. Gardener was saying:

"And so I said to Mr. Gardener, why, I said, sight-seeing is all very well, and I do like to do a place thoroughly. But, after all, I said, we've done England pretty well and all I want now is to get to some quiet spot by the seaside and just relax. That's what I said, wasn't it, Odell? Just *relax*. I feel I must relax, I said. That's so, isn't it, Odell?"

Mr. Gardener, from behind his hat, murmured:

"Yes, darling."

Mrs. Gardener pursued the theme.

"And so, when I mentioned it to Mr. Kelso, at Cook's (He's arranged all our itinerary for us and been *most* helpful in every way. I don't really know what we'd have done without him!)— Well, as I say, when I mentioned it to him, Mr. Kelso said that we couldn't do better than come here. A most picturesque spot, he said, quite out of the world, and at the same time very comfortable and most exclusive in every way. And of course Mr.

Gardener, he chipped in there and said what about the sanitary arrangements? Because, if you'll believe me, Mr. Poirot, a sister of Mr. Gardener's went to stay at a guesthouse once, very exclusive they said it was, and in the heart of the moors, but would you believe me, *nothing but an earth closet!* So naturally that made Mr. Gardener suspicious of these out-of-the-world places, didn't it, Odell?"

"Why, yes, darling," said Mr. Gardener.

"But Mr. Kelso reassured us at once. The sanitation, he said, was absolutely the latest word, and the cooking was excellent. And I'm sure that's so. And what I like about it is, it's *intime* if you know what I mean. Being a small place we all talk to each other and everybody knows everybody. If there is a fault about the British it is that they're inclined to be a bit standoffish until they've known you a couple of years. After that nobody could be nicer. Mr. Kelso said that interesting people came here and I see he was right. There's you, Mr. Poirot and Miss Darnley. Oh! I was just tickled to death when I found out who you were, wasn't I, Odell?"

"You were, darling."

"Ha!" said Miss Brewster, breaking in explosively. "What a thrill, eh, M. Poirot?"

Hercule Poirot raised his hands in deprecation. But it was no more than a polite gesture. Mrs. Gardener flowed smoothly on.

"You see, M. Poirot, I'd heard a lot about you from Cornelia Robson who was. Mr. Gardener and I were at Badenhof in May. And of course Cornelia told us all about that business in Egypt when Linnet Ridgeway was killed. She said you were wonderful and I've always been simply crazy to meet you, haven't I, Odell?"

"Yes, darling."

"And then Miss Darnley, too. I get a lot of my things at Rose Mond's and of course she *is* Rose Mond, isn't she? I think her clothes are ever so clever. Such a marvellous line. That dress I had on last night was one of hers. She's just a lovely woman in every way, I think."

From beyond Miss Brewster, Major Barry who had been sitting with protuberant eyes glued to the bathers grunted out:

"Distinguished lookin' gal!"

Mrs. Gardener clacked her needles.

"I've just got to confess one thing, M. Poirot. It gave me a kind of a *turn* meeting you here—not that I wasn't just thrilled to meet you, because I was. Mr. Gardener knows that. But it just came to me that you might be here—well, *professionally*. You know what I mean? Well, I'm just terribly sensitive, as Mr. Gardener will tell you, and I just couldn't bear it if I was to be mixed up in crime of any kind. You see—"

Mr. Gardener cleared his throat. He said:

"You see, M. Poirot, Mrs. Gardener is very sensitive."

The hands of Hercule Poirot shot into the air.

"But let me assure you, Madame, that I am here simply in the same way that you are here yourselves—to enjoy myself—to spend the holiday. I do not think of crime even."

Miss Brewster said again giving her short gruff bark:

"No bodies on Smugglers' Island."

Hercule Poirot said:

"Ah! but that, it is not strictly true." He pointed downward. "Regard them there, lying out in rows. What are they? They are not men and women. There is nothing personal about them. They are just—bodies!"

Major Barry said appreciatively:

"Good-looking fillies, some of 'em. Bit on the thin side, perhaps."

Poirot cried:

"Yes, but what appeal is there? What mystery? I, I am old, of the old school. When I was young, one saw barely the ankle. The glimpse of a foamy petticoat, how alluring! The gentle swelling of the calf—a knee—a beribboned garter—"

"Naughty, naughty!" said Major Barry hoarsely.

"Much more sensible—the things we wear nowadays," said Miss Brewster.

"Why, yes, M. Poirot," said Mrs. Gardener. "I do think, you know, that our girls and boys nowadays lead a much more natural healthy life. They just romp about together and they—well, they—" Mrs. Gardener blushed slightly for she had a nice mind—"they think nothing *of* it, if you know what I mean?"

"I do know," said Hercule Poirot. "It is deplorable!"

"Deplorable?" squeaked Mrs. Gardener.

"To remove all the romance—all the mystery! To-day everything is *standardized!*" He waved a hand towards the recumbent figures. "That reminds me very much of the Morgue in Paris."

"M. Poirot!" Mrs. Gardener was scandalized.

"Bodies—arranged on slabs—like butcher's meat!"

"But, M. Poirot, isn't that too far-fetched for words?"

Hercule Poirot admitted:

"It may be, yes."

"All the same," Mrs. Gardener knitted with energy, "I'm inclined to agree with you on one point. These girls that lie out like that in the sun will grow hair on their legs and arms. I've said so to Irene—that's my daughter, M. Poirot. Irene, I said to her, if you lie out like that in the sun, you'll have hair all over you, hair on your arms and hair on your legs and hair on your bosom, and what will you look like then? I said to her. Didn't I, Odell?"

"Yes, darling," said Mr. Gardener.

Every one was silent, perhaps making a mental picture of Irene when the worst had happened.

Mrs. Gardener rolled up her knitting and said:

"I wonder now—"

Mr. Gardener said:

"Yes, darling?"

He struggled out of the hammock chair and took Mrs. Gardener's knitting and her book. He asked:

"What about joining us for a drink, Miss Brewster?"

"Not just now, thanks."

The Gardeners went up to the hotel.

Miss Brewster said:

"American husbands are wonderful!"

III

Mrs. Gardener's place was taken by the Reverend Stephen Lane.

Mr. Lane was a tall vigorous clergyman of fifty odd. His face was tanned and his dark grey flannel trousers were holidayfied and disreputable.

He said with enthusiasm:

"Marvellous country! I've been from Leathercombe Bay to Harford and back over the cliffs."

"Warm work walking to-day," said Major Barry who never walked.

"Good exercise," said Miss Brewster. "I haven't been for my row yet. Nothing like rowing for your stomach muscles."

The eyes of Hercule Poirot dropped somewhat ruefully to a certain protuberance in his middle.

Miss Brewster, noting the glance, said kindly:

"You'd soon get that off, M. Poirot, if you took a rowing-boat out every day."

"*Merci, Mademoiselle.* I detest boats!"

"You mean small boats?"

"Boats of all sizes!" He closed his eyes and shuddered. "The movement of the sea, it is not pleasant."

"Bless the man, the sea is as calm as a mill pond to-day."

Poirot replied with conviction:

"There is no such thing as a really calm sea. Always, always, there is motion."

"If you ask me," said Major Barry, "seasickness is nine-tenths nerves."

"There," said the clergyman, smiling a little, "speaks the good sailor—eh, Major?"

"Only been ill once—and that was crossing the channel! Don't think about it, that's my motto."

"Seasickness is really a very odd thing," mused Miss Brewster. "Why should some people be subject to it and not others? It seems so unfair. And nothing to do with one's ordinary health. Quite sickly people are good sailors. Some one told me once it was something to do with one's spine. Then there's the way some people can't stand heights. I'm not very good myself, but Mrs. Redfern is far worse. The other day, on the cliff path to Harford, she turned quite giddy and simply clung to me. She told me she once got stuck halfway down that outside staircase on Milan Cathedral. She'd gone up without thinking but coming down did for her."

"She'd better not go down the ladder to Pixy Cove, then," observed Lane.

Miss Brewster made a face.

"I funk that myself. It's all right for the young. The Cowan boys and the young Mastermans, they run up and down it and enjoy it."

Lane said:

"Here comes Mrs. Redfern now coming up from her bathe."

Miss Brewster remarked:

"M. Poirot ought to approve of her. She's no sunbather."

Young Mrs. Redfern had taken off her rubber cap and was shaking out her hair. She was an ash blonde and her skin was of that dead fairness that goes with that colouring. Her legs and arms were very white.

With a hoarse chuckle, Major Barry said:

"Looks a bit uncooked among the others, doesn't she?"

Wrapping herself in a long bath-robe Christine Redfern came up the beach and mounted the steps towards them.

She had a fair serious face, pretty in a negative way, and small dainty hands and feet.

She smiled at them and dropped down beside them, tucking her bath-wrap round her.

Miss Brewster said:

"You have earned M. Poirot's good opinion. He doesn't like the sun-tanning crowd. Says they're like joints of butcher's meat or words to that effect."

Christine Redfern smiled ruefully.

She said:

"I wish I *could* sun-bathe! But I don't go brown. I only blister and get the most frightful freckles all over my arms."

"Better than getting hair all over them like Mrs. Gardener's Irene," said Miss Brewster. In answer to Christine's inquiring glance she went on: "Mrs. Gardener's been in grand form this morning. Absolutely non stop. 'Isn't that so, Odell?' 'Yes, darling.'" She paused and then said: "I wish, though, M. Poirot, that you'd played up to her a bit. Why didn't you? Why didn't you tell her that you were down here investigating a particularly gruesome murder, and that the murderer, a homicidal maniac, was certainly to be found among the guests of the hotel?"

Hercule Poirot sighed. He said:

"I very much fear she would have believed me."

Major Barry gave a wheezy chuckle. He said:

"She certainly would."

Emily Brewster said:

"No, I don't believe even Mrs. Gardener would have believed in a crime staged here. This isn't the sort of place you'd get a body!"

Hercule Poirot stirred a little in his chair. He protested. He said:

"But why not, Mademoiselle? Why should there not be what you call a 'body' here on Smugglers' Island?"

Emily Brewster said:

"I don't know. I suppose some places *are* more unlikely than others. This isn't the kind of spot—" She broke off, finding it difficult to explain her meaning.

"It is romantic, yes," agreed Hercule Poirot. "It is peaceful. The sun shines. The sea is blue. But you forget, Miss Brewster, there is evil everywhere under the sun."

The clergyman stirred in his chair. He leaned forward. His intensely blue eyes lighted up.

Miss Brewster shrugged her shoulders.

"Oh! of course I realize that, but all the same—"

"But all the same this still seems to you an unlikely setting for crime? You forget one thing, Mademoiselle."

"Human nature, I suppose?"

"That, yes. That, always. But that was not what I was going to say. I was going to point out to you that here every one is on holiday."

Emily Brewster turned a puzzled face to him.

"I don't understand."

Hercule Poirot beamed kindly at her. He made dabs in the air with an emphatic forefinger.

"Let us say, you have an enemy. If you seek him out in his flat, in his office, in the street—*eh bien*, you must have a *reason*—you must account for yourself. But here at the seaside it is necessary for no one to account for himself. You are at Leathercombe Bay, why? *Parbleu!* it is August—one goes to the seaside in August—one is on one's holiday. It is quite natural, you see, for you to be here and for Mr. Lane to be here and for Major Barry to be here and for Mrs. Redfern and her husband to be here. Because it is the custom in England to go to the seaside in August."

"Well," admitted Miss Brewster, "that's certainly a very ingenious idea. But what about the Gardeners? They're American."

Poirot smiled.

"Even Mrs. Gardener, as she told us, feels the need to *relax*. Also, since she is 'doing' England, she must certainly spend a fortnight at the seaside—as a good tourist, if nothing else. She enjoys watching people."

Mrs. Redfern murmured:

"You like watching the people too, I think?"

"Madame, I will confess it. I do."

She said thoughtfully:

"You see—a good deal."

IV

There was a pause. Stephen Lane cleared his throat and said with a trace of self-consciousness:

"I was interested, M. Poirot, in something you said just now. You said that there was evil done everywhere under the sun. It was almost a quotation from Ecclesiastes." He paused and then quoted himself. "*Yea, also the heart of the sons of men is full of evil, and madness is in their heart while they live.*" His face lit up with an almost fanatical light. "I was glad to hear you say that. Nowadays, no one believes in evil. It is considered, at most, a mere negation of good. Evil, people say, is done by those who know no better—who are undeveloped—who are to be pitied rather than blamed. But, M. Poirot, evil is *real!* It is a *fact!* I believe in Evil as I believe in Good. It exists! It is powerful! It walks the earth!"

He stopped. His breath was coming fast. He wiped his forehead with his handkerchief and looked suddenly apologetic.

"I'm sorry. I got carried away."

Poirot said calmly:

"I understand your meaning. Up to a point I agree with you. Evil does walk the earth and can be recognized as such."

Major Barry cleared his throat.

"Talking of that sort of thing, some of these fakir fellers in India—"

Major Barry had been long enough at the Jolly Roger for every one to be on their guard against his fatal tendency to embark on long Indian stories. Both Miss Brewster and Mrs. Redfern burst into speech.

"That's your husband swimming in now, isn't it, Mrs. Redfern? How magnificent his crawl stroke is. He's an awfully good swimmer."

At the same moment Mrs. Redfern said:

"Oh, look! What a lovely little boat that is out there with the red sails. It's Mr. Blatt's, isn't it?"

The sailing boat with the red sails was just crossing the end of the bay. Major Barry grunted:

"Fanciful idea, red sails," but the menace of the story about the fakir was avoided.

Hercule Poirot looked with appreciation at the young man who had just swum to shore. Patrick Redfern was a good specimen of humanity. Lean, bronzed, with broad shoulders and narrow thighs, there was about him a kind of infectious enjoyment and gaiety—a native simplicity that endeared him to all women and most men.

He stood there shaking the water from him and raising a hand in gay salutation to his wife.

She waved back, calling out:

"Come up here, Pat."

"I'm coming."

He went a little way along the beach to retrieve the towel he had left there.

It was then that a woman come down past them from the hotel to the beach.

Her arrival had all the importance of a stage entrance.

Moreover, she walked as though she knew it. There was no self-consciousness apparent. It would seem that she was too used to the invariable effect her presence produced.

She was tall and slender. She wore a simple backless white bathing dress and every inch of her exposed body was tanned a beautiful even shade of bronze. She was as perfect as a statue. Her hair was a rich flaming auburn curling richly and intimately into her neck. Her face had that slight hardness which is seen when thirty years have come and gone, but the whole effect of her was one of youth—of superb and triumphant vitality. There was a Chinese immobility about her face, and an upward slant of the dark blue eyes. On her head she wore a fantastic Chinese hat of jade-green cardboard.

There was that about her which made every other woman on the beach seem faded and insignificant. And with equal inevitability, the eye of every male present was drawn and rivetted on her.

The eyes of Hercule Poirot opened, his moustache quivered appreciatively, Major Barry sat up and his protuberant eyes bulged even further with excitement; on Poirot's left the Reverend Stephen Lane drew in his breath with a little hiss and his figure stiffened.

Major Barry said in a hoarse whisper:

"Arlena Stuart (that's who she was before she married Marshall)—I saw her in *Come and Go* before she left the stage. Something worth looking at, eh?"

Christine Redfern said slowly and her voice was cold:

"She's handsome—yes. I think—she looks rather a beast!"

Emily Brewster said abruptly:

"You talked about evil just now, M. Poirot. Now to my mind that woman's a personification of evil! She's a bad lot through and through. I happen to know a good deal about her."

Major Barry said reminiscently:

"I remember a gal out in Simla. *She* had red hair too. Wife of a subaltern. Did she set the place by the ears? I'll say she did! Men went mad about her! All the women, of course, would have liked to gouge her eyes out! She upset the apple cart in more homes than one."

He chuckled reminiscently.

"Husband was a nice quiet fellow. Worshipped the ground she walked on. Never saw a thing—or made out he didn't."

Stephen Lane said in a low voice full of intense feeling:

"Such women are a menace—a menace to—"

He stopped.

Arlena Stuart had come to the water's edge. Two young men, little more than boys, had sprung up and come eagerly towards her. She stood smiling at them.

Her eyes slid past them to where Patrick Redfern was coming along the beach.

It was, Hercule Poirot thought, like watching the needle of a compass. Patrick Redfern was deflected, his feet changed their direction. The needle, do what it will, must obey the law of magnetism and turn to the North. Patrick Redfern's feet brought him to Arlena Stuart.

She stood smiling at him. Then she moved slowly along the beach by the side of the waves. Patrick Redfern went with her. She stretched herself out by a rock. Redfern dropped to the shingle beside her.

Abruptly, Christine Redfern got up and went into the hotel.

V

There was an uncomfortable little silence after she had left.

Then Emily Brewster said:

"It's rather too bad. She's a nice little thing. They've only been married a year or two."

"Gal I was speaking of," said Major Barry, "the one in Simla. She upset a couple of really happy marriages. Seemed a pity, what?"

"There's a type of woman," said Miss Brewster, "who *likes* smashing up homes." She added after a minute or two, "Patrick Redfern's a fool!"

Hercule Poirot said nothing. He was gazing down the beach, but he was not looking at Patrick Redfern and Arlena Stuart.

Miss Brewster said:

"Well, I'd better go and get hold of my boat."

She left them.

Major Barry turned his boiled gooseberry eyes with mild curiosity on Poirot.

"Well, Poirot," he said. "What are you thinking about? You've not opened your mouth. What do you think of the siren? Pretty hot?"

Poirot said:

"*C'est possible.*"

"Now then, you old dog. I know you Frenchmen!"

Poirot said coldly:

"I am *not* a Frenchman!"

"Well, don't tell me you haven't got an eye for a pretty girl! What do you think of her, eh?"

Hercule Poirot said:

"She is not young."

"What does that matter? A woman's as old as she looks! *Her* looks are all right."

Hercule Poirot nodded. He said:

"Yes, she is beautiful. But it is not beauty that counts in the end. It is not beauty that makes every head (except one) turn on the beach to look at her."

"It's IT, my boy," said the Major. "That's what it is—IT."

Then he said with sudden curiosity:

"What are you looking at so steadily?"

Hercule Poirot replied: "I am looking at the exception. At the one man who did not look up when she passed."

Major Barry followed his gaze to where it rested on a man of about forty, fair-haired and sun-tanned. He had a quiet, pleasant face and was sitting on the beach smoking a pipe and reading the *Times*.

"Oh, *that!*" said Major Barry. "That's the husband, my boy. That's Marshall."

Hercule Poirot said:

"Yes, I know."

Major Barry chuckled. He himself was a bachelor. He was accustomed to think of The Husband in three lights only—as "the Obstacle," "the Inconvenience" or "the Safeguard."

He said:

"Seems a nice fellow. Quiet. Wonder if my *Times* has come?"

He got up and went up towards the hotel.

Poirot's glance shifted slowly to the face of Stephen Lane.

Stephen Lane was watching Arlena Marshall and Patrick Redfern. He turned suddenly to Poirot. There was a stern fanatical light in his eyes.

He said:

"That woman is evil through and through. Do you doubt it?"

Poirot said slowly:

"It is difficult to be sure."

Stephen Lane said:

"But, man alive, don't you feel it in the air? All round you? The presence of Evil."

Slowly, Hercule Poirot nodded his head.

CHAPTER II

WHEN ROSAMUND DARNLEY came and sat down by him, Hercule Poirot made no attempt to disguise his pleasure.

As he has since admitted, he admired Rosamund Darnley as much as any woman he had ever met. He liked her distinction, the graceful lines of her figure, the alert proud carriage of her head. He liked the neat sleek waves of her dark hair and the ironic quality of her smile.

She was wearing a dress of some navy blue material with touches of white. It looked very simple owing to the expensive severity of its line. Rosamund Darnley as Rose Mond Ltd. was one of London's best-known dressmakers.

She said:

"I don't think I like this place. I'm wondering why I came here!"

"You have been here before, have you not?"

"Yes, two years ago, at Easter. There weren't so many people then."

Hercule Poirot looked at her. He said gently:

"Something has occurred to worry you. That is right, is it not?"

She nodded. Her foot swung to and fro. She stared down at it. She said:

"I've met a ghost. That's what it is."

"A ghost, Mademoiselle?"

"Yes."

"The ghost of what? Or of whom?"

"Oh, the ghost of myself."

Poirot asked gently:

"Was it a painful ghost?"

"Unexpectedly painful. It took me back, you know."

She paused, musing. Then she said:

"Imagine my childhood— No, you can't! You're not English!"

Poirot asked:

"Was it a very English childhood?"

"Oh, incredibly so! The country—a big shabby house—horses, dogs—walks in the rain—wood fires—apples in the orchard—lack of money—old tweeds—evening dresses that went on from year to year—a neglected garden—with Michaelmas daisies coming out like great banners in the Autumn . . ."

Poirot asked gently:

"And you want to go back?"

Rosamund Darnley shook her head. She said:

"One can't go back, can one? That—never. But I'd like to have gone on—a different way."

Poirot said:

"I wonder."

Rosamund Darnley laughed.

"So do I really!"

Poirot said:

"When I was young (and that, Mademoiselle, is indeed a long time ago) there was a game entitled '*If not yourself, who would you be?*' One wrote the answer in young ladies' albums. They had gold edges and were bound in blue leather. The answer, Mademoiselle, is not really very easy to find."

Rosamund said:

"No—I suppose not. It would be a big risk. One wouldn't like to take on being a queen or a prime minister. As for one's friends, one knows too much about them. I remember once meeting a charming husband and wife. They were so courteous and delightful to one another and seemed on such good terms after years of marriage that I envied the woman. I'd have changed places with her willingly. Somebody told me afterwards that in private they'd never spoken to each other for eleven years!"

She laughed.

"That shows, doesn't it, that you never know?"

After a moment or two Poirot said:

"Many people, Mademoiselle, must envy you."

Rosamund Darnley said coolly:

"Oh, yes. Naturally."

She thought about it, her lips curved upward in their ironic smile.

"Yes, I'm really the perfect type of the successful woman! I enjoy the artistic satisfaction of the successful creative artist (I really do like designing clothes) and the financial satisfaction of the successful business woman. I'm very well off, I've a good figure, a passable face, and a not too malicious tongue."

She paused. Her smiled widened.

"Of course—I haven't got a husband! I've failed there, haven't I, M. Poirot?"

Poirot said gallantly:

"Mademoiselle, if you are not married, it is because none of my sex have been sufficiently eloquent. It is from choice, not necessity, that you remain single."

Rosamund Darnley said:

"And yet, like all men, I'm sure you believe in your heart that no woman is content unless she is married and has children."

Poirot shrugged his shoulders.

"To marry and have children that is the common lot of women. Only one woman in a hundred—more, in a thousand—can make for herself a name and a position as you have done."

Rosamund grinned at him.

"And yet, all the same, I'm nothing but a wretched old maid! That's what I feel to-day, at any rate. I'd be happier with twopence a year and a big silent brute of a husband and a brood of brats running after me. That's true, isn't it?"

Poirot shrugged his shoulders.

"Since you say so, then, yes, Mademoiselle."

Rosamund laughed, her equilibrium suddenly restored. She took out a cigarette and lit it.

She said:

"You certainly know how to deal with women, M. Poirot. I now feel like taking the opposite point of view and arguing with you in favour of careers for women. Of course I'm damned well off as I am—and I know it!"

"Then everything in the garden—or shall we say at the seaside?—is lovely, Mademoiselle."

"Quite right."

Poirot, in his turn, extracted his cigarette case and lit one of those tiny cigarettes which it was his affectation to smoke.

Regarding the ascending haze with a quizzical eye, he murmured:

"So Mr.—no, Captain—Marshall is an old friend of yours, Mademoiselle?"

Rosamund sat up. She said:

"Now how do you know that? Oh, I suppose Ken told you."

Poirot shook his head.

"Nobody has told me anything. After all, Mademoiselle, I am a detective. It was the obvious conclusion to draw."

Rosamund Darnley said:

"I don't see it."

"But consider!" The little man's hands were eloquent. "You have been here a week. You are lively, gay, without a care. To-day, suddenly, you speak of ghosts, of old times. What has happened? For several days there have been no new arrivals until last night when Captain Marshall and his wife and daughter arrive. To-day the change! It is obvious!"

Rosamund Darnley said:

"Well, it's true enough. Kenneth Marshall and I were more or less children together. The Marshalls lived next door to us. Ken was always nice to me—although condescending, of course, since he was four years older. I've not seen anything of him for a long time. It must be—fifteen years at least."

Poirot said thoughtfully:

"A long time."

Rosamund nodded.

There was a pause and then Hercule Poirot said:

"He is sympathetic, yes?"

Rosamund said warmly:

"Ken's a dear. One of the best. Frightfully quiet and reserved. I'd say his only fault is a *penchant* for making unfortunate marriages."

Poirot said in a tone of great understanding: "Ah . . ."

Rosamund Darnley went on.

"Kenneth's a fool—an utter fool where women are concerned! Do you remember the Martingdale case?"

Poirot frowned.

"Martingdale? Martingdale? Arsenic, was it not?"

"Yes. Seventeen or eighteen years ago. The woman was tried for the murder of her husband."

"And he was proved to have been an arsenic eater and she was acquitted?"

"That's right. Well, after her acquittal, Ken married her. That's the sort of damn silly thing he does."

Hercule Poirot murmured:

"But if she was innocent?"

Rosamund Darnley said impatiently:

"Oh, I daresay she *was* innocent. Nobody really knows! But there are plenty of women to marry in the world without going out of your way to marry one who's stood her trial for murder."

Poirot said nothing. Perhaps he knew that if he kept silence Rosamund Darnley would go on. She did so.

"He was very young, of course, only just twenty-one. He was crazy about her. She died when Linda was born—a year after their marriage. I believe Ken was terribly cut up by her death. Afterwards he racketed around a lot —trying to forget, I suppose."

She paused.

"And then came this business of Arlena Stuart. She was in Revue at the time. There was the Codrington divorce case. Lady Codrington divorced Codrington citing Arlena Stuart. They say Lord Codrington was absolutely infatuated with her. It was understood they were to be married as soon as the decree was made absolute. Actually, when it came to it, he didn't marry her. Turned her down flat. I believe she actually sued him for breach of promise. Anyway, the thing made a big stir at the time. The next thing that happens is that Ken goes and marries her. The fool—the complete fool!"

Hercule Poirot murmured:

"A man might be excused such a folly—she is beautiful, Mademoiselle."

"Yes, there's no doubt of that. There was another scandal about three years ago. Old Sir Robert Erskine left her every penny of his money. I should have thought that would have opened Ken's eyes if anything would."

"And did it not?"

Rosamund Darnley shrugged her shoulders.

"I tell you I've seen nothing of him for years. People say though, that he took it with absolute equanimity. Why, I should like to know? Has he got an absolutely blind belief in her?"

"There might be other reasons."

"Yes. Pride! Keeping a stiff upper lip! I don't know what he really feels about her. Nobody does."

"And she? What does she feel about him?"

Rosamund stared at him. She said:

"She? She's the world's first gold-digger. And a man-eater as well! If anything personable in trousers comes within a hundred yards of her, it's fresh sport for Arlena! She's that kind."

Poirot nodded his head slowly in complete agreement.

"Yes," he said. "That is true what you say. . . . Her eyes look for one thing only—men."

Rosamund said:

"She's got her eye on Patrick Redfern now. He's a good-looking man—and rather the simple kind—you know, fond of his wife, and not a philanderer. That's the kind that's meat and drink to Arlena. I like little Mrs. Redfern—she's nice-looking in her fair washed-out way—but I don't think she'll stand a dog's chance against that man-eating tiger, Arlena."

Poirot said:

"No, it is as you say."

He looked distressed.

Rosamund said:

"Christine Redfern was a school teacher, I believe. She's the kind that thinks that mind has a pull over matter. She's got a rude shock coming to her."

Poirot shook his head vexedly.

Rosamund got up. She said:

"It's a shame, you know." She added vaguely: "Somebody ought to do something about it."

II

Linda Marshall was examining her face dispassionately in her bedroom mirror. She disliked her face very much. At this minute it seemed to her to be mostly bones and freckles. She noted with distaste her heavy bush of red-brown hair (mouse, she called it in her own mind), her greenish-grey eyes, her high cheek-bones and the long aggressive line of the chin. Her mouth and teeth weren't perhaps quite so bad—but what were teeth after all? And was that a spot coming on the side of her nose?

She decided with relief that it wasn't a spot. She thought to herself:

"It's awful to be sixteen—simply *awful*."

One didn't, somehow, know where one was. Linda was as awkward as a young colt and as prickly as a hedgehog. She was conscious the whole time of her ungainliness and of the fact that she was neither one thing nor the other. It hadn't been so bad at school. But now she had left school. Nobody seemed to know quite what she was going to do next. Her father talked vaguely of sending her to Paris next winter. Linda didn't want to go to Paris—but then she didn't want to be at home either. She'd never realized properly, somehow, until now, how very much she disliked Arlena.

Linda's young face grew tense, her green eyes hardened.

Arlena. . . .

She thought to herself:

"She's a beast—a *beast*. . . ."

Stepmothers! It was rotten to have a stepmother, everybody said so. And it was true! Not that Arlena was unkind to her. Most of the time she hardly noticed the girl. But when she did, there was a contemptuous amusement in her glance, in her words. The finished grace and poise of Arlena's movements emphasized Linda's own adolescent clumsiness. With Arlena about, one felt, shamingly, just how immature and crude one was.

But it wasn't that only. No, it wasn't only that.

Linda groped haltingly in the recesses of her mind. She wasn't very good at sorting out her emotions and labelling them. It was something that Arlena *did* to people—to the house—

"She's bad," thought Linda with decision. "She's quite, quite bad."

But you couldn't even leave it at that. You couldn't just elevate your nose with a sniff of moral superiority and dismiss her from your mind.

It was something she did to people. Father, now, Father was quite different. . . .

She puzzled over it. Father coming down to take her out from school. Father taking her once for a cruise. And Father at home—with Arlena there. All—all sort of bottled up and not—and not *there*.

Linda thought:

"And it'll go on like this. Day after day—month after month. I can't bear it."

Life stretched before her—endless—in a series of days darkened and poisoned by Arlena's presence. She was childish enough still to have little sense of proportion. A year, to Linda, seemed like an eternity.

A big dark burning wave of hatred against Arlena surged up in her mind. She thought:

"I'd like to kill her. Oh! I wish she'd die. . . ."

She looked out above the mirror onto the sea below.

This place was really rather fun. Or it could be fun. All those beaches and coves and queer little paths. Lots to explore. And places where one could go off by oneself and muck about. There were caves, too, so the Cowan boys had told her.

Linda thought:

"If only Arlena would go way, I could enjoy myself."

Her mind went back to the evening of their arrival. It had been exciting coming from the mainland. The tide had been up over the causeway. They had come in a boat. The hotel had looked exciting, unusual. And then on the terrace a tall dark woman had jumped up and said:

"Why, Kenneth!"

And her father, looking frightfully surprised, had exclaimed:

"Rosamund!"

Linda considered Rosamund Darnley severely and critically in the manner of youth.

She decided that she approved of Rosamund. Rosamund, she thought, was sensible. And her hair grew nicely—as though it fitted her—most people's hair didn't fit them. And her clothes were nice. And she had a kind of funny amused face—as though it were amused at herself not at you. Rosamund had been nice to her, Linda. She hadn't been gushing or *said* things. (Under the term of "saying things" Linda grouped a mass of miscellaneous dislikes.) And Rosamund hadn't looked as though she thought Linda a fool. In fact she'd treated Linda as though she were a real human being. Linda so seldom felt like a real human being that she was deeply grateful when any one appeared to consider her one.

Father, too, had seemed pleased to see Miss Darnley.

Funny—he'd looked quite different, all of a sudden. He'd looked—he'd looked—Linda puzzled it out—why, *young*, that was it! He'd laughed—a queer boyish laugh. Now Linda came to think of it, she'd very seldom heard him laugh.

She felt puzzled. It was as though she'd got a glimpse of quite a different person. She thought:

"I wonder what Father was like when he was my age. . . ."

But that was too difficult. She gave it up.

An idea just flashed across her mind.

What fun it would have been if they'd come here and found Miss Darnley here—just she and Father.

A vista opened out just for a minute. Father, boyish and laughing, Miss Darnley, herself—and all the fun one could have on the island—bathing—caves—

The blackness shut down again.

Arlena. One couldn't enjoy oneself with Arlena about. Why not? Well, she, Linda, couldn't, anyway. You couldn't be happy when there was a person there you—hated. Yes, hated. She hated Arlena.

Very slowly that black burning wave of hatred rose up again.

Linda's face went very white. Her lips parted a little. The pupils of her eyes contracted. And her fingers stiffened and clenched themselves. . . .

III

Kenneth Marshall tapped on his wife's door. When her voice answered, he opened the door and went in.

Arlena was just putting the finishing touches to her toilet. She was dressed in glittering green and looked a little like a mermaid. She was standing in front of the glass applying mascara to her eyelashes. She said:

"Oh, it's you, Ken."

"Yes. I wondered if you were ready."

"Just a minute."

Kenneth Marshall strolled to the window. He looked out on the sea. His face, as usual, displayed no emotion of any kind. It was pleasant and ordinary.

Turning around, he said:

"Arlena?"

"Yes?"

"You've met Redfern before, I gather?"

Arlena said easily:

"Oh, yes, darling. At a cocktail party somewhere. I thought he was rather a pet."

"So I gather. Did you know that he and his wife were coming down here?"

Arlena opened her eyes very wide.

"Oh, no, darling. It was the *greatest* surprise!"

Kenneth Marshall said quietly:

"I thought, perhaps, that that was what put the idea of this place into your head. You were very keen we should come here."

Arlena put down the mascara. She turned towards him. She smiled—a soft seductive smile. She said:

"Somebody told me about this place. I think it was the Rylands. They said it was simply too marvellous—so unspoilt! Don't you like it?"

Kenneth Marshall said:

"I'm not sure."

"Oh, darling, but you adore bathing and lazing about. I'm sure you'll simply adore it here."

"I can see that you mean to enjoy yourself."

Her eyes widened a little. She looked at him uncertainly.

Kenneth Marshall said:

"I suppose the truth of it is that you told young Redfern that you were coming here?"

Arlena said:

"Kenneth darling, you're not going to be horrid, are you?"

Kenneth Marshall said:

"Look here, Arlena. I know what you're like. That's rather a nice young couple. That boy's fond of his wife really. Must you upset the whole blinking show?"

Arlena said:

"It's so unfair blaming *me*. *I* haven't done anything—anything at all. I can't help it if—"

He prompted her.

"If what?"

Her eyelids fluttered.

"Well, of course, I know people do go crazy about me. But it's not my doing. They just get like that."

"So you do admit that young Redfern is crazy about you?"

Arlena murmured:

"It's really rather stupid of him."

She moved a step towards her husband.

"But you know, don't you, Ken, that I don't really care for any one but you?"

She looked up at him through her darkened lashes.

It was a marvellous look—a look that few men could have resisted.

Kenneth Marshall looked down at her gravely. His face was composed. His voice quiet. He said:

"I think I know you pretty well, Arlena. . . ."

IV

When you came out of the hotel on the south side the terraces and the bathing beach were immediately below you. There was also a path that led off round the cliff on the southwest side of the island. A little way along it, a few steps led down to a series of recesses cut into the cliff and labelled on the hotel map of the island as Sunny Ledge. Here cut out of the cliff were niches with seats in them.

To one of these, immediately after dinner, came Patrick Redfern and his wife. It was a lovely clear night with a bright moon.

The Redferns sat down. For a while they were silent.

At last Patrick Redfern said:

"It's a glorious evening, isn't it, Christine?"

"Yes."

Something in her voice may have made him uneasy. He sat without looking at her.

Christine Redfern asked in her quiet voice:

"Did you know that woman was going to be here?"

He turned sharply. He said:

"I don't know what you mean."

"I think you do."

"Look here, Christine. I don't know what has come over you—"

She interrupted. Her voice held feeling now. It trembled.

"Over *me*? It's what has come over *you!*"

"Nothing's come over me."

"Oh! Patrick! It *has!* You insisted so on coming here. You were quite vehement. I wanted to go to Tintagel again where—where we had our honeymoon. You were bent on coming here."

"Well, why not? It's a fascinating spot."

"Perhaps. But you wanted to come here because *she* was going to be here."

"She? Who is she?"

"Mrs. Marshall. You—you're infatuated with her."

"For God's sake, Christine, don't make a fool of yourself. It's not like you to be jealous."

His bluster was a little uncertain. He exaggerated it.

She said:

"We've been so happy."

"Happy? Of course we've been happy! We *are* happy. But we shan't go on being happy if I can't even speak to another woman without you kicking up a row."

"It's not like that."

"Yes, it is. In marriage one has got to have—well—friendships with other people. This suspicious attitude is all wrong. I—I can't speak to a pretty woman without your jumping to the conclusion that I'm in love with her—"

He stopped. He shrugged his shoulders.

Christine Redfern said:

"You *are* in love with her. . . ."

"Oh, don't be a fool, Christine! I've—I've barely spoken to her."

"That's not true."

"Don't for goodness' sake get into the habit of being jealous of every pretty woman we come across."

Christine Redfern said:

"She's not just any pretty woman! She's—she's *different!* She's a bad lot!

Yes, she is. She'll do you harm. Patrick, please, *give it up*. Let's go away from here."

Patrick Redfern stuck out his chin mutinously. He looked somehow very young as he said defiantly:

"Don't be ridiculous, Christine. And—and don't let's quarrel about it."

"I don't want to quarrel."

"Then behave like a reasonable human being. Come on, let's go back to the hotel."

He got up. There was a pause, then Christine Redfern got up too.

She said:

"Very well . . ."

In the recess adjoining, on the seat there, Hercule Poirot sat and shook his head sorrowfully.

Some people might have scrupulously removed themselves from earshot of a private conversation. But not Hercule Poirot. He had no scruples of that kind.

"Besides," as he explained to his friend Hastings at a later date, "it was a question of murder."

Hastings said, staring:

"But the murder hadn't happened, then."

Hercule Poirot sighed. He said:

"But already, *mon cher,* it was very clearly indicated."

"Then why didn't you stop it?"

And Hercule Poirot, with a sigh, said, as he had said once before in Egypt, that if a person is determined to commit murder it is not easy to prevent them. He does not blame himself for what happened. It was, according to him, inevitable.

CHAPTER III

ROSAMUND DARNLEY AND Kenneth Marshall sat on the short springy turf of the cliff overlooking Gull Cove. This was on the east side of the island. People came here in the morning sometimes to bathe when they wanted to be peaceful.

Rosamund said:

"It's nice to get away from people."

Marshall murmured inaudibly:

"M-m, yes."

He rolled over sniffing at the short turf.

"Smells good. Remember the downs at Shipley?"

"Rather."

"Pretty good, those days."

"Yes."

"You've not changed much, Rosamund."

"Yes, I have. I've changed enormously."

"You've been very successful and you're rich and all that, but you're the same old Rosamund."

Rosamund murmured:

"I wish I were."

"What's that?"

"Nothing. It's a pity, isn't it, Kenneth, that we can't keep the nice natures and high ideals that we had when we were young?"

"I don't know that your nature was ever particularly nice, my child. You used to get into the most frightful rages. You half choked me once when you flew at me in a temper."

Rosamund laughed. She said:

"Do you remember the day that we took Toby down to get water rats?"

They spent some minutes in recalling old adventures.

Then there came a pause.

Rosamund's fingers played with the clasp of her bag.

She said at last:

"Kenneth?"

"Um." His reply was indistinct. He was still lying on his face on the turf.

"If I say something to you that is probably outrageously impertinent, will you never speak to me again?"

He rolled over and sat up.

"I don't think," he said seriously, "that I would ever regard anything you said as impertinent. You see, you *belong*."

She nodded in acceptance of all that last phrase meant. She concealed only the pleasure it gave her.

"Kenneth, why don't you get a divorce from your wife?"

His face altered. It hardened—the happy expression died out of it. He took a pipe from his pocket and began filling it.

Rosamund said:

"I'm sorry if I've offended you."

He said quietly:

"You haven't offended me."

"Well, then, why don't you?"

"You don't understand, my dear girl."

"Are you—so frightfully fond of her?"

"It's not just a question of that. You see, I married her."

"I know. But she's—pretty notorious."

He considered that for a moment, ramming in the tobacco carefully.

"Is she? I suppose she is."

"You *could* divorce her, Ken."

"My dear girl, you've got no business to say a thing like that. Just because men lose their heads about her a bit isn't to say that she loses hers."

Rosamund bit off a rejoinder. Then she said:

"You could fix it so that she divorced you—if you prefer it that way."

"I daresay I could."

"You ought to, Ken. Really, I mean it. There's the child."

"Linda?"

"Yes, Linda."

"What's Linda to do with it?"

"Arlena's not good for Linda. She isn't really. Linda, I think, *feels* things a good deal."

Kenneth Marshall applied a match to his pipe. Between puffs he said:

"Yes—there's something in that. I suppose Arlena and Linda aren't very good for each other. Not the right thing for a girl perhaps. It's a bit worrying."

Rosamund said:

"I like Linda—very much. There's something—fine about her."

Kenneth said:

"She's like her mother. She takes things hard like Ruth did."

Rosamund said:

"Then don't you think—really—that you ought to get rid of Arlena?"

"Fix up a divorce?"

"Yes. People are doing that all the time."

Kenneth Marshall said with sudden vehemence:

"Yes, and that's just what I hate."

"Hate?" She was startled.

"Yes. Sort of attitude to life there is nowadays. If you take on a thing and don't like it, then you get yourself out of it as quick as possible! Dash it all, there's got to be such a thing as good faith. If you marry a woman and engage yourself to look after her, well, it's up to you to do it. It's your show. You've taken it on. I'm sick of quick marriage and easy divorce. Arlena's my wife, that's all there is to it."

Rosamund leaned forward. She said in a low voice:

"So it's like that with you? 'Till death do us part'?"

Kenneth Marshall nodded his head.

He said:

"That's just it."

Rosamund said:

"I see."

II

Mr. Horace Blatt, returning to Leathercombe Bay down a narrow twisting lane, nearly ran down Mrs. Redfern at a corner.

As she flattened herself into the hedge, Mr. Blatt brought his Sunbeam to a halt by applying the brakes vigorously.

"Hullo-ullo-ullo," said Mr. Blatt cheerfully.

He was a large man with a red face and a fringe of reddish hair round a shining bald spot.

It was Mr. Blatt's apparent ambition to be the life and soul of any place he happened to be in. The Jolly Roger Hotel, in his opinion, given somewhat loudly, needed brightening up. He was puzzled at the way people seemed to melt and disappear when he himself arrived on the scene.

"Nearly made you into strawberry jam, didn't I?" said Mr. Blatt gaily.

Christine Redfern said:

"Yes, you did."

"Jump in," said Mr. Blatt.

"Oh, thanks—I think I'll walk."

"Nonsense," said Mr. Blatt. "What's a car for?"

Yielding to necessity Christine Redfern got in.

Mr. Blatt restarted the engine which had stopped owing to the suddenness with which he had previously pulled up.

Mr. Blatt inquired:

"And what are you doing walking about all alone? That's all wrong, a nice-looking girl like you."

Christine said hurriedly:

"Oh! I like being alone."

Mr. Blatt gave her a terrific dig with his elbow, nearly sending the car into the hedge at the same time.

"Girls always say that," he said. "They don't mean it. You know, that place, the Jolly Roger, wants a bit of livening up. Nothing jolly about it. No *life* in it. Of course there's a good amount of duds staying there. A lot of kids, to begin with, and a lot of old fogeys too. There's that old Anglo-Indian bore and that athletic parson and those yapping Americans and that foreigner with the moustache—makes me laugh that moustache of his! I should say he's a hairdresser, something of that sort."

Christine shook her head.

"Oh, no, he's a detective."

Mr. Blatt nearly let the car go into the hedge again.

"A detective? D'you mean he's in *disguise?*"

Christine smiled faintly.

She said:

"Oh, no, he really *is* like that. He's Hercule Poirot. You must have heard of him."

Mr. Blatt said:

"Didn't catch his name properly. Oh, yes, I've *heard* of him. But I thought he was dead. . . . Dash it, he *ought* to be dead. What's he after down here?"

"He's not after anything—he's just on a holiday."

"Well, I suppose that might be so." Mr. Blatt seemed doubtful about it. "Looks a bit of a bounder, doesn't he?"

"Well," said Christine and hesitated. "Perhaps a little peculiar."

"What I say is," said Mr. Blatt, "what's wrong with Scotland Yard? Buy British every time for me."

He reached the bottom of the hill and with a triumphant fanfare of the horn ran the car into the Jolly Roger's garage which was situated, for tidal reasons, on the mainland opposite the hotel.

III

Linda Marshall was in the small shop which catered for the wants of visitors to Leathercombe Bay. One side of it was devoted to shelves on which were books which could be borrowed for the sum of twopence. The newest of them was ten years old, some were twenty years old and others older still.

Linda took first one and then another doubtfully from the shelf and glanced into it. She decided that she couldn't possibly read *The Four Feathers* or *Vice Versa*. She took out a small squat volume in brown calf.

The time passed. . . .

With a start Linda shoved the book back in the shelf as Christine Redfern's voice said:

"What are you reading, Linda?"

Linda said hurriedly:

"Nothing. I'm looking for a book."

She pulled out *The Marriage of William Ashe* at random and advanced to the counter fumbling for twopence.

Christine said:

"Mr. Blatt just drove me home—after nearly running over me first. I really felt I couldn't walk all across the causeway with him, so I said I had to buy some things."

Linda said:

"He's awful, isn't he? Always saying how rich he is and making the most terrible jokes."

Christine said:

"Poor man. One really feels rather sorry for him."

Linda didn't agree. She didn't see anything to be sorry for in Mr. Blatt. She was young and ruthless.

She walked with Christine Redfern out of the shop and down towards the causeway.

She was busy with her own thoughts. She liked Christine Redfern. She and Rosamund Darnley were the only bearable people on the island in Linda's opinion. Neither of them talked much to her for one thing. Now, as they walked, Christine didn't say anything. That, Linda thought, was sensible. If you hadn't anything worth saying why go chattering all the time?

She lost herself in her own perplexities.

She said suddenly:

"Mrs. Redfern, have you ever felt that everything's so awful—so terrible —that you'll—oh, *burst* . . . ?"

The words were almost comic, but Linda's face, drawn and anxious, was not. Christine Redfern, looking at her at first vaguely, with scarcely comprehending eyes, certainly saw nothing to laugh at. . . .

She caught her breath sharply.

She said:

"Yes—yes—I have felt—just that. . . ."

IV

Mr. Blatt said:

"So you're the famous sleuth, eh?"

They were in the cocktail bar, a favourite haunt of Mr. Blatt's.

Hercule Poirot acknowledged the remark with his usual lack of modesty.

Mr. Blatt went on.

"And what are you doing down here—on a job?"

"No, no. I repose myself. I take the holiday."

Mr. Blatt winked.

"You'd say that anyway, wouldn't you?"

Poirot replied:

"Not necessarily."

Horace Blatt said:

"Oh! come now. As a matter of fact you'd be safe enough with *me*. I don't repeat all I hear! Learnt to keep my mouth shut years ago. Shouldn't have got on the way I have if I hadn't known how to do that. But you know what most people are—yap, yap, yap about everything they hear! Now you can't afford that in your trade! That's why you've got to keep it up that you're here holiday-making and nothing else."

Poirot asked:

"And why should you suppose the contrary?"

Mr. Blatt closed one eye.

He said:

"I'm a man of the world. I know the cut of a fellow's jib. A man like you would be at Deauville or Le Touquet or down at Juan les Pins. That's your—what's the phrase?—spiritual home."

Poirot sighed. He looked out of the window. Rain was falling and mist encircled the island. He said:

"It is possible that you are right! There, at least, in wet weather there are the distractions."

"Good old Casino!" said Mr. Blatt. "You know, I've had to work pretty hard most of my life. No time for holidays or kickshaws. I meant to make good and I have made good. Now I can do what I please. My money's as good as any man's. I've seen a bit of life in the last few years, I can tell you."

Poirot murmured:

"Ah, yes?"

"Don't know why I came to this place," Mr. Blatt continued.

Poirot observed:

"I, too, wondered."

"Eh, what's that?"

Poirot waved an eloquent hand.

"I, too, am not without observation. I should have expected *you* most certainly to choose Deauville or Biarritz."

"Instead of which, we're both here, eh?"

Mr. Blatt gave a hoarse chuckle.

"Don't really know why I came here," he mused. "I think, you know, it sounded *romantic*. Jolly Roger Hotel, Smugglers' Island. That kind of address tickles you up, you know. Makes you think of when you were a boy. Pirates, smuggling, all that."

He laughed rather self-consciously.

"I used to sail quite a bit as a boy. Not this part of the world. Off the East coast. Funny how a taste for that sort of thing never quite leaves you. I could have a tip-top yacht if I liked, but somehow I don't really fancy it. I like mucking about in that little yawl of mine. Redfern's keen on sailing, too. He's been out with me once or twice. Can't get hold of him now—always hanging round that red-haired wife of Marshall's."

He paused, then lowering his voice, he went on.

"Mostly a dried-up lot of sticks in this hotel! Mrs. Marshall's about the only lively spot! I should think Marshall's got his hands full looking after her. All sorts of stories about her in her stage days—*and* after! Men go crazy about her. You'll see, there'll be a spot of trouble one of these days."

Poirot asked:

"What kind of trouble?"

Horace Blatt replied:

"That depends. I'd say, looking at Marshall, that he's a man with a funny kind of temper. As a matter of fact, I know he is. Heard something about him. I've met that quiet sort. Never know where you are with that kind. Redfern had better look out—"

He broke off, as the subject of his words came into the bar. He went on speaking loudly and self-consciously.

"And, as I say, sailing round this coast is good fun. Hullo, Redfern, have one with me? What'll you have? Dry Martini? Right. What about you, Mr. Poirot?"

Poirot shook his head.

Patrick Redfern sat down and said:

"Sailing? It's the best fun in the world. Wish I could do more of it. Used to spend most of my time as a boy in a sailing dinghy round this coast."

Poirot said:

"Then you know this part of the world well?"

"Rather! I knew this place before there was a hotel on it. There were just a few fishermen's cottages at Leathercombe Bay and a tumbledown old house, all shut up, on the island."

"There was a house here?"

"Oh, yes, but it hadn't been lived in for years. Was practically falling down. There used to be all sorts of stories of secret passages from the house to Pixy's Cave. We were always looking for that secret passage, I remember."

Horace Blatt spilt his drink. He cursed, mopped himself and asked: "What is this Pixy's Cave?"

Patrick said:

"Oh, don't you know it? It's on Pixy Cove. You can't find the entrance to it easily. It's among a lot of piled-up boulders at one end. Just a long thin crack. You can just squeeze through it. Inside it widens out into quite a big cave. You can imagine what fun it was to a boy! An old fisherman showed it to me. Nowadays, even the fishermen don't know about it. I asked one the other day why the place was called Pixy Cove and he couldn't tell me."

Hercule Poirot said:

"But I still do not understand. What is this Pixy?"

Patrick Redfern said:

"Oh! that's typically Devonshire. There's the Pixy's Cave at Sheepstor on the Moor. You're supposed to leave a pin, you know, as a present for the pixy. A pixy is a kind of moor spirit."

Hercule Poirot said:

"Ah! but it is interesting, that."

Patrick Redfern went on.

"There's a lot of pixy lore on Dartmoor still. There are Tors that are said to be pixy-ridden, and I expect that farmers coming home after a thick night still complain of being pixy-led."

Horace Blatt said:

"You mean when they've had a couple?"

Patrick Redfern said with a smile:

"That's certainly the commonsense explanation!"

Blatt looked at his watch. He said:

"I'm going in to dinner. On the whole, Redfern, pirates are my favourites, not pixies."

Patrick Redfern said with a laugh as the other went out:

"Faith, I'd like to see the old boy pixy-led himself!"

Poirot observed meditatively:

"For a hard-bitten business man, M. Blatt seems to have a very romantic imagination."

Patrick Redfern said:

"That's because he's only half educated. Or so my wife says. Look at what he reads! Nothing but thrillers or Wild West stories."

Poirot said:

"You mean that he has still the mentality of a boy?"

"Well, don't you think so, sir?"

"Me, I have not seen very much of him."

"I haven't really, either. I've been out sailing with him once or twice— but he doesn't really like having any one with him. He prefers to be on his own."

Hercule Poirot said:

"That is indeed curious. It is singularly unlike his practice on land."

Redfern laughed. He said:

"I know. We all have a bit of trouble keeping out of his way. He'd like to turn this place into a cross between Margate and Le Touquet."

Poirot said nothing for a minute or two. He was studying the laughing face of his companion very attentively. He said suddenly and unexpectedly:

"I think, M. Redfern, that you enjoy living."

Patrick stared at him, surprised.

"Indeed I do. Why not?"

"Why not indeed," agreed Poirot. "I make you my felicitation on the fact."

Smiling a little Patrick Redfern said:

"Thank you, sir."

"That is why, as an older man, a very much older man, I venture to offer you a piece of advice."

"Yes, sir?"

"A very wise friend of mine in the Police Force said to me years ago: 'Hercule, my friend, if you would know tranquillity, avoid women.'"

Patrick Redfern said:

"I'm afraid it's a bit late for that, sir. I'm married, you know."

"I do know. Your wife is a very charming, a very accomplished woman. She is, I think, very fond of you."

Patrick Redfern said sharply:

"I'm very fond of her."

"Ah," said Hercule Poirot, "I am delighted to hear it."

Patrick's brow was suddenly like thunder.

"Look here, M. Poirot, what are you getting at?"

"Les femmes." Poirot leaned back and closed his eyes. "I know something of them. They are capable of complicating life unbearably. And the English, they conduct their affairs indescribably. If it was necessary for you to come here, M. Redfern, why, in the name of Heaven, did you bring your wife?"

Patrick Redfern said angrily:

"I don't know what you mean."

Hercule Poirot said calmly:

"You know perfectly. I am not so foolish as to argue with an infatuated man. I utter only the word of caution."

"You've been listening to these damned scandalmongers. Mrs. Gardener, the Brewster woman—nothing to do but to clack their tongues all day. Just because a woman's good-looking—they're down on her like a sack of coals."

Hercule Poirot got up. He murmured:

"Are you really as young as all that?"

Shaking his head, he left the bar. Patrick Redfern stared angrily after him.

V

Hercule Poirot paused in the hall on his way from the dining-room. The doors were open—a breath of soft night air came in.

The rain had stopped and the mist had dispersed. It was a fine night again.

Hercule Poirot found Mrs. Redfern in her favourite seat on the cliff ledge. He stopped by her and said:

"This seat is damp. You should not sit here. You will catch the chill."

"No, I shan't. And what does it matter anyway."

"Tscha, tscha, you are not a child! You are an educated woman. You must look at things sensibly."

She said coldly:

"I can assure you I never take cold."

Poirot said:

"It has been a wet day. The wind blew, the rain came down, and the mist was everywhere so that one could not see through it. *Eh bien*, what is it like now? The mists have rolled away, the sky is clear and up above the stars shine. That is like life, Madame."

Christine said in a low fierce voice:

"Do you know what I am most sick of in this place?"

"What, Madame?"

"Pity."

She brought the word out like the flick of a whip.

She went on:

"Do you think I don't know? That I can't see? All the time people are saying: 'Poor Mrs. Redfern—that poor little woman.' And anyway I'm not little, I'm tall. They say little because they are sorry for me. And I can't bear it!"

Cautiously Hercule Poirot spread his handkerchief on the seat and sat down. He said thoughtfully:

"There is something in that."

She said:

"That woman—" and stopped.

Poirot said gravely:

"Will you allow me to tell you something, Madame? Something that is as true as the stars above us? The Arlena Stuarts—or Arlena Marshalls—of this world—do not count."

Christine Redfern said:

"Nonsense."

"I assure you, it is true. Their Empire is of the moment and for the moment. To count—really and truly to count—a woman must have goodness or brains."

Christine said scornfully:

"Do you think men care for goodness or brains?"

Poirot said gravely:

"Fundamentally, yes."

Christine laughed shortly.

She said:

"I don't agree with you."

Poirot said:

"Your husband loves you, Madame. I know it."

"You can't know it."

"Yes, yes. I know it. I have seen him looking at you."

Suddenly she broke down. She wept stormily and bitterly against Poirot's accommodating shoulder.

She said:

"I can't bear it. . . . I can't bear it. . . ."

Poirot patted her arm. He said soothingly:

"Patience—only patience."

She sat up and pressed her handkerchief to her eyes. She said in a stifled voice:

"It's all right. I'm better now. Leave me. I'd—I'd rather be alone."

He obeyed and left her sitting there while he himself followed the winding path down to the hotel.

He was nearly there when he heard the murmur of voices.

He turned a little aside from the path. There was a gap in the bushes.

He saw Arlena Marshall and Patrick Redfern beside her. He heard the man's voice, with the throb in it of emotion.

"I'm crazy about you—crazy—you've driven me mad. . . . You do care a little—you do care?"

He saw Arlena Marshall's face—it was, he thought, like a sleek happy cat—it was animal, not human. She said softly:

"Of course, Patrick darling, I adore you. You know that. . . ."

For once Hercule Poirot cut his eavesdropping short. He went back to the path and on down to the hotel.

A figure joined him suddenly. It was Captain Marshall.

Marshall said:

"Remarkable night, what? After that foul day." He looked up at the sky. "Looks as though we should have fine weather to-morrow."

CHAPTER IV

THE MORNING OF the 25th of August dawned bright and cloudless. It was a morning to tempt even an inveterate sluggard to rise early.

Several people rose early that morning at the Jolly Roger.

It was eight o'clock when Linda, sitting at her dressing-table, turned a little thick calf-bound volume face downwards, sprawling it open, and looked at her own face in the mirror.

Her lips were set tight together and the pupils of her eyes contracted. She said below her breath:

"I'll do it. . . ."

She slipped out of her pyjamas and into her bathing dress. Over it she flung on a bath-robe and laced espadrilles on her feet.

She went out of her room and along the passage. At the end of it a door on to the balcony led to an outside staircase leading directly down to the rocks below the hotel. There was a small iron ladder clamped onto the rocks leading down into the water which was used by many of the hotel guests for a before breakfast dip as taking up less time than going down to the main bathing beach.

As Linda started down from the balcony she met her father coming up. He said:

"You're up early. Going to have a dip?"

Linda nodded.

They passed each other.

Instead of going on down the rocks, however, Linda skirted round the hotel to the left until she came to the path down to the causeway connecting the hotel with the mainland. The tide was high and the causeway under water, but the boat that took hotel guests across was tied to a little jetty. The man in charge of it was absent at the moment. Linda got in, untied it and rowed herself across.

She tied up the boat on the other side, walked up the slope past the hotel garage and along until she reached the general shop.

The woman had just taken down the shutters and was engaged in sweeping the floor. She looked amazed at the sight of Linda.

"Well, Miss, you *are* up early."

Linda put her hand in the pocket of her bath-wrap and brought out some money. She proceeded to make her purchases.

II

Christine Redfern was standing in Linda's room when the girl returned.

"Oh, there you are," Christine exclaimed. "I thought you couldn't be really up yet."

Linda said:

"No, I've been bathing."

Noticing the parcel in her hand, Christine said with surprise:

"The post has come early to-day."

Linda flushed. With her habitual nervous clumsiness the parcel slipped from her hand. The flimsy string broke and some of the contents rolled over the floor.

Christine exclaimed:

"What have you been buying *candles* for?"

But to Linda's relief she did not wait for an answer, but went on, as she helped to pick the things up from the floor:

"I came in to ask whether you would like to come with me to Gull Cove this morning. I want to sketch there."

Linda accepted with alacrity.

In the last few days she had accompanied Christine Redfern more than once on sketching expeditions. Christine was a most indifferent artist but it is possible that she found the excuse of painting a help to her pride since her husband now spent most of his time with Arlena Marshall.

Linda Marshall had been increasingly morose and bad-tempered. She liked being with Christine who, intent on her work, spoke very little. It was, Linda felt, nearly as good as being by oneself, and in a curious way she craved for company of some kind. There was a subtle kind of sympathy between her and the elder woman, probably based on the fact of their mutual dislike of the same person.

Christine said:

"I'm playing tennis at twelve, so we'd better start fairly early. Half past ten?"

"Right. I'll be ready. Meet you in the hall."

III

Rosamund Darnley, strolling out of the dining-room after a very late breakfast, was cannoned into by Linda as the latter came tearing down the stairs.

"Oh! sorry, Miss Darnley."

Rosamund said:

"Lovely morning, isn't it? One can hardly believe it after yesterday."

"I know. I'm going with Mrs. Redfern to Gull Cove. I said I'd meet her at half past ten. I thought I was late."

"No, it's only twenty-five past."

"Oh! good."

She was panting a little and Rosamund looked at her curiously.

"You're not feverish, are you, Linda?"

The girl's eyes were very bright and she had a vivid patch of colour in each cheek.

"Oh! *no.* I'm never feverish."

Rosamund smiled and said:

"It's such a lovely day I got up for breakfast. Usually I have it in bed. But to-day I came down and faced eggs and bacon like a man."

"I know—it's heavenly after yesterday. Gull Cove is nice in the morning. I shall put a lot of oil on and get really brown."

Rosamund said:

"Yes, Gull Cove is nice in the morning. And it's more peaceful than the beach here."

Linda said, rather shyly:

"Come too."

Rosamund shook her head.

She said:

"Not this morning. I've other fish to fry."

Christine Redfern came down the stairs.

She was wearing beach pyjamas of a loose floppy pattern with long sleeves and wide legs. They were made of some green material with a yellow design. Rosamund's tongue itched to tell her that yellow and green were the most unbecoming colours possible for her fair, slightly anaemic complexion. It always annoyed Rosamund when people had no clothes sense.

She thought: "If I dressed that girl, I'd soon make her husband sit up and take notice. However much of a fool Arlena is, she does know how to dress. This wretched girl looks just like a wilting lettuce."

Aloud she said:

"Have a nice time. I'm going to Sunny Ledge with a book."

IV

Hercule Poirot breakfasted in his room as usual off coffee and rolls.

The beauty of the morning, however, tempted him to leave the hotel earlier than usual. It was ten o'clock, at least half an hour before his usual appearance, when he descended to the bathing beach. The beach itself was empty save for one person.

That person was Arlena Marshall.

Clad in her white bathing-dress, the green Chinese hat on her head, she was trying to launch a white wooden float. Poirot came gallantly to the rescue, completely immersing a pair of white suède shoes in doing so.

She thanked him with one of those sideways glances of hers.

Just as she was pushing off, she called him.

"M. Poirot?"

Poirot leaped to the water's edge.

"Madame."

Arlena Marshall said:

"Do something for me, will you?"

"Anything."

She smiled at him. She murmured:

"Don't tell any one where I am." She made her glance appealing. "Every one *will* follow me about so. I just want for once to be *alone*."

She paddled off vigorously.

Poirot walked up the beach. He murmured to himself:

"*Ah ça, jamais!* That, *par exemple*, I do not believe."

He doubted if Arlena Stuart, to give her her stage name, had ever wanted to be alone in her life.

Hercule Poirot, that man of the world, knew better. Arlena Marshall was doubtless keeping a rendezvous, and Poirot had a very good idea with whom.

Or thought he had, but there he found himself proved wrong.

For just as the float rounded the point of the bay and disappeared out of sight Patrick Redfern closely followed by Kenneth Marshall came striding down the beach from the hotel.

Marshall nodded to Poirot.

"Morning, Poirot. Seen my wife anywhere about?"

Poirot's answer was diplomatic.

"Has Madame then risen so early?"

Marshall said:

"She's not in her room." He looked up at the sky. "Lovely day. I shall have a bathe right away. Got a lot of typing to do this morning."

Patrick Redfern, less openly, was looking up and down the beach. He sat down near Poirot and prepared to wait for the arrival of his lady.

Poirot said:

"And Madame Redfern? Has she too risen early?"

Patrick Redfern said:

"Christine? Oh, she's going off sketching. She's rather keen on art just now."

He spoke impatiently, his mind clearly elsewhere. As time passed he displayed his impatience for Arlena's arrival only too crudely. At every footstep he turned an eager head to see who it was coming down from the hotel.

Disappointment followed disappointment.

First Mr. and Mrs. Gardener complete with knitting and book and then Miss Brewster arrived.

Mrs. Gardener, industrious as ever, settled herself in her chair, and began to knit vigorously and talk at the same time.

"Well, M. Poirot. The beach seems very deserted this morning. Where *is* everybody?"

Poirot replied that the Mastermans and the Cowans, two families with young people in them, had gone off on an all-day sailing excursion.

"Why, that certainly does make all the difference, not having them about laughing and calling out. And only one person bathing, Captain Marshall."

Marshall had just finished his swim. He came up the beach swinging his towel.

"Pretty good in the sea this morning," he said. "Unfortunately I've got a lot of work to do. Must go and get on with it."

"Why, if that isn't too bad, Captain Marshall. On a beautiful day like this, too. My, wasn't yesterday too terrible? I said to Mr. Gardener that if the weather was going to continue like that, we'd just have to leave. It's so melancholy, you know, with the mist right up around the island. Gives you a kind of ghosty feeling, but then I've always been very susceptible to atmosphere ever since I was a child. Sometimes, you know, I'd feel I just had to scream and scream. And that, of course, was very trying to my parents. But my mother was a lovely woman and she said to my father, 'Sinclair, if the child feels like that, we must let her do it. Screaming is her way of expressing herself.' And of course my father agreed. He was devoted to my mother and just did everything she said. They were a perfectly lovely couple, as I'm sure Mr. Gardener will agree. They were a very remarkable couple, weren't they, Odell?"

"Yes, darling," said Mr. Gardener.

"And where's your girl this morning, Captain Marshall?"

"Linda? I don't know. I expect she's mooning round the island somewhere."

"You know, Captain Marshall, that girl looks kind of peaky to me. She needs feeding up and very, very sympathetic treatment."

Kenneth Marshall said curtly:

"Linda's all right."

He went up to the hotel.

Patrick Redfern did not go into the water. He sat about, frankly looking up towards the hotel. He was beginning to look a shade sulky.

Miss Brewster was brisk and cheerful when she arrived.

The conversation was much as it had been on a previous morning. Gentle yapping from Mrs. Gardener and short staccato barks from Miss Brewster.

She remarked at last:

"Beach seems a bit empty. Every one off on excursions?"

Mrs. Gardener said:

"I was saying to Mr. Gardener only this morning that we simply must make an excursion to Dartmoor. It's quite near and the associations are all so romantic. And I'd like to see that convict prison—Princetown, isn't it? I think we'd better fix up right away and go there to-morrow, Odell."

Mr. Gardener said:

"Yes, darling."

Hercule Poirot said to Miss Brewster:

"You are going to bathe, Mademoiselle?"

"Oh, I've had my morning dip before breakfast. Somebody nearly brained me with a bottle, too. Chucked it out of one of the hotel windows."

"Now that's a very dangerous thing to do," said Mrs. Gardener. "I had a dear friend who got concussion by a toothpaste tin falling on him in the street—thrown out of a thirty-fifth storey window it was. A most dangerous thing to do. He got very substantial damages." She began to hunt among her skeins of wool. "Why, Odell, I don't believe I've got that second shade of purple wool. It's in the second drawer of the bureau in our bedroom or it might be the third."

"Yes, darling."

Mr. Gardener rose obediently and departed on his search.

Mrs. Gardener went on:

"Sometimes, you know, I do think that maybe we're going a little too far nowadays. What with all our great discoveries and all the electrical waves there must be in the atmosphere, I do think it leads to a great deal of mental unrest and I just feel that maybe the time has come for a new message to humanity. I don't know, M. Poirot, if you've ever interested yourself in the prophecies from the Pyramids."

"I have not," said Poirot.

"Well, I do assure you that they're very, very interesting. What with Moscow being exactly a thousand miles due North of—now what was it?—Would it be Nineveh?—but anyway you take a circle and it just shows the most surprising things—and one can just see that there must have been special guidance, and that those ancient Egyptians couldn't have thought of what they did all by themselves. And when you've gone into the theory of the numbers and their repetition, why, it's all just so clear that I can't see how any one can doubt the truth of it for a moment."

Mrs. Gardener paused triumphantly but neither Poirot nor Miss Emily Brewster felt moved to argue the point.

Poirot studied his white suède shoes ruefully.

Emily Brewster said:

"You been paddling with your shoes on, M. Poirot?"

Poirot murmured:

"Alas! I was precipitate."

Emily Brewster lowered her voice. She said:

"Where's our Vamp this morning? She's late."

Mrs. Gardener, raising her eyes from her knitting to study Patrick Redfern, murmured:

"He looks just like a thundercloud. Oh! dear, I do feel the whole thing is such a pity. I wonder what Captain Marshall thinks about it all. He's such a nice quiet man—very British and unassuming. You just never know what he's thinking about things."

Patrick Redfern rose and began to pace up and down the beach.

Mrs. Gardener murmured:

"Just like a tiger."

Three pairs of eyes watched his pacing. Their scrutiny seemed to make Patrick Redfern uncomfortable. He looked more than sulky now. He looked in a flaming temper.

In the stillness a faint chime from the mainland came to their ears.

Emily Brewster murmured:

"Wind's from the East again. That's a good sign when you can hear the church clock strike."

Nobody said any more until Mr. Gardener returned with a skein of brilliant magenta wool.

"Why, Odell, what a long time you have been!"

"Sorry, darling, but you see it wasn't in your bureau at all. I found it on your wardrobe shelf."

"Why, isn't that too extraordinary? I could have declared I put it in that bureau drawer. I do think it's fortunate that I've never had to give evidence in a court case. I'd just worry myself to death in case I wasn't remembering a thing just right."

Mr. Gardener said:

"Mrs. Gardener is very conscientious."

V

It was some five minutes later that Patrick Redfern said:

"Going for your row this morning, Miss Brewster? Mind if I come with you?"

Miss Brewster said heartily:

"Delighted."

"Let's row right round the island," proposed Redfern.

Miss Brewster consulted her watch.

"Shall we have time? Oh, yes, it's not half past eleven yet. Come on, then, let's start."

They went down the beach together.

Patrick Redfern took first turn at the oars. He rowed with a powerful stroke. The boat leapt forward.

Emily Brewster said approvingly:

"Good. We'll see if you can keep that up."

He laughed into her eyes. His spirits had improved.

"I shall probably have a fine crop of blisters by the time we get back." He threw up his head tossing back his black hair. "God, it's a marvellous day! If you do get a real summer's day in England there's nothing to beat it."

Emily Brewster said gruffly:

"Can't beat England anyway in my opinion. Only place in the world to live in."

"I'm with you."

They rounded the point of the bay to the west and rowed under the cliffs. Patrick Redfern looked up.

"Any one on Sunny Ledge this morning? Yes, there's a sunshade. Who is it, I wonder?"

Emily Brewster said:

"It's Miss Darnley, I think. She's got one of those Japanese affairs."

They rowed up the coast. On their left was the open sea.

Emily Brewster said:

"We ought to have gone the other way round. This way we've got the current against us."

"There's very little current. I've swum out here and not noticed it. Anyway we couldn't go the other way. The causeway wouldn't be covered."

"Depends on the tide, of course. But they always say that bathing from Pixy Cove is dangerous if you swim out too far."

Patrick was rowing vigorously still. At the same time he was scanning the cliffs attentively.

Emily Brewster thought suddenly:

"He's looking for the Marshall woman. That's why he wanted to come with me. She hasn't shown up this morning and he's wondering what she's up to. Probably she's done it on purpose. Just a move in the game—to make him keener."

They rounded the jutting point of rock to the south of the little bay named Pixy Cove. It was quite a small cove, with rocks dotted fantastically about the beach. It faced nearly northwest and the cliff overhung it a good deal. It was a favourite place for picnic teas. In the morning, when the sun was off it, it was not popular and there was seldom any one there.

On this occasion, however, there was a figure on the beach.

Patrick Redfern's stroke checked and recovered.

He said in a would-be casual tone:

"Hullo, who's that?"

Miss Brewster said drily:

"It looks like Mrs. Marshall."

Patrick Redfern said as though struck by the idea:

"So it does."

He altered his course, rowing inshore.

Emily Brewster protested.

"We don't want to land here, do we?"

Patrick Redfern said quickly:

"Oh, plenty of time."

His eyes looked into hers—something in them, a naïve pleading look rather like that of an importunate dog, silenced Emily Brewster. She thought to herself:

"Poor boy, he's got it badly. Oh, well, it can't be helped. He'll get over it in time."

The boat was fast approaching the beach.

Arlena Marshall was lying face downwards on the shingle her arms outstretched. The white float was drawn up near by.

Something was puzzling Emily Brewster. It was as though she was looking at something she knew quite well but which was in one respect quite wrong.

It was a minute or two before it came to her.

Arlena Marshall's attitude was the attitude of a sunbather. So had she lain many a time on the beach by the hotel, her bronzed body outstretched and the green cardboard hat protecting her head and neck.

But there was no sun on Pixy's Beach and there would be none for some hours yet. The overhanging cliff protected the beach from the sun in the morning. A vague feeling of apprehension came over Emily Brewster.

The boat grounded on the shingle. Patrick Redfern called:

"Hullo, Arlena."

And then Emily Brewster's foreboding took definite shape. For the recumbent figure did not move or answer.

Emily saw Patrick Redfern's face change. He jumped out of the boat and she followed him. They dragged the boat ashore then set off up the beach to where that white figure lay so still and unresponsive near the bottom of the cliff.

Patrick Redfern got there first but Emily Brewster was close behind him.

She saw, as one sees in a dream, the bronzed limbs, the white backless bathing dress—the red curl of hair escaping under the jade-green hat— saw something else too—the curious unnatural angle of the outspread arms. Felt, in that minute, that this body had not *lain* down but had been *thrown*. . . .

She heard Patrick's voice—a mere frightened whisper. He knelt down beside that still form—touched the hand—the arm. . . .

He said in a low shuddering whisper:

"*My God, she's dead.* . . ."

And then, as he lifted the hat a little, peered at the neck:

"*Oh, God, she's been strangled . . . murdered.*"

VI

It was one of those moments when time stands still.

With an odd feeling of unreality Emily Brewster heard herself saying:

"We mustn't touch anything . . . Not until the police come."

Redfern's answer came mechanically:

"No—no—of couse not." And then in a deep agonized whisper: "Who? *Who?* Who could have done that to Arlena. She can't have—have been murdered. It can't be true!"

Emily Brewster shook her head, not knowing quite what to answer.

She heard him draw in his breath—heard the low controlled rage in his voice as he said:

"My God, if I get my hands on the foul fiend who did this."

Emily Brewster shivered. Her imagination pictured a lurking murderer behind one of the boulders. Then she heard her voice saying:

"Whoever did it wouldn't be hanging about. We must get the police. Perhaps"—she hesitated—"one of us ought to stay with—with the body."

Patrick Redfern said:

"I'll stay."

Emily Brewster drew a little sigh of relief. She was not the kind of woman who would ever admit to feeling fear, but she was secretly thankful not to have to remain on that beach alone with the faint possibility of a homicidal maniac lingering close at hand.

She said:

"Good. I'll be as quick as I can. I'll go in the boat. Can't face that ladder. There's a constable at Leathercombe Bay."

Patrick Redfern murmured mechanically:

"Yes—yes, whatever you think best."

As she rowed vigorously away from the shore, Emily Brewster saw Patrick drop down beside the dead woman and bury his head in his hands. There was something so forlorn about his attitude that she felt an unwilling sympathy. He looked like a dog watching by its dead master. Nevertheless her robust common sense was saying to her:

"Best thing that could have happened for him and his wife—and for Marshall and the child—but I don't suppose *he* can see it that way, poor devil."

Emily Brewster was a woman who could always rise to an emergency.

CHAPTER V

INSPECTOR COLGATE STOOD back by the cliff waiting for the police surgeon to finish with Arlena's body. Patrick Redfern and Emily Brewster stood a little to one side.

Dr. Neasdon rose from his knees with a quick deft movement.

He said:

"Strangled—and by a pretty powerful pair of hands. She doesn't seem to have put up much of a struggle. Taken by surprise. H'm—well—nasty business."

Emily Brewster had taken one look and then quickly averted her eyes from the dead woman's face. That horrible purple convulsed countenance.

Inspector Colgate asked:

"What about time of death?"

Neasdon said irritably:

"Can't say definitely without knowing more about her. Lots of factors to take into account. Let's see, it's quarter to one now. What time was it when you found her?"

Patrick Redfern, to whom the question was addressed, said vaguely:

"Some time before twelve. I don't know exactly."

Emily Brewster said:

"It was exactly a quarter to twelve when we found she was dead."

"Ah, and you came here in the boat. What time was it when you caught sight of her lying here?"

Emily Brewster considered.

"I should say we rounded the point about five or six minutes earlier." She turned to Redfern. "Do you agree?"

He said vaguely:

"Yes—yes—about that, I should think."

Neasdon asked the Inspector in a low voice:

"This the husband? Oh! I see, my mistake. Thought it might be. He seems rather done in over it."

He raised his voice officially.

"Let's put it at twenty minutes to twelve. She cannot have been killed very long before that. Say between then and eleven—quarter to eleven at the earliest outside limit."

The Inspector shut his notebook with a snap.

"Thanks," he said. "That ought to help us considerably. Puts it within very narrow limits—less than an hour all told."

He turned to Miss Brewster.

"Now then, I think it's all clear so far. You're Miss Emily Brewster and this is Mr. Patrick Redfern, both staying at the Jolly Roger Hotel. You identify this lady as a fellow guest of yours at the hotel—the wife of a Captain Marshall?"

Emily Brewster nodded.

"Then, I think," said Inspector Colgate, "that we'll adjourn to the hotel." He beckoned to a constable.

"Hawkes, you stay here and don't allow any one onto this cove. I'll be sending Phillips along later."

II

"Upon my soul!" said Colonel Weston. "This is a surprise finding you here!"

Hercule Poirot replied to the Chief Constable's greeting in a suitable manner. He murmured:

"Ah, yes, many years have passed since that affair at St. Loo."

"I haven't forgotten it, though," said Weston. "Biggest surprise of my life. The thing I've never got over, though, is the way you got round me about that funeral business. Absolutely unorthodox, the whole thing. Fantastic!"

"*Tout de même, mon Colonel*," said Poirot. "It produced the goods, did it not?"

"Er—well, possibly. I daresay we should have got there by more orthodox methods."

"It is possible," agreed Poirot diplomatically.

"And here you are in the thick of another murder," said the Chief Constable. "Any ideas about this one?"

Poirot said slowly:

"Nothing definite—but it is interesting."

"Going to give us a hand?"

"You would permit it, yes?"

"My dear fellow, delighted to have you. Don't know enough yet to decide whether it's a case for Scotland Yard or not. Offhand it looks as though our murderer must be pretty well within a limited radius. On the other hand, all these people are strangers down here. To find out about them and their motives you've got to go to London."

Poirot said:

"Yes, that is true."

"First of all," said Weston, "we've got to find out who last saw the dead woman alive. Chambermaid took her her breakfast at nine. Girl in the bureau downstairs saw her pass through the lounge and go out about ten."

"My friend," said Poirot, "I suspect that I am the man you want."

"You saw her this morning? What time?"

"At five minutes past ten. I assisted her to launch her float from the bathing beach."

"And she went off on it?"

"Yes."

"Alone?"

"Yes."

"Did you see which direction she took?"

"She paddled round that point there to the right."

"In the direction of Pixy Cove, that is?"

"Yes."

"And the time then was—?"

"I should say she actually left the beach at a quarter past ten."

Weston considered.

"That fits in well enough. How long should you say that it would take her to paddle round to the Cove?"

"Ah, me, I am not an expert. I do not go in boats or expose myself on floats. Perhaps half an hour?"

"That's about what I think," said the Colonel. "She wouldn't be hurrying, I presume. Well, if she arrived there at a quarter to eleven, that fits in well enough."

"At what time does your doctor suggest she died?"

"Oh, Neasdon doesn't commit himself. He's a cautious chap. A quarter to eleven is his earliest outside limit."

Poirot nodded. He said:

"There is one other point that I must mention. As she left Mrs. Marshall asked me not to say I had seen her."

Weston stared.

He said:

"H'm, that's rather suggestive, isn't it?"

Poirot murmured:

"Yes. I thought so myself."

Weston tugged at his moustache. He said:

"Look here, Poirot. You're a man of the world. What sort of a woman was Mrs. Marshall?"

A faint smile came to Poirot's lips.

He asked:

"Have you not already heard?"

The Chief Constable said drily:

"I know what the women say of her. They would. How much truth is there in it? *Was* she having an affair with this fellow Redfern?"

"I should say undoubtedly *yes*."

"He followed her down here, eh?"

"There is reason to suppose so."

"And the husband? Did he know about it? What did he feel?"

Poirot said slowly:

"It is not easy to know what Captain Marshall feels or thinks. He is a man who does not display his emotions."

Weston said sharply:

"But he might have 'em, all the same."

Poirot nodded. He said:

"Oh, yes, he might have them."

III

The Chief Constable was being as tactful as it was in his nature to be with Mrs. Castle.

Mrs. Castle was the owner and proprietress of the Jolly Roger Hotel. She was a woman of forty odd with a large bust, rather violent henna-red hair, and an almost offensively refined manner of speech.

She was saying:

"That such a thing should happen in my Hotel! Ay am sure it has always been the quayettest place imaginable! The people who come here are such naice people. No *rowdiness*—if you know what Ay mean. Not like the big hotels in St. Loo."

"Quite so, Mrs. Castle," said Colonel Weston. "But accidents happen in the best-regulated—er households."

"Ay'm sure Inspector Colgate will bear me out," said Mrs. Castle, sending an appealing glance towards the Inspector who was sitting looking very official. "As to the laycensing laws, Ay am *most* particular. There has never been *any* irregularity!"

"Quite, quite," said Weston. "We're not blaming you in any way, Mrs. Castle."

"But it does so reflect upon an establishment," said Mrs. Castle, her large bust heaving. "When Ay think of the noisy gaping crowds. Of course no one but hotel guests are allowed upon the island—but all the same they will no doubt come and *point* from the shore."

She shuddered.

Inspector Colgate saw his chance to turn the conversation to good account.

He said:

"In regard to that point you've just raised. Access to the island. How do you keep people off?"

"Ay am *most* particular about it."

"Yes, but what measures do you take? *What* keeps 'em off? Holiday crowds in summer-time swarm everywhere like flies."

Mrs. Castle shuddered slightly again.

She said:

"That is the fault of the charabancs. Ay have seen eighteen at one time parked by the quay at Leathercombe Bay. Eighteen!"

"Just so. How do you stop them coming here?"

"There are notices. And then, of course, at high tide, we are cut off."

"Yes, but at low tide?"

Mrs. Castle explained. At the island end of the causeway there was a gate. This said, "Jolly Roger Hotel. Private. No entry except to Hotel." The rocks rose sheer out of the sea on either side there and could not be climbed.

"Any one could take a boat, though, I suppose, and row round and land on one of the coves? You couldn't stop them doing that. There's a right of access to the foreshore. You can't stop people being on the beach between low and high watermark."

But this, it seemed, very seldom happened. Boats could be obtained at Leathercombe Bay harbour but from there it was a long row to the island and there was also a strong current just outside Leathercombe Bay harbour.

There were notices, too, on both Gull Cove and Pixy Cove by the ladder. She added that George or William was always on the lookout at the bathing beach proper which was the nearest to the mainland.

"Who are George and William?"

"George attends to the bathing beach. He sees to the costumes and the floats. William is the gardener. He keeps the paths and marks the tennis courts and all that."

Colonel Weston said impatiently:

"Well, that seems clear enough. That's not to say that nobody could have come from outside, but any one who did so took a risk—the risk of being noticed. We'll have a word with George and William presently."

Mrs. Castle said:

"Ay do not care for trippers—a very noisy crowd and they frequently leave orange peel and cigarette butts on the causeway and down by the rocks, but all the same Ay never thought one of them would turn out to be a murderer. Oh, dear! it really is too terrible for words. A lady like Mrs. Marshall murdered and what's so horrible, actually—er—strangled. . . ."

Mrs. Castle could hardly bring herself to say the word. She brought it out with the utmost reluctance.

Inspector Colgate said soothingly:

"Yes, it's a nasty business."

"And the newspapers. *My* hotel in the newspapers!"

Colgate said, with a faint grin:

"Oh, well, it's advertisement, in a way."

Mrs. Castle drew herself up. Her bust heaved and whalebone creaked. She said icily:

"That is not the kind of advertisement Ay care about, Mr. Colgate."

Colonel Weston broke in. He said:

"Now then, Mrs. Castle, you've got a list of the guests staying here, as I asked you?"

"Yes, sir."

Colonel Weston pored over the hotel register. He looked over to Poirot who made the fourth member of the group assembled in the Manageress's office.

"This is where you'll probably be able to help us presently."

He read down the names.

"What about servants?"

Mrs. Castle produced a second list.

"There are four chambermaids, the head waiter and three under him and Henry in the bar. William does the boots and shoes. Then there's the cook and two under her."

"What about the waiters?"

"Well, sir, Albert, the Mater Dotel, came to me from the Vincent at Plymouth. He was there for some years. The three under him have been here for three years—one of them four. They are very naice lads and most respectable. Henry has been here since the hotel opened. He is quite an institution."

Weston nodded. He said to Colgate:

"Seems all right. You'll check up on them, of course. Thank you, Mrs. Castle."

"That will be all you require?"

"For the moment, yes."

Mrs. Castle creaked out of the room.

Weston said:

"First thing to do is to talk with Captain Marshall."

IV

Kenneth Marshall sat quietly answering the questions put to him. Apart from a slight hardening of his features he was quite calm. Seen here, with the sunlight falling on him from the window, you realized that he was a handsome man. Those straight features, the steady blue eyes, the firm mouth. His voice was low and pleasant.

Colonel Weston was saying:

"I quite understand, Captain Marshall, what a terrible shock this must be to you. But you realize that I am anxious to get the fullest information as soon as possible."

Marshall nodded.

He said:

"I quite understand. Carry on."

"Mrs. Marshall was your second wife?"

"Yes."

"And you have been married, how long?"

"Just over four years."

"And her name before she was married?"

"Helen Stuart. Her acting name was Arlena Stuart."

"She was an actress?"

"She appeared in Revue and musical shows."

"Did she give up the stage on her marriage?"

"No. She continued to appear. She actually retired only about a year and a half ago."

"Was there any special reason for her retirement?"

Kenneth Marshall appeared to consider.

"No," he said. "She simply said that she was tired of it all."

"It was not—er—in obedience to your special wish?"

Marshall raised his eyebrows.

"Oh, no."

"You were quite content for her to continue acting after your marriage?"

Marshall smiled very faintly.

"I should have preferred her to give it up—that, yes. But I made no fuss about it."

"It caused no point of dissension between you?"

"Certainly not. My wife was free to please herself."

"And—the marriage was a happy one?"

Kenneth Marshall said coldly:

"Certainly."

Colonel Weston paused a minute. Then he said:

"Captain Marshall, have you any idea who could possibly have killed your wife?"

The answer came without the least hesitation.

"None whatever."

"Had she any enemies?"

"Possibly."

"Ah?"

The other went on quickly. He said:

"Don't misunderstand me, sir. My wife was an actress. She was also a very good-looking woman. In both capacities she aroused a certain amount of envy and jealousy. There were fusses over parts—there was rivalry from other women—there was a good deal, shall we say, of general envy, hatred, malice, and all uncharitableness! But that is not to say that there was any one who was capable of deliberately murdering her."

Hercule Poirot spoke for the first time. He said:

"What you really mean, Monsieur, is that her enemies were mostly, or entirely, *women*?"

Kenneth Marshall looked across at him.

"Yes," he said. "That is so."

The Chief Constable said:

"You know of no man who had a grudge against her?"

"No."

"Was she previously acquainted with any one in this hotel?"

"I believe she had met Mr. Redfern before—at some cocktail party. Nobody else to my knowledge."

Weston paused. He seemed to deliberate as to whether to pursue the subject. Then he decided against that course. He said:

"We now come to this morning. When was the last time you saw your wife?"

Marshall paused a minute, then he said:

"I looked in on my way down to breakfast—"

"Excuse me, you occupied separate rooms?"

"Yes."

"And what time was that?"

"It must have been about nine o'clock."

"What was she doing?"

"She was opening her letters."

"Did she say anything?"

"Nothing of any particular interest. Just Good-morning—and that it was a nice day—that sort of thing."

"What was her manner? Unusual at all?"

"No, perfectly normal."

"She did not seem excited, or depressed, or upset in any way?"

"I certainly didn't notice it."

Hercule Poirot said:

"Did she mention at all what were the contents of her letters?"

Again a faint smile appeared on Marshall's lips. He said:

"As far as I can remember, she said they were all bills."

"Your wife breakfasted in bed?"

"Yes."

"Did she always do that?"

"Invariably."

Hercule Poirot said:

"What time did she usually come downstairs?"

"Oh! between ten and eleven—usually nearer eleven."

Poirot went on:

"If she were to descend at ten o'clock exactly, that would be rather surprising?"

"Yes. She wasn't often down as early as that."

"But she was this morning. Why do you think that was, Captain Marshall?"

Marshall said unemotionally:

"Haven't the least idea. Might have been the weather—extra fine day and all that."

"You missed her?"

Kenneth Marshall shifted a little in his chair. He said:

"Looked in on her again after breakfast. Room was empty. I was a bit surprised."

"And then you came down on the beach and asked me if I had seen her?"

"Er—yes." He added with a faint emphasis in his voice, "And you said you hadn't. . . ."

The innocent eyes of Hercule Poirot did not falter. Gently, he caressed his large and flamboyant moustache.

Weston asked:

"Had you any special reason for wanting to find your wife this morning?"

Marshall shifted his glance amiably to the Chief Constable.

He said:

"No, just wondered where she was, that's all."

Weston paused. He moved his chair slightly. His voice fell into a different key. He said:

"Just now, Captain Marshall, you mentioned that your wife had a previous acquaintance with Mr. Patrick Redfern. How well did your wife know Mr. Redfern?"

Kenneth Marshall said:

"Mind if I smoke?" He felt through his pockets. "Dash! I've mislaid my pipe somewhere."

Poirot offered him a cigarette which he accepted. Lighting it, he said:

"You were asking about Redfern. My wife told me she had come across him at some cocktail party or other."

"He was, then, just a casual acquaintance?"

"I believe so."

"Since then—" the Chief Constable paused. "I understand that that acquaintanceship has ripened into something rather closer."

Marshall said sharply:

"You understand that, do you? Who told you so?"

"It is the common gossip of the hotel."

For a moment Marshall's eyes went to Hercule Poirot. They dwelt on him with a kind of cold anger. He said:

"Hotel gossip is usually a tissue of lies!"

"Possibly. But I gather that Mr. Redfern and your wife gave some grounds for the gossip."

"What grounds?"

"They were constantly in each other's company."

"Is that all?"

"You do not deny that that was so?"

"May have been. I really didn't notice."

"You did not—excuse me, Captain Marshall—object to your wife's friendship with Mr. Redfern?"

"I wasn't in the habit of criticizing my wife's conduct."

"You did not protest or object in any way?"

"Certainly not."

"Not even though it was becoming a subject of scandal and an estrangement was growing up between Mr. Redfern and his wife?"

Kenneth Marshall said coldly:

"I mind my own business and I expect other people to mind theirs. I don't listen to gossip and tittle tattle."

"You won't deny that Mr. Redfern admired your wife?"

"He probably did. Most men did. She was a very beautiful woman."

"But you yourself were persuaded that there was nothing serious in the affair?"

"I never thought about it, I tell you."

"And suppose we have a witness who can testify that they were on terms of the greatest intimacy?"

Again those blue eyes went to Hercule Poirot. Again an expression of dislike showed on that usually impassive face.

Marshall said:

"If you want to listen to these tales, listen to 'em. My wife's dead and can't defend herself."

"You mean that you, personally, don't believe them?"

For the first time a faint dew of sweat was observable on Marshall's brow. He said:

"I don't propose to believe anything of the kind."

He went on:

"Aren't you getting a good way from the essentials of this business? What I believe or don't believe is surely not relevant to the plain fact of murder?"

Hercule Poirot answered before either of the others could speak. He said:

"You do not comprehend, Captain Marshall. There is no such thing as a plain fact of murder. Murder springs, nine times out of ten, out of the character and circumstances of the murdered person. *Because* the victim was the kind of person he or she was, *therefore* was he or she murdered! Until we can understand fully and completely *exactly what kind of a per-*

son Arlena Marshall *was,* we shall not be able to see clearly exactly *the kind of person who murdered her.* From that springs the necessity of our questions."

Marshall turned to the Chief Constable. He said:

"That your view, too?"

Weston boggled a little. He said:

"Well, up to a point—that is to say—"

Marshall gave a short laugh. He said:

"Thought you wouldn't agree. This character stuff is M. Poirot's specialty, I believe."

Poirot said, smiling:

"You can at least congratulate yourself on having done nothing to assist me!"

"What do you mean?"

"What have you told us about your wife? Exactly nothing at all. You have told us only what every one could see for themselves. That she was beautiful and admired. Nothing more."

Kenneth Marshall shrugged his shoulders. He said simply:

"You're crazy."

He looked towards the Chief Constable and said with emphasis:

"Anything else, sir, that *you'*d like me to tell you?"

"Yes, Captain Marshall, your own movements this morning, please."

Kenneth Marshall nodded. He had clearly expected this.

He said:

"I breakfasted downstairs about nine o'clock as usual and read the paper. As I told you I went up to my wife's room afterwards and found she had gone out. I came down to the beach, saw M. Poirot and asked if he had seen her. Then I had a quick bathe and went up to the hotel again. It was then, let me see, about twenty to eleven—yes, just about that. I saw the clock in the lounge. It was just after twenty minutes to. I went up to my room, but the chambermaid hadn't quite finished it. I asked her to finish as quickly as she could. I had some letters to type which I wanted to get off by the post. I went downstairs again and had a word or two with Henry in the bar. I went up again to my room at ten minutes to eleven. There I typed my letters. I typed until ten minutes to twelve. I then changed as I had a date to play tennis at twelve. We'd booked the court the day before."

"Who was we?"

"Mrs. Redfern, Miss Darnley, Mr. Gardener and myself. I came down at twelve o'clock and went up to the court. Miss Darnley was there and Mr. Gardener. Mrs. Redfern arrived a few minutes later. We played tennis for an hour. Just as we came into the hotel afterwards I—I—got the news."

"Thank you, Captain Marshall. Just as a matter of form, is there any one who can corroborate the fact that you were typing in your room between —er—ten minutes to eleven and ten minutes to twelve?"

Kenneth Marshall said with a faint smile:

"Have you got some idea that I killed my own wife? Let me see now. The chambermaid was about doing the rooms. She must have heard the typewriter going. And then there are the letters themselves. With all this upset I haven't posted them. I should imagine they are as good evidence as anything."

He took three letters from his pocket. They were addressed, but not stamped. He said:

"Their contents, by the way, are strictly confidential. But when it's a case of murder, one is forced to trust in the discretion of the police. They contain lists of figures and various financial statements. I think you will find that if you put one of your men on to type them out, he won't do it in much under an hour."

He paused.

"Satisfied, I hope?"

Weston said smoothly:

"It is no question of suspicion. Every one on the island will be asked to account for his or her movements between a quarter to eleven and twenty minutes to twelve this morning."

Kenneth Marshall said:

"Quite."

Weston said:

"One more thing, Captain Marshall. Do you know anything about the way your wife was likely to have disposed of any property she had?"

"You mean a will? I don't think she ever made a will."

"But you are not sure?"

"Her solicitors are Barkett, Markett & Applegood, Bedford Square. They saw to all her contracts, etc. But I'm fairly certain she never made a will. She said once that doing a thing like that would give her the shivers."

"In that case, if she has died intestate, you, as her husband, succeed to her property."

"Yes, I suppose I do."

"Had she any near relatives?"

"I don't think so. If she had, she never mentioned them. I know that her father and mother died when she was a child and she had no brothers or sisters."

"In any case, I suppose, she had nothing very much to leave?"

Kenneth Marshall said coolly:

"On the contrary. Only two years ago, Sir Robert Erskine, who was an old friend of hers, died and left her a good deal of his fortune. It amounted, I think, to about fifty thousand pounds."

Inspector Colgate looked up. An alertness came into his glance. Up to now he had been silent. Now he asked:

"Then actually, Captain Marshall, your wife was a rich woman?"

Kenneth Marshall shrugged his shoulders.

"I suppose she was really."

"And you still say she did not make a will?"

"You can ask the solicitors. But I'm pretty certain she didn't. As I tell you, she thought it unlucky."

There was a pause then Marshall added:

"Is there anything further?"

Weston shook his head.

"Don't think so—eh, Colgate? No. Once more, Captain Marshall, let me offer you all my sympathy in your loss."

Marshall blinked. He said jerkily:

"Oh—thanks."

He went out.

V

The three men looked at each other.

Weston said:

"Cool customer. Not giving anything away, is he? What do you make of him, Colgate?"

The Inspector shook his head.

"It's difficult to tell. He's not the kind that shows anything. That sort makes a bad impression in the witness box, and yet it's a bit unfair on them really. Sometimes they're as cut up as anything and yet can't show it. That kind of manner made the jury bring in a verdict of Guilty against Wallace. It wasn't the evidence. They just couldn't believe that a man could lose his wife and talk and act so coolly about it."

Weston turned to Poirot.

"What do you think, Poirot?"

Hercule Poirot raised his hands.

He said:

"What can one say? He is the closed box—the fastened oyster. He has chosen his rôle. He has heard nothing, he has seen nothing, he knows nothing!"

"We've got a choice of motives," said Colgate. "There's jealousy and there's the money motive. Of course, in a way, a husband's the obvious suspect. One naturally thinks of him first. If he knew his missus was carrying on with the other chap—"

Poirot interrupted.

He said:

"I think he knew that."

"Why do you say so?"

"Listen, my friend. Last night I had been talking with Mrs. Redfern on Sunny Ledge. I came down from there to the hotel and on my way I saw those two together—Mrs. Marshall and Patrick Redfern. And a moment or two after I met Captain Marshall. His face was very stiff. It says nothing—but nothing at all! It is almost *too* blank, if you understand me. Oh! he knew all right."

Colgate grunted doubtfully.

He said:

"Oh, well, if you think so—"

"I am sure of it! But even then, what does that tell us? What did Kenneth Marshall *feel* about his wife?"

Colonel Weston said:

"Takes her death coolly enough."

Poirot shook his head in a dissatisfied manner.

Inspector Colgate said:

"Sometimes these quiet ones are the most violent underneath, so to speak. It's all bottled up. He may have been madly fond of her—and madly jealous. But he's not the kind to show it."

Poirot said slowly:

"That is possible—yes. He is a very interesting character, this Captain Marshall. I interest myself in him greatly. And in his *alibi*."

"Alibi by typewriter," said Weston with a short bark of a laugh. "What have you got to say about that, Colgate?"

Inspector Colgate screwed up his eyes. He said:

"Well, you know, sir, I rather fancy that alibi. It's not too good, if you know what I mean. It's—well, it's *natural*. And if we find the chambermaid was about, and did hear the typewriter going, well then, it seems to me that it's all right and that we'll have to look elsewhere."

"H'm," said Colonel Weston. "Where are you going to look?"

VI

For a minute or two the three men pondered the question.

Inspector Colgate spoke first. He said:

"It boils down to this—was it an outsider, or a guest at the hotel? I'm not eliminating the servants entirely, mind, but I don't expect for a minute that we'll find any of them had a hand in it. No, it's a hotel guest, or it's someone from right outside. We've got to look at it this way. First of all—motive. There's gain. The only person to gain by her death was the lady's husband it seems. What other motives are there? First and foremost—jealousy. It seems to me—just looking at it—that if ever you've got a *crime passionnel* [he bowed to Poirot] this is one."

Poirot murmured as he looked up at the ceiling:

"There are so many passions."

Inspector Colgate went on:

"Her husband wouldn't allow that she had any enemies—real enemies, that is, but I don't believe for a minute that that's so! I should say that a lady like her would—well, would make some pretty bad enemies—eh, sir, what do you say?"

Poirot responded. He said:

"*Mais oui,* that is so. Arlena Marshall would make enemies. But in my opinion, the enemy theory is not tenable, for you see, Inspector, Arlena Marshall's enemies would, I think, as I said just now, always be *women.*"

Colonel Weston grunted and said:

"Something in that. It's the women who've got their knife into her here all right."

Poirot went on:

"It seems to be hardly possible that this crime was committed by a woman. What does the medical evidence say?"

Weston grunted again. He said:

"Neasdon's pretty confident that she was strangled by a man. Big hands—powerful grip. It's just possible, of course, that an unusually athletic woman might have done it—but it's damned unlikely."

Poirot nodded.

"Exactly. Arsenic in a cup of tea—a box of poisoned chocolates—a knife—even a pistol—but strangulation—no! It is a man we have to look for.

"And immediately," he went on, "it becomes more difficult. There are two people here in this hotel who have a motive for wishing Arlena Marshall out of the way—but both of them are women."

Colonel Weston asked:

"Redfern's wife is one of them, I suppose?"

"Yes. Mrs. Redfern might have made up her mind to kill Arlena Stuart. She had, let us say, ample cause. I think, too, that it would be possible for Mrs. Redfern to commit a murder. But not this kind of murder. For all her unhappiness and jealousy, she is not, I should say, a woman of strong passions. In love, she would be devoted and loyal—not passionate. As I said just now—arsenic in the teacup—possibly—strangulation, no. I am sure, also, that she is physically incapable of committing this crime and her hands and feet are small below the average."

Weston nodded. He said:

"This isn't a woman's crime. No, a man did this."

Inspector Colgate coughed.

"Let me put forward a solution, sir. Say that prior to meeting this Mr. Redfern the lady had had another affair with someone—call him X. She turns X down for Mr. Redfern. X is mad with rage and jealousy. He follows her down here, stays somewhere in the neighbourhood, comes over to the island and does her in. It's a possibility!"

Weston said:

"It's *possible*, all right. And if it's true, it ought to be easy to prove. Did he come on foot or in a boat? The latter seems more likely. If so, he must have hired a boat somewhere. You'd better make inquiries."

He looked across at Poirot.

"What do you think of Colgate's suggestion?"

Poirot said slowly:

"It leaves, somehow, too much to chance. And besides—somewhere the picture is not true. I cannot, you see, imagine this man . . . the man who is mad with rage and jealousy."

Colgate said:

"People *did* go potty about her, though, sir. Look at Redfern."

"Yes, yes . . . But all the same—"

Colgate looked at him questioningly.

Poirot shook his head.

He said, frowning:

"Somewhere, there is something we have missed. . . ."

CHAPTER VI

Colonel Weston was poring over the hotel register.

He read aloud.

"Major and Mrs. Cowan,
  Miss Pamela Cowan,
  Master Robert Cowan,   Rydal's Mount,
  Master Evan Cowan.   Leatherhead.

Mr. and Mrs. Masterman,
Mr. Edward Masterman,
Miss Jennifer Masterman,   5 Marlborough Avenue,
Mr. Roy Masterman,   London, N.W.
Master Frederick Masterman.

Mr. and Mrs. Gardener.   New York.

Mr. and Mrs. Redfern.   Crossgates, Seldon,
    Princes Risborough.

Major Barry.   18 Cardon Street,
    St. James, London, S.W.1.

Mr. Horace Blatt.   5 Pickersgill Street,
    London, E.C.2.

M. Hercule Poirot.   Whitehaven Mansions,
    London, W.1.

Miss Rosamund Darnley.   8 Cardigan Court, W.1.

Miss Emily Brewster.   Southgates, Sunbury-on-Thames.

Rev. Stephen Lane.   London.

Captain and Mrs. Marshall,   73 Upcott Mansions,
Miss Linda Marshall.   London, S.W.7."

He stopped.

Inspector Colgate said:

"I think, sir, that we can wash out the first two entries. Mrs. Castle tells me that the Mastermans and the Cowans come here regularly every summer with their children. This morning they went off on an all-day excursion sailing, taking lunch with them. They left just after nine o'clock. A man called Andrew Baston took them. We can check up from him, but I think we can put them right out of it."

Weston nodded.

"I agree. Let's eliminate every one we can. Can you give us a pointer on any of the rest of them, Poirot?"

Poirot said:

"Superficially, that is easy. The Gardeners are a middle-aged married couple, pleasant, travelled. All the talking is done by the lady. The husband is acquiescent. He plays tennis and golf and has a form of dry humour that is attractive when one gets him to oneself."

"Sounds quite O.K."

"Next—the Redferns. Mr. Redfern is young, attractive to women, a magnificent swimmer, a good tennis player and accomplished dancer. His wife I have already spoken of to you. She is quiet, pretty in a washed-out way.

She is, I think, devoted to her husband. She has something that Arlena Marshall did not have."

"What is that?"

"Brains."

Inspector Colgate sighed. He said:

"Brains don't count for much when it comes to an infatuation, sir."

"Perhaps not. And yet I do truly believe that in spite of his infatuation for Mrs. Marshall, Patrick Redfern really cares for his wife."

"That may be, sir. It wouldn't be the first time that's happened."

Poirot murmured:

"That is the pity of it! It is always the thing women find it hardest to believe."

He went on:

"Major Barry. Retired Indian Army. An admirer of women. A teller of long and boring stories."

Inspector Colgate sighed.

"You needn't go on. I've met a few, sir."

"Mr. Horace Blatt. He is, apparently, a rich man. He talks a good deal —about Mr. Blatt. He wants to be everybody's friend. It is sad. For nobody likes him very much. And there is something else. Mr. Blatt last night asked me a good many questions. Mr. Blatt was uneasy. Yes, there is something not quite right about Mr. Blatt."

He paused and went on with a change of voice:

"Next comes Miss Rosamund Darnley. Her business name is Rose Mond, Ltd. She is a celebrated dressmaker. What can I say of her? She has brains and charm and chic. She is very pleasing to look at." He paused and added, "And she is a very old friend of Captain Marshall's."

Weston sat up in his chair.

"Oh, she is, is she?"

"Yes. They had not met for some years."

Weston asked:

"Did she know he was going to be down here?"

"She says not."

Poirot paused and then went on:

"Who comes next? Miss Brewster. I find her just a little alarming." He shook his head. "She has a voice like a man's. She is gruff and what you call hearty. She rows boats and has a handicap of four at golf." He paused. "I think, though, that she has a good heart."

Weston said:

"That leaves only the Reverend Stephen Lane. Who's the Reverend Stephen Lane?"

"I can only tell you one thing. He is a man who is in a condition of great nervous tension. Also he is, I think, a fanatic."

Inspector Colgate said:

"Oh, that kind of person."

Weston said:

"And that's the lot!" He looked at Poirot. "You seem very lost in thought, my friend."

Poirot said:

"Yes. Because, you see, when Mrs. Marshall went off this morning and asked me not to tell any one I had seen her, I jumped at once in my own mind to a certain conclusion. I thought that her friendship with Patrick Redfern had made trouble between her and her husband. I thought that she was going to meet Patrick Redfern somewhere and that she did not want her husband to know where she was."

He paused.

"But that, you see, was where I was wrong. Because, although her husband appeared almost immediately on the beach and asked if I had seen her, Patrick Redfern arrived also—and was most patently and obviously looking for her! And therefore, my friends, I am asking myself, *Who was it that Arlena Marshall went off to meet?*"

Inspector Colgate said:

"That fits in with *my* idea. A man from London or somewhere."

Hercule Poirot shook his head. He said:

"But, my friend, according to your theory, Arlena Marshall had broken with this mythical man. Why, then, should she take such trouble and pains to meet him?"

Inspector Colgate shook his head. He said:

"Who do *you* think it was?"

"That is just what I cannot imagine. We have just read through the list of hotel guests. They are all middle-aged—dull. Which of them would Arlena Marshall prefer to Patrick Redfern? No, that is impossible. And yet, all the same, she *did* go to meet someone—and that someone was not Patrick Redfern."

Weston murmured:

"You don't think she just went off by herself?"

Poirot shook his head.

"*Mon cher,*" he said. "It is very evident that you never met the dead woman. Somebody once wrote a learned treatise on the difference that solitary confinement would mean to Beau Brummell or to a man like Newton. Arlena Marshall, my dear friend, would practically not exist in solitude. She only lived in the light of a man's admiration. No, Arlena Marshall went to meet *someone* this morning. *Who was it?*"

II

Colonel Weston sighed, shook his head and said:

"Well, we can go into theories later. Got to get through these interviews now. Got to get it down in black and white where every one was. I suppose we'd better see the Marshall girl now. She might be able to tell us something useful."

Linda Marshall came into the room clumsily, knocking against the doorpost. She was breathing quickly and the pupils of her eyes were dilated. She looked like a startled young colt. Colonel Weston felt a kindly impulse towards her.

He thought:

"Poor kid—she's nothing but a kid after all. This must have been a pretty bad shock to her."

He drew up a chair and said in a reassuring voice:

"Sorry to put you through this, Miss—Linda, isn't it?"

"Yes, Linda."

Her voice had that indrawn breathy quality that is often characteristic of schoolgirls. Her hands rested helplessly on the table in front of him—pathetic hands, big and red, with large bones and long wrists. Weston thought:

"A kid oughtn't to be mixed up in this sort of thing."

He said reassuringly:

"There's nothing very alarming about all this. We just want you to tell us anything you know that might be useful, that's all."

Linda said:

"You mean—about Arlena?"

"Yes. Did you see her this morning at all?"

The girl shook her head.

"No. Arlena always gets down rather late. She has breakfast in bed."

Hercule Poirot said:

"And you, Mademoiselle?"

"Oh, I get up. Breakfast in bed's so *stuffy*."

Weston said:

"Will you tell us just what you did this morning?"

"Well, I had a bathe first and then breakfast and then I went with Mrs. Redfern to Gull Cove."

Weston said:

"What time did you and Mrs. Redfern start?"

"She said she'd be waiting for me in the hall at half past ten. I was afraid

I was going to be late, but it was all right. We started off at about three minutes to the half hour."

Poirot said:

"And what did you do at Gull Cove?"

"Oh, I oiled myself and sunbathed and Mrs. Redfern sketched. Then, later, I went into the sea and Christine went back to the hotel to get changed for tennis."

Weston said, keeping his voice quite casual:

"Do you remember what time that was?"

"When Mrs. Redfern went back to the hotel? Quarter to twelve."

"Sure of that time—quarter to twelve?"

Linda, opening her eyes wide, said:

"Oh, *yes*. I looked at my watch."

"The watch you have on now?"

Linda glanced down at her wrist.

"Yes."

Weston said:

"Mind if I see?"

She held out her wrist. He compared the watch with his own and with the hotel clock on the wall.

He said, smiling:

"Correct to a second. And after that you had a bathe?"

"Yes."

"And you got back to the hotel—when?"

"Just about one o'clock. And—and then—I heard—about Arlena . . ." Her voice changed.

Colonel Weston said:

"Did you—er—get on with your stepmother all right?"

She looked at him for a minute without replying. Then she said:

"Oh, yes."

Poirot asked:

"Did you like her, Mademoiselle?"

Linda said again:

"Oh, yes." She added: "Arlena was quite kind to me."

Weston said with rather uneasy facetiousness:

"Not the cruel stepmother, eh?"

Linda shook her head without smiling.

Weston said:

"That's good. That's good. Sometimes, you know, there's a bit of difficulty in families—jealousy—all that. Girl and her father great pals and then she resents it a bit when he's all wrapped up in the new wife. You didn't feel like that, eh?"

Linda stared at him. She said with obvious sincerity:

"Oh, no."

Weston said:

"I suppose your father was—er—very wrapped up in her?"

Linda said simply:

"I don't know."

Weston went on:

"All sorts of difficulties, as I say, arise in families. Quarrels—rows—that sort of thing. If husband and wife get ratty with each other, that's a bit awkward for a daughter, too. Anything of that sort?"

Linda said clearly:

"Do you mean, did Father and Arlena quarrel?"

"Well—yes."

Weston thought to himself:

"Rotten business—questioning a child about her father. Why is one a policeman? Damn it all, it's got to be done, though."

Linda said positively:

"Oh, no." She added: "Father doesn't quarrel with people. He's not like that at all."

Weston said:

"Now, Miss Linda, I want you to think very carefully. Have you any idea at all who might have killed your stepmother? Is there anything you've ever heard or anything you know that could help us on that point?"

Linda was silent a minute. She seemed to be giving the question a serious unhurried consideration. She said at last:

"No, I don't know who could have wanted to kill Arlena." She added, "Except, of course, Mrs. Redfern."

Weston said:

"You think Mrs. Redfern wanted to kill her? Why?"

Linda said:

"Because her husband was in love with Arlena. But I don't think she would really want to *kill* her. I mean she'd just feel that she wished she was dead—and that isn't the same thing at all, is it?"

Poirot said gently:

"No, it is not at all the same."

Linda nodded. A queer sort of spasm passed across her face. She said:

"And anyway, Mrs. Redfern could never do a thing like that—kill anybody. She isn't—she isn't *violent*, if you know what I mean."

Weston and Poirot nodded. The latter said:

"I know exactly what you mean, my child, and I agree with you. Mrs. Redfern is not of those who, as your saying goes, 'sees red.' She would not be—" He leaned back half closing his eyes, picking his words with care—

"shaken by a storm of feeling—seeing life narrowing in front of her—seeing a hated face—a hated white neck—feeling her hands clench—longing to feel them press into flesh—"

He stopped.

Linda moved jerkily back from the table. She said in a trembling voice: "Can I go now? Is that all?"

Colonel Weston said:

"Yes, yes, that's all. Thank you, Miss Linda."

He got up to open the door for her. Then came back to the table and lit a cigarette.

"Phew," he said. "Not a nice job, ours. I can tell you I felt a bit of a cad questioning that child about the relations between her father and her stepmother. More or less inviting a daughter to put a rope round her father's neck. All the same, it had to be done. Murder is murder. And she's the person most likely to know the truth of things. I'm rather thankful, though, that she'd nothing to tell us in that line."

Poirot said:

"Yes, I thought you were."

Weston said with an embarrassed cough:

"By the way, Poirot, you went a bit far, I thought, at the end. All that hands-sinking-into-flesh business! Not quite the sort of idea to put into a kid's head."

Hercule Poirot looked at him with thoughtful eyes. He said:

"So you thought I put ideas into her head?"

"Well, didn't you? Come now."

Poirot shook his head.

Weston sheered away from the point. He said:

"On the whole we got very little useful stuff out of her. Except a more or less complete alibi for the Redfern woman. If they were together from half past ten to a quarter to twelve that lets Christine Redfern out of it. Exit the jealous wife suspect."

Poirot said:

"There are better reasons than that for leaving Mrs. Redfern out of it. It would, I am convinced, be physically impossible and mentally impossible for her to strangle any one. She is cold rather than warm blooded, capable of deep devotion and unswerving constancy, but not of hot-blooded passion or rage. Moreover, her hands are far too small and delicate."

Colgate said:

"I agree with Mr. Poirot. She's out of it. Dr. Neasdon says it was a full-sized pair of hands throttled that dame."

Weston said:

"Well, I suppose we'd better see the Redferns next. I expect he's recovered a bit from the shock now."

III

Patrick Redfern had recovered full composure by now. He looked pale and haggard and suddenly very young, but his manner was quite composed.

"You are Mr. Patrick Redfern of Crossgates, Seldon, Princes Risborough?"

"Yes."

"How long had you known Mrs. Marshall?"

Patrick Redfern hesitated, then said:

"Three months."

Weston went on:

"Captain Marshall has told us that you and she met casually at a cocktail party. Is that right?"

"Yes, that's how it came about."

Weston said:

"Captain Marshall has implied that until you both met down here you did not know each other well. Is that the truth, Mr. Redfern?"

Again Patrick Redfern hesitated a minute. Then he said:

"Well—not exactly. As a matter of fact I saw a fair amount of her one way and another."

"Without Captain Marshall's knowledge?"

Redfern flushed slightly. He said:

"I don't know whether he knew about it or not."

Hercule Poirot spoke. He murmured:

"And was it also without your wife's knowledge, Mr. Redfern?"

"I believe I mentioned to my wife that I had met the famous Arlena Stuart."

Poirot persisted.

"But she did not know how often you were seeing her?"

"Well, perhaps not."

Weston said:

"Did you and Mrs. Marshall arrange to meet down here?"

Redfern was silent a minute or two. Then he shrugged his shoulders.

"Oh, well," he said. "I suppose it's bound to come out now. It's no good my fencing with you. I was crazy about the woman—mad—infatuated—anything you like. She wanted me to come down here. I demurred a bit and then I agreed. I—I—well, I would have agreed to do any mortal thing she liked. She had that kind of effect on people."

Hercule Poirot murmured:

"You paint a very clear picture of her. She was the eternal Circe. Just that!"

Patrick Redfern said bitterly:

"She turned men into swine all right!" He went on: "I'm being frank with you, gentlemen. I'm not going to hide anything. What's the use? As I say, I was infatuated with her. Whether she cared for me or not, I don't know. She pretended to, but I think she was one of those women who lose interest in a man once they've got him body and soul. She knew she'd got me all right. This morning, when I found her there on the beach, dead, it was as though—" he paused—"as though something had hit me straight between the eyes. I was dazed—knocked out!"

Poirot leaned forward.

"And now?"

Patrick Redfern met his eyes squarely.

He said:

"I've told you the truth. What I want to ask is this—*how much of it has got to be made public?* It's not as though it could have any bearing on her death. And if it all comes out, it's going to be pretty rough on my wife.

"Oh, I know," he went on quickly. "You think I haven't thought much about her up to now? Perhaps that's true. But, though I may sound the worst kind of hypocrite, the real truth is that I care for my wife—care for her very deeply. The other—" he twitched his shoulders—"it was a madness—the kind of idiotic fool thing men do—but Christine is different. She's *real.* Badly as I've treated her, I've known all along, deep down, that she was the person who really counted." He paused—sighed—and said rather pathetically: "I wish I could make you believe that."

Hercule Poirot leaned forward. He said:

"But I do believe it. Yes, yes, I do believe it!"

Patrick Redfern looked at him gratefully. He said:

"Thank you."

Colonel Weston cleared his throat. He said:

"You may take it, Mr. Redfern, that we shall not go into irrelevancies. If your infatuation for Mrs. Marshall played no part in the murder then there will be no point in dragging it into the case. But what you don't seem to realize is that that—er—intimacy—may have a very direct bearing on the murder. It might establish, you understand, a *motive* for the crime."

Patrick Redfern said:

"Motive?"

Weston said:

"Yes, Mr. Redfern, *motive!* Captain Marshall, perhaps, was unaware of the affair. Suppose that he suddenly found out."

Redfern said:

"Oh, God! You mean he got wise and—and killed her?"

The Chief Constable said rather drily:

"That solution had not occurred to you?"

Redfern shook his head. He said:

"No—funny. I never thought of it. You see, Marshall's such a quiet chap. I—oh, it doesn't seem likely."

Weston asked:

"What was Mrs. Marshall's attitude to her husband in all this? Was she —well, uneasy—in case it should come to his ears? Or was she indifferent?"

Redfern said slowly:

"She was—a bit nervous. She didn't want him to suspect anything."

"Did she seem afraid of him?"

"Afraid? No, I wouldn't say that."

Poirot murmured:

"Excuse me, M. Redfern, there was not, at any time, the question of a divorce?"

Patrick Redfern shook his head decisively.

"Oh, no, there was no question of anything like that. There was Christine, you see. And Arlena, I am sure, never thought of such a thing. She was perfectly satisfied married to Marshall. He's—well, rather a big bug in his way—" He smiled suddenly. "County—all that sort of thing, and quite well off. She never thought of me as a possible *husband*. No, I was just one of a succession of poor mutts—just something to pass the time with. I knew that all along, and yet, queerly enough, it didn't alter my feeling towards her. . . ."

His voice trailed off. He sat there thinking.

Weston recalled him to the needs of the moment.

"Now, Mr. Redfern, had you any particular appointment with Mrs. Marshall this morning?"

Patrick Redfern looked slightly puzzled. He said:

"Not a particular appointment, no. We usually met every morning on the beach. We used to paddle about on floats."

"Were you surprised not to find Mrs. Marshall there this morning?"

"Yes, I was. Very surprised. I couldn't understand it at all."

"What did you think?"

"Well, I didn't know what to think. I mean, all the time I thought she would be coming."

"If she were keeping an appointment elsewhere you had no idea with whom that appointment might be?"

Patrick Redfern merely stared and shook his head.

"When you had a rendezvous with Mrs. Marshall, where did you meet?"

"Well, sometimes I'd meet her in the afternoon down at Gull Cove. You see the sun is off Gull Cove in the afternoon and so there aren't usually many people there. We met there once or twice."

"Never on the other cove? Pixy Cove?"

"No. You see Pixy Cove faces west and people go round there in boats or on floats in the afternoon. We never tried to meet in the morning. I would have been too noticeable. In the afternoon people go and have a sleep or mooch around and nobody knows much where any one else is."

Weston nodded.

Patrick Redfern went on:

"After dinner, of course, on the fine nights, we used to go off for a stroll together to different parts of the island."

Hercule Poirot murmured:

"Ah, yes!" and Patrick Redfern shot him an inquiring glance.

Weston said:

"Then you can give us no help whatsoever as to the cause that took Mrs Marshall to Pixy Cove this morning?"

Redfern shook his head. He said, and his voice sounded honestly bewildered:

"I haven't the faintest idea! It wasn't *like* Arlena."

Weston said:

"Had she any friends down here staying in the neighbourhood?"

"Not that I know of. Oh, I'm sure she hadn't."

"Now, Mr. Redfern, I want you to think very carefully. You knew Mrs Marshall in London. You must be acquainted with various members of her circle. Is there any one you know of who could have had a grudge against her? Someone, for instance, whom you may have supplanted in her fancy?"

Patrick Redfern thought for some minutes. Then he shook his head.

"Honestly," he said. "I can't think of any one."

Colonel Weston drummed with his fingers on the table.

He said at last:

"Well, that's that. We seem to be left with three possibilities. That of an unknown killer—some monomaniac—who happened to be in the neighbourhood—and that's a pretty tall order—"

Redfern said, interrupting:

"And yet surely, it's by far the most likely explanation."

Weston shook his head. He said:

"This isn't one of the 'lonely copse' murders. This cove place was pretty inaccessible. Either the man would have to come up from the causeway past the hotel, over the top of the island and down by that ladder contraption, or else he came there by boat. Either way is unlikely for a casual killing."

Patrick Redfern said:

"You said there were three possibilities."

"Um—yes," said the Chief Constable. "That's to say, there were two people on this island who had a motive for killing her. Her husband, for one, and your wife for another."

Redfern stared at him. He looked dumbfounded. He said:

"My wife? Christine? D'you mean that *Christine* had anything to do with this?"

He got up and stood there stammering slightly in his incoherent haste to get the words out.

"You're mad—quite mad— Christine? Why, it's *impossible*. It's laughable!"

Weston said:

"All the same, Mr. Redfern, jealousy is a very powerful motive. Women who are jealous lose control of themselves completely."

Redfern said earnestly:

"Not Christine. She's—oh, she's not like that. She was unhappy, yes. But she's not the kind of person to— Oh, there's no violence in her."

Hercule Poirot nodded thoughtfully. Violence. The same word that Linda Marshall had used. As before, he agreed with the sentiment.

"Besides," went on Redfern confidently. "It would be absurd. Arlena was twice as strong physically as Christine. I doubt if Christine could strangle a kitten—certainly not a strong wiry creature like Arlena. And then Christine could never have got down that ladder to the beach. She has no head for that sort of thing. And—oh, the whole thing is fantastic!"

Colonel Weston scratched his ear tentatively.

"Well," he said. "Put like that it doesn't seem likely. I grant you that. But motive's the first thing we've got to look for." He added: "Motive and opportunity."

IV

When Redfern had left the room, the Chief Constable observed with a slight smile:

"Didn't think it necessary to tell the fellow his wife had got an alibi. Wanted to hear what he'd have to say to the idea. Shook him up a bit, didn't it?"

Hercule Poirot murmured:

"The arguments he advanced were quite as strong as any alibi."

"Yes. Oh! she didn't do it! She couldn't have done it—physically impossible as you said. Marshall *could* have done it—but apparently he didn't."

Inspector Colgate coughed. He said:

"Excuse me, sir, I've been thinking about that alibi. It's possible, you know, if he'd thought this thing out, that those letters were got ready *beforehand.*"

Weston said:

"That's a good idea. We must look into—"

He broke off as Christine Redfern entered the room.

She was, as always, calm and a little precise in manner. She was wearing a white tennis frock and a pale blue pullover. It accentuated her fair, rather anaemic prettiness. Yet, Hercule Poirot thought to himself, it was neither a silly face nor a weak one. It had plenty of resolution, courage and good sense. He nodded appreciatively.

Colonel Weston thought:

"Nice little woman. Bit wishy-washy, perhaps. A lot too good for that philandering young ass of a husband of hers. Oh, well, the boy's young. Women usually make a fool of you once!"

He said:

"Sit down, Mrs. Redfern. We've got to go through a certain amount of routine, you see. Asking everybody for an account of their movements this morning. Just for our records."

Christine Redfern nodded.

She said in her quiet precise voice:

"Oh, yes, I quite understand. Where do you want me to begin?"

Hercule Poirot said:

"As early as possible, Madame. What did you do when you first got up this morning?"

Christine said:

"Let me see. On my way down to breakfast I went into Linda Marshall's room and fixed up with her to go to Gull Cove this morning. We agreed to meet in the lounge at half past ten."

Poirot asked:

"You did not bathe before breakfast, Madame?"

"No. I very seldom do." She smiled. "I like the sea well warmed before I get into it. I'm rather a chilly person."

"But your husband bathes then?"

"Oh, yes. Nearly always."

"And Mrs. Marshall, she also?"

A change came over Christine's voice. It became cold and almost acrid. She said:

"Oh, no, Mrs. Marshall was the sort of person who never made an appearance before the middle of the morning."

With an air of confusion, Hercule Poirot said:

"Pardon, Madame, I interrupted you. You were saying that you went to Miss Linda Marshall's room. What time was that?"

"Let me see—half past eight—no, a little later."

"And was Miss Marshall up then?"

"Oh, yes, she had been out."

"Out?"

"Yes, she said she'd been bathing."

There was a faint—a very faint note of embarrassment in Christine's voice. It puzzled Hercule Poirot.

Weston said:

"And then?"

"Then I went down to breakfast."

"And after breakfast?"

"I went upstairs, collected my sketching box, and sketching book and we started out."

"You and Miss Linda Marshall?"

"Yes."

"What time was that?"

"I think it was just on half past ten."

"And what did you do?"

"We went to Gull Cove. You know, the cove on the east side of the island. We settled ourselves there. I did a sketch and Linda sunbathed."

"What time did you leave the cove?"

"At a quarter to twelve. I was playing tennis at twelve and had to change."

"You had your watch with you?"

"No, as a matter of fact I hadn't. I asked Linda the time."

"I see. And then?"

"I packed up my sketching things and went back to the hotel."

Poirot said:

"And Mademoiselle Linda?"

"Linda? Oh, Linda went into the sea."

Poirot said:

"Were you far from the sea where you were sitting?"

"Well, we were well above high-water mark. Just under the cliff—so that I could be a little in the shade and Linda in the sun."

Poirot said:

"Did Linda Marshall actually enter the sea before you left the beach?"

Christine frowned a little in the effort to remember. She said:

"Let me see. She ran down the beach—I fastened my box— Yes, I heard her splashing in the waves as I was on the path up the cliff."

"You are quite sure of that, Madame? That she really entered the sea?"

"Oh, yes."

She stared at him in surprise.

Colonel Weston also stared at him.

Then he said:

"Go on, Mrs. Redfern."

"I went back to the hotel, changed, and went to the tennis courts where I met the others."

"Who were?"

"Captain Marshall, Mr. Gardener and Miss Darnley. We played two sets. We were just going in again when the news came about—about Mrs. Marshall."

Hercule Poirot leaned forward. He said:

"And what did you think, Madame, when you heard that news?"

"What did I think?"

Her face showed a faint distaste for the question.

"Yes."

Christine Redfern said slowly:

"It was—a horrible thing to happen."

"Ah, yes, your fastidiousness was revolted. I understand that. But what did it mean to *you*—personally?"

She gave him a quick look—a look of appeal. He responded to it. He said in a matter-of-fact voice:

"I am appealing to you, Madame, as a woman of intelligence with plenty of good sense and judgment. You had doubtless during your stay here formed an opinion of Mrs. Marshall, of the kind of woman she was?"

Christine said cautiously:

"I suppose one always does that more or less when one is staying in hotels."

"Certainly, it is the natural thing to do. So I ask you, Madame, were you really very surprised at the manner of her death?"

Christine said slowly:

"I think I see what you mean. No, I was not, perhaps, surprised. Shocked, yes. But she was the kind of woman—"

Poirot finished the sentence for her.

"She was the kind of woman to whom such a thing might happen. . . . Yes, Madame, that is the truest and most significant thing that has been said in this room this morning. Laying all—er—[he stressed it carefully] *personal* feeling aside, what did you really think of the late Mrs. Marshall?"

Christine Redfern said calmly:

"Is it really worth while going into all that now?"

"I think it might be, yes."

"Well, what shall I say?" Her fair skin was suddenly suffused with colour. The careful poise of her manner was relaxed. For a short space the natural raw woman looked out. "She's the kind of woman that to my mind is absolutely worthless! She did nothing to justify her existence. She had no mind—no brains. She thought of nothing but men and clothes and admiration. Useless, a parasite! She was attractive to men, I suppose— Oh, of course she was. And she lived for that kind of life. And so, I suppose, I wasn't really surprised at her coming to a sticky end. She was the sort of woman who would be mixed up with everything sordid—blackmail—jealousy—violence—every kind of crude emotion. She—she appealed to the worst in people."

She stopped, panting a little. Her rather short top lip lifted itself in a kind of fastidious disgust. It occurred to Colonel Weston that you could not have found a more complete contrast to Arlena Stuart than Christine Redfern. It also occurred to him that if you were married to Christine Redfern, the atmosphere might be so rarefied that the Arlena Stuarts of this world would hold a particular attraction for you.

And then, immediately following on these thoughts, a single word out of the words she had spoken fastened on his attention with particular intensity.

He leaned forward and said:

"Mrs. Redfern, why, in speaking of her, did you mention the word *blackmail?*"

CHAPTER VII

CHRISTINE STARED AT him, not seeming at once to take in what he meant. She answered almost mechanically.

"I suppose—because she *was* being blackmailed. She was the sort of person who would be."

Colonel Weston said earnestly:

"But—do you know she was being blackmailed?"

A faint colour rose in the girl's cheeks. She said rather awkwardly:

"As a matter of fact I do happen to know it. I—I overheard something."

"Will you explain, Mrs. Redfern?"

Flushing still more, Christine Redfern said:

"I—I didn't mean to overhear. It was an accident. It was two—no, three nights ago. We were playing bridge." She turned towards Poirot. "You remember? My husband and I, M. Poirot and Miss Darnley. I was dummy. It was very stuffy in the card room, and I slipped out of the window for a breath of fresh air. I went down towards the beach and I suddenly heard voices. One—it was Arlena Marshall's—I knew it at once—said: 'It's no good pressing me. I can't get any more money now. My husband will suspect something.' And then a man's voice said: 'I'm not taking any excuses. You've got to cough up.' And then Arlena Marshall said: 'You blackmailing brute!' And the man said: 'Brute or not, you'll pay up, my lady.'"

Christine paused.

"I'd turned back and a minute after Arlena Marshall rushed past me. She looked—well, frightfully upset."

Weston said:

"And the man? Do you know who he was?"

Christine Redfern shook her head.

She said:

"He was keeping his voice low. I barely heard what he said."

"It didn't suggest the voice to you of any one you knew?"

She thought again, but once more shook her head. She said:

"No, I don't know. It was gruff and low. It—oh, it might have been anybody's."

Colonel Weston said:

"Thank you, Mrs. Redfern."

II

When the door had closed behind Christine Redfern, Inspector Colgate said:

"Now we are getting somewhere!"

Weston said:

"You think so, eh?"

"Well, it's suggestive, sir, you can't get away from it. Somebody in this hotel was blackmailing the lady."

Poirot murmured:

"But it is not the wicked blackmailer who lies dead. It is the victim."

"That's a bit of a setback, I agree," said the Inspector. "Blackmailers aren't in the habit of bumping off their victims. But what it does give us is this, it suggests a reason for Mrs. Marshall's curious behaviour this morning. She'd got a rendezvous with this fellow who was blackmailing her, and she didn't want either her husband or Redfern to know about it."

"It certainly explains that point," agreed Poirot.

Inspector Colgate went on:

"And think of the place chosen. The very spot for the purpose. The lady goes off on her float. That's natural enough. It's what she does every day. She goes round to Pixy Cove where no one ever goes in the morning and which will be a nice quiet place for an interview."

Poirot said:

"But yes, I too was struck by that point. It is, as you say, an ideal spot for a rendezvous. It is deserted, it is only accessible from the land side by descending a vertical steel ladder which is not everybody's money, *bien entendu*. Moreover, most of the beach is invisible from above because of the overhanging cliff. And it has another advantage. Mr. Redfern told me of that one day. There is a cave on it, the entrance to which is not easy to find but where any one could wait unseen."

Weston said:

"Of course, the Pixy's Cave—remember hearing about it."

Inspector Colgate said:

"Haven't heard it spoken of for years, though. We'd better have a look inside it. Never know, we might find a pointer of some kind."

Weston said:

"Yes, you're right, Colgate, we've got the solution to part one of the puzzle. *Why did Mrs. Marshall go to Pixy Cove?* We want the other half of that solution, though. *Who did she go there to meet?* Presumably someone staying in this hotel. None of them fitted as a lover—but a blackmailer's a different proposition."

He drew the register towards him.

"Excluding the waiters, boots, etc., whom I don't think likely, we've got the following: the American—Gardener, Major Barry, Mr. Horace Blatt, and the Reverend Stephen Lane."

Inspector Colgate said:

"We can narrow it down a bit, sir. We might almost rule out the American, I think. He was on the beach all the morning. That's so, isn't it, M. Poirot?"

Poirot replied:

"He was absent for a short time when he fetched a skein of wool for his wife."

Colgate said:

"Oh, well, we needn't count that."

Weston said:

"And what about the other three?"

"Major Barry went out at ten o'clock this morning. He returned at one-thirty. Mr. Lane was earlier still. He breakfasted at eight. Said he was going for a tramp. Mr. Blatt went off for a sail at nine-thirty same as he does most days. Neither of them is back yet?"

"A sail, eh?" Colonel Weston's voice was thoughtful.

Inspector Colgate's voice was responsive. He said:

"Might fit in rather well, sir."

Weston said:

"Well, we'll have a word with this Major bloke—and let me see, who else is there? Rosamund Darnley. And there's the Brewster woman who found the body with Redfern. What's she like, Colgate?"

"Oh, a sensible party, sir. No nonsense about her."

"She didn't express any opinions on the death?"

The Inspector shook his head.

"I don't think she'll have anything more to tell us, sir, but we'll have to make sure. Then there are the Americans."

Colonel Weston nodded. He said: "Let's have 'em all in and get it over as soon as possible. Never know, might learn something. About the blackmailing stunt if about nothing else."

III

Mr. and Mrs. Gardener came into the presence of authority together.

Mrs. Gardener explained immediately.

"I hope you'll understand how it is, Colonel Weston (that is the name, I think?)." Reassured on this point she went on: "But this has been a very bad shock to me and Mr. Gardener is always very, very careful of my health—"

Mr. Gardener here interpolated.

"Mrs. Gardener," he said, "is very sensitive."

"—and he said to me, 'Why, Carrie,' he said, 'naturally I'm coming right along with you.' It's not that we haven't the highest admiration for British police methods, because we have. I've been told that British police procedure is most refined and delicate and I've never doubted it and certainly when I once had a bracelet missing at the Savoy Hotel nothing could have been more lovely and sympathetic than the young man who came to see me about it, and of course I hadn't really lost the bracelet at all, but just mislaid it, that's the worst of rushing about so much, it makes you kind of forgetful where you put things—" Mrs. Gardener paused, inhaled gently and started off again. "And what I say is, and I know Mr. Gardener agrees with me, that we're only too anxious to do anything to help the British police in every way. So go right ahead and ask me anything at all you want to know—"

Colonel Weston opened his mouth to comply with this invitation but had momentarily to postpone speech while Mrs. Gardener went on.

"That's what I said, Odell, isn't it? And that's so, isn't it?"

"Yes, darling," said Mr. Gardener.

Colonel Weston spoke hastily.

"I understand, Mrs. Gardener, that you and your husband were on the beach all the morning?"

For once Mr. Gardener was able to get in first.

"That's so," he said.

"Why, certainly we were," said Mrs. Gardener. "And a lovely peaceful morning it was, just like any other morning, if you get me, perhaps even more so, and not the slightest idea in our minds of what was happening round the corner on that lonely beach."

"Did you see Mrs. Marshall at all to-day?"

"We did not. And I said to Odell, Why, wherever can Mrs. Marshall have got to this morning? I said. And first her husband coming looking for her and then that good-looking young man, Mr. Redfern, and so impatient he was, just sitting there on the beach scowling at every one and everything. And I said to myself, Why, when he has that nice pretty little wife of his own, must he go running after that dreadful woman? Because that's just what I felt she was. I always felt that about her, didn't I, Odell?"

"Yes, darling."

"However that nice Captain Marshall came to marry such a woman I just cannot imagine—and with that nice young daughter growing up, and it's so important for girls to have the right influence. Mrs. Marshall was not at all the right person—no breeding at all—and I should say a very animal nature. Now if Captain Marshall had had any sense he'd have married Miss Darnley who's a very, very charming woman and a very distinguished one. I must say I admire the way she's gone straight ahead and built up a first-class business as she has. It takes brains to do a thing like that—and you've only got to look at Rosamund Darnley to see she's just frantic with brains. She could plan and carry out any mortal thing she liked. I just admire that woman more than I can say. And I said to Mr. Gardener the other day that any one could see she was very much in love with Captain Marshall—crazy about him was what I said, didn't I, Odell?"

"Yes, darling."

"It seems they knew each other as children, and, why, now, who knows, it may all come right after all with that woman out of the way. I'm not a narrow-minded woman, Colonel Weston, and it isn't that I disapprove of the stage as such—why, quite a lot of my best friends are actresses—but I've said to Mr. Gardener all along that there was something evil about that woman. And you see, I've been proved right."

She paused triumphantly.

The lips of Hercule Poirot quivered in a little smile. His eyes met for a minute the shrewd grey eyes of Mr. Gardener.

Colonel Weston said rather desperately:

"Well, thank you, Mrs. Gardener. I suppose there's nothing that either of you has noticed since you've been here that might have a bearing upon the case?"

"Why, no, I don't think so." Mr. Gardener spoke with a slow drawl. "Mrs. Marshall was around with young Redfern most of the time—but everybody can tell you that."

"What about her husband? Did he mind, do you think?"

Mr. Gardener said cautiously:

"Captain Marshall is a very reserved man."

Mrs. Gardener confirmed this by saying:

"Why, yes, he is a real Britisher!"

IV

On the slightly apoplectic countenance of Major Barry various emotions seemed contending for mastery. He was endeavouring to look properly horrified but could not subdue a kind of shamefaced gusto.

He was saying in his hoarse slightly wheezy voice:

"Glad to help you any way I can. 'Course I don't know anythin' about it —nothin' at all. Not acquainted with the parties. But I've knocked about a bit in my time. Lived a lot in the East, you know. And I can tell you that after being in an Indian hill station what you don't know about human nature isn't worth knowin'."

He paused, took a breath and was off again.

"Matter of fact this business reminds me of a case in Simla. Fellow called Robinson or was it Falconer? Anyway he was in the East Wilts or was it the North Surreys? Can't remember now and anyway it doesn't matter. Quiet chap, you know, great reader—mild as milk you'd have said. Went for his wife one evening in their bungalow. Got her by the throat. She'd been carryin' on with some feller or other and he'd got wise to it. By Jove, he nearly did for her! It was touch and go. Surprised us all! Didn't think he had it in him."

Hercule Poirot murmured:

"And you see there an analogy to the death of Mrs. Marshall?"

"Well, what I mean to say—strangled, you know. Same idea. Feller suddenly sees red!"

Poirot said:

"You think that Captain Marshall felt like that?"

"Oh, look here, I never said that." Major Barry's face went even redder. "Never said anything about Marshall. Thoroughly nice chap. Wouldn't say a word against him for the world."

Poirot murmured:

"Ah, *pardon,* but you *did* refer to the natural reactions of a husband."

Major Barry said:

"Well, I mean to say, I should think she'd been pretty hot stuff. Eh? Got young Redfern on a string all right. And there were probably others before him. But the funny thing is, you know, that husbands are a dense lot. Amazin'. I've been surprised by it again and again. They see a feller sweet on their wife but they don't see that *she's* sweet on *him!* Remember a case like that in Poona. Very pretty woman. Jove, she led her husband a dance—"

Colonel Weston stirred a little restively. He said:

"Yes, yes, Major Barry. For the moment we've just got to establish the facts. You don't know of anything personally—that you've seen or noticed that might help us in this case?"

"Well, really, Weston, I can't say I do. Saw her and young Redfern one afternoon on Gull Cove—" here he winked knowingly and gave a deep hoarse chuckle—"Very pretty it was, too. But it's not evidence of that kind you're wanting. Ha, ha."

"You did not see Mrs. Marshall at all this morning?"

"Didn't see anybody this morning. Went over to St. Loo. Just my luck. Sort of place here where nothin' happens for months and when it does you miss it!"

The Major's voice held a ghoulish regret.

Colonel Weston prompted him.

"You went to St. Loo, you say?"

"Yes, wanted to do some telephonin'. No telephone here and that post office place at Leathercombe Bay isn't very private."

"Were your telephone calls of a very private nature?"

The Major winked again cheerfully.

"Well, they were and they weren't. Wanted to get through to a pal of mine and get him to put somethin' on a horse. Couldn't get through to him, worse luck."

"Where did you telephone from?"

"Call box in the G.P.O. at St. Loo. Then on the way back I got lost— these confounded lanes—twistin' and turnin' all over the place. Must have wasted an hour over that at least. Damned confusing part of the world. I only got back half an hour ago."

Colonel Weston said:

"Speak to any one or meet any one in St. Loo?"

Major Barry said with a chuckle:

"Wantin' me to prove an alibi? Can't think of anythin' useful. Saw about fifty thousand people in St. Loo—but that's not to say they'll remember seein' me."

The Chief Constable said:

"We have to ask these things, you know."

"Right you are. Call on me at any time. Glad to help you. Very fetchin' woman, the deceased. Like to help you catch the feller who did it. The Lonely Beach Murder—bet you that's what the papers will call it. Reminds me of the time—"

It was Inspector Colgate who firmly nipped this latest reminiscence in the bud and manœuvred the garrulous Major out of the door.

Coming back he said:

"Difficult to check up on anything in St. Loo. It's the middle of the holiday season."

The Chief Constable said:

"Yes, we can't take him off the list. Not that I seriously believe he's implicated. Dozens of old bores like him going about. Remember one or two of them in my Army days. Still—he's a possibility. I leave all that to you, Colgate. Check what time he took the car out—petrol—all that. It's humanly possible that he parked the car somewhere in a lonely spot, walked back here and went to the cove. But it doesn't seem feasible to me. He'd have run too much risk of being seen."

Colgate nodded.

He said:

"Of course there are a good many charabancs here to-day. Fine day. They start arriving round about half past eleven. High tide was at seven. Low tide would be about one o'clock. People would be spread out over the sands and the causeway."

Weston said:

"Yes. But he'd have to come up from the causeway past the hotel."

"Not right past it. He could branch off on the path that leads up over the top of the island."

Weston said doubtfully:

"I'm not saying that he mightn't have done it without being seen. Practically all the hotel guests were on the bathing beach except for Mrs. Redfern and the Marshall girl who were down in Gull Cove, and the beginning of that path would only be overlooked by a few rooms of the hotel and there are plenty of chances against any one looking out of those windows just at that moment. For the matter of that, I daresay it's possible for a man to walk up to the hotel, through the lounge and out again without any one happening to see him. But what I say is, he couldn't *count* on no one seeing him."

Colgate said:

"He could have gone round to the cove by boat."

Weston nodded. He said:

"That's much sounder. If he'd had a boat handy in one of the coves near by, he could have left the car, rowed or sailed to Pixy Cove, done the murder, rowed back, picked up the car and arrived back with this tale about having been to St. Loo and lost his way—a story that he'd know would be pretty hard to disprove."

"You're right, sir."

The Chief Constable said:

"Well, I leave it to you, Colgate. Comb the neighbourhood thoroughly. You know what to do. We'd better see Miss Brewster now."

V

Emily Brewster was not able to add anything of material value to what they already knew.

Weston said after she had repeated her story:

"And there's nothing you know of that could help us in any way?"

Emily Brewster said shortly:

"Afraid not. It's a distressing business. However I expect you'll soon get to the bottom of it."

Weston said:

"I hope so too."

Emily Brewster said drily:

"Ought not to be difficult."

"Now what do you mean by that, Miss Brewster?"

"Sorry. Wasn't attempting to teach you your business. All I meant was that with a woman of that kind it ought to be easy enough."

Hercule Poirot murmured:

"That is your opinion?"

Emily Brewster snapped out:

"Of course. *De mortuis nil nisi bonum* and all that, but you can't get away from *facts*. That woman was a bad lot through and through. You've only got to hunt round a bit in her unsavoury past."

Hercule Poirot said gently:

"You did not like her?"

"I know a bit too much about her." In answer to the inquiring looks she went on. "My first cousin married one of the Erskines. You've probably heard that that woman induced old Sir Robert when he was in his dotage to leave most of his fortune to her away from his own family."

Colonel Weston said:

"And the family—er—resented that?"

"Naturally. His association with her was a scandal anyway and on top of that to leave her a sum like fifty thousand pounds shows just the kind of woman she was. I daresay I sound hard, but in my opinion the Arlena Stuarts of this world deserve very little sympathy. I know of something else too—a young fellow who lost his head about her completely—he'd always been a bit wild, naturally his association with her pushed him over the edge. He did something rather fishy with some shares—solely to get money to spend on her—and only just managed to escape prosecution. That woman contaminated every one she met. Look at the way she was ruining young Redfern. No, I'm afraid I can't have any regret for her death—though of course it would have been better if she'd drowned herself, or fallen over a cliff. Strangling is rather unpleasant."

"And you think the murderer was someone out of her past?"

"Yes, I do."

"Someone who came from the mainland with no one seeing him?"

"Why should any one see him? We were all on the beach. I gather the Marshall child and Christine Redfern were down on Gull Cove out of the way. Captain Marshall was in his room in the hotel. Then who on earth was there to see him except possibly Miss Darnley."

"Where was Miss Darnley?"

"Sitting up on the cutting at the top of the cliff. Sunny Ledge it's called. We saw her there, Mr. Redfern and I, when we were rowing round the island."

Colonel Weston said:

"You may be right, Miss Brewster."

Emily Brewster said positively:

"I'm sure I'm right. When a woman's neither more nor less than a nasty mess, then she herself will provide the best possible clue. Don't you agree with me, M. Poirot?"

Hercule Poirot looked up. His eyes met her confident grey ones. He said:

"Oh, yes—I agree with that which you have just this minute said. Arlena Marshall herself is the best, the only clue, to her own death."

Miss Brewster said sharply:

"Well, then!"

She stood there, an erect sturdy figure, her cool self-confident glance going from one man to the other.

Colonel Weston said:

"You may be sure, Miss Brewster, that any clue there may be in Mrs. Marshall's past life will not be overlooked."

Emily Brewster went out.

VI

Inspector Colgate shifted his position at the table. He said in a thoughtful voice:

"She's a determined one, she is. And she'd got her knife into the dead lady, proper, she had."

He stopped a minute and said reflectively:

"It's a pity in a way that she's got a cast-iron alibi for the whole morning. Did you notice her hands, sir? As big as a man's. And she's a hefty woman —as strong and stronger than many a man I'd say. . . ."

He paused again. His glance at Poirot was almost pleading.

"And you say she never left the beach this morning, M. Poirot?"

Slowly Poirot shook his head. He said:

"My dear Inspector, she came down to the beach before Mrs. Marshall could have reached Pixy Cove and she was within my sight until she set off with Mr. Redfern in the boat."

Inspector Colgate said gloomily:

"Then that washes her out."

He seemed upset about it.

VII

As always, Hercule Poirot felt a keen sense of pleasure at the sight of Rosamund Darnley.

Even to a bare police inquiry into the ugly facts of murder she brought a distinction of her own.

She sat down opposite Colonel Weston and turned a grave and intelligent face to him.

She said:

"You want my name and address? Rosamund Anne Darnley. I carry on a dressmaking business under the name of Rose Mond, Ltd. at 622 Brook Street."

"Thank you, Miss Darnley. Now can you tell us anything that may help us?"

"I don't really think I can."

"Your own movements—"

"I had breakfast about nine-thirty. Then I went up to my room and collected some books and my sunshade and went out to Sunny Ledge. That must have been about twenty-five past ten. I came back to the hotel about ten minutes to twelve, went up and got my tennis racquet and went out to the tennis courts where I played tennis until lunchtime."

"You were in the cliff recess, called by the hotel, Sunny Ledge, from about half past ten until ten minutes to twelve?"

"Yes."

"Did you see Mrs. Marshall at all this morning?"

"No."

"Did you see her from the cliff as she paddled her float round to Pixy Cove?"

"No, she must have gone by before I got there."

"Did you notice any one on a float or in a boat at all this morning?"

"No, I don't think I did. You see I was reading. Of course I looked up from my book from time to time but as it happened the sea was quite bare each time I did so."

"You didn't even notice Mr. Redfern and Miss Brewster when they went round?"

"No."

"You were, I think, acquainted with Mr. Marshall?"

"Captain Marshall is an old family friend. His family and mine lived next door to each other. I had not seen him, however, for a good many years—it must be something like twelve years."

"And Mrs. Marshall?"

"I'd never exchanged half a dozen words with her until I met her here."

"Were Captain and Mrs. Marshall, as far as you knew, on good terms with each other?"

"On perfectly good terms, I should say."

"Was Captain Marshall very devoted to his wife?"

Rosamund said:

"He may have been. I can't really tell you anything about that. Captain Marshall is rather old-fashioned—he hasn't got the modern habit of shouting matrimonial woes upon the housetop."

"Did you like Mrs. Marshall, Miss Darnley?"

"No."

The monosyllable came quietly and evenly. It sounded what it was—a simple statement of fact.

"Why was that?"

A half smile came to Rosamund's lips. She said:

"Surely you've discovered that Arlena Marshall was not popular with her own sex? She was bored to death with women and showed it. Nevertheless I should like to have had the dressing of her. She had a great gift for clothes. Her clothes were always just right and she wore them well. I should like to have had her as a client."

"She spent a good deal on clothes?"

"She must have done. But then she had money of her own and of course Captain Marshall is quite well off."

"Did you ever hear or did it ever occur to you that Mrs. Marshall was being blackmailed, Miss Darnley?"

A look of intense astonishment came over Rosamund Darnley's expressive face. She said:

"Blackmailed? Arlena?"

"The idea seems to surprise you."

"Well, yes, it does rather. It seems so incongruous."

"But surely it is possible?"

"Everything's possible, isn't it? The world soon teaches one that. But I wondered what any one could blackmail Arlena about?"

"There are certain things, I suppose, that Mrs. Marshall might be anxious should not come to her husband's ears?"

"We-ll, yes."

She explained the doubt in her voice by saying with a half smile:

"I sound sceptical, but then, you see, Arlena was rather notorious in her conduct. She never made much of a pose of respectability."

"You think, then, that her husband was aware of her—intimacies with other people?"

There was a pause. Rosamund was frowning. She spoke at last in a slow reluctant voice. She said:

"You know, I don't really know what to think. I've always assumed that Kenneth Marshall accepted his wife, quite frankly, for what she was. That he had no illusions about her. But it may not be so."

"He may have believed in her absolutely?"

Rosamund said with semi-exasperation:

"Men are such fools. And Kenneth Marshall is unworldly under his sophisticated manner. He *may* have believed in her blindly. He may have thought she was just—admired."

"And you know of no one—that is you have heard of no one who was likely to have had a grudge against Mrs. Marshall?"

Rosamund Darnley smiled. She said:

"Only resentful wives. And I presume since she was strangled, that it was a man who killed her."

"Yes."

Rosamund said thoughtfully:

"No, I can't think of any one. But then I probably shouldn't know. You'll have to ask some one in her own intimate set."

"Thank you, Miss Darnley."

Rosamund turned a little in her chair. She said:

"Hasn't M. Poirot any questions to ask?"

Her faintly ironic smile flashed out at him.

Hercule Poirot smiled and shook his head.

He said:

"I can think of nothing."

Rosamund Darnley got up and went out.

CHAPTER VIII

THEY WERE STANDING in the bedroom that had been Arlena Marshall's.

Two big bay windows gave onto a balcony that overlooked the bathing beach and the sea beyond. Sunshine poured into the room, flashing over the bewildering array of bottles and jars on Arlena's dressing-table.

Here there was every kind of cosmetic and unguent known to beauty parlours. Amongst this panoply of woman's affairs three men moved purposefully. Inspector Colgate went about shutting and opening drawers.

Presently he gave a grunt. He had come upon a packet of folded letters. He and Weston ran through them together.

Hercule Poirot had moved to the wardrobe. He opened the door of the hanging cupboard and looked at the multiplicity of gowns and sports suits that hung there. He opened the other side. Foamy lingerie lay in piles. On a wide shelf were hats. Two more beach cardboard hats in lacquer red and pale yellow—a big Hawaiian straw hat—another of drooping dark blue linen and three or four little absurdities for which, no doubt, several guineas had been paid apiece—a kind of beret in dark blue—a tuft, no more, of black velvet—a pale grey turban.

Hercule Poirot stood scanning them—a faintly indulgent smile came to his lips. He murmured:

"*Les femmes!*"

Colonel Weston was refolding the letters.

"Three from young Redfern," he said. "Damned young ass. He'll learn not to write letters to women in a few more years. Women always keep letters and then swear they've burnt them. There's one other letter here. Same line of country."

He held it out and Poirot took it.

"DARLING ARLENA,

"God, I feel blue. To be going out to China—and perhaps not seeing you again for years and years. I didn't know any man could go on feeling crazy about a woman like I feel about you. Thanks for the cheque. They won't prosecute now. It was a near shave, though, and all because I wanted to make big money for you. Can you forgive me? I wanted to set diamonds in your ears—your lovely lovely ears and clasp great milk-white pearls round your throat only they say pearls are no good nowadays. A fabulous emerald, then? Yes, that's the thing. A great emerald, cool and green and full of hidden fire. Don't forget me—but you won't, I know. You're mine—always.

"Good-bye—good-bye—good-bye.

"J.N."

Inspector Colgate said:

"Might be worth while to find out if J.N. really did go to China. Otherwise—well, he might be the person we're looking for. Crazy about the woman, idealizing her, suddenly finding out he'd been played for a sucker. It sounds to me as though this is the boy Miss Brewster mentioned. Yes, I think this might be useful."

Hercule Poirot nodded. He said:

"Yes, that letter is important. I find it very important."

He turned round and stared at the room—at the bottles on the dressing-table—at the open wardrobe and at a big Pierrot doll that lolled insolently on the bed.

They went into Kenneth Marshall's room.

It was next door to his wife's but with no communicating door and no balcony. It faced the same way and had two windows, but it was much smaller. Between the two windows a gilt mirror hung on the wall. In the corner beyond the right-hand window was the dressing-table. On it were two ivory brushes, a clothes brush and a bottle of hair lotion. In the corner by the left-hand window was a writing-table. An open typewriter stood on it and papers were ranged in a stack beside it.

Colgate went through them rapidly.

He said:

"All seems straightforward enough. Ah, here's the letter he mentioned this morning. Dated the 24th—that's yesterday. And here's the envelope—

postmarked Leathercombe Bay this morning. Seems all square. Now we'll
have an idea if he could have prepared that answer of his beforehand."

He sat down.

Colonel Weston said:

"We'll leave you to it, for a moment. We'll just glance through the rest
of the rooms. Everyone's been kept out of this corridor until now and
they're getting a bit restive about it."

They went next into Linda Marshall's room. It faced east, looking out
over the rocks down to the sea below.

Weston gave a glance round. He murmured:

"Don't suppose there's anything to see here. But it's possible Marshall
might have put something in his daughter's room that he didn't want us to
find. Not likely, though. It isn't as though there had been a weapon or
anything to get rid of."

He went out again.

Hercule Poirot stayed behind. He found something that interested him
in the grate. Something had been burnt there recently. He knelt down,
working patiently. He laid out his finds on a sheet of paper. A large ir-
regular blob of candle grease—some fragments of green paper or cardboard, possibly a pull-off calendar, for with it was an unburnt fragment
bearing a large figure 5 and a scrap of printing . . . *noble deeds.* . . .
There was also an ordinary pin and some burnt animal matter which
might have been hair.

Poirot arranged them neatly in a row and stared at them.

He murmured:

"'Do noble deeds, not dream them all day long.' C'est possible. But what
is one to make of this collection? C'est fantastique!"

And then he picked up the pin and his eyes grew sharp and green.

He murmured:

"Pour l'amour de Dieu! Is it possible?"

Hercule Poirot got up from where he had been kneeling by the grate.

Slowly he looked round the room and this time there was an entirely
new expression on his face. It was grave and almost stern.

To the left of the mantelpiece there were some shelves with a row of
books. Hercule Poirot looked thoughtfully along the titles.

A Bible, a battered copy of Shakespeare's plays. *The Marriage of Wil-
liam Ashe* by Mrs. Humphry Ward. *The Young Stepmother* by Charlotte
Yonge. *The Shropshire Lad.* Eliot's *Murder in the Cathedral.* Bernard
Shaw's *St. Joan. Gone with the Wind* by Margaret Mitchell. *The Burning
Court* by Dickson Carr.

Poirot took out two books, *The Young Stepmother* and *William Ashe*,
and glanced inside at the blurred stamp affixed to the title page. As he

was about to replace them, his eye caught sight of a book that had been shoved behind the other books. It was a small dumpy volume bound in brown calf.

He took it out and opened it. Very slowly he nodded his head.

He murmured:

"*So I was right. . . .* Yes, I was right. But for the other—is that possible too? No, it is not possible, unless . . ."

He stayed there, motionless, stroking his moustaches whilst his mind ranged busily over the problem.

He said again softly:

"*Unless—?*"

II

Colonel Weston looked in at the door.

"Hullo, Poirot, still there?"

"I arrive. I arrive," cried Poirot.

He hurried out into the corridor.

The room next to Linda's was that of the Redferns.

Poirot looked into it, noting automatically the traces of two different individualities—a neatness and tidiness which he associated with Christine and a picturesque disorder which was characteristic of Patrick. Apart from these sidelights on personality the room did not interest him.

Next to it again was Rosamund Darnley's room and here he lingered for a moment in the sheer pleasure of the owner's personality.

He noted the few books that lay on the table next to the bed, the expensive simplicity of the toilet set on the dressing-table. And there came gently to his nostrils the elusive expensive perfume that Rosamund Darnley used.

Next to Rosamund Darnley's room at the northern end of the corridor was an open window leading to a balcony from which an outside stair led down to the rocks below.

Weston said:

"That's the way people go down to bathe before breakfast—that is, if they bathe off the rocks as most of them do."

Interest came into Hercule Poirot's eyes. He stepped outside and looked down.

Below, a path led to steps cut zigzag leading down the rocks to the sea. There was also a path that led round the hotel to the left. He said:

"One could go down these stairs, go to the left round the hotel and join the main path up from the causeway."

Weston nodded. He amplified Poirot's statement.

"One could go right across the island without going through the hotel at all." He added: "But one might still be seen from a window."

"What window?"

"Two of the public bathrooms look out that way—north—and the staff bathroom, and the cloakrooms on the ground floor. Also the billiard room."

Poirot nodded. He said:

"And all the former have frosted glass windows and one does not play billiards on a fine morning."

"Exactly."

Weston paused and said:

"If he did it, that's the way he went."

"You mean Captain Marshall?"

"Yes. Blackmail, or no blackmail, I still feel it points to him. And his manner—well, his manner is unfortunate."

Hercule Poirot said drily:

"Perhaps—but a manner does not make a murderer!"

Weston said:

"Then you think he's out of it?"

Poirot shook his head. He said:

"No, I would not say that."

Weston said:

"We'll see what Colgate can make out of the typewriting alibi. In the meantime I've got the chambermaid of this floor waiting to be interviewed. A good deal may depend on her evidence."

The chambermaid was a woman of thirty, brisk, efficient and intelligent. Her answers came readily.

Captain Marshall had come up to his room not long after ten-thirty. She was then finishing the room. He had asked her to be as quick as possible. She had not seen him come back but she had heard the sound of the typewriter a little later. She put it at about five minutes to eleven. She was then in Mr. and Mrs. Redfern's room. After she had done that she moved on to Miss Darnley's room at the end of the corridor. She could not hear the typewriter from there. She went to Miss Darnley's room, as near as she could say, at just after eleven o'clock. She remembered hearing Leathercombe Church strike the hour as she went in. At a quarter past eleven she had gone downstairs for her eleven o'clock cup of tea and "snack." Afterwards she had gone to do the rooms in the other wing of the hotel. In answer to the Chief Constable's question she explained that she had done the rooms in this corridor in the following order:

Miss Linda Marshall's, the two public bathrooms, Mrs. Marshall's room and private bath, Captain Marshall's room. Mr. and Mrs. Redfern's room and private bath, Miss Darnley's room and private bath. Captain Marshall's and Miss Marshall's rooms had no adjoining bathrooms.

During the time she was in Miss Darnley's room and bathroom she had not heard any one pass the door or go out by the staircase to the rocks, but it was quite likely she wouldn't have heard if any one went quietly.

Weston then directed his questions to the subject of Mrs. Marshall.

No, Mrs. Marshall wasn't one for rising early as a rule. She, Gladys Narracott, had been surprised to find the door open and Mrs. Marshall gone down at just after ten. Something quite unusual, that was.

"Did Mrs. Marshall always have her breakfast in bed?"

"Oh, yes, sir, always. Not very much of it either. Just tea and orange juice and one piece of toast. Slimming like so many ladies."

No, she hadn't noticed anything unusual in Mrs. Marshall's manner that morning. She'd seemed quite as usual.

Hercule Poirot murmured:

"What did you think of Mrs. Marshall, Mademoiselle?"

Gladys Narracott stared at him. She said:

"Well, that's hardly for me to say, is it, sir?"

"But yes, it is for you to say. We are anxious—very anxious—to hear your impression."

Gladys gave a slightly uneasy glance towards the Chief Constable who endeavoured to make his face sympathetic and approving, though actually he felt slightly embarrassed by his foreign colleague's methods of approach. He said:

"Er—yes, certainly. Go ahead."

For the first time Gladys Narracott's brisk efficiency deserted her. Her fingers fumbled with her print dress. She said:

"Well, Mrs. Marshall—she wasn't exactly a lady, as you might say. What I mean is she was more like an actress."

Colonel Weston said:

"She was an actress."

"Yes, sir, that's what I'm saying. She just went on exactly as she felt like it. She didn't—well, she didn't trouble to be polite if she wasn't feeling polite. And she'd be all smiles one minute and then if she couldn't find something or the bell wasn't answered at once or her laundry wasn't back, well, she'd be downright rude and nasty about it. None of us as you might say *liked* her. But her clothes were beautiful, and of course she was a very handsome lady, so it was only natural she should be admired."

Colonel Weston said:

"I am sorry to have to ask you what I am going to ask you, but it is a very vital matter. Can you tell me how things were between her and her husband?"

Gladys Narracott hesitated a minute.

She said:

"You don't—it wasn't—you don't think as *he* did it?"

Hercule Poirot said quickly:

"Do you?"

"Oh! I wouldn't like to think so. He's such a nice gentleman, Captain Marshall. He couldn't do a thing like that—I'm sure he couldn't."

"But you are *not* very sure—I hear it in your voice."

Gladys Narracott said reluctantly:

"You do read such things in the papers! When there's jealousy. If there's been goings on—and of course every one's been talking about it—about her and Mr. Redfern, I mean. And Mrs. Redfern such a nice quiet lady! It does seem a shame! And Mr. Redfern's a nice gentleman too, but it seems men can't help themselves when it's a lady like Mrs. Marshall—one who's used to having her own way. Wives have to put up with a lot, I'm sure." She sighed and paused. "But if Captain Marshall found out about it—"

Colonel Weston said sharply:

"Well?"

Gladys Narracott said slowly:

"I did think sometimes that Mrs. Marshall was frightened of her husband knowing."

"What makes you say that?"

"It wasn't anything definite, sir. It was only I felt—that sometimes she was—afraid of him. He was a very quiet gentleman but he wasn't—he wasn't *easy*."

Weston said:

"But you've nothing definite to go on? Nothing either of them ever said to each other."

Slowly Gladys Narracott shook her head.

Weston sighed. He went on:

"Now, as to letters received by Mrs. Marshall this morning. Can you tell us anything about those?"

"There were about six or seven, sir. I couldn't say exactly."

"Did you take them up to her?"

"Yes, sir. I got them from the office as usual and put them on her breakfast tray."

"Do you remember anything about the look of them?"

The girl shook her head.

"They were just ordinary-looking letters. Some of them were bills and circulars, I think, because they were torn up on the tray."

"What happened to them?"

"They went into the dustbin, sir. One of the police gentlemen is going through that now."

Weston nodded.

"And the contents of the waste-paper baskets, where are they?"

"They'll be in the dustbin too."

Weston said:

"H'm—well, I think that is all at present." He looked inquiringly at Poirot.

Poirot leaned forward.

"When you did Miss Linda Marshall's room this morning, did you do the fireplace?"

"There wasn't anything to do, sir. There had been no fire lit."

"And there was nothing in the fireplace itself?"

"No, sir, it was perfectly all right."

"What time did you do her room?"

"About a quarter past nine, sir, when she'd gone down to breakfast."

"Did she come up to her room after breakfast, do you know?"

"Yes, sir. She came up about a quarter to ten."

"Did she stay in her room?"

"I think so, sir. She came out, hurrying rather, just before half past ten."

"You didn't go into her room again?"

"No, sir. I had finished with it."

Poirot nodded. He said:

"There is another thing I want to know. What people bathed before breakfast this morning?"

"I couldn't say about the other wing and the floor above. Only about this one."

"That is all I want to know."

"Well, sir, Captain Marshall and Mr. Redfern were the only ones this morning, I think. They always go down for an early dip."

"Did you see them?"

"No, sir, but their wet bathing things were hanging over the balcony rail as usual."

"Miss Linda Marshall did not bathe this morning?"

"No, sir. All her bathing dresses were quite dry."

"Ah," said Poirot. "That is what I wanted to know."

Gladys Narracott volunteered:

"She does most mornings, sir."

"And the other three, Miss Darnley, Mrs. Redfern and Mrs. Marshall?"

"Mrs. Marshall never, sir. Miss Darnley has once or twice, I think. Mrs. Redfern doesn't often bathe before breakfast—only when it's very hot, but she didn't this morning."

Again Poirot nodded. Then he asked:

"I wonder if you have noticed whether a bottle is missing from any of the rooms you look after in this wing?"

"A bottle, sir? What kind of a bottle?"

"Unfortunately I do not know. But have you noticed—or would you be likely to notice—if one had gone?"

Gladys said frankly:

"I shouldn't from Mrs. Marshall's room, sir, and that's a fact. She has ever so many."

"And the other rooms?"

"Well, I'm not sure about Miss Darnley. She has a good many creams and lotions. But from the other rooms, yes, I would, sir. I mean if I were to look special. If I were noticing, so to speak."

"But you haven't actually noticed?"

"No, because I wasn't looking special, as I say."

"Perhaps you would go and look now, then."

"Certainly, sir."

She left the room, her print dress rustling. Weston looked at Poirot. He said:

"What's all this?"

Poirot murmured:

"My orderly mind, that is vexed by trifles! Miss Brewster, this morning, was bathing off the rocks before breakfast, and she says that a bottle was thrown from above and nearly hit her. *Eh bien,* I want to know who threw that bottle and why?"

"My dear man, any one may have chucked a bottle away."

"Not at all. To begin with, it could only have been thrown from a window on the east side of the hotel—that is, one of the windows of the rooms we have just examined. Now I ask you, if you have an empty bottle on your dressing-table or in your bathroom, what do you do with it? I will tell you, you drop it into the waste-paper basket. You do not take the trouble to go out on your balcony and hurl it into the sea! For one thing you might hit some one, for another it would be too much trouble. No, you would only do that *if you did not want any one to see that particular bottle.*"

Weston stared at him.

Weston said:

"I know that Chief Inspector Japp, whom I met over a case not long ago, always says you have a damned tortuous mind. You're not going to tell me now that Arlena Marshall wasn't strangled at all, but poisoned out of some mysterious bottle with a mysterious drug?"

"No, no, I do not think there was poison in that bottle."

"Then what was there?"

"I do not know at all. That's why I am interested."

Gladys Narracott came back. She was a little breathless. She said:

"I'm sorry, sir, but I can't find anything missing. I'm sure there's nothing gone from Captain Marshall's room, or Miss Linda Marshall's room or Mr. and Mrs. Redfern's room, and I'm pretty sure there's nothing gone from Miss Darnley's either. But I couldn't say about Mrs. Marshall's. As I say, she's got such a lot."

Poirot shrugged his shoulders.

He said:

"No matter. We will leave it."

Gladys Narracott said:

"Is there anything more, sir?"

She looked from one to the other of them.

Weston said:

"Don't think so. Thank you."

Poirot said:

"I thank you, no. You are sure, are you not, that there is nothing—nothing at all, that you have forgotten to tell us?"

"About Mrs. Marshall, sir?"

"About anything at all. Anything unusual, out of the way, unexplained, slightly peculiar, rather curious—*enfin*, something that has made you say to yourself or to one of your colleagues: 'That's funny!'?"

Gladys said doubtfully:

"Well, not the sort of thing that you would mean, sir."

Hercule Poirot said:

"Never mind what I mean. You do not know what I mean. It is true, then, that you have said to yourself or to a colleague to-day: 'That is funny!'?"

He brought out the three words with ironic detachment.

Gladys said:

"It was nothing really. Just a bath being run. And I did pass the remark to Elsie, downstairs, that it was funny somebody having a bath round about twelve o'clock."

"Whose bath, who had a bath?"

"That I couldn't say, sir. We heard it going down the waste from this wing that's all, and that's when I said what I did to Elsie."

"You're sure it was a bath? Not one of the hand-basins?"

"Oh! quite sure, sir. You can't mistake bath-water running away."

Poirot displaying no further desire to keep her, Gladys Narracott was permitted to depart.

Weston said:

"You don't think this bath question is important, do you, Poirot? I mean, there's no point to it. No bloodstains or anything like that to wash off. That's the—" he hesitated.

Poirot cut in:

"That, you would say, is the advantage of strangulation! No bloodstains, no weapon—nothing to get rid of or conceal! Nothing is needed but physical strength—*and the soul of a killer!*"

His voice was so fierce, so charged with feeling, that Weston recoiled a little.

Hercule Poirot smiled at him apologetically.

"No, no," he said, "the bath is probably of no importance. Any one may have had a bath. Mrs. Redfern before she went to play tennis, Captain Marshall, Miss Darnley. As I say, any one. There is nothing in that."

A police constable knocked at the door, and put in his head.

"It's Miss Darnley, sir. She says she'd like to see you again for a minute. There's something she forgot to tell you, she says."

Weston said:

"We're coming down—now."

III

The first person they saw was Colgate. His face was gloomy.

"Just a minute, sir."

Weston and Poirot followed him into Mrs. Castle's office.

Colgate said:

"I've been checking up with Heald on this typewriting business. Not a doubt of it, it couldn't be done under an hour. Longer, if you had to stop and think here and there. That seems to me pretty well to settle it. And look at this letter."

He held it out.

"MY DEAR MARSHALL,

"Sorry to worry you on your holiday but an entirely unforeseen situation has arisen over the Burley and Tender contracts. . . ."

"Etcetera, etcetera," said Colgate. "Dated the 24th—that's yesterday. Envelope postmarked yesterday evening E.C.1 and Leathercombe Bay this morning. Same typewriter used on envelope and in letter. And by the contents it was clearly impossible for Marshall to prepare his answer beforehand. The figures arise out of the ones in the letter—the whole thing is quite intricate."

"H'm," said Weston gloomily. "That seems to let Marshall out. We'll have to look elsewhere." He added: "I've got to see Miss Darnley again. She's waiting now."

Rosamund came in crisply. Her smile held an apologetic nuance.

She said:

"I'm frightfully sorry. Probably it isn't worth bothering about. But one does forget things so."

"Yes, Miss Darnley?"

The Chief Constable indicated a chair.

She shook her shapely black head.

"Oh, it isn't worth sitting down. It's simply this. I told you that I spent the morning lying out on Sunny Ledge. That isn't quite accurate. I forgot that once during the morning I went back to the hotel and out again."

"What time was that, Miss Darnley?"

"It must have been about a quarter past eleven."

"You went back to the hotel, you said?"

"Yes, I'd forgotten my glare glasses. At first I thought I wouldn't bother and then my eyes got tired and I decided to go in and get them."

"You went straight to your room and out again?"

"Yes. At least, as a matter of fact, I just looked in on Ken—Captain Marshall. I heard his machine going and I thought it was so stupid of him to stay indoors typing on such a lovely day. I thought I'd tell him to come out."

"And what did Captain Marshall say?"

Rosamund smiled rather shamefacedly.

"Well, when I opened the door he was typing so vigorously, and frowning and looking so concentrated that I just went away quietly. I don't think he even saw me come in."

"And that was—at what time, Miss Darnley?"

"Just about twenty past eleven. I noticed the clock in the hall as I went out again."

IV

"And that puts the lid on it finally," said Inspector Colgate. "The chambermaid heard him typing up till five minutes to eleven. Miss Darnley saw him at twenty minutes past, and the woman was dead at a quarter to twelve. He says he spent that hour typing in his room and it seems quite clear that he *was* typing in his room. That washes Captain Marshall right out."

He stopped, then looking at Poirot with some curiosity he asked:

"M. Poirot's looking very serious over something."

Poirot said thoughtfully:

"I was wondering why Miss Darnley suddenly volunteered this extra evidence."

Inspector Colgate cocked his head alertly.

"Think there's something fishy about it? That it isn't just a question of 'forgetting'?"

He considered for a minute or two, then he said slowly:

"Look here, sir, let's look at it this way. Supposing Miss Darnley wasn't on Sunny Ledge this morning as she says. That story's a lie. Now suppose that *after* telling us her story, she finds that somebody saw her somewhere else or alternatively that some one went to the Ledge and didn't find her there. Then she thinks up this story quick and comes and tells it to us to account for her absence. You'll notice that she was careful to say Captain Marshall didn't *see* her when she looked into his room."

Poirot murmured:

"Yes, I noticed that."

Weston said incredulously:

"Are you suggesting that Miss Darnley's mixed up in this? Nonsense, seems absurd to me. Why should she be?"

Inspector Colgate coughed.

He said:

"You'll remember what the American lady, Mrs. Gardener, said. She sort of hinted that Miss Darnley was sweet on Captain Marshall. There'd be a motive there, sir."

Weston said impatiently:

"Arlena Marshall wasn't killed by a woman. It's a man we've got to look for. We've got to stick to the men in the case."

Inspector Colgate sighed. He said:

"Yes, that's true, sir. We always come back to that, don't we?"

Weston went on:

"Better put a constable on to timing one or two things. From the hotel across the island to the top of the ladder. Let him do it running and walking. Same thing with the ladder itself. And somebody had better check the time it takes to go on a float from the bathing beach to the cove."

Inspector Colgate nodded.

"I'll attend to all that, sir," he said confidently.

The Chief Constable said:

"Think I'll go along to the cove now. See if Phillips has found anything. Then there's that Pixy's Cave we've been hearing about. Ought to see if there are any traces of a man waiting in there. Eh? Poirot. What do you think?"

"By all means. It is a possibility."

Weston said:

"If somebody from outside had nipped over to the island that would be a good hiding-place—if he knew about it. I suppose the locals know?"

Colgate said:

"Don't believe the younger generation would. You see, ever since this hotel was started the coves have been private property. Fishermen don't go there, or picnic parties. And the hotel people aren't local. Mrs. Castle's a Londoner."

Weston said:

"We might take Redfern with us. He told us about it. What about you, M. Poirot?"

Hercule Poirot hesitated. He said, his foreign intonation very pronounced:

"No, I am like Miss Brewster and Mrs. Redfern, I do not like to descend perpendicular ladders."

Weston said:

"You can go round by boat."

Again Hercule Poirot sighed.

"My stomach, it is not happy on the sea."

"Nonsense, man, it's a beautiful day. Calm as a mill pond. You can't let us down, you know."

Hercule Poirot hardly looked like responding to this British adjuration. But at that moment, Mrs. Castle poked her ladylike face and elaborate coiffure round the door.

"Ay'm sure Ay hope Ay am not intruding," she said. "But Mr. Lane, the clergyman, you know, has just returned. Ay thought you might like to know."

"Ah, yes, thanks, Mrs. Castle. We'll see him right away."

Mrs. Castle came a little further into the room. She said:

"Ay don't know if it is worth mentioning, but Ay *have* heard that the smallest incident should not be ignored—"

"Yes, yes?" said Weston impatiently.

"It is only that there was a lady and gentleman here about one o'clock. Came over from the mainland. For luncheon. They were informed that there had been an accident and that under the circumstances no luncheons could be served."

"Any idea who they were?"

"Ay couldn't say at all. Naturally no name was given. They expressed disappointment and a certain amount of curiosity as to the nature of the accident. Ay couldn't tell them anything, of course. Ay should say, myself, they were summer visitors of the better class."

Weston said brusquely:

"Ah, well, thank you for telling us. Probably not important but quite right—er—to remember everything."

"Naturally," said Mrs. Castle, "Ay wish to do my Duty!"

"Quite, quite. Ask Mr. Lane to come here."

V

Stephen Lane strode into the room with his usual vigour.

Weston said:

"I'm the Chief Constable of the County, Mr. Lane. I suppose you've been told what has occurred here?"

"Yes—oh, yes—I heard as soon as I got here. Terrible . . . Terrible . . ." His thin frame quivered. He said in a low voice, "All along—ever since I arrived here—I have been conscious—very conscious—of the forces of evil close at hand."

His eyes, burning eager eyes, went to Hercule Poirot.

He said:

"You remember, M. Poirot? Our conversation some days ago? About the reality of evil?"

Weston was studying the tall gaunt figure in some perplexity. He found it difficult to make this man out. Lane's eyes came back to him. The clergyman said with a slight smile:

"I daresay that seems fantastic to you, sir. We have left off believing in evil in these days. We have abolished Hell fire! We no longer believe in the Devil! But Satan and Satan's emissaries were never more powerful than they are to-day!"

Weston said:

"Er—er—yes, perhaps. That, Mr. Lane, is your province. Mine is more prosaic—to clear up a case of murder."

Stephen Lane said:

"An awful word. Murder! One of the earliest sins known on earth—the ruthless shedding of an innocent brother's blood. . . ." He paused, his eyes half closed. Then, in a more ordinary voice he said:

"In what way can I help you?"

"First of all, Mr. Lane, will you tell me your own movements to-day?"

"Willingly. I started off early on one of my usual tramps. I am fond of walking. I have roamed over a good deal of the countryside round here. To-day I went to St. Petrock-in-the-Combe. That is about seven miles from here—a very pleasant walk along winding lanes, up and down the Devon hills and valleys. I took some lunch with me and ate it in a spinney.

I visited the Church—it has some fragments—only fragments, alas, of early glass—also a very interesting painted screen."

"Thank you, Mr. Lane. Did you meet any one on your walk?"

"Not to speak to. A cart passed me once and a couple of boys on bicycles and some cows. However," he smiled, "if you want proof of my statement I wrote my name in the book at the Church. You will find it there."

"You did not see any one at the Church itself—the Vicar, or the verger?" Stephen Lane shook his head. He said:

"No, there was no one about and I was the only visitor. St. Petrock is a very remote spot. The village itself lies on the far side of it about half a mile further on."

Colonel Weston said pleasantly:

"You mustn't think we're—er—doubting what you say. Just a matter of checking up on everybody. Just routine, you know, routine. Have to stick to routine in cases of this kind."

Stephen Lane said gently:

"Oh, yes, I quite understand."

Weston went on:

"Now the next point. Is there anything you know that would assist us at all? Anything about the dead woman? Anything that could give us a pointer as to who murdered her? Anything you heard or saw?"

Stephen Lane said:

"I heard nothing. All I can tell you is this: that I knew instinctively as soon as I saw her that Arlena Marshall was a focus of evil. She *was* Evil! Evil personified! Woman can be man's help and inspiration in life—she can also be man's downfall. She can drag a man down to the level of the beast. The dead woman was just such a woman. She appealed to everything base in a man's nature. She was a woman such as Jezebel and Aholibah. Now—she has been struck down in the middle of her wickedness!"

Hercule Poirot stirred. He said:

"Not struck down—*strangled!* Strangled Mr. Lane, by a pair of human hands."

The clergyman's own hands trembled. The fingers writhed and twitched. He said, and his voice came low and choked:

"That's horrible—horrible— Must you put it like that?"

Hercule Poirot said:

"It is the simple truth. Have you any idea, Mr. Lane, whose hands those were?"

The other shook his head. He said: "I know nothing—nothing . . ."

Weston got up. He said, after a glance at Colgate to which the latter replied by an almost imperceptible nod, "Well, we must get on to the Cove."

Lane said:

"Is that where—it happened?"

Weston nodded.

Lane said:

"Can—can I come with you?"

About to return a curt negative, Weston was forestalled by Poirot.

"But certainly," said Poirot. "Accompany me there in a boat, Mr. Lane. We start immediately."

CHAPTER IX

For the second time that morning Patrick Redfern was rowing a boat into Pixy Cove. The other occupants of the boat were Hercule Poirot, very pale with a hand to his stomach, and Stephen Lane. Colonel Weston had taken the land route. Having been delayed on the way he arrived on the beach at the same time as the boat grounded. A police constable and a plain-clothes sergeant were on the beach already. Weston was questioning the latter as the three from the boat walked up and joined him.

Sergeant Phillips said:

"I think I've been over every inch of the beach, sir."

"Good, what did you find?"

"It's all together here, sir, if you'd like to come and see."

A small collection of objects was laid out neatly on a rock. There were a pair of scissors, an empty Gold Flake packet, five patent bottle tops, a number of used matches, three pieces of string, one or two fragments of newspaper, a fragment of a smashed pipe, four buttons, the drumstick bone of a chicken and an empty bottle of sun-bathing oil.

Weston looked down appraisingly on the objects.

"H'm," he said. "Rather moderate for a beach nowadays! Most people seem to confuse a beach with a public rubbish dump! Empty bottle's been here some time by the way the label's blurred—so have most of the other things, I should say. The scissors are new, though. Bright and shining. *They* weren't out in yesterday's rain! Where were they?"

"Close by the bottom of the ladder, sir. Also this bit of pipe."

"H'm, probably dropped by someone going up or down. Nothing to say who they belong to?"

"No, sir. Quite an ordinary pair of nail scissors. Pipe's a good quality briar—expensive."

Poirot murmured thoughtfully:

"Captain Marshall told us, I think, that he had mislaid his pipe."

Weston said:

"Marshall's out of the picture. Anyway he's not the only person who smokes a pipe."

Hercule Poirot was watching Stephen Lane as the latter's hand went to his pocket and away again. He said pleasantly:

"You also smoke a pipe, do you not, Mr. Lane?"

The clergyman started. He looked at Poirot.

He said:

"Yes. Oh, yes. My pipe is an old friend and companion." Putting his hand into his pocket again he drew out a pipe, filled it with tobacco and lighted it.

Hercule Poirot moved away to where Redfern was standing, his eyes blank.

He said in a low voice:

"I'm glad—they've taken *her* away. . . ."

Stephen Lane asked:

"Where was she found?"

The Sergeant said cheerfully:

"Just about where you're standing, sir."

Lane moved swiftly aside. He stared at the spot he had just vacated.

The Sergeant went on:

"Place where the float was drawn up agrees with putting the time she arrived here at 10.45. That's going by the tide. It's turned now."

Weston said:

"Photography all done?"

"Yes, sir."

Weston turned to Redfern.

"Now then, man, where's the entrance to this cave of yours?"

Patrick Redfern was still staring down at the beach where Lane had been standing. It was as though he was seeing that sprawling body that was no longer there.

Weston's words recalled him to himself.

He said:

"It's over here."

He led the way to where a great mass of tumbled-down rocks were massed picturesquely against the cliffside. He went straight to where two big rocks, side by side, showed a straight narrow cleft between them. He said:

"The entrance is here."

Weston said:

"Here? Doesn't look as though a man could squeeze through."

"It's deceptive, you'll find, sir. It can just be done."

Weston inserted himself gingerly into the cleft. It was not as narrow as it looked. Inside, the space widened and proved to be a fairly roomy recess with room to stand upright and to move about.

Hercule Poirot and Stephen Lane joined the Chief Constable. The others stayed outside. Light filtered in through the opening, but Weston had also got a powerful torch which he played freely over the interior.

He observed:

"Handy place. You'd never suspect it from the outside."

He played the torch carefully over the floor.

Hercule Poirot was delicately sniffing the air.

Noticing this, Weston said:

"Air quite fresh, not fishy or seaweedy, but of course this place is well above high-water mark."

But to Poirot's sensitive nose, the air was more than fresh. It was delicately scented. He knew two people who used that elusive perfume. . . .

Weston's torch came to rest. He said:

"Don't see anything out of the way in here."

Poirot's eyes rose to a ledge a little way above his head. He murmured:

"One might perhaps see that there is nothing up there?"

Weston said:

"If there's anything up there it would have to be deliberately put there. Still, we'd better have a look."

Poirot said to Lane:

"You are, I think, the tallest of us, Monsieur. Could we venture to ask you to make sure there is nothing resting on that ledge?"

Lane stretched up, but he could not quite reach to the back of the shelf. Then, seeing a crevice in the rock, he inserted a toe in it and pulled himself up by one hand.

He said:

"Hullo, there's a box up here."

In a minute or two they were out in the sunshine examining the clergyman's find.

Weston said:

"Careful, don't handle it more than you can help. May be fingerprints."

It was a dark green tin box and bore the word Sandwiches on it.

Sergeant Phillips said:

"Left from some picnic or other, I suppose."

He opened the lid with his handkerchief.

Inside were small tin containers marked salt, pepper, mustard, and two larger square tins evidently for sandwiches. Sergeant Phillips lifted the lid of the salt container. It was full to the brim. He raised the next one, commenting:

"H'm, got salt in the pepper one too."

The mustard compartment also contained salt.

His face suddenly alert, the police sergeant opened one of the bigger square tins. That, too, contained the same white crystalline powder.

Very gingerly, Sergeant Phillips dipped a finger in and applied it to his tongue.

His face changed. He said—and his voice was excited:

"This isn't *salt*, sir. Not by a long way! Bitter taste! Seems to me it's some kind of *drug*."

II

"The third angle," said Colonel Weston with a groan.

They were back at the hotel again.

The Chief Constable went on:

"If by any chance there's a dope gang mixed up in this, it opens up several possibilities. First of all, the dead woman may have been in with the gang herself. Think that's likely?"

Hercule Poirot said cautiously:

"It is possible."

"She may have been a drug addict?"

Poirot shook his head.

He said:

"I should doubt that. She had steady nerves, radiant health, there were no marks of hypodermic injections (not that that proves anything. Some people sniff the stuff.). No, I do not think she took drugs."

"In that case," said Weston, "she may have run into the business accidentally and she was deliberately silenced by the people running the show. We'll know presently just what the stuff is. I've sent it to Neasdon. If we're on to some dope ring, they're not the people to stick at trifles—"

He broke off as the door opened and Mr. Horace Blatt came briskly into the room.

Mr. Blatt was looking hot. He was wiping the perspiration from his forehead. His big hearty voice billowed out and filled the small room.

"Just this minute got back and heard the news! You the Chief Constable? They told me you were in here. My name's Blatt—Horace Blatt. Any way I can help you? Don't suppose so. I've been out in my boat since early this morning. Missed the whole blinking show. The one day that something *does* happen in this out-of-the-way spot, I'm not there. Just like life, that, isn't it? Hullo, Poirot, didn't see you at first. So you're in on this? Oh, well, I suppose you would be. Sherlock Holmes v. the local police, is that it? Ha, ha! Lestrade—all that stuff. I'll enjoy seeing you do a bit of fancy sleuthing."

Mr. Blatt came to anchor in a chair, pulled out a cigarette case and offered it to Colonel Weston who shook his head.

He said, with a slight smile:

"I'm an inveterate pipe smoker."

"Same here. I smoke cigarettes as well—but nothing beats a pipe."

Colonel Weston said with sudden geniality:

"Then light up, man."

Blatt shook his head.

"Not got my pipe on me at the moment. But put me wise about all this. All I've heard so far is that Mrs. Marshall was found murdered on one of the beaches here."

"On Pixy Cove," said Colonel Weston, watching him.

But Mr. Blatt merely asked excitedly:

"And she was strangled?"

"Yes, Mr. Blatt."

"Nasty—very nasty. Mind you, she asked for it! Hot stuff—*trés moutarde* —eh, M. Poirot? Any idea who did it, or mustn't I ask that?"

With a faint smile Colonel Weston said:

"Well, you know, it's we who are supposed to ask the questions."

Mr. Blatt waved his cigarette.

"Sorry—sorry—my mistake. Go ahead."

"You went out sailing this morning. At what time?"

"Left here at a quarter to ten."

"Was any one with you?"

"Not a soul. All on my little lonesome."

"And where did you go?"

"Along the coast in the direction of Plymouth. Took lunch with me. Not much wind so I didn't actually get very far."

After another question or two, Weston asked:

"Now about the Marshalls? Do you know anything that might help us?"

"Well, I've given you my opinion. *Crime passionnel!* All I can tell you is, it wasn't *me!* The fair Arlena had no use for me. Nothing doing in that quarter. She had her own blue-eyed boy! And if you ask me, Marshall was getting wise to it."

"Have you any evidence for that?"

"Saw him give young Redfern a dirty look once or twice. Dark horse,

Marshall. Looks very meek and mild and as though he were half asleep all the time—but that's not his reputation in the City. I've heard a thing or two about him. Nearly had up for assault once. Mind you, the fellow in question had put up a pretty dirty deal. Marshall had trusted him and the fellow had let him down cold. Particularly dirty business, I believe. Marshall went for him and half killed him. Fellow didn't prosecute—too afraid of what might come out. I give you that for what it's worth."

"So you think it possible," said Poirot, "that Captain Marshall strangled his wife?"

"Not at all. Never said anything of the sort. Just letting you know that he's the sort of fellow who could go berserk on occasions."

Poirot said:

"Mr. Blatt, there is reason to believe that Mrs. Marshall went this morning to Pixy Cove to meet someone. Have you any idea who that someone might be?"

Mr. Blatt winked.

"It's not a guess. It's a certainty. Redfern!"

"It was not Mr. Redfern."

Mr. Blatt seemed taken aback. He said hesitatingly:

"Then I don't know . . . No, I can't imagine . . ."

He went on, regaining a little of his aplomb.

"As I said before, it wasn't *me!* No such luck! Let me see, couldn't have been Gardener—his wife keeps far too sharp an eye on him! That old ass Barry? Rot! And it would hardly be the parson. Although, mind you, I've seen his Reverence watching her a good bit. All holy disapproval, but perhaps an eye for the contours all the same! Eh? Lot of hypocrites, most parsons. Did you read that case last month? Parson and the church-warden's daughter? Bit of an eye opener."

Mr. Blatt chuckled.

Colonel Weston said coldly:

"There is nothing you can think of that might help us?"

The other shook his head.

"No. Can't think of a thing." He added: "This will make a bit of a stir, I imagine. The press will be on to it like hot cakes. There won't be quite so much of this high-toned exclusiveness about the Jolly Roger in future. Jolly Roger indeed. Precious little jollity about it."

Hercule Poirot murmured:

"You have not enjoyed your stay here?"

Mr. Blatt's red face got slightly redder. He said:

"Well, no, I haven't. The sailing's all right and the scenery and the service and the food—but there's no *mateyness* in the place, you know what I mean! What I say is, my money's as good as another man's. We're all here to enjoy ourselves. Then why not get together and *do* it? All these cliques and people sitting by themselves and giving you frosty Good-mornings—and Good-evenings—and Yes, very pleasant weather. No joy de viver. Lot of stuck-up dummies!"

Mr. Blatt paused—by now very red indeed.

He wiped his forehead once more and said apologetically:

"Don't pay any attention to me. I get all worked up."

III

Hercule Poirot murmured:

"And what do we think of Mr. Blatt?"

Colonel Weston grinned and said:

"What do *you* think of him? You've seen more of him than I have."

Poirot said softly:

"There are many of your English idioms that describe him. The rough diamond! The self-made man! The social climber! He is, as you choose to look at it, pathetic, ludicrous, blatant! It is a matter of opinion. But I think, too, that he is something else."

"And what is that?"

Hercule Poirot, his eyes raised to the ceiling, murmured:

"I think that he is—*nervous!*"

IV

Inspector Colgate said:

"I've got those times worked out. From the hotel to the ladder down to Pixy Cove three minutes. That's walking till you are out of sight of the hotel and then running like hell."

Weston raised his eyebrows. He said:

"That's quicker than I thought."

"Down ladder to beach one minute and three quarters. Up same two minutes. That's P. C. Flint. He's a bit of an athlete. Walking and taking the ladder in the normal way the whole business takes close on a quarter of an hour."

Weston nodded. He said:

"There's another thing we must go into, the pipe question."

Colgate said:

"Blatt smokes a pipe, so does Marshall, so does the parson. Redfern smokes cigarettes, the American prefers a cigar. Major Barry doesn't smoke at all. There's one pipe in Marshall's room, two in Blatt's, and one in the parson's. Chambermaid says Marshall has two pipes. The other chambermaid isn't a very bright girl. Doesn't know how many pipes the other two have. Says vaguely she's noticed two or three about in their rooms."

Weston nodded.

"Anything else?"

"I've checked up on the staff. They all seem quite O.K. Henry, in the bar, checks Marshall's statement about seeing him at ten to eleven. William, the beach attendant, was down repairing the ladder on the rocks most of the morning. He seems all right. George marked the tennis court and then bedded out some plants round by the dining-room. Neither of them would have seen any one who came across the causeway to the island."

"When was the causeway uncovered?"

"Round about 9.30, sir."

Weston pulled at his moustache.

"It's possible somebody did come that way. We've got a new angle, Colgate."

He told of the discovery of the sandwich box in the cave.

V

There was a tap on the door.

"Come in," said Weston.

It was Captain Marshall.

He said:

"Can you tell me what arrangements I can make about the funeral?"

"I think we shall manage the inquest for the day after to-morrow, Captain Marshall."

"Thank you."

Inspector Colgate said:

"Excuse me, sir, allow me to return you these."

He handed over the three letters.

Kenneth Marshall smiled rather sardonically.

He said:

"Has the police department been testing the speed of my typing? I hope my character is cleared."

Colonel Weston said pleasantly:

"Yes, Captain Marshall, I think we can give you a clean bill of health. Those sheets take fully an hour to type. Moreover, you were heard typing them by the chambermaid up till five minutes to eleven and you were seen by another witness at twenty minutes past."

Captain Marshall murmured:

"Really? That all seems very satisfactory!"

"Yes. Miss Darnley came to your room at twenty minutes past eleven. You were so busy typing that you did not observe her entry."

Kenneth Marshall's face took on an impassive expression. He said:

"Does Miss Darnley say that?" He paused. "As a matter of fact she is wrong. I *did* see her, though she may not be aware of the fact. I saw her in the mirror."

Poirot murmured:

"But you did not interrupt your typing?"

Marshall said shortly:

"No. I wanted to get finished."

He paused a minute, then in an abrupt voice, he said:

"Nothing more I can do for you?"

"No, thank you, Captain Marshall."

Kenneth Marshall nodded and went out.

Weston said with a sigh:

"There goes our most hopeful suspect—cleared! Hullo, here's Neasdon."

The doctor came in with a trace of excitement in his manner. He said:

"That's a nice little death lot you sent me along."

"What is it?"

"What is it? Diamorphine hydrochloride. Stuff that's usually called heroin."

Inspector Colgate whistled. He said:

"Now we're getting places, all right! Depend upon it, this dope stunt is at the bottom of the whole business."

CHAPTER X

THE LITTLE CROWD of people flocked out of The Red Bull. The brief inquest was over—adjourned for a fortnight.

Rosamund Darnley joined Captain Marshall. She said in a low voice:

"That wasn't so bad, was it, Ken?"

He did not answer at once. Perhaps he was conscious of the staring eyes of the villagers, the fingers that nearly pointed to him and only just did not quite do so!

"That's 'im, my dear." "See, that's 'er 'usband." "That be the 'usband." "Look, there 'e goes. . . ."

The murmurs were not loud enough to reach his ears, but he was none the less sensitive to them. This was the modern day pillory. The press he had already encountered—self-confident, persuasive young men, adepts at battering down his wall of silence, of "Nothing to say" that he had endeavoured to erect. Even the curt monosyllables that he had uttered thinking that they at least could not lead to misapprehension had reappeared in this morning's papers in a totally different guise. "Asked whether he agreed that the mystery of his wife's death could only be explained on the assumption that a homicidal murderer had found his way on to the island, Captain Marshall declared that—" and so on and so forth.

Cameras had clicked ceaselessly. Now, at this minute, the well-known sound caught his ear. He half turned—a smiling young man was nodding cheerfully, his purpose accomplished.

Rosamund murmured:

"Captain Marshall and a friend leaving The Red Bull after the inquest."

Marshall winced.

Rosamund said:

"It's no use, Ken! You've got to face it! I don't mean just the fact of Arlena's death—I mean all the attendant beastliness. The staring eyes and gossiping tongues, the fatuous interviews in the papers—and the best way to meet it is to find it funny! Come out with all the old inane clichés and curl a sardonic lip at them."

He said:

"Is that your way?"

"Yes." She paused. "It isn't yours, I know. Protective colouring is your line. Remain rigidly non-active and fade into the background! But you can't do that here—you've no background to fade into. You stand out clear for all to see—like a striped tiger against a white backcloth. *The husband of the murdered woman!*"

"For God's sake, Rosamund—"

She said gently:

"My dear, I'm trying to be good for you!"

They walked for a few steps in silence. Then Marshall said in a different voice:

"I know you are. I'm not really ungrateful, Rosamund."

They had progressed beyond the limits of the village. Eyes followed them but there was no one very near. Rosamund Darnley's voice dropped as she repeated a variant of her first remark.

"It didn't really go so badly, did it?"

He was silent for a moment, then he said:

"I don't know."

"What do the police think?"

"They're non-committal."

After a minute Rosamund said:

"That little man—Poirot—is he really taking an active interest?"

Kenneth Marshall said:

"Seemed to be sitting in the Chief Constable's pocket all right the other day."

"I know—but is he *doing* anything?"

"How the hell should I know, Rosamund?"

She said thoughtfully:

"He's pretty old. Probably more or less ga ga."

"Perhaps."

They came to the causeway. Opposite them, serene in the sun, lay the island.

Rosamund said suddenly:

"Sometimes—things seem unreal. I can't believe, this minute, that it ever happened. . . ."

Marshall said slowly:

"I think I know what you mean. Nature is so—regardless! One ant the less—that's all it is in Nature!"

Rosamund said:

"Yes—and that's the proper way to look at it really."

He gave her one very quick glance. Then he said in a low voice:

"Don't worry, my dear. It's all right. *It's all right.*"

II

Linda came down to the causeway to meet them. She moved with the spasmodic jerkiness of a nervous colt. Her young face was marred by deep black shadows under her eyes. Her lips were dry and rough.

She said breathlessly:

"What happened—what—what did they say?"

Her father said abruptly:

"Inquest adjourned for a fortnight."

"That means they—they haven't decided?"

"Yes. More evidence is needed."

"But—but what do they think?"

Marshall smiled a little in spite of himself.

"Oh, my dear child—who knows? And whom do you mean by they? The

Coroner, the jury, the police, the newspaper reporters, the fishing folk of Leathercombe Bay?"

Linda said slowly:

"I suppose I mean—the police."

Marshall said drily:

"Whatever the police think, they're not giving it away at present."

His lips closed tightly after the sentence. He went into the hotel.

As Rosamund Darnley was about to follow suit, Linda said:

"Rosamund!"

Rosamund turned. The mute appeal in the girl's unhappy face touched her. She linked her arm through Linda's and together they walked away from the hotel, taking the path that led to the extreme end of the island.

Rosamund said gently:

"Try not to mind so much, Linda. I know it's all very terrible and a shock and all that, but it's no use brooding over these things. And it can be only the—the horror of it, that is worrying you. You weren't in the least *fond* of Arlena, you know."

She felt the tremor that ran through the girl's body as Linda answered.

"No, I wasn't fond of her. . . ."

Rosamund went on:

"Sorrow for a person is different—one can't put *that* behind one. But one *can* get over shock and horror by just not letting your mind *dwell* on it all the time."

Linda said sharply:

"You don't understand."

"I think I do, my dear."

Linda shook her head.

"No, you don't. You don't understand in the least—and Christine doesn't understand either! Both of you have been nice to me, but you can't understand what I'm feeling. You just think it's morbid—that I'm dwelling on it all when I needn't."

She paused.

"But it isn't that at all. If you knew what I know—"

Rosamund stopped dead. Her body did not tremble—on the contrary it stiffened. She stood for a minute or two, then she disengaged her arm from Linda's.

She said:

"What is it that you know, Linda?"

The girl gazed at her. Then she shook her head.

She muttered:

"Nothing."

Rosamund caught her by the arm. The grip hurt and Linda winced slightly.

Rosamund said:

"Be careful, Linda. Be damned careful."

Linda had gone dead white.

She said:

"I *am* very careful—all the time."

Rosamund said urgently:

"Listen, Linda, what I said a minute or two ago applies just the same—only a hundred times more so. *Put the whole business out of your mind.* Never think about it. Forget—forget . . . You can if you try! Arlena is dead and nothing can bring her back to life. . . . Forget everything and live in the future. And above all, *hold your tongue.*"

Linda shrank a little. She said:

"You—you seem to know all about it?"

Rosamund said energetically:

"I don't know *anything!* In my opinion a wandering maniac got onto the island and killed Arlena. That's much the most probable solution. I'm fairly sure that the police will have to accept that in the end. That's what *must* have happened! That's what *did* happen!"

Linda said:

"If Father—"

Rosamund interrupted her.

"Don't talk about it."

Linda said:

"I've got to say one thing. My mother—"

"Well, what about her?"

"She—she was tried for murder, wasn't she?"

"Yes."

Linda said slowly:

"And then Father married her. That looks, doesn't it, as though Father didn't really think murder was very wrong—not always, that is."

Rosamund said sharply:

"Don't say things like that—even to me! The police haven't got anything against your father. He's got an alibi—an alibi that they can't break. He's perfectly safe."

Linda whispered:

"Did they think at first that Father—?"

Rosamund cried:

"I don't know what they thought! But they know now *that he couldn't have done it.* Do you understand? *He couldn't have done it.*"

She spoke with authority, her eyes commanded Linda's acquiescence. The girl uttered a long fluttering sigh.

Rosamund said:

"You'll be able to leave here soon. You'll forget everything—everything!"

Linda said with sudden unexpected violence:

"*I shall never forget.*"

She turned abruptly and ran back to the hotel. Rosamund stared after her.

III

"There is something I want to know, Madame?"

Christine Redfern glanced up at Poirot in a slightly abstracted manner. She said:

"Yes?"

Hercule Poirot took very little notice of her abstraction. He had noted the way her eyes followed her husband's figure where he was pacing up and down on the terrace outside the bar, but for the moment he had no interest in purely conjugal problems. He wanted information.

He said:

"Yes, Madame. It was a phrase—a chance phrase of yours the other day which roused my attention."

Christine, her eyes still on Patrick, said:

"Yes? What did I say?"

"It was in answer to a question from the Chief Constable. You described how you went into Miss Linda Marshall's room on the morning of the crime and how you found her absent from it and how she returned there and it was then that the Chief Constable asked you where she had been."

Christine said rather impatiently:

"And I said she had been bathing? Is that it?"

"Ah, but you did not say quite that. You did not say 'she had been bathing.' Your words were 'she said she had been bathing.'"

Christine said:

"It's the same thing, surely."

"No, it is not the same! The form of your answer suggests a certain attitude of mind on your part. Linda Marshall came into the room—she was wearing a bathing-wrap and yet—for some reason—you did not at once assume she had been bathing. That is shown by your words 'she *said* she had been bathing.' What was there about her appearance—was it her manner, or something that she was wearing or something she said, that led you to feel surprised when she said she had been bathing?"

Christine's attention left Patrick and focussed itself entirely on Poirot. She was interested. She said:

"That's clever of you. It's quite true, now I remember . . . I *was*, just faintly, surprised when Linda said she had been bathing."

"But why, Madame, why?"

"Yes, why? That's just what I'm trying to remember. Oh, yes, I think it was the parcel in her hand."

"She had a parcel?"

"Yes."

"You do not know what was in it?"

"Oh, yes, I do. The string broke. It was loosely done up in the way they do in the village. It was *candles*—they were scattered on the floor. I helped her to pick them up."

"Ah," said Poirot. "Candles."

Christine stared at him. She said:

"You seem excited, M. Poirot."

Poirot asked:

"Did Linda say why she had bought candles?"

Christine reflected.

"No, I don't think she did. I suppose it was to read by at night—perhaps the electric light wasn't good."

"On the contrary, Madame, there was a bedside electric lamp in perfect order."

Christine said:

"Then I don't know what she wanted them for."

Poirot said:

"What was her manner—when the string broke and the candles fell out of the parcel?"

Christine said slowly:

"She was—upset—embarrassed."

Poirot nodded his head. Then he asked:

"Did you notice a calendar in her room?"

"A calendar? What kind of a calendar?"

Poirot said:

"Possibly a green calendar—with tear-off leaves."

Christine screwed up her eyes in an effort of memory.

"A green calendar—rather a bright green. Yes, I have seen a calendar like that—but I can't remember where. It may have been in Linda's room, but I can't be sure."

"But you have definitely seen such a thing."

"Yes."

Again Poirot nodded.

Christine said rather sharply:

"What are you hinting at, M. Poirot? What is the meaning of all this?"

For answer Poirot produced a small volume bound in faded brown calf. He said:

"Have you ever seen this before?"

"Why—I think—I'm not sure—yes, Linda was looking into it in the village lending library the other day. But she shut it up and thrust it back quickly when I came up to her. It made me wonder what it was."

Silently Poirot displayed the title.

A History of Witchcraft, Sorcery and of the Compounding of Untraceable Poisons.

Christine said:

"I don't understand. What does all this mean?"

Poirot said gravely:

"It may mean, Madame, a good deal."

She looked at him inquiringly, but he did not go on. Instead he asked:

"One more question, Madame. Did you take a bath that morning before you went out to play tennis?"

Christine stared again.

"A bath? No. I would have had no time and anyway I didn't want a bath—not before tennis. I might have had one after."

"Did you use your bathroom at all when you came in?"

"I sponged my face and hands, that's all."

"You did not turn on the bath at all?"

"No, I'm sure I didn't."

Poirot nodded. He said:

"It is of no importance."

IV

Hercule Poirot stood by the table where Mrs. Gardener was wrestling with a jigsaw. She looked up and jumped.

"Why, M. Poirot, how very quietly you came up beside me! I never heard you. Have you just come back from the inquest? You know, the very thought of that inquest makes me so nervous, I don't know what to do. That's why I'm doing this puzzle. I just felt I couldn't sit outside on the beach as usual. As Mr. Gardener knows, when my nerves are all upset, there's nothing like one of these puzzles for calming me. There now, where *does* this white piece fit in? It must be part of the fur rug, but I don't seem to see . . ."

Gently Poirot's hand took the piece from her. He said:

"It fits, Madame, *here*. It is part of the cat."

"It can't be. It's a black cat."

"A black cat, yes, but you see the tip of the black cat's tail happens to be white."

"Why, so it does! How clever of you! But I do think the people who make puzzles are kind of mean. They just go out of their way to deceive you."

She fitted in another piece and then resumed:

"You know, M. Poirot, I've been watching you this last day or two. I just wanted to watch you detecting if you know what I mean—not that it doesn't sound rather heartless put like that, as though it were all a game—and a poor creature killed. Oh, dear, every time *I* think of it I get the shivers! I told Mr. Gardener this morning I'd just *got* to get away from here, and now the inquest's over he says he thinks we'll be able to leave to-morrow, and that's a blessing, I'm sure. But about detecting, I would so like to know your methods—you know, I'd feel privileged if you'd just *explain* it to me."

Hercule Poirot said:

"It is a little like your puzzle, Madame. One assembles the pieces. It is like a mosaic—many colours and patterns—and every strange-shaped little piece must be fitted into its own place."

"Now isn't that interesting? Why, I'm sure you explain it just too beautifully."

Poirot went on:

"And sometimes it is like that piece of your puzzle just now. One arranges very methodically the pieces of the puzzle—one sorts the colours—and then perhaps a piece of one colour that should fit in with—say, the fur rug, fits in instead in a black cat's tail."

"Why, if that doesn't sound too fascinating! And are there a great many pieces, M. Poirot?"

"Yes, Madame. Almost every one here in this hotel has given me a piece for my puzzle. You amongst them."

"Me?" Mrs. Gardener's tone was shrill.

"Yes, a remark of yours, Madame, was exceedingly helpful. I might say it was illuminating."

"Well, if that isn't too lovely! Can't you tell me some more, M. Poirot?"

"Ah! Madame, I reserve the explanations for the last chapter."

Mrs. Gardener murmured:

"If that isn't just too bad!"

V

Hercule Poirot tapped gently on the door of Captain Marshall's room. Inside there was the sound of a typewriter.

A curt "Come in" came from the room and Poirot entered.

Captain Marshall's back was turned to him. He was sitting typing at the table between the windows. He did not turn his head but his eyes met Poirot's in the mirror that hung on the wall directly in front of him. He said irritably:

"Well, M. Poirot, what is it?"

Poirot said quickly:

"A thousand apologies for intruding. You are busy?"

Marshall said shortly:

"I am rather."

Poirot said:

"It is one little question that I would like to ask you."

Marshall said:

"My God, I'm sick of answering questions. I've answered the police questions. I don't feel called upon to answer yours."

Poirot said:

"Mine is a very simple one. Only this. On the morning of your wife's death, did you have a bath after you finished typing and before you went out to play tennis?"

"A bath? No, of course I didn't! I'd had a bathe only an hour earlier!"

Hercule Poirot said:

"Thank you. That is all."

"But look here— Oh—" the other paused irresolutely.

Poirot withdrew gently closing the door.

Kenneth Marshall said:

"The fellow's crazy!"

VI

Just outside the bar Poirot encountered Mr. Gardener. He was carrying two cocktails and was clearly on his way to where Mrs. Gardener was ensconced with her jigsaw.

He smiled at Poirot in genial fashion.

"Care to join us, M. Poirot?"

Poirot shook his head. He said:

"What did you think of the inquest, Mr. Gardener?"

Mr. Gardener lowered his voice. He said:

"Seemed kind of indeterminate to me. Your police, I gather, have got something up their sleeves."

"It is possible," said Hercule Poirot.

Mr. Gardener lowered his voice still further.

"I shall be glad to get Mrs. Gardener away. She's a very, very sensitive woman, and this affair has got on her nerves. She's very highly strung."

Hercule Poirot said:

"Will you permit me, Mr. Gardener, to ask you one question?"

"Why, certainly, M. Poirot. Delighted to assist in any way I can."

Hercule Poirot said:

"You are a man of the world—a man, I think of considerable acumen. What, frankly, was your opinion of the late Mrs. Marshall?"

Mr. Gardener's eyebrows rose in surprise. He glanced cautiously round and lowered his voice.

"Well, M. Poirot, I've heard a few things that have been kind of going around, if you get me, especially among the women." Poirot nodded. "But if you ask me I'll tell you my candid opinion and that is that that woman was pretty much of a darned fool!"

Hercule Poirot said thoughtfully:

"Now that is very interesting."

VII

Rosamund Darnley said:

"So it's my turn, is it?"

"Pardon?"

She laughed.

"The other day the Chief Constable held his inquisition. You sat by. To-day, I think, you are conducting your own unofficial inquiry. I've been watching you. First Mrs. Redfern, then I caught a glimpse of you through the lounge window where Mrs. Gardener is doing her hateful jigsaw puzzle. Now it's my turn."

Hercule Poirot sat down beside her. They were on Sunny Ledge. Below them the sea showed a deep glowing green. Further out it was a pale dazzling blue.

Poirot said:

"You are very intelligent, Mademoiselle. I have thought so ever since I arrived here. It would be a pleasure to discuss this business with you."

Rosamund Darnley said softly:

"You want to know what I think about the whole thing?"

"It would be most interesting."

Rosamund said:

"I think it's really very simple. The clue is in the woman's past."

"The past? Not the present?"

"Oh! not necessarily the very remote past. I look at it like this. Arlena Marshall was attractive, fatally attractive, to men. It's possible, I think, that she also tired of them rather quickly. Amongst her—followers, shall we say—was one who resented that. Oh, don't misunderstand me, it won't be someone who sticks out a mile. Probably some tepid little man, vain and sensitive—the kind of man who broods. I think he followed her down here, waited his opportunity and killed her."

"You mean that he was an outsider, that he came from the mainland?"

"Yes. He probably hid in that cave until he got his chance."

Poirot shook his head. He said:

"Would she go there to meet such a man as you describe? No, she would laugh and not go."

Rosamund said:

"She mayn't have known she was going to meet him. He may have sent her a message in some other person's name."

Poirot murmured:

"That is possible."

Then he said:

"But you forget one thing, Mademoiselle. A man bent on murder could not risk coming in broad daylight across the causeway and past the hotel. Someone might have seen him."

"They might have—but I don't think that it's certain. I think it's quite possible that he could have come without any one noticing him at all."

"It would be *possible*, yes, that I grant you. But the point is that he could not *count* on that possibility."

Rosamund said:

"Aren't you forgetting something? The weather."

"The weather?"

"Yes. The day of the murder was a glorious day but the day before, remember, there was rain and thick mist. Any one could come onto the island then without being seen. He had only to go down to the beach and spend the night in the cave. That mist, M. Poirot, is important."

Poirot looked at her thoughtfully for a minute or two. He said:

"You know, there is a good deal in what you have just said."

Rosamund flushed. She said:

"That's my theory, for what it is worth. Now tell me yours."

"Ah," said Hercule Poirot. He stared down at the sea.

"*Eh bien*, Mademoiselle. I am a very simple person. I always incline to the belief that the most likely person committed the crime. At the very beginning it seemed to me that one person was very clearly indicated."

Rosamund's voice hardened a little. She said:

"Go on."

Hercule Poirot went on.

"But you see, there is what you call a snag in the way! It seems that it was *impossible* for that person to have committed the crime."

He heard the quick expulsion of her breath. She said rather breathlessly:

"Well?"

Hercule Poirot shrugged his shoulders.

"Well, what do we do about it? That is my problem." He paused and then went on. "May I ask you a question?"

"Certainly."

She faced him, alert and vigilant. But the question that came was an unexpected one.

"When you came in to change for tennis that morning, did you have a bath?"

Rosamund stared at him.

"A bath? What do you mean?"

"That is what I mean. A bath! The receptacle of porcelain, one turns the taps and fills it, one gets in, one gets out and ghoosh—ghoosh—ghoosh, the water goes down the waste-pipe!"

"M. Poirot, are you quite mad?"

"No, I am extremely sane."

"Well, anyway, I *didn't* take a bath."

"Ha!" said Poirot. "So nobody took a bath. That is extremely interesting."

"But why should any one take a bath?"

Hercule Poirot said:

"Why, indeed?"

Rosamund said with some exasperation:

"I suppose this is the Sherlock Holmes touch!"

Hercule Poirot smiled.

Then he sniffed the air delicately.

"Will you permit me to be impertinent, Mademoiselle?"

"I'm sure you couldn't be impertinent, M. Poirot."

"That is very kind of you. Then may I venture to say that the scent you use is delicious—it has a *nuance*—a delicate elusive charm." He waved his hands, and then added in a practical voice, "Gabrielle, No. 8, I think?"

"How clever you are. Yes, I always use it."

"So did the late Mrs. Marshall. It is chic, eh? And very expensive?"

Rosamund shrugged her shoulders with a faint smile.

Poirot said:

"You sat here where we are now, Mademoiselle, on the morning of the crime. You were seen here, or at least your sunshade was seen by Miss Brewster and Mr. Redfern as they passed on the sea. During the morning, Mademoiselle, are you sure you did not happen to go down to Pixy Cove and enter the cave there—the famous Pixy's Cave?"

Rosamund turned her head and stared at him.

She said in a quiet level voice:

"Are you asking me if I killed Arlena Marshall?"

"No. I am asking you if you went into the Pixy's Cave?"

"I don't even know where it is. Why should I go into it? For what reason?"

"On the day of the crime, Mademoiselle, somebody had been in that cave who used Gabrielle No. 8."

Rosamund said sharply:

"You've just said yourself, M. Poirot, that Arlena Marshall used Gabrielle No. 8. She was on the beach there that day. Presumably she went into the cave."

"Why should she go into the cave? It is dark there and narrow and very uncomfortable."

Rosamund said impatiently:

"Don't ask me for reasons. Since she was actually at the cove she was by far the most likely person. I've told you already I never left this place the whole morning."

"Except for the time when you went into the hotel to Captain Marshall's room," Poirot reminded her.

"Yes, of course. I'd forgotten that."

Poirot said:

"And you were wrong, Mademoiselle, when you thought that Captain Marshall did not see you."

Rosamund said incredulously:

"Kenneth did see me? Did—did he say so?"

Poirot nodded.

"He saw you, Mademoiselle, in the mirror that hangs over the table."

Rosamund caught her breath. She said:

"Oh! I see."

Poirot was no longer looking out to sea. He was looking at Rosamund Darnley's hands as they lay folded in her lap. They were well-shaped hands, beautifully moulded with very long fingers.

Rosamund, shooting a quick look at him, followed the direction of hi
eyes. She said sharply:

"What are you looking at my hands for? Do you think—do you think—?

Poirot said:

"Do I think—what, Mademoiselle?"

Rosamund Darnley said:

"Nothing."

VIII

It was perhaps an hour later that Hercule Poirot came to the top of th
path leading to Gull Cove. There was someone sitting on the beach. A
slight figure in a red shirt and dark blue shorts.

Poirot descended the path, stepping carefully in his tight smart shoes.

Linda Marshall turned her head sharply. He thought that she shran
a little.

Her eyes, as he came and lowered himself gingerly to the shingle besid
her, rested on him with the suspicion and alertness of a trapped animal
He realized, with a pang, how young and vulnerable she was.

She said:

"What is it? What do you want?"

Hercule Poirot did not answer for a minute or two. Then he said:

"The other day you told the Chief Constable that you were fond o
your stepmother and that she was kind to you."

"Well?"

"That was not true, was it, Mademoiselle?"

"Yes, it was."

Poirot said:

"She may not have been actively unkind—that I will grant. But you wer
not fond of her—oh, no—I think you disliked her very much. That wa
very plain to see."

Linda said:

"Perhaps I didn't like her very much. But one can't say that when a per
son is dead. It wouldn't be decent."

Poirot sighed. He said:

"They taught you that at your school?"

"More or less, I suppose."

Hercule Poirot said:

"When a person has been murdered, it is more important to be truthfu
than to be decent."

Linda said:

"I suppose you *would* say a thing like that."

"I would say it and I do say it. It is my business, you see, to find out who killed Arlena Marshall."

Linda muttered:

"I want to forget it all. It's so horrible."

Poirot said gently:

"But you can't forget, can you?"

Linda said:

"I suppose some beastly madman killed her."

Hercule Poirot murmured:

"No, I do not think it was quite like that."

Linda caught her breath. She said:

"You sound—as though you *knew?*"

Poirot said:

"Perhaps I do know." He paused and went on, "Will you trust me, my child, to do the best I can for you in your bitter trouble?"

Linda sprang up. She said:

"I haven't any trouble. There is nothing you can do for me. I don't know what you are talking about."

Poirot said, watching her:

"I am talking about *candles.* . . ."

He saw the terror leap into her eyes. She cried:

"I won't listen to you. I won't listen."

She ran across the beach, swift as a young gazelle, and went flying up the zigzag path.

Poirot shook his head. He looked grave and troubled.

CHAPTER XI

INSPECTOR COLGATE WAS reporting to the Chief Constable.

"I've got on to one thing, sir, and something pretty sensational. It's about Mrs. Marshall's money. I've been into it with her lawyers. I'd say it's a bit of a shock to them. I've got proof of the blackmail story. You remember she was left fifty thousand pounds by old Erskine? Well, all that's left of that is about fifteen thousand."

The Chief Constable whistled.

"Whew, what's become of the rest?"

"That's the interesting point, sir. She's sold out stuff from time to time and each time she's handled it in cash or negotiable securities—that's t say she's handed out money to some one that she didn't want traced. Black mail all right."

The Chief Constable nodded.

"Certainly looks like it. And the blackmailer is here in this hotel. Tha means it must be one of those three men. Got anything fresh on any o them?"

"Can't say I've got anything definite, sir. Major Barry's a retired Arm man, as he says. Lives in a small flat, has a pension and a small incom from stocks. *But* he's paid in pretty considerable sums into his account i the last year."

"That sounds promising. What's his explanation?"

"Says they're betting gains. It's perfectly true that he goes to all the larg race meetings. Places his bets on the course too, doesn't run an account.

The Chief Constable nodded.

"Hard to disprove that," he said. "But it's suggestive."

Colgate went on:

"Next, the Reverend Stephen Lane. He's *bona fide* all right—had living at St. Helen's, Whiteridge, Surrey—resigned his living just over year ago owing to ill-health. His ill-health amounted to his going int a nursing home for mental patients. He was there for over a year."

"Interesting," said Weston.

"Yes, sir. I tried to get as much as I could out of the doctor in charge bu you know what these medicos are—it's difficult to pin them down to any thing you can get hold of. But as far as I can make out, his Reverence' trouble was an obsession about the Devil—especially the Devil in th guise of woman—scarlet woman—whore of Babylon."

"H'm," said Weston. "There have been precedents for murder there.

"Yes, sir. It seems to me that Stephen Lane is at least a possibility. Th late Mrs. Marshall was a pretty good example of what a clergyman woul call a Scarlet Woman—hair and goings on and all. Seems to me it's no impossible he may have felt it his appointed task to dispose of her. Tha is if he is really batty."

"Nothing to fit in with the blackmail theory?"

"No, sir, I think we can wash him out as far as that's concerned. Ha some private means of his own, but not very much, and no sudden in crease lately."

"What about his story of his movements on the day of the crime?"

"Can't get any confirmation of them. Nobody remembers meeting a par son in the lanes. As to the book at the church, the last entry was thre days before and nobody had looked at it for about a fortnight. He coul have quite easily gone over the day before, say, or even a couple of days before, and dated his entry the 25th."

Weston nodded. He said:

"And the third man?"

"Horace Blatt? It's my opinion, sir, that there's definitely something fishy there. Pays income tax on a sum far exceeding what he makes out of his hardware business. And mind you, he's a slippery customer. He could probably cook up a reasonable statement—he gambles a bit on the Stock Exchange and he's in with one or two shady deals. Oh, yes, there may be plausible explanations, but there's no getting away from it that he's been making pretty big sums from unexplained sources for some years now."

"In fact," said Weston, "the idea is that Mr. Horace Blatt is a successful blackmailer by profession?"

"Either that, sir, or it's dope. I saw Chief Inspector Ridgeway who's in charge of the dope business, and he was no end keen. Seems there's been a good bit of heroin coming in lately. They're on to the small distributors and they know more or less who's running it the other end, but it's the way it's coming into the country that's baffled them so far."

Weston said:

"If the Marshall woman's death is the result of her getting mixed up, innocently or otherwise, with the dope-running stunt, then we'd better hand the whole thing over to Scotland Yard. It's their pigeon. Eh? What do you say?"

Inspector Colgate said rather regretfully:

"I'm afraid you're right, sir. If it's dope, then it's a case for the Yard."

Weston said after a moment or two's thought:

"It really seems the most likely explanation."

Colgate nodded gloomily.

"Yes, it does. Marshall's right out of it—though I did get some information that might have been useful if his alibi hadn't been so good. Seems his firm is very near the rocks. Not his fault or his partner's, just the general result of the crisis last year and the general state of trade and finance. And as far as he knew, he'd come into fifty thousand pounds if his wife died. And fifty thousand would have been a very useful sum."

He sighed.

"Seems a pity when a man's got two perfectly good motives for murder, that he can be proved to have had nothing to do with it!"

Weston smiled.

"Cheer up, Colgate. There's still a chance we may distinguish ourselves. There's the blackmail angle still and there's the batty parson, but personally I think the dope solution is far the most likely." He added: "And if it was one of the dope gang who put her out we'll have been instrumental in helping Scotland Yard to solve the dope problem. In fact, take it all round, one way or another, we've done pretty well."

An unwilling smile showed on Colgate's face.

He said:

"Well, that's the lot, sir. By the way, I checked up on the writer of that letter we found in her room. The one signed J. N. Nothing doing. He's in China safe enough. Same chap as Miss Brewster was telling us about. Bit of a young scallywag. I've checked up on the rest of Mrs. Marshall's friends. No leads there. Everything there is to get, we've got, sir."

Weston said:

"So now it's up to us." He paused and then added: "Seen anything of our Belgian colleague? Does he know all you've told me?"

Colgate said with a grin:

"He's a queer little cuss, isn't he? D'you know what he asked me day before yesterday? He wanted particulars of any cases of strangulation in the last three years."

Colonel Weston sat up.

"He did, did he? Now I wonder—" he paused a minute. "When did you say the Reverend Stephen Lane went into that mental home?"

"A year ago last Easter, sir."

Colonel Weston was thinking deeply. He said:

"There was a case—body of a young woman found somewhere near Bagshot. Going to meet her husband somewhere and never turned up. And there was what the papers called the Lonely Copse Mystery. Both in Surrey if I remember rightly."

His eyes met those of his Inspector. Colgate said:

"Surrey? My word, sir, it fits, doesn't it? I wonder . . ."

II

Hercule Poirot sat on the turf on the summit of the island.

A little to his left was the beginning of the steel ladder that led down to Pixy Cove. There were several rough boulders near the head of the ladder, he noted, forming easy concealment for any one who proposed to descend to the beach below. Of the beach itself little could be seen from the top owing to the overhang of the cliff.

Hercule Poirot nodded his head gravely.

The pieces of his mosaic were fitting into position.

Mentally he went over those pieces considering each as a detached item.

A morning on the bathing beach some few days before Arlena Marshall's death.

One, two, three, four, five, separate remarks uttered on that morning.

The evening of a bridge game. He, Patrick Redfern and Rosamund Darnley had been at the table. Christine had wandered out while dummy and had overheard a certain conversation. Who else had been in the lounge at that time? Who had been absent?

The evening before the crime. The conversation he had had with Christine on the cliff and the scene he had witnessed on his way back to the hotel.

Gabrielle No. 8.

A pair of scissors.

A broken pipe.

A bottle thrown from a window.

A green calendar.

A packet of candles.

A mirror and a typewriter.

A skein of magenta wool.

A girl's wrist-watch.

Bath-water rushing down the waste-pipe.

Each of these unrelated facts must fit into its appointed place. There must be no loose ends.

And then, with each concrete fact fitted into position, on to the next step: his own belief in the presence of evil on the island. . . .

Evil. . . .

He looked down at a typewritten list in his hands.

Nellie Parsons—found strangled in a lonely copse near Chobham. No clue to her murderer ever discovered.

Nellie Parsons?

Alice Corrigan.

He read very carefully the details of Alice Corrigan's death.

III

To Hercule Poirot, sitting on the ledge overlooking the sea, came Inspector Colgate.

Poirot liked Inspector Colgate. He liked his rugged face, his shrewd eyes, and his slow unhurried manner.

Inspector Colgate sat down. He said, glancing down at the typewritten sheets in Poirot's hand:

"Done anything with those cases, sir?"

"I have studied them—yes."

Colgate got up, he walked along and peered into the next niche. He came back, saying:

"One can't be too careful. Don't want to be overheard."

Poirot said:

"You are wise."

Colgate said:

"I don't mind telling you, M. Poirot, that I've been interested in those cases myself—though perhaps I shouldn't have thought about them if you hadn't asked for them." He paused. "I've been interested in one case in particular."

"Alice Corrigan?"

"Alice Corrigan." He paused. "I've been on to the Surrey police about that case—wanted to get all the ins and outs of it."

"Tell me, my friend. I am interested—very interested."

"I thought you might be. Alice Corrigan was found strangled in Caesar's Grove on Blackridge Heath—not ten miles from Marley Copse where Nellie Parsons was found—and both those places are within twelve miles of Whiteridge where Mr. Lane was vicar."

Poirot said:

"Tell me more about the death of Alice Corrigan."

Colgate said:

"The Surrey police didn't at first connect her death with that of Nellie Parsons. That's because they'd pitched on the husband as the guilty party. Don't quite know why except that he was a bit of what the press calls a 'mystery man'—not much known about him—who he was or where he came from. She'd married him against her people's wishes, she'd a bit of money of her own—and she'd insured her life in his favour—all that was enough to raise suspicion, as I think you'll agree, sir?"

Poirot nodded.

"But when it came down to brass tacks the husband was washed right out of the picture. The body was discovered by one of these women hikers—hefty young woman in shorts. She was an absolutely competent and reliable witness—games mistress at a school in Lancashire. She noted the time when she found the body—it was exactly four fifteen—and gave it as her opinion that the woman had been dead quite a short time—not more than ten minutes. That fitted in well enough with the police surgeon's view when he examined the body at 5.45. She left everything as it was and tramped across country to Bagshot police station where she reported the death. Now from three o'clock to four ten, Edward Corrigan was in the train coming down from London where he'd gone up for the day on business. Four other people were in the carriage with him. From the station he took the local bus, two of his fellow passengers travelling by it also. He got off at the Pine Ridge Café where he'd arranged to meet his wife for tea. Time then was four twenty-five. He ordered tea for them both, but said not to bring it till she came. Then he walked about outside waiting for her. When, by five o'clock she hadn't turned up, he was getting alarmed —thought she might have sprained her ankle. The arrangement was that she was to walk across the moors from the village where they were staying to the Pine Ridge Café and go home by bus. Caesar's Grove is not far from the café and it's thought that as she was ahead of time she sat down there to admire the view for a bit before going on, and that some tramp or madman came upon her there and caught her unawares. Once the husband was proved to be out of it, naturally they connected up her death with that of Nellie Parsons—that rather flighty servant girl who was found strangled in Marley Copse. They decided that the same man was responsible for both crimes but they never caught him—and what's more they never came near to catching him! Drew a blank everywhere."

He paused and then he said slowly:

"And now—here's a third woman strangled—and a certain gentleman we won't name right on the spot."

He stopped.

His small shrewd eyes came round to Poirot. He waited hopefully.

Poirot's lips moved. Inspector Colgate leaned forward.

Poirot was murmuring:

"—so difficult to know which pieces are part of the fur rug and which are the cat's tail."

"I *beg* pardon, sir?" said Inspector Colgate, startled.

Poirot said quickly:

"I apologize. I was following a train of thought of my own."

"What's this about a fur rug and a cat?"

"Nothing—nothing at all." He paused. "Tell me, Inspector Colgate, if you suspected someone of telling lies—many, many lies, but you had no proof, what would you do?"

Inspector Colgate considered.

"It's difficult, that is. But it's my opinion that if any one tells enough lies, they're bound to trip up in the end."

Poirot nodded.

"Yes, that is very true. You see, it is only in my mind that certain statements are lies. I *think* that they are lies, but I cannot *know* that they are lies. But one might perhaps make a test—a test of one little not very noticeable lie. And if that were proved to be a lie—why then, one would know that all the rest were lies, too!"

Inspector Colgate looked at him curiously.

"Your mind works a funny way, doesn't it, sir? But I daresay it comes out all right in the end. If you'll excuse me asking, what put you on to asking about strangulation cases in general?"

Poirot said slowly:

"You have a word in your language—*slick*. This crime seemed to me a very slick crime! It made me wonder if, perhaps, it was not a first attempt."

Inspector Colgate said:

"I see."

Poirot went on:

"I said to myself, let us examine past crimes of a similar kind and if there is a crime that closely resembles this one—*eh bien*, we shall have there a very valuable clue."

"You mean using the same method of death, sir?"

"No, no, I mean more than that. The death of Nellie Parsons for instance tells me nothing. But the death of Alice Corrigan—tell me, Inspector Colgate, do you not notice one striking form of similarity to this crime?"

Inspector Colgate turned the problem over in his mind. He said at last:

"No, sir, I can't say that I do really. Unless it's that in each case the husband has got a cast-iron alibi."

Poirot said softly:

"Ah, so you *have* noticed that?"

IV

"Ha, Poirot. Glad to see you. Come in. Just the man I want."

Hercule Poirot responded to the invitation.

The Chief Constable pushed over a box of cigarettes, took one himself and lighted it. Between puffs he said:

"I've decided, more or less, on a course of action. But I'd like your opinion on it before I act decisively."

Hercule Poirot said:

"Tell me, my friend."

Weston said:

"I've decided to call in Scotland Yard and hand the case over to them. In my opinion, although there have been grounds for suspicion against one or two people, the whole case hinges on dope smuggling. It seems clear to me that that place, Pixy Cove, was a definite rendezvous for the stuff."

Poirot nodded.

"I agree."

"Good man. And I'm pretty certain who our dope smuggler is. Horace Blatt."

Again Poirot assented. He said:

"That, too, is indicated."

"I see our minds have both worked the same way. Blatt used to go sailing in that boat of his. Sometimes he'd invite people to go with him, but most of the time he went out alone. He had some rather conspicuous red sails on that boat but we've found that he had some white sails as well stowed away. I think he sailed out on a good day to an appointed spot, and was met by another boat—sailing boat or motor yacht—something of the kind, and the stuff was handed over. Then Blatt would run ashore into Pixy Cove at a suitable time of day—"

Hercule Poirot smiled:

"Yes, yes, at half past one. The hour of the British lunch when every one is quite sure to be in the dining-room. The island is private. It is not a place where outsiders come for picnics. People take their tea sometimes from the hotel to Pixy Cove in the afternoon when the sun is on it, or if they want a picnic they would go somewhere far afield, many miles away."

The Chief Constable nodded.

"Quite," he said. "Therefore Blatt ran ashore there and stowed the stuff on that ledge in the cave. Somebody else was to pick it up there in due course."

Poirot murmured:

"There was a couple, you remember, who came to the island for lunch on the day of the murder? That would be a way of getting the stuff. Some summer visitors from a hotel on the Moor or at St. Loo come over to Smugglers' Island. They announce that they will have lunch. They walk round the island first. How easy to descend to the beach, pick up the sandwich box, place it, no doubt, in Madame's bathing bag which she carries—and return for lunch to the hotel—a little late, perhaps, say at ten minutes to two, having enjoyed their walk whilst every one else was in the dining-room."

Weston said:

"Yes, it all sounds practicable enough. Now these dope organizations are pretty ruthless. If any one blundered in and got wise to things they wouldn't make any bones about silencing that person. It seems to me that that is the right explanation of Arlena Marshall's death. It's possible that on that morning Blatt was actually at the cove stowing the stuff away. His accomplices were to come for it that very day. Arlena arrives on her float and sees him going into the cave with the box. She asks him about it and he kills her then and there and sheers off in his boat as quick as possible."

Poirot said:

"You think definitely that Blatt is the murderer?"

"It seems the most probable solution. Of course it's possible that Arlena might have got on to the truth earlier, said something to Blatt about it and some other member of the gang fixed a fake appointment with her and did her in. As I say, I think the best course is to hand the case over to Scotland Yard. They've a far better chance than we have of proving Blatt's connection with the gang."

Hercule Poirot nodded thoughtfully.

Weston said:

"You think that's the wise thing to do—eh?"

Poirot was thoughtful. He said at last: "It may be."

"Dash it all, Poirot, have you got something up your sleeve, or haven't you?"

Poirot said gravely:

"If I have, I am not sure that I can prove it."

Weston said:

"Of course, I know that you and Colgate have other ideas. Seems a bit fantastic to me but I'm bound to admit there may be something in it. But even if you're right, I still think it's a case for the Yard. We'll give them the facts and they can work in with the Surrey police. What I feel is that it isn't really a case for us. It's not sufficiently localized."

He paused.

"What do you think, Poirot? What do you feel ought to be done about it?"

Poirot seemed lost in thought. At last he said:

"I know what I should like to do."

"Yes, man."

Poirot murmured:

"I should like to go for a picnic."

Colonel Weston stared at him.

CHAPTER XII

"A picnic, M. Poirot?"

Emily Brewster stared at him as though he were out of his senses.

Poirot said engagingly:

"It sounds to you, does it not, very outrageous? But indeed it seems to me a most admirable idea. We need something of the everyday, the usual, to restore life to the normal. I am most anxious to see something of Dartmoor, the weather is good. It will—how shall I say, it will cheer everybody up! So aid me in this matter. Persuade every one."

The idea met with unexpected success. Every one was at first dubious and then grudgingly admitted it might not be such a bad idea after all.

It was not suggested that Captain Marshall should be asked. He had himself announced that he had to go to Plymouth that day. Mr. Blatt was of the party, enthusiastically so. He was determined to be the life and soul of it. Besides him, there were Emily Brewster, the Redferns, Stephen Lane, the Gardeners who were persuaded to delay their departure by one day, Rosamund Darnley and Linda.

Poirot had been eloquent to Rosamund and had dwelt on the advantage it would be to Linda to have something to take her out of herself. To this Rosamund agreed. She said:

"You're quite right. The shock has been very bad for a child of that age. It has made her terribly jumpy."

"That is only natural, Mademoiselle. But at that age one soon forgets. Persuade her to come. You can, I know."

Major Barry had refused firmly. He said he didn't like picnics. "Lots of baskets to carry," he said. "And darned uncomfortable. Eating my food at a table's good enough for me."

The party assembled at ten o'clock. Three cars had been ordered. Mr. Blatt was loud and cheerful imitating a tourist guide.

"This way, ladies and gentlemen—this way for Dartmoor. Heather and bilberries, Devonshire cream and convicts. Bring your wives, gentlemen, or bring the other thing! Every one welcome! Scenery guaranteed. Walk up. Walk up."

At the last minute Rosamund Darnley came down looking concerned. She said:

"Linda's not coming. She says she's got a frightful headache."

Poirot cried:

"But it will do her good to come. Persuade her, Mademoiselle."

Rosamund said firmly:

"It's no good. She's absolutely determined. I've given her some aspirin and she's gone to bed."

She hesitated and said:

"I think, perhaps, I won't go, either."

"Can't allow that, dear lady, can't allow that," cried Mr. Blatt, seizing her facetiously by the arm. "*La haute Mode* must grace the occasion. No refusals! I've taken you into custody, ha, ha. Sentenced to Dartmoor."

He led her firmly to the first car. Rosamund threw a black look at Hercule Poirot.

"I'll stay with Linda," said Christine Redfern. "I don't mind a bit."

Patrick said:

"Oh, come on, Christine."

And Poirot said:

"No, no, you must come, Madame. With a headache one is better alone. Come, let us start."

The three cars drove off. They went first to the real Pixy's Cave on Sheepstor and had a good deal of fun looking for the entrance and at last finding it, aided by a picture postcard.

It was precarious going on the big boulders and Hercule Poirot did not attempt it. He watched indulgently while Christine Redfern sprang lightly from stone to stone and observed that her husband was never far from her. Rosamund Darnley and Emily Brewster had joined in the search though the latter slipped once and gave a slight twist to her ankle. Stephen Lane was indefatigable, his long lean figure turning and twisting among the boulders. Mr. Blatt contented himself with going a little way and shouting encouragement, also taking photographs of the searchers.

The Gardeners and Poirot remained staidly sitting by the wayside whilst Mrs. Gardener's voice upraised itself in a pleasant even-toned monologue punctuated now and then by the obedient "Yes, darlings" of her spouse.

"—and what I always have felt, M. Poirot, and Mr. Gardener agrees with me—is that snapshots can be very annoying. Unless, that is to say, they are taken among friends. That Mr. Blatt has just no sensitiveness of any kind. He just comes right up to every one and talks away and takes pictures of you and, as I said to Mr. Gardener, that really is very ill-bred. That's what I said, Odell, wasn't it?"

"Yes, darling."

"That group he took of us all sitting on the beach. Well, that's all very well, but he should have asked first. As it was, Miss Brewster was just getting up from the beach and it certainly makes her look a very peculiar shape."

"I'll say it does," said Mr. Gardener with a grin.

"And there's Mr. Blatt giving round copies to everybody without so much as asking first. He gave one to you, M. Poirot, I noticed."

Poirot nodded. He said:

"I value that group very much."

Mrs. Gardener went on:

"And look at his behaviour to-day—so loud and noisy and common. Why, it just makes me shudder. You ought to have arranged to leave that man at home, M. Poirot."

Hercule Poirot murmured:

"Alas, Madame, that would have been difficult."

"I should say it would. That man just pushes his way in anywhere. He's just not sensitive at all."

At this moment the discovery of the Pixy's Cave was hailed from below with loud cries.

The party now drove on, under Hercule Poirot's directions, to a spot where a short walk from the car down a hillside of heather led to a delightful spot by a small river.

A narrow plank bridge crossed the river and Poirot and her husband induced Mrs. Gardener to cross it to where a delightful heathery spot free from prickly furze looked an ideal spot for a picnic lunch.

Talking volubly about her sensations when crossing on a plank bridge Mrs. Gardener sank down. Suddenly there was a slight outcry.

The others had run across the bridge lightly enough, but Emily Brewster was standing in the middle of the plank, her eyes shut, swaying to and fro.

Poirot and Patrick Redfern rushed to the rescue.

Emily Brewster was gruff and ashamed.

"Thanks, thanks. Sorry. Never was good at crossing running water. Get giddy. Stupid, very."

Lunch was spread out and the picnic began.

All the people concerned were secretly surprised to find how much they enjoyed this interlude. It was, perhaps, because it afforded an escape from an atmosphere of suspicion and dread. Here, with the trickling of the water, the soft peaty smell in the air and the warm colouring of bracken and heather, a world of murder and police inquiries and suspicion seemed blotted out as though it had never existed. Even Mr. Blatt forgot to be the life and soul of the party. After lunch he went to sleep a little distance away and subdued snores testified to his blissful unconsciousness.

It was quite a grateful party of people who packed up the picnic baskets and congratulated Hercule Poirot on his good idea.

The sun was sinking as they returned along the narrow winding lanes. From the top of the hill above Leathercombe Bay they had a brief glimpse of the island with the white Hotel on it.

It looked peaceful and innocent in the setting sun.

Mrs. Gardener, not loquacious for once, sighed and said:

"I really do thank you, M. Poirot. I feel so calm. It's just wonderful."

II

Major Barry came out to greet them on arrival.

"Hullo," he said. "Had a good day?"

Mrs. Gardener said:

"Indeed we did. The moors were just too lovely for anything. So English and old world. And the air delicious and invigorating. You ought to be ashamed of yourself for being so lazy as to stay behind."

The Major chuckled.

"I'm too old for that kind of thing—sitting on a patch of bog and eating sandwiches."

A chambermaid had come out of the hotel. She was a little out of breath. She hesitated for a moment, then came swiftly up to Christine Redfern.

Hercule Poirot recognized her as Gladys Narracott. Her voice came quick and uneven.

"Excuse me, Madam, but I'm worried about the young lady. About Miss Marshall. I took her up some tea just now and I couldn't get her to wake and she looks so—so queer somehow."

Christine looked round helplessly. Poirot was at her side in a moment. His hand under her elbow he said quietly:

"We will go up and see."

They hurried up the stairs and along the passage to Linda's room.

One glance at her was enough to tell them both that something was very wrong. She was an odd colour and her breathing was hardly perceptible.

Poirot's hand went to her pulse. At the same time he noticed an envelope stuck up against the lamp on the bedside table. It was addressed to himself.

Captain Marshall came quickly into the room. He said:

"What's this about Linda? What's the matter with her?"

A small frightened sob came from Christine Redfern.

Hercule Poirot turned from the bed. He said to Marshall:

"Get a doctor—as quick as you possibly can. But I'm afraid—very much afraid—it may be too late."

He took the letter with his name on it and ripped open the envelope. Inside were a few lines of writing in Linda's prim schoolgirl hand.

I think this is the best way out. Ask Father to try and forgive me. I killed Arlena. I thought I should be glad—but I'm not. I am very sorry for everything. . . .

III

They were assembled in the lounge—Marshall, the Redferns, Rosamund Darnley and Hercule Poirot.

They sat there silent—waiting. . . .

The door opened and Dr. Neasdon came in. He said curtly:

"I've done all I can. She may pull through—but I'm bound to tell you that there's not much hope."

He paused. Marshall, his face stiff, his eyes a cold frosty blue, asked: "How did she get hold of the stuff?"

Neasdon opened the door again and beckoned.

The chambermaid came into the room. She had been crying.

Neasdon said:

"Just tell us again what you saw?"

Sniffing, the girl said:

"I never thought—I never thought for a minute there was anything wrong—though the young lady did seem rather strange about it." A slight gesture of impatience from the doctor started her off again. "She was in the other lady's room. Mrs. Redfern's. Your room, Madam. Over at the washstand and she took up a little bottle. She did give a bit of a jump when I came in and I thought it was queer her taking things from your room, but then of course it might be something she'd lent you. She just said: 'Oh, this is what I'm looking for—' and went out."

Christine said almost in a whisper:

"My sleeping tablets."

The doctor said brusquely:

"How did she know about them?"

Christine said:

"I gave her one. The night after it happened. She told me she couldn't sleep. She— I remember her saying—'Will one be enough?'—and I said, Oh, yes, they were very strong—that I'd been cautioned never to take more than two at most."

Neasdon nodded.

"She made pretty sure," he said. "Took six of them."

Christine sobbed again.

"Oh, dear, I feel it's my fault. I should have kept them locked up."

The doctor shrugged his shoulders.

"It might have been wiser, Mrs. Redfern."

Christine said despairingly:

"She's dying—and it's my fault. . . ."

Kenneth Marshall stirred in his chair. He said:

"No, you can't blame yourself. Linda knew what she was doing. She took them deliberately. Perhaps—perhaps it was best."

He looked down at the crumpled note in his hand—the note that Poirot had silently handed to him.

Rosamund Darnley cried out:

"I don't believe it. I don't believe Linda killed her. Surely it's impossible —on the evidence!"

Christine said eagerly:

"Yes, she *can't* have done it! She must have got overwrought and imagined it all."

The door opened and Colonel Weston came in. He said:

"What's all this I hear?"

Dr. Neasdon took the note from Marshall's hand and handed it to the Chief Constable. The latter read it. He exclaimed incredulously:

"What? But this is nonsense—absolute nonsense! It's impossible." He repeated with assurance. "Impossible! Isn't it, Poirot?"

Hercule Poirot moved for the first time. He said in a slow sad voice:

"No, I'm afraid it is not impossible."

Christine Redfern said:

"But I was with her, M. Poirot. I was with her up to a quarter to twelve. I told the police so."

Poirot said:

"Your evidence gave her an alibi—yes. But what was your evidence based on? It was based on *Linda Marshall's own wrist-watch.* You do not know *of your own knowledge* that it was a quarter to twelve when you left her—you only know that she told you so. You said yourself the time seemed to have gone very fast."

She stared at him stricken.

He said:

"Now think, Madame, when you left the beach, did you walk back to the hotel fast or slow?"

"I—well, fairly slowly, I think."

"Do you remember much about that walk back?"

"Not very much, I'm afraid. I—I was thinking."

Poirot said:

"I am sorry to ask you this, but will you tell just what you were thinking about during that walk?"

Christine flushed.

"I suppose—if it is necessary . . . I was considering the question of—of leaving here. Just going away without telling my husband. I—I was very unhappy just then, you see."

Patrick Redfern cried:

"Oh, Christine! I know. . . . I know. . . ."

Poirot's precise voice cut in:

"Exactly. You were concerned over taking a step of some importance. You were, I should say, deaf and blind to your surroundings. You probably walked very slowly and occasionally stopped for some minutes whilst you puzzled things out."

Christine nodded.

"How clever you are. It was just like that. I woke up from a kind of dream just outside the hotel and hurried in thinking I should be very late but when I saw the clock in the lounge I realized I had plenty of time."

Hercule Poirot said again:

"Exactly."

He turned to Marshall:

"I must now describe to you certain things I found in your daughter's room after the murder. In the grate was a large blob of melted wax, some burnt hair, fragments of cardboard and paper and an ordinary household pin. The paper and the cardboard might not be relevant but the other three things were suggestive—particularly when I found tucked away in the bookshelf a volume from the local library here dealing with witchcraft and magic. It opened very easily at a certain page. On that page were described various methods of causing death by moulding in wax a figure supposed to represent the victim. This was then slowly roasted till it melted away—or alternatively you would pierce the wax figure to the heart with a pin. Death of the victim would ensue. I later heard from Mrs. Redfern that Linda Marshall had been out early that morning and had bought a packet of candles and had seemed embarrassed when her purchase was revealed. I had no doubt what had happened after that. Linda had made a crude figure of the candle wax—possibly adorning it with a snip of Arlena's red hair to give the magic force—had then stabbed it to the heart with a pin and finally melted the figure away by lighting strips of cardboard under it.

"It was crude, childish, superstitious, but it revealed one thing: the desire to kill.

"Was there any possibility that there had been more than a desire? Could Linda Marshall have *actually* killed her stepmother?

"At first sight it seemed as though she had a perfect alibi—but in actuality, as I have just pointed out, the time evidence was supplied *by Linda herself*. She could easily have declared the time to be a quarter of an hour later than it really was.

"It was quite possible once Mrs. Redfern had left the beach for Linda to follow her up and then strike across the narrow neck of land to the ladder, hurry down it, meet her stepmother there, strangle her and return up the ladder before the boat containing Miss Brewster and Patrick Redfern came in sight. She could then return to Gull Cove, take her bathe and return to the hotel at her leisure.

"But that entailed two things. She must have definite knowledge that Arlena Marshall would be at Pixy Cove and she must be physically capable of the deed.

"Well, the first was quite possible—if Linda Marshall had written a note to Arlena herself in some one else's name. As to the second, Linda has very large strong hands. They are as large as a man's. As to the strength, she is at the age when one is prone to be mentally unbalanced. Mental derangement often is accompanied by unusual strength. There was one other small point. Linda Marshall's mother had actually been accused and tried for murder."

Kenneth Marshall lifted his head. He said fiercely:

"She was also acquitted."

"She was acquitted," Poirot agreed.

Marshall said:

"And I'll tell you this, M. Poirot. Ruth—my wife—was innocent. That I know with complete and absolute certainty. In the intimacy of our life I could not have been deceived. She was an innocent victim of circumstances."

He paused:

"And I don't believe that Linda killed Arlena. It's ridiculous—absurd!"

Poirot said:

"Do you believe that letter, then, to be a forgery?"

Marshall held out his hand for it and Weston gave it to him. Marshall studied it attentively. Then he shook his head.

"No," he said unwillingly. "I believe Linda did write this."

Poirot said:

"Then if she wrote it, there are only two explanations. Either she wrote it in all good faith, knowing herself to be the murderess or—or, I say— *she wrote it deliberately to shield some one else,* some one whom she feared was suspected."

Kenneth Marshall said:

"You mean me?"

"It is possible, is it not?"

Marshall considered for a moment or two, then he said quietly:

"No, I think that idea is absurd. Linda may have realized that I was regarded with suspicion at first. But she knew definitely by now that that was over and done with—that the police had accepted my alibi and turned their attention elsewhere."

Poirot said:

"And supposing that it was not so much that she thought that you were suspected as that she *knew* you were guilty."

Marshall stared at him. He gave a short laugh.

"That's absurd."

Poirot said:

"I wonder. There are, you know, several possibilities about Mrs. Marshall's death. There is the theory that she was being blackmailed, that she went that morning to meet the blackmailer and that the blackmailer killed her. There is the theory that Pixy Cove and Cave were being used for drug-running and that she was killed because she accidentally learned something about that. There is a third possibility—that she was killed by a religious maniac. And there is a fourth possibility—you stood to gain a lot of money by your wife's death, Captain Marshall?"

"I've just told you—"

"Yes, yes—I agree that it is impossible that you could have killed your wife—if you were acting alone. But supposing some one helped you?"

"What the devil do you mean?"

The quiet man was roused at last. He half rose from his chair. His voice was menacing. There was a hard angry light in his eyes.

Poirot said:

"I mean that this is not a crime that was committed single-handed. Two people were in it. It is quite true that you could not have typed that letter and at the same time gone to the cove—but there would have been time for you to have jotted down that letter in shorthand—and for *some one else* to have typed it in your room while you yourself were absent on your murderous errand."

Hercule Poirot looked towards Rosamund Darnley. He said:

"Miss Darnley states that she left Sunny Ledge at ten minutes past eleven and saw you typing in your room. But just about that time Mr. Gardener went up to the hotel to fetch a skein of wool for his wife. He did not meet Miss Darnley or see her. That is rather remarkable. It looks as though either Miss Darnley never left Sunny Ledge, or else she had left it much earlier and was in your room typing industriously. Another point, you stated that when Miss Darnley looked into your room at a quarter past eleven *you saw her in the mirror.* But on the day of the murder your typewriter and papers were all on the writing-desk across the corner of the room, whereas the mirror was between the windows. So that that statement was a deliberate lie. Later, you moved your typewriter to the table under the mirror so as to substantiate your story—but it was too late. I was aware that both you and Miss Darnley had lied."

Rosamund Darnley spoke. Her voice was low and clear.

She said:

"How devilishly ingenious you are!"

Hercule Poirot said, raising his voice:

"But not so devilish and so ingenious as the man who killed Arlena Marshall! Think back for a moment. Who did I think—who did everybody think—that Arlena Marshall had gone to meet that morning? We all jumped to the same conclusion. *Patrick Redfern*. It was not to meet a blackmailer that she went. Her face alone would have told me that. Oh, no, it was a lover she was going to meet—or thought she was going to meet.

"Yes, I was quite sure of that. Arlena Marshall was going to meet Patrick Redfern. But a minute later Patrick Redfern appeared on the beach and was obviously looking for her. So what then?"

Patrick Redfern said with subdued anger:

"Some devil used my name."

Poirot said:

"You were very obviously upset and surprised by her non-appearance. Almost too obviously, perhaps. It is *my* theory, Mr. Redfern, that she went to Pixy Cove to meet *you* and that she *did* meet you and that *you killed her there as you had planned to do*."

Patrick Redfern stared. He said in his high good-humoured Irish voice:

"Is it daft you are? I was with you on the beach until I went round in the boat with Miss Brewster and found her dead."

Hercule Poirot said:

"You killed her after Miss Brewster had gone off in the boat to fetch the police. Arlena Marshall was not dead when you got to the beach. She was waiting hidden in the Cave until the coast should be clear."

"But the body! Miss Brewster and I both saw the body."

"*A* body—yes. But not a *dead* body. The *live* body of the woman who helped you, her arms and legs stained with tan, her face hidden by a green cardboard hat. Christine, your wife (or possibly not your wife—but still your partner), helping you to commit this crime as she helped you to commit that crime in the past when she 'discovered' the body of Alice Corrigan at least twenty minutes before Alice Corrigan died—killed by her husband Edward Corrigan—you!"

Christine spoke. Her voice was sharp—cold. She said:

"Be careful, Patrick, don't lose your temper."

Poirot said:

"You will be interested to hear that both you and your wife Christine were easily recognized and picked out by the Surrey police from a group of people photographed here. They identified you both at once as Edward Corrigan and Christine Deverill, the young woman who found the body."

Patrick Redfern had risen. His handsome face was transformed, suffused with blood, blind with rage. It was the face of a killer—of a tiger. He yelled:

"You damned interfering murdering lousy little worm!"

He hurled himself forward, his fingers stretching and curling, his voice raving curses, as he fastened his fingers round Hercule Poirot's throat. . . .

CHAPTER XIII

Poirot said reflectively:

"It was on a morning when we were sitting out here that we talked of suntanned bodies lying like meat upon a slab and it was then that I reflected how little difference there was between one body and another. If one looked closely and appraisingly—yes—but to the casual glance? One moderately well-made young woman is very like another. Two brown legs, two brown arms, a little piece of bathing suit in between—just a body lying out in the sun. When a woman walks, when she speaks, laughs, turns her head, moves a hand—then, yes, then, there is personality—individuality. But in the sun ritual—no.

"It was that day that we spoke of evil—*evil under the sun*, as Mr. Lane put it. Mr. Lane is a very sensitive person—evil affects him—he perceives its presence—but though he is a good recording instrument, he did not really know exactly where the evil was. To him, evil was focussed in the person of Arlena Marshall and practically every one present agreed with him.

"But to my mind, though evil was present, it was not centralized in Arlena Marshall at all. It was connected with her, yes—but in a totally different way. I saw her, first, last and all the time, as an eternal and predestined *victim*. Because she was beautiful, because she had glamour, because men turned their heads to look at her, it was assumed that she was the type of woman who wrecked lives and destroyed souls. But I saw her very differently. It was not she who fatally attracted men—it was men who fatally attracted her. She was the type of woman whom men care for easily and of whom they as easily tire. And everything that I was told or found out about her strengthened my conviction on this point. The first thing that was mentioned about her was how the man in whose divorce case she had been cited refused to marry her. It was then that Captain Marshall, one of those incurably chivalrous men, stepped in and asked her to marry him. To a shy retiring man of Captain Marshall's type, a public ordeal of any kind would be the worst torture—hence his love and pity for his first wife who was publicly accused and tried for a murder she had not committed. He married her and found himself amply justified in his estimate of her character. After her death another beautiful woman, perhaps something of the same type (since Linda has red hair which she probably inherited from her mother) is held up to public ignominy. Again Marshall performs a rescue act. But this time he finds little to sustain his infatuation. Arlena is stupid, unworthy of his sympathy and protection, mindless. Nevertheless I think he always had a fairly true vision of her. Long after he ceased to love her and was irked by her presence, he remained sorry for her. She was to him like a child who cannot get farther than a certain page in the book of life.

"I saw in Arlena Marshall with her passion for men, a predestined prey for an unscrupulous man of a certain type. In Patrick Redfern, with his good looks, his easy assurance, his undeniable charm for women, I recognized at once that type. The adventurer who makes his living, one way or another, out of women. Looking on from my place on the beach I was quite certain that Arlena was Patrick's victim, not the other way about. And I associated that focus of evil with Patrick Redfern not with Arlena Marshall.

"Arlena had recently come into a large sum of money, left her by an elderly admirer who had not had time to grow tired of her. She was the type of woman who is invariably defrauded of money by some man or other. Miss Brewster mentioned a young man who had been 'ruined' by Arlena, but a letter from him which was found in her room, though it expressed a wish (which cost nothing) to cover her with jewels, in actual *fact* acknowledged a cheque from *her* by means of which he hoped to escape prosecution. A clear case of a young waster sponging on her. I have no doubt that Patrick Redfern found it easy to induce her to hand him large sums from time to time 'for investment.' He probably dazzled her with stories of great opportunities—how he would make her fortune and his own. Unprotected women, living alone, are easy prey to that type of man—and he usually escapes scot-free with the booty. If, however, there is a husband, or a brother, or a father about, things are apt to take an unpleasant turn for the swindler. Once Captain Marshall was to find out what had happened to his wife's fortune, Patrick Redfern might expect short shrift.

"That did not worry him, however, because he contemplated quite calmly doing away with her when he judged it necessary—encouraged by having already got away with one murder—that of a young woman whom he had married in the name of Corrigan and whom he had persuaded to insure her life for a large sum.

"In his plans he was aided and abetted by the young woman who down here passed as his wife and to whom he was genuinely attached. A young woman as unlike the type of his victims as could well be imagined—cool, calm, passionless, but steadfastly loyal to him and an actress of no mean ability. From the time of her arrival here Christine Redfern played a part, the part of the 'poor little wife'—frail, helpless, an intellectual rather than athletic. Think of the points she made one after another. Her tendency to blister in the sun and her consequent white skin, her giddiness at heights—stories of getting stuck on Milan Cathedral, etc. An emphasis on her frailty and delicacy—nearly every one spoke of her as a 'little woman.' She was actually as tall as Arlena Marshall but with very small hands and feet. She spoke of herself as a former school-teacher and thereby emphasized an impression of book learning and lack of athletic prowess. Actually it is quite true that she had worked in a school, but the position she held there was that of *games mistress* and she was an extremely active young woman who could climb like a cat and run like an athlete.

"The crime itself was perfectly planned and timed. It was, as I mentioned before, a very slick crime. The timing was a work of genius.

"First of all there were certain preliminary scenes—one played on the cliff ledge when they knew me to be occupying the next recess—a conventional jealous wife dialogue between her and her husband. Later she played the same part in a scene with me. At the time I remember a vague feeling of having read all this in a book. It did not seem *real*. Because, of course, it was *not* real. Then came the day of the crime. It was a fine day—an essential. Redfern's first act was to slip out very early—by the balcony door which he unlocked from the inside (if found open it would only be thought some one had gone for an early bathe). Under his bathing-wrap he concealed a green Chinese hat, the duplicate of the one Arlena was in the habit of wearing. He slipped across the island, down the ladder and stowed it away in an appointed place behind some rocks. Part I.

"On the previous evening he had arranged a rendezvous with Arlena. They were exercising a good deal of caution about meeting as Arlena was slightly afraid of her husband. She agreed to go round to Pixy Cove early. Nobody went there in the morning. Redfern was to join her there, taking a chance to slip away unobtrusively. If she heard any one descending the ladder or a boat came in sight she was to slip inside the Pixy's Cave, the secret of which he had told her, and wait there until the coast was clear. Part II.

"In the meantime Christine went to Linda's room at a time when she judged Linda would have gone for her early morning dip. She would then alter Linda's watch, putting it on twenty minutes. There was, of course, a risk that Linda might notice her watch was wrong, but it did not much matter if she did. Christine's real alibi was the size of her hands which made it a physical impossibility for her to have committed the crime. Nevertheless an additional alibi would be desirable. When in Linda's room she noticed the book on witchcraft and magic, open at a certain page. She read it and when Linda came in and dropped a parcel of candles she realized what was in Linda's mind. It opened up some new ideas to her. The original idea of the guilty pair had been to cast a reasonable amount of suspicion on Kenneth Marshall, hence the abstracted pipe, a fragment of which was to be planted at the cove underneath the ladder.

"On Linda's return Christine easily arranged an outing together to Gull Cove. She then returned to her own room, took out from a locked suitcase a bottle of artificial suntan, applied it carefully and threw the empty bottle out of the window where it narrowly escaped hitting Emily Brewster who was bathing. Part III successfully accomplished.

"Christine then dressed herself in a white bathing-suit and over it a pair of beach trousers and coat with long floppy sleeves which effectually concealed her newly browned arms and legs.

"At 10.15 Arlena departed for her rendezvous, a minute or two later Patrick Redfern came down and registered surprise, annoyance, etc. Christine's task was easy enough. Keeping her own watch concealed she asked Linda at twenty-five past eleven what time it was. Linda looked at her watch and replied that it was a quarter to twelve. She then starts down to the sea and Christine packs up her sketching things. As soon as Linda's back is turned Christine picks up the girl's watch which she has necessarily discarded before going into the sea and alters it back to the correct time. Then she hurries up the cliff path, runs across the narrow neck of land to the top of the ladder, strips off her pyjamas and shoves them and her sketching box behind a rock and swarms rapidly down the ladder in her best gymnastic fashion.

"Arlena is on the beach below wondering why Patrick is so long in coming. She sees or hears some one on the ladder, takes a cautious observation and to her annoyance sees that inconvenient person—the wife! She hurries along the beach and into the Pixy's Cave.

"Christine takes the hat from its hiding-place, a false red curl pinned underneath the brim at the back, and disposes herself in a sprawling attitude with the hat and curl shielding her face and neck. The timing is perfect. A minute or two later the boat containing Patrick and Emily Brewster comes round the point. Remember it is *Patrick* who bends down and examines the body, *Patrick* who is stunned—shocked—broken down by the death of his lady love! His witness has been carefully chosen. Miss Brewster has not got a good head, she will not attempt to go up the ladder. She will leave the cove by boat, Patrick naturally being the one to remain with the body—'in case the murderer may be still about.' Miss Brewster rows off to fetch the police. Christine, as soon as the boat has disappeared, springs up, cuts the hat into pieces with the scissors Patrick has carefully brought, stuffs them into her bathing suit and swarms up the ladder in double-quick time, slips into her beach pyjamas and runs back to the hotel. Just time to have a quick bath, washing off the brown suntan application, and into her tennis dress. One other thing she does. She burns the pieces of the green cardboard hat and the hair in Linda's grate, adding a leaf of a calendar so that it may be associated with the cardboard. Not a *hat* but a *calendar* has been burnt. As she suspected Linda has been experimenting in magic—the blob of wax and the pin show that.

"Then, down to the tennis court, arriving the last, but showing no signs of flurry or haste.

"And meanwhile Patrick has gone to the Cave. Arlena has seen nothing and heard very little—a boat—voices—she has prudently remained hidden. But now it is Patrick calling.

"'All clear, darling,' and she comes out and his hands fasten round her neck—and that is the end of poor foolish beautiful Arlena Marshall. . . ."

His voice died away.

For a moment there was silence, then Rosamund Darnley said with a little shiver:

"Yes, you make one see it all. But that's the story from the other side. You haven't told us how *you* came to get at the truth?"

Hercule Poirot said:

"I told you once that I had a very simple mind. Always, from the beginning, it seemed to me that *the most likely person* had killed Arlena Marshall. And the most likely person was Patrick Redfern. He was the type, *par excellence*—the type of the man who exploits women like her—and the type of the killer—the kind of man who will take a woman's savings and cut her throat into the bargain. Who was Arlena going to meet that morning? By the evidence of her face, her smile, her manner, her words to me—*Patrick Redfern*. And therefore, in the very nature of things, it should be Patrick Redfern who killed her.

"But at once I came up, as I told you, against impossibility. Patrick Redfern could not have killed her since he was on the beach and in Miss Brewster's company until the actual discovery of the body. So I looked about for other solutions—and there were several. She could have been killed by her husband—with Miss Darnley's connivance. (They too had both lied as to one point which looked suspicious.) She could have been killed as a result of her having stumbled on the secret of the dope smuggling. She could have been killed, as I said, by a religious maniac, and she could have been killed by her stepdaughter. The latter seemed to me at one time to be the real solution. Linda's manner in her very first interview with the police was significant. An interview that I had with her later assured me of one point. Linda considered herself guilty."

"You mean she imagined that she had actually killed Arlena?"

Rosamund's voice was incredulous.

Hercule Poirot nodded.

"Yes. Remember—she is really little more than a child. She read that book on witchcraft and she half believed it. She hated Arlena. She deliberately made the wax doll, cast her spell, pierced it to the heart, melted it away—*and that very day Arlena dies.* Older and wiser people than Linda have believed fervently in magic. Naturally she believed that it was all true—that by using magic she had killed her stepmother."

Rosamund cried:

"Oh, poor child, poor child. And I thought—I imagined—something quite different—that she knew something which would—"

Rosamund stopped. Poirot said:

"I know what it was you thought. Actually your manner frightened Linda still further. She believed that her action had really brought about Arlena's death and that you knew it. Christine Redfern worked on her too, introducing the idea of the sleeping tablets to her mind, showing her the way to a speedy and painless expiation of her crime. You see, once Captain Marshall was proved to have an alibi, it was vital for a new suspect to be found. Neither she nor her husband knew about the dope smuggling. They fixed on Linda to be the scapegoat."

Rosamund said:

"What a devil!"

Poirot nodded.

"Yes, you are right. A cold-blooded and cruel woman. For me, I was in great difficulty. Was Linda guilty only of the childish attempt at witchcraft, or had her hate carried her still further—to the actual act? I tried to get her to confess to me. But it was no good. At that moment I was in grave uncertainty. The Chief Constable was inclined to accept the dope-smuggling explanation. I could let it go at that. I went over the facts again very carefully. I had, you see, a collection of jigsaw puzzle pieces, isolated happenings—plain facts. The whole must fit into a complete and harmonious pattern. There were the scissors found on the beach—a bottle thrown from a window—a bath that no one would admit to having taken—all perfectly harmless occurrences in themselves, but rendered significant by the fact that no one would admit to them. Therefore, they *must* be of significance. Nothing about them fitted in with the theories of either Captain Marshall's or Linda's or of a dope gang's being responsible. And yet they *must* have meaning. I went back again to my first solution—that Patrick Redfern had committed the murder. Was there anything in support of that? Yes, the fact that a very large sum of money was missing from Arlena's account. Who had got that money? Patrick Redfern, of course. She was the type of woman easily swindled by a handsome young man—but she was not at all the type of woman to be blackmailed. She was far too transparent, not good enough at keeping a secret. The blackmailer story had never rung true to my mind. And yet there *had* been that conversation overheard—ah, but overheard by whom? *Patrick Redfern's wife.* It was her story—unsupported by any outside evidence. Why was it invented? The answer came to me like lightning. To account for the absence of Arlena's money!

"Patrick and Christine Redfern. The two of them were in it together. Christine hadn't got the physical strength to strangle her or the mental make-up. No, it was Patrick who had done it—but that was impossible! Every minute of his time was accounted for until the body was found.

"Body—the word body stirred something in my mind—bodies lying on the beach—*all alike.* Patrick Redfern and Emily Brewster had got to the cove and seen *a body* lying there. A body—suppose it was not Arlena's body but somebody else's? The face was hidden by the great Chinese hat.

"But there *was* only one dead body—Arlena's. Then, could it be—a *live* body—someone pretending to be dead? Could it be Arlena herself, inspired by Patrick to play some kind of a joke. I shook my head—no, too risky. A live body—whose? Was there any woman who would help Redfern? Of course—his wife. But she was a white-skinned delicate creature— Ah, yes, but suntan can be applied out of bottles—bottles—a bottle—I had one of my jigsaw pieces. Yes, and afterwards, of course, a bath—to wash that tell-tale stain off before she went out to play tennis. And the scissors? Why, to cut up that duplicate cardboard hat—an unwieldy thing that must be got out of the way, and in the haste the scissors were left behind—the one thing that the pair of murderers forgot.

"But where was Arlena all the time? That again was perfectly clear. Either Rosamund Darnley or Arlena Marshall had been in the Pixy's Cave, the scent they both used told me that. It was certainly not Rosamund Darnley. Then it was Arlena, hiding till the coast should clear.

"When Emily Brewster went off in the boat, Patrick had the beach to himself and full opportunity to commit the crime. Arlena Marshall was killed after a quarter to twelve but the medical evidence was only concerned with the earliest possible time the crime could have been committed. That Arlena was dead at a quarter to twelve was what was told to the doctor, not what he told the police.

"Two more points had to be settled. Linda Marshall's evidence gave Christine Redfern an alibi. Yes, but that evidence depended on Linda Marshall's wrist-watch. All that was needed was to prove that Christine had had two opportunities of tampering with the watch. I found those easily enough. She had been alone in Linda's room that morning—and there was an indirect proof. Linda was heard to say that she was 'afraid she was going to be late,' but when she got down it was only twenty-five past ten by the lounge clock. The second opportunity was easy—she could alter the watch back again as soon as Linda turned her back and went down to bathe.

"Then there was the question of the ladder. Christine had always declared she had no head for heights. Another carefully prepared lie.

"I had my mosaic now—each piece beautifully fitted into its place. But unfortunately I had no definite proof. It was all in my mind.

"It was then that an idea came to me. There was an assurance—a slickness about the crime. I had no doubt that in the future Patrick Redfern would repeat his crime. What about the past? It was remotely possible that this was not his first killing. The method employed, strangulation, was in harmony with his nature—a killer for pleasure as well as for profit. If he was already a murderer I was sure that he would have used the same means. I asked Inspector Colgate for a list of women victims of strangulation. The result filled me with joy. The death of Nellie Parsons found strangled in a lonely copse might or might not be Patrick Redfern's work— it might merely have suggested choice of locality to him, but in Alice Corrigan's death I found exactly what I was looking for. In essence the same method. Juggling with time—a murder committed not, as is the usual way, *before* it is supposed to have happened, but *afterwards*. A body supposedly discovered at a quarter past four. A husband with an alibi up to twenty-five past four.

"What really happened? It was said that Edward Corrigan arrived at the Pine Ridge, found his wife was not there *and went out and walked up and down*. Actually of course he ran full speed to the rendezvous, Caesar's Grove (which you will remember was quite near by), killed her and returned to the café. The girl hiker who reported the crime was a most respectable young lady, games mistress in a well-known girls' school. Apparently she had no connection with Edward Corrigan. She had to walk some way to report the death. The police surgeon only examined the body at a quarter to six. As in this case the time of death was accepted without question.

"I made one final test. I must know definitely if Mrs. Redfern was a liar. I arranged our little excursion to Dartmoor. If any one has a bad head for heights, they are never comfortable crossing a narrow bridge over running water. Miss Brewster, a genuine sufferer, showed giddiness. But Christine Redfern, unconcerned, ran across without a qualm. It was a small point, but it was a definite test. If she had told one unnecessary lie— then all the other lies were possible. In the meantime Colgate had got the photograph identified by the Surrey police. I played my hand in the only way I thought likely to succeed. Having lulled Patrick Redfern into security, I turned on him and did my utmost to make him lose his self-control. The knowledge that he had been identified with Corrigan caused him to lose his head completely."

Hercule Poirot stroked his throat reminiscently.

"What I did," he said with importance, "was exceedingly dangerous—but I do not regret it. I succeeded! I did not suffer in vain."

There was a moment's silence. Then Mrs. Gardener gave a deep sigh.

"Why, M. Poirot," she said. "It's just been too wonderful—hearing just exactly how you got your results. It's every bit as fascinating as a lecture on criminology—in fact it *is* a lecture on criminology. And to think my magenta wool and that sunbathing conversation actually had something to do with it! That really makes me too excited for words and I'm sure Mr. Gardener feels the same, don't you, Odell?"

"Yes, darling," said Mr. Gardener.

Hercule Poirot said:

"Mr. Gardener too was of assistance to me. I wanted the opinion of a sensible man about Mrs. Marshall. I asked Mr. Gardener what he thought of her."

"Is that so," said Mrs. Gardener. "And what did you say about her, Odell?"

Mr. Gardener coughed. He said:

"Well, darling, I never did think very much of her, you know."

"That's the kind of thing men always say to their wives," said Mrs. Gardener. "And if you ask me, even M. Poirot here is what I should call a shade on the indulgent side about her, calling her a natural victim and all that. Of course it's true that she wasn't a cultured woman at all, and as Captain Marshall isn't here I don't mind saying that she always did seem to me kind of dumb. I said so to Mr. Gardener, didn't I, Odell?"

"Yes, darling," said Mr. Gardener.

II

Linda Marshall sat with Hercule Poirot on Gull Cove.

She said:

"Of course I'm glad I didn't die after all. But you know, M. Poirot, it's just the same as if I'd killed her, isn't it? I meant to."

Hercule Poirot said energetically:

"It is not at all the same thing. The wish to kill and the action of killing are two different things. If in your bedroom instead of a little wax figure you had had your stepmother bound and helpless and a dagger in your hand instead of a pin, you would not have pushed it into her heart! Something within you would have said 'no.' It is the same with me. I enrage myself at an imbecile. I say, 'I would like to kick him.' Instead I kick the table. I say, 'This table, it is the imbecile, I kick him so.' And then, if I have not hurt my toe too much, I feel much better and the table it is not usually damaged. But if the imbecile himself was there I should not kick him. To make the wax figures and stick in the pins it is silly, yes, it is childish, yes—but it does something useful too. You took the hate out of yourself and put it into that little figure. And with the pin and the fire you destroyed—not your stepmother—but the hate you bore her. Afterwards, even before you heard of her death, you felt cleansed, did you not—you felt lighter—happier?"

Linda nodded. She said:

"How did you know? That's just how I did feel."

Poirot said:

"Then do not repeat to yourself the imbecilities. Just make up your mind not to hate your next stepmother."

Linda said, startled:

"Do you think I'm going to have another? Oh, I see, you mean Rosamund. I don't mind her." She hesitated a minute. "She's *sensible*."

It was not the adjective that Poirot himself would have selected for Rosamund Darnley, but he realized that it was Linda's idea of high praise.

III

Kenneth Marshall said:

"Rosamund, did you get some extraordinary idea into your head that I'd killed Arlena?"

Rosamund looked rather shamefaced. She said:

"I suppose I was a damned fool."

"Of course you were."

"Yes, but, Ken, you are such an oyster. I never knew what you really felt about Arlena. I didn't know if you accepted her as she was and were just frightfully decent about her, or whether you—well, just believed in her blindly. And I thought if it was that and you suddenly found out that she was letting you down you might go mad with rage. I've heard stories about you. You're always very quiet but you're rather frightening sometimes."

"So you thought I just took her by the throat and throttled the life out of her?"

"Well—yes—that's just exactly what I did think. And your alibi seemed a bit on the light side. That's when I suddenly decided to take a hand and made up that silly story about seeing you typing in your room. And when

I heard that you said you'd seen me look in—well, that made me quite sure you'd done it. That, and Linda's queerness."

Kenneth Marshall said with a sigh:

"Don't you realize that I said I'd seen you in the mirror in order to back up *your* story. I—I thought you needed it corroborated."

Rosamund stared at him.

"You don't mean you thought that I killed your wife?"

Kenneth Marshall shifted uneasily. He mumbled:

"Dash it all, Rosamund, don't you remember how you nearly killed that boy about that dog once? How you hung on to my throat and wouldn't let go."

"But that was years ago."

"Yes, I know—"

Rosamund said sharply:

"What earthly motive do you think I had to kill Arlena?"

His glance shifted. He mumbled something again.

Rosamund cried:

"Ken, you mass of conceit! You thought I killed her out of altruism on your behalf, did you? Or—or did you think I killed her because I wanted you myself?"

"Not at all," said Kenneth Marshall indignantly. "But you know what you said that day—about Linda and everything—and—and you seemed to care what happened to me."

Rosamund said:

"I've always cared about that."

"I believe you have. You know, Rosamund—I can't usually talk about things—I'm not good at talking—but I'd like to get this clear. I didn't care for Arlena—only just a little at first—and living with her day after day was a pretty nerve-racking business. In fact it was absolute hell, but I *was* awfully sorry for her. She was such a damned fool—crazy about men—she just couldn't help it—and they always let her down and treated her rottenly. I simply felt I couldn't be the one to give her the final push. I'd married her and it was up to me to look after her as best I could. I think she knew that and was grateful to me really. She was—she was a pathetic sort of creature really."

Rosamund said gently:

"It's all right, Ken. I understand now."

Without looking at her Kenneth Marshall carefully filled a pipe. He mumbled:

"You're—pretty good at understanding, Rosamund."

A faint smile curved Rosamund's ironic mouth. She said:

"Are you going to ask me to marry you now, Ken, or are you determined to wait six months?"

Kenneth Marshall's pipe dropped from his lips and crashed on the rocks below:

He said:

"Damn, that's the second pipe I've lost down here. And I haven't got another with me. How the devil did you know I'd fixed six months as the proper time?"

"I suppose because it *is* the proper time. But I'd rather have something definite now, please. Because in the intervening months you may come across some other persecuted female and rush to the rescue in chivalrous fashion again."

He laughed.

"You're going to be the persecuted female this time, Rosamund. You're going to give up that damned dressmaking business of yours and we're going to live in the country."

"Don't you know that I make a very handsome income out of my business? Don't you realize that it's *My* business—that I created it and worked it up and that I'm proud of it! And you've got the damned nerve to come along and say, 'Give it all up, dear.'"

"I've got the damned nerve to say it, yes."

"And you think I care enough for you to do it?"

"If you don't," said Kenneth Marshall, "you'd be no good to me."

Rosamund said softly:

"Oh, my dear, I've wanted to live in the country with you all my life. Now—it's going to come true. . . ."